SLEUTHS OF THE CENTURY

SLEUTHS OF THE CENTURY

Edited by

Jon L. Breen and Ed Gorman

CARROLL & GRAF PUBLISHERS, INC.
NEW YORK

First Carroll & Graf edition 2000

Carroll & Graf Publishers, Inc.
19 West 21st Street
New York, NY 10010-6805

Library of Congress Cataloging-in-Publication Data is available.
ISBN: 0-7867-0709-7

Manufactured in the United States of America

Contents

SLEUTHS OF THE CENTURY

Introduction

Since the modern detective story wasn't invented until 1841, when Edgar Allan Poe's "The Murders in the Rue Morgue" introduced gentleman crime-solver C. Auguste Dupin, there is no full century of fictional sleuths to compare to the twentieth. The nineteenth century would bring other memorable detectives to follow in Dupin's footsteps: one-shots like Wilkie Collins' Sergeant Cuff and Charles Dickens' Inspector Bucket plus series characters like Emile Gaboriau's Lecoq, Anna Katharine Green's Ebenezer Gryce, dime-novel heroes Nick Carter and Old King Brady, and the greatest of them all, Arthur Conan Doyle's Sherlock Holmes. But the nineteenth-century sleuths cannot compare in sheer numbers, variety, or quality to those introduced in the twentieth. Given the changing fashions in crime fiction, it's doubtful the twenty-first will outdo the twentieth either. The detective story may turn out to be a twentieth-century art form as surely as silent movies or radio drama, musical comedy, or rock music. (With the exception of silent movies and radio drama, we could be wrong, of course—check with us in 2100.)

In the beginning, the fictional sleuth was a superbrain, with reasoning ability and intuitive brilliance far beyond that of a normal person. For years, most series characters followed this pattern—see for example The Thinking Machine, Hercule Poirot, Ellery Queen, Nero Wolfe—and new detectives of that school still appear occasionally. As the years went by, though, the fictional detective would less and less likely be a super-intelligent freak and more and more likely a recognizably ordinary person with (if professional) solid competence and dogged determination; (if amateur) normal intelligence and overdeveloped curiosity. No one, for example, would call Tony Hillerman's Navajo policeman Jim Chee a supersleuth, though his colleague Joe Leaphorn has a bit of that aura. In the case of the hard-boiled private eyes, their physical durability has usually been more exceptional than their considerable mental prowess.

To represent the twentieth-century detective, we have selected twenty-five. They are male and female; straight and gay; tough and cozy; public, private, and purely amateur. Some of them are obvious consensus choices—who would leave out Wimsey or Queen or Archer or Mason or Wolfe or the cops of the 87th?—while others may be more surprising. They have been arranged chronologically by first appearance in print. Only characters who appeared for the first time in the twentieth century have been considered. Thus, Holmes, though active well into the 1920s, does not qualify.

The selections undoubtedly reflect the editors' personal tastes and biases. (But bear in mind, as any librarian will tell you, bias is not necessarily a pejorative term.) Also, availability for reprint influenced some of the choices. Some famous detectives could not appear because their creators never put them in short stories, e.g. S.S. Van Dine's Philo Vance, Earl Derr Biggers' Charlie Chan, Harry Kemelman's Rabbi David Small, Emma Lathen's John Putnam Thatcher, Patricia Moyes' Henry and Emmy Tibbett, and Elizabeth Peters' Amelia Peabody. Indeed a few of the most famous detectives—Joe Friday, Columbo, Jessica Fletcher—weren't invented for print media at all. And some of the finest crime writers of the century are not represented here because they rarely if ever used series characters, e.g. Cornell Woolrich, Stanley Ellin, Charlotte Armstrong, and Margaret Millar. Grant us those limitations with a small allowance for quirky choices (one per editor should be enough), and we can make a strong argument for our selections.

The statistical-minded will find at least one sleuth representing every decade, with the most productive being the '30s (nine selections), '20s (six), '70s (four), and the least so the teens and '40s (one each). The gender balance among authors is eighteen male to seven female; among detectives, twenty-two male to only three female. This apparent gender gap is *not* a product of the editors' bias. The author disparity may be explained in part by the fact that female writers, being more practical, have historically been less likely than men to expend their energies on short stories. The larger detective disparity reflects the early tendency (with some notable exceptions) of both male and female writers to feature male detectives.

The nationality range represents (we hope) an understandable American bias: among the authors, eighteen American, six British, one Belgian, and coincidentally, among the detectives, eighteen American and six British, one French and one Belgian as well.

Among the categories of detectives, the balance is closer: ten are private, six are professional police, seven are amateurs, and one is a criminal lawyer. Early in the century, the amateurs (albeit brilliant ones) were in the ascendancy, while more recently private eyes and professional cops predominate.

If your favorite crime-solver isn't here, consider that with all the fictional detectives to debut since 1900—there must be thousands—we couldn't even include all of our own favorites, let alone all that might be considered deserving.

The Phantom Motor

Author: Jacques Futrelle (1875–1912)

Detective: The Thinking Machine (1905)

The recent *Titanic* vogue, spurred by James Cameron's great motion picture, has somewhat revived interest in one of that ill-fated voyage's most famous victims. To say Jacques Futrelle must have enjoyed being on the *Titanic* may sound like a sick joke along the lines of, "Other than that, Mrs. Lincoln, how did you like the play?" But the first great American detective story writer of the twentieth century was fascinated by the advanced technology of his time, and the White Star's enormous, modern, and allegedly unsinkable liner certainly represented that. Some writers embrace new technology; others only use it for window dressing. With all the references to computers in recent crime fiction, for example, how many contemporary writers have truly explored the criminous possibilities of the information revolution? While other writers of the early century may have mentioned the growing prominence of the automobile, it was Futrelle who exploited it for fictional mystery in stories like the one that follows.

The best-known story about Professor Augustus S.F.X. Van Dusen (The Thinking Machine) is the much-anthologized "The Problem of Cell 13," which launched his career in some 1905 issues of the *Boston American,* but he had many other memorable cases in a career of explaining the inexplicable.

I

Two dazzling white eyes bulged through the night as an automobile swept suddenly around a curve in the wide road and laid a smooth, glaring pathway ahead. Even at the distance the rhythmical crackling-chug informed Special Constable Baker that it was a gasoline car, and the headlong swoop of the unblinking lights toward him made him instantly aware of the fact that the speed ordinance of Yarborough County was being a little more than broken—it was being obliterated.

Now the County of Yarborough was a wide expanse of summer estates and superbly kept roads, level as a floor and offered distracting temptations to the dangerous pastime of speeding. But against this was the fact that the county was particular about its speed laws, so particular in fact that it had stationed half a hundred men upon its highways to abate the nuisance. Incidentally it had found that keeping record of the infractions of the law was an excellent source of income.

"Forty miles an hour if an inch," remarked Baker to himself.

He arose from a camp stool where he was wont to make himself comfortable from six o'clock until midnight on watch, picked up his lantern, turned up the light and stepped down to the edge of the road. He always remained on watch at the same place—at one end of a long stretch which autoists had unanimously dubbed The Trap. The Trap was singularly tempting—perfectly macadamized road bed lying between two tall stone walls with only enough of a sinuous twist in it to make each end invisible from the other. Another man, Special Constable Bowman, was stationed at the other end of The Trap and there was telephonic communication between the points, enabling the men to check each other and incidentally, if one failed to stop a car or get its number, the other would. That at least was the theory.

So now, with the utmost confidence, Baker waited beside the road. The approaching lights were only a couple of hundred yards away. At the proper instant he would raise his lantern, the car would stop, its occupants would protest and then the county would add a mite to its general fund for making the roads even better and tempting autoists still more. Or sometimes the cars didn't stop. In that event it was part of the Special Constables' duties to get the number as it flew past, and reference to the monthly automobile register would give the name of the owner. An extra fine was always imposed in such cases.

Without the slightest diminution of speed the car came hurtling on toward him and swung wide so as to take the straight path of The Trap at full speed. At the psychological instant Baker stepped out into the road and waved his lantern.

"Stop!" he commanded.

The crackling-chug came on, heedless of the cry. The auto was almost upon him before he leaped out of the road—a feat at which he was particularly expert—then it flashed by and plunged into The Trap. Baker was, at the instant, so busily engaged in getting out of the way that he couldn't read the number, but he was not disconcerted because he knew there was no escape from The Trap. On the one side a solid stone wall eight feet high marked the eastern boundary of the John Phelps Stocker country estate, and on the other side a stone fence nine feet high marked the western boundary of the Thomas Q. Rogers country estate. There was no turnout, no place, no possible way for an auto to get out of The Trap except at one of the two ends guarded by the special constables. So Baker, perfectly confident of results, seized the phone.

"Car coming through sixty miles an hour," he bawled. "It won't stop. I missed the number. Look out."

"All right," answered Special Constable Bowman.

For ten, fifteen, twenty minutes Baker waited expecting a call from Bowman at the other end. It didn't come and finally he picked up the phone again. No answer. He rang several times, battered the box and did some tricks with the receiver. Still no answer. Finally he began to feel worried. He remembered that at that same post one Special Constable had been badly hurt by a reckless chauffeur who refused to stop or turn his car when the officer stepped out into the road. In his mind's eye he saw Bowman now lying helpless, perhaps badly injured. If the car held the pace at which it passed him it would be certain death to whoever might be unlucky enough to get in its path.

With these thoughts running through his head and with genuine solicitude for Bowman, Baker at last walked on along the road of The Trap toward the other end. The feeble rays of the lantern showed the unbroken line of the cold, stone walls on each side. There was no shrubbery of any sort, only a narrow strip of grass close to the wall. The more Baker considered the matter the more anxious he became and he increased his pace a little. As he turned a gentle curve he saw a lantern in the distance coming slowly toward him. It was evidently being carried by someone who was looking carefully along each side of the road.

"Hello!" called Baker, when the lantern came within distance. "That you, Bowman?"

"Yes," came the hallooed response.

The lanterns moved on and met. Baker's solicitude for the other constable was quickly changed to curiosity.

"What're you looking for?" he asked.

"That auto," replied Bowman. "It didn't come through my end and I thought perhaps there had been an accident so I walked along looking for it. Haven't seen anything."

"Didn't come through your end?" repeated Baker in amazement. "Why it must have. It didn't come back my way and I haven't passed it so it must have gone through."

"Well, it didn't," declared Bowman conclusively. "I was on the look-out for it, too, standing beside the road. There hasn't been a car through my end in an hour."

Special Constable Baker raised his lantern until the rays fell full upon the face of Special Constable Bowman and for an instant they stared each at the other. Suspicion glowed from the keen, avaricious eyes of Baker.

"How much did they give you to let 'em by?" he asked.

"Give me?" exclaimed Bowman, in righteous indignation. "Give me nothing. I haven't seen a car."

A slight sneer curled the lips of Special Constable Baker.

"Of course that's all right to report at headquarters," he said, "but I happen to know that the auto came in here, that it didn't go back my way, that it couldn't get out except at the ends, therefore it went your way." He was silent for a moment. "And whatever you got, Jim, seems to me I ought to get half."

Then the worm—i.e., Bowman—turned. A polite curl appeared about his lips and was permitted to show through the grizzled mustache.

"I guess," he said deliberately, "you think because you do that, everybody else does. I haven't seen any autos."

"Don't I always give you half, Jim?" Baker demanded, almost pleadingly.

"Well I haven't seen any car and that's all there is to it. If it didn't go back your way there wasn't any car." There was a pause; Bowman was framing up something particularly unpleasant. "You're seeing things, that's what's the matter."

So was sown discord between two officers of the County of Yarborough. After awhile they separated with mutual sneers and open derision and went back to their respective posts. Each was thoughtful in his own way. At five minutes of midnight when they went off duty Baker called Bowman on the phone again.

"I've been thinking this thing over, Jim, and I guess it would be just as well if we didn't report it or say anything about it when we go in," said Baker slowly. "It seems foolish and if we did say anything about it it would give the boys the laugh on us."

"Just as you say," responded Bowman.

Relations between Special Constable Baker and Special Constable Bowman were strained on the morrow. But they walked along side by side to their respective posts. Baker stopped at his end of The Trap; Bowman didn't even look around.

"You'd better keep your eyes open tonight, Jim," Baker called as a last word.

"I had 'em open last night," was the disgusted retort.

Seven, eight, nine o'clock passed. Two or three cars had gone through The Trap at moderate speed and one had been warned by Baker. At a few minutes past nine he was staring down the road that led into The Trap when he saw something that brought him quickly to his feet. It was a pair of dazzling white eyes, far away. He recognized them—the mysterious car of the night before.

"I'll get it this time," he muttered grimly, between closed teeth.

Then when the onrushing car was a full two hundred yards away Baker planted himself in the middle of the road and began to swing the lantern. The auto seemed, if anything, to be traveling even faster than on the previous night. At a hundred yards Baker began to shout. Still the car didn't lessen speed, merely rushed on. Again at the psychological instant Baker jumped. The auto whisked by as the chauffeur gave it a dextrous twist to prevent running down the Special Constable.

Safely out of its way Baker turned and stared after it, trying to read the number. He could see there was a number because a white board swung from the tail axle, but he could not make out the figures. Dust and a swaying car conspired to defeat him. But he did see that there were four persons in the car dimly silhouetted against the light reflected from the road. It was useless, of course, to conjecture as to sex for even as he looked, the fast receding car swerved around the turn and was lost to sight.

Again he rushed to the telephone; Bowman responded promptly.

"That car's gone in again," Baker called. "Ninety miles an hour. Look out!"

"I'm looking," responded Bowman.

"Let me know what happens," Baker shouted.

With the receiver to his ear he stood for ten or fifteen minutes, then Bowman hallooed from the other end.

"Well?" Baker responded. "Get 'em?"

"No car passed through and there's none in sight," said Bowman.

"But it went in," insisted Baker.

"Well it didn't come out here," declared Bowman. "Walk along the road till I meet you and look out for it."

Then was repeated the search of the night before. When the two men met in the middle of The Trap their faces were blank—blank as the high stone walls which stared at them from each side.

"Nothing!" said Bowman.

"Nothing!" echoed Baker.

Special Constable Bowman perched his head on one side and scratched his grizzly chin.

"You're not trying to put up a job on me?" he inquired coldly. "You did see a car?"

"I certainly did," declared Baker, and a belligerent tone underlay his manner. "I certainly saw it, Jim, and if it didn't come out your end, why—why—"

He paused and glanced quickly behind him. The action inspired a sudden similar caution on Bowman's part.

"Maybe—maybe—" said Bowman after a minute, "maybe it's a—a spook auto?"

"Well it must be," mused Baker. "You know as well as I do that no car can get out of this trap except at the ends. That car came in here, it isn't here now and it didn't go out your end. Now where is it?"

Bowman stared at him a minute, picked up his lantern, shook his head solemnly and wandered along the road back to his post. On his way he glanced around quickly, apprehensively, three times—Baker did the same thing four times.

On the third night the phantom car appeared and disappeared precisely as it had done previously. Again Baker and Bowman met halfway between posts and talked it over.

"I'll tell you what, Baker," said Bowman in conclusion, "maybe you're just imagining that you see a car. Maybe if I was at your end I couldn't see it."

Special Constable Baker was distinctly hurt at the insinuation.

"All right, Jim," he said at last, "if you think that way about it we'll swap posts tomorrow night. We won't have to say anything about it when we report."

"Now that's the talk," exclaimed Bowman with an air approaching enthusiasm. "I'll bet I don't see it."

On the following night Special Constable Bowman made himself comfortable on Special Constable Baker's camp stool. And *he* saw the phantom auto. It came upon him with a rush and a crackling-chug of engine and then sped on leaving him nerveless. He called Baker over the wire and Baker watched half an hour for the phantom. It didn't appear.

Ultimately all things reach the newspapers. So with the story of the phantom auto. Hutchinson Hatch, reporter, smiled incredulously when his City Editor laid aside an inevitable cigar and tersely stated the known facts. The known facts in this instance were meager almost to the disappearing point. They consisted merely of a corroborated statement that an automobile, solid and tangible enough to all appearances, rushed into The Trap each night and totally disappeared.

But there was enough of the bizarre about it to pique the curiosity, to make one wonder, so Hatch journeyed down to Yarborough County, an hour's ride from the city, met and talked to Baker and Bowman and then, in broad daylight strolled along The Trap twice. It was a leisurely, thorough investigation with the end in view of finding out how an automobile once inside might get out again without going out either end.

On the first trip through, Hatch paid particular attention to the Thomas Q. Rogers side of the road. The wall, nine feet high, was an unbroken line of stone with not the slightest indication of a secret wagon-way through it anywhere. Secret wagon-way! Hatch smiled at the phrase. But when he reached the other end—Bowman's end—of The Trap he was perfectly convinced of one thing—that no automobile had left the hard, macadamized road to go over, under, or through the Thomas Q. Rogers wall. Returning, still leisurely, he paid strict attention to the John Phelps Stocker side, and when he reached the other end—Baker's end—he was convinced of another thing—that no automobile had left the road to go over, under, or through the John Phelps Stocker wall. The only opening of any sort was a narrow footpath, not more than sixteen inches wide.

Hatch saw no shrubbery along the road, nothing but a strip of scrupulously cared for grass, therefore the phantom auto could not be hidden any time, night or day. Hatch failed, too, to find any holes in the road so the automobile didn't go down through the earth. At this point he involuntarily glanced up at the blue sky above. Perhaps, he thought whimsically, the automobile was a strange sort of bird, or—or—and he stopped suddenly.

"By George!" he exclaimed. "I wonder if—"

And the remainder of the afternoon he spent systematically making inquiries. He went from house to house, the Stocker house, the Rogers house, both of which were at the time unoccupied, then to cottage, cabin, and hut in turn. But he didn't seem overladen with information when he joined Special Constable Baker at his end of The Trap that evening about seven o'clock.

Together they rehearsed the strange points of the mystery as the shadows grew about them until finally the darkness was so dense that Baker's lantern was the only bright spot in sight. As the chill of the evening closed in a certain awed tone crept into their voices. Occasionally an auto bowled along and each time as it hove in sight Hatch glanced at Baker questioningly. And each time Baker shook his head.

And each time, too, he called Bowman, in this manner accounting for every car that went into The Trap.

"It'll come all right," said Baker after a long silence, "and I'll know it the minute it rounds the curve coming toward us. I'd know its two lights in a thousand."

They sat still and smoked. After awhile two dazzling white lights burst into view far down the road and Baker, in excitement, dropped his pipe.

"That's her," he declared. "Look at her coming!"

And Hatch did look at her coming. The speed of the mysterious car was such as to make one look. Like the eyes of a giant the two lights came on toward them, and Baker perfunctorily went through the motions of attempting to stop it. The car fairly whizzed past them and the rush of air that tugged at their coats was convincing enough proof of its solidity. Hatch strained his eyes to read the number as the auto flashed past. But it was hopeless. The tail of the car was lost in an eddying whirl of dust.

"She certainly does travel," commented Baker, softly.

"She does," Hatch assented.

Then, for the benefit of the newspaper man, Baker called Bowman on the wire.

"Car's coming again," he shouted. "Look out and let me know!"

Bowman, at his end, waited twenty minutes, then made the usual report—the car had not passed. Hutchinson Hatch was a calm, cold, dispassionate young man but now a queer, creepy sensation stole along his spinal column. He lighted a cigarette and pulled himself together with a jerk.

"There's one way to find out where it goes," he declared at last, emphatically, "and that's to place a man in the middle just beyond the bend of The Trap and let him wait and see. If the car goes up, down, or evaporates he'll see and can tell us."

Baker looked at him curiously.

"I'd hate to be the man in the middle," he declared. There was something of uneasiness in his manner.

"I rather think I would, too," responded Hatch.

On the following evening, consequent upon the appearance of the story of the phantom auto in Hatch's paper, there were twelve other reporters on hand. Most of them were openly, flagrantly skeptical; they even insinuated that no one had seen an auto. Hatch smiled wisely.

"Wait!" he advised with deep conviction.

So when the darkness fell that evening the newspaper men of a great city had entered into a conspiracy to capture the phantom auto. Thirteen of them, making a total of fifteen men with Baker and Bowman, were on hand and they agreed to a suggestion for all to take positions along the road of The Trap from Baker's post to Bowman's, watch for the auto, see what happened to it, and compare notes afterward. So they scattered themselves along a few hundred feet apart and waited. That night the phantom auto didn't appear at all and twelve reporters jeered at Hutchinson Hatch and told him to light his pipe with the story. And the next night when Hatch and Baker and Bowman alone were watching the phantom auto reappeared.

II

Like a child with a troublesome problem, Hatch took the entire matter and laid it before Professor Augustus S. F. X. Van Dusen, the master brain. The Thinking Machine, with squint eyes turned steadily upward and long, slender fingers pressed tip to tip, listened to the end.

"Now I know of course that automobiles don't fly," Hatch burst out savagely in conclusion, "and if this one doesn't fly, there is no earthly way for it to get out of The Trap, as they call it. I went over the thing carefully—I even went so far as to examine the ground and the tops of the walls to see if a runway had been let down for the auto to go over."

The Thinking Machine squinted at him inquiringly.

"Are you sure you saw an automobile?" he demanded irritably.

"Certainly I saw it," blurted the reporter. "I not only saw it—I smelled it. Just to convince myself that it was real I tossed my cane in front of the thing and it smashed it to toothpicks."

"Perhaps, then, if everything is as you say, the auto actually *does* fly," remarked the scientist.

The reporter stared into the calm, inscrutable face of The Thinking Machine, fearing first that he had not heard aright. Then he concluded that he had.

"You mean," he inquired eagerly, "that the phantom may be an auto-airplane affair, and that it actually does fly?"

"It's not at all impossible," commented the scientist.

"I had an idea something like that myself," Hatch explained, "and questioned every soul within a mile or so but I didn't get anything."

"The perfect stretch of road there might be the very place for some daring experimenter to get up sufficient speed to soar a short distance in a light machine," continued the scientist.

"Light machine?" Hatch repeated. "Did I tell you that this car had four people in it?"

"Four people!" exclaimed the scientist. "Dear me! Dear me! That makes it very different. Of course four people would be too great a lift for an—"

For ten minutes he sat silent, and tiny, cobwebby lines appeared in his dome-like brow. Then he arose and passed into the adjoining room. After a moment Hatch heard the telephone bell jingle. Five minutes later The Thinking Machine appeared, and scowled upon him unpleasantly.

"I suppose what you really want to learn is if the car is a—a material one, and to whom it belongs?" he queried.

"That's it," agreed the reporter, "and of course, why it does what it does, and how it gets out of The Trap."

"Do you happen to know a fast, long-distance bicycle rider?" demanded the scientist abruptly.

"A dozen of them," replied the reporter promptly. "I think I see the idea, but—"

"You haven't the faintest inkling of the idea," declared The Thinking Machine positively. "If you can arrange with a fast rider who can go a distance—it might be thirty, forty, fifty miles—we may end this little affair without difficulty."

Under these circumstances Professor Augustus S. F. X. Dusen, Ph.D., LL.D., F.R.S., M.D., etc. etc., scientist and logician, met the famous Jimmie Thalhauer, the world's champion long-distance bicyclist. He held every record from five miles up to and including six hours, had twice won the six-day race and was, altogether, a master in his field. He came in chewing a toothpick. There were introductions.

"You ride the bicycle?" inquired the crusty little scientist.

"Well, *some,*" confessed the champion modestly with a wink at Hatch.

"Can you keep up with an automobile for a distance of, say, thirty or forty miles?"

"I can keep up with anything that ain't got wings," was the response.

"Well, to tell you the truth," volunteered The Thinking Machine, "there is a growing belief that this particular automobile has wings. However, if you can keep up with it—"

"Ah, quit your kiddin'," said the champion, easily. "I can ride rings around anything on wheels. I'll start behind it and beat it where it's going."

The Thinking Machine examined the champion, Jimmie Thalhauer, as a curiosity. In the seclusion of his laboratory he had never had an opportunity of meeting just such another worldly young person.

"How fast *can* you ride, Mr. Thalhauer?" he asked at last.

"I'm ashamed to tell you," confided the champion in a hushed voice. "I can ride so fast that I scare myself." He paused a moment. "But it seems to me," he said, "if there's thirty or forty miles to do I ought to do it on a motorcycle."

"Now that's just the point," explained The Thinking Machine. "A motorcycle makes noise and if it could have been used we would have hired a fast automobile. This proposition briefly is: I want you to ride without lights behind an automobile which, may also run without lights and find out where it goes. No occupant of the car must suspect that it is followed."

"Without lights?" repeated the champion. "Gee! Rubber shoe, eh?"

The Thinking Machine looked his bewilderment.

"Yes, that's it," Hatch answered for him.

"I guess it's good for a four-column head? Hunh?" inquired the champion. "Special pictures posed by the champion? Hunh?"

"Yes," Hatch replied.

" 'Tracked on a Bicycle' sounds good to me. Hunh?"

Hatch nodded.

So arrangements were concluded and then and there The Thinking Machine gave definite and conclusive instructions to the champion. While these apparently bore broadly on the problem in hand they conveyed absolutely no inkling of his plan to the reporter. At the end the champion arose to go.

"You're a most extraordinary young man, Mr. Thalhauer," commented The Thinking Machine, not without admiration for the sturdy, powerful figure.

And as Hatch accompanied the champion out the door and down the steps Jimmie smiled with easy grace.

"Nutty old guy, ain't he? Hunh?"

Night! Utter blackness, relieved only by a white, ribbon-like road that winds away mistily under a starless sky. Shadowy hedges line either side and occasionally a tree thrusts itself upward out of the somberness. The murmur of human voices in the shadows, then the crackling-chug of an engine and an automobile moves slowly, without lights, into the road. There is the sudden clatter of an engine at high speed and the car rushes away.

From the hedge comes the faint rustle of leaves as of wind stirring, then a figure moves impalpably. A moment and it becomes a separate entity; a quick movement and the creak of a leather bicycle saddle. Silently the single figure, bent low over the handlebars, moves after the car with ever increasing momentum.

Then a long, desperate race. For mile after mile, mile after mile the auto goes on. The silent cyclist has crept up almost to the rear axle and hangs there doggedly as a racer to his pace. On and on they rush together through the darkness, the chauffeur moving with a perfect knowledge of his road, the single rider behind clinging on grimly with set teeth. The powerful, piston-like legs move up and down to the beat of the engine.

At last, with dust-dry throat and stinging, aching eyes, the cyclist feels the pace slacken and instantly he drops back out of sight. It is only by sound that he follows now. The car stops; the cyclist is lost in the shadows.

For two or three hours the auto stands deserted and silent. At last the voices are heard again, the car stirs, moves away and the cyclist drops in behind. Another race that leads off in another direction. Finally, from a knoll, the lights of a city are seen. Ten minutes elapse, the auto stops, the headlights flare and more leisurely it proceeds on its way.

On the following evening The Thinking Machine and Hutchinson Hatch called upon Fielding Stanwood, President of the Fordyce National Bank. Mr. Stanwood looked at them with interrogative eyes.

"We called to inform you, Mr. Stanwood," explained The Thinking Machine, "that a box of securities, probably United States bonds, is missing from your bank."

"What?" exclaimed Mr. Stanwood, and his face paled. "Robbery?"

"I only know the bonds were taken out of the vault tonight by Joseph Marsh, your assistant cashier," said the scientist, "and that he, together with three other men, left the bank with the box and are now at—a place I can name."

Mr. Stanwood was staring at him in amazement.

"You know where they are?" he demanded.

"I said I did," replied the scientist, shortly.

"Then we must inform the police at once, and—"

"I don't know that there has been an actual crime," interrupted the scientist. "I do know that every night for a week these bonds have been taken out through the connivance of your watchman and in each instance have been returned, intact, before morning. They will be returned tonight. Therefore I would advise, if you act, not to do so until the four men return with the bonds."

It was a singular party that met in the private office of President Stanwood at the bank just after midnight. Marsh and three companions, formally under arrest, were present as were President Stanwood, The Thinking Machine and Hatch, besides detectives. Marsh had the bonds under his arms when he was taken. He talked freely when questioned.

"I will admit," he said without hesitating, "that I have acted beyond my rights in removing the bonds from the vault here, but there is no ground for prosecution. I am a responsible officer of this bank and have violated no trust. Nothing is missing, nothing is stolen. Every bond that went out of the bank is here."

"But why—why did you take the bonds?" demanded Mr. Stanwood.

Marsh shrugged his shoulders.

"It's what has been called a get-rich-quick scheme," said The Thinking Machine. "Mr. Hatch and I made some investigations today. Mr. Marsh and these other three are interested in a business venture that is ethically dishonest but which is within the law. They have sought backing for the scheme amounting to about a million dollars. Those four or five men of means with whom they have discussed the matter have called each night for a week at Marsh's country place. It was necessary to make them believe that there was already a million or so in the scheme, so these bonds were borrowed and represented to be owned by themselves. They were taken to and fro between the bank and his home in a kind of an automobile. This is really what happened, based on knowledge, which Mr. Hatch has gathered and what I myself developed by the use of a little logic."

And his statement of the affair proved to be correct. Marsh and the others admitted the statement to be true. It was while The Thinking Machine was homeward bound that he explained the phantom auto affair to Hatch.

"The phantom auto, as you call it," he said, "is the vehicle in which the bonds were moved about. The phantom idea came merely by chance. On the night the vehicle was first noticed it was rushing along— we'll say to reach Marsh's house in time for an appointment. A road map will show you that the most direct line from the bank to Marsh's was through The Trap. If an automobile should go halfway through there, then out across the Stocker estate to the other road, distance would be lessened by a good five miles. This saving at first was of course valuable, so the car in which they rushed into The Trap was merely taken across the Stocker estate to the road in front."

"But how?" demanded Hatch. "There's no road there."

"I learned by phone from Mr. Stocker that there is a narrow walk from a very narrow foot gate in Stocker's wall on The Trap leading through the grounds to the other road. The phantom auto wasn't really an auto at all—it was merely two motorcycles arranged with seats and a steering apparatus. The French Army has been experimenting with them. The motorcycles are, of course, separate machines and as such it was easy to trundle them through a narrow gate and across to the other road. The seats are light; they can be carried under the arm."

"Oh!" exclaimed Hatch suddenly, then after a minute: "But what did Jimmie Thalhauer do for you?"

"He waited in the road at the other end of the foot-path from The Trap," the scientist explained. "When the auto was brought through and put together he followed it to Marsh's home and from there to the bank. The rest of it you and I worked out today. It's merely logic, Mr. Hatch, logic."

There was a pause.

"That Mr. Thalhauer is really a marvelous young man, Mr. Hatch, don't you think?"

The Secret Garden

Author: G.K. Chesterton (1874–1936)

Detective: Father Brown (1910)

Father Brown, Roman Catholic convert Chesterton's deceptively unassuming clerical sleuth, first appeared in the short story "The Blue Cross" in a 1910 issue of *Storyteller*. The following year, his early cases were collected in *The Innocence of Father Brown,* the first of five collections. Like the much more flamboyant Thinking Machine, Father Brown specializes in bringing rational explanations to seemingly impossible occurrences, meanwhile dispensing trademark Chestertonian paradoxes and drawing moral lessons. More than any other character in British fiction of his time, certainly more than Sherlock Holmes, Father Brown foreshadows the games playing and puzzle designing of the between-World-Wars Golden Age of Detection. John Dickson Carr paid Chesterton the ultimate homage by patterning his most famous detective, Dr. Gideon Fell, after him.

"The Secret Garden," from that first and probably best Father Brown collection, includes all the essential characteristics of the series: an impossible crime, sly satire, exasperatingly cryptic or paradoxical statements by the sleuth, a religiously based motivation, and a brilliant but inevitable solution.

A ristide Valentin, Chief of the Paris Police, was late for his dinner, and some of his guests began to arrive before him. These were, however, reassured by his confidential servant, Ivan, the old man with a scar, and a face almost as gray as his moustaches, who always sat at a table in the entrance hall—a hall hung with weapons. Valentin's house was perhaps as peculiar and celebrated as its master. It was an old house, with high walls and tall poplars almost overhanging the Seine; but the oddity—and perhaps the police value—of its architecture was this: that there was no ultimate exit at all except through this front door, which was guarded by Ivan and the armory. The garden was large and elaborate, and there were many exits from the house into the garden. But there was no exit from the garden into the world outside; all round it ran a tall, smooth, unscalable wall with special spikes at the top; no bad garden, perhaps, for a man to reflect in whom some hundred criminals had sworn to kill.

As Ivan explained to the guests, their host had telephoned that he was detained for ten minutes. He was, in truth, making some last arrangements about executions and such ugly things; and though these duties were rootedly repulsive to him, he always performed them with precision. Ruthless in the pursuit of criminals, he was very mild about their punishment. Since he had been supreme over French—and largely over European—policial methods, his great influence had been honorably used for the mitigation of sentences and the purification of prisons. He was one of the great humanitarian French freethinkers; and the only thing wrong with them is that they make mercy even colder than justice.

When Valentin arrived he was already dressed in black clothes and the red rosette—an elegant figure, his dark beard already streaked with gray. He went straight through his house to his study, which opened on the grounds behind. The garden door of it was open, and after he had carefully locked his box in its official place, he stood for a few seconds at the open door looking out upon the garden. A sharp moon was fighting with the flying rags and tatters of a storm, and Valentin regarded it with a wistfulness unusual in such scientific natures as his. Perhaps such scientific natures have some psychic prevision of the most tremendous problem of their lives. From any such occult mood, at least, he quickly recovered, for he knew he was late, and that his guests had already begun to arrive. A glance at his drawing-room when he entered it was enough to make certain that his principal guest was not there, at any rate. He saw all the other pillars of the little party; he saw Lord Galloway, the English Ambassador—a choleric old man with a russet face like an apple, wearing the blue ribbon of the Garter. He saw Lady Galloway, slim and threadlike, with silver hair and a face sensitive and superior. He saw her daughter, Lady Margaret Graham, a pale and pretty girl with an elfish face and copper-colored hair. He saw the Duchess of Mont St. Michel, black-eyed and opulent, and with her two daughters, black-eyed and opulent also. He saw Dr. Simon, a typical French scientist, with glasses, a pointed brown beard, and a forehead barred with those parallel wrinkles that are the penalty of superciliousness, since they come through constantly elevating the eyebrows. He saw

Father Brown, of Cobhole, in Essex, whom he had recently met in England. He saw—perhaps with more interest than any of these—a tall man in uniform, who had bowed to the Galloways without receiving any very hearty acknowledgment, and who now advanced alone to pay his respects to his host. This was Commandant O'Brien, of the French Foreign Legion. He was a slim yet somewhat swaggering figure, clean-shaven, dark-haired, and blue-eyed, and, as seemed natural in an officer of that famous regiment of victorious failures and successful suicides, he had an air at once dashing and melancholy. He was by birth an Irish gentleman, and in boyhood had known the Galloways—especially Margaret Graham. He had left his country after some crash of debts, and now expressed his complete freedom from British etiquette by swinging about in uniform, sabre, and spurs. When he bowed to the Ambassador's family, Lord and Lady Galloway bent stiffly, and Lady Margaret looked away.

But for whatever old causes such people might be interested in each other, their distinguished host was not specially interested in them. No one of them at least was in his eyes the guest of the evening. Valentin was expecting, for special reasons, a man of world-wide fame, whose friendship he had secured during some of his great detective tours and triumphs in the United States. He was expecting Julius K. Brayne, that multi-millionaire whose colossal and even crushing endowments of small religions have occasioned so much easy sport and easier solemnity for the American and English papers. Nobody could quite make out whether Mr. Brayne was an atheist or a Mormon or a Christian Scientist; but he was ready to pour money into any intellectual vessel, so long as it was an untried vessel. One of his hobbies was to wait for the American Shakespeare—a hobby more patient than angling. He admired Walt Whitman, but thought that Luke P. Tanner, of Paris, Pennsylvania, was more "progressive" than Whitman any day. He liked anything that he thought "progressive." He thought Valentin "progressive," thereby doing him a grave injustice.

The solid appearance of Julius K. Brayne in the room was as decisive as a dinner bell. He had this great quality, which very few of us can claim, that his presence was as big as his absence. He was a huge fellow, as fat as he was tall, clad in complete evening black, without so much relief as a watch-chain or a ring. His hair was white and well brushed back like a German's; his face was red, fierce and cherubic, with one dark tuft under the lower lip that threw up that otherwise infantile visage with an effect theatrical and even Mephisthophelean. Not long, however, did that *salon* merely stare at the celebrated American; his lateness had already become a domestic problem, and he was sent with all speed into the dining-room with Lady Galloway on his arm.

Except on one point the Galloways were genial and casual enough. So long as Lady Margaret did not take the arm of that adventurer O'Brien, her father was quite satisfied; and she had not done so, she had decorously gone in with Dr. Simon. Nevertheless, old Lord Galloway was restless and almost rude. He was diplomatic enough during dinner, but when, over the cigars, three of the younger men—Simon the doctor, Brown the priest, and the detrimental O'Brien, the exile in a foreign uniform—all melted away to mix with the ladies or smoke in the conservatory, then the English diplomatist grew very undiplomatic indeed. He was stung every sixty seconds with the thought that the scamp O'Brien might be signaling to Margaret somehow; he did not attempt to imagine how. He was left over the coffee with Brayne, the hoary Yankee who believed in all religions, and Valentin, the grizzled Frenchman who believed in none. They could argue with each other, but neither could appeal to him. After a time this "progressive" logomachy had reached a crisis of tedium; Lord Galloway got up also and sought the drawing room. He lost his way in long passages for some six or eight minutes: till he heard the high-pitched, didactic voice of the doctor, and then the dull voice of the priest, followed by general laughter. They also, he thought with a curse, were probably arguing about "science and religion." But the instant he opened the *salon* door he saw only one thing—he saw what was not there. He saw that Commandant O'Brien was absent, and that Lady Margaret was absent too.

Rising impatiently from the drawing room, as he had from the dining-room, he stamped along the passage once more. His notion of protecting his daughter from the Irish-Algerian n'er-do-well had become something central and even mad in his mind. As he went toward the back of the house, where was Valentin's study, he was surprised to meet his daughter, who swept past with a white, scornful face, which was a second enigma. If she had been with O'Brien, where was O'Brien? If she had not been with O'Brien, where had she been? With a sort of senile and passionate suspicion he groped his way to the dark back parts of the mansion, and eventually found a servants' entrance that opened on to the garden. The moon with her scimitar had now ripped up and rolled away all the storm-wrack. The argent light lit up all four corners of the garden. A tall figure in blue was striding across the lawn toward the study door; a glint of moonlit silver on his facings picked him out as Commandant O'Brien.

He vanished through the French windows into the house, leaving

Lord Galloway in an indescribable temper, at once virulent and vague. The blue-and-silver garden, like a scene in a theater, seemed to taunt him with all that tyrannic tenderness against which his worldly authority was at war. The length and grace of the Irishman's stride enraged him as if he were a rival instead of a father; the moonlight maddened him. He was trapped as if by magic into a garden of troubadours, a Watteau fairyland; and, willing to shake off such amorous imbecilities by speech, he stepped briskly after his enemy. As he did so he tripped over some tree or stone in the grass; looked down at it first with irritation and then a second time with curiosity. The next instant the moon and the tall poplars looked at an unusual sight—an elderly English diplomatist running hard and crying or bellowing as he ran.

His hoarse shouts brought a pale face to the study door, the beaming glasses and worried brow of Dr. Simon, who heard the nobleman's first clear words. Lord Galloway was crying: "A corpse in the grass—a blood-stained corpse." O'Brien at last had gone utterly out of his mind.

"We must tell Valentin at once," said the doctor, when the other had brokenly described all that he had dared to examine. "It is fortunate that he is here;" and even as he spoke, the great detective entered the study, attracted by the cry. It was almost amusing to note his typical transformation; he had come with the common concern of a host and a gentleman, fearing that some guest or servant was ill. When he was told the gory fact, he turned with all his gravity instantly bright and business-like; for this, however abrupt and awful, was his business.

"Strange, gentlemen," he said as they hurried out into the garden, "that I should have hunted mysteries all over the earth, and now one comes and settles in my own backyard. But where is the place?" They crossed the lawn less easily, as a slight mist had begun to rise from the river; but under the guidance of the shaken Galloway they found the body sunken in deep grass—the body of a very tall and broad-shouldered man. He lay face downward, so they could only see that his big shoulders were clad in black cloth, and that his big head was bald, except for a wisp or two of brown hair that clung to his skull like wet seaweed. A scarlet serpent of blood crawled from under his fallen face.

"At least," said Simon, with a deep and singular intonation, "he is none of our party."

"Examine him, doctor," cried Valentin rather sharply. "He may not be dead."

The doctor bent down. "He is not quite cold, but I am afraid he is dead enough," he answered. "Just help me to lift him up."

They lifted him carefully an inch from the ground, and all doubts as to his being really dead were settled at once and frightfully. The head fell away. It had been entirely sundered from the body; whoever had cut his throat had managed to sever the neck as well. Even Valentin was slightly shocked. "He must have been as strong as a gorilla," he muttered.

Not without a shiver, though he was used to anatomical abortions, Dr. Simon lifted the head. It was slightly slashed about the neck and jaw, but the face was substantially unhurt. It was a ponderous, yellow face, at once sunken and swollen, with a hawk-like nose and heavy lids—a face of a wicked Roman emperor, with, perhaps, a distant touch of a Chinese emperor. All present seemed to look at it with the coldest eye of ignorance. Nothing else could be noted about the man except that, as they had lifted his body, they had seen underneath it the white gleam of a shirt-front defaced with a red gleam of blood. As Dr. Simon said, the man had never been of their party. But he might very well have been trying to join it, for he had come dressed for such an occasion.

Valentin went down on his hands and knees and examined with his closest professional attention the grass and ground for some twenty yards round the body, in which he was assisted less skillfully by the doctor, and quite vaguely by the English lord. Nothing rewarded their grovelings except a few twigs, snapped or chopped into very small lengths, which Valentin lifted for an instant's examination and then tossed away.

"Twigs," he said gravely. "Twigs, and a total stranger with his head cut off; that is all there is on this lawn."

There was an almost creepy stillness, and then the unnerved Galloway called out sharply:

"Who's that? Who's that over there by the garden wall?"

A small figure with a foolishly large head drew waveringly near them in the moonlit haze; looked for an instant like a goblin, but turned out to be the harmless little priest whom they had left in the drawing room.

"I say," he said meekly, "there are no gates to this garden, do you know."

Valentin's black brows had come together somewhat crossly, as they did on principle at the sight of the cassock. But he was far too just a man to deny the relevance of the remark. "You are right," he said. "Before we find out how he came to be killed, we may have to find out how he came to be here. Now listen to me, gentlemen. If it can be done without prejudice to my position and duty, we shall all agree that certain distinguished names might well be kept out of this. There are ladies, gentlemen, and there is a foreign ambassador. If we must mark it down as a crime, then it must be followed up as a crime. But till then I can use my own discretion. I am the head of the police; I am so public that I can afford to be private. Please Heaven, I will clear everyone of my own guests before I call in my men to look for anybody else. Gentlemen, upon your honor, you will none of you leave the house till tomorrow at noon; there are bedrooms for all. Simon, I think you know where to find my man, Ivan, in the front hall; he is a confidential man. Tell him to leave another servant on guard and come to me at once. Lord Galloway, you are certainly the best person to tell fetch ladies what has happened, and prevent a panic. They also must stay. Father Brown and I will remain with the body."

When this spirit of the captain spoke in Valentin he was obeyed like a bugle. Dr. Simon went through to the armory and routed out Ivan, the public detective's private detective. Galloway went to the drawing room and told the terrible news tactfully enough, so that by the time the company assembled there the ladies were already startled and already soothed. Meanwhile the good priest and the good atheist stood at the head and foot of the dead man motionless in the moonlight, like symbolic statues of their two philosophies of death.

Ivan, the confidential man with the scar and the moustache, came out of the house like a cannon ball, and came racing across the lawn to Valentin like a dog to his master. His livid face was quite lively with the glow of this domestic detective story, and it was with almost unpleasant eagerness that he asked his master's permission to examine the remains.

"Yes, look, if you like, Ivan," said Valentin, "but don't be long. We must go in and thrash this out in the house."

Ivan lifted the head, and then almost let it drop.

"Why," he gasped, "it's—no, it isn't; it can't be. Do you know this man, sir?"

"No," said Valentin indifferently. "We had better go inside."

Between them they carried the corpse to a sofa in the study, and then all made their way to the drawing room.

The detective sat down at a desk quietly, and even without hesitation; but his eye was the iron eye of a judge at assize. He made a few rapid notes upon paper in front of him, and then said shortly: "Is everybody here?"

"Not Mr. Brayne," said the Duchess of Mont St. Michel, looking around.

"No," said Lord Galloway in a hoarse, harsh voice. "And not Mr. Neil O'Brien, I fancy. I saw that gentleman walking in the garden when the corpse was still warm."

"Ivan," said the detective, "go and fetch Commandant O'Brien and

Mr. Brayne. Mr. Brayne, I know, is finishing a cigar in the dining-room; Commandant O'Brien, I think, is walking up and down the conservatory. I am not sure."

The faithful attendant flashed from the room, and before anyone could stir or speak Valentin went on with the same soldierly swiftness of exposition.

"Everyone here knows that a dead man has been found in the garden, his head cut clean from his body. Dr. Simon, you have examined it. Do you think that to cut a man's throat like that would need great force? Or, perhaps, only a very sharp knife?"

"I should say that it could not be done with a knife at all," said the pale doctor.

"Have you any thought," resumed Valentin, "of a tool with which it could be done?"

"Speaking within modern probabilities, I really haven't," said the doctor, arching his painful brows. "It's not easy to hack a neck through even clumsily, and this was a very clean cut. It could be done with a battle-ax or an old headsman's ax, or an old two-handed sword."

"But, good heavens!" cried the Duchess, almost in hysterics, "there aren't any two-handed swords and battle-axes round here."

Valentin was still busy with the paper in front of him. "Tell me," he said, still writing rapidly, "could it have been done with a long French cavalry sabre?"

A low knocking came at the door, which, for some unreasonable reason, curdled everyone's blood like the knocking in *Macbeth*. Amid that frozen silence Dr. Simon managed to say: "A sabre—yes, I suppose it could."

"Thank you," said Valentin. "Come in, Ivan."

The confidential Ivan opened the door and ushered in Commandant Neil O'Brien, whom he had found at last pacing the garden again.

The Irish officer stood up disordered and defiant on the threshold. "What do you want with me?" he cried.

"Please sit down," said Valentin in pleasant, level tones. "Why, you aren't wearing your sword. Where is it?"

"I left it on the library table," said O'Brien, his brogue deepening in his disturbed mood. "It was a nuisance, it was getting—"

"Ivan," said Valentin, "please go and get the Commandant's sword from the library." Then, as the servant vanished, "Lord Galloway says he saw you leaving the garden just before he found the corpse. What were you doing in the garden?"

The Commandant flung himself recklessly into a chair. "Oh," he cried in pure Irish, "admirin' the moon. Communing with Nature, me bhoy."

A heavy silence sank and endured, and at the end of it came again that trivial and terrible knocking. Ivan reappeared, carrying an empty steel scabbard. "This is all I can find," he said.

"Put it on the table," said Valentin, without looking up.

There was an inhuman silence in the room, like that sea of inhuman silence round the dock of the condemned murderer. The Duchess' weak exclamations had long ago died away. Lord Galloway's swollen hatred was satisfied and even sobered. The voice that came was quite unexpected.

"I think I can tell you," cried Lady Margaret, in that clear, quivering voice with which a courageous woman speaks publicly. "I can tell you what Mr. O'Brien was doing in the garden, since he is bound to silence. He was asking me to marry him. I refused. I said in my family circumstances I could give him nothing but my respect. He was a little angry at that; he did not seem to think much of my respect. I wonder," she added, with rather a wan smile, "if he will care at all for it now. For I offer it him now. I will swear anywhere that he never did a thing like this."

Lord Galloway had edged up to his daughter, and was intimidating her in what he imagined to be an undertone. "Hold your tongue, Maggie," he said in a thunderous whisper. "Why should you shield the fellow? Where's his sword? Where's his confounded cavalry—"

He stopped because of the singular stare with which his daughter was regarding him, a look that was indeed a lurid magnet for the whole group.

"You old fool!" she said in a low voice without pretense of piety, "what do you suppose you are trying to prove? I tell you this man was innocent while with me. But if he wasn't innocent, he was still with me. If he murdered a man in the garden, who was it who must have seen— who must at least have known? Do you hate Neil so much as to put your own daughter—"

Lady Galloway screamed. Everyone else sat tingling at the touch of those satanic tragedies that have been between lovers before now. They saw the proud, white face of the Scotch aristocrat and her lover, the Irish adventurer, like old portraits in a dark house. The long silence was full of formless historical memories of murdered husbands and poisonous paramours.

In the center of this morbid silence an innocent voice said: "Was it a very long cigar?"

The change of thought was so sharp that they had to look round to see who had spoken.

"I mean," said little Father Brown, from the corner of the room, "I mean that cigar Mr. Brayne is finishing. It seems nearly as long as a walking stick."

Despite the irrelevance there was assent as well as irritation in Valentin's face as he lifted his head.

"Quite right," he remarked sharply. "Ivan, go and see about Mr. Brayne again, and bring him here at once."

The instant the factotum had closed the door, Valentin addressed the girl with an entirely new earnestness.

"Lady Margaret," he said, "we all feel, I am sure, both gratitude and admiration for your act in rising above your lower dignity and explaining the Commandant's conduct. But there is a hiatus still. Lord Galloway, I understand, met you passing from the study to the drawing room, and it was only some minutes afterward that he found the garden and the Commandant still walking there."

"You have to remember," replied Margaret, with a faint irony in her voice, "that I had just refused him, so we should scarcely have come back arm in arm. He is a gentleman, anyhow; and he loitered behind— and so got charged with murder."

"In those few moments," said Valentin gravely, "he might really—"

The knock came again, and Ivan put in his scarred face.

"Beg pardon, sir," he said, "but Mr. Brayne has left the house."

"Left!" cried Valentin, and rose for the first time to his feet.

"Gone. Scooted. Evaporated," replied Ivan in humorous French. "His hat and coat are gone, too, and I'll tell you something to cap it all. I ran outside the house to find any traces of him, and I found one, and a big trace, too."

"What do you mean?" asked Valentin.

"I'll show you," said his servant, and reappeared with a flashing naked cavalry sabre, streaked with blood about the point and edge. Everyone in the room eyed it as if it were a thunderbolt; but the experienced Ivan went on quite quietly:

"I found this," he said, "flung among the bushes fifty yards up the road to Paris. In other words, I found it just where your respectable Mr. Brayne threw it when he ran away."

There was again a silence, but of a new sort. Valentin took the sabre, examined it, reflected with unaffected concentration of thought, and then turned a respectful face to O'Brien. "Commandant," he said, "we trust you will always produce this weapon if it is wanted for police examination. Meanwhile," he added, slapping the steel back in the ringing scabbard, "let me return you your sword."

At the military symbolism of the action the audience could hardly refrain from applause.

For Neil O'Brien, indeed, that gesture was the turning point of existence. By the time he was wandering in the mysterious garden again in the colors of the morning the tragic futility of his ordinary mien had fallen from him; he was a man with many reasons for happiness. Lord Galloway was a gentleman, and had offered him an apology. Lady Margaret was something better than a lady, a woman at least, and had perhaps given him something better than an apology, as they drifted among the old flower beds before breakfast. The whole company was more lighthearted and humane, for though the riddle of the death remained, the load of suspicion was lifted off them all, and sent flying off to Paris with the strange millionaire—a man they hardly knew. The devil was cast out of the house—he had cast himself out.

Still, the riddle remained, and when O'Brien threw himself on a garden seat beside Dr. Simon, that keenly scientific person at once resumed it. He did not get much talk out of O'Brien, whose thoughts were on pleasanter things.

"I can't say it interests me much," said the Irishman frankly, "especially as it seems pretty plain now. Apparently Brayne hated this stranger for some reason; lured him into the garden, and killed him with my sword. Then he fled to the city, tossing the sword away as he went. By the way, Ivan tells me the dead man had a Yankee dollar in his pocket. So he was a countryman of Brayne's, and that seems to clinch it. I don't see any difficulties about the business."

"There are five colossal difficulties," said the doctor quietly, "like high walls within walls. Don't mistake me. I don't doubt that Brayne did it; his flight, I fancy, proves that. But as to how he did it. First difficulty: Why should a man kill another man with a great hulking sabre, when he can almost kill him with a pocket knife and put it back in his pocket? Second difficulty: Why was there no noise or outcry? Does a man commonly see another come up waving a scimitar and offer no remarks? Third difficulty: A servant watched the front door all the evening; and a rat cannot get into Valentin's garden anywhere. How did the dead man get into the garden? Fourth difficulty: Given the same conditions, how did Brayne get out of the garden?"

"And the fifth," said Neil, with eyes fixed on the English priest who was coming slowly up the path.

"Is a trifle, I suppose," said the doctor, "but I think an odd one. When

I first saw how the head had been slashed, I supposed the assassin had struck more than once. But on examination I found many cuts across the truncated section; in other words, they were struck *after* the head was off. Did Brayne hate his foe so fiendishly that he stood sabring his body in the moonlight?"

"Horrible!" said O'Brien, and shuddered.

The little priest, Brown, had arrived while they were talking, and had waited, with characteristic shyness, till they had finished. Then he said awkwardly:

"I say, I'm sorry to interrupt. But I was sent to tell you the news!"

"News?" repeated Simon, and stared at him rather painfully through his glasses.

"Yes, I'm sorry," said Father Brown mildly. "There's been another murder, you know."

Both men on the seat sprang up, leaving it rocking.

"And, what's stranger still," continued the priest, with his dull eye on the rhododendrons, "it's the same disgusting sort; it's another beheading. They found the second head actually bleeding into the river, a few yards along Brayne's road to Paris; so they suppose that he—"

"Great Heaven!" cried O'Brien. "Is Brayne a monomaniac?"

"There are American vendettas," said the priest impassively. Then he added: "They want you to come to the library and see it."

Commandant O'Brien followed the others toward the inquest, feeling decidedly sick. As a soldier, he loathed all this secretive carnage; where were these extravagant amputations going to stop? First one head was hacked off, and then another; in this case (he told himself bitterly) it was not true that two heads were better than one. As he crossed the study he almost staggered at a shocking coincidence. Upon Valentin's table lay the colored picture of yet a third bleeding head; and it was the head of Valentin himself. A second glance showed him it was only a Nationalist paper, called *The Guillotine*, which every week showed one of its political opponents with rolling eyes and writhing features just after execution; for Valentin was an anti-clerical of some note. But O'Brien was an Irishman, with a kind of chastity even in his sins; and his gorge rose against that great brutality of the intellect which belongs only to France. He felt Paris as a whole, from the grotesques on the Gothic churches to the gross caricatures in the newspapers. He remembered the gigantic jests of the Revolution. He saw the whole city as one ugly energy, from the sanguinary sketch lying on Valentin's table up to where, above a mountain and forest of gargoyles, the great devil grins on Notre Dame.

The library was long, low, and dark; what light entered it shot from under low blinds and had still some of the ruddy tinge of morning. Valentin and his servant Ivan were waiting for them at the upper end of a long, slightly-sloping desk, on which lay the mortal remains, looking enormous in the twilight. The big black figure and yellow face of the man found in the garden confronted them essentially unchanged. The second head, which had been fished from among the river reeds that morning, lay streaming and dripping beside it; Valentin's men were still seeking to recover the rest of this second corpse, which was supposed to be afloat. Father Brown, who did not seem to share O'Brien's sensibilities in the least, went up to the second head and examined it with his blinking care. It was little more than a mop of wet white hair, fringed with silver fire in the red and level morning light; the face, which seemed of an ugly, empurpled and perhaps criminal type, had been much battered against trees or stones as it tossed in the water.

"Good morning, Commandant O'Brien," said Valentin, with quiet cordiality. "You have heard of Brayne's last experiment in butchery, I suppose?"

Father Brown was still bending over the head with white hair, and he said, without looking up:

"I suppose it is quite certain that Brayne cut off this head, too."

"Well, it seems common sense," said Valentin, with his hands in his pockets. "Killed in the same way as the other. Found within a few yards of the other. And sliced by the same weapon, which we know he carried away."

"Yes, yes, I know," replied Father Brown submissively. "Yet, you know, I doubt whether Brayne could have cut off this head."

"Why not?" inquired Dr. Simon, with a rational stare.

"Well, doctor," said the priest, looking up blinking, "can a man cut off his own head? I don't know."

O'Brien felt an insane universe crashing about his ears; but the doctor sprang forward with impetuous practicality and pushed back the wet white hair.

"Oh, there's no doubt it's Brayne," said the priest quietly. "He had exactly that chip in the left ear."

The detective, who had been regarding the priest with steady and glittering eyes, opened his clenched mouth and said sharply: "You seem to know a lot about him, Father Brown."

"I do," said the little man simply. "I've been about with him for some weeks. He was thinking of joining our church."

The star of the fanatic sprang into Valentin's eyes; he strode toward the priest with clenched hands. "And, perhaps," he cried, with a blasting sneer, "perhaps he was also thinking of leaving all his money to your church."

"Perhaps he was," said Brown stolidly. "It is possible."

"In that case," cried Valentin, with a dreadful smile, "you may indeed know a great deal about him. About his life and about his—"

Commandant O'Brien laid a hand on Valentin's arm. "Drop that slanderous rubbish, Valentin," he said, "or there may be more swords yet."

But Valentin (under the steady, humble gaze of the priest) had already recovered himself. "Well," he said shortly, "people's private opinions can wait. You gentlemen are still bound by your promise to stay; you must enforce it on yourselves—and on each other. Ivan here will tell you anything more you want to know. I must get to business and write to the authorities. We can't keep this quiet any longer. I shall be writing in my study if there is any more news."

"Is there any more news, Ivan?" asked Dr. Simon, as the chief of police strode out of the room.

"Only one more thing, I think, sir," said Ivan, wrinkling up his gray old face, "but that's important, too, in its way. There's that old buffer you found on the lawn," and he pointed without pretense of reverence at the big black body with the yellow head. "We've found out who he is, anyhow."

"Indeed!" cried the astonished doctor, "and who is he?"

"His name was Arnold Becker," said the under-detective, "though he went by many aliases. He was a wandering sort of scamp, and is known to have been in America; so that was where Brayne got his knife into him. We didn't have much to do with him ourselves, for he worked mostly in Germany. We've communicated, of course, with the German police. But, oddly enough, there was a twin brother of his, named Louis Becker, whom we had a great deal to do with. In fact, we found it necessary to guillotine him only yesterday. Well, it's a rum thing, gentlemen, but when I saw that fellow flat on the lawn I had the greatest jump of my life. If I hadn't seen Louis Becker guillotined with my own eyes, I'd have sworn it was Louis Becker lying there in the grass. Then, of course, I remembered his twin brother in Germany, and following up the clue—"

The explanatory Ivan stopped, for the excellent reason that nobody was listening to him. The Commandant and the doctor were both staring at Father Brown, who had sprung stiffly to his feet, and was holding his temples tight like a man in sudden and violent pain.

"Stop, stop, stop!" he cried. "Stop talking a minute, for I see half. Will God give me strength? Will my brain make the one jump and see all? Heaven help me! I used to be fairly good at thinking. I could para-phrase any page in Aquinas once. Will my head split—or will it see? I see half—I only see half."

He buried his head in his hands, and stood in a sort of rigid torture of thought or prayer, while the other three could only go on staring at this last prodigy of their wild twelve hours.

When Father Brown's hands fell they showed a face quite fresh and serious, like a child's. He heaved a huge sigh, and said: "Let us get this said and done with as quickly as possible. Look here, this will be the quickest way to convince you all of the truth." He turned to the doctor. "Dr. Simon," he said, "you have a strong headpiece, and I heard you this morning asking the five hardest questions about this business. Well, if you will ask them again, I will answer them."

Simon's pince-nez dropped from his nose in his doubt and wonder, but he answered at once. "Well, the first question, you know, is why a man should kill another with a clumsy sabre at all when a man can kill with a bodkin?"

"A man cannot behead with a bodkin," said Brown calmly, "and for *this* murder beheading was absolutely necessary."

"Why?" asked O'Brien, with interest.

"And the next question?" asked Father Brown.

"Well, why didn't the man cry out or anything?" asked the doctor. "Sabres in gardens are certainly unusual."

"Twigs," said the priest gloomily, and turned to the window which looked on the scene of death. "No one saw the point of the twigs. Why should they lie on that lawn (look at it) so far from any tree? They were not snapped off; they were chopped off. The murderer occupied his enemy with some tricks with the sabre, showing how he could cut a branch in mid-air, or what-not. Then, while his enemy bent down to see the result, a silent slash, and the head fell."

"Well," said the doctor slowly, "that seems plausible enough. But my next two questions will stump anyone."

The priest still stood looking critically out of the window and waited.

"You know how all the garden was sealed up like an air-tight cham-ber," went on the doctor. "Well, how did the strange man get into the garden?"

Without turning round, the little priest answered: "There never was any strange man in the garden."

There was a silence, and then a sudden cackle of almost childish laughter relieved the strain. The absurdity of Brown's remark moved Ivan to open taunts.

"Oh!" he cried, "then we didn't lug a great fat corpse on to a sofa last night? He hadn't got into the garden, I suppose?"

"Got into the garden?" repeated Brown reflectively. "No, not entirely."

"Hang it all," cried Simon, "a man gets into a garden, or he doesn't."

"Not necessarily," said the priest, with a faint smile. "What is the next question, doctor?"

"I fancy you're ill," exclaimed Dr. Simon sharply, "but I'll ask the next question if you like. How did Brayne get out of the garden?"

"He didn't get out of the garden," said the priest, still looking out of the window.

"Didn't get out of the garden?" exploded Simon.

"Not completely," said Father Brown.

Simon shook his fists in a frenzy of French logic. "A man gets out of a garden, or he doesn't," he cried.

"Not always," said Father Brown.

Dr. Simon sprang to his feet impatiently. "I have no time to spare on such senseless talk," he cried angrily. "If you can't understand a man being on one side of a wall or the other, I won't trouble you further."

"Doctor," said the cleric very gently, "we have always got on very pleasantly together. If only for the sake of old friendship, stop and tell me your fifth question."

The impatient Simon sank into a chair by the door and said briefly: "The head and shoulders were cut about in a queer way. It seemed to be done after death."

"Yes," said the motionless priest, "it was done so as to make you assume exactly the one simple falsehood that you did assume. It was done to make you take for granted that the head belonged to the body."

The borderland of the brain, where all the monsters are made, moved horribly in the Gaelic O'Brien. He felt the chaotic presence of all the horse-men and fish-women that man's unnatural fancy has begotten. A voice older than his first fathers seemed saying in his ear: "Keep out of the monstrous garden where grows the tree with double fruit. Avoid the evil garden where died the man with two heads." Yet, while these shameful symbolic shapes passed across the ancient mirror of his Irish soul, his Frenchified intellect was quite alert, and was watching the odd priest as closely and incredulously as all the rest.

Father Brown had turned round at last, and stood against the window, with his face in dense shadow; but even in that shadow they could see it was pale as ashes. Nevertheless, he spoke quite sensibly, as if there were no Gaelic souls on earth.

"Gentlemen," he said, "you did not find the strange body of Becker in the garden. You did not find any strange body in the garden. In face of Dr. Simon's rationalism, I still affirm that Becker was only partly present. Look here!" (pointing to the black bulk of the mysterious corpse) "you never saw that man in your lives. Did you ever see this man?"

He rapidly rolled away the bald, yellow head of the unknown, and put in its place the white-maned head beside it. And there, complete, unified, unmistakable, lay Julius K. Brayne.

"The murderer," went on Brown quietly, "hacked off his enemy's head and flung the sword far over the wall. But he was too clever to fling the sword only. He flung the *head* over the wall also. Then he had only to clap on another head to the corpse, and (as he insisted on a private inquest) you all imagined a totally new man."

"Clap on another head!" said O'Brien staring. "What other head? Heads don't grow on garden bushes, do they?"

"No," said Father Brown huskily, and looking at his boots; "there is only one place where they grow. They grow in the basket of the guillotine, beside which the chief of police, Aristide Valentin, was standing not an hour before the murder. Oh, my friends, hear me a minute more before you tear me in pieces. Valentin is an honest man, if being mad for an arguable cause is honesty. But did you never see in that cold, gray eye of his that he is mad? He would do anything, *anything,* to break what he calls the superstition of the Cross. He has fought for it and starved for it, and now he has murdered for it. Brayne's crazy millions had hitherto been scattered among so many sects that they did little to alter the balance of things. But Valentin heard a whisper that Brayne, like so many scatter-brained skeptics, was drifting to us, and that was quite a different thing. Brayne would pour supplies into the impoverished and pugnacious Church of France; he would support six Nationalist newspapers like *The Guillotine.* The battle was already balanced on a point, and the fanatic took flame at the risk. He resolved to destroy the millionaire, and he did it as one would expect the greatest of detectives to commit his only crime. He abstracted the severed head of Becker on some criminological excuse, and took it home in his official box. He had that last argument with Brayne, that Lord Galloway did not hear the end of; that failing, he led him out into the sealed garden, talked about swordsmanship, used twigs and a sabre for illustration, and—"

Ivan of the Scar sprang up. "You lunatic," he yelled; "you'll go to my master now, if I take you by—"

"Why, I was going there," said Brown heavily. "I must ask him to confess, and all that."

Driving the unhappy Brown before them like a hostage or sacrifice, they rushed together into the sudden stillness of Valentin's study.

The great detective sat at his desk apparently too occupied to hear their turbulent entrance. They paused a moment, and then something in the look of that upright and elegant back made the doctor run forward suddenly. A touch and a glance showed him that there was a small box of pills at Valentin's elbow, and that Valentin was dead in his chair; and on the blind face of the suicide was more than the pride of Cato.

Problem at Sea

Author: Agatha Christie (1890–1976)

Detective: Hercule Poirot (1920)

The retired Belgian police detective Hercule Poirot, though born elderly in his creator's 1920 first novel *The Mysterious Affair at Styles,* remained on the scene in new cases for more than half a century. While many would claim another senior-citizen sleuth, Miss Jane Marple, is Christie's greatest character, the Poirot saga contains more brilliant strokes of authorial mendacity (in such novels as *The Murder of Roger Ackroyd* [1926], *Murder on the Orient Express* [1934], *The ABC Murders* [1936], and *Death on the Nile* [1937]) than the shorter skein of Marple adventures.

Unlike the three sleuths who precede him in this volume, but in common with most who follow, Poirot was not primarily a short-story character. The Least Suspected Person solutions he specialized in were most successfully developed at book length, and his creator's best short stories tend to be non-series tales like "Accident," "Philomel Cottage," and "The Witness for the Prosecution." "Problem at Sea," though, embodies the kind of cunning misdirection that marks the longer works, one of which (the 1941 novel *Evil Under the Sun*) opens with a similar situation but proceeds in quite a different direction.

Colonel Clapperton!" said General Forbes. He said it with an effect midway between a snort and a sniff.

Miss Ellie Henderson leaned forward, a strand of her soft gray hair blowing across her face. Her eyes, dark and snapping, gleamed with a wicked pleasure.

"Such a soldierly-looking man!" she said with malicious intent, and smoothed back the lock of hair to await the result.

"Soldierly!" exploded General Forbes. He tugged at his military mustache and his face became bright red.

"In the Guards, wasn't he?" murmured Miss Henderson, completing her work.

"Guards? Guards? Pack of nonsense. Fellow was on the music hall stage! Fact! Joined up and was out in France counting tins of plums and apples. Huns dropped a stray bomb and he went home with a flesh wound in the arm. Somehow or other got into Lady Carrington's hospital."

"So that's how they met."

"Fact! Fellow played the wounded hero. Lady Carrington had no sense and oceans of money. Old Carrington had been in munitions. She'd been a widow only six months. This fellow snaps her up in no time. She wangled him a job at the War Office. Colonel Clapperton! Pah!" he snorted.

"And before the war he was on the music hall stage," mused Miss Henderson, trying to reconcile the distinguished gray-haired Colonel Clapperton with a red-nosed comedian singing mirth-provoking songs.

"Fact!" said General Forbes. "Heard it from old Bassington-french. And lie heard it from old Badger Cotterill, who'd got it from Snooks Parker."

Miss Henderson nodded brightly. "That does seem to settle it!" she said.

A fleeting smile showed for a minute on the face of a small man sitting near them. Miss Henderson noticed the smile. She was observant. It had shown appreciation of the irony underlying her last remark—irony that the General never for a moment suspected.

The General himself did not notice the smile. He glanced at his watch, rose, and remarked: "Exercise. Got to keep oneself fit on a boat," and passed out through the open door onto the deck.

Miss Henderson glanced at the man who had smiled. It was a well-bred glance indicating that she was ready to enter into conversation with a fellow traveler.

"He is energetic—yes?" said the little man.

"He goes round the deck forty-eight times exactly," said Miss Henderson. "What an old gossip! And they say we are the scandal-loving sex."

"What an impoliteness!"

"Frenchmen are always polite," said Miss Henderson—there was the nuance of a question in her voice.

The little man responded promptly. "Belgian, Mademoiselle."

"Oh! Belgian."

"Hercule Poirot. At your service."

The name aroused some memory. Surely she had heard it before? "Are you enjoying this trip, M. Poirot?"

"Frankly, no. It was an imbecility to allow myself to be persuaded to come. I detest *la mer*. Never does it remain tranuil—no, not for a little minute."

"Well, you admit it's quite calm now."

M. Poirot admitted this grudgingly. "*A ce moment,* yes. That is why I revive. I once more interest myself in what passes around me—your very adept handling of the General Forbes, for instance."

"You mean—" Miss Henderson paused.

Hercule Poirot bowed. "Your methods of extracting the scandalous matter. Admirable!"

Miss Henderson laughed in an unashamed manner. "That touch about the Guards? I knew that would bring the old boy up spluttering and gasping." She leaned forward confidentially. "I admit I like scandal—the more ill-natured, the better!"

Poirot looked thoughtfully at her—her slim well-preserved figure, her keen, dark eyes, her gray hair; a woman of forty-five who was content to look her age.

Ellie said abruptly: "I have it! Aren't you the great detective?"

Poirot bowed. "You are too amiable, Mademoiselle." But he made no disclaimer.

"How thrilling," said Miss Henderson. "Are you 'hot on the trail' as they say in books? Have we a criminal secretly in our midst? Or am I being indiscreet?"

"Not at all. Not at all. It pains me to disappoint your expectations, but I am simply here, like everyone else, to amuse myself."

He said it in such a gloomy voice that Miss Henderson laughed.

"Oh! Well, you will be able to get ashore tomorrow at Alexandria. You have been to Egypt before?"

"Never, Mademoiselle."

Miss Henderson rose somewhat abruptly.

"I think I shall join the General on his constitutional," she announced.

Poirot sprang politely to his feet.

She gave him a little nod and passed out onto the deck.

A faint puzzled look showed for a moment in Poirot's eyes, then, a little smile creasing his lips, he rose, put his head through the door and glanced down the deck. Miss Henderson was leaning against the rail talking to a tall, soldierly-looking man.

Poirot's smile deepened. He drew himself back into the smoking room with the same exaggerated care with which a tortoise withdraws itself into its shell. For the moment he had the smoking room to himself, though he rightly conjectured that that would not last long.

It did not. Mrs. Clapperton, her carefully waved platinum head protected with a net, her massaged and dieted form dressed in a smart sports suit, came through the door from the bar with the purposeful air of a woman who has always been able to pay top price for anything she needed.

She said: "John—? Oh! Good morning, M. Poirot—have you seen John?"

"He's on the starboard deck, Madame. Shall I—"

She arrested him with a gesture. "I'll sit here a minute." She sat down in a regal fashion in the chair opposite him. From the distance she had looked a possible twenty-eight. Now, in spite of her exquisitely made-up face, her delicately plucked eyebrows, she looked not her actual forty-nine years, but a possible fifty-five. Her eyes were a hard pale blue with tiny pupils.

"I was sorry not to have seen you at dinner last night," she said. "It was just a shade choppy, of course—"

"*Précisément*," said Poirot with feeling.

"Luckily, I am an excellent sailor," said Mrs. Clapperton. "I say luckily, because, with my weak heart, seasickness would probably be the death of me."

"You have a weak heart, Madame?"

"Yes, I have to be most careful. I must not overtire myself! All the specialists say so!" Mrs. Clapperton had embarked on the-to-her-ever-fascinating topic of her health. "John, poor darling, wears himself out trying to prevent me from doing too much. I live so intensely, if you know what I mean, M. Poirot?"

"Yes, yes."

"He always says to me: 'Try to be more of a vegetable, Adeline.' But I can't. Life was meant to be lived, I feel. As a matter of fact I wore myself out as a girl in the war. My hospital—you've heard of my hospital? Of course I had nurses and matrons and all that—but I actually ran it." She sighed.

"Your vitality is marvelous, dear lady," said Poirot, with the slightly mechanical air of one responding to his cue.

Mrs. Clapperton gave a girlish laugh.

"Everyone tells me how young I am! It's absurd. I never try to pretend I'm a day less than forty-three," she continued with slightly mendacious candor, "but a lot of people find it hard to believe. 'You're so alive, Adeline,' they say to me. But really, M. Poirot, what would one be if one wasn't alive?"

"Dead," said Poirot.

Mrs. Clapperton frowned. The reply was not to her liking. The man, she decided, was trying to be funny. She got up and said coldly: "I must find John."

As she stepped through the door she dropped her handbag. It opened and the contents flew far and wide. Poirot rushed gallantly to the rescue. It was some few minutes before the lipsticks, vanity boxes, cigarette case and lighter, and other odds and ends were collected. Mrs. Clapperton thanked him politely, then she swept down the deck and said, "John—"

Colonel Clapperton was still deep in conversation with Miss Henderson. He swung round and came quickly to meet his wife. He bent over her protectively. Her deck chair—was it in the right place? Wouldn't it be better—? His manner was courteous—full of gentle consideration. Clearly an adored wife spoiled by an adoring husband.

Miss Ellie Henderson looked out at the horizon as though something about it rather disgusted her.

Standing in the smoking-room door, Poirot looked on.

A hoarse quavering voice behind him said:

"I'd take a hatchet to that woman if I were her husband." The old gentleman known disrespectfully among the Younger Set on board as the Grandfather of All the Tea Planters had just shuffled in. "Boy!" he called. "Get me a whiskey peg."

Poirot stooped to retrieve a torn scrap of notepaper, an overlooked item from the contents of Mrs. Clapperton's bag. Part of a prescription, he noted, containing digitalin. He put it in his pocket, meaning to restore it to Mrs. Clapperton later.

"Yes," went on the aged passenger. "Poisonous woman. I remember a woman like that in Poona. In '87 that was."

"Did anyone take a hatchet to her?" inquired Poirot.

The old gentleman shook his head sadly.

"Worried her husband into his grave within the year. Clapperton ought to assert himself. Gives his wife her head too much."

"She holds the purse strings," said Poirot gravely.

"Ha ha!" chuckled the old gentleman. "You've put the matter in a nutshell. Holds the purse strings. Ha ha!"

Two girls burst into the smoking room. One had a round face with freckles and dark hair streaming out in a windswept confusion, the other had freckles and curly chestnut hair.

"A rescue, a rescue!" cried Kitty Mooney. "Pam and I are going to rescue Colonel Clapperton."

"From his wife," gasped Pamela Cregan.

"We think he's a pet. . . ."

"And she's just awful—she won't let him do anything," the two girls exclaimed.

"And if he isn't with her, he's usually grabbed by the Henderson woman. . . .

"Who's quite nice. But terribly old . . ."

They ran out, gasping in between giggles:

"A rescue—rescue . . ."

That the rescue of Colonel Clapperton was no isolated sally, but a fixed project, was made clear that same evening when the eighteen-year-old Pam Cregan came up to Hercule Poirot, and murmured: "Watch us, M. Poirot. He's going to be cut out from under her nose and taken to walk in the moonlight on the boat deck."

It was just at that moment that Colonel Calpperton was saying: "I grant you the price of a Rolls Royce. But it's practically good for a lifetime. Now my car—"

"My car, I think, John." Mrs. Clapperton's voice was shrill and penetrating.

He showed no annoyance at her ungraciousness. Either he was used to it by this time, or else

Or else? thought Poirot and let himself speculate.

"Certainly, my dear, your car," Clapperton bowed to his wife and finished what he had been saying, perfectly unruffled.

Voila ce qu'on appelle le pukka sahib, thought Poirot. "But the General Forbes says that Clapperton is no gentleman at all. I wonder now."

There was a suggestion of bridge. Mrs. Clapperton, General Forbes and a hawkeyed couple sat down to it. Miss Henderson had excused herself and gone out on deck.

"What about your husband?" asked General Forbes, hesitating.

"John won't play," said Mrs. Clapperton. "Most tiresome of him."

The four bridge players began shuffling the cards.

Pam and Kitty advanced on Colonel Clapperton. Each one took an arm.

"You're coming with us!" said Pam. "To the boat deck. There's a moon."

"Don't be foolish, John," said Mrs. Clapperton. "You'll catch a chill."

"Not with us, he won't," said Kitty. "We're hot stuff!"

He went with them, laughing.

Poirot noticed that Mrs. Clapperton said No Bid to her initial bid of two clubs.

He strolled out onto the promenade deck. Miss Henderson was standing by the rail. She looked round expectantly as he came to stand beside her and he saw the drop in her expression.

They chatted for a while. Then presently as he fell silent she asked: "What are you thinking about?"

Poirot replied: "I am wondering about my knowledge of English. Mrs. Clapperton said: 'John won't play bridge.' Is not 'can't play' the usual term?"

"She takes it as a personal insult that he doesn't, I suppose," said Ellie dryly. "The man was a fool ever to have married her."

In the darkness Poirot smiled. "You don't think it's just possible that the marriage may be a success?" he asked diffidently.

"With a woman like that?"

Poirot shrugged his shoulders. "Many odious women have devoted husbands. An enigma of nature. You will admit that nothing she says or does appears to gall him."

Miss Henderson was considering her reply when Mrs. Clapperton's voice floated out through the smoking-room window.

"No, I don't think I will play another rubber. So stuffy. I think I'll go up and get some air on the boat deck."

"Good night," said Miss Henderson. "I'm going to bed." She disappeared abruptly.

Poirot strolled forward to the lounge—deserted save for Colonel Clapperton and the two girls. He was doing card tricks for them, and noting the dexterity of his shuffling and handling of the cards, Poirot rememberd the General's story of a career on the musichall stage.

"I see you enjoy the cards even though you do not play bridge," he remarked.

"I've my reasons for not playing bridge," said Clapperton, his charming smile breaking out. "I'll show you. We'll play one hand."

He dealt the cards rapidly. "Pick up your hands. Well, what about it?" He laughed at the bewildered expression on Kitty's face. He laid down his hand and the others followed suit. Kitty held the entire club suit, M. Poirot the hearts, Pam the diamonds, and Colonel Clapperton the spades.

"You see?" he said. "A man who can deal his partner and his adversaries any hand he pleases had better stand aloof from a friendly game! If the luck goes too much his way, ill-natured things might be said."

"Oh!" gasped Kitty. "How could you do that? It all looked perfectly ordinary."

"The quickness of the hand deceives the eye," said Poirot sententiously—and caught the sudden change in the Colonel's expression.

It was a though he realized that he had been off his guard for a moment or two.

Poirot smiled. The conjuror had shown himself through the mask of the pukka sahib.

The ship reached Alexandria at dawn the following morning.

As Poirot came up from breakfast he found the two girls all ready to go on shore. They were talking to Colonel Clapperton.

"We ought to get off now," urged Kitty. "The passport people will be going off the ship presently. You'll come with us, won't you? You wouldn't let us go ashore all by ourselves? Awful things might happen to us."

"I certainly don't think you ought to go by yourselves," said Clapperton, smiling. "But I'm not sure my wife feels up to it."

"That's too bad," said Pam. "But she can have a nice long rest."

Colonel Clapperton looked a little irresolute. Evidently the desire to play truant was strong upon him. He noticed Poirot.

"Hullo, M. Poirot, you going ashore?"

"No, I think not," M. Poirot replied.

"I'll—I'll—just have a word with Adeline," decided Colonel Clapperton.

"We'll come with you," said Pam. She flashed a wink at Poirot. "Perhaps we can persuade her to come too," she added gravely.

Colonel Clapperton seemed to welcome this suggestion. He looked decidedly relieved.

"Come along then, the pair of you," he said lightly. They all three went along the passage of B deck together.

Poirot, whose cabin was just opposite the Clappertons', followed them out of curiosity.

Colonel Clapperton rapped a little nervously at the cabin door.

"Adeline, my dear, are you up?"

The sleepy voice of Mrs. Clapperton from within replied: "Oh, brother—what is it?"

"It's John. What about going ashore?"

"Certainly not." The voice was shrill and decisive. "I've had a very bad night. I shall stay in bed most of the day."

Pam nipped in quickly, "Oh, Mrs. Clapperton, I'm so sorry. We did so want you to come with us. Are you sure you're not up to it?"

"I'm quite certain." Mrs. Clapperton's voice sounded even shriller.

The Colonel was turning the door handle without result.

"What is it, John? The door's locked. I don't want to be disturbed by the stewards."

"Sorry, my dear, sorry. Just wanted my Baedeker."

"Well, you can't have it," snapped Mrs. Clapperton. "I'm not going to get out of bed. Do go away, John, and let me have a little peace."

"Certainly, certainly, my dear." The Colonel backed away from the door. Pam and Kitty closed in on him.

"Let's start at once. Thank goodness your hat's on your head. Oh! gracious—your passport isn't in the cabin, is it?"

"As a matter of fact it's in my pocket—" began the Colonel.

Kitty squeezed his arm. "Glory be!" she exclaimed. "Now, come on."

Leaning over the rail, Poirot watched the three of them leave the ship.

He heard a faint intake of breath beside him and turned his head to see Miss Henderson. Her eyes were fastened on the three retreating figures.

"So they've gone ashore," she said flatly.

"Yes. Are you going?"

She had a shade hat, he noticed, and a smart bag and shoes. There was a shore-going appearance about her. Nevertheless, after the most infinitesimal of pauses, she shook her head.

"No," she said. "I think I'll stay on board. I have a lot of letters to write."

She turned and left him.

Puffing after his morning tour of forty-eight rounds of the deck, General Forbes took her place. "Aha!" he exclaimed as his eyes noted the retreating figures of the Colonel and the two girls. "So that's the game! Where's the Madam?"

Poirot explained that Mrs. Clapperton was having a quiet day in bed.

"Don't you believe it!" The old warrior closed one knowing eye. "She'll be up for tiffin—and if the poor devil's found to be absent without leave, there'll be ructions."

But the General's prognostications were not fulfilled. Mrs. Clapperton did not appear at lunch and by the time the Colonel and his attendant damsels returned to the ship at four o'clock, she had not shown herself.

Poirot was in his cabin and heard the husband's slightly guilty knock on his cabin door. Heard the knock repeated, the cabin door tried, and finally heard the Colonel's call to a steward.

"Look here, I can't get an answer. Have you a key?"

Poirot rose quickly from his bunk and came out into the passage.

The news went like wildfire round the ship. With horrified incredulity people heard that Mrs. Clapperton had been found dead in her bunk—a native dagger driven through her heart. A string of amber beads was found on the floor of her cabin.

Rumor succeeded rumor. All bead sellers who had been allowed on board that day were being rounded up and questioned! A large sum in cash had disappeared from a drawer in the cabin! The notes had been traced! They had not been traced! Jewelry worth a fortune had been taken! No jewelry had been taken at all! A steward had been arrested and had confessed to the murder!

"What is the truth of it all?" demanded Miss Ellie Henderson, waylaying Poirot. Her face was pale and troubled.

"My dear lady, how should I know?"

"Of course you know," said Miss Henderson.

It was late in the evening. Most people had retired to their cabins. Miss Henderson led Poirot to a couple of deck chairs on the sheltered side of the ship. "Now tell me," she commanded.

Poirot surveyed her thoughtfully. "It's an interesting case," he said.

"Is it true that she had some very valuable jewelry stolen?"

Poirot shook his head. "No. No jewelry was taken. A small amount of loose cash that was in a drawer has disappeared, though."

"I'll never feel safe on a ship again," said Miss Henderson with a shiver. "Any clue as to which of those coffee-colored brutes did it?"

"No," said Hercule Poirot. "The whole thing is rather—strange."

"What do you mean?" asked Ellie sharply.

Poirot spread out his hands. "*Eh bien*—take the facts. Mrs. Clapperton had been dead at least five hours when she was found. Some money had disappeared. A string of beads was on the floor by her bed. The door was locked and the key was missing. The window-*window*, not porthole—gives on the deck and was open."

"Well?" asked the woman impatiently.

"Do you not think it is curious for a murder to be committed under those particular circumstances? Remember that the postcard sellers, money changers, and bead sellers who are allowed on board are all well known to the police."

"The stewards usually lock your cabin, all the same," Ellie pointed out.

"Yes, to prevent any chance of petty pilfering, but this—was murder."

"What exactly are you thinking of, M. Poirot?" Her voice sounded a little breathless.

"I am thinking of the *locked door*."

Miss Henderson considered this. "I don't see anything in that. The man left by the door, locked it and took the key with him so as to avoid having the murder discovered too soon. Quite intelligent of him, for it wasn't discovered until four o'clock in the afternoon."

"No, no, Mademoiselle, you don't appreciate the point I'm trying to make. I'm not worried as to how he got *out*, but as to how he got *in*."

"The window of course."

"*C'est possible.* But it would be a very narrow fit—and there were people passing up and down the deck all the time, remember."

"Then through the door," said Miss Henderson impatiently.

"But you forget, Mademoiselle. Mrs. Clapperton had locked the door on the inside. She had done so before Colonel Clapperton left the boat this morning. He actually tried it—so we *know* that is so."

"Nonsense. It probably stuck—or he didn't turn the handle properly."

"But it does not rest on his word. We actually heard *Mrs. Clapperton herself say so*."

"We?"

"Miss Mooney, Miss Cregan, Colonel Clapperton, and myself."

Ellie Henderson tapped a neatly shod foot. She did not speak for a moment or two, then she said in a slightly irritable tone:

"Well—what exactly do you deduce from that? If Mrs. Clapperton could lock the door she could unlock it too, I suppose."

"Precisely, precisely." Poirot turned a beaming face upon her. "And you see where that leads us. *Mrs. Clapperton unlocked the door and let the murderer in.* Now would she be likely to do that for a bead seller?"

Ellie objected: "She might not have known who it was. He may have knocked—she got up and opened the door—and he forced his way in and killed her."

Poirot shook his head. "*Au contraire.* She was lying peacefully in bed when she was stabbed."

Miss Henderson stared at him. "What's your idea?" she asked abruptly.

Poirot smiled. "Well, it looks, does it not, as though she knew the person she admitted. . . ."

"You mean," said Miss Henderson and her voice sounded a little harsh, *"that the murderer is a passenger on the ship?"*

Poirot nodded. "It seems indicated."

"And the string of beads left on the floor was a blind?"

"Precisely."

"The theft of the money also?"

"Exactly."

There was a pause, then Miss Henderson said slowly: "I thought Mrs. Clapperton a very unpleasant woman and I don't think anyone on board really like her—but there wasn't anyone who had any reason to kill her."

"Except her husband, perhaps," said Poirot.

"You don't really think—" She stopped.

"It is the opinion of ever person on this ship that Colonel Clapperton would have been quite justified in 'taking a hatchet to her.' That was, I think, the expression used."

Ellie Henderson looked at him—waiting.

"But I am bound to say," went on Poirot, "that I myself have not noted any signs of exasperation on the good Colonel's part. Also, what is more important, he had an alibi. He was with those two girls all day and did not return to the ship till four o'clock. By then, Mrs. Clapperton had been dead many hours."

There was another minute of silence. Ellie Henderson said softly: "But you still think—a passenger on the ship?"

Poirot bowed his head.

Ellie Henderson laughed suddenly—a reckless defiant laugh. "Your theory may be difficult to prove, M. Poirot. There are a good many passengers on this ship."

Poirot bowed to her. "I will use a phrase from one of your detective story writers. 'I have my methods, Watson.' "

The following evening, at dinner, every passenger found a typewritten slip by his plate requesting him to be in the main lounge at 8:30. When the company were assembled, the Captain stepped onto the raised platform where the orchestra usually played and addressed them.

"Ladies and gentlemen, you all know of the tragedy that took place yesterday. I am sure you all wish to cooperate in bringing the perpetrator of that foul crime to justice." He paused and cleared his throat. "We have on board with us M. Hercule Poirot, who is probably known to you all as a man who has had wide experience in—er—such matters. I hope you will listen carefully to what he has to say."

It was at this minute that Colonel Clapperton, who had not been at dinner, came in and sat down next to General Forbes. He looked like a man bewildered by sorrow—not at all like a man conscious of great relief. Either he was a very good actor or else he had been genuinely fond of his disagreeable wife.

"M. Hercule Poirot," said the Captain and stepped down. Poirot took his place. He looked comically self-important as he beamed on his audience.

"*Messieurs, Mesdames,*" he began. "It is most kind of you to be so indulgent as to listen to me. M. *le Capitaine* has told you that I have had a certain experience in these matters. I have, it is true, a little idea of my own about how to get to the bottom of this particular case." He made a sign and a steward pushed forward and passed up to him a bulky, shapeless object wrapped in a sheet.

"What I am about to do may surprise you a little," Poirot warned them. "It may occur to you that I am eccentric, perhaps mad. Nevertheless I assure you that behind my madness there is—as you English say— a method."

His eyes met those of Miss Henderson for just a minute. He began unwrapping the bulky object.

"I have here, *Messieurs* and *Mesdames* an important witness to the truth of who killed Mrs. Clapperton." With a deft hand he whisked away the last enveloping cloth, and the object it concealed was revealed—an almost life-sized wooden doll, dressed in a velvet suit and lace collar.

"Now, Arthur," said Poirot and his voice changed subtly—it was no longer foreign—it had instead a confident English, a slightly cockney inflection. "Can you tell me—I repeat—can you tell me—anything at all about the death of Mrs. Clapperton?"

The doll's neck oscillated a little, its wooden lower jaw dropped and wavered and a shrill high-pitched woman's voice spoke:

"*What is it, John? The door's locked. I don't want to be disturbed by the stewards. . . .*"

There was a cry—an overturned chair—a man stood swaying, his hand to his throat—trying to speak—trying. . . . Then suddenly, his figure seemed to crumple up. He pitched headlong.

It was Colonel Clapperton.

Poirot and the ship's doctor rose from their knees by the prostrate figure.

"All over, I'm afraid. Heart," said the doctor briefly.

Poirot nodded. "The shock of having his trick seen through," he said.

He turned to General Forbes. "It was you, General, who gave me a valuable hint with your mention of the music hall stage. I puzzle—think—and then it comes to me. Supposing that before the war Clapperton were a *ventriloquist*. In that case, it would be perfectly possible for three people to hear Mrs. Clapperton speak from inside her cabin *when she was already dead.* . . ."

Ellie Henderson was beside him. Her eyes were dark and full of pain. "Did you know his heart was weak?" she asked.

"I guessed it . . . Mrs. Clapperton talked of her own heart being affected, but she struck me as the type of woman who likes to be thought ill. Then I picked up a torn prescription with a very strong dose of digitalin in it. Digitalin is a heart medicine but it couldn't be Mrs. Clapperton's because digitalin dilates the pupils of the eyes. I had never noticed such a phenomenon with her—but when I looked at his eyes I saw the signs at once."

Ellie murmured: "So you thought—it might end—this way?"

"The best way, don't you think, Mademoiselle?" he said gently.

He saw the tears rise in her eyes. She said: "You've known. You've known all along. . . . That I cared . . . But he didn't do it for me. . . . It was those girls—youth—it made him feel his slavery. He wanted to be free before it was too late. . . . Yes, I'm sure that's how it was . . . When did you guess—that it was he?"

"His self-control was too perfect," said Poirot simply. "No matter how galling his wife's conduct, it never seemed to touch him. That meant either that he was so used to it that it no longer stung him, or else—*eh bien*—I decided on the latter alternative. . . . And I was right. . . .

"And then there was his insistence on his conjuring ability—the evening before the crime. He pretended to give himself away. But a man like Clapperton doesn't give himself away. There must be a reason. So long as people thought he had been a *conjuror* they weren't likely to think of his having been a ventriloquist."

"And the voice we heard—Mrs. Clapperton's voice?"

"One of the stewardesses had a voice not unlike hers. I induced her to hide behind the stage and taught her the words to say."

"It was a trick—a cruel trick," cried out Ellie.

"I do not approve of murder," said Hercule Poirot.

The Piscatorial Farce
of the Stolen Stomach

Author: Dorothy L. Sayers (1893–1957)

Detective: Lord Peter Wimsey (1923)

Dorothy L. Sayers contrasts in many ways with her contemporary Agatha Christie. Though just as fascinated by the detective puzzle, she had broader literary ambitions, and unlike Christie, she eventually abandoned the form in favor of religious drama and Dante translating. But the pair have a couple of things in common. They are the most revered, studied, and reprinted writers of Britain's Golden Age of Detection, and they are equally little prone to squandering a full-scale mystery plot on a short story. Sayers' best short stories are those, like "Suspicion" and "The Inspiration of Mr. Budd," which do *not* involve Lord Peter Wimsey, the aristocratic gentleman detective of most of her novels from *Whose Body?* (1923) through *Busman's Honeymoon* (1937). (A final Wimsey novel, *Thrones, Dominations,* left unfinished by his creator, was completed by Jill Paton Walsh and published in 1998.)

Wimsey is undeniably one of the dozen or so most famous twentieth-century sleuths, and his short-story appearances, if thinly plotted, are as charmingly written as the novels. They also illustrate aspects of the author's character, in this rarely reprinted tale a certain ghoulish sense of humor.

W hat in the world," said Lord Peter Wimsey, "is that?"
Thomas Macpherson disengaged the tall jar from its final swathings of paper and straw and set it tenderly upright beside the coffeepot.

"That," he said, "is Great-Uncle Joseph's legacy."

"And who is Great-Uncle Joseph?"

"He was my mother's uncle. Name of Ferguson. Eccentric old boy. I was rather a favorite of his."

"It looks like it. Was that all he left you?"

"Imph'm. He said a good digestion was the most precious thing a man could have."

"Well, he was right there. Is this his? Was it a good one?"

"Good enough. He lived to be ninety-five, and never had a day's illness."

Wimsey looked at the jar with increased respect.

"What did he die of?"

"Chucked himself out of a sixth-story window. He had a stroke, and the doctors told him—or he guessed for himself—that it was the beginning of the end. He left a letter. Said he had never been ill in his life and wasn't going to begin now. They brought in temporary insanity, of course, but I think he was thoroughly sensible."

"I should say so. What was he when he was functioning?"

"He used to be in business—something to do with shipbuilding, I believe, but he retired long ago. He was what the papers call a recluse. Lived all by himself in a little top flat in Glasgow, and saw nobody. Used to go off by himself for days at a time, nobody knew where or why. I used to look him up about once a year and take him a bottle of whiskey."

"Had he any money?"

"Nobody knew. He ought to have had—he was a rich man when he retired. But, when we came to look into it, it turned out he only had a balance of about five hundred pounds in the Glasgow Bank. Apparently he drew out almost everything he had about twenty years ago. There were one or two big bank failures round about that time, and they thought he must have got the wind up. But what he did with it, goodness only knows."

"Kept it in an old stocking, I expect."

"I should think Cousin Robert devoutly hopes so."

"Cousin Robert?"

"He's the residuary legatee. Distant connection of mine, and the only remaining Ferguson. He was awfully wild when he found he'd only got five hundred. He's rather a bright lad, is Robert, and a few thousands would have come in handy."

"I see. Well, how about a bit of brekker? You might stick Great-Uncle Joseph out of the way somewhere. I don't care about the looks of him."

"I thought you were rather partial to anatomical specimens."

"So I am, but not on the breakfast table. 'A place for everything and everything in its place,' as my grandmother used to say. Besides, it would give Maggie a shock if she saw it."

Macpherson laughed, and transferred the jar to a cupboard.

"Maggie's shock-proof. I brought a few odd bones and things with me, by way of a holiday task. I'm getting near my final, you know. She'll just think this is another of them. Ring the bell, old man, would you? We'll see what the trout's like."

The door opened to admit the housekeeper, with a dish of grilled trout and a plate of fried scones.

"These look good, Maggie," said Wimsey, drawing his chair up and sniffing appreciatively.

"Aye, sir, they're gude, but they're awfu' wee fish."

"Don't grumble at them," said Macpherson. "They're the sole result of a day's purgatory up on Loch Whyneon. What with the sun fit to roast you and an east wind, I'm pretty well flayed alive. I very nearly didn't shave at all this morning." He passed a reminiscent hand over his red and excoriated face. "Ugh! It's a stiff pull up that hill, and the boat was going wallop, wallop all the time, like being in the Bay of Biscay."

"Damnable, I should think. But there's a change coming. The glass is going back. We'll be having some rain before we're many days older."

"Time, too," said Macpherson. "The burns are nearly dry, and there's not much water in the Fleet." He glanced out of the window to where the little river ran tinkling and skinkling over the stones at the bottom of the garden. "If only we get a few days' rain now, there'll be some grand fishing."

"It *would* come just as I've got to go, naturally," remarked Wimsey.

"Yes, can't you stay a bit longer? I want to have a try for some sea-trout."

"Sorry, old man, can't be done. I must be in Town on Wednesday. Never mind. I've had a fine time in the fresh air and got in some good rounds of golf."

"You must come up another time. I'm here for a month—getting my strength up for the exams and all that. If you can't get away before I go, we'll put it off till August and have a shot at the grouse. The cottage is always at your service, you know, Wimsey."

"Many thanks. I may get my business over quicker than I think, and, if I do, I'll turn up here again. When did you say your great-uncle died?"

Macpherson stared at him.

"Some time in April, as far as I can remember. Why?"

"Oh, nothing—I just wondered. You were a favorite of his, didn't you say?"

"In a sense. I think the old boy liked my remembering him from time to time. Old people are pleased by little attentions, you know."

"M'm. Well, it's a queer world. What did you say his name was?"

"Ferguson—Joseph Alexander Ferguson, to be exact. You seem extraordinarily interested in Great-Uncle Joseph."

"I thought, while I was about it, I might look up a man I know in the shipbuilding line, and see if he knows anything about where the money went to."

"If you can do that, Cousin Robert will give you a medal. But, if you really want to exercise your detective powers on the problem, you'd better have a hunt through the flat in Glasgow."

"Yes—what is the address, by the way?"

Macpherson told him the address.

"I'll make a note of it, and, if anything occurs to me, I'll communicate with Cousin Robert. Where does he hang out?"

"Oh, he's in London, in a solicitor's office. Crosbie & Plump, somewhere in Bloomsbury. Robert was studying for the Scottish Bar, you know, but he made rather a mess of things, so they pushed him off among the Sassenachs. His father died a couple of years ago—he was a Writer to the Signet in Edinburgh—and I fancy Robert has rather gone to the bow-wows since then. Got among a cheerful crowd down there, don't you know, and wasted his substance somewhat."

"Terrible! Scotsmen shouldn't be allowed to leave home. What are you going to do with Great-Uncle?"

"Oh, I don't know. Keep him for a bit, I think. I liked the old fellow, and I don't want to throw him away. He'll look rather well in my consulting room, don't you think, when I'm qualified and set up my brass plate. I'll say he was presented by a grateful patient on whom I performed a marvelous operation."

"That's a good idea. Stomach-grafting. Miracle of surgery never before attempted. He'll bring sufferers to your door in flocks."

"Good old Great-Uncle—he may be worth a fortune to me after all."

"So he may. I don't suppose you've got such a thing as a photograph of him, have you?"

"A photograph?" Macpherson stared again. "Great-Uncle seems to be becoming a passion with you. I don't suppose the old man had a photograph taken these thirty years. There was one done then—when he retired from business. I expect Robert's got that."

"Och aye," said Wimsey, in the language of the country.

Wimsey left Scotland that evening, and drove down through the night toward London, thinking hard as he went. He handled the wheel mechanically, swerving now and again to avoid the green eyes of rabbits as they bolted from the roadside to squat fascinated in the glare of his headlamps. He was accustomed to say that his brain worked better when his immediate attention was occupied by the incidents of the road.

Monday morning found him in town with his business finished and his thinking done. A consultation with his shipbuilding friend had put him in possession of some facts about Great-Uncle Joseph's money, together with a copy of Great-Uncle Joseph's photograph, supplied by the London representative of the Glasgow firm to which he had belonged. It appeared that old Ferguson had been a man of mark in his day. The portrait showed a fine, dour old face, long-lipped and high in the cheekbones—one of those faces that alters little in a lifetime. Wimsey looked at the photograph with satisfaction as he slipped it into his pocket and made a beeline for Somerset House.

Here he wandered timidly about the wills department, till a uniformed official took pity on him and inquired what he wanted.

"Oh, thank you," said Wimsey effusively, "thank you so much. Always feel nervous in these places. All these big desks and things, don't you know, so awe-inspiring and businesslike. Yes, I just wanted to have a squint at a will. I'm told you can see anybody's will for a shilling. Is that really so?"

"Yes, sir, certainly. Anybody's will in particular, sir?"

"Oh, yes, of course—how silly of me. Yes. Curious, isn't it, that when you're dead any stranger can come and snoop round your private affairs—see how much you cut up for and who your lady friends were, and all that. Yes. Not at all nice. Horrid lack of privacy, what?"

The attendant laughed.

"I expect it's all one when you're dead, sir."

"That's awfully true. Yes, naturally, you're dead by then and it doesn't matter. May be a bit trying for your relations, of course, to learn what a bad boy you've been. Great fun annoyin' one's relations. Always do it myself. Now, what were we sayin'? Ah! yes—the will. (I'm always so absent-minded.) Whose will, you said? Well, it's an old Scots gentleman called Joseph Alexander Ferguson that died at Glasgow—you know Glasgow, where the accent's so strong that even Scotsmen faint when they hear it—in April, this last April as ever was. If it's not troubling you too much, may I have a bob's-worth of Joseph Alexander Ferguson?"

The attendant assured him that he might, adding the caution that he must memorize the contents of the will and not on any account take notes. Thus warned, Wimsey was conducted into a retired corner, where in a short time the will was placed before him.

It was a commendably brief document, written in holograph, and was dated the previous January. After the usual preamble and the bequest of a few small sums and articles of personal ornament to friends, it proceeded somewhat as follows:

> And I direct that, after my death, the alimentary organs be removed entire with their contents from my body, commencing with the esophagus and ending with the anal canal, and that they be properly secured at both ends with a suitable ligature, and be enclosed in a proper preservative medium in a glass vessel and given to my great-nephew Thomas Macpherson of the Stone Cottage, Gate-house-of-the-Fleet, in Kirkcudbrightshire, now studying medicine in Aberdeen. And I bequeath him these my alimentary organs with their contents for his study and edification, they having served me for ninety-five years without failure or defect, because I wish him to understand that no riches in the world are comparable to the riches of a good digestion. And I desire of him that he will, in the exercise of his medical profession, use his best endeavors to preserve to his patients the blessing of good digestion unimpaired, not needlessly filling their stomachs with drugs out of concern for his own pocket, but exhorting them to a sober and temperate life agreeably to the design of Almighty Providence.

After this remarkable passage, the document went on to make Robert Ferguson residuary legatee without particular specification of any property, and to appoint a firm of lawyers in Glasgow executors of the will.

Wimsey considered the bequest for some time. From the phraseology he concluded that old Mr. Ferguson had drawn up his own will without legal aid, and he was glad of it, for its wording thus afforded a valuable clue to the testator's mood and intention. He mentally noted three points: the "alimentary organs with their contents" were mentioned twice over, with a certain emphasis; they were to be ligatured top and bottom; and the legacy was accompanied by the expression of a wish that the legatee should not allow his financial necessities to interfere with the conscientious exercise of his professional duties. Wimsey chuckled. He felt he rather liked Great-Uncle Joseph.

He got up, collected his hat, gloves and stick, and advanced with the will in his hand to return it to the attendant. The latter was engaged in conversation with a young man, who seemed to be expostulating about something.

"I'm sorry, sir," said the attendant, "but I don't suppose the other gentleman will be very long. Ah!" He turned and saw Wimsey. "Here is the gentleman."

The young man, whose reddish hair, long nose, and slightly sodden eyes gave him the appearance of a dissipated fox, greeted Wimsey with a disagreeable stare.

"What's up? Want me?" asked his lordship airily.

"Yes, sir. Very curious thing, sir; here's a gentleman inquiring for that very same document as you've been studying, sir. I've been in this department fifteen years, and I don't know as I ever remember such a thing happening before."

"No," said Wimsey, "I don't suppose there's much of a run on any of your lines as a rule."

"It's a very curious thing indeed," said the stranger, with marked displeasure in his voice.

"Member of the family?" suggested Wimsey.

"I *am* a member of the family," said the foxy-faced man. "May I ask whether *you* have any connection with us?"

"By all means," replied Wimsey graciously.

"I don't believe it. I don't know you."

"No, no—I meant you might ask, by all means."

The young man positively showed his teeth.

"Do you mind telling me who you are, anyhow, and why you're so damned inquisitive about my great-uncle's will?"

Wimsey extracted a card from his case and presented it with a smile. Mr. Robert Ferguson changed color.

"If you would like a reference as to my respectability," went on Wimsey affably, "Mr. Thomas Macpherson will, I am sure, be happy to tell you about me. I am inquisitive," said his lordship— "a student of humanity. Your cousin mentioned to me the curious clause relating to your esteemed great-uncle's—er—stomach and appurtenances. Curious clauses are a passion with me. I came to look it up and add it to my collection of curious wills. I am engaged in writing a book on the subject—*Clauses and Consequences*. My publishers tell me it should enjoy a ready sale. I regret that my random jottings should have encroached upon your doubtless far more serious studies. I wish you a very good morning."

As he beamed his way out, Wimsey, who had quick ears, heard the attendant informing the indignant Mr. Ferguson that he was "a very funny gentleman—not quite all there, sir." It seemed that his criminological fame had not penetrated to the quiet recesses of Somerset House.

"But," said Wimsey to himself, "I am sadly afraid that Cousin Robert has been given food for thought."

Under the spur of this alarming idea, Wimsey wasted no time, but took a taxi down to Hatton Garden, to call upon a friend of his. This gentleman, rather curly in the nose and fleshy about the eyelids, nevertheless came under Mr. Chesterton's definition of a nice Jew, for his name was neither Montagu nor McDonald, but Nathan Abrahams, and he greeted Lord Peter with a hospitality amounting to enthusiasm.

"So pleased to see you. Sit down and have a drink. You have come at last to select the diamonds for the future Lady Peter, eh?"

"Not yet," said Wimsey.

"No? That's too bad. You should make haste and settle down. It is time you became a family man. Years ago we arranged I should have the privilege of decking the bride for the happy day. That is a promise, you know. I think of it when the fine stones pass through my hands. I say, 'That would be the very thing for my friend Lord Peter.' But I hear nothing, and I sell them to stupid Americans who think only of the price and not of the beauty."

"Time enough to think of the diamonds when I've found the lady."

Mr. Abrahams threw up his hands.

"Oh yes! And then everything will be done in a hurry! 'Quick, Mr. Abrahams! I have fallen in love yesterday and I am being married tomorrow.' But it may take months—years—to find and match perfect stones. It can't be done between today and tomorrow. Your bride will be married in something ready-made from the jeweler's."

"If three days are enough to choose a wife," said Wimsey, laughing, "one day should surely be enough for a necklace."

"That is the way with Christians," replied the diamond merchant resignedly. "You are so casual. You do not think of the future. Three days to choose a wife! No wonder the divorce courts are busy. My son Moses is being married next week. It has been arranged in the family these ten years. Rachel Goldstein, it is. A good girl, and her father is in a very good position. We are all very pleased, I can tell you. Moses is a good son, a very good son, and I am taking him into partnership."

"I congratulate you," said Wimsey heartily. "I hope they will be very happy."

"Thank you, Lord Peter. They will be happy, I am sure. Rachel is a sweet girl and very fond of children. And she is pretty, too. Prettiness is not everything, but it is an advantage for a young man in these days. It is easier for him to behave well to a pretty wife."

"True," said Wimsey. "I will bear it in mind when my time comes. To the health of the happy pair, and may you soon be an ancestor. Talking of ancestors, I've got an old bird here that you may be able to tell me something about."

"Ah, yes! Always delighted to help you in any way, Lord Peter."

"This photograph was taken some thirty years ago, but you may possibly recognize it."

Mr. Abrahams put on a pair of horn-rimmed spectacles, and examined the portrait of Great-Uncle Joseph with serious attention.

"Oh yes, I know him quite well. What do you want to know about him, eh?" He shot a swift and cautious glance at Wimsey.

"Nothing to his disadvantage. He's dead, anyhow. I thought it just possible he had been buying precious stones lately."

"It is not exactly business to give information about a customer," said Mr. Abrahams.

"I'll tell you what I want it for," said Wimsey. He lightly sketched the career of Great-Uncle Joseph, and went on: "You see, I looked at it this way. When a man gets a distrust of banks, what does he do with his money? He puts it into property of some kind. It may be land, it may be houses—but that means rent, and more money to put into banks. He is more likely to keep it in gold or notes, or to put it into precious stones. Gold and notes are comparatively bulky; stones are small. Circumstances in this case led me to think he might have chosen stones. Unless we can discover what he did with the money, there will be a great loss to his heirs."

"I see. Well, if it is as you say, there is no harm in telling you. I know you to be an honorable man, and I will break my rule for you. This gentleman, Mr. Wallace—"

"Wallace, did he call himself?"

"That was not his name? They are funny, these secretive old gentlemen. But that is nothing unusual. Often, when they buy stones, they are afraid of being robbed, so they give another name. Yes, yes. Well, this Mr. Wallace used to come to see me from time to time, and I had instructions to find diamonds for him. He was looking for twelve big stones, all matching perfectly and of superb quality. It took a long time to find them, you know."

"Of course."

"Yes. I supplied him with seven altogether, over a period of twenty years or so. And other dealers supplied him also. He is well known in this street. I found the last one for him—let me see—in last December, I think. A beautiful stone—beautiful! He paid seven thousand pounds for it."

"Some stone. If they were all as good as that, the collection must be worth something."

"Worth anything. It is difficult to tell how much. As you know, the twelve stones, all matched together, would be worth far more than the sum of the twelve separate prices paid for the individual diamonds."

"Naturally they would. Do you mind telling me how he was accustomed to pay for them?"

"In Bank of England notes—always—cash on the nail. He insisted on a discount for cash," added Mr. Abrahams, with a chuckle.

"He was a Scotsman," replied Wimsey. "Well, that's clear enough. He had a safe-deposit somewhere, no doubt. And, having collected the stones, he made his will. That's clear as daylight, too."

"But what has become of the stones?" inquired Mr. Abrahams, with professional anxiety.

"I think I know that too," said Wimsey. "I'm enormously obliged to you, and so, I fancy, will his heir be."

"If they should come into the market again—" suggested Mr. Abrahams.

"I'll see you have the handling of them," said Wimsey promptly.

"That is kind of you," said Mr. Abrahams. "Business is business. Always delighted to oblige you. Beautiful stones—beautiful. If you thought of being the purchaser, I would charge you a special commission, as my friend."

"Thank you," said Wimsey, "but as yet I have no occasion for diamonds, you know."

"Pity, pity," said Mr. Abrahams. "Well, very glad to have been of service to you. You are not interested in rubies? No? Because I have something very pretty here."

He thrust his hand casually into a pocket, and brought out a little pool of crimson fire like a miniature sunset.

"Look nice in a ring, now, wouldn't it?" said Mr. Abrahams. "An engagement ring, eh?"

Wimsey laughed, and made his escape.

He was strongly tempted to return to Scotland and attend personally to the matter of Great-Uncle Joseph, but the thought of an important book sale the next day deterred him. There was a manuscript of Catullus that he was passionately anxious to secure, and he never entrusted his interests to dealers. He contented himself with sending a wire to Thomas Macpherson:

Advise opening up Great-Uncle Joseph immediately.

The girl at the post office repeated the message aloud and rather doubtfully. "Quite right," said Wimsey, and dismissed the affair from his mind.

He had great fun at the sale the next day. He found a ring of dealers in possession, happily engaged in conducting a knockout. Having lain low for an hour in a retired position behind a large piece of statuary, he emerged, just as the hammer was falling upon the Catullus for a price representing the tenth part of its value, with an overbid so large, prompt, and sonorous that the ring gasped with a sense of outrage. Skrymes—a dealer who had sworn an eternal enmity to Wimsey on account of a previous little encounter over a Justinian—pulled himself together and offered a fifty-pound advance. Wimsey promptly doubled his bid. Skrymes overbid him fifty again. Wimsey instantly jumped another hundred, in the tone of a man prepared to go on till Doomsday. Skrymes scowled and was silent. Somebody raised it fifty more; Wimsey made it guineas and the hammer fell. Encouraged by this success, Wimsey, feeling that his hand was in, romped happily into the bidding for the next lot, a *Hypnerotomachia*, which he already possessed, and for which he felt no desire whatever. Skrymes, annoyed by his defeat, set his teeth, determining that, if Wimsey was in the bidding mood, he should pay through the nose for his rashness. Wimsey, entering into the spirit of the thing, skied the bidding with enthusiasm. The dealers, knowing his reputation as a collector, and fancying that there must be some special excellence about the book that they had failed to observe, joined in wholeheartedly, and the fun became fast and furious. Eventually they all dropped out again, leaving Skrymes and Wimsey in together. At which point Wimsey, observing a note of hesitation in the dealer's voice, neatly extricated himself and left Mr. Skrymes with the baby. After this disaster, the ring became sulky and demoralized and refused to bid at all, and a timid little outsider, suddenly flinging himself into the arena, became the owner of a fine fourteenth-century missal at bargain price. Crimson with excitement and surprise, he paid for his purchase and ran out of the room like a rabbit, hugging the missal as though he expected to have it snatched from him. Wimsey thereupon set himself seriously to acquire a few fine early printed books, and, having accomplished this, retired, covered with laurels and hatred.

After this delightful and satisfying day, he felt vaguely hurt at receiving no ecstatic telegram from Macpherson. He refused to imagine that his deductions had been wrong, and supposed rather that the rapture of Macpherson was too great to be confined to telegraphic expression and would come next day by post. However, at eleven next morning the telegram arrived. It said:

> Just got your wire what does it mean Great-Uncle stolen last night burglar escaped please write fully.

Wimsey committed himself to a brief comment in language usually confined to soldiery. Robert had undoubtedly got Great-Uncle Joseph, and, even if they could trace the burglary to him, the legacy was by this time gone forever. He had never felt so furiously helpless. He even cursed the Catullus, which had kept him from going north and dealing with the matter personally.

While he was meditating what to do, a second telegram was brought in. It ran:

> Great-Uncle's bottle found broken in fleet dropped by burglar in flight contents gone what next.

Wimsey pondered this.

"Of course," he said, "if the thief simply emptied the bottle and put Great-Uncle in his pocket, we're done. Or if he's simply emptied Great-Uncle and put the contents in his pocket, we're done. But 'dropped in flight' sounds rather as though Great-Uncle had gone overboard lock, stock, and barrel. Why can't the fool of a Scotsman put a few more details into his wires? It'd only cost him a penny or two. I suppose I'd better go up myself. Meanwhile a little healthy occupation won't hurt him."

He took a telegraph form from the desk and dispatched a further message:

> Was Great-Uncle in bottle when dropped if so drag river if not pursue burglar probably Robert Ferguson spare no pains starting for Scotland tonight hope arrive early tomorrow urgent important put your back into it will explain.

The night express decanted Lord Peter Wimsey at Dumfries early the following morning, and a hired car deposited him at the Stone Cottage in time for breakfast. The door was opened to him by Maggie, who greeted him with hearty cordiality:

"Come awa' in, sir. All's ready for ye, and Mr. Macpherson will be back in a few minutes, I'm thinkin'. Ye'll be tired with your long journey, and hungry, maybe? Aye. Will ye tak' a bit parritch to your eggs and bacon? There's nae troot the day, though yesterday was a gran' day for the fush. Mr. Macpherson has been up and doun, up and doun the river wi' my Jock, lookin' for ane of his specimens, as he ca's them, that was dropped by the thief that cam' in. I dinna ken what the thing may be—my Jock says it's like a calf's pluck to look at, by what Mr. Macpherson tells him."

"Dear me!" said Wimsey. "And how did the burglary happen, Maggie?"

"Indeed, sir, it was a vera' remarkable circumstance. Mr. Macpherson was awa' all day Monday and Tuesday, up at the big loch by the viaduct, fishin'. There was a big rain Saturday and Sunday, ye may remember, and Mr. Macpherson says, "There'll be grand fishin' the morn, Jock," says he. 'We'll go up to the viaduct if it stops rainin' and we'll spend the nicht at the keeper's lodge.' So on Monday it stoppit rainin' and was a grand warm, soft day, so aff they went together. There was a telegram come for him Tuesday mornin', and I set it up on the mantelpiece, where he'd see it when he cam' in, but it's been in my mind since that maybe that telegram had something to do wi' the burglary."

"I wouldn't say but you might be right, Maggie," replied Wimsey gravely.

"Aye, sir, that wadna surprise me." Maggie set down a generous dish of eggs and bacon before the guest and took up her tale again.

"Well, I was sittin' in my kitchen the Tuesday nicht, waitin' for Mr. Macpherson and Jock to come hame, and sair I pitied them, the puir souls, for the rain was peltin' down again, and the nicht was sae dark I was afraid they micht ha' tummelt into a bog-pool. Weel, I was listenin' for the sound o' the door-sneck when I heard something movin' in the front room. The door wasna lockit, ye ken, because Mr. Macpherson was expectit back. So I up from my chair and I thocht they had mebbe came in and I not heard them. I waited a meenute to set the kettle on the fire, and then I heard a crackin' sound. So I cam' out and I called. 'Is't you, Mr. Macpherson?' And there was nae answer, only anither big crackin' noise, so I ran forrit, and a man cam' quickly oot o' the front room, brushin' past me an puttin' me aside wi' his hand, so, and oot o' the front door like a flash o' lightnin'. So, wi' that, I let oot a skelloch, an' Jock's voice answered me fra' the gairden gate. 'Och!' I says, 'Jock!

here's a burrglar been i' the hoose!' An' I heerd him runnin' across the gairden, doun tae the river, tramplin' doun a' the young kail and the stra'berry beds, the blackguard!"

Wimsey expressed his sympathy.

"Aye, that was a bad business. An' the next thing, there was Mr. Macpherson and Jock helter-skelter after him. If Davie Murray's cattle had brokken in, they couldna ha' done mair deevastation. An' then there was a big splashin' an' crashin', an', after a bit, back comes Mr. Macpherson an' he says, 'He's jumpit intil the Fleet,' he says, 'an' he's awa'. What has he taken?' he says. 'I dinna ken,' says I, 'for it all happened sae quickly I couldna see onything.' 'Come awa' ben,' says he, 'an' we'll see what's missin'.' So we lookit high and low, an' all we could find was the cupboard door in the front room broken open, and naething taken but this bottle wi' the specimen."

"Aha!" said Wimsey.

"Ah! an' they baith went oot tegither wi' lichts, but naething could they see of the thief. Sae Mr. Macpherson comes back, and 'I'm gaun to ma bed,' says he, 'for I'm that tired I can dae nae mair the nicht,' says he. 'Oh!' I said, 'I daurna gae tae bed; I'm frichtened.' An' Jock said, 'Hoots, wumman, dinna fash yersel'. There'll be nae mair burglars the nicht, wi' the fricht we've gied 'em.' So we lockit up a' the doors an' windies an' gaed to oor beds, but I couldna sleep a wink."

"Very natural," said Wimsey.

"It wasna till the next mornin'," said Maggie, "that Mr. Macpherson opened yon telegram. Eh! but he was in a taking. An' then the telegrams startit. Back an' forrit, back an' forrit atween the hoose an' the post office. An' then they fund the bits o' the bottle that the specimen was in, stuck between twa stanes i' the river. And aff goes Mr. Macpherson an' Jock wi' their waders on an' a couple o' gaffs, huntin' in a' the pools an' under the stanes to find the specimen. An' they're still at it."

At this point three heavy thumps sounded on the ceiling.

"Gude save us!" ejaculated Maggie, "I was forgettin' the puir gentleman."

"What gentleman?" inquired Wimsey.

"Him that was feshed oot o' the Fleet," replied Maggie. "Excuse me juist a moment, sir."

She fled swiftly upstairs. Wimsey poured himself out a third cup of coffee and lit a pipe.

Presently a thought occurred to him. He finished the coffee—not being a man to deprive himself of his pleasures—and walked quietly upstairs in Maggie's wake. Facing him stood a bedroom door, half open—

the room that he had occupied during his stay at the cottage. He pushed it open. In the bed lay a red-headed gentleman, whose long, foxy countenance was in no way beautified by a white bandage, tilted rakishly across the left temple. A breakfast tray stood on a table by the bed. Wimsey stepped forward with extended hand.

"Good morning, Mr. Ferguson," said he. "This is an unexpected pleasure."

"Good morning," said Mr. Ferguson snappishly.

"I had no idea, when we last met," pursued Wimsey, advancing to the bed and sitting down upon it, "that you were thinking of visiting my friend Macpherson."

"Get off my leg," growled the invalid. "I've broken my kneecap."

"What a nuisance! Frightfully painful, isn't it? And they say it takes years to get right—if it ever does get right. Is it what they call a Potts fracture? I don't know who Potts was, but it sounds impressive. How did you get it? Fishing?"

"Yes. A slip in that damned river."

"Beastly. Sort of thing that might happen to anybody. A keen fisher, Mr. Ferguson?"

"So-so."

"So am I, when I get the opportunity. What kind of fly do you fancy for this part of the country. I rather like a Greenaway's Gadget myself. Every tried it?"

"No," said Mr. Ferguson briefly.

"Some people find a Pink Sisket better, so they tell me. Do you use one? Have you got your fly-book here?"

"Yes—no," said Mr. Ferguson. "I dropped it."

"Pity. But do give me your opinion of the Pink Sisket."

"Not so bad," said Mr. Ferguson. "I've sometimes caught trout with it."

"You surprise me," said Wimsey, not unnaturally, since he had invented the Pink Sisket on the spur of the moment, and had hardly expected his improvisation to pass muster. "Well, I suppose this unlucky accident has put a stop to your sport for the season. Damned bad luck. Otherwise, you might have helped us to have a go at the Patriarch."

"What's that? A trout?"

"Yes—a frightfully wily old fish. Lurks about in the Fleet. You never know where to find him. Any moment he may turn up in some pool or other. I'm going out with Mac to try for him today. He's a jewel of a fellow. We've nicknamed him Great-Uncle Joseph. Hi! don't joggle about like that—you'll hurt that knee of yours. Is there anything I can get for you?"

He grinned amiably, and turned to answer a shout from the stairs.

"Hullo! Wimsey! is that you?"

"It is. How's sport?"

Macpherson came up the stairs four steps at a time, and met Wimsey on the landing as he emerged from the bedroom.

"I say, d'you know who that is? It's Robert."

"I know. I saw him in town. Never mind him. Have you found Great-Uncle?"

"No, we haven't. What's all this mystery about? And what's Robert doing here? What did you mean by saying he was the burglar? And why is Great-Uncle Joseph so important?"

"One thing at a time. Let's find the old boy first. What have you been doing?"

"Well, when I got your extraordinary messages I thought, of course, you were off your rocker." (Wimsey groaned with impatience.) "But then I considered what a funny thing it was that somebody should have thought Great-Uncle worth stealing, and thought there might be some sense in what you said, after all." ("Dashed good of you," said Wimsey.) "So I went out and poked about a bit, you know. Not that I think there's the faintest chance of finding anything, with the river coming down like this. Well, I hadn't got very far—by the way, I took Jock with me. I'm sure he thinks I'm mad, too. Not that he says anything; these people here never commit themselves—"

"Confound Jock! Get on with it."

"Oh—well, before we'd got very far, we saw a fellow wading about in the river with a rod and a creel. I didn't pay much attention, because, you see, I was wondering what you—Yes. Well! Jock noticed him and said to me, 'Yon's a queer kind of fisherman, I'm thinkin'.' So I had a look, and there he was, staggering about among the stones with his fly floating away down the stream in front of him; and he was peering into all the pools he came to, and poking about with a gaff. So I hailed him, and he turned round, and then he put the gaff away in a bit of a hurry and started to reel in his line. He made an awful mess of it," added Macpherson appreciatively.

"I can believe it," said Wimsey. "A man who admits to catching trout with a Pink Sisket would make a mess of anything."

"A pink what?"

"Never mind. I only meant that Robert was no fisher. Get on."

"Well, he got the line hooked round something, and he was pulling and hauling, you know, and splashing about, and then it came out all of a sudden, and he waved it all over the place and got my hat. That made me pretty wild, and I made after him, and he looked round again, and I yelled out, 'Good God, it's Robert!' And he dropped his rod and took to his heels. And of course he slipped on the stones and came down an awful crack. We rushed forward and scooped him up and brought him home. He's got a nasty bang on the head and a fractured patella. Very interesting. I should have liked to have a shot at setting it myself, but it wouldn't do, you know, so I sent for Strachan. He's a good man."

"You've had extraordinary luck about this business so far," said Wimsey. "Now the only thing left is to find Great-Uncle. How far down have you got?"

"Not very far. You see, what with getting Robert home and setting his knee and so on, we couldn't do much yesterday."

"Damn, Robert! Great-Uncle may be away out to sea by this time. Let's get down to it."

He took up a gaff from the umbrella stand ("Robert's," interjected Macpherson), and led the way out. The little river was foaming down in a brown spate, rattling stones and small boulders along in its passage. Every hole, every eddy might be a lurking-place for Great-Uncle Joseph. Wimsey peered irresolutely here and there—then turned suddenly to Jock.

"Where's the nearest spit of land where things usually get washed up?" he demanded.

"Eh, well! there's the Battery Pool, about a mile doon the river. Ye'll whiles find things washed up there. Aye. Imph'm. There's a pool and a bit sand, where the river mak's a bend. Ye'll mebbe find it there, I'm thinkin'. Mebbe no. I couldna say."

"Let's have a look, anyway."

Macpherson, to whom the prospect of searching the stream in detail appeared rather a dreary one, brightened a little at this.

"That's a good idea. If we take the car down to just above Gatehouse, we've only got two fields to cross."

The car was still at the door; the hired driver was enjoying the hospitality of the cottage. They pried him loose from Maggie's scones and slipped down the road to Gatehouse.

"Those gulls seem rather active about something," said Wimsey, as they crossed the second field. The white wings swooped backward and forward in narrowing circles over the yellow shoal. Raucous cries rose on the wind. Wimsey pointed silently with his hand. A long, unseemly object, like a drab purse, lay on the shore. The gulls, indignant, rose higher, squawking at the intruders. Wimsey ran forward, stooped, rose again with the long bag dangling from his fingers.

"Great-Uncle Joseph, I presume," he said, and raised his hat with old-fashioned courtesy.

"The gulls have had a wee peck at it here and there," said Jock. "It'll be tough for them. Aye. They havena done so vera much with it."

"Aren't you going to open it?" said Macpherson impatiently.

"Not here," said Wimsey. "We might lose something." He dropped it into Jock's creel. "We'll take it home first and show it to Robert."

Robert greeted them with ill-disguised irritation.

"We've been fishing," said Wimsey cheerfully. "Look at our bonny wee fush." He weighed the catch in his hand. "What's inside this wee fush, Mr. Ferguson?"

"I haven't the faintest idea," said Robert.

"Then why did you go fishing for it?" asked Wimsey pleasantly. "Have you got a surgical knife there, Mac?"

"Yes—here. Hurry up."

"I'll leave it to you. Be careful. I should begin with the stomach."

Macpherson laid Great-Uncle Joseph on the table, and slit him open with a practiced hand.

"Gude be gracious to us!" cried Maggie, peering over his shoulder. "What'll that be?"

Wimsey inserted a delicate finger and thumb into the cavities of Great-Uncle Joseph. "One—two—three—" The stones glittered like fire as he laid them on the table. "Seven—eight—nine. That seems to be all. Try a little farther down, Mac."

Speechless with astonishment, Mr. Macpherson dissected his legacy.

"Ten—eleven," said Wimsey. "I'm afraid the sea gulls have got number twelve. I'm sorry, Mac."

"But how did they get there?" demanded Robert foolishly.

"Simple as shelling peas. Great-Uncle Joseph makes his will, swallows his diamonds—"

"He must ha' been a grand man for a pill," said Maggie, with respect.

"—and jumps out of the window. It was as clear as crystal to anybody who read the will. He told you, Mac, that the stomach was given you to study."

Robert Ferguson gave a deep groan.

"I knew there was something in it," he said. "That's why I went to look up the will. And when I saw *you* there, I knew I was right. (Curse this leg of mine!) But I never imagined for a moment—"

His eyes appraised the diamonds greedily.

"And what will the value of these same stones be?" inquired Jock.

"About seven thousand pounds apiece, taken separately. More than that, taken together."

"The old man was mad," said Robert angrily. "I shall dispute the will."

"I think not," said Wimsey. "There's such an offense as entering and stealing, you know."

"My God!" said Macpherson, handling the diamonds like a man in a dream. "My God!"

"Seven thousan' pund," said Jock. "Did I unnerstan' ye richtly to say that one o' they gulls is gaun aboot noo wi' seven thousan' punds' worth o' diamonds in his wame? Ech! it's just awfu' to think of. Guid day to you, sirs. I'll be gaun round to Jimmy McTaggart to ask will he send me the loan o' a gun.'

The Adventure of the Glass-Domed Clock

Author: Ellery Queen, pseudonym of Frederic Dannay (1905–1982) and Manfred B. Lee (1905–1971)

Detective: Ellery Queen (1929)

When cousins Dannay and Lee decided to collaborate on a detective novel for submission to a magazine's prize contest, one of the great bylines in mystery fiction was born. No writers ever had a greater allegiance to fair play to the reader than the Queen team, even as they shook off the early influence of S.S. Van Dine and moved into deeper characterization and more ambitious themes.

Ellery Queen (author and character) peaked in the 1940s in such landmark novels as *Calamity Town* (1942) and *Cat of Many Tails* (1949), but the best of the Queen short stories date from the previous decade. Unlike Christie and Sayers, the Queen team had no reluctance to write fully cast, fully clued novels-in-miniature in their early stories. The one that follows, from *The Adventures of Ellery Queen* (1934), still stands as the definitive treatment of a device the Queens turned to again and again: the dying message.

O f all the hundreds of criminal cases in the solution of which Mr. Ellery Queen participated by virtue of his self-imposed authority as son of the famous Inspector Queen of the New York Detective Bureau, he has steadfastly maintained that none offered a simpler diagnosis than the case that he has designated as "The Adventure of the Glass-Domed Clock." "So simple," he likes to say—sincerely!—"that a sophomore student in high school with the most elementary knowledge of algebraic mathematics would find it as easy to solve as the merest equation." He has been asked, as a result of such remarks, what a poor untutored first-grade detective on the regular police force—whose training in algebra might be something less than elementary—could be expected to make of such a "simple" case. His invariably serious response has been: "Amendment accepted. The resolution now reads: Anybody with common sense could have solved this crime. It's as basic as five minus four leaves one."

This was a little cruel, when it is noted that among those who had opportunity—and certainly wishfulness—to solve the crime was Mr. Ellery Queen's own father, the Inspector, certainly not the most stupid of criminal investigators. But then Mr. Ellery Queen, for all his mental prowess, is sometimes prone to confuse his definitions: *viz.,* his uncanny capacity for strict logic is far from the average citizen's common sense. Certainly one would not be inclined to term elementary a problem in which such components as the following figured: a pure purple amethyst, a somewhat bedraggled expatriate from Czarist Russia, a silver loving-cup, a poker game, five birthday encomiums, and of course that peculiarly ugly relic of early Americana catalogued as "the glass-domed clock"—among others! On the surface the thing seems too utterly fantastic, a maniac's howling nightmare. Anybody with Ellery's cherished "common sense" would have said so. Yet when he arranged those weird elements in their proper order and pointed out the "obvious" answer to the riddle—with that almost monastic intellectual innocence of his, as if everybody possessed his genius for piercing the veil of complexities!— Inspector Queen, good Sergeant Velie, and the others figuratively rubbed their eyes, the thing was so clear.

It began, as murders do, with a corpse. From the first, the eeriness of the whole business struck those who stood about in the faintly musked atmosphere of Martin Orr's curio shop and stared down at the shambles that had been Martin Orr. Inspector Queen, for one, refused to credit the evidence of his old senses; and it was not the gory nature of the crime that gave him pause, for he was as familiar with scenes of carnage as a butcher and blood no longer made him squeamish. That Martin Orr, the celebrated little Fifth Avenue curio dealer whose establishment was a treasure-house of authentic rarities, had had his shiny little bald head bashed to red ruin—this was an indifferent if practical detail; the bludgeon, a heavy paperweight spattered with blood but wiped clean of fingerprints, lay not far from the body; so *that* much was clear. No, it was not the assault on Orr that opened their eyes, but what Orr had apparently done, as he lay gasping out his life on the cold cement floor of his shop, *after* the assault.

The reconstruction of events after Orr's assailant had fled the shop, leaving the curio dealer for dead, seemed perfectly legible: having been struck down in the main chamber of his establishment, toward the rear,

Martin Orr had dragged his broken body six feet along a counter—the red trail told the story plainly—had by superhuman effort raised himself to a case of precious and semi-precious stones, had smashed the thin glass with a feeble fist, had groped about among the gem-trays, grasped a large unset amethyst, fallen back to the floor with the stone tightly clutched in his left hand, had then crawled on a tangent five feet past a table of antique clocks to a stone pedestal, raised himself again, and deliberately dragged off the pedestal the object it supported—an old clock with a glass dome over it—so the clock fell to the floor by his side, shattering its fragile case into a thousand pieces. And there Martin Orr had died, in his left fist the amethyst, his bleeding right hand resting on the clock as if in benediction. By some miracle the clock's machinery had not been injured by the fall; it had been one of Martin Orr's fetishes to keep all his magnificent timepieces running; and to the bewildered ears of the little knot of men surrounding Martin Orr's corpse that gray Sunday morning came the pleasant *tick-tick-tick* of the no longer glass-domed clock.

Weird? It was insane!

"There ought to be a law against it," growled Sergeant Velie.

Dr. Samuel Prouty, Assistant Medical Examiner of New York County, rose from his examination of the body and prodded Martin Orr's dead buttocks—the curio dealer was lying face down—with his foot.

"Now here's an old coot," he said grumpily, "sixty if he's a day, with more real stamina than many a youngster. Marvelous powers of resistance! He took a fearful beating about the head and shoulders, his assailant left him for dead, and the old monkey clung to life long enough to make a tour about the place! Many a younger man would have died in his tracks."

"Your professional admiration leaves me cold," said Ellery. He had been awakened out of a pleasantly warm bed not a half-hour before to find Djuna, the Queens' gypsy boy-of-all-work, shaking him. The Inspector had already gone, leaving word for Ellery, if he should be so minded, to follow. Ellery was always so minded when his nose sniffed crime, but he had not had breakfast and he was thoroughly out of temper. So his taxicab had rushed through Fifth Avenue to Martin Orr's shop, and he had found the Inspector and Sergeant Velie already on the cluttered scene interrogating a grief-stunned old woman—Martin Orr's aged widow—and a badly frightened Slavic giant who introduced himself in garbled English as the "ex-Duke Paul." The ex-Duke Paul, it developed, had been one of Nicholas Romanov's innumerable cousins caught in the whirlpool of the Russian revolution who had managed to flee the homeland and was eking out a none too fastidious living in New York as a sort of social curiosity. This was in 1926, when royal Russian expatriates were still something of a novelty in the land of democracy. As Ellery pointed out much later, this was not only 1926, but precisely Sunday, March the seventh, 1926, although at the time it seemed ridiculous to consider the specific date of any importance whatever.

"Who found the body?" demanded Ellery, puffing at his first cigarette of the day.

"His Nibs here," said Sergeant Velie, hunching his colossal shoulders. "*And* the lady. Seems like the Dook or whatever he is has been workin' a racket—been a kind of stooge for the old duck that was murdered. Orr used to give him commissions on the customers he brought in—and I understand he brought in plenty. Anyway, Mrs. Orr here got sort of worried when her hubby didn't come home last night from the poker game. . . ."

"Poker game?"

The Russian's dark face lighted up. "Yuss. Yuss. It is remarkable game. I have learned it since my sojourn in your so amazing country. Meester Orr, myself, and some others here play each week. Yuss." His face fell, and some of his fright returned. He looked fleetingly at the corpse and began to edge away.

"You played last night?" asked Ellery in a savage voice.

The Russian nodded. Inspector Queen said: "We're rounding 'em up. It seems that Orr, the Duke, and four other men had a sort of poker club, and met in Orr's back room there every Saturday night and played till all hours. Looked over that back room, but there's nothing there except the cards and chips. When Orr didn't come home Mrs. Orr got frightened and called up the Duke—he lives at some squirty little hotel in the Forties—the Duke called for her, they came down here this morning. . . . This is what they found." The Inspector eyed Martin Orr's corpse and the debris of glass surrounding him with gloom, almost with resentment. "Crazy, isn't it?"

Ellery glanced at Mrs. Orr; she was leaning against a counter, frozen-faced, tearless, staring down at her husband's body as if she could not believe her eyes. Actually, there was little to see: for Dr. Prouty had flung outspread sheets of a Sunday newspaper over the body, and only the left hand—still clutching the amethyst—was visible.

"Unbelievably so," said Ellery dryly. "I suppose there's a desk in the back room where Orr kept his accounts?"

"Sure."

"Any paper on Orr's body?"

"Paper?" repeated the Inspector in bewilderment. "Why, no."

"Pencil or pen?"

"No. Why, for heaven's sake?"

Before Ellery could reply, a little old man with a face like wrinkled brown papyrus pushed past a detective at the front door; he walked like a man in a dream. His gaze fixed on the shapeless bulk and the bloodstains. Then, incredibly, he blinked four times and began to cry. His wizened frame jerked with sobs. Mrs. Orr awoke from her trance; she cried: "Oh, Sam, Sam!" and putting her arms around the newcomer's racked shoulders, began to weep with him.

Ellery and the Inspector looked at each other, and Sergeant Velie belched his disgust. Then the Inspector grasped the crying man's little arm and shook him. "Here, stop that!" he said gruffly. "Who are you?"

The man raised his tear-stained face from Mrs. Orr's shoulder; he blubbered: "S-Sam Mingo, S-Sam Mingo, Mr. Orr's assistant. Who—who—Oh, I can't believe it!" and he buried his face in Mrs. Orr's shoulder again.

"Got to let him cry himself out, I guess," said the Inspector, shrugging. "Ellery, what the deuce do you make of it? I'm stymied."

Ellery raised his eyebrows eloquently. A detective appeared in the street-door escorting a pale, trembling man. "Here's Arnold Pike, Chief. Dug him out of bed just now."

Pike was a man of powerful physique and jutting jaw; but he was thoroughly unnerved and, somehow, bewildered. He fastened his eyes on the heap that represented Martin Orr's mortal remains and kept mechanically buttoning and unbuttoning his overcoat. The Inspector said: "I understand you and a few others played poker in the back room here last night. With Orr. What time did you break up?"

"Twelve-thirty." Pike's voice wabbled drunkenly.

"What time did you start?"

"Around eleven."

"Cripes," said Inspector Queen, "that's not a poker game, that's a game of tiddledywinks. . . . Who killed Orr, Mr. Pike?"

Arnold Pike tore his eyes from the corpse. "God, sir, I don't know."

"You don't, hey? All friends, were you?"

"Yes. Oh, yes."

"What's your business, Mr. Pike?"

"I'm a stockbroker."

"Why—" began Ellery, and stopped. Under the urging of two detectives, three men advanced into the shop—all frightened, all exhibiting evidences of hasty awakening and hasty dressing, all fixing their eyes at once on the paper-covered bundle on the floor, the streaks of blood, the shattered glass. The three, like the incredible ex-Duke Paul, who was straight and stiff and somehow ridiculous, seemed petrified; men crushed by a sudden blow.

A small fat man with brilliant eyes muttered that he was Stanley Oxman, jeweler. Martin Orr's oldest, closest friend. He could not believe it. It was frightful, unheard of. Martin murdered! No, he could offer no explanation. Martin had been a peculiar man, perhaps, but as far as he, Oxman, knew the curio dealer had not had an enemy in the world. And so on, and so on, as the other two stood by, frozen, waiting their turn.

One was a lean, debauched fellow with the mark of the ex-athlete about him. His slight paunch and yellowed eyeballs could not conceal the signs of a vigorous prime. This was, said Oxman, their mutual friend, Leo Gurney, the newspaper feature writer. The other was J.D. Vincent, said Oxman—developing an unexpected streak of talkativeness, which the Inspector fanned gently—who, like Arnold Pike, was in Wall Street—"a manipulator," whatever that was. Vincent, a stocky man with the gambler's tight face, seemed incapable of speech; as for Gurney, he seemed glad that Oxman had constituted himself spokesman and kept staring at the body on the cement floor.

Ellery sighed, thought of his warm bed, put down the rebellion in his breakfastless stomach, and went to work—keeping an ear cocked for the Inspector's sharp questions and the halting replies. Ellery followed the streaks of blood to the spot where Orr had ravished the case of gems. The case, its glass front smashed, little frazzled splinters framing the orifice, contained more than a dozen metal trays floored with black velvet, set in two rows. Each held scores of gems—a brilliant array of semiprecious and precious stones beautifully variegated in color. Two trays in the center of the front row attracted his eye particularly—one containing highly polished stones of red, brown, yellow, and green; the other a single variety, all of a subtranslucent quality, leek-green in color, and covered with small red spots. Ellery noted that both these trays were in direct line with the place where Orr's hand had smashed the glass case.

He went over to the trembling little assistant, Sam Mingo, who had quieted down and was standing by Mrs. Orr, clutching her hand like a child. "Mingo," he said, touching the man. Mingo started with a leap of his stringy muscles. "Don't be alarmed, Mingo. Just step over here with me for a moment." Ellery smiled reassuringly, took the man's arm, and led him to the shattered case.

And Ellery said: "How is it that Martin Orr bothered with such trifles as these? I see rubies here, and emeralds, but the others. . . . Was he a jeweler as well as a curio dealer?"

Orr's assistant mumbled: "No. N-no, he was not. But he always liked the baubles. The baubles, he called them. Kept them for love. Most of them are birthstones. He sold a few. This is a complete line."

"What are those green stones with the red spots?"

"Bloodstones."

"And this tray of red, brown, yellow, and green ones?"

"All jaspers. The common ones are red, brown, and yellow. The few green ones in the tray are more valuable. . . . The bloodstone is itself a variety of jasper. Beautiful! And . . ."

"Yes, yes," said Ellery hastily. "From which tray did the amethyst in Orr's hand come, Mingo?"

Mingo shivered and pointed a crinkled forefinger to a tray in the rear row, at the corner of the case.

"*All* the amethysts are kept in this one tray?"

"Yes. You can see for yourself—"

"Here!" growled the Inspector, approaching. "Mingo! I want you to look over the stock. Check everything. See if anything's been stolen."

"Yes, sir," said Orr's assistant timidly, and began to potter about the shop with lagging steps. Ellery looked about. The door to the back room was twenty-five feet from the spot where Orr had been assaulted. No desk in the shop itself, he observed, no paper about. . . .

"Well, son," said the Inspector in troubled tones, "it looks as if we're on the trail of something. I don't like it. . . . Finally dragged it out of these birds. I *thought* it was funny, this business of breaking up a weekly Saturday night poker game at half-past twelve. They had a fight!"

"Who engaged in fisticuffs with whom?"

"Oh, don't be funny. It's this Pike feller, the stockbroker. Seems they all had something to drink during the game. They played stud, and Orr, with an ace-king-queen-jack showing, raised the roof off the play. Everybody dropped out except Pike; he had three sixes. Well, Orr gave it everything he had and when Pike threw his cards away on a big over-raise, Orr cackled, showed his hole-card—a deuce!—and raked in the pot. Pike, who'd lost his pile on the hand, began to grumble; he and Orr had words—you know how those things start. They were all pie-eyed, anyway, says the Duke. Almost a fist-fight. The others interfered, but it broke up the game."

"They all left together?"

"Yes. Orr stayed behind to clean up the mess in the backroom. The five others went out together and separated a few blocks away. Any one of 'em could have come back and pulled off the job before Orr shut up shop!"

"And what does Pike say?"

"What the deuce would you expect him to say? That he went right home and to bed, of course."

"The others?"

"They deny any knowledge of what happened after they left here last night. . . . Well, Mingo? Anything missing?"

Mingo said helplessly: "Everything seems all right."

"I thought so," said the Inspector with satisfaction. "This is a grudge kill, son. Well, I want to talk to these fellers some more. . . . What's eating you?"

Ellery lighted a cigarette. "A few random thoughts. Have you decided in your own mind why Orr dragged himself about the shop when he was three-quarters dead, broke the glass-domed clock, pulled an amethyst out of the gem case?"

"That," said the Inspector, the troubled look returning, "is what I'm foggy about. I can't—'Scuse me." He returned hastily to the waiting group of men.

Ellery took Mingo's lax arm. "Get a grip on yourself, man. I want you to look at that smashed clock for a moment. Don't be afraid of Orr—dead men don't bite, Mingo." He pushed the little assistant toward the paper-covered corpse. "Now tell me something about that clock. Has it a history?"

"Not much of one. It's a h-hundred and sixty-nine years old. Not especially valuable. Curious piece because of the glass dome over it. Happens to be the only glass-domed clock we have. That's all."

Ellery polished the lenses of his pince-nez, set the glasses firmly on his nose, and bent over to examine the fallen clock. It had a black wooden base, circular, about nine inches deep, and scarified with age. On this the clock was set—ticking away cozily. The dome of glass had fitted into a groove around the top of the black base, sheathing the clock completely. With the dome unshattered, the entire piece must have stood about two feet high.

Ellery rose, and his lean face was thoughtful. Mingo looked at him in a sort of stupid anxiety. "Did Pike, Oxman, Vincent, Gurney, or Paul ever own this piece?"

Mingo shook his head. "No, sir. We've had it for many years. We couldn't get rid of it. Certainly *those* gentlemen didn't want it."

"Then none of the five ever tried to purchase the clock?"

"Of course not."

"Admirable," said Ellery. "Thank you." Mingo felt that he had been dismissed; he hesitated, shuffled his feet, and finally went over to the silent widow and stood by her side. Ellery knelt on the cement floor and with difficulty loosened the grip of the dead man's fingers about the amethyst. He saw that the stone was a clear glowing purple in color, shook his head as if in perplexity, and rose.

Vincent, the stocky Wall Street gambler with the tight face, was saying to the Inspector in a rusty voice: "—can't see why you suspect any of us. Pike particularly. What's in a little quarrel? We've always been good friends, all of us. Last night we were pickled—"

"Sure," said the Inspector gently. "Last night you were pickled. A drunk sort of forgets himself at times, Vincent. Liquor affects a man's morals as well as his head."

"Nuts!" said the yellow-eyeballed Gurney suddenly. "Stop sleuthing, Inspector. You're barking up the wrong tree. Vincent's right. We're all friends. It was Pike's birthday last week." Ellery stood very still. "We all sent him gifts. Had a celebration, and Orr was the cockiest of us all. Does that look like the preparation for a pay-off?"

Ellery stepped forward, and his eyes were shining. All his temper had fled by now, and his nostrils were quivering with the scent of the chase. "And when was this celebration held, gentlemen?" he asked softly.

Stanley Oxman puffed out his cheeks. "Now they're going to suspect a birthday blowout! Last Monday, mister. This past Monday. What of it?"

"This past Monday," said Ellery. "How nice. Mr. Pike, your gifts—"

"For God's sake. . . ." Pike's eyes were tortured.

"When did you receive them?"

"After the party, during the week. Boys sent them up to me. I didn't see any of them until last night, at the poker game."

The others nodded their heads in concert; the Inspector was looking at Ellery with puzzlement. Ellery grinned, adjusted his pince-nez, and spoke to his father aside. The weight of the Inspector's puzzlement, if his face was a scale, increased. But he said quietly to the white-haired broker: "Mr. Pike, you're going to take a little trip with Mr. Queen and Sergeant Velie. Just for a few moments. The others of you stay here with me. Mr. Pike, please remember not to try anything—foolish."

Pike was incapable of speech; his head twitched sidewise and he buttoned his coat for the twentieth time. Nobody said anything. Sergeant Velie took Pike's arm, and Ellery preceded them into the early-morning peace of Fifth Avenue. On the sidewalk he asked Pike his address, the broker dreamily gave him a street and number, Ellery hailed a taxicab, and the three men were driven in silence to an apartment building a mile farther uptown. They took a self-service elevator to the seventh floor, marched a few steps to a door, Pike fumbled with a key, and they went into his apartment.

"Let me see your gifts, please," said Ellery without expression—the first words uttered since they had stepped into the taxicab. Pike led them to a den-like room. On a table stood four boxes of different shapes, and a handsome silver cup. "There," he said in a cracked voice.

Ellery went swiftly to the table. He picked up the silver cup. On it was engraved the sentimental legend:

> *To a True Friend*
> ARNOLD PIKE
> *March 1, 1876 to—*
> *J.D. Vincent*

"Rather macabre humor, Mr. Pike," said Ellery, setting the cup down, "since Vincent has had space left for the date of your demise." Pike began to speak, then shivered and clamped his pale lips together.

Ellery removed the lid of a tiny black box. Inside, embedded in a cleft between two pieces of purple velvet, there was a man's signet ring, a magnificent and heavy circlet the signet of which revealed the coat-of-arms of royalist Russia. "The tattered old eagle," murmured Ellery. "Let's see what our friend the ex-Duke has to say." On a card in the box, inscribed in minute script, the following was written in French:

> To my good friend Arnold Pike on his 50th birthday. March the first ever makes me sad. I remember that day in 1917—two weeks before the Czar's abdication—the quiet, then the storm. . . . But be merry, Arnold! Accept this signet ring given to me by my royal Cousin, as a token of my esteem. Long life!
>
> *Paul*

Ellery did not comment. He restored ring and card to the box, and picked up another, a large flat packet. Inside there was a gold-tipped Morocco-leather wallet. The card tucked into one of the pockets said:

"Twenty-one years of life's rattle
And men are no longer boys
They gird their loins for the battle
And throw away their toys—

"But here's a cheerful plaything
For a white-haired old mooncalf,
Who may act like any May-thing
For nine years more and a half!"

"Charming verse," chuckled Ellery. "Another misbegotten poet. Only a newspaper man would indite such nonsense. This is Gurney's?"

"Yes," muttered Pike. "It's nice, isn't it?"

"If you'll pardon me," said Ellery, "it's rotten." He threw aside the wallet and seized a larger carton. Inside there was a glittering pair of patent-leather carpet slippers; the card attached read:

Happy Birthday, Arnold! May We Be All Together On as Pleasant a March First to Celebrate Your 100th Anniversary!

Martin

"A poor prophet," said Ellery dryly. "And what's this?" He laid the shoebox down and picked up a small flat box. In it he saw a gold-plated cigarette case, with the initials *A.P.* engraved on the lid. The accompanying card read:

Good luck on your fiftieth birthday. I look forward to your sixtieth on March first, 1936, for another bout of whoopee!

Stanley Oxman

"And Mr. Stanley Oxman," remarked Ellery, putting down the cigarette case, "was a little less sanguine than Martin Orr. His imagination reached no further than sixty, Mr. Pike. A significant point."

"I can't see—" began the broker in a stubborn little mutter, "why you have to bring my friends into it—"

Sergeant Velie gripped his elbow, and he winced. Ellery shook his head disapprovingly at the man-mountain. "And now, Mr. Pike, I think we may return to Martin Orr's shop. Or, as the Sergeant might fastidiously phrase it, the scene of the crime. . . . Very interesting. *Very* interesting. It almost compensates for an empty belly."

"You got something?" whispered Sergeant Velie hoarsely as Pike preceded them into a taxicab downstairs.

"Cyclops," said Ellery, "all God's chillun got something. But *I* got everything."

Sergeant Velie disappeared somewhere *en route* to the curio shop, and Arnold Pike's spirits lifted at once. Ellery eyed him quizzically. "One thing, Mr. Pike," he said as the taxicab turned into Fifth Avenue, "before we disembark. How long have you six men been acquainted?"

The broker sighed. "It's complicated. My only friend of considerable duration is Leo; Gurney, you know. Known each other for fifteen years. But then Orr and the Duke have been friends since 1918, I understand, and of course Stan Oxman and Orr have known each other—knew each other—for many years. I met Vincent about a year ago through my business affiliations and introduced him into our little clique."

"Had you yourself and the others—Oxman, Orr, Paul—been acquainted before this time two years ago?"

Pike looked puzzled. "I don't see . . . Why, no. I met Oxman and the Duke a year and a half ago through Orr."

"And that," murmured Ellery, "is so perfect that I don't care if I *never* have breakfast. Here we are, Mr. Pike."

They found a glum group awaiting their return—nothing had changed, except that Orr's body had disappeared, Dr. Prouty was gone, and some attempt at sweeping up the glass fragments of the domed clock had been made. The Inspector was in a fever of impatience, demanded to know where Sergeant Velie was, what Ellery had sought in Pike's apartment. . . . Ellery whispered something to him, and the old man looked startled. Then he dipped his fingers into his brown snuffbox and partook with grim relish.

The regal expatriate cleared his bull throat. "You have mystery resolved?" he rumbled. "Yuss?"

"Your Highness," said Ellery gravely, "I have indeed mystery resolved." He whirled and clapped his palms together; they jumped. "Attention, please! Piggot," he said to a detective, "stand at that door and don't let anyone in but Sergeant Velie."

The detective nodded. Ellery studied the faces about him. If one of them was apprehensive, he had ample control of his physiognomy. They all seemed merely interested, now that the first shock of the tragedy had passed them by. Mrs. Orr clung to Mingo's fragile hand; her eyes did not once leave Ellery's face. The fat little jeweler, the journalist, the two Wall Street men, the Russian ex-duke . . .

"An absorbing affair," grinned Ellery, "and quite elementary, despite its points of interest. Follow me closely." He went over to the counter and picked up the purple amethyst, which had been clutched in the dead man's hand. He looked at it and smiled. Then he glanced at the other object on the counter—the round-based clock, with the fragments of its glass dome protruding from the circular groove.

"Consider the situation. Martin Orr, brutally beaten about the head, managed in a last desperate living action to crawl to the jewel case on the counter, pick out this gem, then go to the stone pedestal and pull the glass-domed clock from it. Whereupon, his mysterious mission accomplished, he dies.

"Why should a dying man engage in such a baffling procedure? There can be only one general explanation. He knows his assailant and is endeavoring to leave clues to his assailant's identity." At this point the Inspector nodded, and Ellery grinned again behind the curling smoke of his cigarette. "But such clues! Why? Well, what would you expect a dying man to do if he wished to leave behind him the name of his murderer? The answer is obvious: he would write it. But on Orr's body we find no paper, pen, or pencil; and no paper in the immediate vicinity. Where else might he secure writing materials? Well, you will observe that Martin Orr was assaulted at a spot twenty-five feet from the door of the back room. The distance, Orr must have felt, was too great for his failing strength. Then Orr couldn't write the name of his murderer except by the somewhat fantastic method of dipping his finger into his own blood and using the floor as a slate. Such an expedient probably didn't occur to him.

"He must have reasoned with rapidity, life ebbing out of him at every breath. Then—he crawled to the case, broke the glass, took out the amethyst. Then—he crawled to the pedestal and dragged off the glass-domed clock. Then—he died. So the amethyst and the clock were Martin Orr's bequest to the police. You can almost hear him say: 'Don't fail me. This is clear, simple, easy. Punish my murderer.' "

Mrs. Orr gasped, but the expression on her wrinkled face did not alter. Mingo began to sniffle. The others waited in total silence.

"The clock first," said Ellery lazily. "The first thing one thinks of in connection with a timepiece is time. Was Orr trying, then, by dragging the clock off the pedestal, to smash the works and, stopping the clock, to fix the time of his murder? Offhand a possibility, it is true; but if this was his purpose, it failed, because the clock didn't stop running after all. While this circumstance does not invalidate the time-interpretation, further consideration of the whole problem does. For you five gentlemen had left Orr in a body. The time of the assault could not possibly be so checked against your return to your several residences as to point inescapably to one of you as the murderer. Orr must have realized this, if he thought of it at all; in other words, there wouldn't be any particular *point* to such a purpose on Orr's part.

"And there is still another—and more conclusive—consideration that invalidates the time-interpretation; and that is, that Orr crawled *past* a table full of running clocks to get to this glass-domed one. If it had been time he was intending to indicate, he could have preserved his energies by stopping at this table and pulling down one of the many clocks upon it. But no—he deliberately passed that table to get to the *glass-domed* clock. So it wasn't time.

"Very well. Now, since the glass-domed clock is *the only one* of its kind in the shop, it must have been not time in the general sense but this particular timepiece in the specific sense by which Martin Orr was motivated. But what could this particular timepiece possibly indicate? In itself, as Mr. Mingo has informed me, it has no personal connotation with anyone connected with Orr. The idea that Orr was leaving a clue to a clockmaker is unsound; none of you gentlemen follows that delightful craft, and certainly Mr. Oxman, the jeweler, could not have been indicated when so many things in the gem case would have served."

Oxman began to perspire; he fixed his eyes on the jewel in Ellery's hand.

"Then it wasn't a professional meaning from the clock, as a clock," continued Ellery equably, "that Orr was trying to convey. But what is there about this particular clock, which is different from the other clocks in the shop?" Ellery shot his forefinger forward. "This particular clock has a glass dome over it!" He straightened slowly. "Can any of you gentlemen think of a fairly common object almost perfectly suggested by a glass-domed clock?"

No one answered, but Vincent and Pike began to lick their lips. "I see signs of intelligence," said Ellery. "Let me be more specific. What is it—I feel like Sam Lloyd!—that has a base, a glass dome, and ticking machinery inside the dome?" Still no answer. "Well," said Ellery, "I suppose I should have expected reticence. Of course, *it's a stock-ticker!*"

They stared at him, and then all eyes turned to examine the whitening faces of J. D. Vincent and Arnold Pike. "Yes," said Ellery, "you may well gaze upon the countenances of the *Messieurs* Vincent and Pike. For they are the only two of our little cast who are connected with stock-tickers: Mr. Vincent is a Wall Street operator, Mr. Pike is a broker." Quietly two detectives left a wall and approached the two men.

"Whereupon," said Ellery, "we lay aside the glass-domed clock and take up this very fascinating little bauble in my hand." He held up the amethyst. "A purple amethyst—there are bluish-violet ones, you know. What could this purple amethyst have signified to Martin Orr's frantic brain? The obvious thing is that it is a jewel. Mr. Oxman looked disturbed a moment ago; you needn't be, sir. The jewelry significance of this amethyst is eliminated on two counts. The first is that the tray on which the amethysts lie is in a corner at the rear of the shattered case. It was necessary for Orr to reach far into the case. If it were a jewel he sought, why didn't he pick any one of the stones nearer to his palsied hand? For any single one of them would connote 'jeweler.' But no; Orr went to the excruciating trouble of ignoring what was close at hand—as in the business of the clock—and deliberately selected something from an inconvenient place. Then the amethyst did not signify a jeweler, but something else.

"The second is this, Mr. Oxman: certainly Orr knew that the stock-ticker clue would not fix guilt on *one* person; for two of his cronies are connected with stocks. On the other hand, did Orr have two assailants rather than one? Not likely. For if by the amethyst he meant to connote you, Mr. Oxman, and by the glass-domed clock he meant to connote either Mr. Pike or Mr. Vincent, he was still leaving a wabbly trail; for we still would not know whether Mr. Pike or Mr. Vincent was meant. Did he have *three* assailants, then? You see, we are already in the realm of fantasy. No, the major probability is that, since the glass-domed clock cut the possibilities down to two persons, the amethyst was meant to single out one of those two.

"How does the amethyst pin one of these gentlemen down? What significance besides the obvious one of jewelry does the amethyst suggest? Well, it is a rich purple in color. Ah, but one of your coterie fits here: His Highness the ex-Duke is certainly one born to the royal purple, even if it is an ex-ducal purple, as it were. . . ."

The soldierly Russian growled: "I am *not* Highness. You know nothing of royal address!" His dark face became suffused with blood, and he broke into a volley of guttural Russian.

Ellery grinned. "Don't excite yourself—Your Grace, is it? *You* weren't meant. For if we postulate you, we again drag in a third person and leave unsettled the question of which Wall Street man Orr meant to accuse; we're no better off than before. Avaunt, royalty!

"Other possible significances? Yes. There is a species of hummingbird, for instance, known as the amethyst. Out! We have no aviarists here. For another thing, the amethyst was connected with ancient Hebrew ritual—an Orientalist told me this once—breastplate decoration of the high priest, or some such thing. Obviously inapplicable here. No, there is only one other possible application." Ellery turned to the stocky gambler. "Mr. Vincent, what is your birthdate?"

Vincent stammered: "November s-second."

"Splendid. That eliminates *you.*" Ellery stopped abruptly. There was a stir at the door and Sergeant Velie barged in with a very grim face. Ellery smiled. "Well, Sergeant, was my hunch about motive correct?"

Velie said: "And how. He forged Orr's signature to a big check. Money-trouble, all right. Orr hushed the matter up, paid, and said he'd collect from the forger. The banker doesn't even know who the forger is."

"Congratulations are in order, Sergeant. Our murderer evidently wished to evade repayment. Murders have been committed for less vital reasons." Ellery flourished his pince-nez. "I said, Mr. Vincent, that you are eliminated. Eliminated because the only other significance of the amethyst left to us is that it is a *birthstone.* But the November birthstone is a topaz. On the other hand, Mr. Pike has just celebrated a birthday, which. . . ."

And with these words, as Pike gagged and the others broke into excited gabble, Ellery made a little sign to Sergeant Velie, and himself leaped forward. But it was not Arnold Pike who found himself in the crushing grip of Velie and staring into Ellery's amused eyes.

It was the newspaper man, Leo Gurney.

"As I said," explained Ellery later, in the privacy of the Queens' living room and after his belly had been comfortably filled with food, "this has been a ridiculously elementary problem." The Inspector toasted his stockinged feet before the fire, and grunted. Sergeant Velie scratched his head. "You don't think so?"

"But look. It was evident, when I decided what the clues of the clock and the amethyst were intended to convey, that Arnold Pike was the man meant to be indicated. For what is the month of which the amethyst is the birthstone? *February*—in both the Polish and Jewish birthstone systems, the two almost universally recognized. Of the two men indicated by the clock-clue, Vincent was eliminated because his birthstone is a topaz. Was Pike's birthday then in February? Seemingly not, for he celebrated it—this year, 1926—in March! March first, observe. What could this mean? Only one thing: since Pike was the sole remaining possibility, then his birthday *was* in February, but on the *twenty-ninth,* on Leap Day, as it's called, and 1926 not being a Leap Year, Pike chose to celebrate his birthday on the day on which it would ordinarily fall, March first.

"But this meant that Martin Orr, to have left the amethyst, must have known Pike's birthday to be in February, since he seemingly left the February birthstone as a clue. Yet what did I find on the card accompanying Orr's gift of carpet slippers to Pike last week? 'May we all be together on as pleasant a *March first* to celebrate your hundredth anniversary.' But if Pike is fifty years old in 1926, he was born in 1876—a Leap Year—and his hundredth anniversary would be 1976, also a Leap Year. They *wouldn't* celebrate Pike's birthday on his hundredth anniversary on March first! Then Orr *didn't* know Pike's real birthday was February twenty-ninth, or he would have said so on the card. He thought it was March.

"But the person who left the amethyst sign *did* know Pike's birth-month was February, since he left February's birthstone. We've just established that Martin Orr didn't know Pike's birth month was February, but thought it was March. Therefore Martin Orr was not the one who selected the amethyst.

"Any confirmation? Yes. The birthstone for March in the Polish system is the bloodstone; in the Jewish it's the jasper. But both these stones were nearer a groping hand than the amethysts, which lay in a tray at the back of the case. In other words, whoever selected the amethyst deliberately ignored the March stones in favor of the February stone, and therefore knew that Pike was born in February, not in March. But had Orr selected a stone, it would have been bloodstone or jasper, since he believed Pike *was* born in March. Orr eliminated again.

"But if Orr did not select the amethyst, as I've shown, then what have we? Palpably, a frame-up. Someone arranged matters to make us believe that Orr himself had selected the amethyst and smashed the clock. You can see the murderer dragging poor old Orr's dead body around, leaving the blood-trail on purpose. . . ."

Ellery sighed. "I never did believe Orr left those signs. It was all too pat, too slick, too weirdly unreal. It is conceivable that a dying man will leave one clue to his murderer's identity, but *two*. . . ." Ellery shook his head.

"If Orr didn't leave the clues, who did? Obviously the murderer. But the clues deliberately led to Arnold Pike. Then Pike couldn't be the murderer, for certainly he would not leave a trail to himself had he killed Orr.

"Who else? Well, one thing stood out. Whoever killed Orr, framed Pike, and really selected that amethyst, knew Pike's birthday to be in

February. Orr and Pike we have eliminated. Vincent didn't know Pike's birthday was in February, as witness his inscription on the silver cup. Nor did our friend the ex-Duke, who also wrote 'March the first' on his card. Oxman didn't—he said they'd celebrate Pike's sixtieth birthday on March first, 1936—a Leap Year, observe, when Pike's birthday would be celebrated on February twenty-ninth. . . . Don't forget that we may accept these cards' evidence as valid; the cards were sent before the crime, and the crime would have no connection in the murderer's mind with Pike's five birthday cards. The flaw in the murderer's plot was that he assumed—a natural error—that Orr and perhaps the others, too, knew Pike's birthday really fell on Leap Day. And he never did see the cards, which proved the others didn't know, because Pike himself told us that after the party Monday night he did not see any of the others until last night, the night of the murder."

"I'll be fried in lard," muttered Sergeant Velie, shaking his head.

"No doubt," grinned Ellery. "But we've left someone out. How about Leo Gurney, the newspaper feature writer? His stick o' doggerel said that Pike wouldn't reach the age of twenty-one for another nine and a half years. Interesting? Yes, and damning. For this means he considered facetiously that Pike was at the time of writing eleven and a half years old. But how is this possible, even in humorous verse? It's possible only if Gurney knew that Pike's birthday falls on February twenty-ninth, which occurs only once in four years! Fifty divided by four is twelve and a half. But since the year 1900 for some reason I've never been able to discover, was not a Leap Year, Gurney was right, and actually Pike had celebrated only 'eleven and a half' birthdays."

And Ellery drawled: "Being the only one who knew Pike's birthday to be in February, then Gurney was the only one who could have selected the amethyst. Then Gurney arranged matters to make it seem that Orr was accusing Pike. Then Gurney was the murderer of Orr. . . .

"Simple? As a child's sum!"

Madame Maigret's Admirer

Author: Georges Simenon (1903–1989)

Detective: Jules Maigret (1931)

Often known (like his creator) by his surname alone, the Parisian cop Maigret was one of the three or four most famous detective characters of the century. He was also one of the busiest. In 1931, ten of his cases were published in France; the next year, production declined to a mere seven, and after that he slowed down considerably while still out-sleuthing most of his contemporaries. By his final French appearance in 1972, he had appeared in around eighty book-length cases. Not surprisingly, his English-language publishers were constantly playing catch-up.

Simenon was such an economical storyteller that even the novels about Maigret were shorter than average. Like the novels, the short stories vary widely in quality. The story that follows shows us the domestic Maigret and is chosen to celebrate one of detective fiction's good marriages.

I

In the Maigrets' household, as in many others, certain traditions had grown up, which had eventually become as important to them as are religious rites for some people.

Thus, during the many years they had lived in the Place des Vosges, the Superintendent had formed the habit, in summer, of undoing his dark tie as soon as he came in from the courtyard and started up the staircase, completing the process by the time he reached the first floor.

The staircase of the building, which, like all those in the square, had once been a splendid private mansion, ceased at that point to rise majestically between wrought-iron banisters and walls of imitation marble; it became steep and narrow, and Maigret, panting a little, reached the second floor with his shirt collar open.

He still had to go along a poorly lit corridor as far as his own door, the third on the left, and as he put his key into the lock, carrying his jacket over his arm, he invariably called out:

"It's me!"

And he would sniff, so as to guess from the smell what was cooking for lunch, then make his way into the dining room, whose tall window was open on to the dazzling sight of the square where four fountains were plashing musically.

It was June. The weather was particularly hot and at Police Headquarters the talk was all of holidays. There were people in their shirtsleeves on the boulevards and beer was flowing freely on the *terrasse* of every café.

"Have you seen your admirer?" the Superintendent asked, mopping his brow as he settled down by the window.

Nobody would have guessed at that moment that he had just spent hours in that sort of anticrime laboratory known as Police Headquarters, studying the darkest and most sordid recesses of the human heart.

Away from work, he was ready to be amused by trifles, particularly when it was a matter of teasing his naive wife. For the past fortnight the standing joke had been to ask her for news of her admirer.

"Does he still go for his two little turns round the Square? Is he still just as mysterious and distinguished-looking? When I think that you've a weakness for distinguished-looking men and yet you married me!"

Madame Maigret was going back and forth, laying the table, since she would not have a maid, merely a cleaning woman in the mornings for the rough work. She took up the game.

"I never said he was distinguished-looking!"

"But you described him to me: a light gray hat with a bound brim, a small turned-up moustache, probably dyed, a walking stick with a carved ivory knob . . ."

"You may laugh! . . . One of these days you'll realize that I was right . . . I'm convinced that he's no ordinary man and that his behavior means there's something strange going on . . ."

From the window one could automatically watch the comings and goings through the Place des Vosges, which was fairly empty in the mornings but where, in the afternoons, the mothers and nannies of the neighborhood sat on benches watching children at play.

All around the public garden, which, fenced in by its railings, is one of the most formal in Paris, stand identical houses with arcades and steeply sloping roofs.

To begin with, Madame Maigret had paid only casual attention to the stranger, who could scarcely have passed unnoticed, since everything about his dress and attitude was twenty or thirty years out of date, and he reminded one of the typical old dandy only to be seen nowadays in the illustrations of humorous magazines.

It was early in the morning, the time when all the houses had their windows wide open and one could see maids busy with housework in the various homes.

"He seems to be looking out for something," Madame Maigret had commented.

That afternoon she had gone to visit her sister, and next day, at exactly the same time, she had seen the stranger again, walking round the square at a steady pace once and then twice, and finally disappearing in the direction of the Rèpublique district.

"Probably an old fellow who fancies little housemaids and comes to watch them shaking the carpets!" Maigret had said when his wife, in the course of conversation, had mentioned her old dandy.

And at three o'clock that afternoon, to her considerable surprise, she had seen him sitting on a bench immediately opposite her window, motionless, with his hands folded on the knob of his walking stick.

At four o'clock he was still there. At five o'clock he was still there. Not until six o'clock did he get up and take himself off along the Rue des Tournelles, without having spoken a word to anyone or even unfolded a newspaper.

"Don't you think it's odd, Maigret?" For she had always addressed her husband by his surname.

"I've already told you: there must certainly have been some pretty servant girls around him . . ."

And the next day Madame Maigret returned to the attack:

"I watched him carefully, for he spent three hours again sitting on the same bench, in the same place . . ."

"Perhaps he wanted to have a good look at you? From that bench one must be able to see into our apartment, and the gentleman's in love with you . . ."

"Don't talk such nonsense!"

"For one thing, he carries a walking stick, and you've always liked men who use walking sticks . . . I bet he wears pince-nez . . ."

"Why?"

"Because you've a weakness for men with pince-nez!"

They were bickering gently, after twenty years of marriage, enjoying the pleasant peace of their home.

"Listen . . . I looked carefully all round him . . . There was indeed a nursemaid sitting just opposite him, on a chair. A girl I'd already noticed in the fruiterer's shop, for one thing because she's very pretty, and furthermore because she's distinguished-looking . . ."

"There you are!" said Maigret triumphantly. "Your distinguished-looking maid was sitting in front of the old gentleman. You've already noticed that women sometimes sit down without realizing what they're showing, and your admirer spent the afternoon ogling her."

"That's all you think about!"

"So long as I haven't seen your mystery man . . ."

"Can I help it if he only comes when you aren't here?"

And Maigret, who was in constant contact with so many sensational happenings, revived his spirits by such simple pleasantries, and never failed to ask for news of the man whom they had come to describe as Madame Maigret's admirer.

"You can laugh as much as you like! All the same there's something about him, I don't know what, that fascinates and rather frightens me . . . I don't know how to explain . . . When you look at him you can't take your eyes off him. For hours on end he can sit in the same place without stirring, and even his eyes don't move behind his pince-nez . . ."

"Could you see his eyes from here?"

Madame Maigret almost blushed, as though caught in the act.

"I went up to have a closer look . . . I particularly wanted to know if you'd been right . . . Well, the blond nursemaid, who always has two children with her, behaves very properly and there's nothing to be noticed . . ."

"Does she stop there all afternoon too?"

"She arrives about three o'clock, usually after the man. She always has some crochet work with her. They leave at roughly the same time. For hours on end she works at her crochet without raising her head except sometimes to call back the children if they wander off . . ."

"Don't you think, darling, that there are hundreds of nursemaids sitting in the public gardens of Paris doing crochet or knitting for hours on end while they look after their employers' children?"

"Quite possibly!"

"And lots of old retired gentlemen who have nothing to do but warm themselves in the sun, casting lustful glances at pretty girls?"

"This one isn't old . . ."

"You told me yourself that his moustache was certainly dyed and that he must be wearing a wig."

"Yes, but he doesn't seem old."

"The same age as me?"

"Sometimes he seems older and sometimes younger . . ."

And Maigret, pretending to be jealous, grumbled:

"One of these days I shall have to get a close-up view of this admirer of yours!"

He did not give the matter serious thought, and neither did Madame Maigret. In the same way they had once amused themselves for quite a while observing a courting couple who met each evening under the arches, noting their quarrels and reconciliations, until the day when the girl, who worked in the local dairy, had appeared at exactly the same spot with a different young man.

"You know, Maigret . . ."

"What?"

"I've been thinking it over . . . I wonder whether the man couldn't be there to spy on somebody . . ."

Days passed, and the sun grew ever hotter; in the evenings the crowd in the square became denser, as all the working people from neighboring streets came to take the air beside the four fountains.

"What I find so strange is that he never sits down in the mornings. And why does he walk twice round the square, as if he were expecting a signal?"

"What does your pretty blonde do meanwhile?"

"I never see her. She works in a house on the right-hand side and from here one can't see what's happening there. I see her in the market, where she doesn't talk to anyone, except to tell the tradesmen what she wants. She never argues about prices, so that she's cheated of at least twenty percent . . . She always seems to have her mind on something else . . ."

"Well, next time I have a tricky job of watching to be done I'll put you on to it instead of my men."

"You can laugh at me! But sooner or later we shall see whether . . ."

It was eight o'clock. Maigret had dined already, which was unusual, since he was generally kept rather late at the Quai des Orfévres.

He was sitting at the window in his shirtsleeves, his pipe between his lips, gazing absentmindedly at the pink sky that was shortly to be over-run by dusk, and at the Place des Vosges, now crowded with people whom the precocious summer heat had made listless.

Behind him he heard sounds that implied that Madame Maigret was finishing the washing up and would soon come to sit beside him with some piece of needlework.

Evenings such as this, with no unpleasant case to solve, no murderer to discover, no thief to watch, evenings when his thoughts could roam in peace as he watched the pink sky, were rare, and Maigret had never been enjoying his pipe more, when suddenly, without turning round, he called out:

"Henriette?"

"D'you want something?"

"Come and look . . ."

With the stem of his pipe he pointed to a bench just opposite them. At one end of this bench an old fellow who looked like a tramp was taking a nap. At the other end . . .

"It's him!" declared Madame Maigret. "Fancy that!"

It struck her as almost indecent that "her" afternoon stroller should have disrupted his timetable so as to be sitting on the bench at such a time.

"He looks as if he's fallen asleep," muttered Maigret, relighting his pipe. "If there weren't two floors to climb up afterward, I'd go and have a closer look at your admirer, so as to find out what he's really like . . ."

Madame Maigret went back into her kitchen. Maigret watched a squabble between three small boys who ended up by rolling in the dust, while others rushed round them on roller skates.

He stayed there till he had finished his second pipe, and the stranger was still in the same place, whereas the tramp had set off slowly toward the embankment. Madame Maigret settled down with some needlework in her lap, being incapable of spending an hour doing nothing.

"Is he still there?"

"Yes."

"Aren't they going to shut the gates?"

"In a few minutes . . . The attendant has begun driving people toward the exits."

As it happened, the attendant did not notice the stranger, who was sitting there motionless, and three of the gates had already been closed; the attendant was about to turn the key in the lock of the fourth, when Maigret, without a word, picked up his jacket and went downstairs.

From up above, Madame Maigret saw him arguing with the man in green, who took his duties as guardian of the square very seriously. Eventually, however, he let the Superintendent in, and Maigret walked straight up to the man in the pince-nez.

Madame Maigret had sprung to her feet. She realized that something was up, and she signaled to her husband as though to ask:

"Has it happened?"

What, she could not have said exactly; but for many days she had been apprehending some incident. Maigret replied with a nod, got the attendant to stand watch by the gate and came back upstairs.

"My collar and tie . . ."

"Is he dead?"

"As dead as can be! He's been dead for at least two hours, if I'm any judge."

"Do you think he's had a stroke?"

Maigret did not speak; he always had some difficulty tying his tie.

"What are you going to do?"

"Start the inquiry, of course! Inform the D.P.P., the pathologist, and all the rest . . ."

A velvety darkness had fallen over the Place des Vosges, where the tinkle of the fountains rang out more loudly, one of the four, always the same one, having a shriller note than the others.

A few minutes later Maigret was in the tobacconist's shop at the corner of the Rue du Pas-de-la-Mule, where he made a series of phone calls; then he posted a policeman in the attendant's place at the gate of the garden.

Madame Maigret did not want to go down. She knew that her husband hated having her involved in his cases. She also understood that for once he was working undisturbed, since nobody had seen him coming and going or noticed the dead man with the pince-nez.

Furthermore, the square was almost deserted. Only the couple who kept the florist's shop down below were sitting by their door, and the man who sold motor-car accessories, wearing a long gray overall, had come for a chat with them.

They were surprised to see the first car stop at the gate and drive into the garden; they eventually went up to look when they saw a second car and an imposing gentleman who must belong to the Department of Public Prosecution. Finally, by the time the ambulance arrived, the group of onlookers had grown to fifty people, but none of them suspected the cause of this strange gathering, for the crucial scene was concealed by bushes.

Madame Maigret had not switched on the light; she often sat in the dark when she was alone. She kept looking out over the square; she saw windows being opened, but there was no sign of the pretty blond nurse-maid.

The ambulance went off first, toward the Forensic Institute. Then a car with a few passengers . . .

Then she saw Maigret on the pavement; he chatted with some gentlemen for a few minutes before crossing the street on his way home.

"Aren't you going to turn on the light?" he grumbled, peering through the darkness.

She switched on the light.

"Shut the window. It's getting chilly . . ."

He was a different Maigret now, no longer relaxed as he had been so short a while before, but the Maigret whose bursts of ill-temper terrified young detectives at Police Headquarters.

"Stop that sewing! You get on my nerves! Can't you sit for a minute with your hands idle?"

She stopped sewing. He was walking back and forth in the small room, hands behind his back, from time to time casting a peculiar glance at his wife.

"Why did you tell me he sometimes looked old and sometimes young?"

"I don't know . . . I got that impression . . . Why? . . . How old is he?"

"Under thirty, at any rate."

"What are you saying?"

"I'm telling you that your friend is far from being what he seems . . . I'm telling you that he had fair hair hidden under his wig, that his moustache was a false one and that he wore a sort of corset that gave him the stiff look of an old dandy . . ."

"But . . ."

"There's no but about it . . . I'm still wondering by what miracle you happened to smell out this affair."

He seemed almost to hold her responsible for what had occurred, for his spoiled evening, for the work in store for him.

"Do you realize what's been going on? Well, your admirer was murdered on that bench . . ."

"You can't mean it! . . . In front of everybody?"

"Yes, in front of everybody, and probably just when there were most people about . . ."

"Do you think that maid . . . ?"

"I've just sent the bullet to an expert who's going to call me in a few minutes . . ."

"How could anyone have fired a revolver and . . ."

Maigret shrugged his shoulders and waited for the phone call, which, as he expected, came without delay.

"Hello! . . . Yes, that was what I thought . . . But I needed your confirmation."

Madame Maigret was impatient; but he deliberately kept her waiting, and muttered as though the matter did not concern her:

"A compressed air rifle of a special type, extremely uncommon . . ."

"I don't understand . . ."

"It means that the fellow was killed from a distance, possibly by someone in ambush at one of the windows round the square, who had plenty of time to take aim . . . He must have been a first-class marksman, moreover, for the man was shot through the heart and death was instantaneous . . ."

Thus in broad daylight, while the crowd . . ."

Madame Maigret was so upset that she burst into tears, then apologized awkwardly:

"I'm sorry . . . I couldn't help it . . . I feel involved, somehow . . . It's silly, but . . ."

"When you've calmed down, I'll hear your evidence."

"*My* evidence?"

"Of course! You're the only person, so far, who can provide any useful information, since your curiosity led you to . . ."

And Maigret deigned to give her a few details, although still apparently talking to himself.

"The man had no personal papers on him . . . His pockets were practically empty, apart from a few hundred franc notes, a little small change, a tiny key, and a nail file . . . We shall try and identify him nonetheless."

"Only thirty!" Madame Maigret repeated.

It was bewildering! And she understood now why she had been so strangely fascinated by the sight of this young man so rigidly maintaining the pose of an old one, like a waxwork dummy.

"Are you ready to answer?"

"I'm ready!"

"Please observe that I am questioning you in the course of my duties and that tomorrow I shall be obliged to draw up a report of this interrogation . . ."

Madame Maigret smiled wanly, for she was somewhat awestruck.

"Did you notice the man today?"

"I didn't see him in the morning, because I went to the Halles. In the afternoon he was in his usual place . . ."

"And the blond girl?"

"She was there too, as usual."

"Did you ever notice them speaking to each other?"

"They'd have had to speak very loud, for they were more than eight meters apart . . ."

"And they sat motionless like that all afternoon?"

"Except that the girl was doing her crochet . . ."

"Always crochet? For the past fortnight?"

"Yes . . ."

"You didn't notice what stitch she was using?"

"No . . . If it had been knitting I'd have known all about it, but . . ."

"What time did the woman go away?"

"I don't know . . . I was busy preparing a custard . . . Probably about five o'clock, as usual . . ."

"And according to the pathologist, death occurred about five P.M. Only now it's a matter of minutes . . . Did the woman leave before or after five o'clock, before or after the man's death? . . . I wonder what possessed you, today of all days, to make a custard. If one's going to spy on people one may as well do it thoroughly and conscientiously . . ."

"Do you believe that woman . . . ?"

"I don't believe anything at all! I only know that I have nothing to go on for my inquiry but your information, for what it's worth. Do you know, for instance, where the blond girl works?"

"She always goes into number 17B."

"And who lives at number 17B?"

"I don't know that either . . . Some people who have a big American car and a foreign-looking chauffeur . . ."

"And that's all you noticed? Well, you'd make a fine detective, you can take my word for it . . . A big American car and a foreign-looking chauffeur . . ."

He was putting on an act, as he often did in moments of puzzlement, and his anger ended with a warm smile.

"Do you know, old dear, if you hadn't taken an interest in your boyfriend's behavior I should be in a tight corner now? I don't say the situation is very promising, nor that the inquiry will be plain sailing, but all the same we've got something to work on, however slight."

"The pretty blonde?"

"The pretty blonde, as you say! That gives me an idea . . ." He rushed to the telephone and summoned a detective, whom he stationed in front of number 17B, with orders, should a handsome blond girl come out, on no account to lose sight of her.

"And now to bed . . . It'll be time enough tomorrow morning . . .

He was just falling asleep when his wife ventured timidly:

"Don't you think it might be as well to . . ."

"No, no, no!" he shouted, half sitting up in bed. "Just because you almost showed some flair, that doesn't entitle you to start giving me advice! Anyhow, it's time to go to sleep!"

It was the time when the moon was touching the slate roofs of the Place des Vosges with silver, while the four fountains kept up a sort of chamber music in which one of them was always in a hurry and, as it were, out of tune.

II

When Maigret, his face lathered with shaving cream and his braces dangling, cast a first glance through his window at the Place des vosges, there was already a considerable crowd of people around the seat where, the night before, a man had been found dead.

The florist's wife, better informed than the rest since she had witnessed from afar the visit of the Department of Public Prosecution, gave wordy explanations and, even seen from a distance, her emphatic gestures showed that she was speaking with conviction.

The whole neighborhood was there, and women who, a short while before, had been hurrying to get to their workshop or office punctually, had suddenly found time to linger, since a crime was involved.

"Do you know that woman?" asked the Superintendent, pointing with his razor at a youngish lady who stood out among the rest because she wore an extremely elegant light-colored suit of English cut, suitable for morning outings in the Bois de Boulogne.

"I've never seen her . . . At least I don't think so. . . ."

That meant nothing. The first-floor apartments in the Place des Vosges are inhabited by the wealthy middle class and by fashionable people. Nonetheless, the sort of woman whom Maigret was now scrutinizing with some irritation seldom goes for a walk at eight in the morning, unless it be to take her dog for and airing.

"Look here! This morning you must do a lot of shopping . . . You're to go into all the shops. You're to listen to what people are saying and above all you must try to get some information about the blond maid and her employers . . ."

"This time you won't call me a gossip?" Madame Maigret teased him. "When do you expect to be back?"

"How can I tell?"

For while he had been asleep, the inquiry had been going on, and he hoped to find some substantial grounds for his investigation when he reached the Quai des Orfèvres.

Thus, at eleven o'clock last night, Dr. Hébrard, the famous pathologist, had received a message while attending a first night at the Comédie Française, in white tie and tails. He had stayed till the last act, had gone to congratulate an actress friend in her dressing room, and a quarter of an hour later, at the Forensic Institute (which is the same as the new morgue), one of his assistants helped him to slip on his lab coat while another extracted from one of the many drawers lining the walls the body of the unknown man from the Place des Vosges.

At the same moment, on the top floor of the Palais de Justice, where files hold the records of all the criminals in France and most of the criminals in the rest of the world, two men in gray overalls were patiently checking finger-prints.

Not far from these, on the other side of a spiral staircase, the experts on duty in the lab were beginning their meticulous study of various articles: a dark suit of old-fashioned cut, buttoned shoes, a malacca cane with a carved ivory knob, a wig, pince-nez, and a tuft of fair hair cut from the dead man's head.

When Maigret, after shaking hands with his colleagues and having a brief interview with his Chief, went into his office, which, despite the open window, smelled of stale tobacco, three reports were awaiting him, tidily set out on his desk in folders of different colors.

Dr. Hébrard's report first: the victim had died almost immediately on being hit, and the shot had been fired from a distance of more than twenty meters, possibly as much as a hundred, with a small-caliber gun, which nonetheless gave its missiles great penetrative force.

Probable age: twenty-eight.

In view of the absence of professional marks, it was probable that the man had never engaged continuously in manual work. On the other hand he had practiced sport, particularly rowing and boxing.

He was in perfect health, and particularly robust. A scar on the left shoulder showed that about three years previously the young man had been wounded by a revolver bullet that had struck his shoulder blade.

Finally, a certain compression of the fingertips suggested that he must have done a considerable amount of typing.

Maigret read all this slowly, puffing at his pipe and looking up from time to time to watch the Seine flow past in the dazzling morning sunlight. At other moments he would scribble a word or two, comprehensible only to himself, in the notebook, which was notorious not only for its ordinariness but because, during long years of use, it had accumulated comments bewilderingly superimposed on one another in all directions.

The laboratory report was scarcely more sensational.

The garments had been worn by others before belonging to their recent owner, and everything implied that he had bought them in some junk shop or in the Carreau du Temple.

The walking stick and the buttoned shoes seemed to have come from the same source.

The wig, which was of fairly good quality, was of a very ordinary type such as can be found at any wig maker's.

Finally, the examination of the dust found in the garments disclosed a largish quantity of very fine flour, not purified but still mingled with fragments of bran.

The pince-nez were of plain glass, useless as an aid to sight.

There was nothing in the records! No card bearing fingerprints corresponding to those of the victim.

Maigret sat for a few minutes with his elbows on his desk, lost in thought, and possibly overcome by some degree of lethargy. The case promised neither well nor badly, rather badly on the whole, however, since there had been no help at all from chance, which was usually fairly generous.

Finally he rose, put on his hat, and spoke to the janitor on duty in the corridor.

"If anyone wants me, I shall be back in about an hour."

He was too close to the Place des Vosges to take a taxi, and he went there on foot along the Seine; at the fruiterer's shop in the Rue des Tournelles he caught sight of Madame Maigret in animated conversation with three or four gossiping housewives.

He averted his head to conceal a smile and went on his way.

During Maigret's early days in the police force, one of his bosses who had a passion for the scientific methods that had recently been introduced used to tell him:

"Careful, young man! Not so much imagination! Police work is not done with ideas but with facts!"

Which, however, had not prevented Maigret from going on in his own way and carving out a pretty successful career for himself.

Thus, as he reached the Place des Vosges, he was worrying less about the technical details contained in that morning's reports than about what he would have called the atmosphere of the crime.

He tried to imagine the victim, not dead as he had seen him but alive: a young fellow of twenty-eight, fair-haired, strong, and muscular, probably elegant, dressing up every morning in that old dandy's outfit bought at some secondhand market stall, and under which he still wore fine linen . . .

And walking twice around the square before disappearing along the Rue de Turenne.

Where did he go? What did he do until three o'clock in the afternoon? Did he still look like a character from some nineteenth-century comedy, or did he change clothes somewhere in the neighborhood?

How could he then stay motionless for three hours on end, never opening his mouth, never making a gesture, just staring into space?

How long had this performance been going on?

Finally, at night, where did the stranger disappear to? What was his private life? Whom did he see? Whom did he speak to? To whom did he confide the secret of his personality? How was one to account for the flour and the fragments of bran in his clothing, which suggested a mill rather than a bakery? What could he have been doing in a mill?

All this made Maigret forget to stop at number 17B and he had to retrace his steps. He went in under the archway and spoke to the concierge. She showed no surprise when he showed her his police badge.

"What is it you want?"

"I'd like to know which of your tenants employs a rather pretty, smart, fair-haired maid . . ."

She interrupted him to say, without the least hesitation:

"Mademoiselle Rita?"

"Maybe. Every afternoon she looks after two children in the square . . ."

"They're her employers' children: Monsieur and Madame Krofta, who have had the first-floor flat for well over fifteen years . . . They were here even before me. Monsieur Krofta runs an import and export business. He has an office somewhere in the Rue de Quatre-Septembre."

"Is he at home?"

"He's just gone out, but Madame must be upstairs."

"And Rita?"

"I don't know . . . I haven't seen her yet this morning . . . Actually, I've been doing the stairs . . ."

A few minutes later Maigret rang at the door of the first-floor flat, and although he could hear noises going on in the depths of the apartment, he was kept waiting for quite a while at the door. He rang again. Finally the door was half opened, and Maigret saw a youngish woman, trying to disguise her state of undress beneath a pale blue housecoat.

"What do you want?"

"To speak to Monsieur or Madame Krofta. I'm a Superintendent of the Police Judiciaire . . ."

She let him in, resignedly, folding her housecoat about her, and Maigret found himself in a splendid apartment with large high rooms, furnished with great taste and displaying valuable bibelots.

"I apologize for receiving you like this, but I'm alone with the children. How can you have got here so soon? My husband only left a quarter of an hour ago . . ."

She was a foreigner, as was clear from her slight accent and from her typically Central European charm. Maigret had already recognized her as the woman he had noticed that morning, wearing a light-colored suit and listening to the housewives gossiping in the middle of the Place des Vosges.

"Were you expecting me?" he said quietly, trying to conceal his surprise.

"You or somebody else . . . But I must confess I didn't know the police acted so swiftly . . . I suppose my husband will be back soon?"

"I don't know . . ."

"No . . ."

"But then . . ."

There was obviously some misunderstanding, and Maigret, who hoped to gain some information thereby, did nothing to clear it up.

The young woman, meanwhile, possibly in order to give herself time to think, stammered out:

"Will you excuse me a moment? The children are in the bathroom and I wonder if . . . if they're not up to some mischief."

She moved smoothly away; she had real beauty both of face and figure, with a certain majesty in addition to her supple grace.

She could be heard exchanging a few words with her children in the bathroom; then she came back with a slight smile of welcome.

"Forgive me, I never even asked you to sit down . . . I'd rather my husband had been here, for he knows more than I do about the value of the jewels, since it was he who bought them."

To what jewels was she referring? And what was it all about, and why did the young woman appear so tense as she impatiently awaited her husband's return?

It looked as though she were afraid of talking, and was trying to drag out the conversation without giving anything away.

Maigret, who was conscious of all this, was careful not to give her any help; he looked at her with the utmost detachment, assuming what he called his "plain man's" expression.

"One's constantly reading about thefts in the papers, but oddly enough one never imagines such things happening to oneself. And yesterday evening I had no suspicion . . . It was this morning . . ."

"When you came in again?" Maigret suggested.

She gave a start.

"How did you know I'd been out?"

"Because I saw you . . ."

"You were in the neighborhood already?"

"I'm here all the year round, for I'm one of your neighbors."

She was disturbed at this. She was clearly wondering what this mysteriously simple remark might imply.

"I went out, true, as I often do, to take the air before getting the children dressed. That's why you find me in déshabille . . . When I come back I put on my housecoat and . . ."

She could not restrain a sigh of relief. Footsteps had halted on the landing. A key turned in the door.

"It's my husband," she murmured.

And she called out:

"Boris! Come in here . . . There's somebody waiting for you."

The man was good-looking, too; older than his wife, about forty-five years of age, well-dressed and well-groomed, a Hungarian or a Czech, Maigret thought, but speaking perfect, polished French.

"The Superintendent has got here before you, and I was telling him you'd soon be back . . ."

Boris Krofta was scrutinizing Maigret with a polite attention that did not wholly disguise mistrustfulness.

"I beg your pardon," he murmured. "But . . . I don't quite understand . . ."

"Superintendent Maigret of the Police Judiciaire."

"It's odd . . . You wished to speak to me?"

"To the employer of a girl called Rita, who looked after two children in the Place des Vosges every afternoon."

"Yes . . . But . . . you're not going to tell me that you've already traced her, or that you've recovered the jewelry? . . . I know I must strike you as peculiar . . . The coincidence is so strange that I'm trying to understand it. You must realize that I've just got back from the local police station, where I went to lodge a complaint against Rita . . . On my return I find you here, and you tell me . . ."

"What was the subject of your complaint?"

"The theft of the jewelry. The girl disappeared yesterday without warning. I thought she must have run off with a young man, and I decided to put an advertisement in the newspaper. Last night we never left the house. This morning, while my wife was out, it suddenly occurred to me to look in her jewel case . . . That was when I understood why Rita had run away, for the jewel case was empty . . ."

"What time was it when you made this discovery?"

"Barely nine o'clock in the morning. I was in my dressing gown. I dressed quickly and hurried off to the police station . . ."

"And at this point your wife came back?"

"That's right . . . While I was dressing . . . What I still fail to understand is your coming here this morning . . ."

"Just a coincidence!" Maigret murmured, in a tone of the utmost innocence.

"And yet I'd like to be in the picture . . . Did you know, this morning, that the jewels had been stolen?"

Maigret made an evasive gesture that meant nothing and which served to intensify Boris's anxiety.

"At any rate, please do me the favor of telling me the reason for your visit. I don't think it's customary for the French police to enter people's homes, to sit down, and . . ."

"And to listen to what they're told!" Maigret finished. "Admit that it's nothing to do with me. Ever since I came here you've been talking about a theft of jewelry, which doesn't interest me, whereas I came on account of a crime . . ."

"A crime?" the young woman exclaimed.

"Didn't you know that a crime had been committed yesterday in the Place des Vosges?"

He saw her obviously take thought, remembering that Maigret had said he was her neighbor, and instead of saying no as she might have done she murmured with a smile:

"I heard vague rumours of something this morning as I went through the square . . . some housewives were gossiping . . ."

"I don't see how . . ." the husband put in.

"How this business concerns you? I don't know either, so far, but I'm convinced that we shall know sooner or later. At what time did Rita disappear yesterday afternoon?"

"Shortly after five o'clock," replied Boris Krofta without a trace of hesitation. "Isn't that so, Olga?"

"That's right. She came in at five o'clock with the children. She went up into her bedroom and I didn't hear her come down again. About six o'clock I went upstairs, because I was beginning to wonder why she wasn't getting the dinner ready . . . And her room was empty . . ."

"Will you take me up to it?"

"My husband will go up with you. I can hardly do so, dressed as I am . . ."

Maigret was already acquainted with the house, since it was exactly like his own. After the second floor the staircase grew still narrower and darker, and eventually they reached the attic floor. Krofta opened the third door.

"It's here . . . I left the key in the lock . . ."

"Your wife just told me it was she who had gone up!"

"That's true. But I went up myself afterward."

The open door disclosed a maid's bedroom, which would have been quite unremarkable, with its iron bed, its wardrobe, and washstand, but for the view over the Place des Vosges to be seen through the window.

Beside the wardrobe there was a fiber suitcase of a familiar type; inside the wardrobe, some clothes and underwear.

"So your maid must have gone off without any luggage?"

"I suppose she chose to take the jewelry instead; it was worth about two hundred thousand francs . . ."

Maigret's big fingers were fiddling with a small green hat, then he picked up another, trimmed with a yellow ribbon.

"Can you tell me how many hats your maid had?"

"I've no idea . . . My wife may perhaps be able to tell you, but I doubt it . . ."

"How long had she been in your service?"

"Six months . . ."

"Did you find her through an advertisement?"

"Through an employment agency, which had warmly recommended her. For that matter, she was an excellent servant."

"You have no other staff?"

"My wife likes to look after the children herself, so that one maid is quite enough for us. Particularly as we spend a good part of the year on the Riviera, where we have a gardener and his wife to help in the house."

Maigret suddenly felt impelled to blow his nose, in spite of the weather; he dropped his handkerchief and bent down to pick it up.

"That's odd . . ." he muttered as he stood up again.

Then, looking his companion up and down, he opened his mouth and closed it again.

"Did you want to say something?"

"I wanted to ask you one more question. But it's so indiscreet that you may think it uncalled for . . ."

"Please go on!"

"If you insist . . . Well, I wanted to ask you, on the off-chance, whether, your maid being such a pretty girl, you had ever had any relations with her other than those between an employer and his servant? I'm asking you this off the record, and you're quite entitled not to reply."

Oddly enough, Krofta seemed to ponder, suddenly much more preoccupied than he had been. He took his time before replying; he cast a slow glance all around him, and then said with a sigh:

"Must my reply become official?"

"In all probability there will be no question of that."

"In that case I'd rather admit to you that, in fact, I have occasionally . . ."

"In the rooms on the first floor?"

"No . . . That would be difficult because of the children . . ."

"Did you meet outside the house?"

"Never! . . . I came up here from time to time, and . . ."

"I understand the rest!" Maigret said with a smile. "And I'm very glad to have your answer. Actually, I had noticed that a button was missing from the sleeve of your jacket, and I've just picked up that button on the floor, at the foot of the bed. Obviously some violent exertion must have been needed to wrench it off and . . ."

He handed the button to his companion, who seized it with surprising eagerness.

"When was the last time this happened?" Maigret asked casually, as he went toward the door.

"Three or four days ago . . . Wait a minute! . . . Four days, yes . . ."

"And Rita was willing?"

"I think so."

"Was she in love with you?"

"At any rate she let me think she was."

"Have you any rival that you know of?"

"Oh, Superintendent! . . . There was no question of that, and if Rita had had a lover I'd certainly not have considered him as a rival . . . I adore my wife and my children, and I don't know myself why I . . ."

And Maigret, as he went down the stairs, said to himself with a sigh:

"Well, my fine fellow, I have the impression that you've not been telling the truth for a single moment!"

He stopped in the concierge's lodge, and sat down opposite the woman, who was shelling peas.

"So you've been to see them? They're no end upset about that jewelry business!"

"Were you in your lodge yesterday at five o'clock?"

"To be sure I was . . . And my son was sitting just where you are now, doing his homework . . ."

"Did you see Rita and the children come in?"

"As clear as I see you now!"

"And did you see her come down again a few minutes later?"

"That's what Monsieur Krofta came to ask me just now. I told him I hadn't seen anything. He insists that's not possible, that I must have gone out of the lodge or that I wasn't paying attention. After all, so many people go past! Yet I think I'd have noticed her, seeing as it wasn't her usual time of day . . ."

"Have you ever met Monsieur Krofta going up to the third floor?"

"What would he have gone up there for? Oh, I understand . . . You think perhaps he'd have gone up to be with the maid . . . You obviously don't know Mademoiselle Rita . . . They're saying now that she was a thief . . . That's as may be! . . . But she wasn't one for gadding about or letting her master have his way with her . . ."

Maigret, resignedly, lit his pipe and moved off.

III

"Well then, Madame Superintendent Maigret?" he teased her affectionately as he sat down by the window, his shirtsleeves gleaming in the sunlight.

"Well, for lunch today you'll have to make do with some grilled steak and an artichoke. And I bought that ready-cooked to save time. According to gossip . . ."

"What do they say? Come on! Give us the results of your inquiry . . ."

"For one thing, Mademoiselle Rita wasn't really a servant . . ."

"How do you know?"

"All the tradespeople noticed that she didn't know how to count in sous, which implies that she's never had to do the shopping. The first time the butcher tried to give her change for a franc she stared at him, and if she accepted it I'm sure it was in order not to call attention to herself . . ."

"Good! So she was a young lady playing maid at the Kroftas' . . ."

"I think rather she was a student. In the local shops they talk all sorts of languages, Italian, Hungarian, Polish. Apparently she always seemed to understand and when jokes were made in her presence she used to smile . . ."

"And hadn't they anything to say about your admirer?"

"Some people had noticed him, but not to the same extent that I had . . . Oh yes, there's something else. The Gastambides' maid, who often goes to sit in the square of an afternoon, declares that Rita didn't know how to crochet and that it would have been impossible to use the things she made except for floor-cloths . . ."

Maigret's narrowed eyes were twinkling with amusement at the care that his wife had taken to put together her recollections and express them in an orderly and methodical way.

"That's not all! Before Rita, the Kroftas had a maid of their own nationality, but they dismissed her because she became pregnant."

"By Krofta?"

"Oh no! He's too much in love with his wife. Apparently he's so jealous that they don't entertain anybody . . ."

Thus all this petty gossip, these assertions that might be true or untrue, sincere or otherwise, helped to alter and sometimes to complete Maigret's picture of the people concerned.

"Since you've done such good work," Maigret murmured as he lit a fresh pipe, "I'm going to give you a hint myself. The shot that killed our unknown friend in the wig and pince-nez was fired from Rita's attic window, as can easily be proved in a reconstruction of the crime. I checked the angle of fire, which corresponds absolutely with the position of the body and the trajectory of the bullet . . ."

"Do you believe it was she who . . ."

"I've no idea . . . Think it over yourself!"

And with a sigh he resumed his collar and tie; she helped him into his jacket. Half an hour later, he sank into his chair at Police Headquarters and mopped his face, for it was even hotter than on the previous day, and there was thunder in the air.

*   *   *

An hour later, Maigret's three pipes were warm, the ashtray was over-flowing, and the blotter was covered with a tangle of words and scraps of sentences scrawled in all directions. As for the Superintendent, he was yawning, patently drowsy, and staring round-eyed at what he had written in the course of his reverie.

Supposing Krofta had got rid of Rita, the theft of jewelry was a clever invention to divert suspicion from himself.

It was a nice idea, but there was no proof of it and the maid might well have run off with her employer's jewels.

Krofta had hesitated before admitting that he had made love with his servant.

That might mean that it was true and that he was embarrassed by it; it could equally well mean that it was not true, but that he had seen Maigret picking up the button, or that he suspected the Superintendent's question of concealing a trap of this sort.

Could the button have been left for four days on the floor, which seemed to have been recently swept?

And why had Madame Krofta been for an early-morning walk today? Why had she seemed reluctant to admit that she had heard people talking about the crime, when Maigret had seen her spend a considerable time listening to the gossiping housewives?

Why had Krofta asked the concierge if she had seen Rita go out? Was he conducting a personal investigation? Wasn't it more likely that he knew the police would ask the same question, and that by speaking of it beforehand he had the chance of influencing the good woman by suggestion?

Suddenly Maigret sprang up. The final result of this accumulation of trivial facts and observations was not merely to irritate him but to arouse a secret anxiety in him, for it led inevitably to the question: where was Rita?

She was on the run, if she was guilty of theft and murder. But if she was guilty of neither, then . . .

A minute later, he was in the Chief's office where, putting on his surliest air, he demanded:

"Can you let me have a blank search warrant?"

"Things not going right?" the head of the Police Judiciaire chaffed him; he was more familiar than most people with Maigret's moods. "We'll try and get it for you. But you'll have to be prudent, eh?"

As it happened, while the Chief was seeing about the search warrant, Maigret was summoned to the telephone. It was his wife, and there was acute anxiety in her voice.

"I've just thought of something . . . I don't know if I ought to say it over the telephone . . ."

"Say it, anyway!"

"Supposing it wasn't the person you're thinking of who fired the shot . . ."

"I understand. Carry on . . ."

"Supposing, for instance, it was her employer . . . You follow me? . . . I wonder if, by any chance, she could still be in the house? . . . Dead, perhaps? . . . Or else a prisoner? . . ."

It was touching to see Madame Maigret eagerly following a trail for the first time in her life.

But what the Superintendent would not admit was that she had practically reached the same point as himself.

However, he queried ironically: "Is that all?"

"You're making fun of me? . . . You don't believe that . . ."

"In short, you imagine that by searching number 17B from cellar to attic . . ."

"Just think, suppose she were still alive . . ."

"We'll see! Meanwhile, let's hope dinner will be a bit more substantial than lunch . . ."

He hung up, and went back to the Chief's room for the warrant he needed.

"Doesn't this case suggest espionage to you, Maigret?"

The Superintendent, who hated committing himself in such cases, merely shrugged his shoulders.

But as soon as he had left the room he retraced his steps and called out briefly:

"I'll answer that question tonight."

Madame Lecuyer, the concierge of number 17B, was no doubt a worthy woman, who did her best to bring up her children decently, but she had one terrible fault: She panicked readily.

"You understand," she admitted, "with all these people asking me questions from first thing this morning, I don't know if I'm coming or going . . ."

"Keep calm, Madame Lecuyer," said Maigret, as he sat by the window, not far from the small boy who was doing his homework as on the previous day.

"I've never done any harm to anyone and . . ."

"You're not being accused of doing any harm to anyone . . . You're only being asked to try and remember . . . How many tenants have you?"

"Twenty-two, because I must tell you that the flats on the second and third floors are very small, just one or two rooms, so that we have a lot of people . . ."

"Did any of these tenants have anything to do with the Kroftas?"

"How could they? The Kroftas are rich people, with their own car and a chauffeur . . ."

"By the way, do you know where they garage their car?"

"Somewhere along the Boulevard Henri IV . . . The chauffeur hardly ever comes here, for he has his meals out . . ."

"Did he come yesterday afternoon?"

"I can't remember . . . I believe he did . . ."

"With the car?"

"No! The car wasn't parked here yesterday, nor this morning . . . It's true that the Kroftas hardly went out . . ."

"Let's see! Was the chauffeur in the house yesterday at about five o'clock?"

"No! He left again at half past four . . . I remember, because my boy had just come back from school . . ."

"That's true!" confirmed the boy, looking up.

"Now another question: have any large cases been taken out of the house since five o'clock yesterday? For instance, has a removal van been parked in the neighborhood?"

"No, I'm sure of that!"

"Nobody has taken out any cupboards or chests or unwieldy packages?"

"What d'you expect me to say?" she moaned. "How can I tell what you mean by an unwieldy package?"

"One that might, for instance, contain a human body . . ."

"Good heavens! Is that what you're thinking of? Are you supposing now that somebody's been murdered in my house?"

"Go back over your recollections hour by hour . . ."

"No! I saw nothing of the sort . . ."

"No lorry, no cart, not even a handcart, came into the courtyard?"

"I've told you so!"

"There's no empty room in the house? All the flats are occupied?"

"All, without exception! There was just one room on the third floor, and that's been let for the past two months."

At that point the boy raised his head, and with his pen between his lips mumbled:

"What about the piano, Mum?"

"What can that have to do with it? That wasn't a case being taken out, it was a case being brought in . . . and they had a hard job getting it up the stairs!"

"A piano was delivered here?"

"Yesterday at half past six."

"What firm?"

"I don't know . . . There was no name on the van. This one didn't come into the courtyard . . . There was a great big case and three men were at it for a good hour . . ."

"Did they take the case away with them?"

"No . . . Monsieur Lucien went down with the workmen to stand them a drink at the bistro round the corner."

"Who is this Monsieur Lucien?"

"The tenant of the little room I was telling you about . . . He's been there two months . . . He's very quiet and respectable . . . They say he writes music . . ."

"Does he know the Kroftas?"

"I shouldn't think he's even seen them . . ."

"Was he at home at five o'clock yesterday?"

"He came in about half past four . . . about the time the chauffeur left."

"Did he tell you then that he was expecting a piano?"

"No . . . He simply asked if there were any letters for him."

"Did he usually get many?"

"Very few."

"Many thanks, Madame Lecuyer . . . Try to keep calm; there's no need for you to worry yourself . . ."

Maigret went out and gave instructions to two inspectors who were pacing up and down in the Place des Vosges; then he returned to number 17B, going quickly past the lodge lest the concierge should start questioning him again and confiding all her anxiety.

Maigret did not stop on the first floor nor on the second. On the third, bending down, he noticed the scratches made by the piano as the men dragged it along. It seemed to him that the scratches stopped at the fourth door, and he knocked at it; he heard shuffling footsteps, like those of an old woman in slippers, then a cautious voice mumbled:

"Who's there?"

Monsieur Lucien, please?"

"It's next door . . ."

But at the same moment another voice muttered a few words and the door was partially opened; a stout old woman tried to make out Maigret's features in the half-darkness.

"Monsieur Lucien isn't in just now. Can I take a message for him?"

Maigret instinctively leaned forward to try and see the second person who was in the room.

In the dim light, it was difficult to make out anything. The room was cluttered with old furniture, old fabrics, hideous trinkets, and pervaded by the peculiar smell of places where old people live.

Beside the sewing machine a woman was sitting upright as though on a formal call, and the Superintendent was more surprised than he had ever been in his life when he recognized his own wife.

IV

"I heard that Mademoiselle Augustine undertook little sewing jobs," Madame Maigret hurriedly explained. "I came to see her about this. We chatted. Her room happens to be next door to the maid's room, the girl who stole . . ."

Maigret gave a shrug, wondering what his wife was getting at.

"The oddest thing is that yesterday they brought up a piano for the neighbor on the other side, in a huge case that must still be there . . ."

This time Maigret frowned, enraged that his wife should, heaven knows how, have reached the same conclusions as himself.

"Since Monsieur Lucien isn't here I shall have to go downstairs," he announced.

And he did not waste a minute. The two inspectors whom he had left in the Place des Vosges, in front of the house, were now posted in the stairway, not far from the Kroftas' door. A locksmith was sent for, and also the local police superintendent.

The result was that shortly afterward the door of Monsieur Lucien's room had been forced open. In the room there was merely a very ordinary piano, a bed, a chair, a wardrobe, and, standing against the wall, the case that had contained the piano.

"Get this case opened," ordered Maigret, who was playing high and was intensely nervous.

He did not want to touch the case himself, for fear of finding it empty. He filled his pipe with assumed calm, and pretended to be quite unmoved when he heard a shout.

"Superintendent! . . . There's a woman here! . . ."

"I know!"

"She's alive!"

"I know!" he repeated.

Of course! If there was a woman in the packing case, it must be the notorious Rita, and he was practically certain she must be alive, tightly bound and gagged.

"Try to bring her round . . . Send for a doctor . . ."

He walked past his wife, who was in the corridor with Mademoiselle Augustine, and who gave him a smile unparalleled in their domestic history, a smile that suggested that Madame Maigret might be going to exchange her role of docile spouse for that of detective.

As the Superintendent reached the first floor, the door of the Krofta apartment opened. Krofta was there in person, in a state of considerable excitement, yet wholly master of himself.

"Is Monsieur Maigret there?" he asked the two detectives on sentry duty.

"Here I am, Monsieur Krofta."

"You're wanted on the telephone . . . It's the Ministry of the Interior . . ."

Actually, it was the Director of the Police Judiciaire calling his subordinate.

"Is that you, Maigret? . . . I thought I might catch you here . . . While you were up to heaven knows what elsewhere in the house, the person in whose apartment you're now taking this call got in touch with his embassy . . . They contacted the Ministry of Foreign Affairs, who . . ."

"I understand!" growled Maigret.

"Just as I told you! A case of espionage! Our orders are to keep mum, to avoid any leakage to the press . . . Krofta has been for a long time now his country's unofficial agent in France; he centralizes the reports of secret agents . . ."

Krofta, the man in question, was standing in a corner of the room, pale but smiling.

"May I offer you something, Superintendent?"

"No, thanks!"

"I understand you have found my servant?"

And the Superintendent replied, stressing each syllable:

"I found her just in time, yes, Monsieur Krofta! Good day to you!"

"I was so sure," Madame Maigret said as she finished making her chocolate custard, "when I heard that the girl didn't know how to crochet . . ."

"Of course!" her husband agreed.

"They must really have managed to tell each other some interesting things by this system, spending several hours a day at it. If I understand it aright, this girl Rita who had taken a post as domestic servant with the Kroftas actually spent her time spying on her employers."

Maigret was never fond of explaining his cases, but under the circumstances it would have been too cruel to leave Madame Maigret in the dark.

She spied on spies!" he growled. And he added sullenly, shrugging his shoulders:

"That's why, just as I was about to pounce on the gang at last, I got the order: 'Give it up! Silence and discretion!' "

"Indeed, that can't be very pleasant," she sighed as though she thus excused all Maigret's past ill-humor.

"It was a pretty case, though, with strokes of genius. Try to understand the situation. On the one hand the Kroftas, with all the information that passes through their hands and which they transmit to their own government.

"On the other hand the maid Rita and a man, the old gentleman on the bench, your mysterious admirer. For whom were they working? That doesn't concern me now. It's up to Intelligence. They were probably the agents of another power, or perhaps of a dissident faction, since the internal and external policies of certain countries are peculiarly mixed up.

"The fact remains that they needed the information centralized every day by Krofta, and Rita got hold of this without too much difficulty. But how could it be passed on outside? Spies are very vigilant, and any suspicious behavior on her part would have ruined her.

"And so they hit on the idea of the old dandy on the bench! And the idea of the crochet hook which, used by hands more expert than they seemed, might communicate by its jerky movements long messages in Morse code.

"Sitting opposite Rita, her accomplice recorded everything in his memory. It's just one more example of the incredible patience of certain secret agents, for he had to retain everything he had learned, word for word, for hours on end, until the time when, back in his home at Corbeil, near Moulins, he would spend the night typing it out.

"I wonder how the Kroftas discovered this extremely cunning device? They probably learned of it through the chauffeur, when he came in at about four o'clock."

Madame Maigret was so afraid of his stopping that she listened without daring to display the least sign of emotion.

"Now you know as much as I do. The Kroftas had to do away with the man first, and next to question Rita, to get her to say for whom she was working and how much she had already given away.

"For some time past Krofta has been housing a killer, Monsieur Lucien, who's a first-class shot. He rings him up. Lucien wastes no time, and from the girl's bedroom he shoots down his allotted victim.

"Nobody has seen or heard anything, except Rita who has to take the children home and who is forced to keep up a pretence of ignorance on pain of being shot down in her turn.

"She knows what to expect. They try to get her secret from her. She holds out. They threaten her with death, and they have that piano brought up to Monsieur Lucien's room so that the case can be used to remove her body. Besides, who would think of looking for her in the musician's room?

"Krofta has already planned his defensive strategy. He lodges a complaint, reports his maid's disappearance, invents the theft of the jewels, and . . ."

A pause. Night was falling. The blue of the sky was darkening, and the silvery sound of the fountains harmonized with the liquid silver of the moonlight.

"And you coped with it!" Madame Maigret suddenly said with admiration.

He looked at her half seriously, half smiling. She went on:

"How maddening that at the crucial moment they prevented you from finishing the job . . ."

Then he said, with mock indignation:

"D'you know what's even more maddening? To have found you at that Mademoiselle Augustine's! For, after all, you got there before me . . . But then, of course, the victim was your admirer!"

The Wrong Problem

Author: John Dickson Carr (1905–1977)

Detective: Dr. Gideon Fell (1933)

In his fascination with locked rooms and impossible crimes, Carr is a direct literary descendent of Jacques Futrelle and G.K. Chesterton. Carr was an American Anglophile who lived much of his life and set most of his books in Britain. His first series character was a French policeman, Bencolin, hero of some short stories published in college magazines and of his 1930 first novel *It Walks by Night,* and under the barely disguised pseudonym Carter Dickson, he wrote a long series of novels about Sir Henry Merrivale. But his greatest detective creation was Dr. Gideon Fell, who first appeared in *Hag's Nook* (1933) and delivered the famous "Locked Room Lecture" in *The Three Coffins* (1935; British title *The Hollow Man.*

Dr. Gideon Fell was, of course, based on G.K. Chesterton, and of all the stories about him, the one that follows is perhaps the most Chestertonian.

At the Detectives' Club it is still told how Dr. Fell went down into the valley in Somerset that evening and of the man with whom he talked in the twilight by the lake, and of murder that came up as though from the lake itself. The truth about the crime has long been known, but one question must always be asked at the end of it.

The village of Grayling Dene lay a mile away toward the sunset. And the rear windows of the house looked out toward it. This was a long gabled house of red brick, lying in a hollow of the shaggy hills, and its bricks had darkened like an old painting. No lights showed inside, although the lawns were in good order and the hedges trimmed.

Behind the house there was a long gleam of water in the sunset, for the ornamental lake—some fifty yards across—stretched almost to the windows. In the middle of the lake, on an artificial island, stood a summerhouse. A faint breeze had begun to stir, despite the heat, and the valley was alive with a conference of leaves.

The last light showed that all the windows of the house, except one, had little lozenge-shaped panes. The one exception was a window high up in a gable, the highest in the house, looking out over the road to Grayling Dene. It was barred.

Dusk had almost become darkness when two men came down over the crest of the hill. One was large and lean. The other, who wore a shovel hat, was large and immensely stout, and he loomed even more vast against the skyline by reason of the great dark cloak billowing out behind him. Even at that distance you might hear the chuckles that animated his several chins and ran down the ridges of his waistcoat. The two travelers were engaged (as usual) in a violent argument. At intervals, the larger one would stop and hold forth oratorically for some minutes, flourishing his cane. But, as they came down past the lake and the blind house, both of them stopped.

"There's an example," said Superintendent Hadley. "Say what you like, it's a bit too lonely for me. Give me the town—"

"We are not alone," said Dr. Fell.

The whole place had seemed so deserted that Hadley felt a slight start when he saw a man standing at the edge of the lake. Against the reddish glow on the water they could make out that it was a small man in neat dark clothes and a white linen hat. He seemed to be stooping forward, peering out across the water. The wind went rustling again, and the man turned round.

"I don't see any swans," he said. "Can you see any swans?" The quiet water was empty.

"No," said Dr. Fell, with the same gravity. "Should there be any?"

"There should be one," answered the little man, nodding. "Dead. With blood on its neck. Floating there."

"Killed?" asked Dr. Fell, after a pause. He has said afterward that it seemed a foolish thing to say; but that it seemed appropriate to that time between the lights of the day and the brain.

"Oh yes," replied the little man, nodding again. "Killed, like others— human beings. Eye, ear, and throat. Or perhaps I should say ear, eye, and throat, to get them in order."

Hadley spoke with some sharpness.

"I hope we're not trespassing. We knew the land was enclosed, of course, but they told us that the owners were away and wouldn't mind if we took a shortcut. Fell, don't you think we'd better—?"

"I beg your pardon," said the little man, in a voice of such cool sanity that Hadley turned round again. From what they could see in the gloom, he had a good face, a quiet face, a somewhat ascetic face; and he was smiling. "I beg your pardon," he repeated in a curiously apologetic tone. "I should not have said that. You see, I have been far too long with it. I have been trying to find the real answer for thirty years. As for the trespassing, myself, I do not own this land, although I lived here once. There is, or used to be, a bench here somewhere. Can I detain you for a little while?"

Hadley never quite realized afterward how it came about. But such was the spell of the hour, or of the place, or the sincere, serious little man in the white linen hat, that it seemed no time at all before the little man was sitting on a rusty iron chair beside the darkening lake, speaking as though to his fingers.

"I am Joseph Lessing," he said in the same apologetic tone. "If you have not heard of me, I don't suppose you will have heard of my stepfather. But at one time he was rather famous as an eye, ear, and throat specialist. Dr. Harvey Lessing, his name was.

"In those days we—I mean the family—always came down here to spend our summer holidays. It is rather difficult to make biographical details clear. Perhaps I had better do it with dates, as though the matter were really important, like a history book. There were four children. Three of them were Dr. Lessing's children by his first wife, who died in 1899. I was the stepson. He married my mother when I was seventeen, in 1901. I regret to say that *she* died three years later. Dr. Lessing was a kindly man, but he was very unfortunate in the choice of his wives."

The little man appeared to be smiling sadly.

"We were an ordinary, contented and happy group, in spite of Brownrigg's cynicism. Brownrigg was the eldest. Eye, ear, and throat pursued us: he was a dentist. I think he is dead now. He was a stout man, smiling a good deal, and his face had a shine like pale butter. He was an athlete run to seed; he used to claim that he could draw teeth with his fingers. By the way, he was very fond of walnuts. I always seem to remember him sitting between two silver candlesticks at the table, smiling, with a heap of shells in front of him and a little sharp nutpick in his hand.

"Harvey Junior was the next. They were right to call him Junior; he was of the striding sort, brisk and high-colored and likable. He never sat down in a chair without first turning it the wrong way round. He always said 'Ho, my lads!' when he came into a room, and he never went out of it without leaving the door open so that he could come back in again.

Above everything, he was nearly always on the water. We had a skiff and a punt for our little lake—would you believe that it is ten feet deep? Junior always dressed for the part as solemnly as though he had been on the Thames, wearing a red-and-white-striped blazer and a straw hat of the sort that used to be called a boater. I say he was nearly always on the water: but not, of course, after tea. That was when Dr. Lessing went to take his afternoon nap in the summerhouse."

The summerhouse, in its sheath of vines, was almost invisible now. But they all looked at it, very suggestive in the middle of the lake.

"The third child was the girl, Martha. She was almost my own age, and I was very fond of her."

Joseph Lessing pressed his hands together.

"I am not going to introduce an unnecessary love story, gentlemen," he said. "As a matter of fact, Martha was engaged to a young man who had a commission in a line regiment, and she was expecting him down here any day when—the things happened. Arthur Somers, his name was. I knew him well; I was his confidant in the family.

"I want to emphasize what a hot, pleasant summer it was. The place looked then much as it does now, except that I think it was greener then. I was glad to get away from the city. In accordance with Dr. Lessing's passion for 'useful employment,' I had been put to work in the optical department of a jeweler's. I was always skillful with my hands. I dare say I was a spindly, snappish, suspicious lad, but they were all very good to me after my mother died: except butter-faced Brownrigg, perhaps. But for me that summer centers round Martha, with her brown hair piled up on the top of her head, in a white dress with puffed shoulders, playing croquet on a green lawn and laughing. I told you it was a long while ago.

"On the afternoon of the fifteenth of August we had all intended to be out. Even Brownrigg had intended to go out after a sort of lunch-tea that we had at two o'clock in the afternoon. Look to your right, gentlemen. You see that bow window in the middle of the house, overhanging the lake? There was where the table was set.

"Dr. Lessing was the first to leave the table. He was going out early for his nap in the summerhouse. It was a very hot afternoon, as drowsy as the sound of a lawn mower. The sun baked the old bricks and made a flat blaze on the water. Junior had knocked together a sort of miniature landing stage at the side of the lake—it was just about where we are sitting now—and the punt and the rowboat were lying there.

"From the open windows we could all see Dr. Lessing going down to the landing stage with the sun on his bald spot. He had a pillow in one hand and a book in the other. He took the rowboat; he could never manage the punt properly, and it irritated a man of his dignity to try.

"Martha was the next to leave. She laughed and ran away, as she always did. Then Junior said, 'Cheerio, chaps'—or whatever the expression was then—and strode out leaving the door open. I went shortly afterward. Junior had asked Brownrigg whether he intended to go out, and Brownrigg had said yes. But he remained, being lazy, with a pile of walnut shells in front of him. Though he moved back from the table to get out of the glare, he lounged there all afternoon in view of the lake.

"Of course, what Brownrigg said or thought might not have been important. But it happened that a gardener named Robinson had taken it into his head to trim some hedges on this side of the house. He had a full view of the lake. And all that afternoon nothing stirred. The summerhouse, as you can see, has two doors: one facing toward the house, the other in the opposite direction. These openings were closed by sunblinds, striped red and white like Junior's blazer, so that you could not see inside. But all the afternoon the summerhouse remained dead, showing up against the fiery water and that clump of trees at the far side of the lake. No boat put out. No one went in to swim. There was not so much as a ripple, any more than might have been caused by the swans (we had two of them), or by the spring that fed the lake.

"By six o'clock we were all back in the house. When there began to be a few shadows, I think something in the *emptiness* of the afternoon alarmed us. Dr. Lessing should have been there, demanding something. He was not there. We hallooed for him, but he did not answer. The rowboat remained tied up by the summerhouse. Then Brownrigg, in his cool fetch-and-run fashion, told me to go out and wake up the old party. I pointed out that there was only the punt, and that I was a rotten hand at punting, and that whenever I tried it I only went round in circles or upset the boat. But Junior said, 'Come-along-old-chap-you-shall-improve-your-punting-I'll-give-you-a-hand.'

"I have never forgotten how long it took us to get out there while I staggered at the punt pole, and Junior lent a hand.

"Dr. Lessing lay easily on his left side, almost on his stomach, on a long wicker settee. His face was very nearly into the pillow, so that you could not see much except a wisp of sandy side whisker. His right hand hung down to the floor, the fingers trailing into the pages of *Three Men in a Boat*.

"We first noticed that there seemed to be some—that is, something that had come out of his ear. More we did not know, except that he was dead, and in fact the weapon has never been found. He died in his sleep.

The doctor later told us that the wound had been made by some round sharp-pointed instrument, thicker than a hatpin but not so thick as a lead pencil, which had been driven through the right ear into the brain."

Joseph Lessing paused. A mighty swish of wind uprose in the trees beyond the lake, and their tops ruffled under clear starlight. The little man sat nodding to himself in the iron chair. They could see his white hat move.

"Yes?" prompted Dr. Fell in an almost casual tone. Dr. Fell was sitting back, a great bandit shape in cloak and shovel hat. He seemed to be blinking curiously at Lessing over his eyeglasses. "And whom did they suspect?"

"They suspected me," said the little man.

"You see," he went on, in the same apologetic tone, "I was the only one in the group who could swim. It was my one accomplishment. It is too dark to show you now but I won a little medal by it, and I have kept it on my watch chain ever since I received it as a boy."

"But you said," cried Hadley, "that nobody . . ."

"I will explain," said the other, "if you do not interrupt me. Of course, the police believed that the motive must have been money. Dr. Lessing was a wealthy man, and his money was divided almost equally among us. I told you he was always very good to me.

"First they tried to find out where everyone had been in the afternoon. Brownrigg had been sitting, or said he had been sitting, in the dining room. But there was the gardener to prove that not he or anyone else had gone out on the lake. Martha (it was foolish, of course, but they investigated even Martha) had been with a friend of hers—I forget her name now—who came for her in the phaeton and took her away to play croquet. Junior had no alibi, since he had been for a country walk. But," said Lessing, quite simply, "everybody knew *he* would never do a thing like that. I was the changeling, or perhaps I mean ugly duckling, and I admit I was an unpleasant, sarcastic lad.

"This is how Inspector Deering thought I had committed the murder. First, he thought, I had made sure everybody would be away from the house that afternoon. Thus, later, when the crime was discovered, it would be assumed by everyone that the murderer had simply gone out in the punt and come back again. Everybody knew that I could not possibly manage a punt alone. You see?

"Next, the inspector thought, I had come down to the clump of trees across the lake, in line with the summerhouse and the dining room windows. It is shallow there, and there are reeds. He thought that I had taken off my clothes over a bathing suit. He thought that I had crept into the water under cover of the reeds, and that I had simply swum out to the summerhouse under water.

"Twenty-odd yards under water, I admit, are not much to a good swimmer. They thought that Brownrigg could not see me come up out of the water, because the thickness of the summerhouse was between. Robinson had a full view of the lake, but he could not see that one part at the back of the summerhouse. Nor, on the other hand, could I see them. They thought that I had crawled under the sun blind with the weapon in the breast of my bathing suit. Any wetness I might have left would soon be dried by the intense heat. That, I think, was how they believed I had killed the old man who befriended me."

The little man's voice grew petulant and dazed.

"I told them I did not do it," he said with a hopeful air. "Over and over again I told them I did not do it. But I do not think they believed me. That is why for all these years I have wondered—

"It was Brownrigg's idea. They had me before a sort of family council in the library, as though I had stolen jam. Martha was weeping, but I think she was weeping with plain fear. She never stood up well in a crisis, Martha didn't; she turned pettish and even looked softer. All the same, it is not pleasant to think of a murderer coming up to you as you doze in the afternoon heat. Junior, the good fellow, attempted to take my side and call for fair play; but I could see the idea in his face. Brownrigg presided, silkily, and smiled down his nose.

" 'We have either got to believe you killed him,' Brownrigg said, 'or believe in the supernatural. Is the lake haunted? No; I think we may safely discard that.' He pointed his finger at me. 'You damned young snake, you are lazy and wanted that money.'

"But, you see, I had one very strong hold over them—and I used it. I admit it was unscrupulous, but I was trying to demonstrate my innocence and we are told that the devil must be fought with fire. At mention of this hold, even Brownrigg's jowls shook. Brownrigg was a dentist, Harvey was studying medicine. What hold? That is the whole point. Nevertheless, it was not what the family thought I had to fear: it was what Inspector Deering thought.

"They did not arrest me yet, because there was not enough evidence, but every night I feared it would come the next day. Those days after the funeral were too warm; and suspicion acted like woolen underwear under the heat. Martha's tantrums got on even Junior's nerves. Once I thought Brownrigg was going to hit her. She very badly needed her fiancé, Arthur Somers; but, though he wrote that he might be there any day, he still could not get leave of absence from his colonel.

"And then the lake got more food.

"Look at the house, gentlemen. I wonder if the light is strong enough for you to see it from here? Look at the house—the highest window there—under the gable. You see?"

There was a pause, filled with the tumult of the leaves.

"It's got bars," said Hadley.

"Yes," assented the little man. "I must describe the room. It is a little square room. It has one door and one window. At the time I speak of, there was no furniture at all in it. The furniture had been taken out some years before, because it was rather a special kind of furniture. Since then it had been locked up. The key was kept in a box in Dr. Lessing's room; but, of course, nobody ever went up there. One of Dr. Lessing's wives had died there in a certain condition. I told you he had bad luck with his wives. They had not even dared to have a glass window."

Sharply, the little man struck a match. The brief flame seemed to bring his face up toward them out of the dark. They saw that he had a pipe in his left hand. But the flame showed little except the gentle upward turn of his eyes, and the fact that his whitish hair (of such coarse texture that it seemed whitewashed) was worn rather long.

"On the afternoon of the twenty-second of August, we had an unexpected visit from the family solicitor. There was no one to receive him except myself. Brownrigg had locked himself up in his room at the front with a bottle of whiskey; he was drunk or said he was drunk. Junior was out. We had been trying to occupy our minds for the past week, but Junior could not have his boating or I my workshop; this was thought not decent. I believe it was thought that the most decent thing was to get drunk. For some days Martha had been ailing. She was not ill enough to go to bed, but she was lying on a long chair in her bedroom.

"I looked into the room just before I went downstairs to see the solicitor. The room was muffled up with shutters and velvet curtains, as all the rooms decently were. You may imagine that it was very hot in there. Martha was lying back in the chair with a smelling bottle, and there was a white-globed lamp burning on a little round table beside her. I remember that her white dress looked starchy; her hair was piled up on top of her head and she wore a little gold watch on her breast. Also, her eyelids were so puffed that they seemed almost oriental. When I asked her how she was, she began to cry and concluded by throwing a book at me.

"So I went on downstairs. I was talking to the solicitor when it took place. We were in the library, which is at the front of the house, and in consequence we could not hear distinctly. But we heard something. That was why we went upstairs—and even the solicitor ran. Martha was not in her own bedroom. We found out where she was from the fact that the door to the garret stairs was open.

"It was even more intolerably hot up under the roof. The door to the barred room stood halfway open. Just outside stood a housemaid (her name, I think, was Jane Dawson) leaning against the jamb and shaking like the ribbons on her cap. All sound had dried up in her throat, but she pointed inside.

"I told you it was a little, bare, dirty-brown room. The low sun made a blaze through the window, and made shadows of the bars across Martha's white dress. Martha lay nearly in the middle of the room, with her heel twisted under her as though she had turned round before she fell. I lifted her up and tried to talk to her; but a rounded sharp-pointed thing, somewhat thicker than a hatpin, had been driven through the right eye into the brain.

"Yet there was nobody else in the room.

"The maid told a straight story. She had seen Martha come out of Dr. Lessing's bedroom downstairs. Martha was running, running as well as she could in those skirts; once she stumbled, and the maid thought that she was sobbing. Jane Dawson said that Martha made for the garret door as though the devil were after her. Jane Dawson, wishing anything rather than to be alone in the dark hall, followed her. She saw Martha come up here and unlock the door of the little brown room. When Martha ran inside, the maid thought that she did not attempt to close the door; but that it appeared to swing shut after her. You see?

"Whatever had frightened Martha, Jane Dawson did not dare follow her in—for a few seconds, at least, and afterward it was too late. The maid could never afterward describe exactly the sort of sound Martha made. It was something that startled the birds out of the vines and set the swans flapping on the lake. But the maid presently saw straight enough to push the door with one finger and peep round the edge.

"Except for Martha, the room was empty.

"Hence the three of us now looked at each other. The maid's story was not to be shaken in any way, and we all knew she was a truthful witness. Even the police did not doubt her. She said she had seen Martha go into that room, but that she had seen nobody come out of it. She never took her eyes off the door—it was not likely that she would. But when she peeped in to see what had happened, there was nobody except Martha in the room. That was easily established, because there was no place where anyone could have been. Could she have been blinded by the light? No. Could anyone have slipped past her? No. She almost shook her hair loose by her vehemence on this point.

"The window, I need scarcely tell you, was inaccessible. Its bars were firmly set, no farther apart than the breadth of your hand, and in any case the window could not have been reached. There was no way out of the room except the door or the window; and no—what is the word I want?—no mechanical device in it. Our friend Inspector Deering made certain of that. One thing I suppose I should mention. Despite the condition of the walls and ceiling, the floor of the room was swept clean. Martha's white dress with the puffed shoulders had scarcely any dirt when she lay there; it was as white as her face.

"This murder was incredible. I do not mean merely that it was incredible with regard to its physical circumstances, but also that there was Martha dead—on a holiday. Possibly she seemed all the more dead because we had never known her well when she was alive. She was (to me, at least) a laugh, a few coquetries, a pair of brown eyes. You felt her absence more than you would have felt that of a more vital person. And—on a holiday with that warm sun, and the tennis net ready to be put up.

"That evening I walked with Junior here in the dusk by the lake. He was trying to express some of this. He appeared dazed. He did not know why Martha had gone up to that little brown room, and he kept endlessly asking why. He could not even seem to accustom himself to the idea that our holidays were interrupted, much less interrupted by the murders of his father and his sister.

"There was a reddish light on the lake; the trees stood up against it like black lace, and we were walking near that clump by the reeds. The thing I remember most vividly is Junior's face. He had his hat on the back of his head, as he usually did. He was staring down past the reeds, where the water lapped faintly, as though the lake itself were the evil genius and kept its secret. When he spoke I hardly recognized his voice.

" 'God,' he said, 'but it's in the air!'

"There was something white floating by the reeds, very slowly turning round with a snaky discolored talon coming out from it along the water, the talon was the head of a swan, and the swan was dead of a gash across the neck that had very nearly severed it.

"We fished it out with a boat hook," explained the little man as though with an afterthought. And then he was silent.

On the long iron bench Dr. Fell's cape shifted a little; Hadley could hear him wheezing with quiet anger, like a boiling kettle.

"I thought so," rumbled Dr. Fell. He added more sharply: "Look here, this tomfoolery has got to stop."

"I beg your pardon?" said Joseph Lessing, evidently startled.

"With your kind permission," said Dr. Fell, and Hadley has later said that he was never more glad to see that cane flourished or hear that common-sense voice grow fiery with controversy: "with your kind permission, I should like to ask you a question. Will you swear to me by anything you hold sacred (if you have anything, which I rather doubt) that you do not know the real answer?"

"Yes," replied the other seriously, and nodded.

For a little space, Dr. Fell was silent. Then he spoke argumentatively. "I will ask you another question, then. Did you ever shoot an arrow into the air?"

Hadley turned round. "I hear the call of Mumbo-Jumbo," said Hadley with grim feeling. "Hold on, now! You don't think that girl was killed by somebody shooting an arrow into the air, do you?"

"Oh no," said Dr. Fell in a more meditative tone. He looked at Lessing. "I mean it figuratively—like the boy in the verse. Did you ever throw a stone when you were a boy? Did you ever throw a stone, not to hit anything, but for the sheer joy of firing it? Did you ever climb trees? Did you ever like to play pirate and dress up and wave a sword? I don't think so. That's why you live in a dreary, rarefied light; that's why you dislike romance and sentiment and good whiskey and all the noblest things of this world; and it is also why you do not see the unreasonableness of several things in this case.

"To begin with, birds do not commonly rise up in a great cloud from the vines because someone cries out. With the hopping and always-whooping Junior about the premises, I should imagine the birds were used to it. Still less do swans leap up out of the water and flap their wings because of a cry from far away; swans are not so sensitive. But did you ever see a boy throw a stone at a wall? Did you ever see a boy throw a stone at the water? Birds and swans would have been outraged only if something had *struck* both the wall and the water: something, in short, which fell from the barred window.

"Now, frightened women do not in their terror rush up to a garret, especially a garret with such associations. They go downstairs, where there is protection. Martha Lessing was not frightened. She went up to that room for some purpose. What purpose? She could not have been going to get anything, for there was nothing in the room to be got. What could have been on her mind? The only thing we know to have been on her mind was a frantic wish for her fiancé to get there. She had been expecting him for weeks. It is a singular thing about that room: but its window is the highest in the house, and commands the only clear view of the road to the village.

"Now suppose someone had told her that he thought, he rather *thought,* he had glimpsed Arthur Somers coming up the road from the village. It was a long way off, of course, and the someone admitted he might have been mistaken in thinking so. . . .

"H'm, yes. The trap was all set, you see. Martha Lessing waited only long enough to get the key out of the box in her father's room, and she sobbed with relief. But, when she got to the room, there was a strong sun pouring through the bars straight into her face: and the road to the village is a long way off. That, I believe, was the trap. For on the window ledge of that room (which nobody ever used, and which someone had swept so that there should be no footprints) this someone conveniently placed a pair of—eh, Hadley?"

"Field glasses," said Hadley, and got up in the gloom.

"Still," argued Dr. Fell, wheezing argumentatively, "there would be one nuisance. Take a pair of field glasses, and try to use them in a window where the bars are set more closely than the breadth of your hand. The bars get in the way: wherever you turn you bump into them; they confuse sight and irritate you; and, in addition, there is a strong sun to complicate matters. In your impatience, I think you would turn the glasses sideways and pass them out through the bars. Then, holding them firmly against one bar with your hands through the bars on either side, you would look through the eyepieces.

"But," said Dr. Fell, with a ferocious geniality, "those were no ordinary glasses. Martha Lessing had noticed before that the lenses were blurred. Now that they were in position, she tried to adjust the focus by turning the little wheel in the middle. And as she turned the wheel, like the trigger of a pistol it released the spring mechanism and a sharp steel point shot out from the right-hand lens into her eye. She dropped the glasses, which were outside the window. The weight of them tore the point from her eye; and it was this object, falling, which gashed and broke the neck of the swan just before it disappeared into the water below."

He paused. He had taken out a cigar, but he did not light it.

"Busy solicitors do not usually come to a house 'unexpectedly.' They are summoned. Brownrigg was drunk and Junior absent; there was no one at the back of the house to see the glasses fall. For this time the murderer had to have a respectable alibi. Young Martha, the only one who could have been gulled into such a trap, had to be sacrificed—to avert the arrest, which had been threatening someone ever since the police found out how Dr. Lessing really had been murdered.

"There was only one man who admittedly did speak with Martha Lessing only a few minutes before she was murdered. There was only one man who was employed as optician at a jeweler's, and admits he had his 'workshop' here. There was only one man skillful enough with his hands—" Dr. Fell paused, wheezing, and turned to Lessing. "I wonder they didn't arrest you."

"They did," said the little man, nodding. "You see, I was released from Broadmoor only a month ago."

There was a sudden rasp and crackle as he struck another match.

"You—" bellowed Hadley, and stopped. "So it was your mother who died in that room? Then what the hell do you mean by keeping us here with this pack of nightmares?"

"No," said the other peevishly. "You do not understand. I never wanted to know who killed Dr. Lessing or poor Martha. You have got hold of the wrong problem. And yet I tried to tell you what the problem was.

"You see, it was not *my* mother who died mad. It was theirs—Brownrigg's and Harvey's and Martha's. That was why they were so desperately anxious to think I was guilty, for they could not face the alternative. Didn't I tell you I had a hold over them, a hold that made even Brownrigg shake, and that I used it? Do you think they wouldn't have had me clapped into jail straightaway if it had been *my* mother who was mad? Eh?

"Of course," he explained apologetically, "at the trial they had to swear it was my mother who was mad; for I threatened to tell the truth in open court if they didn't. Otherwise I should have been hanged, you see. Only Brownrigg and Junior were left. Brownrigg was a dentist, Junior was to be a doctor, and if it had been known—But that is not the point. That is not the problem. Their mother was mad, but they were harmless. I killed Dr. Lessing. I killed Martha. Yes, I am quite sane. Why did I do it, all those years ago? Why? Is there no rational pattern in the scheme of things, and no answer to the bedeviled of the earth?

The match curled to a red ember, winked and went out. Clearest of all they remembered the coarse hair that was like whitewash on the black, the eyes, and the curiously suggestive hands. Then Joseph Lessing got up from the chair. The last they saw of him was his white hat bobbing and flickering across the lawn under the blowing trees.

The Next Witness

Author: Rex Stout (1886–1975)

Detective: Nero Wolfe (1934)

Nero Wolfe, the corpulent and generally sedentary private detective who appeared first in *Fer-de-Lance* (1934) and last in *A Family Affair* (1875), never had a short-story appearance, but he did star in a long series of novelettes, most of them originally written for the *American* magazine and reprinted three to a volume in book form.

The case that follows may seem atypical, since as a rule Wolfe never left his Manhattan brownstone, allowing that breeziest of Watson characters, Archie Goodwin, to do his legwork. Still, that rule was broken more often than you might think in some of his best and most memorable adventures, including *Some Buried Caesar* (1938), *Too Many Cooks* (1938), *In the Best Families* (1950), and *The Black Mountain* (1954). And wouldn't a high-profile private investigator have to leave his comforting domestic surroundings fairly frequently to testify in court? This story represents the lone recorded example of Wolfe venturing into Perry Mason's territory.

I

I had had previous contacts with Assistant District Attorney Irving Mandelbaum, but had never seen him perform in a courtroom. That morning, watching him at the chore of trying to persuade a jury to clamp it on Leonard Ashe for the murder of Marie Willis, I thought he was pretty good and might be better when he had warmed up. A little plump and a little short, bald in front and big-eared, he wasn't impressive to look at, but he was businesslike and self-assured without being cocky, and he had a neat trick of pausing for a moment to look at the

jury as if he half expected one of them to offer a helpful suggestion.
When he pulled it, not too often, his back was turned to the judge and
the defense counsel, so they couldn't see his face, but I could, from
where I sat in the audience.

It was the third day of the trial, and he had called his fifth witness, a
scared-looking little guy with a pushed-in nose who gave his name,
Clyde Bagby, took the oath, sat down, and fixed his scared brown eyes
on Mandelbaum as if he had abandoned hope.

Mandelbaum's tone was reassuring. "What is your business, Mr.
Bagby?"

The witness swallowed. "I'm the president of Bagby Answers, Inc."

"By 'Inc' you mean 'Incorporated'?"

"Yes, sir."

"Do you own the business?"

"I own half the stock that's been issued, and my wife owns the other
half."

"How long have you been operating that business?"

"Five years now—nearly five and a half."

"And what is the business? Please tell the jury about it."

Bagby's eyes went left for a quick, nervous glance at the jury box but
came right back to the prosecutor. "It's a telephone-answering business,
that's all. You know what that is."

"Yes, but some members of the jury may not be familiar with the
operation. Please describe it."

The witness licked his lips. "Well, you're a person or a firm or an
organization and you have a phone, but you're not always there and you
want to know about calls that come in your absence. So you go to a
telephone-answering service. There are several dozen of them in New
York, some of them spread all over town with neighborhood offices, big
operations. My own operation, Bagby Answers Inc, it's not so big because I specialize in serving individuals, houses and apartments, instead
of firms or organizations. I've got offices in four different exchange
districts—Gramercy, Plaza, Trafalgar, and Rhinelander. I can't work it
from one central office because—"

"Excuse me, Mr. Bagby, but we won't go into technical problems. Is
one of your offices at six-eighteen East Sixty-ninth Street, Manhattan?"

"Yes, sir."

"Describe the operation at that address."

"Well, that's my newest place, opened only a year ago, and my small-
est, so it's not in an office building, it's an apartment—on account of the
labor law. You can't have women working in an office building after

two A.M. unless it's a public service, but I have to give my clients all-night service, so there on Sixty-ninth Street I've got four operators for the three switchboards, and they all live right there in the apartment. That way I can have one at the boards from eight till two at night, and another one from two o'clock on. After nine in the morning three are on, one for each board, for the daytime load."

"Are the switchboards installed in one of the rooms of the apartment?"

"Yes, sir."

"Tell the jury what one of them is like and how it works."

Bagby darted another nervous glance at the jury box and went back to the prosecutor. "It's a good deal like any board in a big office, with rows of holes for the plugs. Of course it's installed by the telephone company, with the special wiring for connections with my clients' phones. Each board has room for sixty clients. For each client there's a little light and a hole and a card strip with the client's name. When someone dials a client's number his light goes on and a buzz synchronizes with the ringing of the client's phone. How many buzzes the girl counts before she plugs in depends on what client it is. Some of them want her to plug in after three buzzes, some want her to wait longer. I've got one client that has her count fifteen buzzes. That's the kind of specialized individualized service I give my clients. The big outfits, the ones with tens of thousands of clients, they won't do that. They've commercialized it. With me every client is a special case and a sacred trust."

"Thank you, Mr. Bagby." Mandelbaum swiveled his head for a swift sympathetic smile at the jury and swiveled it back again. "But I wasn't buzzing for a plug for your business. When a client's light shows on the board, and the girl has heard the prescribed number of buzzes, she plugs in on the line, is that it?"

I thought Mandelbaum's crack was a little out of place for that setting, where a man was on trial for his life, and turned my head right for a glance at Nero Wolfe to see if he agreed, but one glimpse of his profile told me that he was sticking to his role of a morose martyr and so was in no humor to agree with anyone or anything.

That was to be expected. At that hour of the morning, following his hard-and-fast schedule, he would have been up in the plant rooms on the roof of his old brownstone house on West Thirty-fifth Street, bossing Theodore for the glory of his celebrated collection of orchids, even possibly getting his hands dirty. At eleven o'clock, after washing his hands, he would have taken the elevator down to his office on the ground floor, arranged his oversized corpus in his oversized chair behind his desk, rung for Fritz to bring beer, and started bossing Archie Goodwin, me. He would have given me any instructions he thought timely and desirable, for anything from typing a letter to tailing the mayor, which seemed likely to boost his income and add to his reputation as the best private detective east of San Francisco. And he would have been looking forward to lunch by Fritz.

And all that was "would-have-been" because he had been subpoenaed by the State of New York to appear in court and testify at the trial of Leonard Ashe. He hated to leave his house at all, and particularly he hated to leave it for a trip to a witness box. Being a private detective, he had to concede that a summons to testify was an occupational hazard he must accept if he hoped to collect fees from clients, but his cloud didn't even have that silver lining. Leonard Ashe had come to the office one day about two months ago to hire him, but had been turned down. So neither fee nor glory was in prospect. As for me, I had been subpoenaed too, but only for insurance, since I wouldn't be called unless Mandelbaum decided Wolfe's testimony needed corroboration, which wasn't likely.

It was no pleasure to look at Wolfe's gloomy phiz, so I looked back at the performers. Bagby was answering. "Yes, sir, she plugs in and says, 'Mrs. Smith's residence,' or, 'Mr. Jones's apartment,' or whatever she has been told to say for that client. Then she says Mrs. Smith is out and is there any message, and so on, whatever the situation calls for. Sometimes the client has called and given her a message for some particular caller." Bagby flipped a hand. "Just anything. We give specialized service."

Mandelbaum nodded. "I think that gives us a clear picture of the operation. Now, Mr. Bagby, please look at that gentleman in the dark blue suit sitting next to the officer. He is the defendant in this trial. Do you know him?"

"Yes, sir. That's Mr. Leonard Ashe."

"When and where did you meet him?"

"In July he came to my office on Forty-seventh Street. First he phoned, and then he came."

"Can you give the day in July?"

"The twelfth. A Monday."

"What did he say?"

"He asked how my answering service worked, and I told him, and he said he wanted it for his home telephone at his apartment on East Seventy-third Street. He paid cash for a month in advance. He wanted twenty-four-hour service."

"Did he want any special service?"

"He didn't ask me for any, but two days later he contacted Marie Willis and offered her five hundred dollars if she—"

The witness was interrupted from two directions at once. The defense attorney, a champion named Jimmy Donovan whose batting average on big criminal cases had topped the list of the New York bar for ten years, left his chair with his mouth open to object; and Mandelbaum showed the witness a palm to stop him.

"Just a minute, Mr. Bagby. Just answer my questions. Did you accept Leonard Ashe as a client?"

"Sure, there was no reason not to."

"What was the number of his telephone at his home?"

"Rhinelander two-three-eight-three-eight."

"Did you give his name and that number a place on one of your switchboards?"

"Yes, sir, one of the three boards at the apartment on East Sixty-ninth Street. That's the Rhinelander district."

"What was the name of the employee who attended that board—the one with Leonard Ashe's number on it?"

"Marie Willis."

A shadow of stir and murmur rippled across the packed audience, and Judge Corbett on the bench turned his head to give it a frown and then went back to his knitting.

Bagby was going on. "Of course at night there's only one girl on the three boards—they rotate on that—but for daytime I keep a girl at her own board at least five days a week, and six if I can. That way she gets to know her clients."

"And Leonard Ashe's number was on Marie Willis' board?"

"Yes, sir."

"After the routine arrangements for serving Leonard Ashe as a client had been completed, did anything happen to bring him or his number to your personal attention?"

"Yes, sir."

"What and when? First, when?"

Bagby took a second to make sure he had it right before swearing to it. "It was Thursday, three days after Ashe had ordered the service. That was July fifteenth. Marie phoned me at my office and said she wanted to see me privately about something important. I asked if it could wait till she was off the board at six o'clock, and she said yes, and a little after six I went up to Sixty-ninth Street and we went into her room at the apartment. She told me Ashe had phoned her the day before and asked her to meet him somewhere to discuss some details about servicing his number. She told him such a discussion should be with me, but he insisted—"

A pleasant but firm baritone cut in. "If Your Honor pleases." Jimmy Donovan was on his feet. "I submit that the witness may not testify to what Marie Willis and Mr. Ashe said to each other when he was not present."

"Certainly not," Mandelbaum agreed shortly. "He is reporting what Marie Willis told *him* had been said."

Judge Corbett nodded. "That should be kept clear. You understand that, Mr. Bagby?"

"Yes, sir." Bagby bit his lip. "I mean Your Honor."

"Then go ahead. What Miss Willis said to you and you to her."

"Well, she said she had agreed to meet Ashe because he was a theatrical producer and she wanted to be an actress. I hadn't known she was stage-struck but I know it now. So she had gone to his office on Forty-fifth Street as soon as she was off the board, and after he talked some and asked some questions he told her—this is what she told me—he told her he wanted her to listen in on calls to his home number during the daytime. All she would have to do, when his light on her board went on and the buzzes started, if the buzzes stopped and the light went off—that would mean someone had answered the phone at his home—she would plug in and listen to the conversation. Then each evening she would phone him and report. That's what she said Ashe had asked her to do. She said he counted out five hundred dollars in bills and offered them to her and told her he'd give her another thousand if she went along."

Bagby stopped for wind. Mandelbaum prodded him. "Did she say anything else?"

"Yes, sir. She said she knew she should have turned him down flat, but she didn't want to make him sore, so she told him she wanted to think it over for a day or two. Then she said she had slept on it and decided what to do. She said of course she knew that what Ashe was after was phone calls to his wife, and aside from anything else she wouldn't spy on his wife, because his wife was Robina Keane, who had given up her career as an actress two years ago to marry Ashe, and Marie worshiped Robina Keane as her ideal. That's what Marie told me. She said she had decided she must do three things. She must tell me about it because Ashe was my client and she was working for me. She must tell Robina Keane about it, to warn her, because Ashe would probably get someone else to do the spying for him. It occurred to me that her real reason for wanting to tell Robina Keane might be that she hoped—"

Mandelbaum stopped him. "What occurred to you isn't material, Mr. Bagby. Did Marie tell you the third thing she had decided she must do?"

"Yes, sir. That she must tell Ashe that she was going to tell his wife. She said she had to because at the start of her talk with him she had promised Ashe she would keep it confidential, so she had to warn him she was withdrawing her promise."

"Did she say when she intended to do those three things?"

The witness nodded. "She had already done one of them, telling me. She said she had phoned Ashe and told him she would be at his office at seven o'clock. That was crowding it a little, because she had the evening shift that day and would have to be back at the boards at eight o'clock. It crowded me too because it gave me no time to talk her out of it. I went downtown with her in a taxi, to Forty-fifth Street, where Ashe's office was, and did my best but couldn't move her."

"What did you say to her?"

"I tried to get her to lay off. If she went through with her program it might not do any harm to my business, but again it might. I tried to persuade her to let me handle it by going to Ashe and telling him she had told me of his offer and I didn't want him for a client, and then drop it and forget it, but she was dead set on warning Robina Keane, and to do that she had to withdraw her promise to Ashe. I hung on until she entered the elevator to go up to Ashe's office, but I couldn't budge her."

"Did you go up with her?"

"No, that wouldn't have helped any. She was going through with it, and what could I do?"

So, I was thinking to myself, that's how it is. It looked pretty tough to me, and I glanced at Wolfe, but his eyes were closed, so I turned my head the other way to see how the gentleman in the dark blue suit seated next to the officer was taking it. Apparently it looked pretty tough to Leonard Ashe too. With deep creases slanting along the jowls of his dark bony face from the corners of his wide full mouth, and his sunken dark eyes, he was certainly a prime subject for the artists who sketch candidates for the hot seat for the tabloids, and for three days they had been making the most of it. He was no treat for the eyes, and I took mine away from him, to the left, where his wife sat in the front row of the audience.

I had never worshiped Robina Keane as my ideal, but I had liked her fine in a couple of shows, and she was giving a good performance for her first and only courtroom appearance—either being steadfastly loyal to her husband or putting on an act, but good in either case. She was dressed quietly and she sat quietly, but she wasn't trying to pretend she wasn't young and beautiful. Exactly how she and her older and unbeautiful husband stood with each other was anybody's guess, and everybody was guessing. One extreme said he was her whole world and he had been absolutely batty to suspect her of any hoop-rolling; the other extreme said she had quit the stage only to have more time for certain promiscuous activities, and Ashe had been a sap not to know it sooner; and anywhere in between. I wasn't ready to vote. Looking at her, she might have been an angel. Looking at him, it must have taken something drastic to get him that miserable, though I granted that being locked up two months on a charge of murder would have some effect.

Mandelbaum was making sure the jury had got it. "Then you didn't go up to Ashe's office with Marie Willis?"

"No, sir."

"Did you go up later, at any time, after she had gone up?"

"No, sir."

"Did you see Ashe at all that evening?"

"No, sir."

"Did you speak to him on the telephone that evening?"

"No, sir."

Looking at Bagby, and I have looked at a lot of specimens under fire, I decided that either he was telling it straight or he was an expert liar, and he didn't sound like an expert. Mandelbaum went on. "What did you do that evening, after you saw Marie Willis enter the elevator to go up to Ashe's office?"

"I went to keep a dinner date with a friend at a restaurant—Hornby's on Fifty-second Street—and after that, around half-past eight, I went up to my Trafalgar office at Eighty-sixth Street and Broadway. I have six boards there, and a new night girl was on, and I stayed there with her a while and then took a taxi home, across the park to my apartment on East Seventieth Street. Not long after I got home a phone call came from the police to tell me Marie Willis had been found murdered in my Rhinelander office, and I went there as fast as I could go, and there was a crowd out in front, and an officer took me upstairs."

He stopped to swallow, and stuck his chin out a little. "They hadn't moved her. They had taken the plug cord from around her throat, but they hadn't moved her, and there she was, slumped over on the ledge in front of the board. They wanted me to identify her, and I had—"

The witness wasn't interrupted, but I was. There was a tug at my sleeve, and a whisper in my ear—"We're leaving, come on." And Nero

Wolfe arose, sidled past two pairs of knees to the aisle, and headed for the rear of the courtroom. For his bulk he could move quicker and smoother than you would expect, and as I followed him to the door and on out to the corridor we got no attention at all. I was assuming that some vital need had stirred him, like phoning Theodore to tell him or ask him something about an orchid, but he went on past the phone booths to the elevator and pushed the down button. With people all around I asked no questions. He got out at the main floor and made for Centre Street. Out on the sidewalk he backed up against the granite of the courthouse and spoke.

"We want a taxi, but first a word with you."

"No, sir," I said firmly. "First a word *from* me. Mandelbaum may finish with that witness any minute, and the cross-examination may not take long, or Donovan might even reserve it, and you were told you would follow Bagby. If you want a taxi, of course you're going home, and that will just—"

"I'm not going home. I can't."

"Right. If you do you'll merely get hauled back here and also a fat fine for contempt of court. Not to mention me. I'm under subpoena too. I'm going back to the courtroom. Where are you going?"

"To six-eighteen East Sixty-ninth Street."

I goggled at him. "I've always been afraid of this. Does it hurt?"

"Yes. I'll explain on the way."

"I'm going back to the courtroom."

"No. I'll need you."

Like everyone else, I love to feel needed, so I wheeled, crossed the sidewalk, flagged a taxi to the curb, and opened the door. Wolfe came and climbed in, and I followed. After he had got himself braced against the hazards of a carrier on wheels and I had given the driver the address, and we were rolling, I said, "Shoot. I've heard you do a lot of explaining, but this will have to be good."

"It's preposterous," he declared.

"It sure is. Let's go back."

"I mean Mr. Mandelbaum's thesis. I will concede that Mr. Ashe might have murdered that girl. I will concede that his state of mind about his wife might have approached mania, and therefore the motive suggested by that witness might have been adequate provocation. But he's not an imbecile. Under the circumstances as given, and I doubt if Mr. Bagby can be discredited, I refuse to believe he was ass enough to go to that place at that time and kill her. You were present when he called on me that day to hire me. Do you believe it?"

I shook my head. "I pass. You're explaining. However, I read the papers too, and also I've chatted with Lon Cohen of the *Gazette* about it. It doesn't have to be that Ashe went there for the purpose of killing her. His story is that a man phoned him—a voice he didn't recognize— and said if Ashe would meet him at the Bagby place on Sixty-ninth Street he thought they could talk Marie out of it, and Ashe went on the hop, and the door to the office was standing open, and he went in and there she was with a plug cord tight around her throat, and he opened a window and yelled for the police. Of course if you like it that Bagby was lying just now when he said it wasn't him that phoned Ashe, and that Bagby is such a good businessman that he would rather kill an employee than lose a customer—"

"Pfui. It isn't what I like, it's what I don't like. Another thing I didn't like was sitting there on that confounded wooden bench with a smelly woman against me. Soon I was going to be called as a witness, and my testimony would have been effective corroboration of Mr. Bagby's testimony, as you know. It was intolerable. I believe that if Mr. Ashe is convicted of murder on the thesis Mr. Mandelbaum is presenting it will be a justicial transgression, and I will not be a party to it. It wasn't easy to get up and go because I can't go home. If I go home they'll come and drag me out, and into that witness box."

I eyed him. "Let's see if I get you. You can't bear to help convict Ashe of murder because you doubt if he's guilty, so you're scooting. Right?"

The hackie twisted his head around to inform us through the side of his mouth, "Sure he's guilty."

We ignored it. "That's close enough," Wolfe said.

"Not close enough for me. If you expect me to scoot with you and invite a stiff fine for running out on a subpoena, which you will pay, don't try to guff me. Say we doubt if Ashe is guilty, but we think he may get tagged because we know Mandelbaum wouldn't go to trial without a good case. Say also our bank account needs a shot in the arm, which is true. So we decide to see if we can find something that will push Mandelbaum's nose in, thinking that if Ashe is properly grateful a measly little fine will be nothing. The way to proceed would be for you to think up a batch of errands for me, and you to go on home and read a book and have a good lunch, but that's out because they'd come and get you. Therefore we must both do errands. If that's how it stands, it's a fine day and I admit that woman was smelly, but I have a good nose and I think it was Tissot's Passion Flower, which is eighty bucks an ounce. What are we going to do at Sixty-ninth Street?"

"I don't know."
"Good. Neither do I."

II

It was a dump, an old five-story walk-up, brick that had been painted yellow about the time I had started working for Nero Wolfe. In the vestibule I pushed the button that was labeled *Bagby Answers, Inc.,* and when the click came I opened the door and led the way across the crummy little hall to the stairs and up one flight. Mr. Bagby wasn't wasting it on rent. At the front end of the hall a door stood open. As we approached it I stepped aside to let Wolfe go first, since I didn't know whether we were disguised as brush peddlers or as plumbers.

As Wolfe went to speak to a girl at a desk I sent my eyes on a quick survey. It was the scene of the murder. In the front wall of the room three windows overlooked the street. Against the opposite wall were arranged the three switchboards, with three females with headphones seated at them. They had turned their heads for a look at the company.

The girl at the desk, which was near the end window, had only an ordinary desk phone, in addition to a typewriter and other accessories. Wolfe was telling her, "My name is Wolfe and I've just come from the courtroom where Leonard Ashe is being tried." He indicated me with a jerk of his head. "This is my assistant, Mr. Goodwin. We're checking on subpoenas that have been served on witnesses, for both the prosecution and the defense. Have you been served?"

With his air and presence and tone, only one woman in a hundred would have called him, and she wasn't it. Her long, narrow face tilted up to him, she shook her head. "No, I haven't."

"Your name, please?"

"Pearl Fleming."

"Then you weren't working here on July fifteenth."

"No, I was at another office. There was no office desk here then. One of the boards took office calls."

"I see." His tone implied that it was damned lucky for her that he saw. "Are Miss Hart and Miss Velardi and Miss Weltz here?"

My brows wanted to lift, but I kept them down, and anyway there was nothing startling about it. True, it had been weeks since those names had appeared in the papers, but Wolfe never missed a word of an account of a murder, and his skull's filing system was even better than Saul Panzer's.

Pearl Fleming pointed to the switchboards. "That's Miss Hart at the end. Miss Velardi is next to her. Next to Miss Velardi is Miss Yerkes. She came after—she replaced Miss Willis. Miss Weltz isn't here; it's her day off. They've had subpoenas, but—"

She stopped and turned her head. The woman at the end board had removed her headphone, left her seat, and was marching over to us. She was about my age, with sharp brown eyes and flat cheeks and a chin she could have used for an icebreaker if she had been a walrus.

"Aren't you Nero Wolfe, the detective?" she demanded.

"Yes," he assented. "You are Alice Hart?"

She skipped it. "What do you want?"

Wolfe backed up a step. He doesn't like anyone so close to him, especially a woman. "I want information, madam. I want you and Bella Velardi and Helen Weltz to answer some questions."

"We have no information."

"Then I won't get any, but I'm going to try."

"Who sent you here?"

"Autokinesis. There's a cardinal flaw in the assumption that Leonard Ashe killed Marie Willis, and I don't like flaws. It has made me curious, and when I'm curious there is only one cure—the whole truth, and I intend to find it. If I am in time to save Mr. Ashe's life, so much the better; but in any case I have started and will not be stopped. If you and the others refuse to oblige me today there will be other days—and other ways."

From her face it was a toss-up. Her chin stiffened, and for a second she was going to tell him to go soak his head; then her eyes left him for me, and she was going to take it. She turned to the girl at the desk. "Take my board, will you, Pearl? I won't be long." To Wolfe, snapping it: "We'll go to my room. This way." She whirled and started.

"One moment, Miss Hart." Wolfe moved. "A point not covered in the newspaper accounts." He stopped at the boards, behind Bella Velardi at the middle one. "Marie Willis' body was found slumped over on the ledge in front of the switchboard. Presumably she was seated at the switchboard when the murderer arrived. But you live here—you and the others?"

"Yes."

"Then if the murderer was Mr. Ashe, how did he know she was alone on the premises?"

"I don't know. Perhaps she told him she was. Is that the flaw?"

"Good heavens, no. It's conceivable that she did, and they talked, and he waited until a light and buzzes had her busy at the board, with her back to him. It's a minor point, but I prefer someone with surer knowledge that she was alone. Since she was small and slight, even you are not excluded"—he wiggled a finger—"or these others. Not that I am now prepared to charge you with murder."

"I hope not," she snorted, turning. She led the way to a door at the end of the room, on through, and down a narrow hall. As I followed behind Wolfe, I was thinking that the reaction we were getting seemed a little exaggerated. It would have been natural, under the circumstances, for Miss Velardi and Miss Yerkes to turn in their seats for a good look at us, but they hadn't. They had sat, rigid, staring at their boards. As for Alice Hart, either there had been a pinch of relief in her voice when she asked Wolfe if that was the flaw, or I was in the wrong business.

Her room was a surprise. First, it was big, much bigger than the one in front with the switchboards. Second, I am not Bernard Berenson, but I have noticed things here and there, and the framed splash of red and yellow and blue above the mantel was not only a real van Gogh, it was bigger and better than the one Lily Rowan had. I saw Wolfe spotting it as he lowered himself onto a chair actually big enough for him, and I pulled one around to make a group, facing the couch Miss Hart dropped onto.

As she sat she spoke. "What's the flaw?"

He shook his head. "I'm the inquisitor, Miss Hart, not you." He aimed a thumb at the van Gogh. "Where did you get that picture?"

She looked at it, and back at him. "That's none of your business."

"It certainly isn't. But here is the situation. You have of course been questioned by the police and the District Attorney's office, but they were restrained by their assumption that Leonard Ashe was the culprit. Since I reject that assumption and must find another in its stead, there can be no limit to my impertinence with you and others who may be involved. Take you and that picture. If you refuse to say where you got it, or if your answer doesn't satisfy me, I'll put a man on it, a competent man, and he'll find out. You can't escape being badgered, madam; the question is whether you suffer it here and now, by me, or face a prolonged inquiry among your friends and associates by meddlesome men. If you prefer the latter don't waste time with me; I'll go and tackle one of the others."

She was tossing up again. From her look at him it seemed just as well that he had his bodyguard along. She tried stalling. "What does it matter where I got that picture?"

"Probably it doesn't. Possibly nothing about you matters. But the picture is a treasure, and this is an odd address for it. Do you own it?"

"Yes. I bought it."

"When?"

"About a year ago. From a dealer."

"The contents of this room are yours?"

"Yes. I like things that—well, this is my extravagance, my only one."

"How long have you been with this firm?"

"Five years."

"What is your salary?"

She was on a tight rein. "Eighty dollars a week."

"Not enough for your extravagance. An inheritance? Alimony? Other income?"

"I have never married. I had some savings, and I wanted—I wanted these things. If you save for fifteen years you have a right to something."

"You have indeed. Where were you the evening that Marie Willis was killed?"

"I was out in Jersey, in a car with a friend—Bella Velardi. To get cooled off—it was a hot night. We got back after midnight."

"In your car?"

"No, Helen Weltz had let us take hers. She has a Jaguar."

My brows went up, and I spoke. "A Jaguar," I told Wolfe, "is quite a machine. You couldn't squeeze into one. Counting taxes and extras, four thousand bucks isn't enough."

His eyes darted to me and back to her. "Of course the police have asked if you know of anyone who might have had a motive for killing Marie Willis. Do you?"

"No." Her rein wasn't so tight.

"Were you friendly with her?"

"Yes, friendly enough."

"Has any client ever asked you to listen in on calls to his number?"

"Certainly not!"

"Did you know Miss Willis wanted to be an actress?"

"Yes, we all knew that."

"Mr. Bagby says he didn't."

Her chin had relaxed a little. "He was her employer. I don't suppose he knew. When did you talk with Mr. Bagby?"

"I didn't. I heard him on the witness stand. Did you know of Miss Willis' regard for Robina Keane?"

"Yes, we all knew that too. Marie did imitations of Robina Keane in her parts."

"When did she tell you of her decision to tell Robina Keane that her husband was going to monitor her telephone?"

Miss Hart frowned. "I didn't say she told me."

"Did she?"

"No."

"Did anyone?"

"Yes, Miss Velardi. Marie had told her. You can ask her."

"I shall. Do you know Guy Unger?"

"Yes, I know him. Not very well."

Wolfe was playing a game I had often watched him at, tossing balls at random to see how they bounced. It's a good way to try to find a lead if you haven't got one, but it may take all day, and he didn't have it. If one of the females in the front room took a notion to phone the cops or the DA's office about us we might have visitors any minute. As for Guy Unger, that was another name from the newspaper accounts. He had been Marie Willis' boyfriend, or had he? There had been a difference of opinion among the journalists.

Miss Hart's opinion was that Guy Unger and Marie had enjoyed each other's company, but that was as far as it went—I mean her opinion. She knew nothing of any crisis that might have made Unger want to end the friendship with a plug cord. For another five minutes Wolfe went on with the game, tossing different balls from different angles, and then abruptly arose.

"Very well," he said. "For now. I'll try Miss Velardi."

"I'll send her in." Alice Hart was on her feet, eager to cooperate. "Her room is next door." She moved. "This way."

Obviously she didn't want to leave us with her van Gogh. There was a lock on a bureau drawer that I could probably have manipulated in twenty seconds, and I would have liked to try my hand on it, but Wolfe was following her out, so I went along—to the right, down the hall to another door, standing open. Leaving us there, she strode on flat heels toward the front. Wolfe passed through the open door with me behind.

This room was different—somewhat smaller, with no van Gogh and the kind of furniture you might expect. The bed hadn't been made, and Wolfe stood and scowled at it a moment, lowered himself gingerly onto a chair too small for him with worn upholstery, and told me curtly, "Look around."

I did so. Bella Velardi was a crack-lover. A closet door and a majority of the drawers in a dressing table and two chests were open to cracks of various widths. One of the reasons I am still shy a wife is the risk of getting a crack-lover. I went and pulled the closet door open, and, having no machete to hack my way into the jungle of duds, swung it back to its crack and stepped across to the library. It was a stack of paperbacks on a little table, the one on top being entitled *One Mistake Too Many,* with a picture of a double-breasted floozie shrinking in terror from a muscle-bound baboon. There was also a pile of recent editions of *Racing Form* and *Track Dope.*

"She's a philanthropist," I told Wolfe. "She donates dough to the cause of equine genetics."

"Meaning?"

"She bets on horse races."

"Does she lose much?"

"She loses. How much depends on what she bets. Probably tidy sums, since she takes two house journals."

He grunted. "Open drawers. Have one open when she enters. I want to see how much impudence these creatures will tolerate."

I obeyed. The six drawers in the bigger chest all held clothes, and I did no pawing. A good job might have uncovered some giveaway under a pile of nylons, but there wasn't time for it. I closed all the drawers to show her what I thought of cracks. Those in the dressing table were also uninteresting. In the second drawer of the smaller chest, among other items, was a collection of photographs, mostly unmounted snaps, and, running through them, with no expectations, I stopped at one for a second look. It was Bella Velardi and another girl, with a man standing between them, in bathing outfits with the ocean for background. I went and handed it to Wolfe.

"The man?" I asked. "I read newspapers too, and look at the pictures, but it was two months ago, and I could be wrong."

He slanted it to get the best light from a window. He nodded. "Guy Unger." He slipped it into a pocket. "Find more of him."

"If any." I went back to the collection. "But you may not get a chance at her. It's been a good four minutes. Either she's getting a full briefing from Miss Hart, or they've phoned for help, and in that case—"

The sound came of high heels clicking on the uncarpeted hall. I closed the second drawer and pulled the third one open, and was inspecting its contents when the click got to the door and were in the room. Shutting it in no hurry and turning to Bella Velardi, I was ready to meet a yelp of indignation, but didn't have to. With her snappy black eyes and sassy little face she must have been perfectly capable of indignation, but her nerves were too busy with something else. She decided to pretend she hadn't caught me with a drawer open, and that was screwy. Added to other things, it made it a cinch that these phone answerers had something on their minds.

Bella Velardi said in a scratchy little voice, "Miss Hart says you want to ask me something," and went and sat on the edge of the unmade bed, with her fingers twisted together.

Wolfe regarded her with his eyes half closed. "Do you know what a hypothetical question is, Miss Velardi?"

"Of course I do."

"I have one for you. If I put three expert investigators on the job of finding out approximately how much you have lost betting on horse races in the past year, how long do you think it would take them?"

"Why, I—" She blinked at him with a fine set of long lashes. "I don't know."

"I do. With luck, five hours. Without it, five days. It would be simpler for you to tell me. How much have you lost?"

She blinked again. "How do you know I've lost anything?"

"I don't. But Mr. Goodwin, who is himself an expert investigator, concluded from publications he found on that table that you are a chronic bettor. If so, there's a fair chance that you keep a record of your gains and losses." He turned to me. "Archie, your search was interrupted. Resume. See if you can find it." Back to her. "At his elbow if you like, Miss Velardi. There is no question of pilfering."

I went to the smaller chest. He was certainly crowding his luck. If she took this without calling a cop she might not be a murderess, but she sure had a tender spot she didn't want touched.

Actually she didn't just sit and take it. As I got a drawer handle to pull it open she loosened her tongue. "Look, Mr. Wolfe, I'm perfectly willing to tell you anything you want to know. Perfectly!" She was leaning toward him, her fingers still twisted. "Miss Hart said I mustn't be surprised at anything you asked, but I was, so I guess I was flustered. There's no secret about my liking to bet on the races, but the amounts I bet—that's different. You see, I have friends who—well, they don't want people to know they bet, so they give me money to bet for them. So it's about a hundred dollars a week, sometimes more, maybe up to two hundred."

If she liked to bet on any animals other than horses, one would have got her ten that she was a damn liar. Evidently Wolfe would have split it with me, since he didn't even bother to ask her the names of the friends.

He merely nodded. "What is your salary?"

"It's only sixty-five, so of course I can't bet much myself."

"Of course. About the windows in that front room. In summer weather, when one of you is on duty there at night, are the windows open?"

She was concentrating. "When it's hot, yes. Usually the one in the middle. If it's very hot, maybe all of them."

"With the shades up?"

"Yes."

"It was hot July fifteenth. Were the windows open that night?"

"I don't know. I wasn't here."

"Where were you?"

"I was out in Jersey, in a car with a friend—Alice Hart. To get cooled off. We got back after midnight."

Wonderful, I thought. That settled that. One woman might conceivably lie, but surely not two.

Wolfe was eying her. "If the windows were open and the shades up the evening of July fifteenth, as they almost certainly were, would anyone in her senses have proceeded to kill Marie Willis so exposed to view? What do you think?"

She didn't call him on the pronoun. "Why, no," she conceded. "That would have been—no, I don't think so."

"Then she—or he—must have closed the windows and drawn the shades before proceeding. How could Leonard Ashe, in the circumstances as given, have managed that without alarming Miss Willis?"

"I don't know. He might have—no, I don't know."

"He might have what?"

"Nothing. I don't know."

"How well do you know Guy Unger?"

"I know him fairly well."

She had been briefed all right. She was expecting that one.

"Have you seen much of him in the past two months?"

"No, very little."

Wolfe reached in his pocket and got the snapshot and held it out. "When was this taken?"

She left the bed and was going to take it, but he held on to it. After a look she said, "Oh, that," and sat down again. All of a sudden she exploded, indignation finally breaking through. "You took that from my drawer! What else did you take?" She sprang up, trembling all over. "Get out of here! Get out and stay out!"

Wolfe returned the snap to his pocket, arose, said, "Come, Archie, there seems to be a limit after all," and started for the door. I followed.

He was at the sill when she darted past me, grabbed his arm, and took it back. "Wait a minute, I didn't mean that. I flare up like that. I just—I don't care about the damn picture."

Wolfe pulled loose and got a yard of space. "When was it taken?"

"About two weeks ago—two weeks ago Sunday."

"Who is the other woman?"

"Helen Weltz."

"Who took it?"

"A man that was with us."

"His name?"

"His name is Ralph Ingalls."

"Was Guy Unger Miss Weltz's companion, or yours?"

"Why, we—we were just together."

"Nonsense. Two men and two women are never just together. How were you paired?"

"Well—Guy and Helen, and Ralph and me."

Wolfe sent a glance at the chair he had vacated and apparently decided it wasn't worth the trouble of walking back to it. "Then since Miss Willis died Mr. Unger's interest has centered on Miss Weltz?"

"I don't know about 'centered.' They seem to like each other, as far as I know."

"How long have you been working here?"

"At this office, since it opened a year ago. Before that I was at the Trafalgar office for two years."

"When did Miss Willis tell you she was going to tell Robina Keane of her husband's proposal?"

She had expected that one too. "That morning. That Thursday, the fifteenth of July."

"Did you approve?"

"No, I didn't. I thought she ought to just tell him no and forget it. I told her she was asking for trouble and she might get it. But she was so daddled on Robina Keane—" Bella shrugged. "Do you want to sit down?"

"No, thank you. Where is Miss Weltz?"

"This is her day off."

"I know. Where can I find her?"

She opened her mouth and closed it. She opened it again. "I'm not sure. Wait a minute," she said, and went clicking down the hall to the front. It was more like two minutes when she came clicking back and reported, "Miss Hart thinks she's at a little place she rented for the summer up in Westchester. Do you want me to phone and find out?"

"Yes, if you would."

Off she went, and we followed. In the front room the other three were at the boards. While Bella Velardi spoke to Miss Hart, and Miss Hart went to the phone at the desk and got a number and talked, Wolfe stood and frowned around, at the windows, the boards, the phone answerers, and me. When Miss Hart told him Helen Weltz was on the wire he went to the desk and took it.

"Miss Weltz? This is Nero Wolfe. As Miss Hart told you, I'm looking into certain matters connected with the murder of Marie Willis, and would like to see you. I have some other appointments but can adjust them. How long will it take you to get to the city? . . . You can't? . . . I'm afraid I can't wait until tomorrow. . . . No, that's out of the question. . . . I see. You'll be there all afternoon? . . . Very well, I'll do that."

He hung up and asked Miss Hart to tell me how to get to the place in Westchester. She obliged, and beyond Katonah it got so complicated that I got out my notebook. Also I jotted down the phone number. Wolfe had marched out with no amenities, so I thanked her politely and caught up with him halfway down the stairs. When we were out on the sidewalk I inquired, "A taxi to Katonah?"

"No." He was cold with rage. "To the garage for the car."

We headed west.

III

As we stood inside the garage, on Thirty-sixth Street near Tenth Avenue, waiting for Pete to bring the car down, Wolfe came out with something I had been expecting.

"We could walk home," he said, "in four minutes."

I gave him a grin. "Yes, sir. I knew it was coming—while you were on the phone. To go to Katonah we would have to drive. To drive we would have to get the car. To get the car we would have to come to the garage. The garage is so close to home that we might as well go and have lunch first. Once in the house, with the door bolted and not answering the phone, we could reconsider the matter of driving to Westchester. So you told her we would go to Katonah."

"No. It occurred to me in the cab."

"I can't prove it didn't. But I have a suggestion." I nodded at the door to the garage office. "There's a phone in there. Call Fritz first. Or shall I?"

"I suppose so," he muttered, and went to the office door and entered, sat at the desk, and dialed. In a moment he was telling Fritz who and where he was, asking some questions, and getting answers he didn't like. After instructing Fritz to tell callers that he hadn't heard from us and had no idea where we were, and telling him not to expect us home until we got there, he hung up, glared at the phone, and then glared at me.

"There have been four phone calls. One from an officer of the court, one from the District Attorney's office, and two from Inspector Cramer."

"Ouch." I made a face. "The court and the DA, sure, but not Cramer. When you're within a mile of a homicide of his he itches from head to foot. You can imagine what kind of suspicions your walking out under a subpoena would give him. Let's go home. It will be interesting to see whether he has one dick posted out in front, or two or three. Of course he'll collar you and you may get no lunch at all, but what the hell."

"Shut up."

"Yes, sir. Here comes the car."

As we emerged from the office the brown sedan rolled to a stop before us and Pete got out and opened the rear door for Wolfe, who refuses to ride in front because when the crash comes the broken glass will carve him up. I climbed in behind the wheel, released the brake and fingered the lever, and fed gas.

At that time of day the West Side Highway wasn't too crowded, and north of Henry Hudson Bridge, and then on the Sawmill River Parkway, there was nothing to it. I could have let my mind roam if it had had anywhere to roam, but where? I was all for earning a little token of gratitude by jerking Leonard Ashe out from under, but how? It was so damn childish. In his own comfortable chair in his office, Wolfe could usually manage to keep his genius under control, but on the hard courtroom bench, with a perfumed woman crowded against him, knowing he couldn't get up and go home, he had dropped the reins, and now he was stuck. He couldn't call it off and go back to court and apologize because he was too darned pigheaded. He couldn't go home. There was even a chance he couldn't go to Katonah for a wild-goose chase. When I saw in the rearview mirror a parkway police car closing in on us from behind, I tightened my lips, and when he passed on by and shot ahead I relaxed and took a deep breath. It would have been pretty extreme to broadcast a general alarm for a mere witness AWOL, but the way Cramer felt about Wolfe it wouldn't have been fantastic.

As I slowed down for Hawthorne Circle I told Wolfe it was a quarter to two and I was hungry and what about him, and was instructed to stop somewhere and get cheese and crackers and beer, and a little farther on I obeyed. Parked off a side road, he ate the crackers and drank the beer, but rejected the cheese after one taste. I was too hungry to taste.

The dash clock said 2:38 when, having followed Alice Hart's directions, I turned off a dirt road into a narrow rutted driveway, crawled between thick bushes on both sides, and, reaching an open space, stepped on the brake to keep from rubbing a bright yellow Jaguar. To the left was a gravel walk across some grass that needed mowing, leading to a door in the side of a little white house with blue trim. As I climbed out two people appeared around the corner of the house. The one in front was the right age, the right size, and the right shape, with blue eyes and hair that matched the Jaguar, held back smooth with a yellow ribbon.

She came on. "You're Archie Goodwin? I'm Helen Weltz. Mr. Wolfe? It's a pleasure. This is Guy Unger. Come this way. We'll sit in the shade of the old apple tree."

In my dim memory of his picture in the paper two months back, and in the snap I had found in Bella Velardi's drawer, Guy Unger hadn't looked particularly like a murderer, and in the flesh he didn't fill the bill any better. He looked too mean, with mean little eyes in a big round face. His gray suit had been cut by someone who knew how to fit his bulgy shoulders, one a little lower than the other. His mouth, if he had opened it wide, would have been just about big enough to poke his thumb in.

The apple tree was from colonial times, with windfalls of its produce scattered around. Wolfe glowered at the chairs with wooden slats, which had been painted white the year before, but it was either that or squat, so he engineered himself into one. Helen Weltz asked what we would like to drink, naming four choices, and Wolfe said no, thank you, with cold courtesy. It didn't seem to faze her. She took a chair facing him, gave him a bright, friendly smile, and included me with a glance from her lively blue eyes.

"You didn't give me a chance on the phone," she said, not complaining. "I didn't want you to have a trip for nothing. I can't tell you anything about that awful business, what happened to Marie. I really can't, because I don't know anything. I was out on the Sound on a boat. Didn't she tell you?"

Wolfe grunted. "That's not the kind of thing I'm after, Miss Weltz. Such routine matters as checking alibis have certainly been handled competently by the police, to the limit of their interest. My own interest has been engaged late—I hope not too late—and my attack must be eccentric. For instance, when did Mr. Unger get here?"

"Why, he just—"

"Now, wait a minute." Unger had picked up an unfinished highball from a table next to him and was holding it with the fingertips of both hands. His voice wasn't squeaky, as you would expect, but a thick baritone. "Just forget me. I'm looking on, that's all. I can't say I'm an impartial observer, because I'm partial to Miss Weltz, if that's all right with her."

Wolfe didn't even glance at him. "I'll explain, Miss Weltz, why I ask when Mr. Unger got here. I'll explain fully. When I went to that place on Sixty-ninth Street and spoke with Miss Hart and Miss Velardi I was insufferable, both in manner and in matter, and they should have flouted me and ordered me out, but they didn't. Manifestly they were afraid to, and I intend to learn why. I assume that you know why. I assume that, after I left, Miss Hart phoned you again, described the situation, and discussed with you how best to handle me. I surmise that she also phoned Mr. Unger, or you did, and he was enough concerned about me to hurry to get here before I arrived. Naturally I would consider that significant. It would reinforce my suspicion that—"

"Forget it," Unger cut in. "I heard about you being on your way about ten minutes ago, when I got here. Miss Weltz invited me yesterday to come out this afternoon. I took a train to Katonah, and a taxi."

Wolfe looked at him. "I can't challenge that, Mr. Unger, but it doesn't smother my surmise. On the contrary. I'll probably finish sooner with Miss Weltz if you'll withdraw. For twenty minutes, say?"

"I think I'd better stay."

"Then please don't prolong it with interruptions."

"You behave yourself, Guy," Helen scolded him. She smiled at Wolfe. "I'll tell you what I think, I think he just wants to show you how smart he is. When I told him Nero Wolfe was coming, you should have heard him! He said maybe you're famous for brains and he isn't, but he'd like to hear you prove it, something like that. I don't pretend to have brains. I was just scared!"

"Scared of what, Miss Weltz?"

"Scared of you! Wouldn't anybody be scared if they knew you were coming to pump them?" She was appealing to him.

"Not enough to send for help." Wolfe wouldn't enter into the spirit of it. "Certainly not if they had the alternative of snubbing me, as you have. Why don't you choose it? Why do you suffer me?"

"Now *that's* a question." She laughed. "I'll show you why." She got up and took a step, and reached to pat him on the shoulder and then on top of the head. "I didn't want to miss a chance to touch the great Nero Wolfe!" She laughed again, moved to the table and poured herself a healthy dose of bourbon, returned to her chair, and swallowed a good half of it. She shook herself and said, "Brrrrr. That's why!"

Unger was frowning at her. It didn't need the brains of a Nero Wolfe, or even a Guy Unger, to see that her nerves were teetering on an edge as sharp as a knife blade.

"But," Wolfe said dryly, "having touched me, you still suffer me. Of course Miss Hart told you that I reject the thesis that Leonard Ashe killed Marie Willis and propose to discredit it. I'm too late to try any of the conventional lines of inquiry, and anyway they have all been fully and competently explored by the police and the District Attorney on one side and Mr. Ashe's lawyer on the other. Since I can't expect to prove Mr. Ashe's innocence, the best I can hope to establish is a reasonable doubt of his guilt. Can you give it to me?"

"Of course not. How could I?"

"One way would be to suggest someone else with motive and opportunity. Means is no problem, since the plug cord was there at hand. Can you?"

She giggled, and then was shocked, presumably at herself for giggling about murder. "Sorry," she apologized, "but you're funny. The way they had us down there at the District Attorney's office, and the way they kept after us, asking all about Marie and everybody she knew, and of course what they wanted was to find out if there was anybody besides that man Ashe that might have killed her. But now they're trying Ashe for it, and they wouldn't be trying him if they didn't think they could prove it, and here you come and expect to drag it out of me in twenty minutes. Don't you think that's funny for a famous detective like you? I do."

She picked up her glass and drained it, stiffened to control a shudder, and got up and started for the table. Guy Unger reached and beat her to the bottle. "You've had enough, Helen," he told her gruffly. "Take it easy." She stared down at him a moment, dropped the glass on his lap, and went back to her chair.

Wolfe eyed her. "No, Miss Weltz," he said. "No, I didn't expect to drag a disclosure from you in twenty minutes. The most I expected was support for my belief that you people have common knowledge of something that you don't want revealed, and you have given me that. Now I'll go to work, and I confess I'm not too sanguine. It's quite possible that after I've squandered my resources on it, time and thought and money and energy, and enlisted the help of half a dozen able investigators, I'll find that the matter you people are so nervous about has no bearing on the murder of Marie Willis and so is of no use to me, and of no concern. But I can't know that until I know what it is, so I'm going to know. If you think my process of finding out will cause inconvenience to you and the others, or worse, I suggest that you tell me now. It will—"

"I have nothing to tell you!"

"Nonsense. You're at the edge of hysteria."

"I am not!"

"Take it easy, Helen." Guy Unger focused his mean little eyes on Wolfe. "Look, I don't get this. As I understand it, what you're after is an out for Leonard Ashe on the murder. Is that right?"

"Yes."

"And that's all?"

"Yes."

"Would you mind telling me, did Ashe's lawyer hire you?"

"No."

"Who did?"

"Nobody. I developed a distaste for my function as a witness for the prosecution, along with a doubt of Mr. Ashe's guilt."

"Why doubt his guilt?"

Wolfe's shoulders went up a fraction of an inch, and down again. "Divination. Contrariety."

"I see." Unger pursed his midget mouth, which didn't need pursing. "You're shooting at it on spec." He leaned forward. "Understand me, I don't say that's not your privilege. Of course you have no standing at all, since you admit nobody hired you, but if Miss Weltz tells you to go to hell that won't take you off her neck if you've decided to go to town. She'll answer anything you want to ask her that's connected with the murder, and so will I. We've told the police and the District Attorney, why not you? Do you regard me as a suspect?"

"Yes."

"Okay." He leaned back. "I first met Marie Willis about a year ago, a little more. I took her out a few times, maybe once a month, and then later a little oftener, to dinner and a show. We weren't engaged to be married, nothing like that. The last week in June, just two weeks before her death, she was on vacation, and four of us went for a cruise on my boat, up the Hudson and Lake Champlain. The other two were friends of mine, a man and a woman—do you want their names?"

"No."

"Well, that was what got me in the murder picture, that week's cruise she had taken on my boat so recently. There was nothing to it, we had just gone to have a good time, but when she was murdered the cops naturally thought I was a good prospect. There was absolutely nothing in my relations with Marie that could possibly have made me want to kill her. Any questions?"

"No."

"And if they had dug up a motive they would have been stuck with it, because I certainly didn't kill her the evening of July fifteenth. That was a Thursday, and at five o'clock that afternoon I was taking my boat through the Harlem River and into the sound, and at ten o'clock that night I was asleep on her at an anchorage near New Haven. My friend Ralph Ingalls was with me, and his wife, and Miss Helen Weltz. Of course the police have checked it, but maybe you don't like the way they check alibis. You're welcome to check it yourself if you care to. Any questions?"

"One or two." Wolfe shifted his fanny on the board slats. "What is your occupation?"

"For God's sake. You haven't even read the papers."

"Yes, I have, but that was weeks ago, and as I remember it they were vague. 'Broker,' I believe. Stockbroker?"

"No, I'm a freewheeler. I'll handle almost anything."

"Have you an office?"

"I don't need one."

"Have you handled any transactions for anyone connected with that business, Bagby Answers, Incorporated? Any kind of transaction?"

Unger cocked his head. "Now that's a funny question. Why do you ask that?"

"Because I suspect the answer is yes."

"Why? Just for curiosity."

"Now, Mr. Unger." Wolfe turned a palm up. "Since apparently you had heard of me, you may know that I dislike riding in cars, even when Mr. Goodwin is driving. Do you suppose I would have made this excursion completely at random? If you find the question embarrassing, don't answer it."

"It's not embarrassing." Unger turned to the table, poured an inch of bourbon in his glass, added two inches of water from a pitcher, gave it a couple of swirls, took a sip, and another one, and finally put the glass down and turned back to Wolfe.

"I'll tell you," he said in a new tone. "This whole business is pretty damn silly. I think you've got hold of some crazy idea somewhere, God knows what, and I want to speak with you privately." He arose. "Let's take a little walk."

Wolfe shook his head. "I don't like conversing on my feet. If you want to say something without a witness, Miss Weltz and Mr. Goodwin can leave us. Archie?"

I stood up. Helen Weltz looked up at Unger, and at me, and then slowly lifted herself from her chair. "Let's go and pick flowers," I suggested. "Mr. Unger will want me in sight and out of hearing."

She moved. We picked our way through the windfalls of the apple tree, and of two more trees, and went on into a meadow where the grass and other stuff was up to our knees. She was in the lead. "Goldenrod I know," I told her back, "but what are the blue ones?"

No answer. In another hundred yards I tried again. "This is far enough unless he uses a megaphone."

She kept going. "Last call!" I told her. "I admit he would be a maniac to jump Mr. Wolfe under the circumstances, but maybe he is one. I learned long ago that with people involved in a murder case nothing is impossible."

She wheeled on me. "He's not involved in a murder case!"

"He will be before Mr. Wolfe gets through with him."

She plumped down in the grass, crossed her legs, buried her face in her hands, and started to shake. I stood and looked down at her, expecting the appropriate sound effect, but it didn't come. She just went on shaking, which wasn't wholesome. After half a minute of it I squatted in front of her, made contact by taking a firm grip on her bare ankle, and spoke with authority.

"That's no way to do it. Open a valve and let it out. Stretch out and kick and scream. If Unger thinks it's me and flies to the rescue that will give me an excuse to plug him."

She mumbled something. Her hands muffled it, but it sounded like "God help me." The shakes turned into shivers and were tapering off. When she spoke again it came through much better. "You're hurting me," she said, and I loosened my grip on her ankle and in a moment took my hand away, when her hands dropped and she lifted her head.

Her face was flushed, but her eyes were dry. "My God," she said, "it would be wonderful if you put your arms around me tight and told me, 'All right, my darling, I'll take care of everything, just leave it to me.' Oh, that would be wonderful!"

"I may try it," I offered, "if you'll brief me on what I'd have to take care of. The arms around you tight are no problem. Then what?"

She skipped over it. "God," she said bitterly, "am I a fool! You saw my car. My Jaguar."

"Yeah, I saw it. Very fine."

"I'm going to burn it. How do you set fire to a car?"

"Pour gasoline on it, all over inside, toss a match in, and jump back fast. Be careful what you tell the insurance company or you'll end up in the can."

She skipped again. "It wasn't only the car, it was other things too. I had to have them. Why didn't I get me a man? I could have had a dozen, but no, not me. I was going to do it all myself. It was going to be *my* Jaguar. And now here I am, and you, a man I never saw before—it would be heaven if you'd just take me over. I'm telling you, you'd be getting a bargain!"

"I might, at that." I was sympathetic but not mealy. "Don't be too sure you're a bad buy. What are the liabilities?"

She twisted her neck to look across the meadow toward the house. Wolfe and Unger were in their chairs under the apple tree, evidently keeping their voices down, since no sound came, and my ears are good.

She turned back to me. "Is it a bluff? Is he just trying to scare something out of us?"

"No, not just. If he scares something out, fine. If not, he'll get it the hard way. If there's anything to get he'll get it. If you're sitting on a lid you don't want opened, my advice is to move, the sooner the better, or you may get hurt."

"I'm already hurt!"

"Then hurt worse."

"I guess I can be." She reached for one of the blue flowers and pulled it off with no stem. "You asked what these are. They're wild asters, just the color of my eyes." She crushed it with her fingers and dropped it. "I already know what I'm going to do. I decided walking over here with you. What time is it?"

I looked at my wrist. "Quarter past three."

"Let's see, four hours—five. Where can I see Nero Wolfe around nine o'clock in town?"

From long habit I started to say at his office, but remembered it was out of bounds. "His address and number are in the phone book," I told her, "but he may not be there this evening. Phone and ask for Fritz. Tell him you are the Queen of Hearts, and he'll tell you where Mr. Wolfe is. If you don't say you're the Queen of Hearts he won't tell you anything because Mr. Wolfe hates to be disturbed when he's out. But why not save time and trouble? Evidently you've decided to tell him something, and there he is. Come on and tell him now."

She shook her head. "I can't. I don't dare."

"On account of Unger?"

"Yes."

"If he can ask to speak privately with Mr. Wolfe, why can't you?"

"I tell you I don't dare!"

"We'll go and come back as soon as Unger leaves."

"He's not going to leave. He's going to ride to town with me."

"Then record it on tape and use me for tape. You can trust my memory. I guarantee to repeat it to Mr. Wolfe word for word. Then when you phone this evening he will have had time—"

"Helen! *Helen!*" Unger was calling her.

She started to scramble up, and I got upright and gave her a hand. As we headed across the meadow she spoke, barely above a whisper. "If you tell him I'll deny it. Are you going to tell him?"

"Wolfe, yes. Unger, no."

"If you do I'll deny it."

"Then I won't."

As we approached they left their chairs. Their expressions indicated that they had not signed a mutual nonaggression pact, but there were no scars of battle. Wolfe said, "We're through here, Archie," and was going. Nobody else said anything, which made it rather stiff. Following Wolfe around the house to the open space, I saw that it would take a lot of maneuvering to turn around without scraping the Jaguar, so I had to back out through the bushes to the dirt road, where I swung the rear around to head the way we had come.

When we had gone half a mile I called back to my rearseat passenger, "I have a little item for you!"

"Stop somewhere," he ordered, louder than necessary. "I can't talk like this."

A little farther on there was roadside room under a tree, and I pulled over and parked.

I twisted around in the seat to face him. "We got a nibble," I said, and reported on Helen Weltz. He started frowning, and when I finished he was frowning more.

"Confound it," he growled, "she was in a panic, and it'll wear off."

"It may," I conceded. "And so? I'll go back and do it over if you'll write me a script."

"Pfui. I don't say I could better it. You are a connoisseur of comely young women. Is she a murderess in a funk trying to wriggle out? Or what is she?"

I shook my head. "I pass. She's trying to wriggle all right, but for out of what I would need six guesses. What did Unger want privately? Is he trying to wriggle too?"

"Yes. He offered me money—five thousand dollars, and then ten thousand."

"For what?"

"Not clearly defined. A retaining fee for investigative services. He was crude about it for a man with brains."

"I'll be damned." I grinned at him. "I've often thought you ought to get around more. Only five hours ago you marched out of that court-room in the interest of justice, and already you've scared up an offer of ten grand. Of course it may have nothing to do with the murder. What did you tell him?"

"That I resented and scorned his attempt to suborn me."

My brows went up. "He was in a panic, and it'll wear off. Why not string him along?"

"It would take time, and I haven't any. I told him I intend to appear in court tomorrow morning."

"Tomorrow?" I stared. "With what, for God's sake?"

"At the least, with a diversion. If Miss Weltz's panic endures, possibly with something better, though I didn't know that when I was talking with Mr. Unger."

I looked it over. "Uh-huh," I said finally. "You've had a hard day, and soon it will be dark and dinnertime, and then bedtime, and deciding to go back to court tomorrow makes it possible for you to go home. Okay, I'll get you there by five o'clock."

I turned and reached for the ignition key, but had barely touched it when his voice stopped me. "We're not going home. Mr. Cramer will have a man posted there all night, probably with a warrant, and I'm not going to risk it. I had thought of a hotel, but that might be risky too, and now that Miss Weltz may want to see me it's out of the question. Isn't Saul's apartment conveniently located?"

"Yes, but he has only one bed. Lily Rowan has plenty of room in her penthouse, and we'd be welcome, especially you. You remember the time she squirted perfume on you."

"I do," he said coldly. "We'll manage somehow at Saul's. Besides, we have errands to do and may need him. We must of course phone him first. Go ahead. To the city."

He gripped the strap. I started the engine.

IV

For more years than I have fingers Inspector Cramer of Homicide had been dreaming of locking Wolfe up, at least overnight, and that day he darned near made it. He probably would have if I hadn't spent an extra dime. Having phoned Saul Panzer, and also Fritz, from a booth in a drugstore in Washington Heights, I called the *Gazette* office and got Lon Cohen. When he heard my voice he said, "Well, well. Are you calling from your cell?"

"No. If I told you where I am you'd be an accomplice. Has our absence been noticed?"

"Certainly, the town's in an uproar. A raging mob has torn the court-house down. We're running a fairly good picture of Wolfe, but we need a new one of you. Could you drop in at the studio, say in five minutes?"

"Sure, glad to. But I'm calling to settle a bet. Is there a warrant for us?"

"You're damn right there is. Judge Corbett signed it first thing after lunch. Look, Archie, let me send a man—"

I told him much obliged and hung up. If I hadn't spent that dime and learned there was a warrant, we wouldn't have taken any special precaution as we approached Saul's address on East Thirty-eighth Street and would have run smack into Sergeant Purley Stebbins, and the question of where to spend the night would have been taken off our hands.

It was nearly eight o'clock. Wolfe and I had each disposed of three orders of chili con carne at a little dump on 170th Street where a guy named Dixie knows how to make it, and I had made at least a dozen phone calls trying to get hold of Jimmy Donovan, Leonard Ashe's attorney. That might not have been difficult if I could have left word that Nero Wolfe had something urgent for him, and given a number for him to call, but that wouldn't have been practical, since an attorney is a sworn officer of the law, and he knew there was a warrant out for Wolfe, not to mention me. So I hadn't got him, and as we crawled with the traffic through East Thirty-eighth Street the sight of Wolfe's scowl in the rearview mirror didn't make the scene any gayer.

My program was to let him out at Saul's address between Lexington and Third, find a place to park the car, and join him at Saul's. But just as I swung over and was braking I saw a familiar broad-shouldered figure on the sidewalk, switched from the brake to the gas pedal, and kept going. Luckily a gap had opened, and the light was green at Third

Avenue, so I rolled on through, found a place to stop without blocking traffic, and turned in the seat to tell Wolfe, "I came on by because I decided we don't want to see Saul."

"You did." He was grim. "What flummery is this?"

"No flummery. Sergeant Purley Stebbins was just turning in at the entrance. Thank God it's dark or he would have seen us. Now where?"

"At the entrance of Saul's address?"

"Yes."

A short silence. "You're enjoying this," he said bitterly.

"I am like hell. I'm a fugitive from justice, and I was going to spend the evening at the Polo Grounds watching a ball game. Where now?"

"Confound it. You told Saul about Miss Weltz."

"Yes, sir. I told Fritz that if the Queen of Hearts phones she is to call Saul's number, and I told Saul that you'd rather have an hour alone with her than a blue orchid. You know Saul."

Another silence. He broke it. "You have Mr. Donovan's home address."

"Right. East Seventy-seventh Street."

"How long will it take to drive there?"

"Ten minutes."

"Go ahead."

"Yes, sir. Sit back and relax." I fed gas.

It took only nine minutes at that time of evening, and I found space to park right in the block, between Madison and Park. As we walked to the number a cop gave us a second glance, but Wolfe's size and carriage rated that much notice without any special stimulation. It was just my nerves. There were a canopy and a doorman, and rugs in the lobby. I told the doorman casually, "Donovan. We're expected," but he hung on.

"Yes, sir, but I have orders—Your name, please?"

"Judge Wolfe," Wolfe told him.

"One moment, please."

He disappeared through a door. It was more like five moments before he came back, looking questions but not asking them, and directed us to the elevator. Twelve B, he said.

Getting off at the twelfth floor, we didn't have to look for B because a door at the end of the foyer was standing open, and on the sill was Jimmy Donovan himself. In his shirt sleeves, with no necktie, he looked more like a janitor than a champion of the bar, and he sounded more like one when he blurted, "It's you, huh? What kind of a trick is this? *Judge* Wolfe!"

"No trick." Wolfe was courteous but curt. "I merely evaded vulgar curiosity. I had to see you."

"You can't see me. It's highly improper. You're a witness for the prosecution. Also a warrant has been issued for you, and I'll have to report this."

He was absolutely right. The only thing for him to do was shut the door on us and go to his phone and call the DA's office. My one guess why he didn't, which was all I needed, was that he would have given his shirt, and thrown in a necktie, to know what Wolfe was up to. He didn't shut the door.

"I'm not here," Wolfe said, "as a witness for the prosecution. I don't intend to discuss my testimony with you. As you know, your client, Leonard Ashe, came to me one day in July and wanted to hire me, and I refused. I have become aware of certain facts connected with what he told me that day, which I think he should know about, and I want to tell him. I suppose it would be improper for me to tell you more than that, but it wouldn't be improper to tell him. He is on trial for first-degree murder."

I had the feeling I could see Donovan's brain working at it behind his eyes. "It's preposterous," he declared. "You know damn well you can't see him."

"I can if you'll arrange it. That's what I'm here for. You're his counsel. Early tomorrow morning will do, before the court sits. You may of course be present if you wish, but I suppose you would prefer not to. Twenty minutes with him will be enough."

Donovan was chewing his lip. "I can't ask you what you want to tell him."

"I understand that. I won't be on the witness stand, where you can cross-examine me, until tomorrow."

"No." The lawyer's eyes narrowed. "No, you won't. I can't arrange for you to see him; it's out of the question. I shouldn't be talking to you. It will be my duty to report this to Judge Corbett in the morning. Good evening, gentlemen."

He backed up and swung the door shut, but didn't bang it, which was gracious of him. We rang for the elevator, were taken down, and went out and back to the car.

"You'll phone Saul," Wolfe said.

"Yes, sir. His saying he'll report to the judge in the morning meant he didn't intend to phone the DA now, but he might change his mind. I'd rather move a few blocks before phoning."

"Very well. Do you know the address of Mrs. Leonard Ashe's apartment?"

"Yes, Seventy-third Street."

"Go in that direction. I have to see her, and you'd better phone and arrange it."

"You mean now."

"Yes."

"That should be a cinch. She's probably sitting there hoping a couple of strange detectives will drop in. Do I have to be Judge Goodwin?"

"No. We are ourselves."

As I drove downtown on Park, and east on Seventy-fourth to Third Avenue, and down a block, and west on Seventy-third, I considered the approach to Robina Keane. By not specifying it Wolfe had left it to me, so it was my problem. I thought of a couple of fancy strategies, but by the time I got the car maneuvered to the curb in the only vacant spot between Lexington and Madison I had decided that the simplest was the best. After asking Wolfe if he had any suggestions and getting a no, I walked to Lexington and found a booth in a drugstore.

First I called Saul Panzer. There had been no word from the Queen of Hearts, but she had said around nine o'clock and it was only eight-forty. Sergeant Stebbins had been and gone. What he had said was that the police were concerned about the disappearance of Nero Wolfe because he was an important witness in a murder case, and they were afraid something might have happened to him, especially since Archie Goodwin was also gone. What he had not said was that Inspector Cramer suspected that Wolfe had tramped out of the courtroom hell-bent on messing the case up, and he wanted to get his hands on him quick. Had Wolfe communicated with Saul, and did Saul know where he was? There was a warrant out for both Wolfe and Goodwin. Saul had said no, naturally, and Purley had made some cutting remarks and left.

I dialed another number, and when a female voice answered I told it I would like to speak to Mrs. Ashe. It said Mrs. Ashe was resting and couldn't come to the phone. I said I was speaking for Nero Wolfe and it was urgent and vital. It said Mrs. Ashe absolutely would not come to the phone. I asked it if it had ever heard of Nero Wolfe, and it said of course. All right, I said, tell Mrs. Ashe that he must see her immediately and he can be there in five minutes. That's all I can tell you on the phone, I said, except that if she doesn't see him she'll never stop regretting it. The voice told me to hold the wire, and was gone so long I began to wish I had tried a fancy one, but just as I was reaching for the handle of the booth door to let in some air it came back and said Mrs. Ashe would see Mr. Wolfe. I asked it to instruct the lobby guardians to admit us, hung up, went out and back to the car, and told Wolfe, "Okay. You'd better make it good after what I told her. No word from Helen Weltz. Stebbins only asked some foolish questions and got the answers he deserved."

He climbed out, and we walked to the number. This one was smaller and more elegant, too elegant for rugs. The doorman was practically Laurence Olivier, and the elevator man was his older brother. They were chilly but nothing personal. When we were let out at the sixth floor the elevator man stayed at his open door until we had pushed a button and the apartment door had opened and we had been told to enter.

The woman admitting us wasn't practically Phyllis Jay, she was Phyllis Jay. Having paid $4.40 or $5.50 several times to see her from an orchestra seat, I would have appreciated this free close-up of her on a better occasion, but my mind was occupied. So was hers. Of course she was acting, since actresses always are, but the glamour was turned off because the part didn't call for it. She was playing a support for a friend in need, and kept strictly in character as she relieved Wolfe of his hat and cane and then escorted us into a big living room, across it, and through an arch into a smaller room.

Robina Keane was sitting on a couch, patting at her hair. Wolfe stopped three paces off and bowed. She looked up at him, shook her head as if to dislodge a fly; pressed her fingertips to her eyes, and looked at him again. Phyllis Jay said, "I'll be in the study, Robbie," waited precisely the right interval for a request to stay, didn't get it, and turned and went. Mrs. Ashe invited us to sit, and, after moving a chair around for Wolfe, I took one off at the side.

"I'm dead tired," she said. "I'm so empty, completely empty. I don't think I ever—But what is it? Of course it's something about my husband?"

Either the celebrated lilt of her voice was born in, or she had used it so much and so long that it might as well have been. She looked all in, no doubt of that, but the lilt was there.

"I'll make it as brief as I can," Wolfe told her. "Do you know that I have met your husband? That he called on me one day in July?"

"Yes, I know. I know all about it—now."

"It was to testify about our conversation that day that I was summoned to appear at his trial, by the State. In court this morning, waiting to be called, an idea came to me which I thought merited exploration, and if it was to bring any advantage to your husband the exploration could not wait. So I walked out, with Mr. Goodwin, my assistant, and we have spent the day on that idea."

"What idea?" Her hands were fists, on the couch for props.

"Later for that. We have made some progress, and we may make more tonight. Whether we do or not, I have information that will be of considerable value to your husband. It may not exculpate him, but at least it should raise sufficient doubt in the minds of the jury to get him acquitted. The problem is to get the information to the jury. It would take intricate and prolonged investigation to get it in the form of admissible evidence, and I have in mind a shortcut. To take it I must have a talk with your husband."

"But he—How can you?"

"I must. I have just called on Mr. Donovan, his attorney, and asked him to arrange it, but I knew he wouldn't; that was merely to anticipate you. I knew that if I came to you, you would insist on consulting him, and I have already demonstrated the futility of that. I am in contempt of the court, and a warrant has been issued for my arrest. Also I am under subpoena as a witness for the prosecution, and it is improper for the defense counsel even to talk with me, let alone arrange an interview for me with his client. You, as the wife of a man on trial for his life, are under no such prescription. You have wide acquaintance and great personal charm. It would not be too difficult, certainly not impossible, for you to get permission to talk with your husband tomorrow morning before the court convenes; and you can take me with you. Twenty minutes would be ample, and even ten would do. Don't mention me in getting the permission; that's important; simply take me with you and we'll see. If it doesn't work there's another possible expedient. Will you do it?"

She was frowning. "I don't see—You just want to talk with him?"

"Yes."

"What do you want to tell him?"

"You'll hear it tomorrow morning when he does. It's complicated and conjectural. To tell you now might compromise my plan to get it to the jury, and I won't risk it."

"But tell me what it's about. Is it about me?"

Wolfe lifted his shoulders to take in a deep breath, and let them sag again. "You say you're dead tired, madam. So am I. I would be interested in you only if I thought you were implicated in the murder of Marie Willis, and I don't. At considerable risk to my reputation, my self-esteem, and possibly even my bodily freedom, I am undertaking a step that should be useful to your husband and am asking your help; but I am not asking you to risk anything. You have nothing to lose, but I have. Of course I have made an assumption that may not be valid: that, whether you are sincerely devoted to your husband or not, you don't want him convicted of murder. I can't guarantee that I have the key that will free him, but I'm not a novice in these matters."

Her jaw was working. "You didn't have to say that." The lilt was gone. "Whether I'm devoted to my husband. My husband's not a fool, but he acted like one. I love him very dearly, and I want—" Her jaw worked. "I love him very much. No, I don't want him convicted of murder. You're right, I have nothing to lose, nothing more to lose. But if I do this I'll have to tell Mr. Donovan."

"No. You must not. Not only would he forbid it, he would prevent it. This is for you alone."

She abandoned the prop of her fists and straightened her back. "I thought I was too tired to live," she said, lilting again, "and I am, but it's going to be a relief to do something." She left the couch and was on her feet. "I'm going to do it. As you say, I have a wide acquaintance, and I'll do it all right. You go on and make some more progress and leave this to me. Where can I reach you?"

Wolfe turned. "Saul's number, Archie."

I wrote it on a leaf of my notebook and went and handed it to her. Wolfe arose. "I'll be there all night, Mrs. Ashe, up to nine in the morning, but I hope it will be before that."

I doubted if she heard him. Her mind was so glad to have a job that it had left us entirely. She did go with us to the foyer to see us out, but she wasn't there. I was barely across the threshold when she shut the door.

We went back to the car and headed downtown on Park Avenue. It seemed unlikely that Purley Stebbins had taken it into his head to pay Saul a second call, but a couple of blocks away I stopped to phone, and Saul said no, he was alone. It seemed even more unlikely that Stebbins had posted a man out front, but I stopped twenty yards short of the number and took a good long look. There was a curb space a little further down, and I squeezed the car into it and looked some more before opening the door for Wolfe to climb out. We crossed the street and entered the vestibule, and I pushed the button.

When we left the self-service elevator at the fifth floor, Saul was there to greet us. I suppose to some people Saul Panzer is just a little guy with a big nose who always seems to need a shave, but to others, including Wolfe and me, he's the best free-for-all operative that ever tailed a subject. Wolfe had never been at his place before, but I had, many times over the years, mostly on Saturday nights with three or four others for some friendly and ferocious poker. Inside, Wolfe stood and looked around. It was a big room, lighted with two floor lamps and two table lamps. One wall had windows, another was solid with books, and the other two had pictures and shelves that were cluttered with everything from chunks of minerals to walrus tusks. In the far corner was a grand piano.

"A good room," Wolfe said. "Satisfactory. I congratulate you." He crossed to a chair, the nearest thing to his idea of a chair he had seen all day, and sat. "What time is it?"

"Twenty minutes to ten."

"Have you heard from that woman?"

"No, sir. Will you have some beer?"

"I will indeed. If you please."

In the next three hours he accounted for seven bottles. He also handled his share of liver pâté, herring, sturgeon, pickled mushrooms, Tunisian melon, and three kinds of cheese. Saul was certainly prancing as a host, though he is not a prancer. Naturally, the first time Wolfe ate under his roof, and possibly the last, he wanted to give him good grub, that was okay, but I thought the three kinds of cheese was piling it on a little. He sure would be sick of cheese by Saturday. He wasn't equipped to be so fancy about sleeping. Since he was the host it was his problem, and his arrangement was Wolfe in the bedroom, me on the couch in the big room, and him on the floor, which seemed reasonable.

However, at a quarter to one in the morning we were still up. Though time hadn't dragged too heavily, what with talking and eating and drinking and three hot games of checkers between Wolfe and Saul, all draws, we were all yawning. We hadn't turned in because we hadn't heard from Helen Weltz, and there was still a dim hope. The other thing was all set. Just after midnight Robina Keane had phoned and told Wolfe she had it fixed. He was to meet her in Room 917 at 100 Centre Street at half-past eight. He asked me if I knew what Room 917 was, and I didn't. After that came he leaned back in his chair and sat with his eyes closed for a while, then straightened up and told Saul he was ready for the third game of checkers.

At a quarter to one he left his chair, yawned and stretched, and announced, "Her panic wore off. I'm going to bed."

"I'm afraid," Saul apologized, "I have no pajamas you could get into, but I've got—"

The phone rang. I was nearest, and turned and got it. "This is Jackson four-three-one-oh-nine."

"I want— This is the Queen of Hearts."

"It sure is. I recognize your voice. This is Archie Goodwin. Where are you?"

"In a booth at Grand Central. I couldn't get rid of him, and then—but that doesn't matter now. Where are you?"

"In an apartment on Thirty-eighth Street with Mr. Wolfe, waiting for you. It's a short walk. I'll meet you at the information booth, upper level, in five minutes. Will you be there?"

"Yes."

"Sure?"

"Of course I will!"

I hung up, turned, and said loftily, "If it wore off it wore on again. Make some coffee, will you, Saul? She'll need either that or bourbon. And maybe she likes cheese."

I departed.

V

At six minutes past ten in the morning Assistant District Attorney Mandelbaum was standing at the end of his table in the courtroom to address Judge Corbett. The room was packed. The jury was in the box. Jimmy Donovan, defense attorney, looking not at all like a janitor, was fingering through some papers his assistant had handed him.

"Your Honor," Mandelbaum said, "I wish to call a witness whom I called yesterday, but he was not available. I learned only a few minutes ago that he is present. You will remember that on my application you issued a warrant for Mr. Nero Wolfe."

"Yes, I do." The judge cleared his throat. "Is he here?"

"He is." Mandelbaum turned and called, "Nero Wolfe!"

Having arrived at one minute to ten, we wouldn't have been able to get in if we hadn't pushed through to the officer at the door and told him who we were and that we were wanted. He had stared at Wolfe and admitted he recognized him, and let us in, and the attendant had managed to make room for us on a bench just as Judge Corbett entered. When Wolfe was called by Mandelbaum and got up to go forward I had enough space.

He walked down the aisle, through the gate, mounted the stand, turned to face the judge, and stood.

"I have some questions for you, Mr. Wolfe," the judge said, "after you are sworn."

The attendant extended the Book and administered the oath, and

Wolfe sat. A witness chair is supposed to take any size, but that one just barely made it.

The judge spoke. "You knew you were to be called yesterday. You were present, but you left and could not be found, and a warrant was issued for you. Are you represented by counsel?"

"No, sir."

"Why did you leave? You are under oath."

"I was impelled to leave by a motive that I thought imperative. I will of course expound it now if you so order, but I respectfully ask your indulgence. I understand that if my reason for leaving is unsatisfactory I will be in contempt of court and will suffer a penalty. But I ask, Your Honor, does it matter whether I am adjudged in contempt now, or later, after I have testified? Because my reason for leaving is inherent in my testimony, and therefore I would rather plead on the charge of contempt afterward, if the court will permit. I'll still be here."

"Indeed you will. You're under arrest."

"No, I'm not."

"You're not under arrest?"

"No, sir. I came here voluntarily."

"Well, you are now." The judge turned his head. "Officer, this man is under arrest." He turned back. "Very well. You will answer to the contempt charge later. Proceed, Mr. Mandelbaum."

Mandelbaum approached the chair. "Please tell the jury your name, occupation, and address."

Wolfe turned to the jury box. "I am Nero Wolfe, a licensed private detective, with my office in my house at nine-eighteen West Thirty-fifth Street, Manhattan, New York City."

"Have you ever met the defendant in this case?" Mandelbaum pointed. "That gentleman."

"Yes, sir. Mr. Leonard Ashe."

"Where and under what circumstances did you meet him?"

"He called on me at my office, by appointment, at eleven o'clock on the morning of Tuesday, July thirteenth, this year."

"What did he say to you on that occasion?"

"That he wished to engage my professional services. That he had, the preceding day, arranged for an answering service for the telephone at his residence on Seventy-third Street in New York. That he had learned, upon inquiry, that one of the employees of the answering service would be assigned to his number and would serve it five or six days a week. That he wanted to hire me to learn the identity of that employee, and to propose to her that she eavesdrop on calls made during the daytime to his number, and report on them either to him or to me—I can't say definitely which, because he wasn't clear on that point."

"Did he say why he wanted to make that arrangement?"

"No. He didn't get that far."

Donovan was up. "Objection, Your Honor. Conclusion of the witness as to the intention of the defendant."

"Strike it," Mandelbaum said amiably. "Strike all of his answer except the word 'No.' Your answer is 'No,' Mr. Wolfe?"

"Yes, sir."

"Did the defendant suggest any inducement to be offered to the employee to get her to do the eavesdropping?"

"He didn't name a sum, but he indicated that—"

"Not what he indicated. What he said."

I allowed myself a grin. Wolfe, who always insisted on precision, who loved to ride others, especially me, for loose talk, and who certainly knew the rules of evidence, had been caught twice. I promised myself to find occasion later to comment on it.

He was unruffled. "He said that he would make it worth her while, meaning the employee, but stated no amount."

"What else did he say?"

"That was about all. The entire conversation was only a few minutes. As soon as I understood clearly what he wanted to hire me to do, I refused to do it."

"Did you tell him why you refused?"

"Yes, sir."

"What did you say?"

"I said that while it is the function of a detective to pry into people's affairs, I excluded from my field anything connected with marital difficulties and therefore declined his job."

"Had he told you that what he wanted was to spy on his wife?"

"No, sir."

"Then why did you mention marital difficulties to him?"

"Because I had concluded that that was the nature of his concern."

"What else did you say to him?"

Wolfe shifted in the chair. "I would like to be sure I understand the question. Do you mean what I said to him that day, or on a later occasion?"

"I mean that day. There was no later occasion, was there?"

"Yes, sir."

"Are you saying that you had another meeting with the defendant, on another day?"

"Yes, sir."

Mandelbaum held a pose. Since his back was to me I couldn't see his look of surprise, but I didn't have to. In his file was Wolfe's signed statement, saying among other things that he had not seen Leonard Ashe before or since July 13. His voice went up a notch. "When and where did this meeting take place?"

"Shortly after nine o'clock this morning, in this building."

"You met and spoke with the defendant in this building today?"

"Yes, sir."

"Under what circumstances?"

"His wife had arranged to see and speak with him, and she allowed me to accompany her."

"How did she arrange it? With whom?"

"I don't know."

"Was Mr. Donovan, the defense counsel, present?"

"No, sir."

"Who was?"

"Mrs. Ashe, Mr. Ashe, myself, and two armed guards, one at the door and one at the end of the room."

"What room was it?"

"I don't know. There was no number on the door. I think I could lead you to it."

Mandelbaum whirled around and looked at Robina Keane, seated on the front bench. Not being a lawyer, I didn't know whether he could get her to the stand or not. Of course a wife couldn't be summoned to testify against her husband, but I didn't know if this would have come under that ban. Anyway, he either skipped it or postponed it. He asked the judge to allow him a moment and went to the table to speak in an undertone to a colleague. I looked around. I had already spotted Guy Unger, in the middle of the audience on the left. Bella Velardi and Alice Hart were on the other side, next to the aisle. Apparently the Sixty-ninth Street office of Bagby Answers, Inc., was being womaned for the day from other offices. Clyde Bagby, the boss, was a couple of rows in front of Unger. Helen Weltz, the Queen of Hearts, whom I had driven from Saul's address to a hotel seven hours ago, was in the back, not far from me.

The colleague got up and left, in a hurry, and Mandelbaum went back to Wolfe.

"Don't you know," he demanded, "that it is a misdemeanor for a witness for the State to talk with the defendant charged with a felony?"

"No, sir, I don't. I understand it would depend on what was said. I didn't discuss my testimony with Mr. Ashe."

"What did you discuss?"

"Certain matters that I thought would be of interest to him."

"What matters? Exactly what did you say?"

I took a deep breath, spread and stretched my fingers, and relaxed. The fat son-of-a-gun had put it over. Having asked that question, Mandelbaum couldn't possibly keep it from the jury unless Jimmy Donovan was a sap, and he wasn't.

Wolfe testified. "I said that yesterday, seated in this room awaiting your convenience, I had formed a surmise that certain questions raised by the murder of Marie Willis had not been sufficiently considered and investigated, and that therefore my role as a witness for the prosecution was an uncomfortable one. I said that I had determined to satisfy myself on certain points; that I knew that in leaving the courtroom I would become liable to a penalty for contempt of court, but that the integrity of justice was more important than my personal ease; that I had been confident that Judge Corbett would—"

"If you please, Mr. Wolfe. You are not now pleading to a charge of contempt."

"No, sir. You asked what I said to Mr. Ashe. He asked what surmise I had formed, and I told him—that it was a double surmise. First, that as one with long experience in the investigation of crime and culprits, I had an appreciable doubt of his guilt. Second, that the police had been so taken by the circumstances pointing to Mr. Ashe—his obvious motive and his discovery of the body—that their attention in other directions had possibly been somewhat dulled. For example, an experienced investigator always has a special eye and ear for any person occupying a privileged position. Such persons are doctors, lawyers, trusted servants, intimate friends, and, of course, close relatives. If one in those categories is a rogue he has peculiar opportunities for his scoundrelism. It occurred to me that—"

"You said all this to Mr. Ashe?"

"Yes, sir. It occurred to me that a telephone-answering service was in the same kind of category as those I have mentioned, as I sat in this room yesterday and heard Mr. Bagby describe the operation of the switchboards. An unscrupulous operator might, by listening in on conversations, obtain various kinds of information that could be turned to account—for instance, about the stock market, about business or professional plans, about a multitude of things. The possibilities would be limitless. Certainly one, and perhaps the most promising, would be the discovery of personal secrets. Most people are wary about discussing or disclosing vital secrets on the telephone, but many are not, and in emergencies caution is often forgotten. It struck me that for getting the kind of information, or at least hints of it, that is most useful and profitable for a blackmailer, a telephone-answering service has potentialities equal to those of a doctor or lawyer or trusted servant. Any operator at the switchboard could simply—"

"This is mere idle speculation, Mr. Wolfe. Did you say all that to the defendant?"

"Yes, sir."

"How long were you with him?"

"Nearly half an hour. I can say a great deal in half an hour."

"No doubt. But the time of the court and jury should not be spent on irrelevancies." Mandelbaum treated the jury to one of his understanding glances, and went back to Wolfe. "You didn't discuss your testimony with the defendant?"

"No, sir."

"Did you make any suggestions to him regarding the conduct of his defense?"

"No, sir. I made no suggestions to him of any kind."

"Did you offer to make any kind of investigation for him as a contribution to his defense?"

"No, sir."

"Then why did you seek this interview with him?"

"One moment." Donovan was on his feet. "I submit, Your Honor, that this is the State's witness, and this is not proper direct examination. Surely it is cross-examination, and I object to it."

Judge Corbett nodded. "The objection is sustained. Mr. Mandelbaum, you know the rules of evidence."

"But I am confronted by an unforeseen contingency."

"He is still your witness. Examine him upon the merits."

"Also, Your Honor, he is in contempt."

"Not yet. That is in abeyance. Proceed."

Mandelbaum looked at Wolfe, glanced at the jury, went to the table and stood a moment gazing down at it, lifted his head, said, "No more questions," and sat down.

Jimmy Donovan arose and stepped forward, but addressed the bench instead of the witness stand. "Your Honor, I wish to state that I knew nothing of the meeting this morning, of the witness with my client, either before or after it took place. I only learned of it here and now. If you think it desirable, I will take the stand to be questioned about it under oath."

Judge Corbett shook his head. "I don't think so, Mr. Donovan. Not unless developments suggest it."

"At any time, of course." Donovan turned. "Mr. Wolfe, why did you seek an interview this morning with Mr. Ashe?"

Wolfe was relaxed but not smug. "Because I had acquired information that cast a reasonable doubt on his guilt, and I wanted to get it before the court and the jury without delay. As a witness for the prosecution, with a warrant out for my arrest, I was in a difficult situation. It occurred to me that if I saw and talked with Mr. Ashe the fact would probably be disclosed in the course of my examination by Mr. Mandelbaum; and if so, he would almost certainly ask me what had been said. Therefore I wanted to tell Mr. Ashe what I had surmised and what I had discovered. If Mr. Mandelbaum allowed me to tell all I had said to Mr. Ashe, that would do it. If he dismissed me before I finished, I thought it likely that on cross-examination the defense attorney would give me an opportunity to go on." He turned a palm up. "So I sought an interview with Mr. Ashe."

The judge was frowning. One of the jurors made a noise, and the others looked at him. The audience stirred, and someone tittered. I was thinking Wolfe had one hell of a nerve, but he hadn't violated any law I had ever heard of, and Donovan had asked him a plain question and got a plain answer. I would have given a ream of foolscap to see Donovan's face.

If his face showed any reaction to the suggestion given him, his voice didn't. "Did you say more to Mr. Ashe than you have already testified to?"

"Yes, sir."

"Please tell the jury what you said to him."

"I said that I left this room yesterday morning, deliberately risking a penalty for contempt of court, to explore my surmises. I said that, taking my assistant, Mr. Archie Goodwin, with me, I went to the office of Bagby Answers, Incorporated, on Sixty-ninth Street, where Marie Willis was murdered. I said that from a look at the switchboards I concluded that it would be impossible for any one operator—"

Mandelbaum was up. "Objection, Your Honor. Conclusions of the witness are not admissible."

"He is merely relating," Donovan submitted, "what he said to Mr. Ashe. The Assistant District Attorney asked him to."

"The objection is overruled," Judge Corbett said dryly.

Wolfe resumed. "I said I had concluded that it would be impossible for any one operator to eavesdrop frequently on her lines without the others becoming aware of it, and therefore it must be done collusively if at all. I said that I had spoken at some length with two of the operators, Alice Hart and Bella Velardi, who had been working and living there along with Marie Willis, and had received two encouragements for my surmise: one, that they were visibly disturbed at my declared intention of investigating them fully and ruthlessly, and tolerated my rudeness beyond reason; and two, that it was evident that their personal expenditures greatly exceeded their salaries. I said—may I ask, sir, is it necessary for me to go on repeating that phrase, 'I said'?"

"I think not," Donovan told him. "Not if you confine yourself strictly to what you said to Mr. Ashe this morning."

"I shall do so. The extravagance in personal expenditures was true also of the third operator who had lived and worked there with Marie Willis, Helen Weltz. It was her day off, and Mr. Goodwin and I drove to her place in the country, near Katonah in Westchester County. She was more disturbed even than the other two; she was almost hysterical. With her was a man named Guy Unger, and he too was disturbed. After I had stated my intention to investigate everyone connected with Bagby Answers, Incorporated, he asked to speak with me privately and offered me ten thousand dollars for services that he did not specify. I gathered that he was trying to bribe me to keep my hands off, and I declined the offer."

"You said all that to Mr. Ashe?"

"Yes, sir. Meanwhile Helen Weltz had spoken privately with Mr. Goodwin, and had told him she wanted to speak with me, but must first get rid of Mr. Unger. She said she would phone my office later. Back in the city, I dared not go to my home, I was subject to arrest and detention, so Mr. Goodwin and I went to the home of a friend, and Helen Weltz came to us there sometime after midnight. My attack had broken her completely, and she was in terror. She confessed that for years the operation had been used precisely as I had surmised. All of the switchboard operators had been parties to it, including Marie Willis. Their dean, Alice Hart, collected information—"

There was an interruption. Alice Hart, on the aisle, with Bella Velardi next to her, got up and headed for the door, and Bella followed her. Eyes went to them from all directions, including Judge Corbett's, but nobody said or did anything, and when they were five steps from the door I sang out to the guard, "That's Alice Hart in front!"

He blocked them off. Judge Corbett called, "Officer, no one is to leave the room!"

The audience stirred and muttered, and some stood up. The judge banged his gavel and demanded order, but he couldn't very well threaten to have the room cleared. Miss Hart and Miss Velardi gave it up and went back to their seats.

When the room was still the judge spoke to Wolfe. "Go ahead."

He did so. "Alice Hart collected information from them and gave them cash from time to time, in addition to their salaries. Guy Unger and Clyde Bagby also gave them cash occasionally. The largest single amount ever received by Helen Weltz was fifteen hundred dollars, given her about a year ago by Guy Unger. In three years she received a total of approximately fifteen thousand dollars, not counting her salary. She didn't know what use was made of the information she passed on to Alice Hart. She wouldn't admit that she had knowledge that any of it had been used for blackmailing, but she did admit that some of it could have been so used."

"Do you know," Judge Corbett asked him, "where Helen Weltz is now?"

"Yes, sir. She is present. I told her that if she came and faced it the District Attorney might show appreciation for her help."

"Have you anything to add that you told Mr. Ashe this morning?"

"I have, Your Honor. Do you wish me to differentiate clearly between what Helen Weltz told me and my own exposition?"

"No. Anything whatever that you said to Mr. Ashe."

"I told him that the fact that he had tried to hire me to learn the identity of the Bagby operator who would service his number, and to bribe her to eavesdrop on his line, was one of the points that had caused me to doubt his guilt; that I had questioned whether a man who was reluctant to undertake such a chore for himself would be likely to strangle the life out of a woman and then open a window and yell for the police. Also I asked him about the man who telephoned him to say that if Ashe would meet him at the Bagby office on Sixty-ninth Street he thought they could talk Miss Willis out of it. I asked if it was quite possible, but if so he had disguised his voice."

"Had you any evidence that Mr. Bagby made that phone call?"

"No, Your Honor. All I had, besides my assumptions from known facts and my own observations, was what Miss Weltz had told me. One thing she had told me was that Marie Willis had become an imminent threat to the whole conspiracy. She had been ordered by both Unger and Bagby to accept Ashe's proposal to eavesdrop on his line, and not to tell

Mrs. Ashe, whom Miss Willis idolized; and she had refused and announced that she was going to quit. Of course that made her an intolerable peril to everyone concerned. The success and security of the operation hinged on the fact that no victim ever had any reason to suspect that Bagby Answers, Incorporated, was responsible for his distress. It was Bagby who got the information, but it was Unger who used it, and the tormented under the screw could not know where the tormentor had got the screw. So Miss Willis's rebellion and decision to quit—combined, according to Miss Weltz, with an implied threat to expose the whole business—were a mortal menace to any and all of them, ample provocation for murder to one willing to risk that extreme. I told Mr. Ashe that all this certainly established a reasonable doubt of his guilt, but I also went beyond that and considered briefly the most likely candidate to replace him. Do you wish that too?"

The judge was intent on him. "Yes. Proceed."

"I told Mr. Ashe that I greatly preferred Mr. Bagby. The mutual alibi of Miss Hart and Miss Velardi might be successfully impeached, but they have it, and besides I have seen and talked with them and was not impressed. I exclude Miss Weltz because when she came to me last evening she had been jolted by consternation into utter candor, or I am a witless gull; and that excludes Mr. Unger too, because Miss Weltz claims certain knowledge that he was on his boat in the Sound all of that evening. As for Mr. Bagby, he had most at stake. He admits that he went to his apartment around the time of the murder, and his apartment is on Seventieth Street, not far from where the murder occurred. I leave the timetable to the police; they are extremely efficient with timetables. Regarding the telephone call, Mr. Ashe said it could have been his voice."

Wolfe pursed his lips. "I think that's all—no, I also told Mr. Ashe that this morning I sent a man, Saul Panzer, to keep an eye on Mr. Bagby's office on Forty-seventh Street, to see that no records are removed or destroyed. I believe that covers it adequately, Your Honor. I would now like to plead to the charge of contempt, both on behalf of Mr. Goodwin and myself. If I may—"

"No." Judge Corbett was curt. "You know quite well you have made that charge frivolous by the situation you have created. The charge is dismissed. Are you through with the witness, Mr. Donovan?"

"Yes, Your Honor. No more questions."

"Mr. Mandelbaum?"

The Assistant District Attorney got up and approached the bench. "Your Honor will appreciate that I find myself in an extraordinary predicament." He sounded like a man with a major grievance. "I feel that I am entitled to ask for a recess until the afternoon session, to consider the situation and consult with my colleagues. If my request is granted, I also ask that I be given time, before the recess is called, to arrange for five persons in the room to be taken into custody as material witnesses— Alice Hart, Bella Velardi, Helen Weltz, Guy Unger, and Clyde Bagby."

"Very well." The judge raised his eyes and his voice. "The five persons just named will come forward. The rest of you will keep your seats and preserve order."

All of them obeyed but two. Nero Wolfe left the witness chair and stepped down to the floor, and as he did so Robina Keane sprang up from her place on the front bench, ran to him, threw her arms around his neck, and pressed her cheek against his. As I said before, actresses always act, but I admit that was unrehearsed and may have been artless. In any case, I thoroughly approved, since it indicated that the Ashe family would prove to be properly grateful, which after all was the main point.

VI

The thought may have occurred to you, that's all very nice, and no doubt Ashe sent a handsome check, but after all one reason Wolfe walked out was because he hated to sit against a perfumed woman on a wooden bench waiting for his turn to testify, and he had to do it all over again when the State was ready with its case, against the real murderer. It did look for a while as if he might have to face up to that, but a week before the trial opened he was informed that he wouldn't be needed, and he wasn't. They had plenty without him to persuade a jury to bring in a verdict of guilty against Clyde Bagby.

The Case of the Irate Witness

Author: Erle Stanley Gardner (1889–1970)

Detective: Perry Mason (1933)

Gardner created a long list of series characters and wrote many short stories and novelettes for both pulp and slick magazine markets. But the detectives of his novels appear rarely in shorter form. The favorites of many readers, the team of Donald Lam and Bertha Cool, whom he wrote about as A.A. Fair, never appeared in a short story. His most famous sleuth, maverick trial lawyer Perry Mason, starred in more than eighty novels between *The Case of the Velvet Claws* (1933) and the posthumously published *The Case of the Postponed Murder* (1973) but only a single short story plus a couple of *American* magazine novelettes.

Fortunately for anthologists, the lone Perry Mason short story, widely reprinted since its appearance in a 1953 issue of *Collier's*, has all of the attributes—tricky plotting, fast pace, legal legerdemain—that make the novels so addictive.

The early-morning shadows cast by the mountains still lay heavily on the town's main street as the big siren on the roof of the Jebson Commercial Company began to scream shrilly.

The danger of fire was always present, and at the sound, men at breakfast rose and pushed their chairs back from the table, others who were shaving barely paused to wipe lather from their faces, and those who had been sleeping grabbed the first available garments. All of them ran to places where they could look for the first telltale wisps of smoke.

There was no smoke.

The big siren was still screaming urgently as the men formed into streaming lines, like ants whose hill has been attacked. The lines all moved toward the Jebson Commercial Company.

There the men were told that the doors of the big vault had been found wide open. A jagged hole had been cut into one door with an acetylene torch.

This was the fifteenth of the month. The big, twice-a-month payroll, which had been brought up from the Ivanhoe National Bank the day before, had been the prize. The men looked at one another silently.

Frank Bernal, manager of the company's mine, the man who ruled Jebson City with an iron hand, arrived and took charge. The responsibility was his, and what he found was alarming.

Tom Munson, the night watchman, was lying on the floor in a back room, snoring in drunken slumber. The burglar alarm, which had been installed within the last six months, had been bypassed by means of an electrical device. This device was so ingenious that it was apparent that, if the work were that of a gang, at least one of the burglars was an expert electrician.

Ralph Nesbitt, the company accountant, was significantly silent. When Frank Bernal had been appointed manager a year earlier, Nesbitt had pointed out that the big vault was obsolete.

Bernal, determined to prove himself in his new job, had avoided the expense of tearing out the old vault and installing a new one by investing in an up-to-date burglar alarm and putting a special night watchman on duty.

Now the safe had been looted of $100,000 and Frank Bernal had to make a report to the main office in Chicago, with the disquieting knowledge that Ralph Nesbitt's memo stating the antiquated vault was a pushover was at this moment reposing in the company files.

Some distance out of Jebson City, Perry Mason, the famous trial lawyer, was driving fast along a mountain road. He had had plans for a weekend fishing trip for some time, but a jury, which had waited until midnight before reaching its verdict had delayed Mason's departure and it was now eight-thirty in the morning.

His fishing clothes, rod, wading boots, and creel were all in the trunk. He was wearing the suit in which he had stepped from the courtroom, and having driven all night, he was eager for the cool, piny mountains.

A blazing red light, shining directly at him as he rounded a turn in the canyon road, dazzled his road-weary eyes. A sign, STOP—POLICE, had been placed in the middle of the road. Two men, a grim-faced man with a .30–30 rifle in his hands and a silver badge on his shirt and a uniformed motorcycle officer, stood beside the sign.

Mason stopped his car.

The man with the badge, a deputy sheriff, said, "We'd better take a look at your driving license. There's been a big robbery at Jebson City."

"That so?" Mason said. "I went through Jebson City an hour ago and everything seemed quiet."

"Where you been since then?"

"I stopped at a little service station and restaurant for breakfast."

"Let's take a look at your driving license."

Mason handed it to him.

The man started to return it, then looked at it again. "Say," he said, "you're Perry Mason, the big criminal lawyer!"

"Not a criminal lawyer," Mason said patiently, "a trial lawyer. I sometimes defend men who are accused of crime."

"What are you doing up in this country?"

"Going fishing."

The deputy looked at him suspiciously. "Why aren't you wearing your fishing clothes?"

"Because," Mason said, and smiled, "I'm not fishing."

"You said you were going fishing."

"I also intend," Mason said, "to go to bed tonight. According to you, I should be wearing my pajamas."

The deputy frowned. The traffic officer laughed and waved Mason on.

The deputy nodded at the departing car. "Looks like a live clue to me," he said, "but I can't find it in that conversation."

"There isn't any," the traffic officer said.

The deputy remained dubious, and later on, when a news-hungry reporter from the local paper asked the deputy if he knew of anything that would make a good story, the deputy said that he did.

And that was why Della Street, Perry Mason's confidential secretary, was surprised to read stories in the metropolitan papers stating that Perry Mason, the noted trial lawyer, was rumored to have been retained to represent the person or persons who had looted the vault of the Jebson Commercial Company. All this had been arranged, it would seem, before Mason's "client" had even been apprehended.

When Perry Mason called his office by long distance the next afternoon, Della said, "I thought you were going to the mountains for a vacation."

"That's right. Why?"

"The papers claim you're representing whoever robbed the Jebson Commercial Company."

"First I've heard of it," Mason said. "I went through Jebson City before they discovered the robbery, stopped for breakfast a little farther on, and then got caught in a roadblock. In the eyes of some officious deputy, that seems to have made me an accessory after the fact."

"Well," Della Street said, "they've caught a man by the name of Harvey L. Corbin and apparently have quite a case against him. They're hinting at mysterious evidence, which won't be disclosed until the time of trial."

"Was he the one who committed the crime?" Mason asked.

"The police think so. He has a criminal record. When his employers at Jebson City found out about it, they told him to leave town. That was the evening before the robbery."

"Just like that, eh?" Mason asked.

"Well, you see, Jebson City is a one-industry town, and the company owns all the houses. They're leased to the employees. I understand Corbin's wife and daughter were told they could stay on until Corbin got located in a new place, but Corbin was told to leave town at once. You aren't interested, are you?"

"Not in the least," Mason said, "except that when I drive back, I'll be going through Jebson City, and I'll probably stop to pick up the local gossip."

"Don't do it," she warned. "This man Corbin has all the earmarks of being an underdog, and you know how you feel about underdogs."

A quality in her voice made Perry suspicious. "You haven't been approached, have you, Della?"

"Well," she said, "in a way. Mrs. Corbin read in the papers that you were going to represent her husband, and she was overjoyed. It seems that she thinks her husband's implication in this is a raw deal. She hadn't known anything about his criminal record, but she loves him and is going to stand by him."

"You've talked with her?" Mason asked.

"Several times. I tried to break it to her gently. I told her it was probably nothing but a newspaper story. You see, Chief, they have Corbin dead to rights. They took some money from his wife as evidence. It was part of the loot."

"And she has nothing?"

"Nothing. Corbin left her forty dollars, and they took it all as evidence."

"I'll drive all night," he said. "Tell her I'll be back tomorrow."

"I was afraid of that," Della Street said. "Why did you have to call up? Why couldn't you have stayed up there fishing? Why did you have to get your name in the papers?"

Mason laughed and hung up.

Paul Drake, of the Drake Detective Agency, came in and sat in the big chair in Mason's office and said, "You have a bear by the tail, Perry."

"What's the matter, Paul? Didn't your detective work in Jebson City pan out?"

"It panned out all right, but the stuff in the pan isn't what you want, Perry," Drake explained.

"How come?"

"Your client's guilty."

"Go on," Mason said.

"The money he gave his wife was some of what was stolen from the vault."

"How do they know it was the stolen money?" Mason asked.

Drake pulled a notebook from his pocket. "Here's the whole picture. The plant manager runs Jebson City. There isn't any private property. The Jebson company controls everything."

"Not a single small business?"

Drake shook his head. "Not unless you want to consider garbage collecting as small business. An old coot by the name of George Addey lives five miles down the canyon; he has a hog ranch and collects the garbage. He's supposed to have the first nickel he ever earned. Buries his money in cans. There's no bank nearer than Ivanhoe City."

"What about the burglary? The men who did it must have moved in acetylene tanks and—"

"They took them right out of the company store," Drake said. And then he went on: "Munson, the watchman, likes to take a pull out of a flask of whiskey along about midnight. He says it keeps him awake. Of course, he's not supposed to do it, and no one was supposed to know about the whiskey, but someone did know about it. They doped the whiskey with a barbiturate. The watchman took his usual swig, went to sleep, and stayed asleep."

"What's the evidence against Corbin?" Mason asked.

"Corbin had a previous burglary record. It's a policy of the company not to hire anyone with a criminal record. Corbin lied about his past and got a job. Frank Bernal, the manager, found out about it, sent for Corbin about eight o'clock the night the burglary took place, and ordered him out of town. Bernal agreed to let Corbin's wife and child stay on in the house until Corbin could get located in another city. Corbin pulled out in the morning and gave his wife this money. It was part of the money from the burglary."

"How do they know?" Mason asked.

"Now there's something I don't know," Drake said. "This fellow Bernal is pretty smart, and the story is that he can prove Corbin's money was from the vault."

Drake paused, then continued: "As I told you, the nearest bank is at Ivanhoe City, and the mine pays off in cash twice a month. Ralph Nesbitt, the cashier, wanted to install a new vault. Bernal refused to okay the expense. So the company has ordered both Bernal and Nesbitt back to its main office at Chicago to report. The rumor is that they may fire Bernal as manager and give Nesbitt the job. A couple of the directors don't like Bernal, and this thing has given them their chance. They dug out a report Nesbitt had made showing the vault was a pushover. Bernal didn't act on that report." He sighed and then asked, "When's the trial, Perry?"

"The preliminary hearing is set for Friday morning. I'll see then what they've got against Corbin."

"They're lying for you up there," Paul Drake warned. "Better watch out, Perry. That district attorney has something up his sleeve, some sort of surprise that's going to knock you for a loop."

In spite of his long experience as a prosecutor, Vernon Flasher, the district attorney of Ivanhoe County, showed a certain nervousness at being called upon to oppose Perry Mason. There was, however, a secret assurance underneath that nervousness.

Judge Haswell, realizing that the eyes of the community were upon him, adhered to legal technicalities to the point of being pompous both in rulings and mannerisms.

But what irritated Perry Mason was the attitude of the spectators. He sensed that they did not regard him as an attorney trying to safeguard the interests of a client, but as a legal magician with a cloven hoof. The looting of the vault had shocked the community, and there was a tight-lipped determination that no legal tricks were going to do Mason any good *this* time.

Vernon Flasher didn't try to save his surprise evidence for a whirlwind finish. He used it right at the start of the case.

Frank Bernal, called as a witness, described the location of the vault, identified photographs, and then leaned back as the district attorney said abruptly, "You had reason to believe this vault was obsolete?"

"Yes, sir."

"It had been pointed out to you by one of your fellow employees, Mr. Ralph Nesbitt?"

"Yes, sir."

"And what did you do about it?"

"Are you," Mason asked in some surprise, "trying to cross-examine your own witness?"

"Just let him answer the question, and you'll see," Flasher replied grimly.

"Go right ahead and answer," Mason said to the witness.

Bernal assumed a more comfortable position. "I did three things," he said, "to safeguard the payrolls and to avoid the expense of tearing out the old vault and installing a new vault in its place."

"What were those three things?"

"I employed a special night watchman, I installed the best burglar alarm money could buy, and I made arrangements with the Ivanhoe National Bank, where we have our payrolls made up, to list the number of each twenty-dollar bill that was a part of each payroll."

Mason suddenly sat up straight.

Flasher gave him a glance of gloating triumph. "Do you wish the court to understand, Mr. Bernal," he said smugly, "that you have the numbers of the bills in the payroll that were made up for delivery on the fifteenth?"

"Yes, sir. Not *all* the bills, you understand. That would have taken too much time. But I have the numbers of all the twenty-dollar bills."

"And who recorded those numbers?" the prosecutor asked.

"The bank."

"And do you have that list of numbers with you?"

"I do. Yes, sir." Bernal produced a list. "I felt," he said, glancing coldly at Nesbitt, "that these precautions would be cheaper than a new vault."

"I move the list be introduced in evidence," Flasher said.

"Just a moment," Mason objected. "I have a couple of questions. You say this list is not in your handwriting, Mr. Bernal?"

"Yes, sir."

"Whose handwriting is it, do you know?" Mason asked.

"The assistant cashier of the Ivanhoe National Bank."

"Oh, all right," Flasher said. "We'll do it the hard way, if we have to. Stand down, Mr. Bernal, and I'll call the assistant cashier."

Harry Reedy, assistant cashier of the Ivanhoe Bank, had the mechanical assurance of an adding machine. He identified the list of numbers as being in his handwriting. He stated that he had listed the numbers of the twenty-dollar bills and put that list in an envelope, which had been sealed and sent up with the money for the payroll.

"Cross-examine," Flasher said.

Mason studied the list. "These numbers are all in your handwriting?" he asked Reedy.

"Yes, sir."

"Did you yourself compare the numbers you wrote down with the numbers on the twenty-dollar bills?"

"No, sir. I didn't personally do that. Two assistants did that. One checked the numbers as they were read off, one as I wrote them down."

"The payrolls are for approximately a hundred thousand dollars, twice each month?"

"That's right. And ever since Mr. Bernal took charge, we have taken this means to identify payrolls. No attempt is made to list the bills in numerical order. The serial numbers are simply read off and written down. Unless a robbery occurs, there is no need to do anything further. In the event of a robbery, we can reclassify the numbers and list the bills in numerical order."

"These numbers are in your handwriting—every number?"

"Yes, sir. More than that, you will notice that at the bottom of each page I have signed my initials."

"That's all," Mason said.

"I now offer once more to introduce this list in evidence," Flasher said.

"So ordered," Judge Haswell ruled.

"My next witness is Charles J. Oswald, the sheriff," the district attorney announced.

The sheriff, a long, lanky man with a quiet manner, took the stand. "You're acquainted with Harvey L. Corbin, the defendant in this case?" the district attorney asked.

"I am."

"Are you acquainted with his wife?"

"Yes, sir."

"Now, on the morning of the fifteenth of this month, the morning of the robbery at the Jebson Commercial Company, did you have any conversation with Mrs. Corbin?"

"I did. Yes, sir."

"Did you ask her about her husband's activities the night before?"

"Just a moment," Mason said. "I object to this on the ground that any conversation the sheriff had with Mrs. Corbin is not admissible against the defendant, Corbin; furthermore, that in this state a wife cannot testify against her husband. Therefore, any statement she might make would be an indirect violation of that rule. Furthermore, I object on the ground that the question calls for hearsay."

Judge Haswell looked ponderously thoughtful, then said, "It seems to me Mr. Mason is correct."

"I'll put it this way, Mr. Sheriff," the district attorney said. "Did you, on the morning of the fifteenth, take any money from Mrs. Corbin?"

"Objected to as incompetent, irrelevant, and immaterial," Mason said.

"Your Honor," Flasher said irritably, "that's the very gist of our case. We propose to show that two of the stolen twenty-dollar bills were in the possession of Mrs. Corbin."

Mason said, "Unless the prosecution can prove the bills were given to Mrs. Corbin by her husband, the evidence is inadmissible."

"That's just the point," Flasher said. "Those bills *were* given to her by the defendant."

"How do you know?" Mason asked.

"She told the sheriff so."

"That's hearsay," Mason snapped.

Judge Haswell fidgeted on the bench. "It seems to me we're getting into a peculiar situation here. You can't call the wife as a witness, and I don't think her statement to the sheriff is admissible."

"Well," Flasher said desperately, "in this state, Your Honor, we have a community-property law. Mrs. Corbin had this money. Since she is the wife of the defendant, it was community property. Therefore, it's partially his property."

"Well now, there," Judge Haswell said, "I think I can agree with you. You introduce the twenty-dollar bills. I'll overrule the objection made by the defense."

"Produce the twenty-dollar bills, Sheriff," Flasher said triumphantly.

The bills were produced and received in evidence.

"Cross-examine," Flasher said curtly.

"No questions of this witness," Mason said, "but I have a few questions to ask Mr. Bernal on cross-examination. You took him off the stand to lay the foundation for introducing the bank list, and I didn't have an opportunity to cross-examine him."

"I beg your pardon," Flasher said. "Resume the stand, Mr. Bernal."

His tone, now that he had the twenty-dollar bills safely introduced in evidence, was excessively polite.

Mason said, "This list that has been introduced in evidence is on the stationery of the Ivanhoe National Bank?"

"That's right. Yes, sir."

"It consists of several pages, and at the end there is the signature of the assistant cashier?"

"Yes, sir."

"And each page is initialed by the assistant cashier?"

"Yes, sir."

"This was the scheme that you thought of in order to safeguard the company against a payroll robbery?"

"Not to safeguard the company against a payroll robbery, Mr. Mason, but to assist us in recovering the money in the event there was a holdup."

"This was your plan to answer Mr. Nesbitt's objections that the vault was an outmoded model?"

"A part of my plan, yes. I may say that Mr. Nesbitt's objections had never been voiced until I took office. I felt he was trying to embarrass me by making my administration show less net returns than expected." Bernal tightened his lips and added, "Mr. Nesbitt had, I believe, been expecting to be appointed manager. He was disappointed. I believe he still expects to be manager."

In the spectators' section of the courtroom, Ralph Nesbitt glared at Bernal.

"You had a conversation with the defendant on the night of the fourteenth?" Mason asked Bernal.

"I did. Yes, sir."

"You told him that for reasons that you deemed sufficient you were discharging him immediately and wanted him to leave the premises at once?"

"Yes, sir. I did."

"And you paid him his wages in cash?"

"Mr. Nesbit paid him in my presence, with money he took from the petty-cash drawer of the vault."

"Now, as part of the wages due him, wasn't Corbin given these two twenty-dollar bills that have been introduced in evidence?"

Bernal shook his head. "I had thought of that," he said, "but it would have been impossible. Those bills weren't available to us at that time. The payroll is received from the bank in a sealed package. Those two twenty-dollar bills were in that package."

"And the list of the numbers of the twenty-dollar bills?"

"That's in a sealed envelope. The money is placed in the vault. I lock the list of numbers in my desk."

"Are you prepared to swear that neither you nor Mr. Nesbitt had access to these two twenty-dollar bills on the night of the fourteenth?"

"That is correct."

"That's all," Mason said. "No further cross-examination."

"I now call Ralph Nesbitt to the stand," District Attorney Flasher said. "I want to fix the time of these events definitely, Your Honor."

"Very well," Judge Haswell said. "Mr. Nesbitt, come forward."

Ralph Nesbitt, after answering the usual preliminary questions, sat down in the witness chair.

"Were you present at a conversation that took place between the defendant, Harvey L. Corbin, and Frank Bernal on the fourteenth of this month?" the district attorney asked.

"I was. Yes, sir."

"What time did that conversation take place?"

"About eight o'clock in the evening."

"And, without going into the details of that conversation, I will ask you if the general effect of it was that the defendant was discharged and ordered to leave the company's property?"

"Yes, sir."

"And he was paid the money that was due him?"

"In cash. Yes, sir. I took the cash from the safe myself."

"Where was the payroll then?"

"In the sealed package in a compartment in the safe. As cashier, I had the only key to that compartment. Earlier in the afternoon I had gone to Ivanhoe City and received the sealed package of money and the envelope containing the list of numbers. I personally locked the package of money in the vault."

"And the list of numbers?"

"Mr. Bernal locked that in his desk."

"Cross-examine," Flasher said.

"No questions," Mason said.

"That's our case, Your Honor," Flasher observed.

"May we have a few minutes' indulgence?" Mason asked Judge Haswell.

"Very well, Make it brief," the judge agreed.

Mason turned to Paul Drake and Della Street. "Well, there you are," Drake said. "You're confronted with the proof, Perry."

"Are you going to put the defendant on the stand?" Della Street asked.

Mason shook his head. "It would be suicidal. He has a record of a prior criminal conviction. Also, it's a rule of law that if one asks about any part of a conversation on direct examination, the other side can bring out all the conversation. That conversation, when Corbin was discharged, was to the effect that he had lied about his past record. And I guess there's no question that he did."

"And he's lying now," Drake said. "This is one case where you're licked. I think you'd better cop a plea and see what kind of a deal you can make with Flasher."

"Probably not any," Mason said. "Flasher wants to have the reputation of having given me a licking—Wait a minute, Paul. I have an idea."

Mason turned abruptly, walked away to where he could stand by himself, his back to the crowded courtroom.

"Are you ready?" the judge asked.

Mason turned. "I am quite ready, Your Honor. I have one witness whom I wish to put on the stand. I wish a subpoena *duces tecum* issued for that witness. I want him to bring certain documents that are in his possession."

"Who is the witness, and what are the documents?" the judge asked.

Mason walked quickly over to Paul Drake. "What's the name of that character who has the garbage-collecting business," he said softly, "the one who has the first nickel he's ever made?"

"George Addey."

The lawyer turned to the judge. "The witness that I want is George Addey, and the documents that I want him to bring to court with him are all the twenty-dollar bills that he has received during the past sixty days."

"Your Honor," Flasher protested, "this is an outrage. This is making a travesty out of justice. It is exposing the court to ridicule."

Mason said, "I give Your Honor my assurance that I think this witness is material and that the documents are material. I will make an affidavit to that effect if necessary. As attorney for the defendant, may I point out that if the court refuses to grant this subpoena, it will be denying the defendant due process of law."

"I'm going to issue the subpoena," Judge Haswell said testily, "and for your own good, Mr. Mason, the testimony had better be relevant."

George Addey, unshaven and bristling with indignation, held up his right hand to be sworn. He glared at Perry Mason.

"Mr. Addey," Mason said, "You have the contract to collect garbage from Jebson City?"

"I do."

"How long have you been collecting garbage there?"

"For over five years, and I want to tell you—"

Judge Haswell banged his gavel. "The witness will answer questions and not interpolate any comments."

"I'll interpolate anything I dang please," Addey said.

"That'll do," the judge said. "Do you wish to be jailed for contempt of court, Mr. Addey?"

"I don't want to go to jail, but I—"

"Then you'll remember the respect that is due the court," the judge said. "Now you sit there and answer questions. This is a court of law. You're in this court as a citizen, and I'm here as a judge, and I propose to see that the respect due to the court is enforced." There was a moment's silence while the judge glared angrily at the witness. "All right, go ahead, Mr. Mason," Judge Haswell said.

Mason said, "During the thirty days prior to the fifteenth of this month, did you deposit any money in any banking institution?"

"I did not."

"Do you have with you all the twenty-dollar bills that you received during the last sixty days?"

"I have, and I think making me bring them here is just like inviting some crook to come and rob me and—"

Judge Haswell banged with his gavel. "Any more comments of that sort from the witness and there will be a sentence imposed for contempt of court. Now you get out those twenty-dollar bills, Mr. Addey, and put them right up here on the clerk's desk."

Addey, mumbling under his breath, slammed a roll of twenty-dollar bills down on the desk in front of the clerk.

"Now," Mason said, "I'm going to need a little clerical assistance. I would like to have my secretary, Miss Street, and the clerk help me check through the numbers on these bills. I will select a few at random."

Mason picked up three of the twenty-dollar bills and said, "I am going to ask my assistants to check the list of numbers introduced in evidence. In my hand is a twenty-dollar bill that has the number L 07083274 A. Is that bill on the list? The next bill that I pick up is number L 07579190 A. Are either of those bills on the list?"

The courtroom was silent. Suddenly Della Street said, "Yes, here's one that's on the list—bill number L 07579190 A. It's on the list, on page eight."

"What?" the prosecutor shouted.

"Exactly," Mason said, smiling. "So, if a case is to be made against a person merely because he has possession of the money that was stolen on the fifteenth of this month, then your office should prefer charges against this witness, George Addey, Mr. District Attorney."

Addey jumped from the witness stand and shook his fist in Mason's face. "You're a cockeyed liar!" he screamed. "There ain't a one of those bills but what I didn't have it before the fifteenth. The company cashier changes my money into twenties, because I like big bills. I bury 'em in cans, and I put the date on the side of the can."

"Here's the list," Mason said. "Check it for yourself."

A tense silence gripped the courtroom as the judge and the spectators waited.

"I'm afraid I don't understand this, Mr. Mason," Judge Haswell said after a moment.

"I think it's quite simple," Mason said. "And I now suggest the court take a recess for an hour and check these other bills against this list. I think the district attorney may be surprised."

And Mason sat down and proceeded to put papers in his briefcase.

Della Street, Paul Drake, and Perry Mason were sitting in the lobby of the Ivanhoe Hotel.

"When are you going to tell us?" Della Street asked fiercely. "Or do we tear you limb from limb? How could the garbage man have . . . ?"

"Wait a minute," Mason said. "I think we're about to get results. Here comes the esteemed district attorney, Vernon Flasher, and he's accompanied by Judge Haswell."

The two strode over to Mason's group and bowed with cold formality.

Mason got up.

Judge Haswell began in his best courtroom voice. "A most deplorable situation has occurred. It seems that Mr. Frank Bernal has—well—"

"Been detained somewhere," Vernon Flasher said.

"Disappeared," Judge Haswell said. "He's gone."

"I expected as much," Mason said.

"Now will you kindly tell me just what sort of pressure you brought to bear on Mr. Bernal to . . . ?"

"Just a moment, Judge," Mason said. "The only pressure I brought to bear on him was to cross-examine him."

"Did you know that there had been a mistake in the dates on those lists?"

"There was no mistake. When you find Bernal, I'm sure you will discover there was a deliberate falsification. He was short in his accounts, and he knew he was about to be demoted. He had a desperate need for a hundred thousand dollars in ready cash. He had evidently been planning this burglary, or, rather, this embezzlement, for some time. He learned that Corbin had a criminal record. He arranged to have these lists furnished by the bank. He installed a burglar alarm and, naturally, knew how to circumvent it. He employed a watchman he knew was addicted to drink. He only needed to stage his coup at the right time. He fired Corbin and paid him off with bills that had been recorded by the bank on page eight of the list of bills *in the payroll on the first of the month.*

"Then he removed page eight from the list of bills contained in the payroll *of the fifteenth,* before he showed it to the police, and substituted page eight of the list for the *first-of-the-month* payroll. It was that simple.

"Then he drugged the watchman's whiskey, took an acetylene torch, burned through the vault doors, and took all the money."

"May I ask how you knew all this?" Judge Haswell demanded.

"Certainly," Mason said. "My client told me he received those bills from Nesbitt, who took them from the petty-cash drawer in the safe. He also told the sheriff that. I happened to be the only one who believed him. It sometimes pays, Your Honor, to have faith in a man, even if he has made a previous mistake. Assuming my client was innocent, I knew either Bernal or Nesbitt must be guilty. I then realized that only Bernal had custody of the *previous* lists of numbers.

"As an employee, Bernal had been paid on the first of the month. He looked at the numbers on the twenty-dollar bills in his pay envelope and found that they had been listed on page eight of the payroll for the first.

"Bernal only needed to extract all the twenty-dollar bills from the petty-cash drawer, substitute twenty-dollar bills from his own pay envelope, call in Corbin, and fire him. His trap was set.

"I let him know I knew what had been done by bringing Addey into court and proving my point. Then I asked for a recess. That was so Bernal would have a chance to skip out. You see, flight may be received as evidence of guilt. It was a professional courtesy to the district attorney. It will help him when Bernal is arrested."

The King in Yellow

Author: Raymond Chandler (1888–1959)

Detective: Steve Grayce (1934)

The origins of Chandler's seminal detective character Philip Marlowe can be traced back through the short stories he wrote in the 1930s. Back then, in stories such as "Finger Man," the private-eye narrator was unnamed, but later he became Marlowe's forerunner, John Dalmas, and in the following instance, Steve Grayce. By the time "The King in Yellow" appeared in 1938, Chandler's pulp apprenticeship was drawing to a close. He had it all together: the similes, the crisp, smart-ass dialogue, the jaundiced social observations, the sharply economical scene-setting, the complex mystery puzzle. Chandler has been most often criticized for messy plotting, but in contrast to some of his minimalist descendants, he as least deigned to do a plot, and, with all its other attributes, "The King in Yellow" has a good one.

I

George Millar, night auditor at the Carlton Hotel, was a dapper wiry little man, with a soft deep voice like a torch singer's. He kept it low, but his eyes were sharp and angry, as he said into the PBX mouthpiece: "I'm very sorry. It won't happen again. I'll send him up at once."

He tore off the headpiece, dropped it on the keys of the switchboard and marched swiftly from behind the pebbled screen and out into the entrance lobby. It was past one and the Carlton was two thirds residential. In the main lobby, down three shallow steps, lamps were dimmed and the night porter had finished tidying up. The place was deserted—a wide space of dim furniture, rich carpet. Faintly in the distance a radio

193

sounded. Millar went down the steps and walked quickly toward the sound, turned through an archway, and looked at a man stretched out on a pale green davenport and what looked like all the loose cushions in the hotel. He lay on his side dreamy-eyed and listened to the radio two yards away from him.

Millar barked: "Hey, you! Are you the house dick here or the house cat?"

Steve Grayce turned his head slowly and looked at Millar. He was a long black-haired man, about twenty-eight with deep-set silent eyes and a rather gentle mouth. He jerked a thumb at the radio and smiled. "King Leopardi, George. Hear that trumpet tone. Smooth as an angel's wing, boy."

"Swell! Go on back upstairs and get him out of the corridor!"

Steve Grayce looked shocked. "What—again? I thought I had those birds put to bed long ago." He swung his feet to the floor and stood up. He was at least a foot taller than Millar.

"Well, Eight-sixteen says no. Eight-sixteen says he's out in the hall with two of his stooges. He's dressed in yellow satin shorts and a trombone and he and his pals are putting on a jam session. And one of those hustlers Quillan registered in Eight-eleven is out there truckin' for them. Now get on to it, Steve—and this time make it stick."

Steve Grayce smiled wryly. He said: "Leopardi doesn't belong here anyway. Can I use chloroform or just my blackjack?"

He stepped long legs over the pale-green carpet, through the arch and across the main lobby to the single elevator that was open and lighted. He slid the doors shut and ran it up to Eight, stopped it roughly and stepped out into the corridor.

The noise hit him like a sudden wind. The walls echoed with it. Half a dozen doors were open and angry guests in night robes stood in them peering.

"It's O.K., folks," Steve Grayce said rapidly. "This is absolutely the last act. Just relax."

He rounded a corner and the hot music almost took him off his feet. Three men were lined up against the wall, near an open door from which light streamed. The middle one, the one with the trombone, was six feet tall, powerful and graceful, with a hairline mustache. His face was flushed and his eyes had an alcoholic glitter. He wore yellow satin shorts with large initials embroidered in black on the left leg—nothing more. His torso was tanned and naked.

The two with him were in pajamas, the usual halfway good-looking band boys, both drunk, but not staggering drunk. One jittered madly on a clarinet and the other on a tenor saxophone.

Back and forth in front of them, strutting, trucking, preening herself like a magpie, arching her arms and her eyebrows, bending her fingers back until the carmine nails almost touched her arms, a metallic blonde swayed and went to town on the music. Her voice was a throaty screech, without melody, as false as her eyebrows and as sharp as her nails. She wore high-heeled slippers and black pajamas with a long purple sash.

Steve Grayce stopped dead and made a sharp downward motion with his hand. "Wrap it up!" he snapped. "Can it. Put it on ice. Take it away and bury it. The show's out. Scram, now—scram!"

King Leopardi took the trombone from his lips and bellowed: "Fanfare to a house dick!"

The three drunks blew a stuttering note that shook the walls. The girl laughed foolishly and kicked out. Her slipper caught Steve Grayce in the chest. He picked it out of the air, jumped toward the girl and took hold of her wrist.

"Tough, eh?" he grinned. "I'll take you first."

"Get him!" Leopardi yelled. "Sock him low! Dance the gum-heel on his neck!"

Steve swept the girl off her feet, tucked her under his arm and ran. He carried her as easily as a parcel. She tried to kick his legs. He laughed and shot a glance through a lighted doorway. A man's brown brogues lay under a bureau. He went on past that to a second lighted doorway, slammed through and kicked the door shut, turned far enough to twist the tabbed key in the lock. Almost at once a fist hit the door. He paid no attention to it.

He pushed the girl along the short passage past the bathroom, and let her go. She reeled away from him and put her back to the bureau, panting, her eyes furious. A lock of damp gold-dipped hair swung down over one eye. She shook her head violently and bared her teeth.

"How would you like to get vagged, sister?"

"Go to hell!" she spit out. "The King's a friend of mine, see? You better keep your paws off me, copper."

"You run the circuit with the boys?"

She spat at him again.

"How'd you know they'd be here?"

Another girl was sprawled across the bed, her head to the wall, tousled black hair over a white face. There was a tear in the leg of her pajamas. She lay limp and groaned.

Steve said harshly: "Oh, oh, the torn-pajama act. It flops here, sister, it flops hard. Now listen, you kids. You can go to bed and stay till morning or you can take the bounce. Make up your minds."

The black-haired girl groaned. The blonde said: "You get out of my room, you damned gum-heel!"

She reached behind her and threw a hand mirror. Steve ducked. The mirror slammed against the wall and fell without breaking. The black-haired girl rolled over on the bed and said wearily: "Oh lay off. I'm sick."

She lay with her eyes closed, the lids fluttering.

The blonde swiveled her hips across the room to a desk by the window, poured herself a full half-glass of Scotch in a water glass and gurgled it down before Steve could get to her. She choked violently, dropped the glass, and went down on her hands and knees.

Steve said grimly: "That's the one that kicks you in the face, sister."

The girl crouched, shaking her head. She gagged once, lifted the carmine nails to paw at her mouth. She tried to get up, and her foot skidded out from under her and she fell down on her side and went fast asleep.

Steve sighed, went over and shut the window and fastened it. He rolled the black-haired girl over and straightened her on the bed and got the bedclothes from under her, tucked a pillow under her head. He picked the blonde bodily off the floor and dumped her on the bed and covered both girls to the chin. He opened the transom, switched off the ceiling light and unlocked the door. He relocked it from the outside, with a master key on a chain.

"Hotel business," he said under his breath. "Phooey."

The corridor was empty now. One lighted door still stood open. Its number was 815, two doors from the room the girls were in. Trombone music came from it softly—but not softly enough for 1:25 A.M.

Steve Grayce turned into the room, crowded the door shut with his shoulder and went along past the bathroom. King Leopardi was alone in the room.

The bandleader was sprawled out in an easy chair, with a tall misted glass at his elbow. He swung the trombone in a tight circle as he played it and the lights danced in the horn.

Steve lit a cigarette, blew a plume of smoke and stared through it at Leopardi with a queer, half-admiring, half-contemptuous expression.

He said softly: "Lights out, yellow pants. You play a sweet trumpet and your trombone don't hurt either. But we can't use it here. I already told you that once. Lay off. Put that thing away."

Leopardi smiled nastily and blew a stuttering raspberry that sounded like a devil laughing.

"Says you," he sneered. "Leopardi does what he likes, where he likes, when he likes. Nobody's stopped him yet, gum shoe. Take the air."

Steve hunched his shoulders and went close to the tall dark man. He said patiently: "Put that bazooka down, big stuff. People are trying to sleep. They're funny that way. You're a great guy on a band shell. Everywhere else you're just a guy with a lot of jack and a personal reputation that stinks from here to Miami and back. I've got a job to do and I'm doing it. Blow that thing again and I'll wrap it around your neck."

Leopardi lowered the trombone and took a long drink from the glass at his elbow. His eyes glinted nastily. He lifted the trombone to his lips again, filled his lungs with air and blew a blast that rocked the walls. Then he stood up very suddenly and smoothly and smashed the instrument down on Steve's head.

"I never did like house peepers," he sneered. "They smell like public toilets."

Steve took a short step back and shook his head. He leered, slid forward on one foot and smacked Leopardi open-handed. The blow looked light, but Leopardi reeled all the way across the room and sprawled at the foot of the bed, sitting on the floor, his right arm draped in an open suitcase.

For a moment neither man moved. Then Steve kicked the trombone away from him and squashed his cigarette in a glass tray. His black eyes were empty but his mouth grinned whitely.

"If you want trouble," he said, "I come from where they make it."

Leopardi smiled, thinly, tautly, and his right hand came up out of the suitcase with a gun in it. His thumb snicked the safety catch. He held the gun steady, pointing.

"Make some with this," he said, and fired.

The bitter roar of the gun seemed a tremendous sound in the closed room. The bureau mirror splintered and glass flew. A sliver cut Steve's cheek like a razor blade. Blood oozed in a small narrow line on his skin.

He let his feet in a dive. His right shoulder crushed against Leopardi's bare chest and his left hand brushed the gun away from him, under the bed. He rolled swiftly to his right and came up on his knees spinning.

He said thickly, harshly: "You picked the wrong gee, brother."

He swarmed on Leopardi and dragged him to his feet by his hair, by main strength. Leopardi yelled and hit him twice on the jaw and Steve grinned and kept his left hand twisted in the bandleader's long sleek black hair. He turned his hand and the head twisted with it and Leopardi's third punch landed on Steve's shoulder. Steve took hold of the wrist behind the punch and twisted that and the bandleader went down on his knees yowling. Steve lifted him by the hair again, let go of his wrist and punched him three times in the stomach, short terrific jabs. He let go of the hair then as he sank the fourth punch almost to his wrist.

Leopardi sagged blindly to his knees and vomited.

Steve stepped away from him and went into the bathroom and got a towel off the rack. He threw it at Leopardi, jerked the open suitcase onto the bed and started throwing things into it.

Leopardi wiped his face and got to his feet still gagging. He swayed, braced himself on the end of the bureau. He was white as a sheet.

Steve Grayce said: "Get dressed, Leopardi. Or go out the way you are. It's all one to me."

Leopardi stumbled into the bathroom, pawing the wall like a blind man.

II

Millar stood very still behind the desk as the elevator opened. His face was white and scared and his cropped black mustache was a smudge across his upper lip. Leopardi came out of the elevator first, a muffler around his neck, a lightweight coat tossed over his arm, a hat tilted on his head. He walked stiffly, bent forward a little, his eyes vacant. His face had a greenish pallor.

Steve Grayce stepped out behind him carrying a suitcase, and Carl, the night porter, came last with two more suitcases and two instrument cases in black leather. Steve marched over to the desk and said harshly: "Mr. Leopardi's bill—if any. He's checking out."

Millar goggled at him across the marble desk. "I—I don't think, Steve—"

"O.K. I thought not."

Leopardi smiled very thinly and unpleasantly and walked out through the brass-edged swing doors the porter held open for him. There were two nighthawk cabs in the line. One of them came to life and pulled up to the canopy and the porter loaded Leopardi's stuff into it. Leopardi got into the cab and leaned forward to put his head to the open window. He said slowly and thickly: "I'm sorry for you, gum heel, I mean sorry."

Steve Grayce stepped back and looked at him woodenly. The cab moved off down the street, rounded a corner and was gone. Steve turned on his heel, took a quarter from his pocket and tossed it up in the air. He slapped it into the night porter's hand.

"From the King," he said. "Keep it to show your grandchildren."

He went back into the hotel, got into the elevator without looking at Millar, shot it up to Eight again and went along the corridor, master-keyed his way into Leopardi's room. He relocked it from the inside, pulled the bed out from the wall and went in behind it. He got a .32 automatic off the carpet, put it in his pocket, and prowled the floor with his eyes looking for the ejected shell. He found it against the wastebasket, reached to pick it up, and stayed bent over, staring into the basket. His mouth tightened. He picked up the shell and dropped it absently into his pocket, then reached a questing finger into the basket and lifted out a torn scrap of paper on which a piece of newsprint had been pasted. Then he picked up the basket, pushed the bed back against the wall and dumped the contents of the basket out on it.

From the trash of torn papers and matches he separated a number of pieces with newsprint pasted to them. He went over to the desk with them and sat down. A few minutes later he had the torn scraps put together like a jigsaw puzzle and could read the message that had been made by cutting words and letters from magazines and pasting them on a sheet.

TEN GRAND BY TH U RS DAY NI GHT,
LEO PAR DI. DAY AFTER *YOU* OPEN AT
T HE CL U B SHAL OTTE. OR EL SE—
CURTAINS. FROM HER BROTHER.

Steve Grayce said: "Huh." He scooped the torn pieces into a hotel envelope, put that in his inside breast pocket and lit a cigarette. "The guy had guts," he said. "I'll grant him that—and his trumpet."

He locked the room, listened a moment in the now silent corridor, then went along to the room occupied by the two girls. He knocked softly and put his ear to the panel. A chair squeaked and feet came toward the door.

"What is it?" The girl's voice was cool, wide awake. It was not the blond's voice.

"The house man. Can I speak to you a minute?"

"You're speaking to me."

"Without the door between, lady."

"You've got a passkey. Help yourself." The steps went away. He unlocked the door with his master key, stepped quietly inside, and shut it. There was a dim light in a lamp with a shirred shade on the desk. On the bed the blonde snored heavily, one hand clutched in her brilliant metallic hair. The black-haired girl sat in the chair by the window, her legs crossed at right angles like a man's and stared at Steve emptily.

He went close to her and pointed to the long tear in her pajama leg. He said softly: "You're not sick. You were not drunk. That tear was done a long time ago. What's the racket? A shakedown on the King?"

The girl stared at him coolly, puffed at a cigarette, and said nothing.

"He checked out." Steve said. "Nothing doing in that direction now, sister." He watched her like a hawk, his black eyes hard and steady on her face.

"Aw, you house dicks make me sick!" the girl said with sudden anger. She surged to her feet and went past him into the bathroom, shut and locked the door.

Steve shrugged and felt the pulse of the girl asleep in the bed—a thumpy, draggy pulse, a liquor pulse.

"Poor damn hustlers," he said under his breath.

He looked at a large purple bag that lay on the bureau, lifted it idly and let it fall. His face stiffened again. The bag made a heavy sound on the glass top, as if there were a lump of lead inside it. He snapped it open quickly and plunged a hand in. His fingers touched the cold metal of a gun. He opened the bag wide and stared down into it at a small .25 automatic. A scrap of white paper caught his eye. He fished it out and held it to the light—a rent receipt with a name and address. He stuffed it into his pocket, closed the bag and was standing by the window when the girl came out of the bathroom.

"Hell, are you still haunting me?" she snapped. "You know what happens to hotel dicks that master-key their way into ladies' bedrooms at night?"

Steve said loosely: "Yeah. They get in trouble. They might even get shot at."

The girl's face became set, but her eyes crawled sideways and looked at the purple bag. Steve looked at her. "Know Leopardi in Frisco?" he asked. "He hasn't played here in two years. Then he was just a trumpet player in Vane Utigore's band—a cheap outfit."

The girl curled her lip, went past him and sat down by the window again. Her face was white, stiff. She said dully: "Blossom did. That's Blossom on the bed."

"Know he was coming to this hotel tonight?"

"What makes it your business?"

"I can't figure him coming here at all," Steve said. "This is a quiet place. So I can't figure anybody coming here to put the bite on him."

"Go somewhere else and figure. I need sleep."

Steve said: "Good night, sweetheart—and keep your door locked."

A thin man with thin blond hair and thin face was standing by the desk, tapping on the marble with thin fingers. Millar was still behind the desk and he still looked white and scared. The thin man wore a dark gray suit with a scarf inside the collar of the coat. He had a look of having just got up. He turned sea-green eyes slowly on Steve as he got out of the elevator, waited for him to come up to the desk and throw a tabbed key on it.

Steve said: "Leopardi's key, George. There's a busted mirror in his room and the carpet has his dinner on it—mostly Scotch." He turned to the thin man.

"You want to see me, Mr. Peters?"

"What happened, Grayce?" The thin man had a tight voice that expected to be lied to.

"Leopardi and two of his boys were on Eight, the rest of the gang on Five. The bunch on Five went to bed. A couple of obvious hustlers managed to get themselves registered just two rooms from Leopardi. They managed to contact him and everybody was having a lot of nice noisy fun out in the hall. I could only stop it by getting a little tough."

"There's blood on your cheek," Peters said coldly. "Wipe it off."

Steve scratched at his cheek with a handkerchief. The thin thread of blood had dried. "I got the girls tucked away in their room," he said. "The two stooges took the hint and holed up, but Leopardi still thought the guests wanted to hear trombone music. I threatened to wrap it around his neck and he beaned me with it. I slapped him open-handed and he pulled a gun and took a shot at me. Here's the gun."

He took the .32 automatic out of his pocket and laid it on the desk. He put the used shell beside it. "So I beat some sense into him and threw him out," he added.

Peters tapped on the marble. "Your usual tact seems to have been well in evidence."

Steve stared at him. "He shot at me," he repeated quietly. "With a gun. This gun. I'm tender to bullets. He missed, but suppose he hadn't? I like my stomach the way it is, with just one way in and one way out."

Peters narrowed his tawny eyebrows. He said very politely: "We have you down on the payroll here as a night clerk, because we don't like the name house detective. But neither night clerks nor house detectives put guests out of the hotel without consulting me. Not ever, Mr. Grayce."

Steve said: "The guy shot at me, pal. With a gun. Catch on? I don't have to take that without a kickback, do I?" His face was a little white.

Peters said: "Another point for your consideration. The controlling interest in this hotel is owned by Mr. Halsey G. Walters. Mr. Walters also owns the Club Shalotte, where King Leopardi is opening on Wednesday night. And that, Mr. Grayce, is why Leopardi was good enough to give us his business. Can you think of anything else I should like to say to you?"

"Yeah. I'm canned," Steve said mirthlessly.

"Very correct, Mr. Grayce. Good night, Mr. Grayce."

The thin blond man moved to the elevator and the night porter took him up.

Steve looked at Millar.

"Jumbo Walters, huh?" he said softly. "A tough, smart guy. Much too smart to think this dump and the Club Shalotte belong to the same sort of customers. Did Peters write Leopardi to come here?"

"I guess he did, Steve." Millar's voice was low and gloomy.

"Then why wasn't he put in the tower suite with a private balcony to dance on, at twenty-eight bucks a day? Why was he put on a medium-priced transient floor? And why did Quillan let those girls get so close to him?"

Millar pulled at his black mustache. "Tight with money—as well as with Scotch, I suppose. As to the girls, I don't know."

Steve slapped the counter open-handed. "Well, I'm canned, for not letting a drunken heel make a parlor house and a shooting gallery out of the eighth floor. Nuts! Well, I'll miss the joint at that."

"I'll miss you too, Steve," Millar said gently. "But not for a week. I take a week off starting tomorrow. My brother has a cabin at Crestline."

"Didn't know you had a brother," Steve said absently. He opened and closed his fist on the marble desktop.

"He doesn't come into town much. A big guy. Used to be a fighter."

Steve nodded and straightened from the counter. "Well, I might as well finish out my night," he said. "On my back. Put this gun away somewhere, George."

He grinned coldly and walked away, down the steps into the dim main lobby and across to the room where the radio was. He punched the pillows into shape on the pale-green davenport, then suddenly reached into his pocket and took out the scrap of white paper he had lifted from the black-haired girl's purple handbag. It was a receipt for a week's rent, to a Miss Marilyn Delorme, Apt. 211, Ridgeland Apartments, 118 Court Street.

He tucked it into his wallet and stood staring at the silent radio. "Steve, I think you got another job," he said under his breath. "Something about this set-up smells."

He slipped into a closetlike phone booth in the corner of the room, dropped a nickel and dialed an all-night radio station. He had to dial four times before he got a clear line to the Owl Program announcer.

"How's to play King Leopardi's record of 'Solitude' again?" he asked him.

"Got a lot of requests piled up. Played it twice already. Who's calling?"

"Steve Grayce, night man at the Carlton Hotel."

"Oh, a sober guy on his job. For you, pal, anything."

Steve went back to the davenport, snapped the radio on and lay down on his back, with his hands clasped behind his head.

Ten minutes later the high, piercingly sweet trumpet notes of King Leopardi came softly from the radio, muted almost to a whisper, and sustaining E above high C for an almost incredible period of time.

"Shucks," Steve grumbled, when the record ended. "A guy that can play like that—maybe I was too tough with him."

III

Court street was old town, wop town, crook town, arty town. It lay across the top of Bunker Hill and you could find anything there from down-at-heels ex-Greenwich-villagers to crooks on the lam, from ladies of anybody's evening to County Relief clients brawling with haggard landladies in grand old houses with scrolled porches, parquetry floors, and immense sweeping banisters of white oak, mahogany and Circassian walnut.

It had been a nice place once, had Bunker Hill, and from the days of its niceness there still remained the funny little funicular railway, called the Angel's Flight, which crawled up and down a yellow clay bank from Hill Street. It was afternoon when Steve Grayce got off the car at the top, its only passenger. He walked along in the sun, a tall, wide-shouldered, rangy-looking man in a well-cut blue suit.

He turned west at Court and began to read the numbers. The one he wanted was two from the corner, across the street from a red brick funeral parlor with a sign in gold over it: Paolo Perrugini Funeral Home.

A swarthy iron-gray Italian in a cutaway coat stood in front of the curtained door of the red brick building, smoking a cigar and waiting for somebody to die.

One-eighteen was a three-storied frame apartment house. It had a glass door, well masked by a dirty net curtain, a hall runner eighteen inches wide, dim doors with numbers painted on them with dim-paint, a staircase halfway back. Brass stair rods glittered in the dimness of the hallway.

Steve Grayce went up the stairs and prowled back to the front. Apartment 211, Miss Marilyn Delorme, was on the right, a front apartment. He tapped lightly on the wood, waited, tapped again. Nothing moved beyond the silent door, or in the hallway. Behind another door across the hall somebody coughed and kept on coughing.

Standing there in the half-light Steve Grayce wondered why he had come. Miss Delorme had carried a gun. Leopardi had received some kind of a threat letter and torn it up and thrown it away. Miss Delorme had checked out of the Carlton about an hour after Steve told her Leopardi was gone. Even at that—

He took out a leather keyholder and studied the lock of the door. It looked as if it would listen to reason. He tried a pick on it, snicked the bolt back and stepped softly into the room. He shut the door, but the pick wouldn't lock it.

The room was dim with drawn shades across two front windows. The air smelled of face powder. There was light-painted furniture, a pull-down double bed, which was pulled down but had been made up. There was a magazine on it, a glass tray full of cigarette butts, a pint bottle half full of whiskey, and a glass on a chair beside the bed. Two pillows had been used for a backrest and were still crushed in the middle.

On the dresser there was a composition toilet set, neither cheap nor expensive, a comb with black hair in it, a tray of manicuring stuff, plenty of spilled powder—in the bathroom, nothing. In a closet behind the bed a lot of clothes and two suitcases. The shoes were all one size.

Steve stood beside the bed and pinched his chin. "Blossom, the spitting blonde, doesn't live here," he said under his breath. "Just Marilyn the torn-pants brunette."

He went back to the dresser and pulled drawers out. In the bottom drawer, under the piece of wallpaper that lined it, he found a box of .25 copper-nickel automatic shells. He poked at the butts in the ashtray. All had lipstick on them. He pinched his chin again, then feathered the air with the palm of his hand, like an oarsman with a scull.

"Bunk," he said softly. "Wasting your time, Stevie."

He walked over to the door and reached for the knob, then turned back to the bed and lifted it by the footrail.

Miss Marilyn Delorme was in.

She lay on her side on the floor under the bed, long legs scissored out as if in running. One mule was on, one off. Garters and skin showed at the tops of her stockings, and a blue rose on something pink. She wore a square-necked, short-sleeved dress that was not too clean. Her neck above the dress was blotched with purple bruises.

Her face was a dark plum color, her eyes had the faint stale glitter of death, and her mouth was open so far that it foreshortened her face. She was colder than ice, and still quite limp. She had been dead two or three hours at least, and six hours at most.

The purple bag was beside her, gaping like her mouth. Steve didn't touch any of the stuff that had been emptied out on the floor. There was no gun and there were no papers.

He let the bed down over her again, then made the rounds of the apartment, wiping everything he had touched and a lot of things he couldn't remember whether he had touched or not.

He listened at the door and stepped out. The hall was still empty. The man behind the opposite door still coughed. Steve went down the stairs, looked at the mailboxes, and went back along the lower hall to a door.

Behind this door a chair creaked monotonously. He knocked and a woman's sharp voice called out. Steve opened the door with is handkerchief and stepped in.

In the middle of the room a woman rocked in an old Boston rocker, her body in the slack boneless attitude of exhaustion. She had a mud-colored face, stringy hair, gray cotton stockings—everything a Bunker Hill landlady should have. She looked at Steve with the interested eye of a dead goldfish.

"Are you the manager?"

The woman stopped rocking, screamed, "Hi, Jake! Company!" at the top of her voice, and started rocking again.

An icebox door thudded shut behind a partly open inner door and a very big man came into the room carrying a can of beer. He had a doughy mooncalf face, a tuft of fuzz on top of an otherwise bald head, a thick brutal neck and chin, and brown pig eyes about as expressionless as the woman's. He needed a shave—had needed one the day before—and his collarless shirt gaped over a big hard hairy chest. He wore scarlet suspenders with large gilt buckles on them.

He held the can of beer out to the woman. She clawed it out of his hand and said bitterly: "I'm so tired I ain't got no sense."

The man said: "Yah. You ain't done the halls so good at that."

The woman snarled: "I done 'em as good as I aim to." She sucked the beer thirstily.

Steve looked at the man and said: "Manager?"

"Yah. 'S me. Jake Stoyanoff. Two hun'erd eighty-six stripped, and still plenty tough."

Steve said: "Who lives in Two-eleven?"

The big man leaned forward a little from the waist and snapped his suspenders. Nothing changed in his eyes. The skin along his big jaw may have tightened a little. "A dame," he said.

"Alone?"

"Go on—ask me," the big man said. He stuck his hand out and lifted a cigar off the edge of a stained-wood table. The cigar was burning unevenly and it smelled as if somebody had set fire to the doormat. He pushed it into his mouth with a hard, thrusting motion, as if he expected his mouth wouldn't want it to go in.

"I'm asking you," Steve said.

"Ask me out in the kitchen," the big man drawled.

He turned and held the door open. Steve went past him.

The big man kicked the door shut against the squeak of the rocking chair, opened up the icebox and got out two cans of beer. He opened them and handed one to Steve.

"Dick?"

Steve drank some of the beer, put the can down on the sink, got a brand-new card out of his wallet—a business card printed that morning. He handed it to the man.

The man read it, put it down on the sink, picked it up and read it again. "One of them guys," he growled over his beer. "What's she pulled this time?"

Steve shrugged and said: "I guess it's the usual. The torn-pajama act. Only there's a kickback this time."

"How come? You handling it, huh? Must be a nice cozy one."

Steve nodded. The big man blew smoke from his mouth. "Go ahead and handle it," he said.

"You don't mind a pinch here?"

The big man laughed heartily. "Nuts to you, brother," he said pleasantly enough. "You're a private dick. So it's a hush. O.K. Go out and hush it. And if it *was* a pinch—that bothers me like a quart of milk. Go into your act. Take all the room you want. Cops don't bother Jake Stoyanoff."

Steve stared at the man. He didn't say anything. The big man talked it up some more, seemed to get more interested. "Besides," he went on, making motions with the cigar, "I'm softhearted. I never turn up a dame. I never put a frill in the middle." He finished his beer and threw the can in a basket under the sink, and pushed his hand out in front of him, revolving the large thumb slowly against the next two fingers. "Unless there's some of that," he added.

Steve said softly: "You've got big hands. You could have done it."

"Huh?" His small brown leathery eyes got silent and stared.

Steve said: "Yeah. You might be clean. But with those hands the cops'd go round and round with you just the same."

The big man moved a little to his left, away from the sink. He let his right hand hang down at his side, loosely. His mouth got so tight that the cigar almost touched his nose.

"What's the beef, huh?" he barked. "What you shovin' at me, guy? What—"

"Cut it," Steve drawled. "She's been croaked. Strangled. Upstairs, on the floor under her bed. About midmorning, I'd say. Big hands did it— hands like yours."

The big man did a nice job of getting the gun off his hip. It arrived so suddenly that it seemed to have grown in his and and been there all the time.

Steve frowned at the gun and didn't move. The big man looked him over. "You're tough," he said. "I been in the ring long enough to size up a guy's meat. You're plenty hard, boy. But you ain't as hard as lead. Talk it up fast."

"I knocked at her door. No answer. The lock was a pushover. I went in. I almost missed her because the bed was pulled down and she had been sitting on it, reading a magazine. There was no sign of struggle. I lifted the bed just before I left—and there she was. Very dead, Mr. Stoyanoff. Put the gat away. Cops don't bother you, you said a minute ago."

The big man whispered: "Yes and no. They don't make me happy neither. I get a bump once'n a while. Mostly a Dutch. You said something about my hands, mister."

Steve shook his head. "That was a gag," he said. "Her neck has nail marks. You bite your nails down close. You're clean."

The big man didn't look at his fingers. He was very pale. There was sweat on his lower lip, in the black stubble of his beard. He was still leaning forward, still motionless, when there was a knocking beyond the kitchen door, the door from the living room to the hallway. The creaking chair stopped and the woman's sharp voice screamed: "Hi, Jake! Company!"

The big man cocked his head. "That old slut wouldn't climb off'n her fanny if the house caught fire," he said thickly.

He stepped to the door and slipped through it, locking it behind him.

Steve ranged the kitchen swiftly with his eyes. There was a small high window beyond the sink, a trap low down for a garbage pail and parcels, but no other door. He reached for his card Stoyanoff had left lying on the drain board and slipped it back into his pocket. Then he took a short-barreled Detective Special out of his left breast pocket where he wore it nose down, as in a holster.

He had got that far when the shots roared beyond the wall—muffled a little, but still loud—four of them blended in a blast of sound.

Steve stepped back and hit the kitchen door with his leg out straight. It held and jarred him to the top of his head and in his hip joint. He swore, took the whole width of the kitchen and slammed into it with his left shoulder. It gave this time. He pitched into the living room. The mud-faced woman sat leaning forward in her rocker, her head to one side and a lock of mousy hair smeared down over her bony forehead.

"Backfire, huh?" she said stupidly. "Sounded kinda close. Musta been in the alley."

Steve jumped across the room, yanked the outer door open and plunged out into the hall.

The big man was still on his feet, a dozen feet down the hallway, in the direction of a screen door that opened flush on an alley. He was clawing at the wall. His gun lay at this feet. His left knee buckled and he went down on it.

A door was flung open and a hard-looking woman peered out, and instantly slammed her door shut again. A radio suddenly gained in volume beyond her door.

The big man got up off his left knee and the leg shook violently inside his trousers. He went down on both knees and got the gun into his hand and began to crawl toward the screen door. Then, suddenly he went down flat on his face and tried to crawl that way, grinding his face into the narrow hall runner.

Then he stopped crawling and stopped moving altogether. His body went limp and the hand holding the gun opened and the gun rolled out of it.

Steve hit the screen door and was out in the alley. A gray sedan was speeding toward the far end of it. He stopped, steadied himself and brought his gun up level, and the sedan whisked out of sight around the corner.

A man boiled out of another apartment house across the alley. Steve ran on, gesticulating back at him and pointing ahead. As he ran he slipped the gun back into his pocket. When he reached the end of the alley, the gray sedan was out of sight. Steve skidded around the wall onto the sidewalk, slowed to a walk and then stopped.

Half a block down a man finished parking a car, got out and went across the sidewalk to a lunchroom. Steve watched him go in, then straightened his hat and walked along the wall to the lunchroom.

He went in, sat at the counter, and ordered coffee. In a little while there were sirens.

Steve drank his coffee, asked for another cup and drank that. He lit a cigarette and walked down the long hill to Fifth, across to Hill, back to the foot of the Angel's Flight, and got his convertible out of a parking lot.

He drove out west, beyond Vermont, to the small hotel where he had taken a room that morning.

IV

Bill Dockery, floor manager of the Club Shalotte, teetered on his heels and yawned in the unlighted entrance to the dining room. It was a dead hour for business, late cocktail time, too early for dinner, and much too early for the real business of the club, which was high-class gambling.

Dockery was a handsome mug in a midnight-blue dinner jacket and a maroon carnation. He had a two-inch forehead under black lacquer hair, good features a little on the heavy side, alert brown eyes, and very long curly eyelashes, which he liked to let down over his eyes, to fool troublesome drunks into taking a swing at him.

The entrance door of the foyer was opened by the uniformed doorman and Steve Grayce came in.

Dockery said, "Ho-hum," tapped his teeth and leaned his weight forward. He walked across the lobby slowly to meet the guest. Steve stood just inside the doors and ranged his eyes over the high foyer walled with milky glass, lighted softly from behind. Molded in the glass were etchings of sailing ships, beasts of the jungle, Siamese pagodas, temples of Yucatan. The doors were square frames of chromium, like photo frames. The Club Shalotte had all the class there was, and the mutter of voices from the bar lounge on the left was not noisy. The faint Spanish music behind the voices was delicate as a carved fan.

Dockery came up and leaned his sleek head forward an inch. "May I help you?"

"King Leopardi around?"

Dockery leaned back again. He looked less interested. "The band-leader? He opens tomorrow night."

"I thought he might be around—rehearsing or something."

"Friend of his?"

"I know him. I'm not job-hunting, and I'm not a song plugger if that's what you mean."

Dockery teetered on his heels. He was tone-deaf and Leopardi meant no more to him than a bag of peanuts. He half smiled. "He was in the bar lounge a while ago." He pointed with his square rock-like chin. Steve Grayce went into the bar lounge.

It was about a third full, warm and comfortable and not too dark nor too light. The little Spanish orchestra was in an archway, playing with muted strings small seductive melodies that were more like memories than sounds. There was no dance floor. There was a long bar with comfortable seats, and there were small round composition-top tables, not too close together. A wall seat ran around three sides of the room. Waiters flitted among the tables like moths.

Steve Grayce saw Leopardi in the far corner, with a girl. There was an empty table on each side of him. The girl was a knockout.

She looked tall and her hair was the color of a brushfire seen through a dust cloud. On it, at the ultimate rakish angle, she wore a black velvet double-pointed beret with two artificial butterflies made of polka-dot feathers and fastened on with tall silver pins. Her dress was burgundy-red wool and the blue fox draped over one shoulder was at least two feet wide. Her eyes were large, smoke-blue, and looked bored. She slowly turned a small glass on the table top with a gloved left hand.

Leopardi faced her, leaning forward, talking. His shoulders looked very big in a shaggy, cream-colored sports coat. Above the neck of it his hair made a point on his brown neck. He laughed across the table as Steve came up and his laugh had a confident, sneering sound.

Steve stopped, then moved behind the next table. The movement caught Leopardi's eye. His head turned, he looked annoyed, and then his eyes got very wide and brilliant and his whole body turned slowly, like a mechanical toy.

Leopardi put both his rather small well-shaped hands down on the table, on either side of a highball glass. He smiled. Then he pushed his chair back and stood up. He put one finger up and touched his hairline mustache, with theatrical delicacy. Then he said drawlingly, but distinctly: "You son of a bitch!"

A man at a nearby table turned his head and scowled. A waiter who had started to come over stopped in his tracks, then faded back among the tables. The girl looked at Steve Grayce and then leaned back against the cushions of the wall seat and moistened the end of one bare finger on her right hand and smoothed a chestnut eyebrow.

Steve stood quite still. There was a sudden high flush on his cheekbones. He said softly: "You left something at the hotel last night. I think you ought to do something about it. Here."

He reached a folded paper out of his pocket and held it out. Leopardi took it, still smiling, opened it and read it. It was a sheet of yellow paper with torn pieces of white paper pasted on it. Leopardi crumpled the sheet and let it drop at his feet.

He took a smooth step toward Steve and repeated more loudly: "You son of a bitch!"

The man who had first looked around stood up sharply and turned. He said clearly: "I don't like that sort of language in front of my wife."

Without even looking at the man Leopardi said: "To hell with you and your wife."

The man's face got a dusky red. The woman with him stood up and grabbed a bag and a coat and walked away. After a moment's indecision the man followed her. Everybody in the place was staring now. The waiter who had faded back among the tables went through the doorway into the entrance foyer, walking very quickly.

Leopardi took another, longer step and slammed Steve Grayce on the jaw. Steve rolled with the punch and stepped back and put his hand down on another table and upset a glass. He turned to apologize to the couple at the table. Leopardi jumped forward very fast and hit him behind the ear.

Dockery came through the doorway, split two waiters like a banana skin and started down the room showing all his teeth.

Steve gagged a little and ducked away. He turned and said thickly: "Wait a minute, you fool—that isn't all of it—there's—"

Leopardi closed in fast and smashed him full on the mouth. Blood oozed from Steve's lip and crawled down the line at the corner of his mouth and glistened on his chin. The girl with the red hair reached for her bag, white-faced with anger, and started to get up from behind her table.

Leopardi turned abruptly on his heel and walked away. Dockery put out a hand to stop him. Leopardi brushed it aside and went on, went out of the lounge.

The tall red-haired girl put her bag down on the table again and dropped her handkerchief on the floor. She looked at Steve quietly, spoke quietly. "Wipe the blood off your chin before it drips on your shirt." She had a soft husky voice with a trill in it.

Dockery came up harsh-faced, took Steve by the arm and put weight on the arm. "All right, you! Let's go!"

Steve stood quite still, his feet planted, staring at the girl. He dabbed at his mouth with a handkerchief. He half smiled. Dockery couldn't move him an inch. Dockery dropped his hand, signaled two waiters and they jumped behind Steve, but didn't touch him.

Steve felt his lip carefully and looked at the blood on his handkerchief. He turned to the people at the table behind him and said: "I'm terribly sorry. I lost my balance."

The girl whose drink he had spilled was mopping her dress with a small fringed napkin. She smiled up at him and said: "It wasn't your fault."

The two waiters suddenly grabbed Steve's arms from behind. Dockery shook his head and they let go again. Dockery said tightly: "You hit him?"

"No."

"You say anything to make him hit you?"

"No."

The girl at the corner table bent down to get her fallen handkerchief. It took her quite a time. She finally got it and slid into the corner behind the table again. She spoke coldly.

"Quite right, Bill. It was just some more of King's sweet way with his public."

Dockery said, "Huh?" and swiveled his head on his thick hard neck. Then he grinned and looked back at Steve.

Steve said grimly: "He gave me three good punches, one from behind, without a return. You look pretty hard. See can you do it."

Dockery measured him with his eyes. He said evenly: "You win. I couldn't . . . Beat it!" he added sharply to the waiters. They went away. Dockery sniffed his carnation, and said quietly: "We don't go for brawls in here." He smiled at the girl again and went away, saying a word here and there at the tables. He went out through the foyer doors.

Steve tapped his lip, put his handkerchief in his pocket and stood searching the floor with his eyes.

The red-haired girl said calmly: "I think I have what you want—in my handkerchief. Won't you sit down?"

Her voice had a remembered quality, as if he had heard it before.

He sat down opposite her, in the chair where Leopardi had been sitting.

The red-haired girl said: "The drink's on me. I was with him."

Steve said, "Coke with a dash of bitters," to the waiter.

The waiter said: "Madame?"

"Brandy and soda. Light on the brandy, please." The waiter bowed and drifted away. The girl said amusedly: "Coke with a dash of bitters. That's what I love about Hollywood. You meet so many neurotics."

Steve stared into her eyes and said softly: "I'm an occasional drinker, the kind of guy who goes out for a beer and wakes up in Singapore with a full beard."

"I don't believe a word of it. Have you known the King long?"

"I met him last night. I didn't get along with him."

"I sort of noticed that." She laughed. She had a rich low laugh too.

"Give me that paper, lady."

"Oh, one of these impatient men. Plenty of time." The handkerchief with the crumpled yellow sheet inside it was clasped tightly in her gloved hand. Her middle right finger played with an eyebrow. "You're not in pictures, are you?"

"Hell, no."

"Same here. Me, I'm too tall. The beautiful men have to wear stilts in order to clasp me to their bosoms."

The waiter set the drinks down in front of them, made a grace note in the air with his napkin and went away.

Steve said quietly, stubbornly: "Give me that paper, lady."

"I don't like that 'lady' stuff. It sounds like cop to me."

"I don't know your name."

"I don't know yours. Where did you meet Leopardi?"

Steve sighed. The music from the little Spanish orchestra had a melancholy minor sound now and the muffled clicking of gourds dominated it.

Steve listened to it with his head on one side. He said: "The E string is a half-tone flat. Rather cute effect."

The girl stared at him with new interest. "I'd never have noticed that," she said. "And I'm supposed to be a pretty good singer. But you haven't answered my question."

He said slowly: "Last night I was house dick at the Carlton Hotel. They called me night clerk, but house dick was what I was. Leopardi stayed there and cut up too rough. I threw him out and got canned."

The girl said: "Ah. I begin to get the idea. He was being the King and you were being—if I might guess—a pretty tough order of house detective."

"Something like that. Now will you please—"

"You still haven't told me your name."

He reached for his wallet, took one of the brand-new cards out of it and passed it across the table. He sipped his drink while she read it.

"A nice name," she said slowly. "But not a very good address. And *Private investigator* is bad. It should have been *Investigations,* very small, in the lower left-hand corner."

"They'll be small enough," Steve grinned. "Now will you please—"

She reached suddenly across the table and dropped the crumpled ball of paper in his hand.

"Of course I haven't read it—and of course I'd like to. You do give me that much credit, I hope"—she looked at the card again, and added—"Steve. Yes, and your office should be in a Georgian or very modernistic building in the Sunset Eighties. Suite Something-or-other. And your clothes should be very jazzy. Very jazzy indeed, Steve. To be inconspicuous in this town is to be a busted flush."

He grinned at her. His deep-set black eyes had lights in them. She put the card away in her bag, gave her fur piece a yank, and drank about half of her drink. "I have to go." She signaled the waiter and paid the check. The waiter went away and she stood up.

Steve said sharply: "Sit down."

She stared at him wonderingly. Then she sat down again and leaned against the wall, still staring at him. Steve leaned across the table, asked "How well do *you* know Leopardi?"

"Off and on for years. If it's any of your business. Don't go masterful on me, for God's sake. I loathe masterful men. I once sang for him, but not for long. You can't just sing for Leopardi—if you get what I mean."

"You were having a drink with him."

She nodded slightly and shrugged. "He opens here tomorrow night. He was trying to talk me into singing for him again. I said no, but I may have to, for a week or two anyway. The man who owns the Club Shalotte also owns my contract—and the radio station where I work a good deal."

"Jumbo Walters," Steve said. "They say he's tough but square. I never met him, but I'd like to. After all I've got a living to get. Here."

He reached back across the table and dropped the crumpled paper. "The name was—"

"Dolores Chiozza."

Steve repeated it lingeringly. "I like it. I like your singing too. I've heard a lot of it. You don't oversell a song, like most of these high-money torchers." His eyes glistened.

The girl spread the paper on the table and read it slowly, without expression. Then she said quietly: "Who tore it up?"

"Leopardi, I guess. The pieces were in his wastebasket last night. I put them together, after he was gone. The guy has guts—or else he gets these things so often they don't register any more."

"Or else he thought it was a gag." She looked across the table levelly, then folded the paper and handed it back.

"Maybe. But if he's the kind of guy I hear he is—one of them is going to be on the level and the guy behind it is going to do more than just shake him down."

Dolores Chiozza said: "He's the kind of guy you hear he is."

"It wouldn't be hard for a woman to get to him then—would it—a woman with a gun?"

She went on staring at him. "No. And everybody would give her a big hand, if you ask me. If I were you, I'd just forget the whole thing. If he wants protection—Walters can throw more around him than the police. If he doesn't—who cares? I don't. I'm damn sure I don't."

"You're kind of tough yourself, Miss Chiozza—over some things."

She said nothing. Her face was a little white and more than a little hard.

Steve finished his drink, pushed his chair back, and reached for his hat. He stood up. "Thank you very much for the drink, Miss Chiozza. Now that I've met you I'll look forward all the more to hearing you sing again."

"You're damn formal all of a sudden," she said.

He grinned. "So long, Dolores."

"So long, Steve. Good luck—in the sleuth racket. If I hear of anything—"

He turned and walked among the tables out of the bar lounge.

V

In the crisp fall evening the lights of Hollywood and Los Angeles winked at him. Searchlight beams probed the cloudless sky as if searching for bombing planes.

Steve got his convertible out of the parking lot and drove it east along Sunset. At Sunset and Fairfax he bought an evening paper and pulled over to the curb to look through it. There was nothing in the paper about 118 Court Street.

He drove on and ate dinner at the little coffee shop beside his hotel and went to a movie. When he came out he bought a Home Edition of the *Tribune,* a morning sheet. They were in that—both of them.

Police thought Jake Stoyanoff might have strangled the girl, but she had not been attacked. She was described as a stenographer, unemployed at the moment. There was no picture of her. There was a picture of Stoyanoff that looked like a touched-up police photo. Police were looking for a man who had been talking to Stoyanoff just before he was shot. Several people said he was a tall man in a dark suit. That was all the description the police got—or gave out.

Steve grinned sourly, stopped at the coffee shop for a good-night cup of coffee and then went up to his room. It was a few minutes to eleven o'clock. As he unlocked his door the telephone started to ring.

He shut the door and stood in the darkness remembering where the phone was. Then he walked straight to it, catlike in the dark room, sat in an easy chair, and reached the phone up from the lower shelf of a small table. He held the one-piece to his ear and said: "Hello."

"Is this Steve? It was a rich, husky voice, low, vibrant. It held a note of strain.

"Yeah, this is Steve. I can hear you. I know who you are."

There was a faint dry laugh. "You'll make a detective after all. And it seems I'm to give you your first case. Will you come over to my place at once? Twenty-four-twelve Renfrew—North, there isn't any South—just half a block below Fountain. It's a sort of bungalow court. My house is the last in line, at the back."

Steve said: "Yes. Sure. What's the matter?"

There was a pause. A horn blared in the street outside the hotel. A wave of white light went across the ceiling from some car rounding the corner uphill. The low voice said very slowly: "Leopardi. I can't get rid of him. He's—he's passed out in my bedroom." Then a tinny laugh that didn't go with the voice at all.

Steve held the phone so tight his hand ached. His teeth clicked in the darkness. He said flatly, in a dull, brittle voice: "Yeah. It'll cost you twenty bucks."

"Of course. Hurry, please."

He hung up, sat there in the dark room breathing hard. He pushed his hat back on his head, then yanked it forward again with a vicious jerk and laughed out loud. "Hell," he said, "*That* kind of a dame."

Twenty-four-twelve Renfrew was not strictly a bungalow court. It was a staggered row of six bungalows, all facing the same way, but so arranged that no two of their front entrances overlooked each other. There was a brick wall at the back and beyond the brick wall a church. There was a long smooth lawn, moon-silvered.

The door was up two steps, with lanterns on each side and an iron-work grill over the peep hole. This opened to his knock and a girl's face looked out, a small oval face with a Cupid's-bow mouth, arched and plucked eyebrows, wavy brown hair. The eyes were like two fresh and shiny chestnuts.

Steve dropped a cigarette and put his foot on it. "Miss Chiozza. She's expecting me. Steve Grayce."

"Miss Chiozza has retired, sir," the girl said with a half-insolent twist to her lips.

"Break it up, kid. You heard me, I'm expected."

The wicket slammed shut. He waited, scowling back along the narrow moonlit lawn toward the street. O.K. So it was like that—well, twenty bucks was worth a ride in the moonlight anyway.

The lock clicked and the door opened wide. Steve went past the maid into a warm cheerful room, old-fashioned with chintz. The lamps were neither old nor new and there were enough of them—in the right places. There was a hearth behind a paneled copper screen, a davenport close to it, a bar-top radio in the corner.

The maid said stiffly: "I'm sorry, sir. Miss Chiozza forgot to tell me. Please have a chair." The voice was soft, and it might be cagey. The girl went off down the room—short skirt, sheer silk stockings, and four-inch spike heels.

Steve sat down and held his hat on his knee and scowled at the wall. A swing door creaked shut. He got a cigarette out and rolled it between his fingers and then deliberately squeezed it to a shapeless flatness of white paper and ragged tobacco. He threw it away from him, at the fire screen.

Dolores Chiozza came toward him. She wore green velvet lounging pajamas with a long gold-fringed sash. She spun the end of the sash as if she might be going to throw a loop with it. She smiled a slight artificial smile. Her face had a clean scrubbed look and her eyelids were bluish and they twitched.

Steve stood up and watched the green morocco slippers peep out under the pajamas as she walked. When she was close to him he lifted his eyes to her face and said dully: "Hello."

She looked at him very steadily, then spoke in a high, carrying voice. "I know it's late, but I knew you were used to being up all night. So I thought what we had to talk over—Won't you sit down?"

She turned her head very slightly, seemed to be listening for something.

Steve said: "I never go to bed before two. Quite all right."

She went over and pushed a bell beside the hearth. After a moment the maid came through the arch.

"Bring some ice cubes, Agatha. Then go along home. It's getting pretty late."

"Yes'm." The girl disappeared.

There was a silence then that almost howled till the tall girl took a cigarette absently out of a box, put it between her lips and Steve struck a match clumsily on his shoe. She pushed the end of the cigarette into the flame and her smoke-blue eyes were very steady on his black ones. She shook her head very slightly.

The maid came back with a copper ice bucket. She pulled a low Indian-brass tray-table between them before the davenport, put the ice-bucket on it, then a siphon, glasses, and spoons, and a triangular bottle that looked like good Scotch had come in it except that it was covered with silver filigree work and fitted with a stopper.

Dolores Chiozza said, "Will you mix a drink?" in a formal voice.

He mixed two drinks, stirred them, handed her one. She sipped it, shook her head. "Too light," she said. He put more whiskey in it and handed it back. She said, "Better," and leaned back against the corner of the davenport.

The maid came into the room again. She had a small rakish red hat on her wavy brown hair and was wearing a gray coat trimmed with nice fur. She carried a black brocade bag that could have cleaned out a fair-sized icebox. She said: "Good night, Miss Dolores."

"Good night, Agatha."

The girl went out the front door, closed it softly. Her heels clicked down the walk. A car door opened and shut distantly and a motor started. Its sound soon dwindled away. It was a very quiet neighborhood.

Steve put his drink down on the brass tray and looked levelly at the tall girl, said harshly: "That means she's out of the way?"

"Yes. She goes home in her own car. She drives me home from the studio in mine—when I go to the studio, which I did tonight. I don't like to drive a car myself."

"Well, what are you waiting for?"

The red-haired girl looked steadily at the paneled fire screen and the unlit log fire behind it. A muscle twitched in her cheek.

After a moment she said: "Funny that I called you instead of Walters.

He'd have protected me better than you can. Only he wouldn't have believed me. I thought perhaps you would. I didn't invite Leopardi here. So far as I know—we two are the only people in the world who know he's here."

Something in her voice jerked Steve upright.

She took a small crisp handkerchief from the breast pocket of the green velvet pajama-suit, dropped it on the floor, picked it up swiftly, and pressed it against her mouth. Suddenly, without making a sound, she began to shake like a leaf.

Steve said swiftly: "What the hell—I can handle that heel in my hip pocket. I did last night—and last night he had a gun and took a shot at me."

Her head turned. Her eyes were very wide and staring. "But it couldn't have been my gun," she said in a dead voice.

"Huh? Of course not—what—?"

"It's my gun tonight," she said and stared at him. "You said a woman could get to him with a gun very easily."

He just stared at her. His face was white now and he made a vague sound in his throat.

"He's not drunk, Steve," she said gently. "He's dead. In yellow pajamas—in my bed. With my gun in his hand. You didn't think he was just drunk—did you, Steve?"

He stood up in a swift lunge, then became absolutely motionless, staring down at her. He moved his tongue on his lips and after a long time he formed words with it. "Let's go look at him," he said in a hushed voice.

VI

The room was at the back of the house to the left. The girl took a key out of her pocket and unlocked the door. There was a low light on a table, and the venetian blinds were drawn. Steve went in past her silently, on cat feet.

Leopardi lay squarely in the middle of the bed, a large smooth silent man, waxy and artificial in death. Even his mustache looked phony. His half-open eyes, sightless as marbles, looked as if they had never seen. He lay on his back, on the sheet, and the bedclothes were thrown over the foot of the bed.

The King wore yellow silk pajamas, the slip-on kind, with a turned collar. They were loose and thin. Over his breast they were dark with blood that had seeped into the silk as if into blotting paper. There was a little blood on his bare brown neck.

Steve stared at him and said tonelessly: "The King in Yellow. I read a book with that title once. He liked yellow, I guess. I packed some of his stuff last night. And he wasn't yellow either. Guys like him usually are— or are they?"

The girl went over to the corner and sat down in a slipper chair and looked at the floor. It was a nice room, as modernistic as the living room was casual. It had a chenille rug, café-au-lait color, severely angled furniture in inlaid wood, and a trick dresser with a mirror for a top, a kneehole and drawers like a desk. It had a box mirror above and a semi-cylindrical frosted wall light set above the mirror. In the corner there was a glass table with a crystal greyhound on top of it, and a lamp with the deepest drum shade Steve had ever seen.

He stopped looking at all this and looked at Leopardi again. He pulled the King's pajamas up gently and examined the wound. It was directly over the heart and the skin was scorched and mottled there. There was not so very much blood. He had died in a fraction of a second.

A small Mauser automatic lay cuddled in his right hand, on top of the bed's second pillow.

"That's artistic," Steve said and pointed. "Yeah, that's a nice touch. Typical contact wound, I guess. He even pulled his pajama shirt up. I've heard they do that. A Mauser seven-six-three about. Sure it's your gun?"

"Yes." She kept on looking at the floor. "It was in a desk in the living room—not loaded. But there were shells. I don't know why. Somebody gave it to me once. I didn't even know how to load it."

Steve smiled. Her eyes lifted suddenly and she saw his smile and shuddered. "I don't expect anybody to believe that," she said. "We may as well call the police, I suppose."

Steve nodded absently, put a cigarette in his mouth and flipped it up and down with his lips that were still puffy from Leopardi's punch. He lit a match on his thumbnail, puffed a small plume of smoke and said quietly: "No cops. Not yet. Just tell it."

The red-haired girl said: "I sing at KFQC, you know. Three nights a week—on a quarter-hour automobile program. This was one of the nights. Agatha and I got home—oh, close to half-past ten. At the door I remembered there was no fizz-water in the house, so I sent her back to the liquor store three blocks away, and came in alone. There was a queer smell in the house. I don't know what it was. As if several men had been in here, somehow. When I came in the bedroom—he was exactly as he is now. I saw the gun and I went and looked and then I knew I was sunk. I didn't know what to do. Even if the police cleared me, everywhere I went from now on—"

Steve said sharply: "He got in here—how?"

"I don't know."

"Go on," he said.

"I locked the door. Then I undressed—with that on my bed. I went into the bathroom to shower and collect my brains, if any. I locked the door when I left the room and took the key. Agatha was back then, but I don't think she saw me. Well, I took the shower and it braced me up a bit. Then I had a drink and then I came in here and called you."

She stopped and moistened the end of a finger and smoothed the end of her left eyebrow with it. "That's all, Steve—absolutely all."

"Domestic help can be pretty nosy. This Agatha's nosier than most— or I miss my guess." He walked over to the door and looked at the lock. "I bet there are three or four keys in the house that knock this over." He went to the windows and felt the catches, looked down at the screens through the glass. He said over his shoulder, casually: "Was the King in love with you?"

Her voice was sharp, almost angry. "He never was in love with any woman. A couple of years back in San Francisco, when I was with his band for a while, there was some slap-silly publicity about us. Nothing to it. It's been revived here in the hand-outs to the press, to build up his opening. I was telling him this afternoon I wouldn't stand for it, that I wouldn't be linked with him in anybody's mind. His private life was filthy. It reeked. Everybody in the business knows that. And it's not a business where daisies grow very often."

Steve said: "Yours was the only bedroom he couldn't make?"

The girl flushed to the roots of her dusky red hair.

"That sounds lousy," he said. "But I have to figure the angles. That's about true, isn't it?"

"Yes—I suppose so. I wouldn't say the only one."

"Go on out in the other room and buy yourself a drink."

She stood up and looked at him squarely across the bed. "I didn't kill him, Steve. I didn't let him into this house tonight. I didn't know he was coming here, or had any reason to come here. Believe that or not. But something about this is wrong. Leopardi was the last man in the world to take his lovely life himself."

Steve said: "He didn't, angel. Go buy that drink. He was murdered. The whole thing is a frame—to get a cover-up from Jumbo Walters. Go on out."

He stood silent, motionless, until sounds he heard from the living room told him she was out there. Then he took out his handkerchief and loosened the gun from Leopardi's right hand and wiped it over carefully on the outside, broke out the magazine and wiped that off, spilled out the shells and wiped every one, ejected the one in the breech and wiped that. He reloaded the gun and put it back in Leopardi's dead hand and closed his fingers around it and pushed his index finger against the trigger. Then he let the hand fall naturally back on the bed.

He pawed through the bedclothes and found an ejected shell and wiped that off, put it back were he had found it. He put the handkerchief to his nose, sniffed it wryly, went around the bed to a clothes closet and opened the door.

"Careless of your clothes, boy," he said softly.

The rough cream-colored coat hung in there, on a hook, over dark gray slacks with a lizard-skin belt. A yellow satin shirt and a wine-colored tie dangled alongside. A handkerchief to match the tie flowed loosely four inches from the breast pocket of the coat. On the floor lay a pair of gazelle-leather nutmeg-brown sports shoes, and socks with garters. And there were yellow satin shorts with heavy black initials on them lying close by.

Steve felt carefully in the gray slacks and got out a leather keyholder. He left the room, went along the cross-hall and into the kitchen. It had a solid door, a good spring lock with a key stuck in it. He took it out and tried keys from the bunch in the keyholder, found none that fitted, put the other key back and went into the living room. He opened the front door, went outside and shut it again without looking at the girl huddled in a corner of the davenport. He tried keys in the lock, finally found the right one. He let himself back into the house, returned to the bedroom and put the keyholder back in the pocket of the gray slacks again. Then he went to the living room.

The girl was still huddled motionless, staring at him.

He put his back to the mantel and puffed a cigarette. "Agatha with you all the time at the studio?"

She nodded. "I suppose so. So he had a key. That was what you were doing, wasn't it?"

"Yes. Had Agatha long?"

"About a year."

"She steal from you? Small stuff, I mean?"

Dolores Chiozza shrugged wearily. "What does it matter? Most of them do. A little face cream or powder, a handkerchief, a pair of stockings once in a while. Yes, I think she stole from me. They look on that sort of thing as more or less legitimate."

"Not the nice ones, angel."

"Well—the hours were a little trying. I work at night, often get home very late. She's a dresser as well as a maid."

"Anything else about her? She use cocaine or weed? Hit the bottle? Ever have laughing fits?"

"I don't think so. What has she got to do with it, Steve?"

"Lady, she sold somebody a key to your apartment. That's obvious. You didn't give him one, the landlord wouldn't give him one, but Agatha had one. Check?"

Her eyes had a stricken look. Her mouth trembled a little, not much. A drink was untasted at her elbow. Steve bent over and drank some of it.

She said slowly: "We're wasting time, Steve. We have to call the police. There's nothing anybody can do. I'm done for as a nice person, even if not as a lady at large. They'll think it was a lovers' quarrel and I shot him and that's that. If I could convince them I didn't, then he shot himself in my bed, and I'm still ruined. So I might as well make up my mind to face the music."

Steve said softly: "Watch this. My mother used to do it."

He put a finger to his mouth, bent down, and touched her lips at the same spot with the same finger. He smiled, said: "We'll go to Walters— or you will. He'll pick his cops and the ones he picks won't go screaming through the night with reporters sitting in their laps. They'll sneak in quiet, like process servers. Walters can handle this. That was what was counted on. Me, I'm going to collect Agatha. Because I want a description of the guy she sold that key to—and I want it fast. And by the way, you owe me twenty bucks for coming over here. Don't let that slip your memory."

The tall girl stood up, smiling. "You're a kick, you are," she said. "What makes you so sure he was murdered?"

"He's not wearing his own pajamas. His have his initials on them. I packed his stuff last night—before I threw him out of the Carlton. Get dressed, angel—and get me Agatha's address."

He went into the bedroom and pulled a sheet over Leopardi's body, held it a moment above the still, waxen face before letting it fall.

"So long, guy," he said gently. "You were a louse—but you sure had music in you."

It was a small frame house on Brighton Avenue near Jefferson, in a block of small frame houses, all old-fashioned, with front porches. This one had a narrow concrete walk that the moon made whiter than it was.

Steve mounted the steps and looked at the light-edged shade of the wide front window. He knocked. There were shuffling steps and a woman opened the door and looked at him through the hooked screen—a dumpy elderly woman with frizzled gray hair. Her body was shapeless in a wrapper and her feet slithered in loose slippers. A man with a polished bald head and milky eyes sat in a wicker chair beside a table. He held his hands in his lap and twisted the knuckles aimlessly. He didn't look toward the door.

Steve said: "I'm from Miss Chiozza. Are you Agatha's mother?"

The woman said dully: "I reckon. But she ain't home, mister." The man in the chair got a handkerchief from somewhere and blew his nose. He snickered darkly.

Steve said: "Miss Chiozza's not feeling so well tonight. She was hoping Agatha would come back and stay the night with her."

The milky-eyed man snickered again, sharply. The woman said: "We dunno where she is. She don't come home. Pa'n me waits up for her to come home. She stays out till we're sick."

The old man snapped in a reedy voice: "She'll stay out till the cops get her one of these times."

"Pa's half blind," the woman said. "Makes him kinda mean. Won't you step in?"

Steve shook his head and turned his hat around in his hands like a bashful cowpuncher in a horse opera. "I've got to find her," he said. "Where would she go?"

"Out drinkin' liquor with cheap spenders," Pa cackled. "Pantywaists with silk handkerchiefs 'stead of neckties. If I had eyes, I'd strap her till she dropped." He grabbed the arms of his chair and the muscles knotted on the backs of his hands. Then he began to cry. Tears welled from his milky eyes and started through the white stubble on his cheeks. The woman went across and took the handkerchief out of his fist and wiped his face with it. Then she blew her nose on it and came back to the door.

"Might be anywhere," she said to Steve. "This is a big town, mister. I dunno where at to say."

Steve said dully: "I'll call back. If she comes in, will you hang onto her? What's your phone number?"

"What's the phone number, Pa?" the woman called back over her shoulder.

"I ain't sayin'," Pa snorted.

The woman said: "I remember now. South Two-four-five-four. Call any time. Pa'n me ain't got nothing to do."

Steve thanked her and went back down the white walk to the street and along the walk half a block to where he had left his car. He glanced idly across the way and started to get into his car, then stopped moving suddenly with his hand gripping the car door. He let go of that, took three steps sideways and stood looking across the street tight-mouthed.

All the houses in the block were much the same, but the one opposite had a FOR RENT placard stuck in the front window and a real-estate sign spiked into the small patch of front lawn. The house itself looked neglected, utterly empty, but in its little driveway stood a small neat black coupe.

Steve said under his breath: "Hunch. Play it up, Steve."

He walked almost delicately across the wide dusty street, his hand touching the hard metal of the gun in his pocket, and came up behind the little car, stood and listened. He moved silently along its left side, glanced back across the street, then looked in the car's open left-front window.

The girl sat almost as if driving, except that her head was tipped a little too much into the corner. The little red hat was still on her head, the gray coat, trimmed with fur, still around her body. In the reflected moonlight her mouth was strained open. Her tongue stuck out. And her chestnut eyes stared at the roof of the car.

Steve didn't touch her. He didn't have to touch her to look any closer to know there would be heavy bruises on her neck.

"Tough on women, these guys," he muttered.

The girl's big black brocade bag lay on the seat beside her, gaping open like her mouth—like Miss Marilyn Delorme's mouth, and Miss Marilyn Delorme's purple bag.

"Yeah—tough on women."

He backed away till he stood under a small palm tree by the entrance to the driveway. The street was as empty and deserted as a closed theater. He crossed silently to his car, got into it and drove away.

Nothing to it. A girl coming home alone late at night, stuck up and strangled a few doors from her own home by some tough guy. Very simple. The first prowl car that cruised that block—if the boys were half awake—would take a look the minute they spotted the FOR RENT sign. Steve tramped hard on the throttle and went away from there.

At Washington and Figueroa he went into an all-night drugstore and pulled shut the door of the phone booth at the back. He dropped his nickel and dialed the number of police headquarters.

He asked for the desk and said: "Write this down, will you sergeant? Brighton Avenue, thirty-two-hundred block, west side, in driveway of empty house. Got that much?"

"Yeah. So what?"

"Car with dead woman in it," Steve said, and hung up.

VII

Quillan, head day clerk and assistant manager of the Carlton Hotel, was on night duty, because Millar, the night auditor, was off for a week. It was half-past one and things were dead and Quillan was bored. He had done everything there was to do long ago, because he had been a hotel man for twenty years and there was nothing to it.

The night porter had finished cleaning up and was in his room beside the elevator bank. One elevator was lighted and open, as usual. The main lobby had been tidied up and the lights had been properly dimmed. Everything was exactly as usual.

Quillan was a rather short, rather thick-set man with clear bright toadlike eyes that seemed to hold a friendly expression without really having any expression at all. He had pale sandy hair and not much of it. His pale hands were clasped in front of him on the marble top of the desk. He was just the right height to put his weight on the desk without looking as if he were sprawling. He was looking at the wall across the entrance lobby, but he wasn't seeing it. He was half asleep, even though his eyes were wide open, and if the night porter struck a match behind his door, Quillan would know it and bang on his bell.

The brass-trimmed swing doors at the street entrance pushed open and Steve Grayce came in, a summer-weight coat turned up around his neck, his hat yanked low and a cigarette wisping smoke at the corner of his mouth. He looked very casual, very alert, and very much at ease. He strolled over to the desk and rapped on it.

"Wake up!" he snorted.

Quillan moved his eyes an inch and said: "All outside rooms with bath. But positively no parties on the eighth floor. Hiyah, Steve. So you finally got the ax. And for the wrong thing. That's life."

Steve said: "O.K. Have you got a new night man here?"

"Don't need one, Steve. Never did, in my opinion."

"You'll need one as long as old hotel men like you register floozies on the same corridor with people like Leopardi."

Quillan half-closed his eyes and then opened them to where they had been before. He said indifferently: "Not me, pal. But anybody can make a mistake. Millar's really an accountant—not a desk man."

Steve leaned back and his face became very still. The smoke almost hung at the tip of his cigarette. His eyes were like black glass now. He smiled a little dishonestly.

"And why was Leopardi put in an eight-dollar room on Eight instead of in a tower suite at twenty-eight per?"

Quillan smiled back at him. "I didn't register Leopardi, old sock. There were reservations in. I supposed they were what he wanted. Some guys don't spend. Any other questions, Mr. Grayce?"

"Yeah. Was Eight-fourteen empty last night?"

"It was on change, so it was empty. Something about the plumbing. Proceed."

"Who marked it on change?"

Quillan's bright fathomless eyes turned and became curiously fixed. He didn't answer.

Steve said: "Here's why. Leopardi was in Eight-fifteen and the two girls in Eight-eleven. Just Eight-thirteen between. A lad with a passkey could have gone into Eight-thirteen and turned both the bolt locks on the communicating doors. Then, if the folks in the two other rooms had done the same thing on their side, they'd have a suite set up."

"So what?" Quillan asked. "We got chiseled out of eight bucks, eh? Well, it happens, in better hotels than this." His eyes looked sleepy now.

Steve said: "Millar could have done that. But hell, it doesn't make sense. Millar's not that kind of a guy. Risk a job for a buck tip—phooey. Millar's no dollar pimp."

Quillan said: "All right, policeman. Tell me what's really on your mind."

"One of the girls in Eight-eleven had a gun. Leopardi got a threat letter yesterday—I don't know where or how. It didn't faze him, though. He tore it up. That's how I know. I collected the pieces from his basket. I suppose Leopardi's boys all checked out of here."

"Of course. They went to the Normandy."

"Call the Normandy, and ask to speak to Leopardi. If he's there, he'll still be at the bottle. Probably with a gang."

"Why?" Quillan asked gently.

"Because you're a nice guy. If Leopardi answers—just hang up." Steve paused and pinched his chin hard. "If he went out, try to find out where."

Quillan straightened, gave Steve another long quiet look and went behind the pebbled-glass screen. Steve stood very still, listening, one hand clenched at his side, the other tapping noiselessly on the marble desk.

In about three minutes Quillan came back and leaned on the desk again and said: "Not there. Party going on in his suite—they sold him a big one—and sounds loud. I talked to a guy who was fairly sober. He said Leopardi got a call around ten—some girl. He went out preening himself, as the fellow says. Hinting about a very juicy date. The guy was just lit enough to hand me all this."

Steve said: "You're a real pal. I hate not to tell you the rest. Well, I liked working here. Not much work at that."

He started toward the entrance doors again. Quillan let him get his hand on the brass handle before he called out. Steve turned and came back slowly.

Quillan said: "I heard Leopardi took a shot at you. I don't think it was noticed. It wasn't reported down here. And I don't think Peters fully realized that until he saw the mirror in Eight-fifteen. If you care to come back, Steve—"

Steve shook his head. "Thanks for the thought."

"And hearing about that shot," Quillan added, "made me remember something. Two years ago a girl shot herself in Eight-fifteen."

Steve straightened his back so sharply that he almost jumped. "What girl?"

Quillan looked surprised. "I don't know. I don't remember her real name. Some girl who had been kicked around all she could stand and wanted to die in a clean bed—alone."

Steve reached across and took hold of Quillan's arm. "The hotel files," he rasped. "The clippings, whatever there was in the papers will be in them. I want to see those clippings."

Quillan stared at him for a long moment. Then he said: "Whatever game you're playing, kid—you're playing it damn close to your vest. I will say that for you. And me bored stiff with a night to kill."

He reached along the desk and thumped the call bell. The door of the night porter's room opened and the porter came across the entrance lobby. He nodded and smiled at Steve.

Quillan said: "Take the board, Carl. I'll be in Mr. Peters's office for a little while."

He went to the safe and got keys out of it.

VIII

The cabin was high up on the side of the mountain, against a thick growth of digger pine, oak, and incense cedar. It was solidly built, with a stone chimney, shingled all over and heavily braced against the slope of the hill. By daylight the roof was green and the sides dark reddish brown and the window frames and draw curtains red. In the uncanny brightness of an all-night mid-October moon in the mountains, it stood out sharply in every detail, except color.

It was at the end of a road, a quarter of a mile from any other cabin. Steve rounded the bend toward it without lights, at five in the morning. He stopped his car at once, when he was sure it was the right cabin, got out and walked soundlessly along the side of the gravel road, on a carpet of wild iris.

On the road level there was a rough pine board garage, and from this a path went up to the cabin porch. The garage was unlocked. Steve swung the door open carefully, groped in past the dark bulk of a car and felt the top of the radiator. It was still warmish. He got a small flash out of his pocket and played it over the car. A gray sedan, dusty, the gas gauge low. He snapped the flash off, shut the garage door carefully and slipped into place the piece of wood that served for a hasp. Then he climbed the path to the house.

There was light behind the drawn red curtains. The porch was high and juniper logs were piled on it, with the bark still on them. The front door had a thumb latch and a rustic door handle above.

He went up, neither too softly nor too noisily, lifted his hand, sighed deep in his throat, and knocked. His hand touched the butt of the gun in the inside pocket of his coat, once, then came away empty.

A chair creaked and steps padded across the floor and a voice called out softly: "What is it?" Millar's voice.

Steve put his lips close to the wood and said: "This is Steve, George. You up already?"

They key turned, and the door opened. George Millar, the dapper night auditor of the Carlton House, didn't look dapper now. He was dressed in old trousers and a thick blue sweater with a roll collar. His feet were in ribbed wool socks and fleece-lined slippers. His clipped black mustache was a curved smudge across his pale face. Two electric bulbs burned in their sockets in a low beam across the room, below the slope of the high roof. A table lamp was lit and its shade was tilted to throw light on a big Morris chair with a leather seat and back-cushion. A fire burned lazily in a heap of soft ash on the big open hearth.

Millar said in his low, husky voice: "Hell's sake, Steve. Glad to see you. How'd you find us anyway? Come on in, guy."

Steve stepped through the door and Millar locked it. "City habit," he said grinning. "Nobody locks anything in the mountains. Have a chair. Warm your toes. Cold out at this time of night."

Steve said: "Yeah. Plenty cold."

He sat down in the Morris chair and put his hat and coat on the end of the solid wood table behind it. He leaned forward and held his hands out to the fire.

Millar said: "How the hell did you find us, Steve?"

Steve didn't look at him. He said quietly: "Not so easy at that. You told me last night your brother had a cabin up here—remember? So I had nothing to do, so I thought I'd drive up and bum some breakfast. The guy in the inn at Crestline didn't know who had cabins where. His trade is with people passing through. I rang up a garage man and he didn't know any Millar cabin. Then I saw a light come on down the street in a coal-and-wood yard and a little guy who is forest ranger and deputy sheriff and wood-and-gas dealer and half a dozen other things was getting his car out to go down to San Bernardino for some tank gas. A very smart little guy. The minute I said your brother had been a fighter he wised up. So here I am."

Millar pawed at his mustache. Bedsprings creaked at the back of the cabin somewhere. "Sure, he still goes under his fighting name—Gaff Talley. I'll get him up and we'll have some coffee. I guess you and me are both in the same boat. Used to working at night and can't sleep. I haven't been to bed at all."

Steve looked at him slowly and looked away. A burly voice behind them said: "Gaff is up. Who's your pal, George?"

Steve stood up casually and turned. He looked at the man's hands first. He couldn't help himself. They were large hands, well kept as to cleanliness, but coarse and ugly. One knuckle had been broken badly. He was a big man with reddish hair. He wore a sloppy bathrobe over outing-flannel pajamas. He had a leathery expressionless face, scarred over the cheekbones. There were fine white scars over his eyebrows and at the corners of his mouth. His nose was spread and thick. His whole face looked as if it had caught a lot of gloves. His eyes alone looked vaguely like Millar's eyes.

Millar said: "Steve Grayce. Night man at the hotel—until last night." His grin was a little vague.

Gaff Talley came over and shook hands. "Glad to meet you," he said. "I'll get some duds on and we'll scrape a breakfast off the shelves. I slept enough. George ain't slept any, the poor sap."

He went back across the room toward the door through which he'd come. He stopped there and leaned on an old photograph, put his big hand down behind a pile of records in paper envelopes. He stayed just like that, without moving.

Millar said: "Any luck on a job, Steve? Or did you try yet?"

"Yeah, In a way. I guess I'm a sap, but I'm going to have a shot at the private-agency racket. Not much in it unless I can land some publicity." He shrugged. Then he said very quietly: "King Leopardi's been bumped off."

Millar's mouth snapped wide open. He stayed like that for almost a minute—perfectly still, with his mouth open. Gaff Talley leaned against the wall and stared without showing anything in his face. Millar finally said: "Bumped off? Where? Don't tell me—"

"Not in the hotel, George. Too bad, wasn't it? In a girl's apartment. Nice girl too. She didn't entice him there. The old suicide gag—only it won't work. And the girl is my client."

Millar didn't move. Neither did the big man. Steve leaned his shoulders against the stone mantel. He said softly: "I went out to the Club Shalotte this afternoon to apologize to Leopardi. Silly idea, because I didn't owe him an apology. There was a girl there in the bar lounge with him. He took three socks at me and left. The girl didn't like that. We got rather clubby. Had a drink together. Then late tonight—last night—she called me up and said Leopardi was over at her place and—he was drunk and she couldn't get rid of him. I went there. Only he wasn't drunk. He was dead, in her bed, in yellow pajamas."

The big man lifted his left hand and roughed back his hair. Millar leaned slowly against the edge of the table, as if he were afraid the edge might be sharp enough to cut him. His mouth twitched under the clipped black mustache.

He said huskily: "That's lousy."

The big man said: "Well, for cryin' into a milk bottle."

Steve said: "Only they weren't Leopardi's pajamas. His had initials on them—big black initials. And his were satin, not silk. And although he had a gun in his hand—this girl's gun by the way—*he* didn't shoot himself in the heart. The cops will determine that. Maybe you birds never heard of the Lund test, with paraffin wax, to find out who did or didn't fire a gun recently. The killer ought to have been pulled in the hotel last night, in Room Eight-fifteen. I spoiled that by heaving him out on his neck before that black-haired girl in Eight-eleven could get to him. Didn't I, George?"

Millar said: "I guess you did—if I know what you're talking about."

Steve said slowly: "I think you know what I'm talking about, George. It would have been a kind of poetic justice if King Leopardi had been knocked off in Room Eight-fifteen. Because that was the room where a girl shot herself two years ago. A girl who registered as Mary Smith—but whose usual name was Eve Talley. And whose real name was Eve Millar."

The big man leaned heavily on the victrola and said thickly: "Maybe I ain't woke up yet. That sounds like it might grow up to be a dirty crack. We had a sister named Eve that shot herself in the Carlton. So what?"

Steve smiled a little crookedly. He said: "Listen, George. You told me Quillan registered those girls in Eight-eleven. *You* did. You told me Leopardi registered on Eight, instead of in a good suite, because he was tight. He wasn't tight. He just didn't care where he was put, as long as female company was handy. And you saw to that. You planned the whole thing, George. You even got Peters to write Leopardi at the Raleigh in Frisco and ask him to use the Carlton when he came down—because the same man owned it who owned the Club Shalotte. As if a guy like Jumbo Walters would care where a bandleader registered."

Millar's face was dead white, expressionless. His voice cracked. "Steve—for God's sake, Steve, what are you talking about? How the hell could I—"

"Sorry, kid. I liked working with you. I liked you a lot. I guess I still like you. But I don't like people who strangle women—or people who smear women in order to cover up a revenge murder."

"His hand shot up—and stopped. The big man said: "Take it easy—and look at this one."

Gaff's hand had come up from behind the pile of records. A Colt .45 was in it. He said between his teeth: "I always thought house dicks were just a bunch of cheap grafters. I guess I missed out on you. You got a few brains. Hell, I bet you even run out to One-eighteen Court Street. Right?"

Steve let his hand fall empty and looked straight at the big Colt. "Right. I saw the girl—dead—with your fingers marked into her neck. They can measure those, fella. Killing Dolores Chiozza's maid the same way was a mistake. They'll match up the two sets of marks, find out that your black-haired gun girl was at the Carlton last night, and piece the whole story together. With the information they get at the hotel they can't miss. I give you two weeks, if you beat it quick. And I mean quick."

Millar licked his dry lips and said softly: "There's no hurry, Steve. No hurry at all. Our job is done. Maybe not the best way, maybe not the nicest way, but it wasn't a nice job. And Leopardi was the worst kind of a louse. We loved our sister, and he made a tramp out of her. She was a wide-eyed kid that fell for a flashy greaseball, and the greaseball went up in the world and threw her out on her ear for a red-headed torcher who was more his kind. He threw her out and broke her heart and she killed herself."

Steve said harshly: "Yeah—and what were you doing all that time—manicuring your nails?"

"We weren't around when it happened. It took us a little time to find out the why of it."

Steve said: "So that was worth killing four people for, was it? And as for Dolores Chiozza, she wouldn't have wiped her feet on Leopardi—then, or any time since. But you had to put her in the middle too, with your rotten little revenge murder. You make me sick, George. Tell your big tough brother to get on with his murder party."

The big man grinned and said: "Nuff talk, George. See has he a gat—and don't get behind him or in front of him. This bean-shooter goes on through."

Steve stared at the big man's .45. His face was hard as white bone. There was a thin cold sneer on his lips and his eyes were cold and dark.

Millar moved softly in his fleece-lined slippers. He came around the end of the table and went close to Steve's side and reached out a hand to tap his pockets. He stepped back and pointed: "In there."

Steve said softly: "I must be nuts. I could have taken you then, George."

Gaff Talley barked: "Stand away from him."

He walked solidly across the room and put the big Colt against Steve's stomach hard. He reached up with his left hand and worked the Detective Special from the inside breast pocket. His eyes were sharp on Steve's eyes. He held Steve's gun out behind him. "Take this, George."

Millar took the gun and went over beyond the big table again and stood at the far corner of it. Gaff Talley backed away from Steve.

"You're through, wise guy," he said. "You got to know that. There's only two ways outa these mountains and we gotta have time. And maybe you didn't tell nobody. See?"

Steve stood like a rock, his face white, a twisted half-smile working at the corners of his lips. He stared hard at the big man's gun and his stare was faintly puzzled.

Millar said: "Does it have to be that way, Gaff?" His voice was a croak now, without tone, without its usual pleasant huskiness.

Steve turned his head a little and looked at Millar. "Sure it has, George. You're just a couple of cheap hoodlums after all. A couple of nasty-minded sadists playing at being revengers of wronged girlhood. Hillbilly stuff. And right this minute you're practically cold meat—cold, rotten meat."

Gaff Talley laughed and cocked the big revolver with his thumb. "Say your prayers, guy," he jeered.

Steve said grimly: "What makes you think you're going to bump me off with that thing? No shells in it, strangler. Better try to take me the way you handle women—with your hands."

The big man's eyes flicked down, clouded. Then he roared with laughter. "Geez, the dust on that one must be a foot thick," he chuckled. "Watch."

He pointed the big gun at the floor and squeezed the trigger. The firing pin clicked dryly—on an empty chamber. The big man's face convulsed.

For a short moment nobody moved. Then Gaff turned slowly on the balls of his feet and looked at his brother. He said almost gently: "You, George?"

Millar licked his lips and gulped. He had to move his mouth in and out before he could speak.

"Me, Gaff. I was standing by the window when Steve got out of his car down the road, I saw him go into the garage. I knew the car would still be warm. There's been enough killing, Gaff. Too much. So I took the shells out of your gun."

Millar's thumb moved back the hammer on the Detective Special. Gaff's eyes bulged. He stared fascinated at the snub-nosed gun. Then he lunged violently toward it, flailing with the empty Colt. Millar braced himself and stood very still and said dimly, like an old man: "Good-bye, Gaff."

The gun jumped three times in his small neat hand. Smoke curled lazily from its muzzle. A piece of burned log fell over in the fireplace.

Gaff Talley smiled queerly and stooped and stood perfectly still. The gun dropped at his feet. He put his big heavy hands against his stomach, said slowly, thickly: " 'S all right, kid. 'S all right, I guess . . . I guess I . . ."

His voice trailed off and his legs began to twist under him. Steve took three long quick silent steps, and slammed Millar hard on the angle of the jaw. The big man was still falling—as slowly as a tree falls.

Millar spun across the room and crashed against the end wall and a blue-and-white plate fell off the plate-molding and broke. The gun sailed from his fingers. Steve dived for it and came up with it. Millar crouched and watched his brother.

Gaff Talley bent his head to the floor and braced his hands and then lay down quietly, on his stomach, like a man who was very tired. He made no sound of any kind.

Daylight showed at the windows, around the red glass-curtains. The piece of broken log smoked against the side of the hearth and the rest of the fire was a heap of soft gray ash with a glow at its heart.

Steve said dully: "You saved my life, George—or at least you saved a lot of shooting. I took the chance because what I wanted was evidence. Step over there to the desk and write it all out and sign it."

Millar said: "Is he dead?"

"He's dead, George. You killed him. Write that too."

Millar said quietly: "It's funny. I wanted to finish Leopardi myself, with my own hands, when he was at the top, when he had the farthest to fall. Just finish him and then take what came. But Gaff was the guy who wanted it done cute. Gaff, the tough mug who never had any education and never dodged a punch in his life, wanted to do it smart and figure angles. Well, maybe that's why he owned property, like that apartment house on Court Street that Jake Stoyanoff managed for him. I don't know how he got to Dolores Chiozza's maid. It doesn't matter that much, does it?"

Steve said: "Go and write it. You were the one called Leopardi up and pretended to be the girl, huh?"

Millar said: "Yes. I'll write it all down, Steve. I'll sign it and then you'll let me go—just for an hour. Won't you, Steve? Just an hour's start. That's not much to ask of an old friend, is it, Steve?"

Millar smiled. It was a small, frail, ghostly smile. Steve bent beside the big sprawled man and felt his neck artery. He looked up, said: "Quite dead . . . Yes, you get an hour's start, George—if you write it all out."

Millar walked softly over to a tall oak highboy desk, studded with tarnished brass nails. He opened the flap and sat down and reached for a pen. He unscrewed the top from a bottle of ink and began to write in his neat, clear accountant's handwriting.

Steve Grayce sat down in front of the fire and lit a cigarette and stared at the ashes. He held the gun with his left hand on his knee. Outside the cabin, birds began to sing. Inside there was no sound but the scratching pen.

IX

The sun was well up when Steve left the cabin, locked it up, walked down the steep path and along the narrow gravel road to his car. The garage was empty now. The gray sedan was gone. Smoke from another cabin floated lazily above the pines and oaks half a mile away. He started his car, drove it around a bend, past two old boxcars that had been converted into cabins, then on to a main road with a stripe down the middle and so up the hill to Crestline.

He parked on the main street before the Rim-of-the-World Inn, had a cup of coffee at the counter, then shut himself in a phone booth at the back of the empty lounge. He had the long-distance operator get Jumbo Walters' number in Los Angeles, then called the owner of the Club Shalotte.

A voice said silkily: "This is Mr. Walters' residence."

"Steve Grayce. Put him on, if you please."

"One moment, please." A click, another voice, not so smooth and much harder. "Yeah?"

"Steve Grayce. I want to speak to Mr. Walters."

"Sorry. I don't seem to know you. It's a little early, amigo. What's your business?"

"Did he go to Miss Chiozza's place?"

"Oh." A pause. "The shamus. I get it. Hold the line, pal."

Another voice now—lazy, with the faintest color of Irish in it. "You can talk, son. This is Walters."

"I'm Steve Grayce. I'm the man—"

"I know all about that, son. The lady is O.K., by the way. I think she's asleep upstairs. Go on."

"I'm at Crestline—top of the Arrowhead grade. Two men murdered Leopardi. One was George Millar, night auditor at the Carlton Hotel. The other his brother, an ex-fighter named Gaff Talley. Talley's dead— shot by his brother. Millar got away—but he left me a full confession signed, detailed, complete."

Walters said slowly: "You're a fast worker, son—unless you're just plain crazy. Better come in here fast. Why did they do it?"

"They had a sister."

Walters repeated quietly: "They had a sister . . . What about this fellow that got away? We don't want some hick sheriff or publicity-hungry county attorney to get ideas—"

Steve broke in quietly: "I don't think you'll have to worry about that, Mr. Walters. I think I know where he's gone."

He ate breakfast at the inn, not because he was hungry, but because he was weak. He got into his car again and started down the long smooth grade from Crestline to San Bernardino, a broad paved boulevard skirting the edge of a sheer drop into the deep valley. There were places where the road went close to the edge, white guard-fences alongside.

Two miles below Crestline was the place. The road made a sharp turn around a shoulder of the mountain. Cars were parked on the gravel off the pavement—several private cars, an official car, and a wrecking car. The white fence was broken through and men stood around the broken place looking down.

Eight hundred feet below, what was left of a gray sedan lay silent and crumpled in the morning sunshine.

The Pink Caterpillar

Author: Anthony Boucher (1911–1968)

Detective: Fergus O'Breen (1939)

In 1970, when the first Anthony Boucher Memorial Mystery Convention was held, no one present needed to be told who Anthony Boucher was. Born William Anthony Parker White, he had written novels, short stories, and radio plays in the mystery field; he had been the founding editor of *The Magazine of Fantasy and Science Fiction;* and perhaps most significantly, he had been the most influential American critic of detective fiction via his long-running "Criminals at Large" column in the *New York Times Book Review.* With Bouchercon having become a bigger and bigger event, thirty years later some of the attendees probably have a much looser grasp of whom this annual event was named after.

Boucher was almost equally important in the mystery and fantasy/science-fiction fields. Appropriately, he was one of the few writers to confront a fictional detective created for "mundane" mysteries with fantastic or science-fictional problems. Most of the short-story appearances of private eye Fergus O'Breen, who appeared in Boucher's *The Case of the Crumpled Knave* (1939) and two subsequent novels, make this genre crossover. "The Pink Caterpillar" may be the best of these.

A nd their medicine men can do time travel, too," Norm Harker said. "At least, that's the firm belief everywhere on the island: a *tualala* can go forward in time and bring you back any single item you specify, for a price. We used to spend the night watches speculating on what would be the one best thing to order."

Norman hadn't told us the name of the island. The stripe and a half on his sleeve lent him discretion, and Tokyo hadn't learned yet what secret installations the Navy had been busy with on that minute portion of the South Pacific. He couldn't talk about the installations, of course;

but the island had provided him with plenty of other matters to keep us entertained, sitting up there in the Top of the Mark.

"What would you order, Tony," he asked, "with a carte blanche like that on the future?"

"How far future?"

"They say a *tualala* goes to one hundred years from date: no more, no less."

"Money wouldn't work," I mused. "Jewels maybe. Or a gadget—any gadget—and you could invent it as of now and make a fortune. But then it might depend on principles not yet worked out . . . Or the *Gone With the Wind* of the twenty-first century—but publish it now and it might lay an egg. Can you imagine today's bestsellers trying to compete with Dickens? No . . . it's a tricky question. What did you try?"

"We finally settled on Hitler's tombstone. Think of the admission tickets we could sell to see that!"

"And—?"

"And nothing. We couldn't pay the *tualala*'s price. For each article fetched through time he wanted one virgin from the neighboring island. We felt the staff somehow might not understand if we went collecting them. There's always a catch to magic," Norman concluded lightly.

Fergus said "Uh-huh" and nodded gravely. He hadn't been saying much all evening—just sitting there and looking out over the panorama of the bay by night, a glistening joy now that the dimout was over, and listening. I still don't know the sort of work he's been doing, but it's changing him, toning him down.

But even a toned-down Irishman can stand only so much silence, and there was obviously a story on his lips. Norm asked, "You've been running into magic too?"

"Not lately." He held his glass up to the light and watched his drink. "Damned if I know why writers call a highball an amber liquid," he observed. "Start a cliché and it sticks . . . Like about detectives being hardheaded realists. Didn't you ever stop to think that there's hardly another profession outside the clergy that's so apt to run up against the things beyond realism? Why do you call in a detective? Because something screwy's going on and you need an explanation. And if there isn't an explanation . . .

"This was back a ways. Back when I didn't have anything worse to deal with than murderers and, once, a werewolf. But he was a hell of a swell guy. The murderers I used to think were pretty thorough low-lifes, but now . . . Anyway, this was back then. I was down in Mexico putting the finishing touches on that wacky business of the Aztec Calendar when I heard from Dan Rafetti. I think you know him, Tony; he's an investigator for Southwest National Life Insurance, and he's thrown some business my way now and then, like the Solid Key case.

"This one sounded interesting. Nothing spectacular, you understand, and probably no money to speak of. But the kind of crazy unexplained little detail that stirs up the O'Breen curiosity. Very simple: Southwest gets a claim from a beneficiary. One of their customers died down in Mexico and his sister wants the cash. They send to the Mexican authorities for a report on his death and it was heart failure and that's that. Only the policy is made out to Mr. Frank Miller and the Mexican report refers to him as *Dr.* F. Miller. They ask the sister and she's certain he hasn't any right to such a title. So I happen to be right near Tlichotl, where he died, and would I please kind of nose around and see was there anything phony, like maybe an imposture. Photographs and fingerprints, from a Civil Service application he once made, enclosed."

"Nice businesslike beginning," Norman said.

Fergus nodded. "That's the way it started: all very routine, yours-of-the-27th-*ult*. Prosaic, like. And Tlichotl was prosaic enough too. Maybe to a tourist it'd be picturesque, but I'd been kicking around these Mexican mountain towns long enough so one seemed as commonplace as another. Sort of a montage of flat houses and white trousers and dogs and children and an old church and an almost-as-old pulquería and one guy who plays a hell of a guitar on Saturday nights.

"Tlichotl wasn't much different. There was a mine near it, and just out of town was a bunch of drab new frame houses for the American engineers. Everybody in town worked in the mine—all pure Indians, with those chaste profiles straight off of the Aztec murals that begin to seem like the only right and normal human face when you've seen 'em long enough.

"I went to the doctor first. He was the government sanitation agent and health instructor, and the town looked like he was doing a good job. His English was better than my Spanish, and he was glad I liked tequila. Yes, he remembered Dr. Miller. He checked up his records and announced that Dr. M. died on November 2. It was January when I talked to him. Simple death: heart failure. He'd had several attacks in past weeks, and the doctor had expected him to go any day. All of a sudden a friend he hadn't seen in years showed up in town unannounced, and the shock did it. Any little thing might have.

"The doctor wasn't a stupid man, or a careless one. I was willing to take his word that the death had been natural. And maybe I ought to put in here, before your devious minds start getting ahead of me, that as far as I ever learned he was absolutely right. Common-or-garden heart failure, and that didn't fit into any picture of insurance fraud. But there was still the inconsistency of the title, and I went on, 'Must've been kind of nice for you to have a colleague here to talk with?'

"The doctor frowned a little at that. It seemed he'd been sort of hurt by Dr. Miller's attitude. Had tried to interest him in some researches he was doing with an endemic variant of undulant fever, which he'd practically succeeded in wiping out. But the North American 'doctor' just didn't give a damn. No fraternal spirit; no scientific curiosity; nothing.

"I gathered they hadn't been very friendly, my doctor and 'Dr.' Miller. In fact, Miller hadn't been intimate with anybody, not even the other North Americans at the mine. He liked the Indians and they liked him, though they were a little scared of him on account of the skeleton— apparently an anatomical specimen and the first thing I'd heard of to go with his assumed doctorate. He had a good short-wave radio, and he listened to music on that and sketched a little and read and went for short hikes. It sounded like a good life, if you like a lonely one. They might know a little more about him at the pulquería; he stopped there for a drink sometimes. And the widow Sánchez had kept house for him; she might know something.

"I tried the widow first. She wore a shapeless black dress that looked as though she'd started mourning Mr. Sánchez ten years before, but her youngest child wasn't quite walking yet. She'd liked her late employer, might he rest in peace. He had been a good man, and so little trouble. No, he never gave medicine to anybody; that was the job of the señor médico from Mexico City. No, he never did anything with bottles. No, he never received much mail and surely not with money in it, for she had often seen him open his few letters. yes, indeed he was a médico; did he not have the bones, the *esquéleto,* to prove it?

"And if the señor interested himself so much for el doctor Miller, perhaps the señor would care to see his house? It was untouched, as he'd left it. No one lived there now. No, it was not haunted—at least, not that anyone knew, though no man knows such things. It was only that no one new ever comes to live in Tlichotl, and an empty house stays empty.

"I looked the house over. It had two rooms and a kitchen and a tiny patio. 'Dr.' Miller's things were undisturbed; no one had claimed them and it was up to time and heat and insects to take care of them. There was a radio and beside it the sketching materials. One wall was a bookcase, well filled, mostly with sixteenth- and seventeenth-century literature in English and Spanish. The books had been faithfully read. There

were a few recent volumes, mostly on travel or on Mexican Indian culture, and a few magazines. No medical books or periodicals.

"Food, cooking utensils, clothing, a pile of sketches (good enough so
you'd feel all right when you'd done them and bad enough so you
wouldn't feel urged to exhibit them), pipes and tobacco—these just
about made up the inventory. No papers to speak of, just a few personal
letters, mostly from his sister (and beneficiary). No instruments or medi-
cines of any kind. Nothing whatsoever out of the way—not even the
skeleton.

"I'd heard about that twice, so I asked what had become of it. The
sons of the mining engineers, the young demons, had stolen it to celebrate a gringo holiday, which I gathered had been Halloween. They had
built an enormous bonfire, and the skeleton had fallen in and been
consumed. The doctor Miller had been very angry; he had suffered one
of his attacks then, almost as bad as the one that gave him death, may
the Lord hold him in His kindness. But now it was time for a mother to
return and feed her brood; and her house was mine, and would the
señor join in her poor supper?

"The beans were good and the tortillas wonderful; and the youngest
children hadn't ever seen red hair before and had some pointed questions to ask me about mine. And in the middle of the meal something
suddenly went *click* in my brain and I knew why Frank Miller had called
himself 'doctor.' "

Fergus paused and beckoned to a waiter.

Norman said, "Is that all?"

"For the moment. I'm giving you boys a chance to scintillate. There
you have all the factors up to that point. All right: *Why* was Miller
calling himself 'doctor'?"

"He wasn't practicing," Norman said slowly. "And he wasn't even
running a fake medical racket by mail, as people have done from Mexico to avoid the U.S. Post Office Department."

"And," I added, "he hadn't assumed the title to impress people, to
attain social standing, because he had nothing to do with his neighbors.
And he wasn't carrying on any experiments or research, which he might
have needed the title in writing up. So he gained nothing in cash or
prestige. All right, what other reason is there for posing as a doctor?"

"Answer," said Fergus leisurely: "He wasn't posing as a doctor.
Look; you might pose as a doctor with no props at all, thinking no one
would come in your house but the housekeeper. Or you might stage an
elaborate front complete with instrument cabinets and five-pound

books. But you wouldn't try it with just one prop, an anatomical skeleton."

Norman and I looked at each other and nodded. It made sense. "Well then?" I asked.

The fresh drinks came, and Fergus said, "My round. Well then, the skeleton was not a prop for the medical pose. Quite the reverse. Turn it around and it makes sense. He called himself a doctor *to account for the skeleton.*"

I choked on my first sip, and Norman spluttered a little, too. Fergus went on eagerly, with that keen light in his green eyes, "You can't hide a skeleton in a tiny house. The housekeeper's bound to see it, and word gets around. Miller liked the Indians and he liked peace. He had to account for the skeleton. So he became a 'doctor.' "

"But that—" Norman objected. "That's no answer. That's just another question."

"I know," said Fergus. "But that's the first step in detection: to find the right question. And that's it: *Why does a man live with a skeleton?*"

We were silent for a bit. The Top of the Mark was full of glasses and smoke and uniforms; and despite the uniforms it seemed a room set aside that was not a part of a world at war—still less of a world in which a man might live with a skeleton.

"Of course you checked the obvious answer," I said at last.

Fergus nodded. "He couldn't very well have been a black magician, if that's what you mean, or white either. Not a book or a note in the whole place dealing with the subject. No wax, chalk, incense, or what-have-you. The skeleton doesn't fit any more into a magical pattern than into a medical."

"The Dead Beloved?" Norman suggested, hesitantly uttering the phrase in mocking capitals. "Rose-for-Emily stuff? A bit grisly, but not inconceivable."

"The Mexican doctor saw the skeleton. It was a man's, and not a young one."

"Then he was planning an insurance fraud—burn the house down and let the bones be found while he vanished."

"A, you don't burn adobe. B, you don't let the skeleton be seen by the doctor who'll examine it later. C, it was that of a much shorter man than Miller."

"A writer?" I ventured wildly. "I've sometimes thought myself a skeleton might be useful in the study—check where to inflict skull wounds and such."

"With no typewriter, no manuscripts, and very little mail?"

Norman's face lit up. "You said he sketched. Maybe he was working on a modern *Totentanz*—Dance of Death allegory. Holbein and Dürer must have had a skeleton or two around."

"I saw his sketches. Landscapes only."

I lit my pipe and settled back. "All right. We've stooged and we don't know. Now tell us why a man keeps house with a set of bones." My tone was lighter than necessary.

Fergus said, "I won't go into all the details of my investigation. I saw damned near every adult in Tlichotl and most of the kids. And I pieced out what I think is the answer. But I think you can gather it from the evidence of four people.

"First, Jim Reilly, mining engineer. Witness deposeth and saith he was on the main street, if you can call it that, of Tlichotl on November 2. He saw a stranger, 'swarthy but not a Mex,' walk up to Miller and say, 'Frank!' Miller looked up and was astonished. The stranger said, 'Sorry for the delay. But it took me a little time to get here.' And he hadn't finished the sentence before Miller dropped dead. Queried about the stranger, witness says he gave his name as Humbert Targ; he stayed around town for a few days for the funeral and then left. Said he'd known Miller a long time ago—never quite clear where, but seemingly in the South Seas, as we used to say before we learned to call it the South Pacific. Asked for description, witness proved pretty useless: medium height, medium age, dark complexion . . . Only helpful details: stranger wore old clothes ('Shabby?' 'No, just old.' 'Out-of-date?' 'I guess so.' 'How long ago? What kind?' 'I don't know. Just old—funny-looking') and had only one foot ('One leg?' 'No, two legs, just one foot.' 'Wooden peg?' 'No, just empty trouser cuff. Walked with crutches').

"Second witness, Father Gonzaga, and it's a funny sensation to be talking to a priest who wears just a plain business suit. He hadn't known 'Dr.' Miller well, though he'd said a mass for his soul. But one night Miller had come from the pulquería and insisted on talking to him. He wanted to know how you could ever get right with God and yourself if you'd done someone a great wrong and there was no conceivable way you could make it up to him. The padre asked why, was the injured person dead? Miller hesitated and didn't answer. He's alive, then? Oh no, no! Restitution could surely be made to the next of kin if it were a money matter? No, it was . . . personal. Father's advice was to pray for the injured party's soul and for grace to avoid such temptation another time. I don't much see what else he could have suggested, but Miller wasn't satisfied."

I wasn't hearing the noise around us any more. Norman was leaning forward too, and I saw in his eyes that he too was beginning to feel the essential *wrong*ness of the case the detective had stumbled on.

"Third witness, the widow Sánchez. She told me about the skeleton when I came back for more beans and brought a bottle of red wine to go with them—which it did, magnificently. 'Dr.' Miller had treasured his skeleton very highly. She was not even supposed to dust it. But once she forgot, and a finger came off. This was in October. She thought he might not notice a missing finger, where she knew she'd catch it if he found a loose one, so she burned the bones in the charcoal brazier over which she fried her tortillas. Two days later she was serving the doctor his dinner when she saw a pink caterpillar crawling near his place. She'd never seen a pink caterpillar before. She flicked it away with a napkin; but not before the 'doctor' saw it. He jumped up from the table and ran to look at the skeleton and gave her a terrific bawling out. After that she saw the caterpillar several times. It was about then that Miller started having those heart attacks. Whenever she saw the caterpillar it was crawling around the 'doctor.' I looked at her a long time while she finished the wine, and then I said, 'Was it a caterpillar?' She crossed herself and said 'No.' She said it very softly, and that was all she said that night."

I looked down at the table. My hand lay there, and the index finger was tapping gently. We seemed to be sitting in quite a draft, and I shuddered.

"Fourth witness, Timmy Reilly, twelve-year-old son to Jim. He thought it was a great lark that they'd stolen the old boy's bones for Halloween. Fun and games. These dopes down here didn't know from nothin' about Halloween, but him and the gang, they sure showed 'em. But I could see he was holding something back. I made a swap. He could wear my detective badge (which I've never worn yet) for a whole day if he'd tell me what else he knew. So he showed it to me: the foot that he'd rescued when the skeleton was burned up. He'd tried to grab the bones as they toppled over and all he could reach was the heel. He had the whole foot, well articulated and lousy with tarsals and stuff. So I made a better deal: he could have the badge for keeps (with the numbers scratched out a little) if he'd let me burn the foot. He let me."

Fergus paused, and it all began to click into place. The pattern was clear, and it was a pattern that should not be.

"You've got it now?" Fergus asked quietly. "All I needed to make it perfect was Norm's story. There had to be such a thing as *tualala*, with such powers as theirs. I'd deduced them, but it's satisfying to have them confirmed.

"Miller had had an enemy, many years before, a man who had sworn to kill him. And Miller had known a *tualala,* back there in the South Seas. And when he'd asked himself what would be the best single item to bring back from the future, he knew the answer: *his enemy's skeleton.*

It wasn't murder. He probably had scruples about that. He sounded like a good enough guy in a way, and maybe his *tualala* asked a more possible price. The skeleton was the skeleton that would exist a hundred years from now, no matter how or when the enemy had died. But bring that skeleton back here and the enemy can no longer exist. His skeleton can't be two places at once. You've got the dry dead bones. What becomes of the live ones with flesh on them? You don't know. You don't care. You're safe. You're free to lead the peaceful life you want with Indians and mountain scenery and your scratch pad and your radio. And your skeleton.

"You've got to be careful of that skeleton. If it ceases to exist in time, the full-fleshed living skeleton might return. You mustn't even take a chance on the destruction of a little piece. You lose a finger, and a finger returns—a pink thing that crawls, and always toward you.

"Then the skeleton itself is destroyed. You're in mortal terror, but nothing happens. Two days go by and it's November 2. You know what the Second of November is in Latin America? It's All Souls' Day in the Church, and they call it the *Día de los difuntos*—the Day of the Dead. But it isn't a sad day outside of church. You go to the cemetery and it's picnic. There are skeletons everywhere, same like Halloween—bright, funny skeletons that never hurt anybody. And there are skulls to wear and skulls to drink out of and bright white sugar skulls with pink and green trimmings to eat. All along every street are vendors with skulls and skeletons for every purpose, and every kid you see has a sugar skull to suck. Then at night you go to the theater to see *Don Juan Tenorio* where the graves open and the skeletons dance, while back home the kids are howling themselves to sleep because death is so indigestible.

"Of course, there's no theater in Tlichotl, but you can bet there'd be skulls and skeletons—some of them dressed up like Indian gods for the Christian feast, some of them dancing on wires, some of them vanishing down small gullets. And there you are in the midst of skeletons, skeletons everywhere, and your skeleton is gone and all your safety with it. And there on the street with all the skulls staring at you, you see him and he isn't a skull any more. He's Humbert Targ and he's explaining that it took him a little time to get here.

"Wouldn't *you* drop dead?" Fergus concluded simply.

My throat felt dry as I asked, "What did you tell the insurance company?"

"Much like Norm's theory. Man was an artist, had an anatomical model, gave out he was a doctor to keep the natives from conniption fits. Collected expenses, but no bonus: the prints they sent me fitted what I found in his home, and they had to pay the sister."

Norman cleared his throat. "I'm beginning to hope they don't send me back to the island."

"Afraid you might get too tempted by a *tualala?*"

"No. But on the island we really do have pink caterpillars. I'm not sure I could face them."

"There's one thing I still wonder," Fergus said reflectively. "Where was Humbert Targ while his skeleton hung at Miller's side? Or should I say, *when* was he? He said, 'It took a little time to get here.' From where? From when? And what kind of time?"

There are some questions you don't even try to answer.

The Suicide

Author: Ross Macdonald (1915–1983)

Detective: Lew Archer (1946)

Lew Archer presents the same kind of dating problem as Philip Marlowe. In "Find the Woman" (*Ellery Queen's Mystery Magazine*, June 1946), published under the author's birth name Kenneth Millar, the detective narrator is named Rogers, and the name Archer appears in print for the first time in *The Moving Target* (1949), as by John Macdonald, a pseudonym later amended to avoid confusion with John D. MacDonald. But when "Find the Woman" was reprinted in the collection *The Name Is Archer* (1955), Rogers became Archer.

The short stories about Lew Archer are all solidly professional work, though they generally lack the depth and complexity of the detective's book-length cases. As Tom Nolan points out in his outstanding *Ross Macdonald: A Biography* (1999), events in the Archer novels and stories not only reflected their author's life experiences but sometimes forecast them. Apart from its qualities as a story, "The Suicide" (first published as "The Beat-Up Sister" in *Manhunt*, October 1953) has some striking parallels with Macdonald's well-publicized search in 1959 for his troubled daughter Linda, an event described in detail in Nolan's biography.

I picked her up on the Daylight. Or maybe she picked me up. With some of the nicest girls, you never know.

She seemed to be very nice, and very young. She had a flippant nose and wide blue eyes, the kind that men like to call innocent. Her hair bubbled like boiling gold around her small blue hat. When she turned from the window to hear my deathless comments on the landscape and the weather, she wafted spring odors toward me.

She laughed in the right places, a little hectically. But in between, when the conversation lagged, I could see a certain somberness in her eyes, a pinched look around her mouth like the effects of an early frost. When I asked her to join me in the buffet car for a drink, she said:

"Oh, no. Thank you. I couldn't possibly."

"Why not?"

"I'm not quite twenty-one, for one thing. You wouldn't want to contribute to the delinquency of a minor?"

"It sounds like a pleasant enterprise."

She veiled her eyes and turned away. The green hills plunged backward past the train window like giant dolphins against the flat blue background of the sea. The afternoon sun was bright on her hair. I hoped I hadn't offended her.

I hadn't. After a while she leaned toward me and touched my arm with hesitant fingertips.

"Since you're so kind, I'll tell you what I would like." She wrinkled her nose in an anxious way. "A sandwich? Would it cost so very much more than a drink?"

"A sandwich it is."

On the way to the diner, she caught the eye of every man on the train who wasn't asleep. Even some of the sleeping ones stirred, as if her passing had induced a dream. I censored my personal dream. She was too young for me, too innocent. I told myself that my interest was strictly paternal.

She asked me to order her a turkey sandwich, all white meat, and drummed on the tablecloth until it arrived. It disappeared in no time. She was ravenous.

"Have another," I said.

She gave me a look that wasn't exactly calculating, just questioning. "Do you really think I should?"

"Why not? You're pretty hungry."

"Yes, I am. But—" She blushed. "I hate to ask a stranger—you know?"

"No personal obligation. I like to see hungry people eat."

"You're awfully generous. And I am awfully hungry. Are you sure you can afford it?"

"Money is no object. I just collected a thousand-dollar fee in San Francisco. If you can use a full-course dinner, say so."

"Oh no, I couldn't accept that. But I will confess that I could eat another sandwich."

I signaled to the waiter. The second sandwich went the way of the first while I drank coffee. She ate the olives and slices of pickle, too.

"Feeling better now? You were looking a little peaked."

"Much better, thank you. I'm ashamed to admit it, but I hadn't eaten all day. And I've been on short rations for a week."

I looked her over deliberately. Her dark blue suit was new, and expensively cut. Her bag was fine calfskin. Tiny diamonds winked in the white-gold case of her wristwatch.

"I know what you're thinking," she said. "I could have pawned something. Only I couldn't *bear* to. I spent my last cent on my ticket—I waited till the very last minute, when I had just enough to pay my fare."

"What were you waiting for?"

"To hear from Ethel. But we won't go into that." Her eyes shuttered themselves, and her pretty mouth became less pretty. "It's my worry."

"All right."

"I don't mean to be rude, or ungrateful. I thought I could hold out until I got to Los Angeles. I would have, too, if you hadn't broken me down with kindness."

"Forget about my kindness. I hope there's a job waiting for you in Los Angeles. Or maybe a husband?"

"No." The idea of a husband, or possibly a job, appealed to her sense of humor. She giggled like a schoolgirl. "You have one more guess."

"Okay. You flunked out of school, and couldn't face the family."

"You're half right. But I'm still enrolled at Berkeley, and I have no intention of flunking out. I'm doing very well in my courses."

"What are you taking?"

"Psychology and sociology, mostly. I plan to be a psychiatric social worker."

"You don't look the type."

"I am, though." The signs of early frost showed on her face again. I couldn't keep up with her moods. She was suddenly very serious. "I'm interested in helping people in trouble. I've seen a great deal of trouble. And so many people need help in the modern world."

"You can say that again."

Her clear gaze came up to my face. "You're interested in people, too, aren't you? Are you a doctor, or a lawyer?"

"What gave you that idea?"

"You mentioned a fee you earned, a thousand-dollar fee. It sounded as if you were a professional man."

"I don't know if you'd call my job a profession. I'm a private detective. My name is Archer."

Her reaction was disconcerting. She gripped the edge of the table with her hands, and pushed herself away from it. She said in a whisper as thin and sharp as a razor:

"Did Edward hire you? To spy on me?"

"Of course. Naturally. It's why I mentioned the fact that I'm a detective. I'm very cunning. And who in hell is Edward?"

"Edward Illman." She was breathing fast. "Are you sure he didn't employ you to pick me—to contact me? Cross your heart?"

The colored waiter edged toward our table, drawn by the urgent note in her voice. "Anything the matter, lady?"

"No. It's all right, thank you. The sandwiches were fine."

She managed to give him a strained smile, and he went away with a backward look.

"I'll make a clean breast of everything," I said. "Edward employed me to feed you drugged sandwiches. The kitchen staff is in my pay, and you'll soon begin to feel the effects of the drug. After that comes the abduction by helicopter."

"Please. You mustn't joke about such things. I wouldn't put it past him, after what he did to Ethel."

"Ethel?"

"My sister, my older sister. Ethel's a darling. But Edward doesn't think so. He hates her—he hates us both. I wouldn't be surprised if he's responsible for all this."

"All what?" I said. "We seem to be getting nowhere. Obviously you're in some sort of a bind. You want to tell me about it, I want to hear about it. Now take a deep breath and start over, from the beginning. Bear in mind that I don't know these people from Adam. I don't even know your name."

"I'm sorry, my name is Clare Larrabee." Dutifully, she inhaled. "I've been talking like a silly fool, haven't I? It's because I'm so anxious about Ethel. I haven't heard from her for several weeks. I have no idea where she is or what's happened to her. Last week, when my allowance didn't come, I began to get really worried. I phoned her house in West Hollywood and got no answer. Since then I've been phoning at least once a day, with never an answer. So finally I swallowed my pride and got in touch with Edward. He said he hasn't seen her since she went to Nevada. Not that I believe him, necessarily. He'd just as soon lie as tell the truth. He perjured himself right and left when they arranged the settlement."

"Let's get Edward straight," I said. "Is he your sister's husband?"

"He was. Ethel divorced him last month. And she's well rid of him, even if he did cheat her out of her fair share of the property. He claimed to be a pauper, practically, but I know better. He's a very successful real estate operator—you must have heard of the Illman Tracts."

"This is the same Illman?"

"Yes. Do you know him?"

"Not personally. I used to see his name in the columns. He's quite a Casanova, isn't he?"

"Edward is a dreadful man. Why Ethel ever married him . . . Of course she wanted security, to be able to send me to college, and everything. But I'd have gone to work, gladly, if I could have stopped the marriage. I could see what kind of a husband he'd make. He even had the nerve to make a—make advances to me at the wedding reception." Her mouth pouted out in girlish indignation.

"And now you're thinking he had something to do with your sister's disappearance?"

"Either that, or she did away with—No, I'm sure it's Edward. He sounded so smug on the long-distance telephone yesterday, as if he'd just swallowed the canary. I tell you, that man is capable of anything. If something's happened to Ethel, I know who's responsible."

"Probably nothing has. She could have gone off on a little trip by herself."

"You don't know Ethel. We've always kept in close touch, and she's been so punctual with my allowance. She'd never dream of going away and leaving me stranded at school without any money. I held out as long as I could, expecting to hear from her. When I got down below twenty dollars, I decided to take the train home."

"To Ethel's house in West Hollywood?"

"Yes. It's the only home I have since Daddy passed away. Ethel's the only family I have. I couldn't bear to lose Ethel." Her eyes filmed with tears.

"Do you have taxi fare?"

She shook her head, shamefaced.

"I'll drive you out. I don't live far from there myself. My car's stashed in a garage near Union Station."

"You're being good to me." Her hand crept out across the tablecloth and pressed the back of mine. "Forgive me for saying those silly things, about Edward hiring you."

I told her that would be easy.

We drove out Sunset and up into the hills. Afternoon was changing into evening. The late sunlight flashed like intermittent searchlights from the western windows of the hillside apartment buildings. Clare huddled anxiously in the far corner of the seat. She didn't speak, except to direct me to her sister's house.

It was a flat-roofed building set high on a sloping lot. The walls were redwood and glass, and the redwood had not yet weathered gray. I parked on the slanting blacktop drive and got out. Both stalls of the carport under the house were empty. The draperies were pulled over the picture windows that overlooked the valley.

I knocked on the front door. The noise resounded emptily through the building. I tried it. It was locked. So was the service door at the side.

I turned to the girl at my elbow. She was clutching the handle of her overnight bag with both hands, and looking pinched again. I thought that it was a cold homecoming for her.

"Nobody home," I said.

"It's what I was afraid of. What shall I do now?"

"You share this house with your sister?"

"When I'm home from school."

"And it belongs to her?"

"Since the divorce it does."

"Then you can give me permission to break in."

"All right. But please don't damage anything if you can help it. Ethel is very proud of her house."

The side door had a spring-type lock. I took a rectangle of plastic out of my wallet, and slipped it into the crack between the door and the frame. The lock slid back easily.

"You're quite a burglar," she said in a dismal attempt at humor.

I stepped inside without answering her. The kitchen was bright and clean, but it had a slightly musty, disused odor. The bread in the breadbox was stale. The refrigerator needed defrosting. There was a piece of ham moldering on one shelf, and on another a half-empty bottle of milk, which had gone sour.

"She's been gone for some time," I said. "At least a week. We should check her clothes."

"Why?"

"She'd take some along if she left to go on a trip, under her own power."

She led me through the living room, which was simply and expensively furnished in black iron and net, into the master bedroom. The huge square bed was neatly made, and covered with a pink quilted silk spread. Clare avoided looking at it, as though the conjunction of a man and a bed gave her a guilty feeling. While she went through the closet, I searched the vanity and the chest of drawers.

They were barer than they should have been. Cosmetics were conspicuous by their absence. I found one thing of interest in the top drawer of the vanity, hidden under a tangle of stockings: a bankbook issued by the Las Vegas branch of the Bank of Southern California. Ethel Illman had deposited $30,000 on March 14 of this year. On March 17 she had withdrawn $5,000. On March 20 she had withdrawn $6,000. On March 22 she had withdrawn $18,995. There was a balance in her account, after service charges, of $3.65.

Clare said from the closet in a muffled voice:

"A lot of her things are gone. Her mink stole, her good suits and shoes, a lot of her best summer clothes."

"Then she's probably on a vacation." I tried to keep the doubt out of my voice. A woman wandering around with $30,000 in cash was taking a big chance. I decided not to worry Clare with that, and put the little bankbook in my pocket.

"Without telling me? Ethel wouldn't do that." She came out of the closet, pushing her fine light hair back from her forehead. "You don't understand how close we are to each other, closer than sisters usually are. Ever since Father died—"

"Does she drive her own car?"

"Of course. It's a last year's Buick convertible, robin's-egg blue."

"If you're badly worried, go to Missing Persons."

"No. Ethel wouldn't like that. She's a very proud person, and shy. Anyway, I have a better idea." She gave me that questioning-calculating look of hers.

"Involving me?"

"Please." Her eyes in the darkening room were like great soft center-less pansies, purple or black. "You're a detective, and evidently a good one. And you're a man. You can stand up to Edward and make him answer questions. He just laughs at me. Of course I can't pay you in advance . . ."

"Forget the money for now. What makes you so certain that Illman is in on this?"

"I just know he is. He threatened her in the lawyer's office the day they made the settlement. She told me so herself. Edward said that he was going to get that money back if he had to take it out of her hide. He wasn't fooling, either. He's beaten her more than once."

"How much was the settlement?"

"Thirty thousand dollars and the house and the car. She could have collected much more, hundreds of thousands, if she'd stayed in California and fought it through the courts. But she was too anxious to get free from him. So she let him cheat her, and got a Nevada divorce instead. And even then he wasn't satisfied."

She looked around the abandoned bedroom, fighting back tears. Her skin was so pale that it seemed to be phosphorescent in the gloom. With a little cry, she flung herself face down on the bed and gave herself over to grief. I said to her shaking back:

"You win. Where do I find him?"

He lived in a cottage hotel on the outskirts of Bel-Air. The gates of the walled pueblo were standing open, and I went in. A few couples were strolling on the gravel paths among the palm-shaded cottages, walking off the effects of the cocktail hour or working up an appetite for dinner. The women were blonde, and had money on their backs. The men were noticeably older than the women, except for one, who was noticeably younger. They paid no attention to me.

I passed an oval swimming pool, and found Edward Illman's cottage, number twelve. Light streamed from its open French windows onto a flagstone terrace. A young woman in a narrow-waisted, billowing black gown lay on a chrome chaise at the edge of the light. With her arms hanging loose from her naked shoulders, she looked like an expensive French doll that somebody had accidentally dropped there. Her face was polished and plucked and painted, expressionless as a doll's. But her eyes snapped open at the sound of my footsteps.

"Who goes there?" she said with a slight Martini accent. "Halt and give the password or I'll shoot you dead with my atomic wonder-weapon." She pointed a wavering finger at me and said: "Bing. Am I supposed to know you? I have a terrible memory for faces."

"I have a terrible face for memories. Is Mr. Illman home?"

"Uh-huh. He's in the shower. He's always taking showers. I told him he's got a scour-and-scrub neurosis, his mother was frightened by a washing machine." Her laughter rang like cracked bells. "If it's about business, you can tell me."

"Are you his confidential secretary?"

"I was." She sat up on the chaise, looked pleased with herself. "I'm his fiancée, at the moment."

"Congratulations."

"Uh-huh. He's loaded." Smiling to herself, she got to her feet. "Are you loaded?"

"Not so it gets in my way."

She pointed her finger at me and said bing again and laughed, teetering on her four-inch heels. She started to fall forward on her face. I caught her under the armpits.

"Too bad," she said to my chest. "I don't think you have a terrible face for memories at all. You're much prettier than old Teddy-bear."

"Thanks. I'll treasure the compliment."

I set her down on the chaise, but her arms twined round my neck like smooth white snakes and her body arched against me. She clung to me like a drowning child. I had to use force to detach myself.

"What's the matter?" she said with an up-and-under look. "You a fairy?"

A man appeared in the French windows, blotting out most of the light. In a white terry-cloth bathrobe, he had the shape and bulk of a Kodiak bear. The top of his head was as bald as an ostrich egg. He carried a chip on each shoulder, like epaulets.

"What goes on?"

"Your fiancée swooned, slightly."

"Fiancée hell. I saw what happened." Moving very quickly and lightly for a man of his age and weight, he pounced on the girl on the chaise and began to shake her. "Can't you keep your hands off anything in pants?"

Her head bobbed back and forth. Her teeth clicked like castanets.

I put a rough hand on his shoulder. "Leave her be."

He turned on me. "Who do you think you're talking to?"

"Edward Illman, I presume."

"And who are you?"

"The name is Archer. I'm looking into the matter of your wife's disappearance."

"I'm not married. And I have no intention of getting married. I've been burned once." He looked down sideways at the girl. She peered up at him in silence, hugging her shoulders.

"Your ex-wife, then," I said.

"Has something happened to Ethel?"

"I thought you might be able to tell me."

"Where did you get that idea? Have you been talking to Clare?"

I nodded.

"Don't believe her. She's got a down on me, just like her sister. Because I had the misfortune to marry Ethel, they both think I'm fair game for anything they want to pull. I wouldn't touch either one of them with an insulated pole. They're a couple of hustlers, if you want the truth. They took me for sixty grand, and what did I get out of it but headaches?"

"I thought it was thirty."

"Sixty," he said, with the money light in his eyes. "Thirty in cash, and the house is worth another thirty, easily."

I looked around the place, which must have cost him fifty dollars a day. Above the palms, the first few stars sparkled like solitaire diamonds.

"You seem to have some left."

"Sure I have. But I work for my money. Ethel was strictly from nothing when I met her. She owned the clothes on her back and what was under them and that was all. So she gives me a bad time for three years and I pay off at the rate of twenty grand a year. I ask you, is that fair?"

"I hear you threatened to get it back from her."

"You have been talking to Clare, eh? All right, so I threatened her. It didn't mean a thing. I talk too much sometimes, and I have a bad temper."

"I'd never have guessed."

The girl said: "You hurt me, Teddy. I need another drink. Get me another drink, Teddy."

"Get it yourself."

She called him several bad names and wandered into the cottage, walking awkwardly like an animated doll.

He grasped my arm. "What's the trouble about Ethel? You said she disappeared. You think something's happened to her?"

I removed his hand. "She's missing. Thirty thousand in cash is also missing. There are creeps in Vegas who would knock her off for one big bill, or less."

"Didn't she bank the money? She wouldn't cash a draft for that amount and carry it around. She's crazy, but not that way."

"She banked it all right, on March fourteenth. Then she drew it all out again in the course of the following week. When did you send her the draft?"

"The twelfth or the thirteenth. That was the agreement. She got her final divorce on March eleventh."

"And you haven't seen her since?"

"I have not. Frieda has, though."

"Frieda?"

"My secretary." He jerked a thumb toward the cottage. "Frieda went over to the house last week to pick up some of my clothes I'd left behind. Ethel was there, and she was all right then. Apparently she's taken up with another man."

"Do you know his name?"

"No, and I couldn't care less."

"Do you have a picture of Ethel?"

"I did have some. I tore them up. She's a well-stacked blonde, natural blonde. She looks very much like Clare, same coloring, but three or four years older. You should be able to get a picture from Clare. And while you're at it, tell her for me she's got a lot of gall setting the police on me. I'm a respectable businessman in this town." He puffed out his chest under the bathrobe. It was thickly matted with brown hair, which was beginning to grizzle.

"No doubt," I said. "Incidentally, I'm not the police. I run a private agency. My name is Archer."

"So that's how it is, eh?" The planes of his broad face gleamed angrily in the light. He cocked a fat red fist. "You come here pumping me. Get out, by God, or I'll throw you out!"

"Calm down. I could break you in half."

His face swelled with blood, and his eyes popped. He swung a round-house right at my head. I stepped inside of it and tied him up. "I said calm down, old man. You'll break a vein."

I pushed him off balance and released him. He sat down very suddenly on the chaise. Frieda was watching us from the edge of the terrace. She laughed so heartily that she spilled her drink.

Illman looked old and tired, and he was breathing raucously through his mouth. He didn't try to get up. Frieda came over to me and leaned her weight on my arm. I could feel her small sharp breasts.

"Why didn't you hit him," she whispered, "when you had the chance? He's always hitting other people." Her voice rose. "Teddy-bear thinks he can get away with murder."

"Shut your yap," he said, "or I'll shut it for you."

"Button yours, muscle-man. You'll lay a hand on me once too often."

"You're fired."

"I already quit."

They were a charming couple. I was on the point of tearing myself away when a bellboy popped out of the darkness, like a gnome in uniform.

"A gentleman to see you, Mr. Illman."

The gentleman was a brown-faced young Highway Patrolman, who stepped forward rather diffidently into the light. "Sorry to trouble you, sir. Our San Diego office asked me to contact you as soon as possible."

Frieda looked from me to him, and began to gravitate in his direction. Illman got up heavily and stepped between them.

"What is it?"

The patrolman unfolded a teletype flimsy and held it up to the light.

"Are you the owner of a blue Buick convertible, last year's model?" He read off the license number.

"It was mine," Illman said. "It belongs to my ex-wife now. Did she forget to change the registration?"

"Evidently she did, Mr. Illman. In fact, she seems to've forgotten the car entirely. She left it in a parking space above the public beach in La Jolla. It's been sitting there for the last week, until we hauled it in. Where can I get in touch with Mrs. Illman?"

"I don't know. I haven't seen her for some time."

The patrolman's face lengthened and turned grim. "You mean she's dropped out of sight?"

"Out of my sight, at least. Why?"

"I hate to have to say this, Mr. Illman. There's a considerable quantity of blood on the front seat of the Buick, according to this report. They haven't determined yet if it's human blood, but it raises the suspicion of foul play."

"Good heavens! It's what we've been afraid of, isn't it, Archer?" His voice was thick as corn syrup with phony emotion. "You and Clare were right after all."

"Right about what, Mr. Illman?" The patrolman looked slightly puzzled.

"About poor Ethel," he said. "I've been discussing her disappearance with Mr. Archer here. Mr. Archer is a private detective, and I was just about to engage his services to make a search for Ethel." He turned to me with a painful smile pulling his mouth to one side. "How much did you say you wanted in advance? Five hundred?"

"Make it two. That will buy my services for four days. It doesn't buy anything else, though."

"I understand that, Mr. Archer. I'm sincerely interested in finding Ethel for a variety of reasons, as you know."

He was a suave old fox. I almost laughed in his face. But I played along with him. I liked the idea of using his money to hang him, if possible.

"Yeah. This is a tragic occurrence for you."

He took a silver money clip shaped like a dollar sign out of his bathrobe pocket. I wondered if he didn't trust his roommate. Two bills changed hands. After a further exchange of information, the patrolman went away.

"Well," Illman said. "It looks like a pretty serious business. If you think I had anything to do with it, you're off your rocker."

"Speaking of rockers, you said your wife was crazy. What kind of crazy?"

"I was her husband, not her analyst. I wouldn't know."

"Did she need an analyst?"

"Sometimes I thought so. One week she'd be flying, full of big plans to make money. Then she'd go into a black mood and talk about killing herself." He shrugged. "It ran in her family."

"This could be an afterthought on your part."

His face reddened.

I turned to Frieda, who looked as if the news had sobered her. "Who was this fellow you saw at Ethel's house last week?"

"I dunno. She called him Owen, I think. Maybe it was his first name, maybe it was his last name. She didn't introduce us." She said it as if she felt cheated.

"Describe him?"

"Sure. A big guy, over six feet, wide in the shoulders, narrow in the beam. A smooth hunk of male. And young," with a malicious glance at Illman. "Black hair, and he had all of it, dreamy dark eyes, a cute little hairline moustache. I tabbed him for a gin-mill cowboy from Vegas, but he could be a movie star if I was a producer."

"Thank God you're not," Illman said.

"What made you think she'd taken up with him?"

"The way he moved around the house, like he owned it. He poured himself a drink while I was there. And he was in his shirtsleeves. A real sharp dresser, though. Custom-made stuff."

"You have a good eye."

"For men, she has," Illman said.

"Lay off me," she said in a hard voice, with no trace of the Martini drawl. "Or I'll really walk out on you, and then where will you be?"

"Right where I am now. Sitting pretty."

"That's what you think."

I interrupted their communion. "Do you know anything about this Owen character, Illman?"

"Not a thing. He's probably some jerk she picked up in Nevada while she was sweating out the divorce."

"Have you been to San Diego recently?"

"Not for months."

"That's true," Frieda said. "I've been keeping close track of Teddy. I have to. Incidentally, it's getting late and I'm hungry. Go and put on some clothes, darling. You're prettier with clothes on."

"More than I'd say for you," he leered.

I left them and drove back to West Hollywood. The night-blooming girls and their escorts had begun to appear on the Strip. Gusts of music came from the doors that opened for them. But when I turned off Sunset, the streets were deserted, emptied by the television curfew.

All the lights were on in the redwood house on the hillside. I parked in the driveway and knocked on the front door. The draperies over the window beside it were pulled to one side, then fell back into place. A thin voice drifted out to me.

"Is that you, Mr. Archer?"

I said that it was. Clare opened the door inch by inch. Her face was almost haggard.

"I'm so relieved to see you."

"What's the trouble?"

"A man was watching the house. He was sitting there at the curb in a long black car. It looked like an undertaker's car. And it had a Nevada license."

"Are you sure?"

"Yes. It lighted up when he drove away. I saw it through the window. He left only a couple of minutes ago."

"Did you get a look at his face?"

"I'm afraid not. I didn't go out. I was petrified. He shone a searchlight on the window."

"Take it easy. There are plenty of big black cars in town, and quite a few Nevada licenses. He was probably looking for some other address."

"No. I had a—a kind of fatal feeling when I saw him. I just *know* that he's connected in some way with Ethel's disappearance. I'm scared."

She leaned against the door, breathing quickly. She looked very young and vulnerable. I said:

"What am I going to do with you, kid? I can't leave you here alone."

"Are you going away?"

"I have to. I saw Edward. While I was there, he had a visitor from the HP. They found your sister's car abandoned near San Diego." I didn't mention the blood. She had enough on her mind.

"Edward killed her!" she cried. "I knew it."

"That I doubt. She may not even be dead. I'm going to San Diego to find out."

"Take me along, won't you?"

"It wouldn't be good for your reputation. Besides, you'd be in the way."

"No, I wouldn't. I promise. I have friends in San Diego. Just let me drive down there with you, and I can stay with them."

"You wouldn't be making this up?"

"Honest, I have friends there. Gretchen Falk and her husband, they're good friends of Ethel's and mine. We lived in San Diego for a while, before she married Edward. The Falks will be glad to let me stay with them."

"Hadn't you better phone them first?"

"I can't. The phone's disconnected. I tried it."

"Are you sure these people exist?"

"Of course," she said urgently.

I gave in. I turned out the lights and locked the door and put her bag in my car. Clare stayed very close to me.

As I was backing out, a car pulled in behind me, blocking the entrance to the driveway. I opened the door and got out. It was a black Lincoln with a searchlight mounted over the windshield.

Clare said: "He's come back."

The searchlight flashed on. Its bright beam swiveled toward me. I reached for the gun in my shoulder holster and got a firm grip on nothing. Holster and gun were packed in the suitcase in the trunk of my car. The searchlight blinded me.

A black gun emerged from the dazzle, towing a hand and an arm. They belonged to a quick-stepping cube-shaped man in a double-breasted flannel suit. A snap-brim hat was pulled down over his eyes. His mouth was as full of teeth as a barracuda's. It said:

"Where's Dewar?"

"Never heard of him."

"Owen Dewar. You've heard of him."

The gun dragged him forward another step and collided with my breastbone. His free hand palmed my flanks. All I could see was his unchanging smile, framed in brilliant light. I felt a keen desire to do some orthodontic work on it. But the gun was an inhibiting factor.

"You must be thinking of two other parties," I said.

"No dice. This is the house, and that's the broad. Out of the car, lady."

"I will not," she said in a tiny voice behind me.

"Out, or I'll blow a hole in your boyfriend here."

Reluctantly, she clambered out. The teeth looked down at her ankles as if they wanted to chew them. I made a move for the gun. It dived into my solar plexus, doubling me over. Its muzzle flicked the side of my head. It pushed me back against the fender of my car. I felt a worm of blood crawling past my ear.

"You coward! Leave him alone." Clare flung herself at him. He side-stepped neatly, moving on the steady pivot of the gun against my chest. She went to her knees on the blacktop.

"Get up, lady, but keep your voice down. How many boyfriends you keep on the string, anyway?"

She got to her feet. "He isn't my boyfriend. Who are you? Where is Ethel?"

"That's a hot one." The smile intensified. "You're Ethel. The question is, where's Dewar?"

"I don't know any Dewar."

"Sure you do, Ethel. You know him well enough to marry him. Now tell me where he is, and nobody gets theirselves hurt." The flat voice dropped, and added huskily: "Only I haven't got much time to waste."

"You're wrong," she said. "You're completely mistaken. I'm not Ethel. I'm Clare. Ethel's my older sister."

He stepped back and swung the gun in a quarter-circle, covering us both. "Turn your face to the light. Let's have a good look at you."

She did as she was told, striking a rigid pose. He shifted the gun to his left hand, and brought a photograph out of his inside pocket. Looking from it to her face, he shook his head doubtfully.

"I guess you're leveling at that. You're younger than this one, and thinner." He handed her the photograph. "She your sister?"

"Yes. It's Ethel."

I caught a glimpse of the picture over her shoulder. It was a blown-up candid shot of two people. One was a pretty blonde who looked like Clare five years from now. She was leaning on the arm of a tall dark man with a hairline moustache. They were smirking at each other, and there was a flower-decked altar in the background.

"Who's the man?" I said.

"Dewar. Who else?" said the teeth behind the gun. "They got married in Vegas last month. I got this picture from the Chaparral Chapel. It goes with the twenty-five-dollar wedding." He snatched it out of Clare's hands and put it back in his pocket. "It took me a couple of weeks to run her down. She used her maiden name, see."

"Where did you catch up with her? San Diego?"

"I didn't catch up with her. Would I be here if I did?"

"What do you want her for?"

"I don't want her. I got nothing against the broad, except that she tied up with Dewar. He's the boy I want."

"What for?"

"You wouldn't be inarested. He worked for me at one time." The gun swiveled brightly toward Clare. "You know where your sister is?"

"No, I don't. I wouldn't tell you if I did."

"That's no way to talk now, lady. My motto's cooperation. From other people."

I said: "Her sister's been missing for a week. The HP found her car in San Diego. It had bloodstains on the front seat. Are you sure you didn't catch up with her?"

"I'm asking you the questions, punk." But there was a trace of uncertainty in his voice. "What happened to Dewar if the blonde is missing?"

"I think he ran out with her money."

Clare turned to me. "You didn't tell me all this."

"I'm telling you now."

The teeth said: "She had money?"

"Plenty."

"The bastard. The bastard took us both, eh?"

"Dewar took you for money?"

"You ask too many questions, punk. You'll talk yourself to death one of these days. Now stay where you are for ten minutes, both of you. Don't move, don't yell, don't telephone. I might decide to drive around the block and come back and make sure."

He backed down the brilliant alley of the searchlight beam. The door of his car slammed. All of its lights went off together. It rolled away into darkness, and didn't come back.

It was past midnight when we got to San Diego, but there was still a light in the Falks' house. It was a stucco cottage on a street of identical cottages in Pacific Beach.

"We lived here once," Clare said. "When I was going to high school. That house, second from the corner." Her voice was nostalgic, and she looked around the jerry-built tract as if it represented something precious to her. The pre-Illman era in her young life.

I knocked on the front door. A big henna-head in a housecoat opened it on a chain. But when she saw Clare beside me, she flung the door wide.

"Clare honey, where you been? I've been trying to phone you in Berkeley, and here you are. How are you, honey?"

She opened her arms and the younger woman walked into them.

"Oh, Gretchen," she said with her face on the redhead's breast. "Something's happened to Ethel, something terrible."

"I know it, honey, but it could be worse."

"Worse than murder?"

"She isn't murdered. Put that out of your mind. She's pretty badly hurt, but she isn't murdered."

Clare stood back to look at her face. "You've seen her? Is she here?"

The redhead put a finger to her mouth, which was big and generous-looking, like the rest of her. "Hush, Clare. Jake's asleep, he has to get up early, go to work. Yeah, I've seen her, but she isn't here. She's in a nursing home over on the other side of town."

"You said she's badly hurt?"

"Pretty badly beaten, yeah, poor dear. But the doctor told me she's pulling out of it fine. A little plastic surgery, and she'll be good as new."

"Plastic surgery?"

"Yeah, I'm afraid she'll need it. I got a look at her face tonight, when they changed the bandages. Now take it easy, honey. It could be worse."

"Who did it to her?"

"That lousy husband of hers."

"Edward?"

"Heck, no. The other one. The one that calls himself Dewar, Owen Dewar."

I said: "Have you seen Dewar?"

"I saw him a week ago, the night he beat her up, the dirty rotten bully." Her deep contralto growled in her throat. "I'd like to get my hands on him just for five minutes."

"So would a lot of people, Mrs. Falk."

She glanced inquiringly at Clare. "Who's your friend? You haven't introduced us."

"I'm sorry. Mr. Archer, Mrs. Falk. Mr. Archer is a detective, Gretchen."

"I was wondering. Ethel didn't want me to call the police. I told her she ought to, but she said no. The poor darling's so ashamed of herself, getting mixed up with that kind of a louse. She didn't even get in touch with *me* until tonight. Then she saw in the paper about her car being picked up, and she thought maybe I could get it back for her without any publicity. Publicity is what she doesn't want most. I guess it's a tragic thing for a beautiful girl like Ethel to lose her looks."

I said: "There won't be any publicity if I can help it. Did you go to see the police about her car?"

"Jake advised me not to. He said it would blow the whole thing wide open. And the doctor told me he was kind of breaking the law by not reporting the beating she took. So I dropped it."

"How did this thing happen?"

"I'll tell you all I know about it. Come on into the living room, kids, let me fix you something to drink."

Clare said: "You're awfully kind, Gretchen, but I must go to Ethel. Where is she?"

"The Mission Rest Home. Only don't you think you better wait till morning? It's a private hospital, but it's awful late for visitors."

"I've got to see her," Clare said. "I couldn't sleep a wink if I didn't. I've been so worried about her."

Gretchen heaved a sigh. "Whatever you say, honey. We can try, anyway. Give me a second to put on a dress and I'll show you where the place is."

She led us into the darkened living room, turned the television set off and the lights on. A quart of beer, nearly full, stood on a coffee table beside the scuffed davenport. She offered me a glass, which I accepted gratefully. Clare refused. She was so tense she couldn't even sit down.

We stood and looked at each other for a minute. Then Gretchen came back, struggling with a zipper on one massive hip.

"All set, kids. You better drive, Mr. Archer. I had a couple of quarts to settle my nerves. You wouldn't believe it, but I've gained five pounds since Ethel came down here. I always gain weight when I'm anxious."

We went out to my car, and turned toward the banked lights of San Diego. The women rode in the front seat. Gretchen's opulent flesh was warm against me.

"Was Ethel here before it happened?" I asked.

"Sure she was, for a day. Ethel turned up here eight or nine days ago, Tuesday of last week it was. I hadn't heard from her for several months, since she wrote me that she was going to Nevada for a divorce. It was early in the morning when she drove up; in fact, she got me out of bed. The minute I saw her, I knew that something was wrong. The poor kid was scared, really scared. She was as cold as a corpse, and her teeth were chattering. So I fed her some coffee and put her in a hot tub, and after that she told me what it was that'd got her down."

"Dewar?"

"You said it, mister. Ethel never was much of a picker. When she was hostessing at the Grant coffee shop back in the old days, she was always falling for the world's worst phonies. Speaking of phonies, this Dewar takes the cake. She met him in Las Vegas when she was waiting for her divorce from Illman. He was a big promoter, to hear him tell it. She fell for the story, and she fell for him. A few days after she got her final decree, she married him. Big romance. Big deal. They were going to be business partners, too. He said he had some money to invest, twenty-five thousand or so, and he knew of a swell little hotel in Acapulco that they could buy at a steal for fifty thousand. The idea was that they should each put up half, and go and live in Mexico in the lap of luxury for the rest of their lives. He didn't show her any of his money, but she believed him. She drew her settlement money out of the bank and came to L.A. with him to close up her house and get set for the Mexican deal."

"He must have hypnotized her," Clare said. "Ethel's a smart business-woman."

"Not with something tall, dark, and handsome, honey. I give him that much. He's got the looks. Well, they lived in L.A. for a couple of weeks, on Ethel's money of course, and he kept putting off the Mexican trip. He didn't want to go anywhere, in fact, just sit around the house and drink her liquor and eat her good cooking."

"He was hiding out," I said.

"From what? The police?"

"Worse than that. Some gangster pal from Nevada was gunning for him; still is. Ethel wasn't the only one he fleeced."

"Nice guy, eh? Anyway, Ethel started to get restless. She didn't like sitting around with all that money in the house, waiting for nothing. Last Monday night, a week ago Monday that is, she had a showdown with him. Then it all came out. He didn't have any money or anything else. He wasn't a promoter, he didn't know of any hotel in Acapulco. His whole buildup was as queer as a three-dollar bill. Apparently he made his living gambling, but he was even all washed up with that. Nothing. But she was married to him now, he said, and she was going to sit still and like it or he'd knock her block off.

"He meant it, too, Ethel said. She's got the proof of it now. She waited until he drank himself to sleep that night, then she threw some things in a bag, including her twenty-five thousand, and came down here. She was on her way to get a quickie divorce in Mexico, but Jake and me talked her into staying for a while and thinking it over. Jake said she could probably get an annulment right in California, and that would be more legal."

"He was probably right."

"Yeah? Maybe it wasn't such a bright idea after all. We kept her here just long enough for Dewar to catch up with her. Apparently she left some letters behind, and he ran down the list of her friends until he found her at our place. He talked her into going for a drive to talk it over. I didn't hear what was said—they were in her room—but he must have used some powerful persuasion. She went out of the house with him as meek as a lamb, and they drove away in her car. That was the last I saw of her, until she got in touch with me tonight. When she didn't come back, I wanted to call the police, but Jake wouldn't let me. He said I had no business coming between a man and his wife, and all that guff. I gave Jake a piece of my mind tonight on that score. I ought to've called the cops as soon as Dewar showed his sneaking face on our front porch."

"What exactly did he do to her?"

"He gave her a bad clobbering, that's obvious. Ethel didn't want to talk about it much tonight. The subject was painful to her in more ways than one."

"Did he take her money?"

"He must have. It's gone. So is he."

We were on the freeway, which curved past the hills of Balboa Park. The trees of its man-made jungle were restless against the sky. Below us on the other side, the city sloped like a frozen cascade of lights down to the black concavity of the bay.

The Mission Rest Home was in the eastern suburbs, an old stucco mansion that had been converted into a private hospital. The windows in its thick stucco walls were small and barred, and there were lights in some of them.

I rang the doorbell. Clare was so close to my back I could feel her breath. A woman in a purple flannelette wrapper opened the door. Her hair hung in two gray braids, which were ruler-straight. Her hard black eyes surveyed the three of us, and stayed on Gretchen.

"What is it now, Mrs. Falk?" she said brusquely.

"This is Mrs.—Miss Larrabee's sister, Clare."

"Miss Larrabee is probably sleeping. She shouldn't be disturbed."

"I know it's late," Clare said in a tremulous voice. "But I've come all the way from San Francisco to see her."

"She's doing well, I assure you of that. She's completely out of danger."

"Can't I just go in for a teensy visit? Ethel will want to see me, and Mr. Archer has some questions to ask her. Mr. Archer is a private detective."

"This is very irregular." Reluctantly, she opened the door. "Wait here, and I'll see if she is awake. Please keep your voices down. We have other patients."

We waited in a dim high-ceilinged room that had once been the reception room of the mansion. The odors of mustiness and medication blended depressingly in the stagnant air.

"I wonder what brought her here," I said.

"She knew old lady Lestina," Gretchen said. "She stayed with her at one time, when Mrs. Lestina was running a boardinghouse."

"Of course," Clare said. "I remember the name. That was when Ethel was going to San Diego State. Then Daddy—got killed, and she had to drop out of school and go to work." Tears glimmered in her eyes. "Poor Ethel. She's always tried so hard, and been so good to me."

Gretchen patted her shoulder. "You bet she has, honey. Now you have a chance to be good to her."

"Oh, I will. I'll do everything I can."

Mrs. Lestina appeared in the arched doorway. "She's not asleep. I guess you can talk to her for a very few minutes."

We followed her to a room at the end of one wing of the house. A white-uniformed nurse was waiting at the door. "Don't say anything to upset her, will you? She's always fighting sedation as it is."

The room was large but poorly furnished, with a mirrorless bureau, a couple of rickety chairs, a brown-enameled hospital bed. The head on the raised pillow was swathed in bandages through which tufts of blond hair were visible. The woman sat up and spread her arms. The whites of her eyes were red, suffused with blood from broken vessels. Her swollen lips opened and said, "Clare!" in a tone of incredulous joy.

The sisters hugged each other, with tears and laughter. "It's wonderful to see you," the older one said through broken teeth. "How did you get here so fast?"

"I came to stay with Gretchen. Why didn't you call me, Ethel? I've been worried sick about you."

"I'm dreadfully sorry, darling. I should have, shouldn't I? I didn't want you to see me like this. And I've been so ashamed of myself. I've been such a terrible fool. I've lost our money."

The nurse was standing against the door, torn between her duty and her feelings. "Now you promised not to get excited, Miss Larrabee."

"She's right," Clare said. "Don't give it a second thought. I'm going to leave school and get a job and look after you. You need some looking after for a change."

"Nuts. I'll be fine in a couple of weeks." The brave voice issuing from the mask was deep and vibrant. "Don't make any rash decisions, kiddo. The head is bloody but unbowed." The sisters looked at each other in the silence of deep affection.

I stepped forward to the bedside and introduced myself. "How did this happen to you, Miss Larrabee?"

"It's a long story," she lisped, "and a sordid one."

"Mrs. Falk has told me most of it up to the point when Dewar made you drive away with him. Where did he take you?"

"To the beach, I think it was in La Jolla. It was late and there was nobody there and the tide was coming in. And Owen had a gun. I was terrified. I didn't know what more he wanted from me. He already had my twenty-five thousand."

"He had the money?"

"Yes. It was in my room at Gretchen's house. He made me give it to him before we left there. But it didn't satisfy him. He said I hurt his pride by leaving him. He said he had to satisfy his pride." Contempt ran through her voice like a thin steel thread.

"By beating you up?"

"Apparently. He hit me again and again. I think he left me for dead. When I came to, the waves were splashing on me. I managed somehow to get up to the car. It wasn't any good to me, though, because Owen had the keys. It's funny he didn't take it."

"Too easily traced," I said. "What did you do then?"

"I hardly know. I think I sat in the car for a while, wondering what to do. Then a taxi went by and I stopped him and told him to bring me here."

"You weren't very wise not to call the police. They might have got your money back. Now it's a cold trail."

"Did you come here to lecture me?"

"I'm sorry. I didn't mean—"

"I was half crazy with the pain," she said. "I hardly knew what I was doing. I couldn't bear to have anybody see me."

Her fingers were active among the folds of the sheets. Clare reached out and stroked her hands into quietness. "Now, now, darling," she crooned. "Nobody's criticizing you. You take things nice and easy for a while, and Clare will look after you."

The masked head rolled on the pillow. The nurse came forward, her face solicitous. "I think Miss Larrabee has had enough, don't you?"

She showed us out. Clare lingered with her sister for a moment, then followed us to the car. She sat between us in brooding silence all the way to Pacific Beach. Before I dropped them off at Gretchen's house, I asked for her permission to go to the police. She wouldn't give it to me, and nothing I could say would change her mind.

I spent the rest of the night in a motor court, trying to crawl over the threshold of sleep. Shortly after dawn I disentangled myself from the twisted sheets and drove out to La Jolla. La Jolla is a semidetached suburb of San Diego, a small resort town half surrounded by sea. It was a gray morning. The slanting streets were scoured with the sea's cold breath, and the sea itself looked like hammered pewter.

I warmed myself with a short-order breakfast and went the rounds of the hotels and motels. No one resembling Dewar had registered in the past week. I tried the bus and taxi companies, in vain. Dewar had slipped out of town unnoticed. But I did get a lead on the taxi driver who had taken Ethel to the Mission Rest Home. He had mentioned the injured woman to his dispatcher, and the dispatcher gave me his name and address. Stanley Simpson, 38 Calle Laureles.

Simpson was a paunchy, defeated-looking man who hadn't shaved for a couple of days. He came to the door of his tiny bungalow in his underwear, rubbing sleep out of his eyes. "What's the pitch, bub? If you got me up to try and sell me something, you're in for a disappointment."

I told him who I was and why I was there. "Do you remember the woman?"

"I hope to tell you I do. She was bleeding like a stuck pig, all over the backseat. It took me a couple of hours to clean it off. Somebody pistol-whipped her, if you ask me. I wanted to take her to the hospital, but she said no. Hell, I couldn't argue with her in that condition. Did I do wrong?" His slack mouth twisted sideways in a self-doubting grimace.

"If you did, it doesn't matter. She's being taken good care of. I thought you might have got a glimpse of the man that did it to her."

"Not me, mister. She was all by herself, nobody else in sight. She got out of a parked car and staggered out into the road. I couldn't just leave her there, could I?"

"Of course not. You're a Good Samaritan, Simpson. Exactly where did you pick her up?"

"Down by the Cove. She was sitting in this Buick. I dropped a party off at the beach club and I was on my way back, kind of cruising along—"

"What time?"

"Around ten o'clock, I guess it was. I can check my schedule."

"It isn't important. Incidentally, did she pay you for the ride?"

"Yeah, she had a buck and some change in her purse. She had a hard time making it. No tip," he added gloomily.

"Tough cheese."

His fogged eyes brightened. "You're a friend of hers, aren't you? Wouldn't you say I rate a tip on a run like that? I always say, better late than never."

"Is that what you always say?" I handed him a dollar.

The Cove was a roughly semicircular inlet at the foot of a steep hill surmounted by a couple of hotels. Its narrow curving beach and the street above it were both deserted. An offshore wind had swept away the early-morning mist, but the sky was still cloudy, and the sea grim. The long swells slammed the beach like stone walls falling, and broke in foam on the rocks that framed the entrance to the Cove.

I sat in my car and watched them. I was at a dead end. This seaswept place, under this iron sky, was like the world's dead end. Far out at sea, a carrier floated like a chip on the horizon. A Navy jet took off from it and scrawled tremendous nothings on the distance.

Something bright caught my eye. It was in the trough of a wave a couple of hundred yards outside the Cove. Then it was on a crest: the aluminum air-bottle of an Aqua-lung strapped to a naked brown back. Its wearer was prone on a surfboard, kicking with black-finned feet towards the shore. He was kicking hard, and paddling with one arm, but he was making slow progress. His other arm dragged in the opaque water. He seemed to be towing something, something heavy. I wondered if he had speared a shark or a porpoise. His face was inscrutable behind its glass mask.

I left my car and climbed down to the beach. The man on the surfboard came toward me with his tiring one-armed stroke, climbing the walled waves and sliding down them. A final surge picked him up and set him on the sand, almost at my feet. I dragged his board out of the backwash, and helped him to pull in the line that he was holding in one hand. His catch was nothing native to the sea. It was a man.

The end of the line was looped around his body under the armpits. He lay face down like an exhausted runner, a big man, fully clothed in soggy tweeds. I turned him over and saw the aquiline profile, the hairline moustache over the blue mouth, the dark eyes clogged with sand. Owen Dewar had made his escape by water.

The skin-diver took off his mask and sat down heavily, his chest working like a great furred bellows. "I go down for abalone," he said between breaths. "I find this. Caught between two rocks at thirty–forty feet."

"How long has he been in the water?"

"It's hard to tell. I'd say a couple of days, anyway. Look at his color. Poor stiff. But I wish they wouldn't drown themselves in my hunting grounds."

"Do you know him?"

"Nope. Do you?"

"Never saw him before," I said, with truth.

"How about you phoning the police, Mac? I'm pooped. And unless I make a catch, I don't eat today. There's no pay in fishing for corpses."

"In a minute."

I went through the dead man's pockets. There was a set of car keys in his jacket pocket, and an alligator wallet on his hip. It contained no money, but the driver's license was decipherable: Owen Demar, Mesa Court, Las Vegas. I put the wallet back, and let go of the body. The head rolled sideways. I saw the small hole in his neck, washed clean by the sea.

"Holy Mother!" the diver said. "He was shot."

I got back to the Falk house around midmorning. The sun had burned off the clouds, and the day was turning hot. By daylight the long, treeless street of identical houses looked cheap and rundown. It was part of the miles of suburban slums that the war had scattered all over Southern California.

Gretchen was sprinkling the brown front lawn with a desultory hose. She looked too big for the pocket-handkerchief yard. The sunsuit that barely covered her various bulges made her look even bigger. She turned off the water when I got out of my car.

"What gives? You've got trouble on your face if I ever saw trouble."

"Dewar is dead. Murdered. A skin-diver found him in the sea off La Jolla."

She took it calmly. "That's not such bad news, is it? He had it coming. Who killed him?"

"I told you a gunman from Nevada was on his trail. Maybe he caught him. Anyway, Dewar was shot and bled to death from a neck wound. Then he was dumped in the ocean. I had to lay the whole thing on the line for the police, since there's murder in it."

"You told them what happened to Ethel?"

"I had to. They're at the rest home talking to her now."

"What about Ethel's money? Was the money on him?"

"Not a trace of it. And he didn't live to spend it. The police pathologist thinks he's been dead for a week. Whoever got Dewar got the money at the same time."

"Will she ever get it back, do you think?"

"If we can catch the murderer, and he still has it with him. That's a big if. Where's Clare, by the way? With her sister?"

"Clare went back to L.A."

"What for?"

"Don't ask me." She shrugged her rosy shoulders. "She got Jake to drive her down to the station before he went to work. I wasn't up. She didn't even tell me she was going." Gretchen seemed peeved.

"Did she get a telegram, or a phone call?"

"Nothing. All I know is what Jake told me. She talked him into lending her ten bucks. I wouldn't mind so much, but it was all the ready cash we had, until payday. Oh well, I guess we'll get it back, if Ethel recovers her money."

"You'll get it back," I said. "Clare seems to be a straight kid."

"That's what I always used to think. When they lived here, before Ethel met Illman and got into the chips, Clare was just about the nicest kid on the block. In spite of all the trouble in her family."

"What trouble was that?"

"Her father shot himself. Didn't you know? They said it was an accident, but the people on the street—we knew different. Mr. Larrabee was never the same after his wife left him. He spent his time brooding, drinking, and brooding. Clare reminded me of him, the way she behaved last night after you left. She wouldn't talk to me or look at me. She shut herself up in her room and acted real cold. If you want the honest truth, I don't like her using my home as if it were a motel and Jake was a taxi service. The least she could of done was say good-bye to me."

"It sounds as if she had something on her mind."

All the way back to Los Angeles, I wondered what it was. It took me a little over two hours to drive from San Diego to West Hollywood. The black Lincoln with the searchlight and the Nevada license plates was standing at the curb below the redwood house. The front door of the house was standing open.

I transferred my automatic from the suitcase to my jacket pocket, making sure that it was ready to fire. I climbed the terraced lawn beside the driveway. My feet made no sound in the grass. When I reached the porch, I heard voices from inside. One was the gunman's hoarse and deathly monotone:

"I'm taking it, sister. It belongs to me."

"You're a liar."

"Sure, but not about this. The money is mine."

"It's my sister's money. What right have you got to it?"

"This. Dewar stole it from me. He ran a poker game for me in Vegas, a high-stakes game in various hotels around town. He was a good dealer, and I trusted him with the house take. I let it pile up for a week, that was my mistake. I should've kept a closer watch on him. He ran out on me with twenty-five grand or more. That's the money you're holding, lady."

"I don't believe it. You can't prove that story. It's fantastic."

"I don't have to prove it. Gelt talks, but iron talks louder. So hand it over, eh?"

"I'll die first."

"Maybe you will at that."

I edged along the wall to the open door. Clare was standing flat against the opposite wall of the hallway. She was clutching a sheaf of bills to her breast. The gunman's broad flannel back was to me, and he was advancing on her.

"Stay away from me, you." Her cry was thin and desperate. She was trying to merge with the wall, pressed by an orgastic terror.

"I don't like taking candy from a baby," he said in a very reasonable tone. "Only I'm going to have that money back."

"You can't have it. It's Ethel's. It's all she has."

"—you, lady. You and your sister both."

He raised his armed right hand and slapped the side of her face with the gun barrel, lightly. Fingering the welt it left, she said in a kind of despairing stupor:

"You're the one that hurt Ethel, aren't you? Now you're hurting me. You like hurting people, don't you?"

"Listen to reason, lady. It ain't just the money, it's a matter of business. I let it happen once, it'll happen again. I can't afford to let anybody get away with nothing. I got a reputation to live up to."

I said from the doorway: "Is that why you killed Dewar?"

He let out an animal sound, and whirled in my direction. I shot before he did, twice. The first slug rocked him back on his heels. His bullet went wild, plowed the ceiling. My second slug took him off balance and slammed him against the wall. His blood spattered Clare and the money in her hands. She screamed once, very loudly.

The man from Las Vegas dropped his gun. It clattered on the parquetry. His hands clasped his perforated chest, trying to hold the blood in. He slid down the wall slowly, his face a mask of smiling pain, and sat with a bump on the floor. He blew red bubbles and said:

"You got me wrong. I didn't kill Dewar. I didn't know he was dead. The money belongs to me. You made a big mistake, punk."

"So did you."

He went on smiling, as if in fierce appreciation of the joke. Then his red grin changed to a rictus, and he slumped sideways.

Clare looked from him to me, her eyes wide and dark with the sight of death. "I don't know how to thank you. He was going to kill me."

"I doubt that. He was just combining a little pleasure with business."

"But he shot at you."

"It's just as well he did. It leaves no doubt that it was self-defense."

"Is it true what you said? That Dewar's dead? He killed him?"

"You tell me."

"What do you mean?"

"You've got the money that Dewar took from your sister. Where did you get it?"

"It was here, right in this house. I found it in the kitchen."

"That's kind of hard to swallow, Clare."

"It's true." She looked down at the blood-spattered money in her hands. The outside bill was a hundred. Unconsciously, she tried to wipe it clean on the front of her dress. "He had it hidden here. He must have come back and hid it."

"Show me where."

"You're not being very nice to me. And I'm not feeling well."

"Neither is Dewar. You didn't shoot him yourself, by any chance?"

"How could I? I was in Berkeley when it happened. I wish I was back there now."

"You know when it happened, do you?"

"No." She bit her lip. "I don't mean that. I mean I was in Berkeley all along. You're a witness, you were with me on the train coming down."

"Trains run both ways."

She regarded me with loathing. "You're not nice at all. To think that yesterday I thought you were nice."

"You're wasting time, Clare. I have to call the police. But first I want to see where you found the money. Or where you say you did."

"In the kitchen. You've got to believe me. It took me a long time to get here from the station on the bus. I'd only just found it when he walked in on me."

"I'll believe the physical evidence, if any."

To my surprise, the physical evidence was there. A red-enameled flour canister was standing open on the board beside the kitchen sink. There were fingerprints on the flour, and a floury piece of oilskin wrapping in the sink.

"He hid the money under the flour," Clare said. "I guess he thought it would be safer here than if he carried it around with him."

It wasn't a likely story. On the other hand, the criminal mind is capable of strange things. Whose criminal mind, I wondered: Clare's, or Owen Dewar's, or somebody else's? I said:

"Where did you get the bright idea of coming back here and looking for it?"

"Ethel suggested it last night, just before I left her. She told me this was his favorite hiding place while she was living with him. She discovered it by accident one day."

"Hiding place for what?"

"Some kind of drug he took. He was a drug addict. Do you still think I'm lying?"

"Somebody is. But I suppose I've got to take your word, until I get something better. What are you going to do with the money?"

"Ethel said if I found it, that I was to go down and put it in the bank."

"There's no time for that now. You better let me hold it for you. I have a safe in my office."

"No. You don't trust me. Why should I trust you?"

"Because you can trust me, and you know it. If the cops impound it, you'll have to prove ownership to get it back."

She was too spent to argue. She let me take it out of her hands. I riffled through the bills and got a rough idea of their sum. There was easily twenty-five thousand there. I gave her a receipt for that amount, and put the sheaf of bills in my inside pocket.

It was after dark when the cops got through with me. By that time I was equipped to do a comparative study on the San Diego and Los Angeles P.D.'s. With the help of a friend in the D.A.'s office, Clare's eyewitness account, and the bullet in the ceiling, I got away from them without being booked. The dead man's record also helped. He had been widely suspected of shooting Bugsy Siegel, and had fallen heir to some of Siegel's holdings. His name was Jack Fidelis. R.I.P.

I drove out Sunset to my office. The Strip was lighting up for business again. The stars looked down on its neon conflagration like hard bright knowing eyes. I pulled the Venetian blinds and locked the doors and counted the money: $26,380. I wrapped it up in brown paper, sealed it with wax and tucked it away in the safe. I would have preferred to tear it in little pieces and flush the green confetti down the drain. Two men had died for it. I wasn't eager to become the third.

I had a steak in the restaurant at International Airport, and hopped a shuttle plane to Las Vegas. There I spent a rough night in various gambling joints, watching the suckers blow their vacation money, pinching my own pennies, and talking to some of the guys and girls that raked the money in. The rest of Illman's two hundred dollars bought me the facts I needed.

I flew back to Los Angeles in the morning, picked up my car and headed for San Diego. I was tired enough to sleep standing up, like a horse. But something heavier than sleep or tiredness sat on the back of my neck and pressed the gas pedal down to the floorboards. It was the thought of Clare.

Clare was with her sister in the Mission Rest Home. She was waiting outside the closed door of Ethel's room when Mrs. Lestina took me down the hall. She looked as if she had passed a rougher night than mine. Her grooming was careless, hair uncombed, mouth unpainted. The welt from Fidelis' gun had turned blue and spread to one puffed eye. And I thought how very little it took to break a young girl down into a tramp, if she was vulnerable, or twist her into something worse than a tramp.

"Did you bring it with you?" she said as soon as Mrs. Lestina was out of earshot. "Ethel's angry with me for turning it over to you."

"I'm not surprised."

"Give it to me. Please." Her hand clawed at my sleeve. "Isn't that what you came for, to give it back to me?"

"It's in the safe in my office in Los Angeles. That is, if you're talking about the money."

"What else would I be talking about? You'll simply have to go back there and get it. Ethel can't leave here without it. She needs it to pay her bill."

"Is Ethel planning to go some place?"

"I persuaded her to come back to Berkeley with me. She'll have better care in the hospital there, and I know of a good plastic surgeon—"

"It'll take more than that to put Ethel together again."

"What do you mean?"

"You should be able to guess. You're not a stupid girl, or are you? Has she got you fooled the way she had me fooled?"

"I don't know what you're talking about. But I don't like it. Every time I see you, you seem to get nastier."

"This is a nasty business. It's rubbing off on all of us, isn't it, kid?"

She looked at me vaguely through a fog of doubt. "Don't you dare call me kid. I thought you were a real friend for a while, but you don't even like me. You've said some dreadful things. You probably think you can scare me into letting you keep our money. Well, you can't."

"That's my problem," I said. "What to do with the money."

"You'll give it back to Ethel and me, that's what you'll do. There are laws to deal with people like you—"

"And people like Ethel. I want to talk to her."

"I won't let you. My sister's suffered enough already."

She spread her arms across the width of the door. I was tempted to go away and send her the money and forget the whole thing. But the need to finish it pushed me, imperative as a gun at my back.

I lifted her by the waist and tried to set her aside. Her entire body was rigid and jerking galvanically. Her hands slid under my arms and around my neck and held on. Her head rolled on my shoulder and was still. Suddenly, like delayed rain after lightning, her tears came. I stood and held her vibrating body, trying to quench the dangerous heat that was rising in my veins, and wondering what in hell I was going to do.

"Ethel did it for me," she sobbed. "She wanted me to have a good start in life."

"Some start she's giving you. Did she tell you that?"

"She didn't have to. I knew. I tried to pretend to myself, but I knew. When she told me where to look for the money last night—the night before last."

"You knew Ethel took it from Dewar and hid it in her house?"

"Yes. The thought went through my mind, and I couldn't get rid of it. Ethel's always taken terrible chances, and money means so much to her. Not for herself. For me."

"She wasn't thinking of you when she gambled away the money she got from Illman. She went through it in a week."

"Is that what happened to it?"

"That's it. I flew to Las Vegas last night and talked to some of the people that got her money, dealers and stickmen. They remembered her. She had a bad case of gambling fever that week. It didn't leave her until the money was gone. Then maybe she thought of you."

"Poor Ethel. I've seen her before when she had a gambling streak."

"Poor Dewar," I said.

The door beside us creaked open. The muzzle of a blue revolver looked out. Above it, Ethel's eyes glared red from her bandaged face.

"Come in here, both of you."

Clare stretched out her hands toward her sister. "No, Ethel. Darling, you mustn't. Give me that gun."

"I have a use for it. I know what I'm doing."

She backed away, supporting herself on the doorknob.

I said to Clare: "We better do as she says. She won't hurt you."

"Nor you unless you make me. Don't reach for your gun, and don't try anything funny. You know what happened to Dewar."

"Not as well as you do."

"Don't waste any tears on that one. Save them for yourself. Now get in here." The gun wagged peremptorily.

I edged past her with Clare at my back. Ethel shut the door and moved to the bed, her eyes never leaving mine. She sat on its edge, and supported the elbow of her gun arm on her knee, hunched far over like an aged wreck of a woman.

It was strange to see the fine naked legs dangling below her hospital gown, the red polish flaking off her toenails. Her voice was low and resonant.

"I don't like to do this. But how am I going to make you see it my way if I don't? I want Clare to see it, too. It was self-defense, understand. I didn't intend to kill him. I never expected to see him again. Fidelis was after him, and it was only a matter of time until he caught up with Owen. Owen knew that. He told me himself he wouldn't live out the year. He was so sure of it he was paralyzed. He got so he wouldn't even go out of the house.

"Somebody had to make a move, and I decided it might as well be me. Why should I sit and wait for Fidelis to come and take the money back and blow Owen's head off for him? It was really my money, anyway, mine and Clare's."

"Leave me out of this," Clare said.

"But you don't understand, honey," the damaged mouth insisted. "It really was my money. We were legally married, what was his was mine. I talked him into taking it in the first place. He'd never have had the guts to do it alone. He thought Fidelis was God himself. I didn't. But I didn't want to be there when Jack Fidelis found him. So I left him. I took the money out of his pillow when he was asleep and hid it where he'd never look for it. Then I drove down here. I guess you know the rest. He found a letter from Gretchen in the house, and traced me through it. He thought I was carrying the money. When it turned out that I wasn't, he took me out to the beach and beat me up. I wouldn't tell him where it was. He threatened to shoot me then. I fought him for the gun, and it went off. It was a clear case of self-defense."

"Maybe it was. You'll never get a jury to believe it, though. Innocent people don't dump their shooting victims in the drink."

"But I didn't. The tide was coming in. I didn't even touch him after he died. He just lay there, and the water took him."

"While you stood and watched?"

"I couldn't get away. I was so weak I couldn't move for a long time. Then when I finally could, it was too late. He was gone, and he had the keys to the car."

"He drove you out to La Jolla, did he?"

"Yes."

"And held a gun on you at the same time. That's quite a trick."

"He did, though," she said. "That is the way it happened."

"I hear you telling me, Mrs. Dewar."

She winced behind her mask at the sound of her name. "I'm not Mrs. Dewar," she said. "I've taken back my maiden name. I'm Ethel Larrabee."

"We won't argue about the name. You'll be trading it in for a number, anyway."

"I don't think I will. The shooting was self-defense, and once he was dead the money belonged to me. There's no way of proving he stole it, now that Fidelis is gone. I guess I owe you a little thanks for that."

"Put down your gun, then."

"I'm not that grateful," she said.

Clare moved across the room toward her. "Let me look at the gun, Ethel. It's father's revolver, isn't it?"

"Be quiet, you little fool."

"I won't be quiet. These things have to be said. You're way off by yourself, Ethel I'm not with you. I want no part of this, or the money. You don't understand how strange and dreadful—" Her voice broke. She stood a few feet from her sister, held back by the gun's menace, yet strangely drawn toward it. "That's father's revolver, isn't it? The one he shot himself with?"

"What if it is?"

"I'll tell you, Ethel Larrabee," I said. "Dewar didn't pull a gun on you. You were the one that had the gun. You forced him to drive you out to the beach and shot him in cold blood. But he didn't die right away. He lived long enough to leave his marks on you. Isn't that how it happened?"

The bandaged face was silent. I looked into the terrible eyes for assent. They were lost and wild, like an animal's. "Is that true, Ethel? Did you murder him?" Clare looked down at her sister with pity and terror.

"I did it for you," the masked face said. "I always tried to do what was best for you. Don't you believe me? Don't you know I love you? Ever since father killed himself I've tried—"

Clare turned and walked to the wall and stood with her forehead against it. Ethel put the muzzle of the gun in her mouth. Her broken teeth clenched on it the way a smoker bites on a pipe stem. The bones and flesh of her head muffled its roar.

I laid her body out on the bed and pulled a sheet up over it.

The Empty Hours

Author: Ed McBain (1926–   )

Detectives: 87th Precinct (1956)

Ed McBain, also and for a time better known as Evan Hunter, didn't really invent the police procedural with the first 87th Precinct novel, *Cop Hater* (1956). He'd been preceded by Lawrence Treat, Hillary Waugh, Jonathan Craig, and others, not to mention the radio-TV series that did most to popularize the form, *Dragnet*. But McBain may have brought the procedural to its highest level, and more than forty years later new novels of the 87th, most recently *The Big Bad City* (1999), continue to raise the bar.

A personal note from editor Jon L. Breen: "My first story to appear in print was a parody of the 87th Precinct series in *Ellery Queen's Mystery Magazine*, May 1967. I'd called it 'The Cutter,' but to present it in tandem with the novelette that follows, editor Ellery Queen (Frederic Dannay) retitled it 'The Crowded Hours.' Another reason for choosing it is that it is one of the few 87th Precinct novelettes not to have been expanded or incorporated into a novel."

I

They thought she was colored at first.

The patrolman who investigated the complaint didn't expect to find a dead woman. This was the first time he'd seen a corpse, and he was somewhat shaken by the ludicrously relaxed grotesqueness of the girl lying on her back on the rug, and his hand trembled a little as he made out his report. But when he came to the blank line calling for an identification of RACE, he unhesitatingly wrote "Negro."

The call had been taken at Headquarters by a patrolman in the central Complaint Bureau. He sat at a desk with a pad of printed forms before him, and he copied down the information, shrugged because this seemed like a routine squeal, rolled the form, and slipped it into a metal carrier, and then shot it by pneumatic tube to the radio room. A dispatcher there read the complaint form, shrugged because this seemed like a routine squeal, studied the precinct map on the wall opposite his desk, and then dispatched car eleven of the 87th Precinct to the scene.

The girl was dead.

She may have been a pretty girl, but she was hideous in death, distorted by the expanding gases inside her skin case. She was wearing a sweater and skirt, and she was barefoot, and her skirt had pulled back when she fell to the rug. Her head was twisted at a curious angle, the short black hair cradled by the rug, her eyes open and brown in a bloated face. The patrolman felt a sudden impulse to pull the girl's skirt down over her knees. He knew, suddenly, she would have wanted this. Death had caught her in this indecent posture, robbing her of female instinct. There were things this girl would never do again, so many things, all of which must have seemed enormously important to the girl herself. But the single universal thing was an infinitesimal detail, magnified now by death: she would never again perform the simple feminine and somehow beautiful act of pulling her skirt down over her knees.

The patrolman sighed and finished his report. The image of the dead girl remained in his mind all the way down to the squad car.

It was hot in the squadroom on that night in early August. The men working the graveyard shift had reported for duty at 6:00 P.M., and they would not go home until eight the following morning. They were all detectives and perhaps privileged members of the police force, but there were many policemen—Detective Meyer Meyer among them—who maintained that a uniformed cop's life made a hell of a lot more sense than a detective's.

"Sure, it does," Meyer insisted now, sitting at his desk in his shirt sleeves. "A patrolman's schedule provides regularity and security. It gives a man a home life."

"This squadroom is your home, Meyer," Carella said. "Admit it."

"Sure," Meyer answered, grinning. "I can't wait to come to work each day." He passed a hand over his bald pate. "You know what I like especially about this place? The interior decoration. The décor. It's very restful."

"Oh, you don't like your fellow workers, huh?" Carella said. He slid off the desk and winked at Cotton Hawes, who was standing at one of the filing cabinets. Then he walked toward the water cooler at the other end of the room, just inside the slatted railing that divided squadroom from corridor. He moved with a nonchalant ease that was deceptive. Steve Carella had never been one of those weight-lifting goons, and the image he presented was hardly one of bulging muscular power. But there was a quiet strength about the man and the way he moved, a confidence in the way he casually accepted the capabilities and limitations of his body. He stopped at the water cooler, filled a paper cup, and turned to look at Meyer again.

"No, I like my colleagues," Meyer said. "In fact, Steve, if I had my choice in all the world of who to work with, I would choose you honorable, decent guys. Sure." Meyer nodded, building steam. "In fact, I'm thinking of having some medals cast off, so I can hand them out to you guys. Boy, am I lucky to have this job! I may come to work without pay from now on. I may just refuse my salary, this job is so enriching. I want to thank you guys. You make me recognize the real values in life."

"He makes a nice speech," Hawes said.

"He should run the lineup. It would break the monotony. How come you don't run the lineup, Meyer?"

"Steve, I been offered the job," Meyer said seriously. "I told them I'm needed right here at the Eighty-seventh, the garden spot of all the precincts. Why, they offered me chief of detectives, and when I said no, they offered me commissioner, but I was loyal to the squad."

"Let's give *him* a medal," Hawes said, and the telephone rang.

Meyer lifted the receiver. "Eighty-seventh Squad, Detective Meyer. What? Yeah, just a second." He pulled a pad into place and began writing. "Yeah, I got it. Right. Right. Right. Okay." He hung up. Carella had walked to his desk. "A little colored girl," Meyer said.

"Yeah?"

"In a furnished room on South Eleventh."

"Yeah?"

"Dead," Meyer said.

II

The city doesn't seem to be itself in the very early hours of the morning.

She is a woman, of course, and time will never change that. She awakes as a woman, tentatively touching the day in a yawning, smiling stretch, her lips free of color, her hair tousled, warm from sleep, her body richer, an innocent girlish quality about her as sunlight stains the eastern sky and covers her with early heat. She dresses in furnished rooms in crumby rundown slums, and she dresses in Hall Avenue penthouses, and in the countless apartments that crowd the buildings of Isola and Riverhead and Calm's Point, in the private houses that line the streets of Bethtown and Majesta, and she emerges a different woman, sleek and businesslike, attractive but not sexy, a look of utter competence about her, manicured and polished, but with no time for nonsense, there is a long working day ahead of her. At five o'clock a metamorphosis takes place. She does not change her costume, this city, this woman, she wears the same frock or the same suit, the same high-heeled pumps or the same suburban loafers, but something breaks through that immaculate shell, a mood, a tone, an undercurrent. She is a different woman who sits in the bars and cocktail lounges, who relaxes on the patios or on the terraces shelving the skyscrapers, a different woman with a somewhat lazily inviting grin, a somewhat tired expression, an impenetrable knowledge on her face and in her eyes: she lifts her glass, she laughs gently, the evening sits expectantly on the skyline, the sky is awash with the purple of day's end.

She turns female in the night.

She drops her femininity and turns female. The polish is gone, the mechanized competence; she becomes a little scatterbrained and a little cuddly; she crosses her legs recklessly and allows her lipstick to be kissed clear off her mouth, and she responds to the male hands on her body, and she turns soft and inviting and miraculously primitive. The night is a female time, and the city is nothing but a woman.

And in the empty hours she sleeps, and she does not seem to be herself.

In the morning she will awake again and touch the silent air in a yawn, spreading her arms, the contented smile on her naked mouth. Her hair will be mussed, we will know her, we have seen her this way often.

But now she sleeps. She sleeps silently, this city. Oh, an eye open in the buildings of the night here and there, winking on, off again, silence. She rests. In sleep we do not recognize her. Her sleep is not like death, for we can hear and sense the murmur of life beneath the warm bedclothes. But she is a strange woman whom we have known intimately, loved passionately, and now she curls into an unresponsive ball beneath the sheets, and our hand is on her rich hip. We can feel life there, but we do not know her. She is faceless and featureless in the dark. She could be any city, any woman, anywhere. We touch her uncertainly. She has pulled the black nightgown of early morning around her, and we do not know her. She is a stranger, and her eyes are closed.

The landlady was frightened by the presence of policemen, even though she had summoned them. The taller one, the one who called himself Detective Hawes, was a redheaded giant with a white streak in his hair, a horror if she'd ever seen one. The landlady stood in the apartment where the girl lay dead on the rug, and she talked to the detectives in whispers, not because she was in the presence of death, but only because it was three o'clock in the morning. The landlady was wearing a bathrobe over her gown. There was an intimacy to the scene, the same intimacy that hangs alike over an impending fishing trip or a completed tragedy. Three A.M. is a time for slumber, and those who are awake while the city sleeps share a common bond that makes them friendly aliens.

"What's the girl's name?" Carella asked. It was three o'clock in the morning, and he had not shaved since 5:00 P.M. the day before, but his chin looked smooth. His eyes slanted slightly downward, combining with his clean-shaven face to give him a curiously oriental appearance. The landlady liked him. He was a nice boy, she thought. In her lexicon the men of the world were either "nice boys" or "louses." She wasn't sure about Cotton Hawes yet, but she imagined he was a parasitic insect.

"Claudia Davis," she answered, directing the answer to Carella whom she liked, and totally ignoring Hawes who had no right to be so big a man with a frightening white streak in his hair.

"Do you know how old she was?" Carella asked.

"Twenty-eight or twenty-nine, I think."

"Had she been living here long?"

"Since June," the landlady said.

"That short a time, huh?"

"And *this* has to happen," the landlady said. "She seemed like such a nice girl. Who do you suppose did it?"

"I don't know," Carella said.

"Or do you think it was suicide? I don't smell no gas, do you?"

"No," Carella said. "Do you know where she lived before this, Mrs. Mauder?"

"No, I don't."

"You didn't ask for references when she took the apartment?"

"It's only a furnished room," Mrs. Mauder said, shrugging. "She paid me a month's rent in advance."

"How much was that, Mrs. Mauder?"

"Sixty dollars. She paid it in cash. I never take checks from strangers."

"But you have no idea whether she's from this city, or out of town, or whatever. Am I right?"

"Yes, that's right."

"Davis," Hawes said, shaking his head. "That'll be a tough name to track down, Steve. Must be a thousand of them in the phone book."

"Why is your hair white?" the landlady asked.

"Huh?"

"That streak."

"Oh." Hawes unconsciously touched his left temple. "I got knifed once," he said, dismissing the question abruptly. "Mrs. Mauder, was the girl living alone?"

"I don't know. I mind my own business."

"Well, surely you would have seen . . ."

"I think she was living alone. I don't pry, and I don't spy. She gave me a month's rent in advance."

Hawes sighed. He could feel the woman's hostility. He decided to leave the questioning to Carella. "I'll take a look through the drawers and closets," he said, and moved off without waiting for Carella's answer.

"It's awfully hot in here," Carella said.

"The patrolman said we shouldn't touch anything until you got here," Mrs. Mauder said. "That's why I didn't open the windows or nothing."

"That was very thoughtful of you," Carella said, smiling. "But I think we can open the window now, don't you?"

"If you like. It does smell in here. Is . . . is that her? Smelling?"

"Yes," Carella answered. He pulled open the window. "There. That's a little better."

"Doesn't help much," the landlady said. "The weather's been terrible—just terrible. Body can't sleep at all." She looked down at the dead girl. "She looks just awful, doesn't she?"

"Yes. Mrs. Mauder, would you know where she worked, or if she had a job?"

"No, I'm sorry."

"Anyone ever come by asking for her? Friends? Relatives?"

"No, I'm sorry. I never saw any."

"Can you tell me anything about her habits? When she left the house in the morning? When she returned at night?"

"I'm sorry; I never noticed."

"Well, what made you think something was wrong in here?"

"The milk. Outside the door. I was out with some friends tonight, you

see, and when I came back a man on the third floor called down to say
his neighbor was playing the radio very loud and would I tell him to
shut up, please. So I went upstairs and asked him to turn down the
radio, and then I passed Miss Davis' apartment and saw the milk standing outside the door, and I thought this was kind of funny in such hot
weather, but I figured it was *her* milk, you know, and I don't like to pry.
So I came down and went to bed, but I couldn't stop thinking about that
milk standing outside in the hallway. So I put on a robe and came
upstairs and knocked on the door, and she didn't answer. So I called out
to her, and she still didn't answer. So I figured something must be
wrong. I don't know why. I just figured . . . I don't know. If she was in
here, why didn't she answer?"

"How'd you know she was here?"

"I didn't."

"Was the door locked?"

"Yes."

"You tried it?"

"Yes. It was locked."

"I see," Carella said.

"Couple of cars just pulled up downstairs," Hawes said, walking
over. "Probably the lab. And Homicide South."

"They know the squeal is ours," Carella said. "Why do they bother?"

"Make it look good," Hawes said. "Homicide's got the title on the
door, so they figure they ought to go out and earn their salaries."

"Did you find anything?"

"A brand-new set of luggage in the closet, six pieces. The drawers and
closets are full of clothes. Most of them look new. Lots of resort stuff,
Steve. Found some brand-new books, too."

"What else?"

"Some mail on the dresser top."

"Anything we can use?"

Hawes shrugged. "A statement from the girl's bank. Bunch of canceled checks. Might help us."

"Maybe," Carella said. "Let's see what the lab comes up with."

The laboratory report came the next day, together with a necropsy
report from the assistant medical examiner. In combination, the reports
were fairly valuable. The first thing the detectives learned was that the
girl was a white Caucasian of approximately thirty years of age.

Yes, white.

The news came as something of a surprise to the cops because the girl
lying on the rug had certainly looked like a Negress. After all, her skin

was black. Not tan, not coffee-colored, not brown, but black—that intensely black coloration found on primitive tribes who spend a good deal of their time in the sun. The conclusion seemed to be a logical one, but death is a great equalizer not without a whimsical humor all its own, and the funniest kind of joke is a sight gag. Death changes white to black, and when that grisly old man comes marching in, there's no question of who's going to school with whom. There's no longer any question of pigmentation, friend. That girl on the floor looked black, but she was white, and whatever else she was she was also stone-cold dead, and that's the worst you can do to anybody.

The report explained that the girl's body was in a state of advanced putrefaction, and it went into such esoteric terms as "general distention of the body cavities, tissues, and blood vessels with gas," and "black discoloration of the skin, mucous membranes, and irides caused by hemolysis and action of hydrogen sulfide on the blood pigment," all of which broke down to the simple fact that it was a damn hot week in August and the girl had been lying on a rug that retained heat and speeded the post-mortem putrefaction. From what they could tell, and in weather like this, it was mostly a guess, the girl had been dead and decomposing for at least forty-eight hours, which set the time of her demise as August first or thereabouts.

One of the reports went on to say that the clothes she'd been wearing had been purchased in one of the city's larger department stores. All of her clothes—those she wore and those she found in her apartment—were rather expensive, but someone at the lab thought it necessary to note that all her panties were trimmed with Belgian lace and retailed for twenty-five dollars a pair. Someone else at the lab mentioned that a thorough examination of her garments and her body had revealed no traces of blood, semen, or oil stains.

The coroner fixed the cause of death as strangulation.

III

It is amazing how much an apartment can sometimes yield to science. It is equally amazing, and more than a little disappointing, to get nothing from the scene of a murder when you are desperately seeking a clue. The furnished room in which Claudia Davis had been strangled to death was full of juicy surfaces conceivably carrying hundreds of latent fingerprints. The closets and drawers contained piles of clothing that might have carried traces of anything from gunpowder to face powder.

But the lab boys went around lifting their prints and sifting their dust and vacuuming with a Söderman-Heuberger filter, and they went down to the morgue and studied the girl's skin and came up with a total of nothing. Zero. Oh, not quite zero. They got a lot of prints belonging to Claudia Davis, and a lot of dust collected from all over the city and clinging to her shoes and her furniture. They also found some documents belonging to the dead girl—a birth certificate, a diploma of graduation from a high school in Santa Monica, and an expired library card. And, oh yes, a key. The key didn't seem to fit any of the locks in the room. They sent all the junk over to the 87th, and Sam Grossman called Carella personally later that day to apologize for the lack of results.

The squadroom was hot and noisy when Carella took the call from the lab. The conversation was a curiously one-sided affair. Carella, who had dumped the contents of the laboratory envelope onto his desk, merely grunted or nodded every now and then. He thanked Grossman at last, hung up, and stared at the window facing the street and Grover Park.

"Get anything?" Meyer asked.

"Yeah. Grossman thinks the killer was wearing gloves."

"That's nice," Meyer said.

"Also, I think I know what this key is for." He lifted it from the desk.

"Yeah? What?"

"Well, did you see these canceled checks?"

"No."

"Take a look," Carella said.

He opened the brown bank envelope addressed to Claudia Davis, spread the canceled checks on his desk top, and then unfolded the yellow bank statement. Meyer studied the display silently.

"Cotton found the envelope in her room," Carella said. "The statement covers the month of July. Those are all the checks she wrote, or at least everything that cleared the bank by the thirty-first."

"Lots of checks here," Meyer said.

"Twenty-five, to be exact. What do you think?"

"I know what *I* think," Carella said.

"What's that?"

"I look at those checks, I can see a life. It's like reading somebody's diary. Everything she did last month is right here, Meyer. All the department stores she went to, look, a florist, her hairdresser, a candy shop, even her shoemaker, and look at this. A check made out to a funeral home. Now who died, Meyer, huh? And look here. She was living at Mrs. Mauder's place, but here's a check made out to a swank apartment building on the South Side, in Stewart City. And some of these checks are just made out to names, *people*. This case is crying for some people."

"You want me to get the phone book?"

"No, wait a minute. Look at this bank statement. She opened the account on July fifth with a thousand bucks. All of a sudden, bam, she deposits a thousand bucks in the Seaboard Bank of America."

"What's so odd about that?"

"Nothing, maybe. But Cotton called the other banks in the city, and Claudia Davis has a very healthy account at the Highland Trust on Cromwell Avenue. And I mean *very* healthy."

"How healthy?"

"Close to sixty grand."

"What!"

"You heard me. And the Highland Trust lists no withdrawals for the month of July. So where'd she get the money to put into Seaboard?"

"Was that the only deposit?"

"Take a look."

Meyer picked up the statement.

"The initial deposit was on July fifth," Carella said. "A thousand bucks. She made another thousand-dollar deposit on July twelfth. And another on the nineteenth. And another on the twenty-seventh."

Meyer raised his eyebrows. "Four grand. That's a lot of loot."

"And all deposited in less than a month's time. I've got to work almost a full year to make that kind of money."

"Not to mention the sixty grand in the other bank. Where do you suppose she got it, Steve?"

"I don't know. It just doesn't make sense. She wears underpants trimmed with Belgian lace, but she lives in a crumby room-and-a-half with bath. How the hell do you figure that? Two bank accounts, twenty-five bucks to cover her ass, and all she pays is sixty bucks a month for a flophouse."

"Maybe she's hot, Steve."

"No." Carella shook his head. "I ran a make with C.B.I. She hasn't got a record, and she's not wanted for anything. I haven't heard from the feds yet, but I imagine it'll be the same story."

"What about that key? You said . . ."

"Oh yeah. That's pretty simple, thank God. Look at this."

He reached into the pile of checks and sorted out a yellow slip, larger than the checks. He handed it to Meyer. The slip read:

THE SEABOARD BANK OF AMERICA

Isola Branch   P 1698

July 5

We are charging your account as per items below. Please see that the amount is deducted on your books so that our accounts may agree.

FOR	Safe deposit rental #375		5	00
	U.S. Tax			50
	AMOUNT OF CHARGE		5	50

CHARGE Claudia Davis   ENTERED BY

1263 South Eleventh   *BPR*

Isola

"She rented a safe-deposit box the same day she opened the new checking account, huh?" Meyer said.

"Right."

"What's in it?"

"That's a good question."

"Look, do you want to save some time, Steve?"

"Sure."

"Let's get the court order *before* we go to the bank."

IV

The manager of the Seaboard Bank of America was a bald-headed man in his early fifties. Working on the theory that similar physical types are *simpático,* Carella allowed Meyer to do most of the questioning. It was not easy to elicit answers from Mr. Anderson, the manager of the bank, because he was by nature a reticent man. But Detective Meyer Meyer was the most patient man in the city, if not the entire world. His patience was an acquired trait, rather than an inherited one. Oh, he had inherited a few things from his father, a jovial man named Max Meyer, but patience was not one of them. If anything, Max Meyer had been a very impatient if not downright short-tempered sort of fellow. When his wife, for example, came to him with the news that she was expecting a baby, Max nearly hit the ceiling. He enjoyed little jokes immensely, was perhaps the biggest practical joker in all Riverhead, but this particular prank of nature failed to amuse him. He had thought his wife was long past the age when bearing children was even a remote possibility. He never thought of himself as approaching dotage, but he was after all getting on in years, and a change-of-life baby was hardly what the doctor had ordered. He allowed the impending birth to simmer inside him, planning his revenge all the while, plotting the practical joke to end all practical jokes.

When the baby was born, he named it Meyer, a delightful handle, which when coupled with the family name provided the infant with a double-barreled monicker: Meyer Meyer.

Now that's pretty funny. Admit it. You can split your sides laughing over that one, unless you happen to be a pretty sensitive kid who also happens to be an Orthodox Jew, and who happens to live in a predominately Gentile neighborhood. The kids in the neighborhood thought Meyer Meyer had been invented solely for their own pleasure. If they needed further provocation for beating up the Jew boy, and they didn't need any, his name provided excellent motivational fuel. "Meyer Meyer, Jew on fire!" they would shout, and then they would chase him down the street and beat the hell out of him.

Meyer learned patience. It is not very often that one kid, or even one grown man, can successfully defend himself against a gang. But sometimes you can talk yourself out of a beating. Sometimes, if you're patient, if you just wait long enough, you can catch one of them alone and stand up to him face to face, man to man, and know the exultation of a fair fight without the frustration of overwhelming odds.

Listen, Max Meyer's joke was a harmless one. You can't deny an old man his pleasure. But Mr. Anderson, the manager of the bank, was fifty-four years old and totally bald. Meyer Meyer, the detective second grade who sat opposite him and asked questions, was also totally bald. Maybe a lifetime of sublimation, a lifetime of devoted patience, doesn't leave any scars. Maybe not. But Meyer Meyer was only thirty-seven years old.

Patiently he said, "Didn't you find these large deposits rather odd, Mr. Anderson?"

"No," Anderson said. "A thousand dollars is not a lot of money."

"Mr. Anderson," Meyer said patiently, "you are aware, of course, that banks in this city are required to report to the police any unusually large sums of money deposited at one time. You are aware of that, are you not?"

"Yes, I am."

"Miss Davis deposited four thousand dollars in three weeks' time. Didn't that seem unusual to you?"

"No. The deposits were spaced. A thousand dollars is not a lot of money, and not an unusually large deposit."

"To me," Meyer said, "a thousand dollars is a lot of money. You can buy a lot of beer with a thousand dollars."

"I don't drink beer," Anderson said flatly.

"Neither do I," Meyer answered.

"Besides, we *do* call the police whenever we get a very large deposit, unless the depositor is one of our regular customers. I did not feel that these deposits warranted such a call."

"Thank you, Mr. Anderson," Meyer said. "We have a court order here. We'd like to open the box Miss Davis rented."

"May I see the order, please?" Anderson said. Meyer showed it to him. Anderson sighed and said, "Very well. Do you have Miss Davis' key?"

Carella reached into his pocket. "Would this be it?" he said. He put a key on the desk. It was the key that had come to him from the lab together with the documents they'd found in the apartment.

"Yes, that's it," Mr. Anderson said. "There are two different keys to every box, you see. The bank keeps one, and the renter keeps the other. The box cannot be opened without both keys. Will you come with me, please?"

He collected the bank key to safety-deposit box number 375 and led the detectives to the rear of the bank. The room seemed to be lined with shining metal. The boxes, row upon row, reminded Carella of the morgue and the refrigerated shelves that slid in and out of the wall on squeaking rollers. Anderson pushed the bank key into a slot and turned it, and then he put Claudia Davis' key into a second slot and turned that. He pulled the long, thin box out of the wall and handed it to Meyer. Meyer carried it to the counter on the opposite wall and lifted the catch.

"Okay?" he said to Carella.

"Go ahead."

Meyer raised the lid of the box.

There was $16,000 in the box. There was also a slip of note paper. The $16,000 was neatly divided into four stacks of bills. Three of the stacks held $5,000 each. The fourth stack held only $1,000. Carella picked up the slip of paper. Someone, presumably Claudia Davis, had made some annotations on it in pencil.

$$
\begin{array}{ll}
7/5 & 20,000 \\
7/5 & -1,000 \\
\hline
& 19,000 \\
7/12 & -1,000 \\
\hline
& 18,000 \\
7/19 & -1,000 \\
\hline
& 17,000 \\
7/27 & -1,000 \\
\hline
& 16,000
\end{array}
$$

"Make any sense to you, Mr. Anderson?"

"No. I'm afraid not."

"She came into this bank on July fifth with twenty thousand dollars in cash, Mr. Anderson. She put a thousand of that into a checking account and the remainder into this box. The dates on this slip of paper show exactly when she took cash from the box and transferred it to the checking account. She knew the rules, Mr. Anderson. She knew that twenty grand deposited in one lump would bring a call to the police. This way was a lot safer."

"We'd better get a list of these serial numbers," Meyer said.

"Would you have one of your people do that for us, Mr. Anderson?"

Anderson seemed ready to protest. Instead, he looked at Carella, sighed, and said, "Of course."

The serial numbers didn't help them at all. They compared them against their own lists, and the out-of-town lists, and the FBI lists, but none of those bills was hot.

Only August was.

V

Stewart City hangs in the hair of Isola like a jeweled tiara. Not really a city, not even a town, merely a collection of swank apartment buildings overlooking the River Dix, the community had been named after British royalty and remained one of the most exclusive neighborhoods in town. If you could boast of a Stewart City address, you could also boast of a high income, a country place on Sands Spit, and a Mercedes Benz in the garage under the apartment building. You could give your address with a measure of snobbery and pride—you were, after all, one of the elite.

The dead girl named Claudia Davis had made out a check to Management Enterprise, Inc., at 13 Stewart Place South, to the tune of $750. The check had been dated July nine, four days after she'd opened the Seaboard account.

A cool breeze was blowing in off the river as Carella and Hawes pulled up. Late-afternoon sunlight dappled the polluted water of the Dix. The bridges connecting Calm's Point with Isola hung against a sky awaiting the assault of dusk.

"Want to pull down the sun visor?" Carella asked.

Hawes reached up and turned down the visor. Clipped to the visor so that it showed through the windshield of the car was a hand-lettered card that read POLICEMAN ON DUTY CALL—87TH PRECINCT. The car, a 1956 Chevrolet, was Carella's own.

"I've got to make a sign for my car," Hawes said. "Some bastard tagged it last week."

"What did you do?"

"I went to court and pleaded not guilty. On my day off."

"Did you get out of it?"

"Sure. I was answering a squeal. It's bad enough I had to use my own car, but for Pete's sake, to get a ticket!"

"I prefer my own car," Carella said. "Those three cars belonging to the squad are ready for the junk heap."

"*Two,*" Hawes corrected. "One of them's been in the police garage for a month now."

"Meyer went down to see about it the other day."

"What'd they say? Was it ready?"

"No, the mechanic told him there were four patrol cars ahead of the sedan, and they took precedence. Now how about that?"

"Sure, it figures. I've still got a chit in for the gas I used, you know that?"

"Forget it. I've never got back a cent I laid out for gas."

"What'd Meyer do about the car?"

"He slipped the mechanic five bucks. Maybe that'll speed him up."

"You know what the city ought to do?" Hawes said. "They ought to buy some of those used taxicabs. Pick them up for two or three hundred bucks, paint them over, and give them out to the squads. Some of them are still in pretty good condition."

"Well, it's an idea," Carella said dubiously, and they entered the building. They found Mrs. Miller, the manager, in an office at the rear of the ornate entrance lobby. She was a woman in her early forties with a well-preserved figure and a very husky voice. She wore her hair piled on the top of her head, a pencil stuck rakishly into the reddish-brown heap. She looked at the photostated check and said, "Oh yes, of course."

"You knew Miss Davis?"

"Yes, she lived here for a long time."

"How long?"

"Five years."

"When did she move out?"

"At the end of June." Mrs. Miller crossed her splendid legs and smiled graciously. The legs were remarkable for a woman of her age, and the smile was almost radiant. She moved with an expert femininity, a calculated, conscious fluidity of flesh that suggested availability and yet was totally respectable. She seemed to have devoted a lifetime to learning the ways and wiles of the female and now practiced them with facility and charm. She was pleasant to be with, this woman, pleasant to watch and to hear, and to think of touching. Carella and Hawes, charmed to their shoes, found themselves relaxing in her presence.

"This check," Carella said, tapping the photostat. "What was it for?"

"June's rent. I received it on the tenth of July. Claudia always paid her rent by the tenth of the month. She was a very good tenant."

"The apartment cost seven hundred and fifty dollars a month?"

"Yes."

"Isn't that high for an apartment?"

"Not in Stewart City," Mrs. Miller said gently. "And this was a riverfront apartment."

"I see. I take it Miss Davis had a good job."

"No, no, she doesn't have a job at all."

"Then how could she afford . . . ?"

"Well, she's rather well off, you know."

"Where does she get the money, Mrs. Miller?"

"Well . . ." Mrs. Miller shrugged. "I really think you should ask *her,* don't you? I mean, if this is something concerning Claudia, shouldn't you . . . ?"

"Mrs. Miller," Carella said, "Claudia Davis is dead."

"What?"

"She's . . ."

"What? No. No." She shook her head. "Claudia? But the check . . . I . . . the check came only last month." She shook her head again. "No. No."

"She's dead, Mrs. Miller," Carella said gently. "She was strangled."

The charm faltered for just an instant. Revulsion knifed the eyes of Mrs. Miller, the eyelids flickered, it seemed for an instant that the pupils would turn shining and wet, that the carefully lipsticked mouth would crumble. And then something inside took over, something that demanded control, something that reminded her that a charming woman does not weep and cause her fashionable eye makeup to run.

"I'm sorry," she said, almost in a whisper. "I am really, really sorry. She was a nice person."

"Can you tell us what you know about her, Mrs. Miller?"

"Yes. Yes, of course." She shook her head again, unwilling to accept the idea. "That's terrible. That's terrible. Why, she was only a baby."

"We figured her for thirty, Mrs. Miller. Are we wrong?"

"She seemed younger, but perhaps that was because . . . well, she was a rather shy person. Even when she first came here, there was an air of—well, lostness about her. Of course, that was right after her parents died, so . . ."

"Where did she come from, Mrs. Miller?"

"California. Santa Monica."

Carella nodded. "You were starting to tell us . . . you said she was rather well off. Could you . . . ?"

"Well, the stock, you know."

"What stock?"

"Her parents had set up a securities trust account for her. When they died, Claudia began receiving the income from the stock. She was an only child, you know."

"And she lived on stock dividends alone?"

"They amounted to quite a bit. Which she saved, I might add. She was a very systematic person, not at all frivolous. When she received a dividend check, she would endorse it and take it straight to the bank. Claudia was a very sensible girl."

"Which bank, Mrs. Miller?"

"The Highland Trust. Right down the street. On Cromwell Avenue."

"I see," Carella said. "Was she dating many men? Would you know?"

"I don't think so. She kept pretty much to herself. Even after Josie came."

Carella leaned forward. "Josie? Who's Josie?"

"Josie Thompson. Josephine, actually. Her cousin."

"And where did *she* come from?"

"California. They both came from California."

"And how can we get in touch with this Josie Thompson?"

"Well, she . . . Don't you know? Haven't you . . . ?"

"What, Mrs. Miller?"

"Why, Josie is dead. Josie passed on in June. That's why Claudia moved, I suppose. I suppose she couldn't bear the thought of living in that apartment without Josie. It *is* a little frightening, isn't it?"

"Yes," Carella said.

DETECTIVE DIVISION SUPPLEMENTARY REPORT	SQUAD	PRECINCT	PRECINCT REPORT	DETECTIVE DIVISION REPORT NUMBER
pdcn 360 rev 25m	87	87	32-101	DD 60 R-42

NAME AND ADDRESS OF PERSON REPORTING	DATE ORIGINAL REPORT
Miller Irene (Mrs. John) 13 Stewart Place S.	8-4-60
SURNAME GIVEN NAME INITIALS NUMBER STREET	

DETAILS

Summary of interview with Irene (Mrs. John) Miller at office of Management Enterprises, Inc., address above, in re homicide Claudia Davis. Mrs. Miller states:

Claudia Davis came to this city in June of 1955, took $750-a-month apartment above address, lived there alone. Rarely seen in company of friends, male or female. Young recluse type living on substantial income of inherited securities. Parents, Mr. and Mrs. Carter Davis, killed on San Diego Freeway in head-on collision with station wagon, April 14, 1955. L.A.P.D. confirms traffic accident, driver of other vehicle convicted for negligent operation. Mrs. Miller describes girl as medium height and weight, close-cropped brunette hair, brown eyes, no scars or birthmarks she can remember, tallies with what we have on corpse. Further says Claudia Davis was quiet, unobtrusive tenant, paid rent and all service bills punctually, was gentle, sweet, plain, childlike, shy, meticulous in money matters, well liked but unapproachable.

In April or May of 1959, Josie Thompson, cousin of deceased, arrived from Brentwood, California. (Routine check with Criminal Bureau Identification negative, no record. Check-

ing now with L.A.P.D., and FBI.) Described as
slightly older than Claudia, rather different in
looks and personality. ''They were like black and
white,'' Mrs. Miller says, ''but they hit it off
exceptionally well.'' Josie moved into the apartment with cousin. Words used to describe relationship between two were ''like the closest
sisters,'' and ''really in tune,'' and ''the best of
friends,'' etc. Girls did not date much, were
constantly in each other's company, Josie seeming
to pick up recluse habits from Claudia. Went on
frequent trips together. Spent summer of '59 on
Tortoise Island in the bay, returned Labor Day.
Went away again at Christmas time to ski Sun
Valley, and again in March this year to Kingston,
Jamaica, for three weeks, returning at beginning
of April. Source of income was fairly standard
securities-income account. Claudia did not own
the stock, but income on it was hers for as long
as she lived. Trust specified that upon her death
the stock and the income be turned over to
U.C.L.A. (father's alma mater). In any case,
Claudia was assured of a very, very substantial
lifetime income (see Highland Trust bank account)
and was apparently supporting Josie as well,
since Mrs. Miller claims neither girl worked.
Brought up question of possible lesbianism, but
Mrs. Miller, who is knowledgeable and hip, says
no, neither girl was a dike.

On June 3, Josie and Claudia left for
another weekend trip. Doorman reports having
helped them pack valises into trunk of Claudia's
car, 1960 Cadillac convertible. Claudia did the
driving. Girls did not return on Monday morning
as they had indicated they would. Claudia called
on Wednesday, crying on telephone. Told Mrs.
Miller that Josie had had a terrible accident and
was dead. Mrs. Miller remembers asking Claudia if
she could help in any way. Claudia said, quote,
No, everything's been taken care of already,
unquote.

On June 17, Mrs. Miller received a letter
from Claudia (letter attached—handwriting com-
pares positive with checks Claudia signed) stating she could not possibly return to apartment,
not after what had happened to her cousin. She
reminded Mrs. Miller lease expired on July 4,
told her she would send check for June's rent

before July 10. Said moving company would pack
and pick up her belongings, delivering all valu-
ables and documents to her, and storing rest.
(See Claudia Davis' check number 010, 7/14,
made payable to Allora Brothers, Inc., ''in payment for packing, moving, and storage.'') Claudia
Davis never returned to the apartment. Mrs.
Miller had not seen her and knew nothing of her
whereabouts until we informed her of the
homicide.

DATE OF THIS REPORT
August 6

Det 2/gr	Carella	S.L.	714-56-32	Det/Lt. Peter Byrnes
RANK	SURNAME	INITIALS	SHIELD NUMBER	COMMANDING OFFICER

VI

The drive upstate to Triangle Lake was a particularly scenic one, and since it was August, and since Sunday was supposed to be Carella's day off, he thought he might just as well combine a little business with pleasure. So he put the top of the car down, and he packed Teddy into the front seat together with a picnic lunch and a gallon Thermos of iced coffee, and he forgot all about Claudia Davis on the drive up through the mountains. Carella found it easy to forget about almost anything when he was with his wife.

Teddy, as far as he was concerned—and his astute judgment had been backed up by many a street-corner whistle—was only the most beautiful woman in the world. He could never understand how he, a hairy, corny, ugly, stupid, clumsy cop, had managed to capture anyone as wonderful as Theodora Franklin. But capture her he had, and he sat beside her now in the open car and stole sidelong glances at her as he drove, excited as always by her very presence.

Her black hair, always wild, seemed to capture something of the wind's frenzy as it whipped about the oval of her face. Her brown eyes were partially squinted against the rush of air over the windshield. She wore a white blouse emphatically curved over a full bosom, black tapered slacks form-fitted over generous hips and good legs. She had kicked off her sandals and folded her knees against her breasts, her bare feet pressed against the glove-compartment panel. There was about her, Carella realized, a curious combination of savage and sophisticate. You never knew whether she was going to kiss you or slug you, and the uncertainty kept her eternally desirable and exciting.

Teddy watched her husband as he drove, his big-knuckled hands on the wheel of the car. She watched him not only because it gave her pleasure to watch him, but also because he was speaking. And since she could not hear, since she had been born a deaf mute, it was essential that she look at his mouth when he spoke. He did not discuss the case at all. She knew that one of the Claudia Davis checks had been made out to the Fancher Funeral Home in Triangle Lake and she knew that Carella wanted to talk to the proprietor of the place personally. She further knew that this was very important or he wouldn't be spending his Sunday driving all the way upstate. But he had promised her he'd combine business with pleasure. This was the pleasure part of the trip, and in deference to his promise and his wife, he refrained from discussing the case, which was really foremost in his mind. He talked, instead, about the scenery, and their plans for the fall, and the way the twins were growing, and how pretty Teddy looked, and how she'd better button that top button of her blouse before they got out of the car, but he never once mentioned Claudia Davis until they were standing in the office of the Fancher Funeral Home and looking into the gloomy eyes of a man who called himself Barton Scoles.

Scoles was tall and thin and he wore a black suit that he had probably worn to his own confirmation back in 1912. He was so much the stereotype of a small-town undertaker that Carella almost burst out laughing when he met him. Somehow, though, the environment was not conducive to hilarity. There was a strange smell hovering over the thick rugs and the papered walls and the hanging chandeliers. It was a while before Carella recognized it as formaldehyde and then made the automatic association and, curious for a man who had stared into the eyes of death so often, suddenly felt like retching.

"Miss Davis made out a check to you on July fifteenth," Carella said. "Can you tell me what it was for?"

"Sure can," Scoles said. "Had to wait a long time for that check. She give me only a twenty-five dollar deposit. Usually take fifty, you know. I got stuck many a time, believe me."

"How do you mean?" Carella asked.

"People. You bury their dead, and then sometimes they don't pay you for your work. This business isn't *all* fun, you know. Many's the time I handled the whole funeral and the service and the burial and all, and never did get paid. Makes you lose your faith in human nature."

"But Miss Davis finally *did* pay you."

"Oh, sure. But I can tell you I was sweating that one out. I can tell you that. After all, she was a strange gal from the city, has the funeral here, nobody comes to it but her, sitting in the chapel out there and watching the body as if someone's going to steal it away, just her and the departed. I tell you, Mr. Carella . . . Is that your name?"

"Yes, Carella."

"I tell you, it was kind of spooky. Lay there two days, she did, her cousin. And then Miss Davis asked that we bury the girl right here in the local cemetery, so I done that for her, too—all on the strength of a twenty-five-dollar deposit. That's trust, Mr. Carella, with a capital T."

"When was this, Mr. Scoles?"

"The girl drowned the first weekend in June," Scoles said. "Had no business being out on the lake so early, anyways. That water's still icy-cold in June. Don't really warm up none till the latter part July. She fell over the side of the boat—she was out there rowing, you know—and that icy water probably froze her solid, or give her cramps or something, drowned her, anyways." Scoles shook his head. "Had no business being out on the lake so early."

"Did you see a death certificate?"

"Yep, Dr. Donneli made it out. Cause of death was drowning, all right, no question about it. We had an inquest, too, you know. The Tuesday after she drowned. They said it was accidental."

"You said she was out rowing in a boat. Alone?"

"Yep. Her cousin, Miss Davis, was on the shore watching. Jumped in when she fell overboard, tried to reach her, but couldn't make it in time. That water's plenty cold, believe me. Ain't too warm even now, and here it is August already."

"But it didn't seem to affect Miss Davis, did it?"

"Well, she was probably a strong swimmer. Been my experience most pretty girls are strong girls, too. I'll bet your wife here is a strong girl. She sure is a pretty one."

Scoles smiled, and Teddy smiled, and squeezed Carella's hand.

"About the payment," Carella said, "for the funeral and the burial. Do you have any idea why it took Miss Davis so long to send her check?"

"Nope. I wrote her twice. First time was just a friendly little reminder. Second time, I made it a little stronger. Attorney friend of mine in town wrote it on his stationery; that always impresses them. Didn't get an answer either time. Finally, right out of the blue, the check came, payment in full. Beats me. Maybe she was affected by the death. Or maybe she's always slow paying her debts. I'm just happy the check came, that's all. Sometimes the live ones can give you more trouble than them who's dead, believe me."

They strolled down to the lake together, Carella and his wife, and ate their picnic lunch on its shores. Carella was strangely silent. Teddy dangled her bare feet in the water. The water, as Scoles had promised, was very cold even though it was August. On the way back from the lake Carella said, "Honey, would you mind if I make one more stop?"

Teddy turned her eyes to him inquisitively.

"I want to see the chief of police here."

Teddy frowned. The question was in her eyes, and he answered it immediately.

"To find out whether or not there were any witnesses to that drowning. *Besides* Claudia Davis, I mean. From the way Scoles was talking, I get the impression that lake was pretty deserted in June."

The chief of police was a short man with a pot belly and big feet. He kept his feet propped up on his desk all the while he spoke to Carella. Carella watched him and wondered why everybody in this damned town seemed to be on vacation from an MGM movie. A row of rifles in a locked rack was behind the chief's desk. A host of WANTED fliers covered a bulletin board to the right of the rack. The chief had a hole in the sole of his left shoe.

"Yep," he said, "there was a witness, all right."

Carella felt a pang of disappointment. "Who?" he asked.

"Fellow fishing at the lake. Saw the whole thing. Testified before the coroner's jury."

"What'd he say?"

"Said he was fishing there when Josie Thompson took the boat out. Said Claudia Davis stayed behind, on the shore. Said Miss Thompson fell overboard and went under like a stone. Said Miss Davis jumped in the water and began swimming toward her. Didn't make it in time. That's what he said."

"What else did he say?"

"Well, he drove Miss Davis back to town in her car. A 1960 Caddy convertible, I believe. She could hardly speak. She was sobbing and mumbling and wringing her hands, oh, in a hell of a mess. Why, we had to get the whole story out of that fishing fellow. Wasn't until the next day that Miss Davis could make any kind of sense."

"When did you hold the inquest?"

"Tuesday. Day before they buried the cousin. Coroner did the dissection on Monday. We got authorization from Miss Davis, Penal Law

2213, next of kin being charged by law with the duty of burial may authorize dissection for the sole purpose of ascertaining the cause of death."

"And the coroner reported the cause of death as drowning?"

"That's right. Said so right before the jury."

"Why'd you have an inquest? Did you suspect something more than accidental drowning?"

"Not necessarily. But that fellow who was fishing, well, *he* was from the city, too, you know. And for all we knew, him and Miss Davis could have been in this together, you know, shoved the cousin over the side of the boat, and then faked up a whole story, you know. They both coulda been lying in their teeth."

"Were they?"

"Not so we could tell. You never seen anybody so grief-stricken as Miss Davis was when the fishing fellow drove her into town. Girl would have to be a hell of an actress to behave that way. Calmed down the next day, but you shoulda seen her when it happened. And at the inquest it was plain this fishing fellow had never met her before that day at the lake. Convinced the jury he had no prior knowledge of or connection with either of the two girls. Convinced me, too, for that matter."

"What's his name?" Carella asked. "This fishing fellow."

"Courtenoy."

"What did you say?"

"Courtenoy. Sidney Courtenoy."

"Thanks," Carella answered, and he rose suddenly. "Come on, Teddy. I want to get back to the city."

VII

Courtenoy lived in a one-family clapboard house in Riverhead. He was rolling up the door of his garage when Carella and Meyer pulled into his driveway early Monday morning. He turned to look at the car curiously, one hand on the rising garage door. The door stopped, halfway up, halfway down. Carella stepped into the driveway.

"Mr. Courtenoy?" he asked.

"Yes?" He stared at Carella, puzzlement on his face, the puzzlement that is always there when a perfect stranger addresses you by name. Courtenoy was a man in his late forties, wearing a cap and a badly fitted sports jacket and dark flannel slacks in the month of August. His hair was graying at the temples. He looked tired, very tired, and his weariness had nothing whatever to do with the fact that it was only seven o'clock in the morning. A lunch box was at his feet where he had apparently put it when he began rolling up the garage door. The car in the garage was a 1953 Ford.

"We're police officers," Carella said. "Mind if we ask you a few questions?"

"I'd like to see your badge," Courtenoy said. Carella showed it to him. Courtenoy nodded as if he had performed a precautionary public duty. "What are your questions?" he asked. "I'm on my way to work. Is this about that damn building permit again?"

"What building permit?"

"For extending the garage. I'm buying my son a little jalopy, don't want to leave it out on the street. Been having a hell of a time getting a building permit. Can you imagine that? All I want to do is add another twelve feet to the garage. You'd think I was trying to build a city park or something. Is that what this is about?"

From inside the house a woman's voice called, "Who is it, Sid?"

"Nothing, nothing," Courtenoy said impatiently. "Nobody. Never mind, Bett." He looked at Carella. "My wife. You married?"

"Yes, sir, I'm married," Carella said.

"Then you know," Courtenoy said cryptically. "What are your questions?"

"Ever see this before?" Carella asked. He handed a photostated copy of the check to Courtenoy, who looked at it briefly and handed it back.

"Sure."

"Want to explain it, Mr. Courtenoy?"

"Explain what?"

"Explain why Claudia Davis sent you a check for a hundred and twenty dollars.

"As recompense," Courtenoy said unhesitatingly.

"Oh, recompense, huh?" Meyer said. "For what, Mr. Courtenoy? For a little cock-and-bull story?"

"Huh? What are you talking about?"

"Recompense for *what,* Mr. Courtenoy?"

"For missing three days' work, what the hell did you think?"

"How's that again?"

"No, what did you *think?*" Courtenoy said angrily, waving his finger at Meyer. "What did you think it was for? Some kind of payoff or something? Is that what you thought?"

"Mr. Courtenoy . . ."

"I lost three days' work because of that damn inquest. I had to stay up at Triangle Lake all day Monday and Tuesday and then again on Wednesday waiting for the jury decision. I'm a bricklayer. I get five bucks an hour and I lost three days' work, eight hours a day, and so Miss Davis was good enough to send me a check for a hundred and twenty bucks. Now just what the hell did you think, would you mind telling me?"

"Did you know Miss Davis before that day at Triangle Lake, Mr. Courtenoy?"

"Never saw her before in my life. What is this? Am I on trial here? What is this?"

From inside the house the woman's voice came again, sharply, "Sidney! Is something wrong? Are you all right?"

"Nothing's wrong. Shut up, will you?"

There was an aggrieved silence from within the clapboard structure. Courtenoy muttered something under his breath and then turned to face the detectives again. "You finished?" he asked.

"Not quite, Mr. Courtenoy. We'd like you to tell us what you saw that day at the lake."

"What the hell for? Go read the minutes of the inquest if you're so damn interested. I've got to get to work."

"That can wait, Mr. Courtenoy."

"Like hell it can. This job is away over in . . ."

"Mr. Courtenoy, we don't want to have to go all the way downtown and come back with a warrant for your arrest."

"My *arrest!* For what? Listen, what did I . . . ?"

"Sidney? Sidney, shall I call the police?" the woman shouted from inside the house.

"Oh, shut the hell up!" Courtenoy answered. "Call the police," he mumbled. "I'm up to my ears in cops, and she wants to call the police. What do you want from me? I'm an honest bricklayer. I saw a girl drown. I told it just the way I saw it. Is that a crime? Why are you bothering me?"

"Just tell it again, Mr. Courtenoy. Just the way you saw it."

"She was out in the boat," Courtenoy said, sighing. "I was fishing. Her cousin was on the shore. She fell over the side."

"Josie Thompson."

"Yes, Josie Thompson, whatever the hell her name was."

"She was alone in the boat?"

"Yes. She was alone in the boat."

"Go on."

"The other one—Miss Davis—screamed and ran into the water, and began swimming toward her." He shook his head. "She didn't make it in time. That boat was a long way out. When she got there, the lake was still. She dove under and came up, and then dove under again, but it was too late, it was just too late. Then, as she was swimming back, I thought *she* was going to drown, too. She faltered and sank below the surface, and I waited and I thought sure she was gone. Then there was a patch of yellow that broke through the water, and I saw she was all right."

"Why didn't you jump in to help her, Mr. Courtenoy?"

"I don't know how to swim."

"All right. What happened next?"

"She came out of the water—Miss Davis. She was exhausted and hysterical. I tried to calm her down, but she kept yelling and crying, not making any sense at all. I dragged her over to the car, and I asked her for the car keys. She didn't seem to know what I was talking about at first. 'The keys!' I said, and she just stared at me. 'Your car keys!' I yelled. 'The keys to the car.' Finally she reached in her purse and handed me the keys."

"Go on."

"I drove her into town. It was me who told the story to the police. She couldn't talk, all she could do was babble and scream and cry. It was a terrible thing to watch. I'd never before seen a woman so completely off her nut. We couldn't get two straight words out of her until the next day. Then she was all right. Told the police who she was, explained what I'd already told them the day before, and told them the dead girl was her cousin, Josie Thompson. They dragged the lake and got her out of the water. A shame. A real shame. Nice young girl like that."

"What was the dead girl wearing?"

"Cotton dress. Loafers, I think. Or sandals. Little thin sweater over the dress. A cardigan."

"Any jewelry?"

"I don't think so. No."

"Was she carrying a purse?"

"No. Her purse was in the car with Miss Davis'."

"What was Miss Davis wearing?"

"When? The day of the drowning? Or when they pulled her cousin out of the lake?"

"Was she there then?"

"Sure. Identified the body."

"No, I wanted to know what she was wearing on the day of the accident, Mr. Courtenoy."

"Oh, skirt and a blouse, I think. Ribbon in her hair. Loafers. I'm not sure."

"What color blouse? Yellow?"

"No. Blue."

"You said yellow."

"No, blue. I didn't say yellow."

Carella frowned. "I thought you said yellow earlier." He shrugged. "All right, what happened after the inquest?"

"Nothing much. Miss Davis thanked me for being so kind and said she would send me a check for the time I'd missed. I refused at first and then I thought, What the hell, I'm a hard-working man, and money doesn't grow on trees. So I gave her my address. I figured she could afford it. Driving a Caddy, and hiring a fellow to take it back to the city."

"Why didn't she drive it back herself?"

"I don't know. I guess she was still a little shaken. Listen, that was a terrible experience. Did you ever see anyone die up close?"

"Yes," Carella said.

From inside the house Courtenoy's wife yelled, "Sidney, tell those men to get out of our driveway!"

"You heard her," Courtenoy said, and finished rolling up his garage door.

VIII

Nobody likes Monday morning.

It was invented for hang-overs. It is really not the beginning of a new week, but only the tail end of the week before. Nobody likes it, and it doesn't have to be rainy or gloomy or blue in order to provoke disaffection. It can be bright and sunny and the beginning of August. It can start with a driveway interview at seven A.M. and grow progressively worse by nine-thirty that same morning. Monday is Monday and legislation will never change its personality. Monday is Monday, and it stinks.

By nine-thirty that Monday morning, Detective Steve Carella was on the edge of total bewilderment and, like any normal person, he blamed it on Monday. He had come back to the squadroom and painstakingly gone over the pile of checks Claudia Davis had written during the month of July, a total of twenty-five, searching them for some clue to her strangulation, studying them with the scrutiny of a typographer in a print shop. Several things seemed evident from the cheeks, but nothing seemed pertinent. He could recall having said: "I look at those checks, I can see a life. It's like reading somebody's diary," and he was beginning to believe he had uttered some famous last words in those two succinct sentences. For if this was the diary of Claudia Davis, it was a singularly unprovocative account that would never make the nation's bestseller lists.

Most of the checks had been made out to clothing or department stores. Claudia, true to the species, seemed to have a penchant for shopping and a checkbook that yielded to her spending urge. Calls to the various stores represented revealed that her taste ranged through a wide variety of items. A check of sales slips showed that she had purchased during the month of July alone three baby doll nightgowns, two half slips, a trenchcoat, a wrist watch, four pairs of tapered slacks in various colors, two pairs of walking shoes, a pair of sunglasses, four bikini swimsuits, eight wash-and-wear frocks, two skirts, two cashmere sweaters, half-a dozen bestselling novels, a large bottle of aspirin, two bottles of Dramamine, six pieces of luggage, and four boxes of cleansing tissue. The most expensive thing she had purchased was an evening gown costing $500. These purchases accounted for most of the checks she had drawn in July. There were also checks to a hairdresser, a florist, a shoemaker, a candy shop, and three unexplained checks that were drawn to individuals, two men and a woman.

The first was made out to George Badueck.

The second was made out to David Oblinsky.

The third was made out to Martha Feldelson.

Someone on the squad had attacked the telephone directory and come up with addresses for two of the three. The third, Oblinsky; had an unlisted number, but a half-hour's argument with a supervisor had finally netted an address for him. The completed list was now on Carella's desk together with all the canceled checks. He should have begun tracking down those names, he knew, but something still was bugging him.

"Why did Courtenoy lie to me and Meyer?" he asked Cotton Hawes. "Why did he lie about something as simple as what Claudia Davis was wearing on the day of the drowning?"

"How did he lie?"

"First he said she was wearing yellow, said he saw a patch of yellow break the surface of the lake. Then he changed it to blue. Why did he do that, Cotton?"

"I don't know."

"And if he lied about that, why couldn't he have been lying about everything? Why couldn't he and Claudia have done in little Josie together."

"I don't know," Hawes said.

"Where'd that twenty thousand bucks come from, Cotton?"

"Maybe it was a stock dividend."

"Maybe. Then why didn't she simply deposit the check? This was cash, Cotton, *cash*. Now where did it come from? That's a nice piece of change. You don't pick twenty grand out of the gutter."

"I suppose not."

"I know where you can get twenty grand, Cotton."

"Where?"

"From an insurance company. When someone dies." Carella nodded once, sharply. "I'm going to make some calls. Damnit, that money had to come from *some*place."

He hit pay dirt on his sixth call. The man he spoke to was named Jeremiah Dodd and was a representative of the Security Insurance Corporation, Inc. He recognized Josie Thompson's name at once.

"Oh yes," he said. "We settled that claim in July."

"Who made the claim, Mr. Dodd?"

"The beneficiary, of course. Just a moment. Let me get the folder on this. Will you hold on, please?"

Carella waited impatiently. Over at the insurance company on the other end of the line he could hear muted voices. A girl giggled suddenly, and he wondered who was kissing whom over by the water cooler. At last Dodd came back on the line.

"Here it is," he said. "Josephine Thompson. Beneficiary was her cousin, Miss Claudia Davis. Oh yes, now it's all coming back. Yes, this is the one."

"What one?"

"Where the girls were mutual beneficiaries."

"What do you mean?"

"The cousins," Dodd said. "There were two life policies. One for Miss Davis and one for Miss Thompson. And they were mutual beneficiaries."

"You mean Miss Davis was the beneficiary of Miss Thompson's policy and vice versa?"

"Yes, that's right."

"That's very interesting. How large were the policies?"

"Oh, very small."

"Well, how *small* then?"

"I believe they were both insured for twelve thousand five hundred. Just a moment; let me check. Yes, that's right."

"And Miss Davis applied for payment on the policy after her cousin died, huh?"

"Yes. Here it is, right here. Josephine Thompson drowned at Lake Triangle on June fourth. That's right. Claudia Davis sent in the policy and the certificate of death and also a coroner's jury verdict."

"She didn't miss a trick, did she?"

"Sir? I'm sorry, I . . ."

"Did you pay her?"

"Yes. It was a perfectly legitimate claim. We began processing it at once."

"Did you send anyone up to Lake Triangle to investigate the circumstances of Miss Thompson's death?"

"Yes, but it was merely a routine investigation. A coroner's inquest is good enough for us, Detective Carella."

"When did you pay Miss Davis?"

"On July first."

"You sent her a check for twelve thousand five hundred dollars, is that right?"

"No, sir."

"Didn't you say . . . ?"

"The policy insured her for twelve-five, that's correct. But there was a double-indemnity clause, you see, and Josephine Thompson's death was accidental. No, we had to pay the policy's limit, Detective Carella. On July first we sent Claudia Davis a check for twenty-five thousand dollars."

IX

There are no mysteries in police work.

Nothing fits into a carefully preconceived scheme. The high point of any given case is very often the corpse that opens the case. There is no climactic progression; suspense is for the movies. There are only people and curiously twisted motives, and small unexplained details, and coincidence, and the unexpected, and they combine to form a sequence of events, but there is no real mystery, there never is. There is only life, and sometimes death, and neither follows a rule book. Policemen hate mystery stories because they recognize in them a control that is lacking in their own very real, sometimes routine, sometimes spectacular, sometimes tedious investigation of a case. It is very nice and very clever and very convenient to have all the pieces fit together neatly. It is very kind to think of detectives as master mathematicians working on an algebraic problem whose constants are death and a victim, whose unknown is a murderer. But many of these mastermind detectives have trouble adding up the deductions on their twice-monthly paychecks. The world is full of wizards, for sure, but hardly any of them work for the city police.

There was one big mathematical discrepancy in the Claudia Davis case.

There seemed to be $5,000 unaccounted for.

Twenty-five grand had been mailed to Claudia Davis on July 1, and she presumably received the check after the Fourth of July holiday, cashed it someplace, and then took her money to the Seaboard Bank of America, opened a new checking account, and rented a safety-deposit box. But her total deposit at Seaboard had been $20,000 whereas the check had been for $25,000, so where was the laggard five? And who had cashed the check for her? Mr. Dodd of the Security Insurance Corporation, Inc., explained the company's rather complicated accounting system to Carella. A check was kept in the local office for several days after it was cashed in order to close out the policy, after which it was sent to the main office in Chicago where it sometimes stayed for several weeks until the master files were closed out. It was then sent to the company's accounting and auditing firm in San Francisco. It was Dodd's guess that the canceled check had already been sent to the California accountants, and he promised to put a tracer on it at once. Carella asked him to please hurry. Someone had cashed that check for Claudia and, supposedly, someone also had one-fifth of the check's face value.

The very fact that Claudia had not taken the check itself to Seaboard seemed to indicate that she had something to hide. Presumably, she did not want anyone asking questions about insurance company checks, or insurance policies, or double indemnities, or accidental drownings, or especially her cousin Josie. The check was a perfectly good one, and yet she had chosen to cash it *before* opening a new account. Why? And why, for that matter, had she bothered opening a new account when she had a rather well-stuffed and active account at another bank?

There are only whys in police work, but they do not add up to mystery. They add up to work, and nobody in the world likes work. The bulls of the 87th would have preferred to sit on their backsides and sip at gin-and-tonics, but the whys were there, so they put on their hats and their holsters and tried to find some becauses.

Cotton Hawes systematically interrogated each and every tenant in the rooming house where Claudia Davis had been killed. They all had alibis tighter than the closed fist of an Arabian stablekeeper. In his report to the lieutenant, Hawes expressed the belief that none of the tenants was guilty of homicide. As far as he was concerned, they were all clean.

Meyer Meyer attacked the 87th's stool pigeons. There were money-changers galore in the precinct and the city, men who turned hot loot into cold cash—for a price. If someone had cashed a $25,000 check for Claudia and kept $5,000 of it during the process, couldn't that person conceivably be one of the money-changers? He put the precinct stoolies on the ear, asked them to sound around for word of a Security Insurance Corporation check. The stoolies came up with nothing.

Detective Lieutenant Sam Grossman took his laboratory boys to the murder room and went over it again. And again. And again. He reported that the lock on the door was a snap lock, the kind that clicks shut automatically when the door is slammed. Whoever killed Claudia Davis could have done so without performing any locked-room gymnastics. All he had to do was close the door behind him when he left. Grossman also reported that Claudia's bed had apparently not been slept in on the night of the murder. A pair of shoes had been found at the foot of a large easy chair in the bedroom and a novel was wedged open on the arm of the chair. He suggested that Claudia had fallen asleep while reading, had awakened, and gone into the other room where she had met her murderer and her death. He had no suggestion as to just who that murderer might have been.

Steve Carella was hot and impatient and overloaded. There were other things happening in the precinct, things like burglaries and muggings and knifings and assaults and kids with summertime on their hands hitting other kids with ball bats because they didn't like the way they pronounced the word *"señor."* There were telephones jangling, and reports to be typed in triplicate, and people filing into the squadroom day and night with complaints against the citizenry of that fair city, and the Claudia Davis case was beginning to be a big fat pain in the keester. Carella wondered what it was like to be a shoemaker. And while he was wondering, he began to chase down the checks made out to George Badueck, David Oblinsky, and Martha Fedelson.

Happily, Bert Kling had nothing whatsoever to do with the Claudia Davis case. He hadn't even discussed it with any of the men on the squad. He was a young detective and a new detective, and the things that happened in that precinct were enough to drive a guy nuts and keep him busy forty-eight hours every day, so he didn't go around sticking his nose into other people's cases. He had enough troubles of his own. One of those troubles was the lineup.

On Wednesday morning Bert Kling's name appeared on the lineup duty chart.

X

The lineup was held in the gym downtown at Headquarters on High Street. It was held four days a week, Monday to Thursday, and the purpose of the parade was to acquaint the city's detectives with the people who were committing crime, the premise being that crime is a repetitive profession and that a crook will always be a crook, and it's good to know who your adversaries are should you happen to come face to face with them on the street. Timely recognition of a thief had helped crack many a case and had, on some occasions, even saved a detective's life. So the lineup was a pretty valuable in-group custom. This didn't mean that detectives enjoyed the trip downtown. They drew lineup perhaps once every two weeks and, often as not, lineup duty fell on their day off, and nobody appreciated rubbing elbows with criminals on his day off.

The lineup that Wednesday morning followed the classic pattern of all lineups. The detectives sat in the gymnasium on folding chairs, and the chief of detectives sat behind a high podium at the back of the gym. The green shades were drawn and the stage illuminated, and the offenders who'd been arrested the day before were marched before the assembled bulls while their chief read off the charges and handled the interrogation. The pattern was a simple one. The arresting officer, uniformed or plain-clothes, would join the chief at the rear of the gym when his arrest came up. The chief would read off the felon's name, and then the section of the city in which he'd been arrested, and then a number. He would say, for example, "Jones, John, Riverhead, three." The "three" would simply indicate that this was the third arrest in Riverhead that day. Only felonies and special types of misdemeanors were handled at the lineup, so this narrowed the list of performers on any given day. Following the case number, the chief would read off the offense, and then say either "Statement" or "No statement," telling the assembled cops that the thief either had or had not said anything when they'd put the collar on him. If there had been a statement, the chief would limit his questions to rather general topics since he didn't want to lead the felon into saying anything that might contradict his usually incriminating initial statement, words that could be used against him in court. If there had been *no* statement, the chief would pull out all the stops. He was generally armed with whatever police records were available on the man who stood under the blinding lights, and it was the smart thief who understood the purpose of the lineup and who knew he was not bound to answer a goddamned thing they asked him. The chief of detectives was something like a deadly earnest Mike Wallace, but the stakes were slightly higher here because this involved something a little more important than a novelist plugging his new book or a senator explaining the stand he had taken on a farm bill. These were truly "interviews in depth," and the booby prize was very often a long stretch up the river in a cozy one-windowed room.

The lineup bored the hell out of Kling. It always did. It was like seeing a stage show for the hundredth time. Every now and then somebody stopped the show with a really good routine. But usually it was the same old song and dance. It wasn't any different that Wednesday. By the time the eighth offender had been paraded and subjected to the chief's bludgeoning interrogation, Kling was beginning to doze. The detective sitting next to him nudged him gently in the ribs.

". . . Reynolds, Ralph," the chief was saying, "Isola, four. Caught burgling an apartment on North Third. No statement. How about it, Ralph?"

"How about what?"

"You do this sort of thing often?"

"What sort of thing?"

"Burglary."

"I'm no burglar," Reynolds said.

"I've got his B-sheet here," the chief said. "Arrested for burglary in 1948, witness withdrew her testimony, claimed she had mistakenly identified him. Arrested again for burglary in 1952, convicted for Burglary One, sentenced to ten at Castleview, paroled in '58 on good behavior. You're back at the old stand, huh, Ralph?"

"No, not me. I've been straight ever since I got out."

"Then what were you doing in that apartment during the middle of the night?"

"I was a little drunk. I must have walked into the wrong building."

"What do you mean?"

"I thought it was my apartment."

"Where do you live, Ralph?"

"On . . . uh . . . well . . ."

"Come on, Ralph."

"Well, I live on South Fifth."

"And the apartment you were in last night is on North Third. You must have been pretty drunk to wander that far off course."

"Yeah, I guess I was pretty drunk."

"Woman in that apartment said you hit her when she woke up. Is that true, Ralph?"

"No. No, hey, I never hit her."

"She says so, Ralph."

"Well, she's mistaken."

"Well, now, a doctor's report says somebody clipped her on the jaw, Ralph, now how about that?"

"Well, maybe."

"Yes or no?"

"Well, maybe when she started screaming she got me nervous. I mean, you know, I thought it was my apartment and all."

"Ralph, you were burgling that apartment. How about telling us the truth?"

"No, I got in there by mistake."

"How'd you get in?"

"The door was open."

"In the middle of the night, huh? The door was open?"

"Yeah."

"You sure you didn't pick the lock or something, huh?"

"No, no. Why would I do that? I thought it was my apartment."

"Ralph, what were you doing with burglar's tools?"

"Who? Who me? Those weren't burglar's tools."

"Then what were they? You had a glass cutter, and a bunch of jimmics, and some punches, and a drill and bits, and three celluloid strips, and some lock-picking tools, and eight skeleton keys. Those sound like burglar's tools to me, Ralph."

"No. I'm a carpenter."

"Yeah, you're a carpenter all right, Ralph. We searched your apartment, Ralph, and found a couple of things we're curious about. Do you always keep sixteen wrist watches and four typewriters and twelve bracelets and eight rings and a mink stole and three sets of silverware, Ralph?"

"Yeah. I'm a collector."

"Of other people's things. We also found four hundred dollars in American currency and five thousand dollars in French francs. Where'd you get that money, Ralph?"

"Which?"

"Whichever you feel like telling us about."

"Well, the U.S. stuff I . . . I won at the track. And the other, well, a Frenchman owed me some gold, and so he paid me in francs. That's all."

"We're checking our stolen-goods list right this minute, Ralph."

"So check!" Reynolds said, suddenly angry. "What the hell do you want from me? Work for your goddamn living! You want it all on a platter! Like fun! I told you everything I'm gonna . . ."

"Get him out of here," the chief said. "Next, Blake, Donald, Bethtown, two. Attempted rape. No statement . . ."

Bert Kling made himself comfortable on the folding chair and began to doze again.

XI

The check made out to George Badueck was numbered 018. It was a small check, five dollars. It did not seem very important to Carella, but it was one of the unexplained three, and he decided to give it a whirl.

Badueck, as it turned out, was a photographer. His shop was directly across the street from the County Court Building in Isola. A sign in his window advised that he took photographs for chauffeurs' licenses, hunting licenses, passports, taxicab permits, pistol permits, and the like. The shop was small and crowded. Badueck fitted into the shop like a beetle in an ant trap. He was a huge man with thick, unruly black hair and the smell of developing fluid on him.

"Who remembers?" he said. "I get millions of people in here every day of the week. They pay me in cash, they pay me with checks, they're ugly, they're pretty, they're skinny, they're fat, they all look the same on the pictures I take. Lousy. They all look like I'm photographing them for you guys. You never see any of these official-type pictures? Man, they look like mug shots, all of them. So who remembers this . . . what's her name? Claudia Davis, yeah. Another face that's all. Another mug shot. Why? Is the check bad or something?"

"No, it's a good check."

"So what's the fuss?"

"No fuss," Carella said. "Thanks a lot."

He sighed and went out into the August heat. The County Court Building across the street was white and Gothic in the sunshine. He wiped a handkerchief across his forehead and thought, *Another face, that's all*. Sighing, he crossed the street and entered the building. It was cool in the high vaulted corridors. He consulted the directory and went up to the Bureau of Motor Vehicles first. He asked the clerk there if anyone named Claudia Davis had applied for a license requiring a photograph.

"We only require pictures on chauffeurs' licenses," the clerk said.

"Well, would you check?" Carella asked.

"Sure. Might take a few minutes, though. Would you have a seat?"

Carella sat. It was very cool. It felt like October. He looked at his watch. It was almost time for lunch, and he was getting hungry. The clerk came back and motioned him over.

"We've got a Claudia Davis listed," he said, "but she's already got a license, and she didn't apply for a new one."

"What kind of license?"

"Operator's."

"When does it expire?"

"Next September."

"And she hasn't applied for anything needing a photo?"

"Nope. Sorry."

"That's all right. Thanks," Carella said.

He went out into the corridor again. He hardly thought it likely that Claudia Davis had applied for a permit to own or operate a taxicab, so he skipped the Hack Bureau and went upstairs to Pistol Permits. The woman he spoke to there was very kind and very efficient. She checked her files and told him that no one named Claudia Davis had ever applied for either a carry or a premises pistol permit. Carella thanked her and went into the hall again. He was very hungry. His stomach was beginning to growl. He debated having lunch and then returning and decided, *Hell, I'd better get it done now.*

The man behind the counter in the Passport Bureau was old and thin and he wore a green eyeshade. Carella asked his question, and the old man went to his files and creakingly returned to the window.

"That's right," he said.

"What's right?"

"She did. Claudia Davis. She applied for a passport."

"When?"

The old man checked the slip of paper in his trembling hands. "July twentieth," he said.

"Did you give it to her?"

"We accepted her application, sure. Isn't us who issues the passports. We've got to send the application on to Washington."

"But you did accept it?"

"Sure, why not? Had all the necessary stuff. Why shouldn't we accept it?"

"What was the necessary stuff?"

"Two photos, proof of citizenship, filled-out application, and cash."

"What did she show as proof of citizenship?"

"Her birth certificate."

"Where was she born?"

"California."

"She paid you in cash?"

"That's right."

"Not a check?"

"Nope. She started to write a check, but the blamed pen was on the blink. We use ballpoints, you know, and it gave out after she filled in the application. So she paid me in cash. It's not all that much money, you know."

"I see. Thank you," Carella said.

"Not at all," the old man replied, and he creaked back to his files to replace the record on Claudia Davis.

The check was numbered 007, and it was dated July twelfth, and it was made out to a woman named Martha Fedelson.

Miss Fedelson adjusted her pince-nez and looked at the check. Then she moved some papers aside on the small desk in the cluttered office, and put the check down, and leaned closer to it, and studied it again.

"Yes," she said, "that check was made out to me. Claudia Davis wrote it right in this office." Miss Fedelson smiled. "If you can call it an office. Desk space and a telephone. But then, I'm just starting, you know."

"How long have you been a travel agent, Miss Fedelson?"

"Six months now. It's very exciting work."

"Had you ever booked a trip for Miss Davis before?"

"No. This was the first time."

"Did someone refer her to you?"

"No. She picked my name out of the phone book."

"And asked you to arrange this trip for her, is that right?"

"Yes."

"And this check? What's it for?"

"Her airline tickets, and deposits at several hotels."

"Hotels *where*?"

"In Paris and Dijon. And then another in Lausanne, Switzerland."

"She was going to Europe?"

"Yes. From Lausanne she was heading down to the Italian Riviera. I was working on that for her, too. Getting transportation and the hotels, you know."

"When did she plan to leave?"

"September first."

"Well, that explains the luggage and the clothes," Carella said aloud.

"I'm sorry," Miss Fedelson said, and she smiled and raised her eyebrows.

"Nothing, nothing," Carella said. "What was your impression of Miss Davis?"

"Oh, that's hard to say. She was only here once, you understand." Miss Fedelson thought for a moment, and then said, "I suppose she *could* have been a pretty girl if she tried, but she wasn't trying. Her hair was short and dark, and she seemed rather—well, withdrawn, I guess. She didn't take her sunglasses off all the while she was here. I suppose you would call her shy. Or frightened. I don't know." Miss Fedelson smiled again. "Have I helped you any?"

"Well, now we know she was going abroad," Carella said.

"September is a good time to go," Miss Fedelson answered. "In September the tourists have all gone home." There was a wistful sound to her voice. Carella thanked her for her time and left the small office with its travel folders on the cluttered desk top.

XII

He was running out of checks and running out of ideas. Everything seemed to point toward a girl in flight, a girl in hiding, but what was there to hide, what was there to run from? Josie Thompson had been in that boat alone. The coroner's jury had labeled it accidental drowning. The insurance company hadn't contested Claudia's claim, and they'd given her a legitimate check that she could have cashed anywhere in the world. And yet there *was* hiding, and there *was* flight—and he couldn't understand why.

He took the list of remaining checks from his pocket. The girl's shoemaker, the girl's hairdresser, a florist, a candy shop. None of them truly important. And the remaining check made out to an individual, the check numbered 006 and dated July eleventh, and written to a man named David Oblinsky in the amount of $45.75. Carella had his lunch at two-thirty and then went downtown. He found Oblinsky in a diner near the bus terminal. Oblinsky was sitting on one of the counter stools, and he was drinking a cup of coffee. He asked Carella to join him, and Carella did.

"You traced me through that check, huh?" he said. "The phone company gave you my number and my address, huh? I'm unlisted, you know. They ain't supposed to give out my number."

"Well, they made a special concession because it was police business."

"Yeah, well, suppose the cops called and asked for Marlon Brando's number? You think they'd give it out? Like hell they would. I don't like that. No, sir, I don't like it one damn bit."

"What do you do, Mr. Oblinsky? Is there a reason for the unlisted number?"

"I drive a cab is what I do. Sure there's a reason. It's classy to have an unlisted number. Didn't you know that?"

Carella smiled. "No, I didn't."

"Sure, it is."

"Why did Claudia Davis give you this check?" Carella asked.

"Well, I work for a cab company here in this city, you see. But usually on weekends or on my day off I use my own car and I take people on long trips, you know what I mean? Like to the country, or the mountains, or the beach, wherever they want to go. I don't care. I'll take them wherever they want to go."

"I see."

"Sure. So in June sometime, the beginning of June it was, I get a call from this guy I know up at Triangle Lake, he tells me there's a rich broad there who needs somebody to drive her Caddy back to the city for her. He said it was worth thirty bucks if I was willing to take the train up and the heap back. I told him, no sir, I wanted forty-five or it was no deal. I knew I had him over a barrel, you understand? He'd already told me he checked with the local hicks and none of them felt like making the ride. So he said he would talk it over with her and get back to me. Well, he called again . . . you know, it burns me up about the phone company. They ain't supposed to give out my number like that. Suppose it was Marilyn Monroe? You think they'd give out her number? I'm gonna raise a stink about this, believe me."

"What happened when he called you back?"

"Well, he said she was willing to pay forty-five, but like could I wait until July sometime when she would send me a check because she was a little short right at the moment. So I figured what the hell, am I going to get stiffed by a dame who's driving a 1960 Caddy? I figured I could trust her until July. But I also told him, if that was the case, then I also wanted her to pay the tolls on the way back, which I don't ordinarily ask my customers to do. That's what the seventy-five cents was for. The tolls."

"So you took the train up there and then drove Miss Davis and the Cadillac back to the city, is that right?"

"Yeah."

"I suppose she was pretty distraught on the trip home."

"Huh?"

"You know. Not too coherent."

"Huh?"

"Broken up. Crying. Hysterical," Carella said.

"No. No, she was okay."

"Well, what I mean is . . ." Carella hesitated. "I assumed she wasn't capable of driving the car back herself."

"Yeah, that's right. That's why she hired me."

"Well, then . . ."

"But not because she was broken up or anything."

"Then why?" Carella frowned. "Was there a lot of luggage? Did she need your help with that?"

"Yeah, sure. Both hers and her cousin's. Her cousin drowned, you know."

"Yes. I know that."

"But anybody coulda helped her with her luggage," Oblinsky said. "No, that wasn't why she hired me. She really *needed* me, mister."

"Why?"

"Why? Because she don't know how to drive, that's why."

Carella stared at him. "You're wrong," he said.

"Oh, no," Oblinsky said. "She can't drive, believe me. While I was putting the luggage in the trunk, I asked her to start the car, and she didn't even know how to do that. Hey, you think I ought to raise a fuss with the phone company?"

"I don't know," Carella said, rising suddenly. All at once the check made out to Claudia Davis' hairdresser seemed terribly important to him. He had almost run out of checks, but all at once he had an idea.

XIII

The hairdresser's salon was on South Twenty-third, just off Jefferson Avenue. A green canopy covered the sidewalk outside the salon. The words Arturo Manfredi, Inc., were lettered discreetly in white on the canopy. A glass plaque in the window repeated the name of the establishment and added, for the benefit of those who did not read either *Vogue* or *Harper's Bazaar,* that there were two branches of the shop, one here in Isola and another in "Nassau, the Bahamas." Beneath that, in smaller, more modest letters, were the words "Internationally Renowned." Carella and Hawes went into the shop at four-thirty in the afternoon. Two meticulously coifed and manicured women were sitting in the small reception room, their expensively sleek legs crossed, apparently awaiting either their chauffeurs, their husbands, or their lovers. They both looked up expectantly when the detectives entered, expressed mild disappointment by only slightly raising newly plucked eyebrows, and went back to reading their fashion magazines. Carella and Hawes walked to the desk. The girl behind the desk was a blonde with a brilliant shellacked look and an English finishing school voice.

"Yes?" she said. "May I help you?"

She lost a tiny trace of her poise when Carella flashed his buzzer. She read the raised lettering on the shield, glanced at the photo on the plastic-encased I.D. card, quickly regained her polished calm, and said coolly and unemotionally, "Yes, what can I do for you?"

"We wonder if you can tell us anything about the girl who wrote this check?" Carella said. He reached into his jacket pocket, took out a folded photostat of the check, unfolded it, and put it on the desk before the blonde. The blonde looked at it casually.

"What is the name?" she asked. "I can't make it out."

"Claudia Davis."

"D-A-V-I-S?"

"Yes."

"I don't recognize the name," the blonde said. "She's not one of our regular customers."

"But she did make out a check to your salon," Carella said. "She wrote this on July seventh. Would you please check your records and find out why she was here and who took care of her?"

"I'm sorry," the blonde said.

"What?"

"I'm sorry, but we close at five o'clock, and this is the busiest time of the day for us. I'm sure you can understand that. If you'd care to come back a little later . . ."

"No, we wouldn't care to come back a little later," Carella said. "Because if we came back a little later, it would be with a search warrant and possibly a warrant for the seizure of your books, and sometimes that can cause a little commotion among the gossip columnists, and that kind of commotion might add to your international renown a little bit. We've had a long day, miss, and this is important, so how about it?"

"Of course. We're always delighted to cooperate with the police," the blonde said frigidly. "Especially when they're so well mannered."

"Yes, we're all of that," Carella answered.

"Yes. July seventh, did you say?"

"July seventh."

The blonde left the desk and went into the back of the salon. A brunette came out front and said, "Has Miss Marie left for the evening?"

"Who's Miss Marie?" Hawes asked.

"The blond girl."

"No. She's getting something for us."

"That white streak is very attractive," the brunette said. "I'm Miss Olga."

"How do you do."

"Fine, thank you," Miss Olga said. "When she comes back, would you tell her there's something wrong with one of the dryers on the third floor?"

"Yes, I will," Hawes said.

Miss Olga smiled, waved, and vanished into the rear of the salon again. Miss Marie reappeared not a moment later. She looked at Carella and said, "A Miss Claudia Davis was here on July seventh. Mr. Sam worked on her. Would you like to talk to him?"

"Yes, we would."

"Then follow me, please," she said curtly.

They followed her into the back of the salon past women who sat with crossed legs, wearing smocks, their heads in hair dryers.

"Oh, by the way," Hawes said, "Miss Olga said to tell you there's something wrong with one of the third-floor dryers."

"Thank you," Miss Marie said.

Hawes felt particularly clumsy in this world of women's machines. There was an air of delicate efficiency about the place, and Hawes—six feet two inches tall in his bare soles, weighing in at a hundred and ninety pounds—was certain he would knock over a bottle of nail polish or a pail of hair rinse. As they entered the second-floor salon, as he looked down that long line of humming space helmets at women with crossed legs and what looked like barbers' aprons covering their nylon slips, he became aware of a new phenomenon. The women were slowly turning their heads inside the dryers to look at the white streak over his left temple. He suddenly felt like a horse's ass. For whereas the streak was the legitimate result of a knifing—they had shaved his red hair to get at the wound, and it had grown back this way—he realized all at once that many of these women had shelled out hard-earned dollars to simulate identical white streaks in their own hair, and he no longer felt like a cop making a business call. Instead, he felt like a customer who had come to have his goddamned streak touched up a little.

"This is Mr. Sam," Miss Marie said, and Hawes turned to see Carella shaking hands with a rather elongated man. The man wasn't particularly tall, he was simply elongated. He gave the impression of being seen from the side seats in a movie theater, stretched out of true proportion, curiously two-dimensional. He wore a white smock, and there were three narrow combs in the breast pocket. He carried a pair of scissors in one thin, sensitive-looking hand.

"How do you do?" he said to Carella, and he executed a half-bow, European in origin, American in execution. He turned to Hawes, took his hand, shook it, and again said, "How do you do?"

"They're from the police," Miss Marie said briskly, releasing Mr. Sam from any obligation to be polite, and then left the men alone.

"A woman named Claudia Davis was here on July seventh," Carella said. "Apparently she had her hair done by you. Can you tell us what you remember about her?"

"Miss Davis, Miss Davis," Mr. Sam said, touching his high forehead in an attempt at visual shorthand, trying to convey the concept of thought without having to do the accompanying brainwork. "Let me see, Miss Davis, Miss Davis."

"Yes."

"Yes, Miss Davis. A very pretty blonde."

"No," Carella said. He shook his head. "A brunette. You're thinking of the wrong person."

"No, I'm thinking of the right person," Mr. Sam said. He tapped his temple with one extended forefinger, another piece of visual abbreviation. "I remember. Claudia Davis. A blonde."

"A brunette," Carella insisted, and he kept watching Mr. Sam.

"When she left. But when she came, a blonde."

"What?" Hawes said.

"She was a blonde, a very pretty, natural blonde. It is rare. Natural blondness, I mean. I couldn't understand why she wanted to change the color."

"You dyed her hair?" Hawes asked.

"That is correct."

"Did she say *why* she wanted to be a brunette?"

"No, sir. I argued with her. I said, 'You have *beau*tiful hair, I can do *mar*-velous things with this hair of yours. You are a *blonde,* my dear, there are drab women who come in here every day of the week and *beg* to be turned into blondes.' No. She would not listen. I dyed it for her." Mr. Sam seemed to become offended by the idea all over again. He looked at the detectives as if they had been responsible for the stubbornness of Claudia Davis.

"What else did you do for her, Mr. Sam?" Carella asked.

"The dye, a cut, and a set. And I believe one of the girls gave her a facial and a manicure."

"What do you mean by a cut? Was her hair long when she came here?"

"Yes, beautiful long blond hair. She wanted it cut. I cut it." Mr. Sam shook his head. "A pity. She looked terrible. I don't usually say this about someone I work on, but she walked out of here looking terrible. You would hardly recognize her as the same pretty blonde who came in not three hours before."

"Maybe that was the idea," Carella said.

"I beg your pardon?"

"Forget it. Thank you, Mr. Sam. We know you're busy."

In the street outside Hawes said, "You knew before we went in there, didn't you, Mr. Steve?"

"I suspected, Mr. Cotton, I suspected. Come on, let's get back to the squad."

XIV

They kicked it around like a bunch of advertising executives. They sat in Lieutenant Byrnes' office and tried to find out how the cookie crumbled and which way the Tootsie rolled. They were just throwing out a life preserver to see if anyone grabbed at it, that's all. What they were doing, you see, was running up the flag to see if anyone saluted, that's all. The lieutenant's office was a four-window office because he was top man in this particular combine. It was a very elegant office. It had an electric fan all its own, and a big wide desk. It got cross ventilation from the street. It was really very pleasant. Well, to tell the truth, it was a pretty ratty office in which to be holding a top-level meeting, but it was the best the precinct had to offer. And after a while you got used to the chipping paint and the soiled walls and the bad lighting and the stench of urine from the men's room down the hall. Peter Byrnes didn't work for B.B.D. & O. He worked for the city. Somehow, there was a difference.

"I just put in a call to Irene Miller," Carella said. "I asked her to describe Claudia Davis to me, and she went through it all over again. Short, dark hair, shy, plain. Then I asked her to describe the cousin, Josie Thompson." Carella nodded glumly. "Guess what?"

"A pretty girl," Hawes said. "A pretty girl with long blond hair."

"Sure. Why, Mrs. Miller practically spelled it out the first time we talked to her. It's all there in the report. She said they were like black and white in looks and personality. Black and white, sure. A brunette and a goddamn blonde!"

"That explains the yellow," Hawes said.

"What yellow?"

"Courtenoy. He said he saw a patch of yellow breaking the surface. He wasn't talking about her clothes, Steve. He was talking about her *hair*."

"It explains a lot of things," Carella said. "It explains why shy Claudia Davis was preparing for her European trip by purchasing baby doll nightgowns and bikini bathing suits. And it explains why the undertaker up there referred to Claudia as a pretty girl. And it explains why our necropsy report said she was thirty when everybody talked about her as if she were much younger."

"The girl who drowned wasn't Josie, huh?" Meyer said. "You figure she was Claudia."

"Damn right I figure she was Claudia."

"And you figure she cut her hair afterward, and dyed it, and took her cousin's name, and tried to pass as her cousin until she could get out of the country, huh?" Meyer said.

"Why?" Byrnes said. He was a compact man with a compact bullet head and a chunky economical body. He did not like to waste time or words.

"Because the trust income was in Claudia's name. Because Josie didn't have a dime of her own."

"She could have collected on her cousin's insurance policy," Meyer said.

"Sure, but that would have been the end of it. The trust called for those stocks to be turned over to U.C.L.A. if Claudia died. A college, for God's sake! How do you suppose Josie felt about that? Look, I'm not trying to hang a homicide on her. I just think she took advantage of a damn good situation. Claudia was in that boat alone. When she fell over the side, Josie really tried to rescue her, no question about it. But she missed, and Claudia drowned. Okay. Josie went all to pieces, couldn't talk straight, crying, sobbing, real hysterical woman, we've seen them before. But came the dawn. And with the dawn, Josie began thinking. They were away from the city, strangers in a strange town. Claudia had drowned but no one *knew* that she was Claudia. No one but Josie. She had no identification on her, remember? Her purse was in the car. Okay. If Josie identified her cousin correctly, she'd collect twenty-five grand on the insurance policy, and then all that stock would be turned over to the college, and that would be the end of the gravy train. But suppose, just suppose Josie told the police the girl in the lake was Josie Thompson? Suppose she said, 'I, Claudia Davis, tell you that girl who drowned is my cousin, Josie Thompson'?"

Hawes nodded. "Then she'd still collect on an insurance policy, and also fall heir to those fat security dividends coming in."

"Right. What does it take to cash a dividend check? A bank account, that's all. A bank account with an established signature. So all she had to do was open one, sign her name as Claudia Davis, and then endorse every dividend check that came in exactly the same way."

"Which explains the new account," Meyer said. "She couldn't use Claudia's old account because the bank undoubtedly knew both Claudia *and* her signature. So Josie had to forfeit the sixty grand at Highland Trust and start from scratch."

"And while she was building a new identity and a new fortune," Hawes said, "just to make sure Claudia's few friends forgot all about her, Josie was running off to Europe. She may have planned to stay there for years."

"It all ties in," Carella said. "Claudia had a driver's license. She was the one who drove the car away from Stewart City. But Josie had to hire a chauffeur to take her back?"

"And would Claudia, who was so meticulous about money matters, have kept so many people waiting for payment?" Hawes said. "No, sir. That was Josie. And Josie was broke, Josie was waiting for that insurance policy to pay off so she could settle those debts and get the hell out of the country."

"Well, I admit it adds up," Meyer said.

Peter Byrnes never wasted words. "Who cashed that twenty-five thousand-dollar check for Josie?" he said.

There was silence in the room.

"Who's got that missing five grand?" he said.

There was another silence.

"Who *killed* Josie?" he said.

XV

Jeremiah Dodd of the Security Insurance Corporation, Inc., did not call until two days later. He asked to speak to Detective Carella, and when he got him on the phone, he said, "Mr. Carella, I've just heard from San Francisco on that check."

"What check?" Carella asked. He had been interrogating a witness to a knifing in a grocery store on Culver Avenue. The Claudia Davis or rather the Josie Thompson case was not quite yet in the Open File, but it was ready to be dumped there, and was truly the farthest thing from Carella's mind at the moment.

"The check was paid to Claudia Davis," Dodd said.

"Oh, yes. Who cashed it?"

"Well, there are two endorsements on the back. One was made by Claudia Davis, of course. The other was made by an outfit called Leslie Summers, Inc. It's a regular company stamp marked 'For Deposit Only' and signed by one of the officers."

"Have any idea what sort of a company that is?" Carella asked.

"Yes," Dodd said. "They handle foreign exchange."

"Thank you," Carella said.

He went there with Bert Kling later that afternoon. He went with Kling completely by chance and only because Kling was heading downtown to buy his mother a birthday gift and offered Carella a ride. When they parked the car, Kling asked, "How long will this take, Steve?"

"Few minutes, I guess."

"Want to meet me back here?"

"Well, I'll be at 720 Hall, Leslie Summers, Inc. If you're through before me, come on over."

"Okay, I'll see you," Kling said.

They parted on Hall Avenue without shaking hands. Carella found the street-level office of Leslie Summers, Inc., and walked in. A counter ran the length of the room, and there were several girls behind it. One of the girls was speaking to a customer in French and another was talking Italian to a man who wanted lire in exchange for dollars. A board behind the desk quoted the current exchange rate for countries all over the world. Carella got in line and waited. When he reached the counter, the girl who'd been speaking French said, "Yes, sir?"

"I'm a detective," Carella said. He opened his wallet to where his shield was pinned to the leather. "You cashed a check for Miss Claudia

Davis sometime in July. An insurance-company check for twenty-five thousand dollars. Would you happen to remember it?"

"No, sir, I don't think I handled it."

"Would you check around and see who did, please?"

The girl held a brief consultation with the other girls, and then walked to a desk behind which sat a corpulent, balding man with a razor-thin mustache. They talked with each other for a full five minutes. The man kept waving his hands. The girl kept trying to explain about the insurance-company check. The bell over the front door sounded. Bert Kling came in, looked around, saw Carella, and joined him at the counter.

"All done?" Carella asked.

"Yeah, I bought her a charm for her bracelet. How about you?"

"They're holding a summit meeting," Carella said.

The fat man waddled over to the counter. "What is the trouble?" he asked Carella.

"No trouble. Did you cash a check for twenty-five thousand dollars?"

"Yes. Is the check no good?"

"It's a good check."

"It looked like a good check. It was an insurance-company check. The young lady waited while we called the company. They said it was bona fide and we should accept it. Was it a bad check?"

"No, no, it was fine."

"She had identification. It all seemed very proper."

"What did she show you?"

"A driver's license or a passport is what we usually require. But she had neither. We accepted her birth certificate. After all, we *did* call the company. Is the check no good?"

"It's fine. But the check was for twenty-five thousand, and we're trying to find out what happened to five thousand of . . ."

"Oh, yes. The francs."

"What?"

"She bought five thousand dollars' worth of French francs," the fat man said. "She was going abroad?"

"Yes, she was going abroad," Carella said. He sighed heavily. "Well, that's that, I guess."

"It all seemed very proper," the fat man insisted.

"Oh, it was, it was. Thank you. Come on, Bert."

They walked down Hall Avenue in silence.

"Beats me," Carella said.

"What's that, Steve?"

"This case." He sighed again. "Oh, what the hell!"

"Yeah, let's get some coffee. What was all that business about the francs?"

"She bought five thousand dollars' worth of francs," Carella said.

"The French are getting a big play lately, huh?" Kling said, smiling. "Here's a place. This look okay?"

"Yeah, fine." Carella pulled open the door of the luncheonette. "What do you mean, Bert?"

"With the francs."

"What about them?"

"The exchange rate must be very good."

"I don't get you."

"You know. All those francs kicking around."

"Bert, what the hell are you talking about?"

"Weren't you with me? Last Wednesday?"

"With you where?"

"The lineup. I thought you were with me."

"No, I wasn't," Carella said tiredly.

"Oh, well, that's why."

"That's why what? Bert, for the love of . . ."

"That's why you don't remember him."

"Who?"

"The punk they brought in on that burglary pickup. They found five grand in French francs in his apartment."

Carella felt as if he'd just been hit by a truck.

XVI

It had been crazy from the beginning. Some of them are like that. The girl had looked black, but she was really white. They thought she was Claudia Davis, but she was Josie Thompson. And they had been looking for a murderer when all there happened to be was a burglar.

They brought him up from his cell where he was awaiting trial for Burglary One. He came up in an elevator with a police escort. The police van had dropped him off at the side door of the Criminal Courts Building, and he had entered the corridor under guard and been marched down through the connecting tunnel and into the building that housed the district attorney's office, and then taken into the elevator. The door of the elevator opened into a tiny room upstairs. The other door of the room was locked from the outside and a sign on it read NO ADMITTANCE.

The patrolman who'd brought Ralph Reynolds up to the interrogation room stood with his back against the elevator door all the while the detectives talked to him, and his right hand was on the butt of his Police Special.

"I never heard of her," Reynolds said.

"Claudia Davis," Carella said. "Or Josie Thompson. Take your choice."

"I don't know either one of them. What the hell *is* this? You got me on a burglary rap, now you try to pull in everything was ever done in this city?"

"Who said anything was done, Reynolds?"

"If nothing was done, why'd you drag me up here?"

"They found five thousand bucks in French francs in your pad, Reynolds. Where'd you get it?"

"Who wants to know?"

"Don't get snotty, Reynolds! Where'd you get that money?"

"A guy owed it to me. He paid me in francs. He was a French guy."

"What's his name?"

"I can't remember."

"You'd better start trying."

"Pierre something."

"Pierre what?" Meyer said.

"Pierre La Salle, something like that. I didn't know him too good."

"But you lent him five grand, huh?"

"Yeah."

"What were you doing on the night of August first?"

"Why? What happened on August first?"

"You tell us."

"I don't know what I was doing."

"Were you working?"

"I'm unemployed."

"You know what we mean!"

"No. What do you mean?"

"Were you breaking into apartments?"

"No."

"Speak up! Yes or no?"

"I said no."

"He's lying, Steve," Meyer said.

"Sure he is."

"Yeah, sure I am. Look, cop, you got nothing on me but Burglary

One, if that. And that you gotta prove in court. So stop trying to hang anything else on me. You ain't got a chance."

"Not unless those prints check out," Carella said quickly.

"What prints?"

"The prints we found on the dead girl's throat," Carella lied.

"I was wearing . . . !"

The small room went as still as death.

Reynolds sighed heavily. He looked at the floor.

"You want to tell us?"

"No," he said. "Go to hell."

He finally told them. After twelve hours of repeated questioning he finally broke down. He hadn't meant to kill her, he said. He didn't even know anybody was in the apartment. He had looked in the bedroom, and the bed was empty. He hadn't seen her asleep in one of the chairs, fully dressed. He had found the French money in a big jar on one of the shelves over the sink. He had taken the money and then accidentally dropped the jar, and she woke up and came into the room and saw him and began screaming. So he grabbed her by the throat. He only meant to shut her up. But she kept struggling. She was very strong. He kept holding on, but only to shut her up. She kept struggling, so he had to hold on. She kept struggling as if . . . as if he'd really been trying to kill her, as if she didn't want to lose her life. But that was manslaughter, wasn't it? He wasn't trying to kill her. That wasn't homicide, was it?

"I didn't mean to kill her!" he shouted as they took him into the elevator. "She began screaming! I'm not a killer! Look at me! Do I look like a killer?" And then, as the elevator began dropping to the basement, he shouted, "I'm a burglar!" as if proud of his profession, as if stating that he was something more than a common thief, a trained workman, a skilled artisan. "I'm not a killer! I'm a burglar!" he screamed. "I'm not a killer! I'm not a killer!" And his voice echoed down the elevator shaft as the car dropped to the basement and the waiting van.

They sat in the small room for several moments after he was gone.

"Hot in here," Meyer said.

"Yeah." Carella nodded.

"What's the matter?"

"Nothing."

"Maybe he's right," Meyer said. "Maybe he's only a burglar."

"He stopped being that the minute he stole a life, Meyer."

"Josie Thompson stole a life, too."

"No," Carella said. He shook his head. "She only borrowed one. There's a difference, Meyer."

The room went silent.

"You feel like some coffee?" Meyer asked.

"Sure."

They took the elevator down and then walked out into the brilliant August sunshine. The streets were teeming with life. They walked into the human swarm, but they were curiously silent.

At last Carella said, "I guess I think she shouldn't be dead. I guess I think that someone who tried so hard to make a life shouldn't have had it taken away from her."

Meyer put his hand on Carella's shoulder. "Listen," he said earnestly. "It's a job. It's only a job."

"Sure," Carella said. "It's only a job."

The Heroine

Author: Patricia Highsmith (1921–1995)

The closest Patricia Highsmith ever came to writing with a series character was when she wrote four novels about a young urban psychopath named Tom Ripley. This should come as no surprise, however, because in her other novels and short fiction, she was known for turning the conventional mystery story upside down. Either by showing the world through the eyes of a criminal or starting with an (relatively) innocent man or woman and showing their gradual descent into crime (*Strangers on a Train*) or madness (*Edith's Diary*), Highsmith redefined the suspense story, combining subtle social or political commentary in her elegantly plotted stories.

Her work attracted interest from Hollywood, most notable *Strangers on a Train*, which was adapted and filmed by Alfred Hitchcock. The movie has been hailed as a masterpiece of taut, white-knuckled suspense. The Ripley novels have also garnered interest, with a version of *The Talented Mr. Ripley* released in the year 2000.

The girl was so sure she would get the job, she had unabashedly come out to Westchester with her suitcase. She sat in a comfortable chair in the living room of the Christiansens' house, looking in her navy-blue coat and beret even younger than twenty-one, and replied earnestly to their questions.

"Have you worked as a governess before?" Mr. Christiansen asked. He sat beside his wife on the sofa, his elbows on the knees of his gray flannel trousers, and his hands clasped. "Any references, I mean?"

"I was a maid in Mrs. Dwight Howell's house in New York for the last seven months." Lucille looked at him with suddenly wide gray eyes.

"I could get a reference from there if you like . . . But when I saw your advertisement this morning, I didn't want to wait. I've always wanted a place where there were children."

Mrs. Christiansen smiled, but mainly to herself, at the girl's enthusiasm. She took a silver box from the coffee table, stood up, and offered it to the girl. "Will you have one?"

"No, thank you. I don't smoke."

"Well," Mrs. Christiansen said, lighting her own cigarette, "we might call them, of course, but my husband and I set more store by appearances than references . . . What do you say, Ronald? You told me you wanted someone who really liked children."

And fifteen minutes later, Lucille Smith was standing in her room in the servant's quarters back of the house, buttoning the belt of her new white uniform. She touched her mouth lightly with lipstick. "You're starting all over again, Lucille," she told herself in the mirror. "You're going to have a happy, useful life from now on, and forget everything that was before."

But there went her eyes too wide again, as if to deny her words. Her eyes looked much like her mother's when they opened like that, and her mother was part of what she must forget. She must overcome that habit of stretching her eyes. It made her look surprised and uncertain, too, which was not at all the way to look around children. Her hand trembled as she set the lipstick down. She recomposed her face in the mirror, smoothed the starched front of her uniform. There were only a few things like the eyes to remember, a few silly habits, really, like burning little bits of paper in ashtrays, forgetting time sometimes—little things that many people did, but that she must remember not to do. With practice the remembering would come automatically. Because she was just like other people (had the psychiatrist not told her so?), and other people never thought of them at all.

She crossed the room, sank on to the window seat under the blue curtains, and looked out on the garden and lawn that lay between the servants' house and the big house. The yard was longer than it was wide, with a round fountain in the center and two flagstone walks lying like a crooked cross in the grass. There were benches here and there, against a tree, under an arbor, that seemed to be made of white lace. A beautiful yard!

And the house was the house of her dreams! A white, two-story house with dark-red shutters, with oaken doors and brass knockers and latches that opened with a press of the thumb . . . and broad lawns and poplar trees so dense and high one could not see through, so that

one did not have to admit or believe that there was another house somewhere beyond . . . The rain-streaked Howell house in New York,
granite pillared and heavily ornamented, had looked, Lucille thought,
like a stale wedding cake in a row of other stale wedding cakes . . .

She rose suddenly from her seat. The Christiansen house was
blooming, friendly, and alive! There were children in it. Thank God for
the children! But she had not even met them yet.

She hurried downstairs, crossed the yard on the path that ran from
the door, lingered a few seconds to watch the plump faun blowing water
from his reeds into the rock pond . . . What was it the Christiansens
had agreed to pay her? She did not remember and she did not care. She
would have worked for nothing just to live in such a place.

Mrs. Christiansen took her upstairs to the nursery. She opened the
door of a room whose walls were decorated with bright peasant designs,
dancing couples and dancing animals, and twisting trees in blossom.
There were twin beds of buff-colored oak, and the floor was yellow
linoleum, spotlessly clean.

The two children lay on the floor in one corner, amid scattered cray-
ons and picture books.

"Children this is your new nurse," their mother said. "Her name is
Lucille."

The little boy stood up and said, "How do you do," as he solemnly
held out a crayon-stained hand.

Lucille took it, and with a slow nod of her head repeated his greeting.

"And Heloise," Mrs. Christiansen said, leading the second child, who
was smaller, toward Lucille.

Heloise stared up at the figure in white and said, "How do you do."

"Nicky is nine and Heloise six," Mrs. Christiansen told her.

"Yes," Lucille said. She noticed that both children had a touch of red
in their blond hair, like their father. Both wore blue overalls without
shirts, and their backs and shoulders were sun-brown beneath the
straps. Lucille could not take her eyes from them. They were the perfect
children of her perfect house. They looked up at her frankly, with no
mistrust, no hostility. Only love, and some childlike curiosity.

". . . and most people do prefer living where there's more country,"
Mrs. Christiansen was saying.

"Oh yes . . . yes, ma'am. It's ever so much nicer here than in the
city."

Mrs. Christiansen was smoothing the little girl's hair with a tenderness that fascinated Lucille. "It's just about time for their lunch," she

said. "You'll have your meals up here, Lucille. And would you like tea or coffee or milk?"

"I'd like coffee, please."

"All right, Lisabeth will be up with the lunch in a few minutes." She paused at the door. "You aren't nervous about anything, are you, Lucille?" she asked in a low voice.

"Oh no, ma'am."

"Well, you mustn't be." She seemed about to say something else, but she only smiled and went out.

Lucille stared after her, wondering what that something else might have been.

"You're a lot prettier than Catherine," Nicky told her.

She turned around. "Who's Catherine?" Lucille seated herself on a hassock, and as she gave all her attention to the two children who still gazed at her, she felt her shoulders relax their tension.

"Catherine was our nurse before. She went back to Scotland . . . I'm glad you're here. We didn't like Catherine."

Heloise stood with her hands behind her back, swaying from side to side as she regarded Lucille. "No," she said, "we didn't like Catherine."

Nicky stared at his sister. "You shouldn't say that. That's what I said!"

Lucille laughed and hugged her knees. Then Nicky and Heloise laughed, too.

A colored maid entered with a steaming tray and set it on the blond wood table in the center of the room. She was slender and of indefinite age. "I'm Lisabeth Jenkins, miss," she said shyly as she laid some paper napkins at three places.

"My name's Lucille Smith," the girl said.

"Well, I'll just leave you to do the rest, miss. If you need anything else, just holler." She went out, her hips small and hard-looking under the blue uniform.

The three sat down at the table, and Lucille lifted the cover from the large dish, exposing three parsley-garnished omelettes, bright yellow in the bar of sunlight that crossed the table. But first there was tomato soup for her to ladle out, and triangles of buttered toast to pass. Her coffee was in a silver pot, and the children had two large glasses of milk. The table was low for Lucille, but she did not mind. It was so wonderful merely to be sitting here with these children, with the sun warm and cheerful on the yellow linoleum floor, on the table, on Heloise's ruddy face opposite her. How pleasant not to be in the Howell house! She had always been clumsy there. But here it would not matter if she dropped a pewter cover or let a gravy spoon fall in someone's lap. The children would only laugh.

Lucille sipped her coffee.

"Aren't you going to eat?" Heloise asked, with her mouth already full.

The cup slipped in Lucille's fingers, and she spilled half her coffee on the cloth. No, it was not cloth, thank goodness, but oilcloth. She could get it up with a paper towel, and Lisabeth would never know.

"Piggy!" laughed Heloise.

"Heloise!" Nicky admonished, and went to fetch some paper towels from the bathroom.

They mopped up together.

"Dad always gives us a little bit of his coffee," Nicky remarked as he took his place again.

Lucille had been wondering whether the children would mention the accident to their mother. She sensed that Nicky was offering her a bribe. "Does he?" she asked.

"He pours a little in our milk," Nicky went on, "just so you can see the color."

"Like this?" And Lucille poured a bit from the graceful silver spout into each glass.

The children gasped with pleasure. "Yes!"

"Mother doesn't like us to have coffee," Nicky explained, "But when she's not looking, Dad let's us have a little like you did. Dad says his day wouldn't be any good without his coffee, and I'm the same way . . . Gosh, Catherine wouldn't give us any coffee like that, would she, Heloise?"

"Not her!" Heloise took a long, delicious draught from her glass, which she held with both hands.

Lucille felt a glow rise from deep inside her until it settled in her face and burned there. The children liked her, there was no doubt of that. She remembered how often she had gone to the public parks in the city, during the three years she had worked as a maid in various houses (to be a maid was all she was fit for, she used to think), merely to sit on a bench and watch the children play. But the children there had usually been dirty or foul-mouthed, and she herself had always been an outsider. Once she had seen a mother slap her own child across the face. She remembered how she had fled in pain and horror . . .

"Why do you have such big eyes?" Heloise demanded.

Lucille started. "My mother had big eyes, too," she said deliberately, like a confession.

"Oh," Heloise replied, satisfied.

Lucille cut slowly into the omelette she did not want. Her mother had been dead three weeks now. Only three weeks and it seemed much, much longer. That was because she was forgetting, she thought, forgetting all the hopeless hope of the last three years, that her mother might recover in the sanatorium. But recover to what? The illness was something separate, something that had killed her. It had been senseless to hope for a complete sanity, which she knew her mother had never had. Even the doctors had told her that. And they had told her other things, too, about herself. Good, encouraging things they were, that she was as normal as her father had been. Looking at Heloise's friendly little face across from her, Lucille felt the comforting glow return. Yes, in this perfect house, closed from all the world, she could forget and start anew.

"Are we ready for some Jell-O?" she asked.

Nicky pointed to her plate. "You're not finished eating."

"I wasn't very hungry." Lucille divided the extra dessert between them.

"We could go out to the sandbox now," Nicky suggested. "We always go just in the mornings, but I want you to see our castle."

The sandbox was in the back of the house in a corner made by a projecting ell. Lucille seated herself on the wooden rim of the box while the children began piling and patting like gnomes.

"I must be the captured princess!" Heloise shouted.

"Yes, and I'll rescue her, Lucille. You'll see!"

The castle of moist sand rose rapidly. There were turrets with tin flags sticking from their tops, a moat, and a drawbridge made of the lid of a cigar box covered with sand. Lucille watched, fascinated. She remembered vividly the story of Brian de Bois-Guilbert and Rebecca. She had read *Ivanhoe* through at one long sitting, oblivious of time and place just as she was now.

When the castle was done, Nicky put half a dozen marbles inside it just behind the drawbridge. "These are good soldiers imprisoned," he told her. He held another cigar box lid in front of them until he had packed up a barrier of sand. Then he lifted the lid and the sand door stood like a porte-cochere.

Meanwhile Heloise gathered ammunition of small pebbles from the ground next to the house. "We break the door down and the good soldiers come down the hill across the bridge. Then I'm saved!"

"Don't tell her! She'll see!"

Seriously Nicky thumped the pebbles from the rim of the sandbox opposite the castle door, while Heloise behind the castle thrust a hand forth to repair the destruction as much as she could between shots, for besides being the captured princess she was the defending army.

Suddenly Nicky stopped and looked at Lucille. "Dad knows how to shoot with a stick. He puts the rock on one end and hits the other. That's a balliska."

"Ballista," Lucille said.

"Golly, how did *you* know?"

"I read about it in a book—about castles."

"Golly!" Nicky went back to his thumping, embarrassed that he had pronounced the word wrong. "We got to get the good soldiers out fast. They're captured, see? Then when they're released that means we can all fight together and *take the castle!*"

"And save the princess!" Heloise put in.

As she watched, Lucille found herself wishing for some real catastrophe, something dangerous and terrible to befall Heloise, so that she might throw herself between her and the attacker, and prove her great courage and devotion . . . She would be seriously wounded herself, perhaps with a bullet or a knife, but she would beat off the assailant. Then the Christiansens would love her and keep her with them always. If some madman were to come upon them suddenly now, someone with a loose mouth and bloodshot eyes, she would not be afraid for an instant.

She watched the sand wall crumble and the first good soldier marble struggled free and came wobbling down the hill. Nicky and Heloise whooped with joy. The wall gave way completely, and two, three, four soldiers followed the first, their stripes turning gaily over the sand. Lucille leaned forward. Now she understood! She was like the good soldiers imprisoned in the castle. The castle was the Howell house in the city, and Nicky and Heloise had set her free. She was free to do good deeds. And now if only something would happen . . .

"O-o-ow!"

It was Heloise. Nicky had mashed one of her fingers against the edge of the box as they struggled to get the same marble.

Lucille seized the child's hand, her heart thumping at the sight of the blood that rose from many little points in the scraped flesh. "Heloise, does it hurt very much?"

"Oh, she wasn't supposed to touch the marbles in the first place!" Disgruntled, Nicky sat in the sand.

Lucille held her handkerchief over the finger and half carried her into the house, frantic lest Lisabeth or Mrs. Christiansen see them. She took

Heloise into the bathroom that adjoined the nursery, and in the medicine cabinet found Mercurochrome and gauze. Gently she washed the
finger. It was only a small scrape, and Heloise stopped her tears when
she saw how slight it was.

"See, it's just a little scratch!" Lucille said, but that was only to calm
the child. To her it was not a little scratch. It was a terrible thing to
happen the first afternoon she was in charge, a catastrophe she had
failed to prevent. She wished over and over that the hurt might be on her
own hand, twice as severe.

Heloise smiled as she let the bandage be tied. "Don't punish Nicky,"
she said. "He didn't mean to do it. He just plays rough."

But Lucille had no idea of punishing Nicky. She wanted only to punish herself, to seize a stick and thrust it into her own palm.

"Why do you make your teeth like that?"

"I—I thought it might be hurting you."

"It doesn't hurt anymore." And Heloise went skipping out of the
bathroom. She leaped on to her bed and lay on the tan cover that fitted
the corners and came all the way to the floor. Her bandaged finger
showed startlingly white against the brown of her arm. "We have to
take a nap now," she told Lucille, and closed her eyes. "Good-bye."

"Good-bye," Lucille answered, and tried to smile.

She went down to get Nicky and when they came up the stairs Mrs.
Christiansen was at the nursery door.

Lucille blanched. "I don't think it's bad, ma'am. It—It's a scratch
from the sandbox."

"Heloise's finger? Oh, no, don't worry, my dear. They're always getting little scratches. It does them good. Makes them more careful."

Mrs. Christiansen went in and sat on the edge of Nicky's bed. "Nicky,
dear, you must learn to be more gentle. Just see how you frightened
Lucille!" She laughed and ruffled his hair.

Lucille watched from the doorway. Again she felt herself an outsider,
but this time because of her incompetence. Yet how different this was
from the scenes she had watched in the parks!

Mrs. Christiansen patted Lucille's shoulder as she went out. "They'll
forget all about it by nightfall."

"Nightfall," Lucille whispered as she went back into the nursery.
"What a beautiful word!"

While the children slept, Lucille looked through an illustrated book of
Pinocchio. She was avid for stories, any kind of stories, but most of all
adventure stories and fairy tales. And at her elbow on the children's
shelf there were scores of them. It would take her months to read them

all. It did not matter that they were for children. In fact, she found that kind more to her liking, because such stories were illustrated with pictures of animals dressed up, and tables and houses and all sorts of things come to life.

Now she turned the pages of *Pinocchio* with a sense of contentment and happiness so strong that it intruded upon the story she was reading. The doctor at the sanatorium had encouraged her reading, she remembered, and had told her to go to movies, too. "Be with normal people and forget all about your mother's difficulties . . ." (Difficulties, he had called it then, but all other times he had said strain. Strain it was, like a thread, running through the generations. She had thought, through her.) Lucille could still see the psychiatrist's face, his head turned a little to one side, his glasses in his hand as he spoke, just as she had thought a psychiatrist should look. "Just because your mother had a strain, there's no reason why you should not be as normal as your father was. I have every reason to believe you are. You are an intelligent girl, Lucille . . . Get yourself a job out of the city . . . relax . . . enjoy life . . . I want you to forget even the house your family lived in . . . After a year in the country . . ."

That, too, was three weeks ago just after her mother had died in the ward. And what the doctor had said was true. In this house where there was peace and love, beauty and children, she could feel the moils of the city sloughing off her like a snake's outworn skin. Already, in this one half day! In a week she would forget forever her mother's face.

With a little gasp of joy that was almost ecstasy she turned to the bookshelf and chose at random six or seven tall, slender, brightly colored books. One she laid open, face down, in her lap. Another she opened and leaned against her breast. Still holding the rest in one hand, she pressed her face into *Pinocchio*'s pages, her eyes half closed. Slowly she rocked back and forth in the chair, conscious of nothing but her own happiness and gratitude. The chimes downstairs struck three times, but she did not hear them.

"What are you doing?" Nicky asked, his voice politely curious.

Lucille brought the book down from her face. When the meaning of his question struck her, she flushed and smiled like a happy but guilty child. "Reading!" she laughed.

Nicky laughed, too. "You read awful close."

"Ya-yuss," said Heloise, who had also sat up.

Nicky came over and examined the books in her lap. "We get up at three o'clock. Would you read to us now? Catherine always read to us until dinner."

"Shall I read to you out of *Pinocchio*?" Lucille suggested, happy that she might possibly share with them the happiness she had gained from the first pages of its story. She sat down on the floor so they could see the pictures as she read.

Nicky and Heloise pushed their eager faces over the pictures, and sometimes Lucille could hardly see to read. She did not realize that she read with a tense interest that communicated itself to the two children, and that this was why they enjoyed it so much. For two hours she read, and the time slipped by almost like so many minutes.

Just after five Lisabeth brought in the tray with their dinner, and when the meal was over Nicky and Heloise demanded more reading until their bedtime at seven. Lucille gladly began another book, but when Lisabeth returned to remove the tray, she told Lucille that it was time for the children's bath, and that Mrs. Christiansen would be up to say good night in a little while.

Mrs. Christiansen was up at seven, but the two children by that time were in their robes, freshly bathed, and deep in another story with Lucille on the floor.

"You know," Nicky said to his mother, "we've read all these books before with Catherine, but when Lucille reads them they seem like *new* books!"

Lucille flushed with pleasure. When the children were in bed, she went downstairs with Mrs. Christiansen.

"Is everything fine, Lucille? . . . I thought there might be something you'd like to ask me about the running of things."

"No, ma'am, except . . . might I come up once in the night to see how the children are doing?"

"Oh, I wouldn't want you to break your sleep, Lucille. That's very thoughtful, but it's really unnecessary."

Lucille was silent.

"And I'm afraid the evenings are going to seem long to you. If you'd ever like to go to a picture in town, Alfred, that's the chauffeur, he'll be glad to take you in the car."

"Thank you, ma'am."

"Then good night, Lucille."

"Good night, ma'am."

She went out the back way, across the garden where the fountain was still playing. And when she put her hand on the knob of her door, she wished that it were the nursery door, that it were eight o'clock in the morning and time to begin another day.

Still she was tired, pleasantly tired. How very pleasant it was, she thought, as she turned out the light, to feel properly tired in the evening (although it was only nine o'clock) instead of bursting with energy, instead of being unable to sleep for thinking of her mother or worrying about herself . . . She remembered one day not so long ago when for fifteen minutes she had been unable to think of her name. She had run in panic to the doctor . . .

That was past! She might even ask Alfred to buy her a pack of cigarettes in town—a luxury she had denied herself for months.

She took a last look at the house from her window. The curtains in the nursery billowed out now and then and were swept back again. The wind spoke in the nodding tops of the poplars like friendly voices, like the high-pitched, ever rippling voices of children . . .

The second day was like the first, except that there was no mishap, no scraped hand—and the third and the fourth. Regular and identical like the row of Nicky's lead soldiers on the play table in the nursery. The only thing that changed was Lucille's love for the family and the children—a blind and passionate devotion that seemed to redouble each morning. She noticed and loved many things: the way Heloise drank her milk in little gulps at the back of her throat, how the blond down on their backs swirled up to meet the hair on the napes of their necks, and when she bathed them the painful vulnerability of their bodies.

Saturday evening she found an envelope addressed to herself in the mailbox at the door of the servants' house. Inside was a blank sheet of paper and inside that a couple of new twenty-dollar bills. Lucille held one of them by its crisp edges. Its value meant nothing to her. To use it she would have to go to stores where other people were. What use had she for money if she were never to leave the Christiansen home? It would simply pile up, forty dollars each week. In a year's time she would have two thousand and eighty dollars, and in two years' time twice that. Eventually she might have as much as the Christiansens themselves and that would not be right.

Would they think it very strange if she asked to work for nothing? Or for ten dollars perhaps?

She had to speak to Mrs. Christiansen, and she went to her the next morning. It was an inopportune time. Mrs. Christiansen was making up a menu for a dinner.

"Yes?" Mrs. Christiansen said in her pleasant voice.

Lucille watched the yellow pencil in her hand moving swiftly over the paper. "It's too much for me, ma'am."

The pencil stopped. Mrs. Christiansen's lips parted slightly in surprise. "You *are* such a funny girl, Lucille!"

How do you mean—funny?" Lucille asked curiously.

"Well, first you want to be practically day and night with the children. You never even want your afternoon off. You're always talking about doing something 'Important' for us, though what that could be I can't imagine . . . And now your salary's too much! We've never had a girl like you, Lucille. I can assure you, you're different!" She laughed, and the laugh was full of ease and relaxation that contrasted with the tension of the girl who stood before her.

Lucille was rapt by the conversation. "How do you mean different, ma'am?"

"Why, I've just told you, my dear. And I refuse to lower your salary because that would be sheer exploitation. In fact, if you ever change your mind and want a raise—"

"Oh no, ma'am . . . but I just wish there was something more I could do for you . . . all of you . . ."

"Lucille! You're working for us, aren't you? Taking care of our children. What could be more important than that?"

"But I mean something bigger—I mean more—"

"Nonsense, Lucille," Mrs. Christiansen interrupted. "Just because the people you were with before were not so—friendly as we are doesn't mean you have to work your fingers to the bone for us." She waited for the girl to make some move to go, but she still stood by the desk, her face puzzled. "Mr. Christiansen and I are very well pleased with you, Lucille."

"Thank you, ma'am."

She went back to the nursery where the children were playing. She had not made Mrs. Christiansen understand. If she could just go back and explain what she felt, tell her about her mother and her fear of herself for so many months, how she had never dared take a drink or even a cigarette . . . and how just being with the family in this beautiful house had made her well again . . . telling her all that might relieve her. She turned toward the door, but the thought of disturbing her or boring her with the story, a servant girl's story, made her stop. So during the rest of the day she carried her unexpressed gratitude like a great weight in her breast.

That night she sat in her room with the light on until after twelve o'clock. She had her cigarettes now, and she allowed herself three in the evening, but even those were sufficient to set her blood fingling, to relax her mind, to make her dream heroic dreams. And when the three cigarettes were smoked, and she would have liked another, she rose very light in the head and put the cigarette pack in her top drawer to close away temptation. Just as she slid the drawer she noticed on her handkerchief box the two twenty-dollar bills the Christiansens had given her. She took them now, and sat down again in her chair.

From the book of matches she took a match, struck it, and leaned it, burning end down, against the side of her ashtray. Slowly she struck matches one after another and laid them strategically to make a tiny, flickering, well-controlled fire. When the matches were gone, she tore the pasteboard cover into little bits and dropped them in slowly. Finally she took the twenty-dollar bills and with some effort tore bits from them of the same size. These, too, she meted to the fire.

Mrs. Christiansen did not understand, but if she saw *this,* she might. Still *this* was not enough. Mere faithful service was not enough either. Anyone would give that, for money. She was different. Had not Mrs. Christiansen herself told her that? Then she remembered what else she had said: "Mr. Christiansen and I are very well pleased with you, Lucille."

The memory of those words brought her up from her chair with an enchanted smile upon her lips. She felt wonderfully strong and secure in her own strength of mind and her position in the household. *Mr. Christiansen and I are very well pleased with you, Lucille.* There was really only one thing lacking in her happiness. She had to prove herself in crisis.

If only a plague like those she had read of in the Bible . . . "And it came to pass that there was a great plague over all the land." That was how the Bible would say it. She imagined waters lapping higher against the big house, until they swept almost into the nursery. She would rescue the children and swim with them to safety, wherever that might be.

She moved restlessly about the room.

Or if there came an earthquake . . . She would rush in among falling walls and drag the children out. Perhaps she would go back for some trifle, like Nicky's lead soldiers or Heloise's paint set, and be crushed to death. Then the Christiansens would know her devotion.

Or if there might be a fire. Anyone might have a fire. Fires were common things and needed no wrathful visitations from the upper world. There might be a terrible fire just with the gasoline in the garage and a match.

She went downstairs, through the inside door that opened to the garage. The tank was three feet high and entirely full, so that unless she had been inspired with the necessity and importance of her deed, she would not have been able to lift the thing over the threshold of the garage and of the servants' house, too. She rolled the tank across the yard in the same manner as she had seen men roll beer barrels and ash cans. It made no noise on the grass and only a brief bump and rumble over one of the flagstone paths, lost in the night.

No lights shone at any of the windows, but if they had, Lucille would not have been deterred. She would not have been deterred had Mr. Christiansen himself been standing there by the fountain, for probably she would not have seen him. And if she had, was she not about to do a noble thing? No, she would have seen only the house and the children's faces in the room upstairs.

She unscrewed the cap and poured some gasoline on a corner of the house, rolled the tank farther, poured more against the white shingles, and so on until she reached the far corner. Then she struck her match and walked back the way she had come, touching off the wet places. Without a backward glance she went to stand at the door of the servants' house and watch.

The flames were first pale and eager, then they became yellow with touches of red. As Lucille watched, all the tension that was left in her, in body or mind, flowed evenly upward and was lifted from her forever, leaving her muscles and brain free for the voluntary tension of an athlete before a starting gun. She would let the flames leap tall, even to the nursery window, before she rushed in, so that the danger might be at its highest. A smile like that of a saint settled on her mouth, and anyone seeing her there in the doorway, her face glowing in the lambent light, would certainly have thought her a beautiful young woman.

She had lit the fire at five places, and these now crept up the house like the fingers of a hand, warm and flickering, gentle and caressing. Lucille smiled and held herself in check. Then suddenly the gasoline tank, having grown too warm, exploded with a sound like a cannon and lighted the entire scene for an instant.

As though this had been the signal for which she waited, Lucille went confidently forward.

The Death of a Bum

Author: Donald E. Westlake (1933–   )

Detective: Abraham Levine (1959)

In his long and varied career, Westlake has created few series detectives. His best-known recurring characters, the risibly ill-starred designer of big capers Dortmunder and (in decidedly non-comic novels signed by Robert Stark) professional thief Parker, are both criminals. Of his series sleuths, the most interesting is Abraham Levine, whose cases were collected in an eponymous 1984 volume.

Levine usually appeared in *Alfred Hitchcock's Mystery Magazine,* but the story that follows, the only previously unanthologized Levine, found its home in a lesser market, *Mike Shayne Mystery Magazine* for June 1965, for reasons unrelated to quality. As Westlake explains in his introduction to *Levine,* he was trying to do something different with the series, something that did not agree with the normal demands of detective fiction magazine markets. "The Death of a Bum" was part of that plan, and he knew it would be difficult to sell. When you've read the story, you'll know why it was problematic, but you'll probably also agree it's one of its author's finest achievements.

Abraham Levine of Brooklyn's Forty-third Precinct sat at his desk in the squadroom and wished Jack Crawley would get well soon. Crawley, his usual tour partner, was in the hospital recovering from a bullet in the leg, and Levine was working now with a youngster recently assigned to the squad, a college graduate named Andy Stettin. Levine liked the boy—though he sometimes had the feeling Stettin was picking his brains—but there was an awkwardness in the work without Crawley.

He was sitting now at the desk, thinking about Jack Crawley, when the telephone rang. He answered, saying, "Forty-third Precinct. Levine."

It was a woman's voice, middle-aged, very excited. "There's a man been murdered! You've got to come right away!"

Levine pulled pencil and paper close, then said, "Your name, please?"

"There's been a murder! Don't you understand—"

"Yes, ma'am. May I have your name, please?"

"Mrs. Francis Temple. He's lying right upstairs."

"The address, please?"

"One ninety-eight Third Street. I told all this to the other man, I don't see—"

"And you say there's a dead man there?"

"He's been shot! I just went in to change the linen, and he was lying there!"

"Someone will be there right away." He hung up as she was starting another sentence, and looked up to see Stettin, a tall athletic young man with dark-rimmed glasses and a blond crewcut, standing by the door, already wearing his coat.

"Just a second," Levine said, and dialed for Mulvane, on the desk downstairs. "This is Abe. Did you just transfer a call from Mrs. Francis Temple to my office?"

"I did. The beat car's on the way."

"All right. Andy and I are taking it."

Levine cradled the phone and got to his feet. He went over and took his coat from the rack and shrugged into it, then followed the impatient Stettin downstairs to the car.

That was another thing. Crawley had always driven the Chevy. But Stettin drove too fast, was too quick to hit the siren and gun through busy intersections, so now Levine had to do the driving, a chore he didn't enjoy.

The address was on a block of ornate nineteenth-century brownstones, now all converted either into furnished apartments or boardinghouses. One ninety-eight was furnished apartments, and Mrs. Francis Temple was its landlady. She was waiting on the top step of the stoop, wringing her hands, a buxom fiftyish woman in a black dress and open black sweater, a maroon knit shawl over her head to keep out the cold.

The prowl car was double-parked in front of the house, and Levine braked the Chevy to a stop behind it. He and Stettin climbed out, crossed the sidewalk, and went up the stoop.

Mrs. Temple was on the verge of panic. Her hands kept washing each other, she kept shifting her weight back and forth from one foot to the other, and she stared bug-eyed as the detectives came up the stoop toward her.

"Are you police?" she demanded, her voice shrill.

Levine dragged out his wallet, showed her the badge. "Are the patrolmen up there?" he asked.

She nodded, stepping aside to let him move past her. "I went in to change the linen, and there he was, lying in the bed, all covered with blood. It was terrible, terrible."

Levine went on in, Stettin after him, and Mrs. Temple brought up the rear, still talking. Levine interrupted her to ask, "Which room?"

"The third floor front," she said, and went back to repeating how terrible it had been when she'd gone in there and seen him on the bed, covered with blood.

Stettin was too eager for conscious politeness. He bounded on up the maroon-carpeted stairs, while Levine plodded up after him, the woman one step behind all the way, the shawl still over her head.

One of the patrolmen was standing in the open doorway at the other end of the third-floor hall. As was usual in this type of brownstone, the upper floors consisted of two large rooms rented separately, each with a small kitchenette but both sharing the same bath. The dead man was in the front room.

Levine said to the woman, "Wait out here, please," nodded to the patrolman, and went on through into the room.

Stettin and the second patrolman were over to the right, by the studio couch, talking together. Their forms obscured Levine's view of the couch as he came through the doorway, and he got the feeling, as he had had more than once with the energetic Stettin, that he was Stettin's assistant rather than the other way around.

Which was ridiculous, of course. Stettin turned, clearing Levine's view, saying, "How's it look to you, Abe?"

The studio couch had been opened up and was now in its other guise, that of a linen-covered bed. Between the sheets the corpse lay peaceably on its back with the covers tucked up around the sheets and rested stiffly on its chest.

Levine came over and stood by the bed, looking down at it. The bullet had struck the bridge of the nose, smashing bone and cartilage, and discoloring the flesh around it. There was hardly any nose left. The mouth hung open, and the top front teeth had been jarred partially out of their sockets by the force of the bullet.

The slain man had bled profusely, and the pillow and the turned-down sheet around his throat were drenched with blood.

The top blanket was blue, and was now scattered with smallish chunks of white stuff. Levine reached down and picked up one of the white chunks, feeling it between his fingers.

"Potato," he said, more to himself than to the cop at his side.

Stettin said, "What's that?"

"Potato. That stuff on the bed. He used a potato for a silencer."

Stettin smiled blankly. "I don't follow you, Abe."

Levine moved his hands in demonstration as he described what he meant. "The killer took a raw potato, and jammed the barrel of the gun into it. Then, when he fired, the bullet smashed through the potato, muffling the sound. It's a kind of homemade silencer."

Stettin nodded, and glanced again at the body. "Think it was a gang killing, then?"

"I don't know," Levine replied, frowning. He turned to the patrolman. "What have you got?"

The patrolman dragged a flat black notebook out of his hip pocket, and flipped it open. "He's the guy that rented the place. The landlady identified him. He gave his name as Maurice Gold."

Excited, Stettin said, "Morry Gold?" He came closer to the bed, squinting down at the face remnant as though he could see it better that way. "Yeah, by God, it is," he said, his expression grim. "It *was* a gang killing, Abe!"

"You know him?"

"I saw him once. On the lineup downtown, maybe—two months ago."

Levine smiled thinly. Leave it to Stettin, he thought. Most detectives considered the lineup a chore and a waste of time, and grumbled every time their turn came around to go downtown and attend. The lineup was supposed to familiarize the precinct detectives with the faces of known felons, but it took a go-getter like Stettin to make the theory work. Levine had been attending the lineup twice a month for fifteen years and hadn't once recognized one of the felons later on.

Stettin was turning his head this way and that, squinting at the body again. "Yeah, sure," he said. "Morry Gold. He had a funny way of talking—a Cockney accent, maybe. That's him, all right."

"What was he brought in for?"

"Possession of stolen goods. He was a fence. I remember the Chief talking to him. I guess he'd been brought in lots of times before." He shook his head. "Apparently he managed to wriggle out of it."

The patrolman said, "He'd have been much better off if he hadn't."

"A falling out among thieves," said Stettin. "Think so, Abe?"

"It could be." To the patrolman, he said, "Anything else?"

"He lived here not quite two years. That's what the landlady told me. She found him at quarter after four, and the last time she saw him alive was yesterday, around seven o'clock in the evening. He went out then. He must have come back some time after eleven o'clock, when the landlady went to bed. Otherwise, she'd have seen him come in." He grinned without humor. "She's one of those," he said.

"I'll go talk to her." Levine looked over at the body again, and averted his eyes. An old English epitaph flickered through his mind: *As you are, so was I; as I am, so you will be.* Twenty-four years as a cop hadn't hardened him to the tragic and depressing finality of death, and in the last few years, as he had moved steadily into the heart-attack range and as the inevitability of his own end had become more and more real to him, he had grown steadily more vulnerable to the dread implicit in the sight of death.

He turned away, saying, "Andy, give the place a going-over. Address book, phone numbers, somebody's name in the flyleaf of a book. You know the kind of thing."

"Sure." Stettin glanced around, eager to get at it. "Do you think he'd have any of the swag here?"

The word sounded strange on Stettin's tongue, odd and archaic. Levine smiled, as the death-dread wore off, and said, "I doubt it. Stick around here for the M.E. and the technical crew. Get the time of death and whatever else they can give you."

"Sure thing."

Mrs. Francis Temple was still outside in the hall, jabbering now at the second patrolman, who was making no attempt to hide his boredom. Levine took her away, much to the patrolman's relief, and they went downstairs to her cellar apartment, the living room of which was Gay Nineties from end to end, from the fringed beaded lampshades to the marble porcelain vases on the mantle.

In these surroundings, Mrs. Temple's wordiness switched from the terrible details of her discovery of the body to the nostalgic details of her life with her late husband, who had been a newspaperman.

Levine, by main force, wrestled the conversation back to the present, in order to ask his questions about Maurice Gold. "What did he do for a living," he asked. "Do you know?"

"He said he was a salesman. Sometimes he was gone nearly a week at a time."

"Do you know what he sold?"

She shook her head. "There were never any samples or anything in his room," she said. "I would have noticed them." She shivered suddenly, hugging herself, and said, "What a terrible thing. You don't know what it was like to come into the room and see him—"

Levine thought he knew. He thought he knew better than Mrs. Temple. He said, "Did he have many visitors? Close friends, that you know about?"

"Well—There were two or three men who came by sometimes in the evenings. I believe they played cards."

"Do you know their names?"

"No, I'm sorry. I really didn't know Mr. Gold very well—not as a friend. He was a very close-mouthed man." One hand fluttered to her lips. "Oh, listen to me. The poor man is lying dead, and listen to me talking about him."

"Did anyone else ever come by?" Levine persisted. "Besides these three men he played cards with."

She shook her head. "Not that I remember. I think he was a lonely man. Lonely people can recognize one another, and I've been lonely, too, since Alfred died. These last few years have been difficult for me, Mr. Levine."

It took Levine ten minutes to break away from the woman gently, without learning anything more. "We'd like to try to identify his card-playing friends," he said. "Would you have time to come look at pictures this afternoon?"

"Well, yes, of course. It was a terrible thing, Mr. Levine, an absolutely terrible—"

"Yes, ma'am."

Levine escaped, to find Stettin coming back downstairs, loose-limbed and athletic. Feeling a little bit guilty at palming the voluble Mrs. Temple off on his partner, Levine said, "Take Mrs. Temple to look at some mug shots, will you? Known former acquaintances of Gold—or anyone she recognizes. She says there were two or three men who used to come here to play cards."

"Will do." Stettin paused at the foot of the steps. "Uh, Abe," he said, "we don't have to break our humps over this one, do we?"

"What do you mean?"

"Well—" Stettin shrugged, and nodded his head at the stairs. "He was just a bum, you know. A small-time crook. The world's better off without him."

"He was alive," said Levine. "And now he's dead."

"Okay, okay. For Pete's sake, I wasn't saying we should forget the whole thing—just that we shouldn't break our humps over it."

"We'll do our job," Levine told him, "just as though he'd had the keys to the city and money in fifty-seven banks."

"Okay. You didn't have to get sore, Abe."

"I'm not sore. Take Mrs. Temple in the car. I'm going to stay here a while and ask some more questions. Mrs. Temple's in her apartment there."

"Okay."

"Oh, by the way. When you get out to the car, call in and have somebody get us the dope on that arrest two months ago. Find out if you can whether there was anybody else involved, and if by chance the arresting officer knows any of Gold's friends. Anything like that."

"Will do."

Levine went on upstairs to ask questions.

The other tenants knew even less than Mrs. Temple. Levine was interrupted for a while by a reporter, and by the time he'd finished questioning the tenants it was past four o'clock, and late enough for him to go off duty. He phoned the precinct, and then went on home.

The following morning he arrived at the precinct at eight o'clock for his third and last day-shift on this cycle. Stettin was already there, sitting at Levine's desk and looking through a folder. He leaped to his feet, grinning and ebullient as ever, saying, "Hiya, Abe. We got us some names."

"Good."

Levine eased himself into his chair, and Stettin hovered over him, opening the folder. "The arresting officer was a Patrolman Michaels, out of the Thirtieth. I couldn't find out why the charge didn't stick, because Michaels was kind of touchy about that. I guess he made some kind of procedural goof. But anyhow, he gave me some names. Gold has a brother, Abner, who runs a pawnshop in East New York. Michaels says Gold was a kind of go-between for his brother. Morry would buy the stolen goods, cache it, and then transfer it to Abner's store."

Levine nodded. "Anything else?"

"Well, Gold took one fall, about nine years ago. He was caught accepting a crate full of stolen furs. The thief was caught with him." Stettin pointed to a name and address. "That's him—Elly Kapp. Kapp got out last year, and that's his last known address."

"You've been doing good work," Levine told him. He grinned up at Stettin and said, "Been breaking your hump?"

Stettin grinned back, in embarrassment. "I can't help it," he said. "You know me, old Stettin Fetchit."

Levine nodded. He'd heard Stettin use the line before. It was his half-joking apology for being a boy on the way up, surrounded by stodgy plodders like Abe Levine.

"Okay," said Levine. "Anything from Mrs. Temple?"

"One positive identification, and a dozen maybes. The positive is a guy named Sal Casetta. He's a small-time bookie."

Levine got to his feet. "Let's go talk to these three," he said. "The brother first."

Twenty-two minutes later they were in the East New York pawnshop. Abner Gold was a stocky man with thinning hair and thick spectacles. He was also—once Levine had flashed the police identification—very nervous.

"Come into the office," he said. "Please, please. Come into the office."

Levine noticed that the thick accent Gold had worn when they'd first come in had suddenly vanished.

Gold unlocked the door to the cage, relocked it after them, and led the way back past the bins to his office, a small and crowded room full of ledgers. There was a rolltop desk, a metal filing cabinet and four sagging leather chairs.

"Sit down, sit down," he said. "You've come about my brother."

"You've been notified?"

"I read about it in the *News*. A terrible way to hear, believe me."

"I'm sure it must be," Levine said.

He hesitated. Usually, Jack Crawley handled the questioning, while Levine observed silently from a corner. But Jack was still laid up with the bad leg, and Levine wasn't sure Stettin—eager though he might be—would know the right questions or how to ask them. So it was up to him.

Levine sighed, and said, "When was the last time you saw your brother, Mr. Gold?"

Gold held his hands out to the sides, in a noncommittal shrug. "A week ago? Two weeks?"

"You're not sure."

"I think two weeks. You must understand, my brother and I—we'd drifted apart."

"Because of his trouble with the law?"

Gold nodded. "A part of it, yes. God rest his soul, Mister—?"

"Levine."

"Yes. God rest his soul, Mr. Levine, but I must tell you what's in my heart. You have to know the truth. Maurice was not a good man. Do you understand me? He was my brother, and now he's been murdered, but still I must say it. His life went badly for him, Mr. Levine, and he became sour. When he was young—" He shrugged again. "He became very bitter, I think. He lost his belief."

"His faith, you mean?"

"Oh, that, too. Maurice was not a religious man. But even more than that, do you follow me? He lost his *belief*. In the goodness of man—in *life*. Do you understand me?"

"I think so." Levine watched Gold's face carefully. Stettin had said that the brothers had worked together in the buying and selling of stolen goods, but Abner Gold was trying very hard to convince them of his own innocence. Levine wasn't sure yet whether or not he could be convinced.

"The last time you saw him," he said, "did he act nervous at all? As though he was expecting trouble?"

"Maurice always expected trouble. But I do know what you mean. No, nothing like that, nothing more than his usual pessimism."

"Do you yourself know of any enemies he might have made?"

"Ever since I read the article in the paper, I've been asking myself exactly that question. Did anyone hate my brother enough to want to kill him. But I can think of no one. You must understand me, I didn't know my brother's associates. We—drifted apart."

"You didn't know any of his friends at all?"

"I don't believe so, no."

"Not Sal Casetta?"

"An Italian? No, I don't know him." Gold glanced at Stettin, then leaned forward to say to Levine, "Excuse me, do you mind? Could I speak to you alone for a moment?"

"Sure," said Stettin promptly. "I'll wait outside."

"Thank you. Thank you very much." Gold beamed at Stettin until he left, then leaned toward Levine again. "I can talk to you," he said. "Not in front of the other policeman."

Levine frowned, but said nothing.

"Listen to me," said Gold. His eyes were dark, and deep-set. "Maurice was my brother. If anyone has the right to say what I am going to say now it is me, the brother. Maurice is better dead. Better for everyone. The police are shorthanded, I know this. You have so much work; forget Maurice. No one wants vengeance. Listen to me, I am his brother. Who has a better right to talk?"

You're talking to the wrong man, Levine thought. *Stettin's the one who thinks your way.* But he kept quiet, and waited.

Gold paused, his hands out as though in offering, presenting his ideas to Levine. Then he lowered his hands and leaned back and said, "You understand me. That's why I wanted to talk to you alone. You are a policeman, sworn to uphold the law, this new law in this new country. But I am speaking to you now from the old law. You follow me, Levine. And if I say to you, I don't want vengeance for the slaying of my brother, I speak within a law that is older and deeper."

"A law that says murder should be ignored and forgotten? A law that says life doesn't matter? I never heard of it."

"Levine, you know what law I'm talking about! I'm his brother, and I—"

"You're a fool, Gold, and that's the damnedest bribe I've ever been offered."

"Bribe?" Gold seemed shocked at the thought. "I didn't offer you any—"

"What do I do to belong, Gold? I send in the label from a package of Passover candles, and then what do I get? I learn all about the secret handshake, and I get the ring with the secret compartment, and I get the magic decodifier so we can send each other messages others won't understand. Is that it?"

"You shouldn't mock what—"

"Is there anything you wouldn't use, Gold? Do you have respect for anything at all?"

Gold looked away, his expression stony. "I thought I could talk to you," he said. "I thought you would understand."

"I do understnad," Levine told him. "Get on your feet."

"What?"

"You're coming back to the precinct to answer some more questions."

"But—but I've *told* you—" Gold started to say.

"You told me you didn't want your brother's murderer found. After a while, you'll tell me why. On your feet."

"For God's sake, Levine—"

"Get on your feet!"

It was a small room. The echoes of his shout came back to his ears, and he suddenly realized he'd lost his temper despite himself, and his left hand jerked automatically to his chest, pressing there to feel for the heartbeat. He had a skip, every eighth beat or so, and when he allowed himself to get excited the skipping came closer together. That irregularity of rhythm was the most pronounced symptom he had to support his fear of heart trouble and it was never very far from his consciousness. He pressed his hand to his chest now, feeling the thumping within, and the skip, and counted from there to the next skip . . . seven.

He took a deep breath. Quietly he said, "Come along, Gold. Don't make me call in the other policeman to carry you."

Abraham Levine couldn't bring himself to grill Gold personally after all; he was afraid he'd lose control. So he simply filled Stettin in on what had been said, and what he wanted to know. Stettin took care of the questioning, with assists from Andrews and Campbell, two of the other detectives now on duty, while Levine left the precinct again, to find Sal Casetta.

Casetta lived in the New Utrecht section of Brooklyn, in a brick tenement on 79th Street. It was a walk-up, and the bookmaker's apartment was on the fourth floor. Levine climbed the stairs slowly, stopping to rest at each landing. When he got to the fourth floor, he paused to catch his breath, and light a cigarette before knocking on the door marked 14.

A woman answered—a short blowsy woman in a loose sweater and a tight black skirt. She was barefooted, and her feet were dirty, her toenails enameled a deep red. She looked challengingly at Levine.

Levine said, "I'm looking for Sal Casetta."

"He ain't home."

"Where can I find him?"

"What do you want him for?"

"Police," said Levine. "I don't want to talk to him about bookmaking. A friend of his was killed; maybe he could help us."

"What makes you think he wants to help you?"

"It was a friend of his that was killed."

"So what? You ain't a friend of his."

"If Sal were killed," Levine said, "and I was looking for his murderer, would you help me?"

The woman grimaced, and shrugged uneasily. "I told you he wasn't here," she said.

"Just tell me where I can find him."

She thought it over. She was chewing gum, and her jaw moved continuously for a full minute. Finally, she shrugged again and said, "Come on in. I'll go get him for you."

"Thank you."

She led the way into a small living room, with soiled drapes at the windows, and not enough furniture. "Grab a seat any place," she said. "Look out for roaches."

Levine thanked her again, and sat down gingerly on an unpainted wooden chair.

"What was the name of the friend?" she asked.

"Morry Gold."

"Oh, *that* bum." Her mouth twisted around its wad of gum. "Why waste time on him?"

"Because he was killed," said Levine.

"You want to make work for yourself," she told him, "it's no skin off my nose. Wait here, I'll be right back."

While he waited Levine's thoughts kept reverting to Morry Gold. After about ten minutes, he heard the front door open, and a few seconds later the woman came back accompanied by a short, heavyset man with bushy black hair and rather shifty eyes.

He came in nodding his head jerkily, saying, "I read about it in the papers. I read about it this morning."

"You're Sal Casetta?"

"Yeah, yeah, that's right, that's me. You're a cop, huh?"

Levine showed his badge, then said, "You used to play cards with Morry Gold?"

"Yeah, sure, that's right. Poker. Quarter, half-dollar. Friendly game, you know."

"Who were the other players?" Levine asked.

"Well, uh—" Casetta glanced nervously at the woman, and rubbed the back of his hand across his nose. "Well, you know how it is. You don't feel right about giving out names."

"Why? Do you think one of them killed Gold?"

"Hey now—Listen. We're all friends. Nothing like that. *I* wouldn't want to bump Morry, and neither would those guys. We're all buddies."

"Then give me their names."

Casetta cleared his throat, and glanced at the woman again, and scuffed his feet on the floor. Finally, he said, "Well, all right. But don't tell them you got it from me, huh?"

"Gold's landlady identified you," Levine told him. "She could have identified the other two."

"Yeah, sure, that's right. So it's Jake Mosca—that's like Moscow, only with an 'a'—and Barney Feldman. Okay?"

Levine copied the names down. "You know where they live?"

"Naw, not me."

"We'll leave that a blank, then. When was the last game?"

"At Morry's? That was on Saturday. Right, baby?"

The woman nodded. "Saturday," she said.

"Did Gold act nervous or depressed Saturday?"

"You mean, did he know he was gonna get it? Not a bit. Calm like always, you know?"

"Do you have any idea who might have wanted to kill him?"

"Not me. I know Morry from when we used to live in the same neighborhood, that's all. His business is his business."

"You wouldn't know who his enemies were."

"That's right. If Morry had enemies, he never said nothing to me."

"What about other friends?"

"Friends?" Casetta rubbed his nose again, then said, "We didn't see each other that much since we moved away. Just for the games. Uh, wait a second. There was another guy came in the game for a while, Arnie something. A fish, a real fish. So after a while he quit."

"You don't remember his last name?"

Casetta shook his head. "Just Arnie something. Maybe Jake or Barney knows."

"All right. Do you know Gold's brother, Abner?"

"Naw, I never met him. Morry talked about him sometimes. They didn't get along."

Levine got to his feet. "Thank you very much," he said.

"Yeah, sure. Morry was okay."

"Oh, one thing more. What about women? Did he have any woman friends that you know about?"

"I never seen him with a woman," Casetta said.

"Saturday at the game, did he seem to have an unusual amount of money on him? Or did he seem very broke? How did he seem to be fixed?"

"Like always. Nothing special, pretty well heeled but nothing spectacular, you know?" Casetta looked around, at the woman, at the apartment. "Like me," he said.

Elly Kapp's last known address was in Gravesend, off Avenue X, and since Kapp had once been caught turning stolen goods over to Morry Gold it occurred to Levine that the man might know whom Gold had been dealing with lately. He might even be still selling to Gold himself.

There was no Kapp listed among the mailboxes at the address. Levine pressed the bell-button beneath the metal plate reading *Superintendent,* and several minutes later a slow-rolling fat woman with receding gray hair appeared in the doorway, holding the door open a scant three inches. She said nothing, only stared mistrustfully, so Levine dragged out his wallet and showed his identification.

"I'm looking for Elly Kapp," he said.

"Don't live here no more."

"Where does he live now?"

"I don't know." She started to close the door, but Levine held it open with the palm of his hand. "When did he move?" he demanded.

The woman shrugged. "Who remembers?" Her eyes were dull, and watched his mouth rather than his eyes. "Who cares where he went, or what he's done?"

Levine moved his hand away, and allowed the woman to close the door. He watched through the glass as she turned and rolled slowly back across the inner vestibule. Her ankles were swollen like sausages. When she disappeared in the gloom just beyond Levine turned away and went back down the stoop to the Chevy.

He drove slowly back to the precinct. Indifference breathed in the air all around him, sullen and surly. *No man is important,* the streets seemed to be saying. *Man is only useful as long as he breathes. Once the breathing stops, he is forgotten. Time stretches away beyond him, smooth and slick and with no handholds. The man is dead, and almost as swiftly as a dropped heartbeat, the space that he occupied yawns emptily and there is nothing left of him but a name.*

At times, another man is paid to remember the name long enough to carve it on stone, and the stone is set in the earth, and immediately it begins to sink. But the man is gone long since. What does it matter if he stopped a second ago or a century ago or a millenium ago? He stopped, he is no more, he is forgotten. Who cares?

Levine saw the red light just in time, and jammed on the brakes. He sat hunched over the wheel, unnerved at having almost run the light, and strove to calm himself. His breathing was labored, as though he'd been running, and he knew that the beating of his heart was erratic and heavy. He inhaled, very slowly, and let his breath out even more slowly while he waited for the light to change.

The instant it became green he drove on across the intersection. He was calmer now. The death of Morry Gold had affected him too much, and he told himself he had to snap out of it. He knew, after all, the reason he was so affected. It was because Morry Gold's death had been greeted by such universal indifference.

Almost always, the victim of a homicide is survived by relatives and friends who are passionately concerned with his end, and make a nuisance of themselves by badgering the police for quick results. With such rallying, the dead man doesn't seem quite so forlorn, quite so totally alone and forgotten.

In the interrogation room down the hall from the squadroom, Stettin and Andrews and Campbell were questioning Abner Gold. Levine stuck his head in, nodded at Stettin, avoided looking at Gold, and immediately shut the door again. He turned away and walked slowly back down the hall toward the squadroom. He heard the door behind him open and close, and then Stettin, in long easy strides, had come up even with him.

Stettin shook his head. "Nothing, Abe," he said.

"No explanation?"

"Not from him. He won't say a word anymore. Not until he calls a lawyer."

Levine shook his head tiredly. He knew the type. Abner Gold's one virtue would be patience. He would sit in silence, and wait, and wait until eventually the detectives found his stubborn silence intolerable, and then he knew he would be allowed to go home.

"I have an explanation," Stettin said. "He's afraid of an investigation. He's afraid if we dig too deep we'll come up with proof he worked with his brother."

"Maybe," said Levine. "Or maybe he's afraid we'll come up with proof he killed his brother."

"What for?"

"I don't know. For cheating him on some kind of deal. For blackmailing him. Your guess is as good as mine."

Stettin shrugged. "We can keep asking," he said. "But he can keep right on not answering until we can no longer stand the sight of him."

Levine glanced at his watch. Quarter to one. He'd stopped off for lunch on the way back. He said, "I'll go talk to him for a while."

"That's up to you."

The way he said it, Levine was reminded that Stettin didn't want to break his hump over this one. Levine walked over to his desk and sat down and said, "I got two more names. From Casetta. Jake Mosca and Barney Feldman. No addresses. See what you can dig up on them, will you? And go talk to them."

"Sure. How was Casetta?"

"I don't know. Maybe Gold cheated him at poker. Maybe Gold was playing around with his wife. He didn't act nervous or worried." Levine rubbed a hand wearily across his face. "I'll go talk to Gold now," he said. "Did we get the M.E.'s report?"

"It's right there on your desk."

Levine didn't open it. He didn't want to read about Morry Gold's corpse. He said, "What kind of gun?"

"A thirty-eight. You look tired, Abe."

"I guess I am. I can sleep late tomorrow."

"Sure."

"Oh, one more thing. Elly Kapp isn't at that address anymore. See what you can find there, will you?"

"Will do."

Levine walked down the hall again and took over the questioning of Gold. After Andrews and Campbell had left the room, Levine looked at Gold and said, "What did Morry do to you?"

Gold shook his head.

"You're a cautious man, Gold." Levine's voice rose impatiently. "It had to be something strong to make you kill him. Did he cheat you?"

Humor flickered at the corners of Gold's mouth. "He cheated me always," he said. "For years. I was used to it, Abraham."

Levine shrugged off the use of the first name. It wasn't important enough to be angry about. "So he was blackmailing you," he said, "and finally you'd had enough. But didn't you know someone would hear the sound of the shot? Mrs. Temple saw you go out."

"A false identification," said Gold. "I would risk nothing for Maurice. He was not worth the danger of killing him."

Levine shrugged. If Gold knew a potato silencer had been used, he hadn't mentioned it. Not that Levine had expected the trick to work. Tricks like that work only in the movies. And killers go to the movies, too.

Levine asked questions for over two hours. Sometimes Gold answered, and sometimes he didn't. As the time wore on, Levine grew more and more tired, more and more heavy and depressed, but Gold remained unchanged, displaying only the same solid patience.

Finally, at three-thirty, Levine told him he could leave. Gold thanked him, with muted sardonicism, and left. Levine went back down the hall to the squadroom.

There was a note from Stettin. Elly Kapp was being held in a precinct in west Brooklyn. Last night, he'd been caught halfway through the window of a warehouse near the Brooklyn piers, and tomorrow morning he would be transferred downtown.

Levine phoned the precinct and got permission from the Lieutenant of Detectives there to come over and question the prisoner. Stettin had taken the Chevy, so Levine had to drive an unfamiliar car, newer and stiffer.

Kapp had very little useful to say. At first, he said, "Morry Gold? I ain't seen him since we took the fall. I'm a very superstitious guy, mister. I don't go near anyone who is with me when a job goes sour. That guy by me is a jinx."

Levine questioned him further, wanting to know the names of other thieves with whom Gold had had dealings, whether or not Gold had been known to cheat thieves in the past, whether or not Kapp knew of anyone who harbored a grudge against Gold. Kapp pleaded ignorance for a while, and then gradually began to look crafty.

"Maybe I could help you out," he said finally. "I don't promise you nothing, but maybe I could. If we could work out maybe a deal?"

Levine shook his head, and left the room. Kapp called after him, but Levine didn't listen to what he was saying. Kapp didn't know anything; his information would be useless. He would implicate anybody, make up any kind of story he thought Levine wanted to hear, if it would help him get a lighter sentence for the attempted robbery of the warehouse.

It was four o'clock. Levine brought the unfamiliar car back to the precinct, signed out, and went home.

The third day of the case, Levine came to work at four in the afternoon, starting a three-day tour on the night shift. As usual, Stettin was already there when he arrived.

"Hi, Abe," Stettin greeted. "I talked to Feldman yesterday. He owns a grocery store in Brownsville. Like everybody else, he didn't know Morry Gold all that well. But he did give me a couple more names."

"Good," said Levine. He had been about to shrug out of his coat, but now he kept it on.

"One of them's a woman," said Stettin. "May Torasch. She was possibly Gold's girlfriend. Feldman didn't know for sure."

"What about Feldman?"

"I don't think so, Abe. He and Gold just know each other from the old days, that's all."

"All right."

"I tried to see the other one, Jake Mosca, but he wasn't home."

"Maybe he'll be home now." Levine started to button his coat again. Stettin said, "Want me to come along?"

Levine was going to say no, tell him to check out the other names he had, but then he changed his mind. Stettin would be his partner for a while, so they ought to start learning how to work together. Besides, Stettin was only half-hearted in this case, and he might miss something important. Levine wished he'd questioned the grocer himself.

"Come on along," Levine said.

Mosca lived way out Flatbush Avenue toward Floyd Bennett. There were old two-family houses out that way, in disrepair, and small apartment buildings that weren't quite tenements. It was in one of the latter that Mosca lived, on the second floor.

The hall was full of smells, and badly lit. A small boy who needed a haircut stood down at the far end of the hall and watched them as Levine knocked on the door.

There were sounds of movement inside, but that was all. Levine knocked again, and this time a voice called, "Who is it?"

"Police," called Levine.

Inside, a bureau drawer opened, and Levine heard cursing. His eyes widening, he jumped quickly to one side, away from the door, shouting, "Andy! Get out of the way!"

From inside, there were sounds like wood cracking, and a series of punched-out holes appeared in the door just as Stettin started to obey.

Levine was clawing on his hip for his gun. The shots, sounding like wood cracking, kept resounding in the apartment, and the holes kept appearing in the door. Plaster was breaking in small chunks in the opposite wall now.

The door was thin, and Levine could hear the clicking when the gun was empty and the man inside kept pulling the trigger. He stepped in front of the door, raised his foot, kicked it just under the knob. The lock splintered away and the door swung open. The man inside was goggle-eyed with rage and fear.

The instant the door came open he threw the empty gun at Levine and spun away for the window. Levine ducked and ran into the apartment, shouting to Mosca to stop. Mosca went over the sill headfirst, out onto the fire escape. Levine fired at him, trying to hit him in the leg, but the bullet went wild. But before he could fire again Mosca went clattering down the fire escape.

Levine got to the window in time to see the man reach the ground. He ran across the weedy backyard, over the wooden fence, and went dodging into a junkyard piled high with rusting parts of automobiles.

Levine was trying to do everything at once. He started out the window, then realized Mosca had too much of a headstart on him. Then he remembered Andy and, as he descended to the floor, he realized that Stettin hadn't followed him into the room and wondered why.

The moment he emerged into the hallway the reason became clear. Andy was lying on his side a yard from the door, his entire left shoulder drenched with blood and his knees drawn up sharply. He was no longer moving. Levine bent over him for an instant, then swung about, ran down the stairs and out to the Chevy and called in.

Everyone seemed to show up at once. Ambulance and patrolmen and detectives, suddenly filling the corridor. Lieutenant Barker, chief of the precinct's detective squad, came with the rest and stood looking down at

Andy Stettin, his face cold with rage. He listened to Levine's report of what had happened, saying nothing until Levine had finished.

Then he said, "He may pull through, Abe. He still has a chance. You mustn't blame yourself for this."

Should I have been able to tell him? Levine wondered. *He was new, and I was more or less breaking him in, showing him the ropes, so shouldn't I have told him that when you hear the cursing, when you hear the bureau drawer opening, get away from the door?*

But how could I have told him everything, all the different things you learn? You learn by trial and error, the same as in any other walk of life. But here, sometimes, they only give you one error.

It isn't fair.

The apartment was swarming with police, and soon they found out why Mosca had fired eight times through the door. A shoebox in a closet was a quarter full of heroin, cut and capsuled, ready for the retail trade. Mosca had a record, but for theft, not for narcotics, so there was no way Levine and Stettin could have known.

For an hour or two, Levine was confused. The world swirled around him at a mad pace, but he couldn't really concentrate on any of it. People talked to him, and he answered one way and another, without really understanding what was being said to him or what he was replying. He walked in a shocked daze, not comprehending.

He came out of it back at the precinct. The entire detective squad was there, all the off-duty men having been called in, and Lieutenant Barker was talking to them. They filled the squadroom, sitting on the desks and leaning against the walls, and Lieutenant Barker stood facing them.

"We're going to get this Jake Mosca," he was saying. "We're going to get him because Andy Stettin is damn close to death. Do you know why we have to get a cop-killer? It's because the cop is a *symbol*. He's a symbol of the law, the most solid symbol of the law the average citizen ever sees. Our society is held together by law, and we cannot let the symbol of the law be treated with arrogance and contempt.

"I want the man who shot Stettin. You'll get to everyone this Mosca knows, every place he might think of going. You'll get him because Andy Stettin is dying—and he is a cop."

No, thought Levine, *that's wrong. Andy Stettin is a man, and that's why we have to get Jake Mosca. He was alive, and now he may die. He is a living human being, and that's why we have to get his would-be killer. There shouldn't be any other reasons, there shouldn't have to be any other reasons.*

But he didn't say anything.

Apparently, the Lieutenant could see that Levine was still dazed, because he had him switch with Rizzo, who was catching at the squad-room phone this tour. For the rest of the tour, Levine sat by the phone in the empty squadroom, and tried to understand.

Andrews and Campbell brought Mosca in a little after eleven. They'd found him hiding in a girlfriend's apartment, and when they brought him in he was bruised and semiconscious. Campbell explained he'd tried to resist arrest, and no one argued with him.

Levine joined the early part of the questioning, and got Mosca's alibi for the night Morry Gold was killed. He made four phone calls, and the alibi checked out. Jake Mosca had not murdered Morry Gold.

The fourth day, Levine again arrived at the precinct at four o'clock. He was scheduled to catch this tour, so he spent another eight hours at the telephone, and got nothing done on the Morry Gold killing. The fifth day, working alone now, he went on with the investigation.

May Torasch, the woman whose name Andy Stettin had learned, worked in the credit department of a Brooklyn department store. Levine went to her apartment, on the fringe of Sunset, at seven o'clock, and found her home. She was another blowsy woman, reminding him strongly of Sal Casetta's wife. But she was affable, and seemed to want to help, though she assured Levine that she and Morry Gold had never been close friends.

"Face it," she said, "he was a bum. He wasn't going nowhere, so I never wasted much time on him."

She had seen Morry two days before his death; they'd gone to a bar off Flatbush Avenue and had a few drinks. But she hadn't gone back to his apartment with him. She hadn't been in the mood.

"I was kind of low that night," she said.

"Was Morry low?" Levine asked.

"No, not him. He was the same as ever. He'd talk about the weather all the time, and his lousy landlady. I wouldn't have gone out with him, but I was feeling so low I didn't want to go home."

She didn't have any idea who might have murdered him. "He was just a bum, just a small-timer. Nobody paid any attention to him." Nor could she add to the names of Gold's acquaintances.

From her apartment, Levine went to the bar where she and Morry had last been together. It was called The Green Lantern, and was nearly empty when Levine walked in shortly before nine. He showed his identification to the bartender and asked about Morry Gold. But the bartender knew very few of his customers by name.

"I might know this guy by sight," he explained, "But the name don't mean a thing." And the same was true of May Torasch.

There were still two more names on the list, Joe Whistler and Arnie Hendricks, the latter being the Arnie Sal Casetta had mentioned. Joe Whistler was another bartender, so Levine went looking for him first, and found him at work, tending bar in a place called Robert's, in Canarsie, not more than a dozen blocks from Levine's home.

Whistler knew Gold only casually, and could add nothing. Levine spent half an hour with him, and then went in search of Arnie Hendricks.

Arnie Hendricks was a small-time fight manager, originally from Detroit. He wasn't at home, and the gym where he usually hung out was closed this time of night. Levine went back to the precinct, sat down at his desk, and looked at his notes.

He had eight names relating to Morry Gold. There were one brother, one woman, and six casual friends. None of them had offered any reasons for Morry's murder, none of them had suggested any suspects who might have hated Morry enough to kill him, and none of them had given any real cause to be considered a suspect himself, with the possible exception of Abner Gold.

But the more Levine thought about Abner Gold, the more he was willing to go along with Andy Stettin's idea. The man was afraid of an investigation not because he had murdered his brother, but because he was afraid the police would be able to link him to his brother's traffic in stolen goods.

Eight names. One of them, Arnie Hendricks, was still an unknown, but the other seven had been dead ends.

Someone had murdered Morry Gold. Somewhere in the world, the murderer still lived. He had a name and a face; and he had a connection somehow with Morry Gold. And he was practically unsought. Of the hundreds of millions of human beings on the face of the earth, only one, Abraham Levine, who had never known Morry Gold in life, was striving to find the man who had brought about Morry Gold's death.

After a while, wearily, he put his notes away and pecked out his daily report on one of the office Remingtons. Then it was midnight, and he went home. And that was when he got some good news from the hospital—Andy Stettin was going to live.

The sixth day, he went to the precinct, reported in, got the Chevy, and went out looking for Arnie Hendricks. He spent seven hours on it, stopping off only to eat, but he couldn't find Hendricks anywhere. People he talked to had seen Hendricks during the day, so the man wasn't in hiding, but Levine couldn't seem to catch up with him. It was suggested that Hendricks might be off at a poker game somewhere in Manhattan, but Levine couldn't find out exactly where the poker game was being held.

He got back to the precinct at eleven-thirty, and started typing out his daily report. There wasn't much to report. He'd looked for Hendricks, and had failed to find him. He would look again tomorrow.

Lieutenant Barker came in at a quarter to twelve. That was unusual; the Lieutenant was rarely around later than eight or nine at night, unless something really important had happened in the precinct. He came into the squadroom and said, "Abe, can I talk to you? Bring that report along."

Levine pulled the incomplete report from the typewriter and followed the Lieutenant into his ofice. The Lieutenant sat down, and motioned for Levine to do the same, then held out his hand.

"Could I see that report?" he asked.

"It isn't finished."

"That's all right."

The Lieutenant glanced at the report, and then dropped it on his desk. "Abe," he said, "do you know what our full complement is supposed to be?"

"Twenty men, isn't it?"

"Right. And we have fifteen. With Crawley out, fourteen. Abe, here's your reports for the last six days. What have you been doing, man? We're understaffed, we're having trouble keeping up with the necessary stuff, and look what you've been doing. For six days you've been running around in circles. And for what? For a small-time punk who got a small-time punk's end."

"He was murdered, Lieutenant."

"Lots of people are murdered, Abe. When we can, we find out who did the job, and we turn him over to the DA. But we don't make an obsession out of it. Abe, for almost a week now you haven't been pulling your weight around here. There've been three complaints about how long it took us to respond to urgent calls. We're understaffed, but we're not *that* understaffed."

Barker tapped the little pile of reports. "This man Gold was a fence, and a cheap crook. He isn't worth it, Abe. We can't waste any more time on him. When you finish up this report, I want you to recommend we switch the case to Pending. And tomorrow I want you to get back with the team."

"Lieutenant, I've got one more man to—"

"And tomorrow there'll be one more, and the day after that one more. Abe, you've been working on nothing else at *all*. Forget it, will you? This is a cheap penny-ante bum. Even his brother doesn't care who killed him. Let it go, Abe."

He leaned forward over the desk. "Abe, some cases don't get solved right away. That's what the Pending file is for. So six weeks from now, or six months from now, or six years from now, while we're working on something else, when the break finally does come, we can pull that case out and hit it hot and heavy again. But it's *cold* now, Abe, so let it lie."

Speeches roiled around inside Levine's head, but they were only words so he didn't say them. He nodded, reluctantly. "Yes, sir," he said.

"The man was a bum," said the Lieutenant, "pure and simple. Forget him, he isn't worth your time."

"Yes, sir," said Levine.

He went back to the squadroom and finished typing the report, recommending that the Morry Gold case be switched to the Pending file. Then it was twelve o'clock, and he left the precinct and walked to the subway station. The underground platform was cold and deserted. He stood shivering on the concrete, his hands jammed deep into his pockets. He waited twenty minutes before a train came. Then it did come, crashed into the station and squealed to a stop. The doors in front of Levine slid back with no hands touching them, and he stepped aboard.

The car was empty, with a few newspapers abandoned on the seats. The doors slid shut behind him and the train started forward. He was the only one in the car. He was the only one in the car and all the seats were empty, but he didn't sit down.

The train rocked and jolted as it hurtled through the cold hole under Brooklyn, and Abraham Levine stood swaying in the middle of the empty car, a short man, bulky in his overcoat, hulk-shouldered, crying.

Breathe No More

Author: John D. MacDonald (1916–1986)

Detective: Park Falkner (1950)

Of course, John D. MacDonald's most famous detective was Travis McGee, but the "salvage expert" who investigated his way through twenty-one novels never appeared in any of MacDonald's hundreds of thousands of words of short fiction. However, as with Raymond Chandler, the evolution of McGee can be traced to his short fiction of the 1950s. One character in particular, Park Falkner, was mentioned by MacDonald himself in the introduction to volume one of his short-story collection *The Good Old Stuff*: "This story intrigues me because it deals with Park Falkner, who in some aspects seems like a precursor of Travis McGee."

Precursor indeed. While there are superficial differences between the two characters, the personality and motivations of the two are practically identical. McGee pursued justice and championed the helpless from his boat *The Busted Flush*; Falkner did the same on his private island, bringing people there and uncovering the crimes they think they've gotten away with.

While it is the McGee novels that MacDonald will be remembered for, his short mystery fiction exemplified the genre during the late 1940s and early 1950s. He wrote with wit, color, wryness, style, and reality, and that is what he will always be remembered for.

He looked like a fat child as he walked gingerly down the beach. He winced, sat down, picked a wicked little sand burr from the pink pad of his foot. For a time he sat there, pouting and petulant, his fat tummy and thick shoulders an angry pink from the mid-afternoon Florida sun. A porpoise chasing sand sharks made a lazy arc a hundred yards out. The Gulf was oily and torpid. The fat man wore spectacular swimming trunks. He was semi-bald, with rimless glasses pinched into the bridge of his soft nose. He sat and looked dully at the small waves, tasting again the sense of utter defeat that had been with him these past two days on Grouper Island. Defeat. Everything gone. Not much more time left. How would it be to wade out and start swimming? Swim until there was nothing but exhaustion, strangling, and death.

He shivered in the sun's heat. No.

Slowly he stood up. Sweat trickled down through the gray mat of hair on his chest. He walked back toward the house of his odd host, toward the gleaming-white terraced fortress of the man called Park Falkner.

Twenty feet farther along he angled up across the dry sand. He saw her, bronze, oiled, and gleaming in the sun. She lay on a blanket, her hair wrapped, turban fashion, in a towel, her eyes covered with odd little plastic cups joined together with a nose band. She was in a hollow in the sand, her scanty bathing suit hiding little of her firm, tanned flesh.

The hate for her shuddered up in him, tightening his throat, making him feel weak and trembling. She had done this to him. She had lost everything for him. He knew it was useless, but he had to plead with her again, plead for her silence. He remembered the last time, remembered her evil amusement.

"Laura!" he said softly. "Laura, are you awake?"

She didn't move. He saw the slow rise and fall of her breathing. Asleep. The wish to do her harm came with an almost frightening suddenness. He looked at the big white house three hundred yards away. No sign of movement on any of the terraces. They would be napping after the large lunch, after the cocktails.

He moved close to her. He knew, suddenly and with satisfaction, that he was going to try to kill Laura Hale. But how? There could be no marks on her throat. No bruise of violence. He squatted beside her. Her underlip sagged a bit away from the even white teeth. Her breathing merged with the husky whisper of the sea. A gull wheeled and called hoarsely, startling him. Sandpipers ran and pecked along the sand.

Methodically, as though he were a fat child playing, he began to heap up the dry white sand, removing the shell fragments. He piled it on the edge of the blanket, near her head. Sweat ran from him as he worked. The conical pile grew higher and higher. The widening base of it moved closer to her head. He stopped when it was over two feet high and again he watched the white house. So far he had done nothing. He forced himself to breathe slowly. He held his hands hard against his thighs to steady them.

Laura slept on. The plastic cups over her eyes gave her a look of blindness.

It had to be done quickly. He went over every step. The pile of sand towered over her face. With an awkward, splay-fingered push, he shoved the tiny mountain over and across her face, burying it deep. He followed it over, resting his chest on the pile that covered her face, grabbing her wrists as they flashed up. He held her down as she made her soundless struggle. Surely she knew who was doing this thing to her. Surely she cursed her own stupidity in sleeping out here alone before the ultimate panic just before death came to her. Her hard, slim body arched convulsively and her hips thudded down against the blanket. She writhed and once nearly broke his grip on her wrist. Then her long legs straightened out slowly, moved aimlessly, and were still. He lay there, pressed against the sand that covered her head, feeling an almost sensual excitement. He released her hand. The arm flopped down as though it were boneless. He squatted back and watched her for a moment. Then, with care, he brushed the sand from her face. Grotesquely, the eye cups were still in place. The sand stuck to the lotion she had used. She did not breathe. The white teeth were packed and caked with sand, the nostrils filled.

Filled with a desperate exaltation, he glanced at the house, sleeping in the white sun glare, then took her wrists and dragged her down to the sea. Her feet made two grooves in the wet sand. He dragged her through the surf and into the stiller water. He weight in the water was as nothing. He yanked the towel from her head, and her long black hair floated out. He tied the towel around his neck. The sand was washed from her dead face. It was unmarked. He worked her out into deeper water, got behind her, and wrapped his thick arms around her, contracting her lungs and then letting them expand, contracting them again. They would fill with seawater. There would be sand in her lungs also. But that would be a normal thing for one who had died in the sea. If they found her.

He floated and looked at the house again. Safe so far. He wound his hand in her black hair and with a determined sidestroke took her on out, pausing to rest from time to time. When he thought he was far enough out, he stopped. He let her go, and she seemed to sink, but the process was so slow that he lost patience. Her face was a few inches below the surface and her eyes, half open, seemed to watch him. He thrust her down, got his feet against her body and pushed her farther. He was gasping with weariness, and the beach suddenly seemed to be an alarming distance away. As he tried to float a wave broke in his face. He coughed and avoided panic. When rested, he began to work his way back to the beach. He scuffed out the marks of her dragging feet, walked up to the blanket. The eye cups lay there. He spread the towel out to dry, picked up the eye cups and then the blanket, to shake it. He shook it once and then it slipped from his fingers. Her bathing cap had been under the blanket. Why hadn't he thought of that? He trembled. He picked up the blanket again, shook it, put the eye cups on it next to the bottle of suntan lotion.

With the cap in his hand, balled tightly, he walked back to the sea. He swam out, but he could not be sure of the place. When he knew that he could not find her, he left the cap in the sea and swam slowly back.

He walked to the showers behind the house and stood under the cold water for a long time. He went up to his room, meeting no one. He stripped, laid a towel across himself, and stared up at the high ceiling.

He cried for a little while and did not know why.

There was a feeling of having lost his identity. As though the act of murder had made him into another person. The old fear was gone, and now there was a new fear. "I am Carl Branneck," he whispered. "Now they can't do anything to me. They can't do anything. Anything. Anything."

He repeated the word like an incantation until he fell asleep.

Park Falkner was awakened from his nap by the sound of low voices, of a woman's laugh. He stretched like a big lean cat and came silently to his feet. He was tall and hard and fit, a man in his mid-thirties, his naked body marked with a half-dozen violent scars. He was sun-darkened to a mahogany shade. A tropical disease had taken, forever, hair, eyebrows, and lashes, but the bald well-shaped head seemed to accentuate the youthfulness of his face. The lack of eyebrows and lashes gave his face an expressionless look, but there was rapacity in the strong beaked nose, both humor and cruelty in the set of the mouth. He stepped into the faded tubular Singhalese sarong, pulled it up, and knotted it at his waist with a practiced motion. Except for the monastic simplicity of his bed, the room was planned for a Sybarite: two massive built-in couches with pillows and handy bookshelves; a fireplace of gray stone that reached up to the black-beamed ceiling; a built-in record player and record library that took up half of one wall, complete with panel control to the amplifiers located all over the house and grounds; and adjoining bath with a special shower stall, large enough for a platoon. The four paintings, in lighted niches, had been done on the property by guest artists. Stimulated by a certain freedom that existed on Falkner's Grouper Island, they were pictures that the rather prominent artists would prefer not to show publicly.

One whole wall of the bedroom was of glass, looking out over a small private terrace and over the sea. Park Falkner padded out across is terrace and looked down to the next one below. It extended farther out than did his own.

The conversation below had ceased. The two wheeled chaise longues were side by side. The little waitress from Winter Haven, Pamela, lay glassy and stunned by the heat of the sun, her lips swollen. Carlos Berreda, his brown and perfect body burnished by the sun, insistently stroked her wrist and the back of her hand. He leaned closer and closer to her lips. Park Falkner went quickly back into his bedroom and returned with the silver-and-mahogany thermos jug. He lifted the cap and upended it over the two below. Slivers of ice sparkled out with the water.

Carlos gave a hoarse and angry shout and Pamela screamed. Park held the empty jug and smiled down at them. They were both standing, their faces upturned. Pamela was pink with embarrassment.

"Have you forgotten?" Park said in Spanish. "Tomorrow in Monterrey you will meet two friends, Carlos. Friends that weigh five hundred kilos apiece and have long horns. This is not time for indoor sports."

The angry look left Carlos's face, and he gave Park a shamefaced grin. "*Muy correcto, jefe.* But the little one is so . . . is so . . ."

"She's all of eighteen, Señor Wolf."

"What're you saying about me?" Pamela demanded.

"That you're a sweet child, and we want you to come and watch the practice."

They went down to the patio behind the house. Carlos's sword handler brought the capes, laid them out on a long table, and, with weary tread, went over to the corner and came back trundling the practice device, the bull's head and horns mounted at the proper height on a two-wheeled carriage propelled by two long handles.

Carlos grinned at Pamela. "Watch thees, *Muñequita.*" He snapped the big cape, took his stance, made a slow and perfect and lazy veronica as the horns rolled by. The sweating assistant wheeled the horns and came back from the other direction. Carlos performed a classic gaonera. Pamela sat on the table by the capes and swung her legs.

She frowned. "But it isn't like having a real bull, is it?" she said.

Park laughed, and Carlos flashed the girl a look of hot anger. "Not exactly, *niña.*" The sword handler guffawed.

After Carlos went through his repertoire with the big cape, Park Falkner took the muleta and sword and, under Carlos's critical eye, performed a series of natural passes, topping them off with *manoletinas* to the right and to the left.

"How was it?" Park asked.

Carlos grinned. "The sword hand on the natural passes. Eet ees not quite *correcto,* señor, but eet ees good. You could have been a *torero* had you started when young."

"Let me try!" Pamela said.

Park moved over into the shade. Carlos had to reach around her to show her the correct positions of the hands on the cape. Three more of the houseguests came out to the patio. Taffy Angus, a hard-voiced, silver-haired ex-model, over forty but still exceedigly lovely. Johnny Loomis, the loud, burly, red-faced sports reporter from Chicago, ex-All American, current alcoholic. Steve Townsend, the small, wry, pale man who had arrived in response to Park Falkner's enigmatic wire.

Park pushed a handy button and a few moments later Mick Rogers, wearing his look of chronic disgust on his battered face, appeared in the opposite doorway, which opened into the kitchen. He winked at Park, disappeared, returned almost immediately, pushing a pale blue bar decorated with coral-colored elephants in various poses of abandon. The glassed clinked as he rolled it over into the shade in the opposite corner.

The others moved over toward the bar in response to Mick's nasal chant: "Step right up and get it. Give yourself a package, folks. That cocktail hour has been on for five minutes."

Taffy stayed next to Park. "What is it this time?" she asked in a low voice.

He clicked open her purse and took out her cigarettes and lighter. "What do you think it is?"

"Damn you, Park! One of these times you're going to go too far. Why can't you just relax and enjoy it?"

"Baby mine, I'd go mad in a month. Don't ask me to give up my hobby."

"Twisting people's lives around is a hell of a hobby, if you ask me. I don't know what you're doing this time, but it has something to do with that horrid puffy little man named Branneck and the unwholesome Laura Hale and that Steve Townsend."

"How sensitive you are to situations, Taffy!" Park said mockingly.

"Sensitive? I saw Branneck when he got his first look at Laura Hale five minutes after he arrived. He changed from a smug little fat man into a nervous wreck. And she looked as though she had just found a million dollars. I'm just not going to come her to this private island of yours anymore."

"You'll keep coming, Taffy, every time I ask you. You have a woman's curiosity. And deep down in that rugged old heart of yours, you have a hunch that I'm doing right."

"Are you, Park?"

He shrugged. "Who can tell? I'll be serious for a second or two. Don't be too shocked, lambie. My esteemed ancestors had the golden touch. Even if there were any point in making more money, it would bore me. The company of my Big Rich friends and relatives bores the hell out of me. So I have some clever young men who dig around in disorderly pasts. When they come up barking, carrying a bone, I just mix some human ingredients together and see what happens. A tossed salad of emotions, call it."

"Or dirty laundry."

"Don't scoff. I just make like fate, and certain people get what my grandmother called their comeuppance."

"It always makes me feel ill, Park."

"And—admit it—fascinated, Taffy."

She sighed. "All right. You win. Fascinated. Like looking at an open wound. But someday one of your salad ingredients is going to kill you."

"One day a *toro* may kill Carlos. The profession gives his life a certain spice. And I'm too old to take up bullfighting."

She gave him a flat, long, brown-eyed stare. "I wouldn't want you dead, Park."

"After this shindig is over, Taffy, can you stay here for a few days when the others have left?"

"Have I ever said no?" She grinned. "Goodness! I blushed. I'd better rush right up and put that in my diary. Say, are you flying Carlos to Mexico in the morning?"

"I can't leave now, the way things are shaping up. I'll have Lew earn his keep by flying Carlos and his man over."

"And the little girl too?"

"No. I don't throw canaries to cats, my love. This evening I'm having Mick drive her back to Winter Haven."

Taffy whispered, "Here it comes!"

Carl Branneck came slowly out onto the patio. He wore pale blue shorts and a white nylon sleeveless shirt. He was lobster red from the sun and his glasses were polished and glittering. His stubby hairy legs quivered fleshily as he walked. He gave Park a meek smile.

"Guess I overslept, eh?"

"Not at all, Mr. Branneck. Festivities are just starting. Step over and tell Mick what you want."

Branneck moved away uncertainly. Taffy said, "By tonight that poor little man is going to be one large blister."

Lew Cherezack, Park's pilot and driver, came in at a trot He was young and he had the wrinkled, anxious face of a boxer pup. He grinned and said, "Hello Taff! Why didn't I meet you before the war?"

"Which war?" Taffy asked coldly.

"What's up?" Park asked.

"Well, I see this car boiling out across our causeway, and so I go over to the gate. This large young guy jumps out with a look like he wants to take a punch at me. He tells me he's come after his girl, Laura Hale, and, damn it, he wants to see her right away and no kidding around. He says his name is Thomas O'Day. I got him pacing around out there."

O'Day spun around as Park approached. He glanced at the sarong, and a faint look of contempt appeared on his square, handsome face. "Are you Falkner?"

"It seems possible."

"Okay. I don't know what the hell you told Laura to get her to come down here without a word to me. I traced her as far as the Tampa airport, and today I found out that your driver picked her up there and brought her here. I want an explanation."

"Is she your wife?"

"No. We're engaged."

"I didn't notice any ring."

"Well, almost engaged. And what the hell business is that of yours? I took time off from my job, Falkner, and I can't stand her arguing with you. I want to see Laura and I want to see her right now. Go get her."

"You're annoying the hell out of me, O'Day," Park said mildly.

O'Day tensed and launched a large, determined right fist at Park's face. Park leaned away from it, grabbed the thick wrist with both hands, let himself fall backward, pulled O'Day with him. He got both bare feet against O'Day's middle and pushed up hard. The imprisoned wrist was like the hub of a wheel, with O'Day's heels traversing the rim. He hit flat on his back on the sand with an impressive thud. Park stood and watched him. O'Day gagged and fought for breath. He sat up and coughed and knuckled his right shoulder. He looked up at Park and glared, then grinned.

"So I had it coming, Mr. Falkner."

"Come on in and have a drink. I'll send somebody after your girl."

He took O'Day in with him, made a group introduction. O'Day asked

Mick for a Collins as Park sent Lew to find Laura. O'Day watched Townsend, finally went over and said, "I've got a feeling I've seen you before, Mr. Townsend."

"That could be."

"Are you from Chicago?"

"I've been there," Townsend said and turned away, terminating the conversation.

Pamela was working the cape and Carlos was charging her with the wheeled horns. She was very serious about it, her underlip caught behind her upper teeth, a frown of concentration on her brow.

"A second Conchita Cintrón!" Carlos called as she made a fairly acceptable veronica. Johnny Loomis, his tongue already thickened, began a braying discourse on the art of the matador.

Lew appeared and caught Park's eye. He left. Park caught him outside. Lew looked upset. "Park, she isn't in her room and I'll be damned if she's on the island. Come on. I want to show you something."

The two men stood and looked down at the blanket. The sun was far enough down so that their shadows across the sand were very long.

Park sighed heavily. "I don't like the way it looks. Break out the Lambertson lungs and be quick about it. Tide's on the change."

"How about O'Day?"

"If he can swim, fix him up. It'll give him something to do."

The sun rested on the rim of the horizon, a hot rivet sinking into the steel plate of the sea. The angle made visibility bad. Park Falkner was forty feet down, the pressure painful against his earplugs, the lead weights tight around him in the canvas belt. It was a shadow world. He saw the dim shape of a sand shark stirring the loose sand as it sped away. A stingray, nearly a yard in diameter, drifted lazily, its tail grooving the bottom. The oxygen mixture from the back tank hissed and bubbled. He swam with a froglike motion of his legs, using a wide breaststroke.

The last faint visibility was gone. He jettisoned some of the lead and rose slowly to the surface. The sun was gone and the dusk was gray-blue. He pulled out the earplugs and heard Mick's shout. Mick was far down the beach. He squinted. Mick and Lew and Townsend were standing by something on the sand. O'Day was running toward them. Park shoved the face mask up onto his forehead and went toward the shore in a long, powerful, eight-beat crawl.

He walked over and looked down at her. She was as blue as the early dusk.

Mick said in a half whisper, "The crabs got her a little on the arm but that's all."

"Wrap her in a blanket and take her over to the old icehouse. Lew, you phone it in. Take O'Day with you."

O'Day stood and looked down at Laura's body. He didn't move. Lew Cherezack tugged at his arm. Park stepped over and slapped O'Day across the face. The big man turned without a word and went back toward the house with long strides.

Mrs. Mick Rogers had laid out a buffet supper, but no one had eaten much. The certificate stating accidental death by drowning had been signed. Mrs. Rogers had packed Laura Hale's suitcase and placed it in the station wagon. The undertaker had said, over the phone, that he couldn't pick up the body until midnight.

Johnny Loomis had passed out and Mick had put him to bed, just before leaving for Winter Haven with a subdued and depressed Pamela. Carlos had complained bitterly about the death, saying that it was bad luck before tomorrow's corrida. He had gone nervously to bed after the arrangements had been made for Lew to fly him and his helper to Monterrey at dawn. Park Falkner sat on the lowest terrace facing the sea. Taffy was in the next chair. Townsend, Branneck, and O'Day were at the other end of the terrace. A subdued light shone on the small self-service bar. O'Day, with an almost monotonous regularity, stepped over and mixed himself a Scotch and water. It seemed not to affect him.

The other three were far enough away so that Park and Taffy could talk without being overheard.

"Satisfied?" Taffy asked in a low tone.

"Please shut up."

"What was she, twenty-seven? Twenty-eight? Think of the wasted years, Park. Having fun with your tossed salad?"

"I didn't figure it this way, Taffy. Believe me."

"Suppose you tell me how you figured it."

"Not yet. Later. I have to think."

"I've been thinking. The little gal was vain, you know. Careful of her looks. You know what seawater will do to a woman's hair, don't you?"

"Keep going."

"I know she had a bathing cap. She didn't wear it. So she drowned by accident on purpose. Suicide. That's a woman's logic speaking, Park."

"I noticed the same thing, but I didn't arrive at the same answer."

"What . . . do . . . you . . . mean?" Taffy demanded, each word spaced.

"You wouldn't know unless I told you the whole story. And I don't want to do that yet."

Branneck stood up and yawned. "Night, all. Don't know if I can sleep with this burn, but I'm sure going to try." The others murmured good night, and he went into the house.

O'Day said thickly but carefully, "I haven't asked you, Falkner. Can I stay until . . . they take her?"

"Stay the night. That'll be better. I've had a room fixed for you. Go up to the second floor. Second door on the left. Mick took your bag up out of your car before he left."

"I don't want to impose on—"

"Don't talk rot. Go to bed. You'll find a sleeping pill on the nightstand. Take it."

Only Taffy, Townsend, and Park Falkner were left. After O'Day had gone, Townsend said dryly, "This is quite a production. Lights, camera, action."

"Stick around for the floor show," Taffy said, her tone bitter.

"I can hardly wait. Good night, folks," Townsend said. He left the terrace.

Taffy stood up and walked over toward the railing. She wore a white Mexican off-the-shoulder blouse. Her slim midriff was bare, her hand-blocked skirt long and full. She was outlined against the meager moonlight, her silver hair falling an unfashionable length to her shoulder blades. In the night light she looked no more than twenty. In the hardest light she looked almost thirty.

Park went to her. "We've known each other a long time, Taff. Do you want to help me? It won't be . . . pleasant."

She shrugged. "When you ask me like that. . . ."

"Go on up to your room and get one of your swimsuits. Meet me by the garages."

She came toward him through the night. He took her wrist, and together they went into the icehouse. When the door was shut behind them, he turned on the powerful flashlight, directed it at the blanket-wrapped body on the table. Taffy shuddered.

"I want to show you something, Taff. Be a brave girl."

He uncovered the head, held the flashlight close, and thumbed up an eyelid. "See?" he said. "A ring of small hemorrhages against the white of the eye. Something was pressed hard there."

"I—I don't understand."

"I found it right after they examined her. Both eyes are the same. Other than that, and the sea damage, there's not a mark on her."

"Wouldn't contact lenses do that?" Taffy asked.

"They might, if they didn't fit properly, or if they had been inserted clumsily. But I don't think she wore them. She was grateful to me for having her come down here. She . . . attempted to show her gratitude. The offer was refused, but in the process of refusing it, I had a good close look at her eyes. I'd say no. I have another answer."

"But what?"

He took the plastic cups out and held them in the flashlight glow.

Taffy gasped. "No, Park. Someone would have had to—"

"Exactly. Pressed them down quite hard on the eyes. No point in it unless the pressure also served some other purpose. Smothering her. Evidently she was smothered while in the sun, while on her back. Maybe she was sleeping. The smotherer dragged her into the sea, forgetting the cap or ignoring it."

"Did he use a towel to do it?"

"I wouldn't think so. A little air would get through. She'd struggle longer and the plastic cups would have slipped and made other marks. And I don't think a pillow was used. Look."

He curled back her upper lip. Up above the ridge of the gum was a fine dark line of damp sand.

"No," Taffy said in a whisper. "No."

"It wouldn't be hard to do. Taffy, maybe I won't ask you to do what I originally planned."

She straightened up. "Try me."

"I want that swimsuit. She'll have to be dressed in yours. You go on along. Leave your suit here. I'll change it."

Taffy said tonelessly, "Go on outside, Park." She pushed him gently.

Outside he lit a cigarette, cupped his hands around the glow. The luminous dial of his wristwatch told him that it was after eleven. The sea sighed as though with some vast, half-forgotten regret. The stars were cool and withdrawn. He rubbed the cigarette out with his toe. She came out into the darkness and silently leaned her forehead against his shoulder. He held her for a moment, and then they walked back to the house together. He took the damp swimsuit from her. When the door shut he went up the stairs to his own room. He sat in the darkness and thought of Laura Hale, of the way the hard core of her showed beneath the blue of her eyes.

* * *

Mick came back after driving Pamela home, and later he heard another car, heard Mick speak to a stranger. Soon the strange car drove back across the causeway, the motor noise lost in the sound of the sea.

Mick knocked and came in. "Sitting in the dark, hey? They took her off with 'em. I delivered Pamela. She thinks Carlos is coming back to see her after he fights."

"He might. Go get Branneck. Don't let him give you an argument or make any noise. Get him up here."

The lights were on and Park was sitting cross-legged on his bed when Mick Rogers shoved Branneck through the door. Branneck's pajamas were yellow-and-white vertical stripes. His eyes were puffy. He sputtered with indignation.

"I demand to know why—"

"Shut up," said Park. He smiled amiably at Branneck. "Sit down."

Branneck remained standing. "I want to know why your man—"

"Because seven years and three months ago, in a very beautiful and very complicated variation of the old badger game, a wealthy Chicago citizen named Myron C. Cauldfeldt was bled white to the tune of two hundred and twenty-five thousand dollars. He was in no position to complain to the police until he was visited by the girl in the case. She explained to him that her partner, or one of her partners, had run out with the entire take. She was angry. She went with Cauldfeldt to the police and made a confession. In view of her age—twenty—she was given a suspended sentence and put on probation. The man who had run out with the take disappeared completely. Now am I making any sense?" He paused, waiting.

Branneck gave a blind man's look toward the chair. He stumbled over and sat down. He breathed hard through his open mouth.

Park Falkner stood up. "Someday, Branneck," he said lightly, "you ought to do some research into the lives of people who run out with large bundles of dough. They hide in shabby little rooms and slowly confidence comes back. A year passes. Two. They slowly come out of cover and take up the threads of a new life. Sometimes they are able to almost forget the source of their money."

Branneck had slowly gained control. He said, "I haven't the faintest idea what you're talking about, Falkner. It wasn't true, was it, what you said about wanting to buy some of my properties? That was just to get me to come down here."

Mick leaned against the closed door, cleaning his fingernails with a broken match. He gave Branneck a look of disgust.

"Let's review, Branneck. Or should I call you Roger Krindall?" Park said.

"My name is Branneck," the man said huskily.

"Okay. Branneck, then. You are a respected citizen of Biloxi. You arrived there about six years ago and made yourself agreeable. You did some smart dealing in shore properties. My investigator estimates that you're worth a few million. You belong to the proper clubs. Two years ago you married a widow of good social standing. Your stepdaughter is now sixteen. You are respected. A nice life, isn't it?"

"What are you trying to say?"

"You came here thinking that I was a customer for the Coast Drive Motel that you just finished building. Selling it would be a nice stroke of business. I might be willing to buy it. I'll give you ten thousand for it."

Branneck jumped up, his face greenish pale under the fresh burn. "Ten thousand! Are you crazy? I've got two hundred thousand in it and a mortgage of three hundred and twenty thousand outstanding!"

"He won't sell, Park," Mick said.

"No imagination, I guess, Mick."

Branneck stared hard at Park and then at Mick. "I see what you're getting at. Very nice little scheme. Now I can figure how you got a layout like this. Well, you're wrong. Dead wrong. If I was all chump you could have made it stick. But I'll take my chances on what you can do to me. You've got me mixed up with somebody named Krindall. You can't prove a damn thing. And if you start to spread on little rumor in Biloxi you'll get slapped in the face with a slander suit so fast your head'll swim. I'm going back to bed, and I'm pulling out of here first thing in the morning."

He strode toward the door. Mick glanced at Park for instructions and then stepped aside. Branneck slammed the door.

"He knows Cauldfeldt is dead," Park said. "And I think he knows that too much time has passed for the Chicago police to do anything to him, even if they could get hold of Laura Hale for a positive identification. I had him going for a minute, but he made a nice recovery."

"So it blows up in our face?" Mick asked.

"I wouldn't say so. He killed Laura Hale."

The match slipped out of Mick's fingers. He bent and picked it up. "Give me some warning next time, Park. That's a jolt."

Park began to pace back and forth. "Yes, he killed her, and he got his chance because I was stupid. And so was she. Neither of us figured him as having the nerve for that kind of violence. She was a tramp all the way through. She thought I had arranged it so we could bleed Branneck, alias Krindall, and split the proceeds. Finding out that I had other plans was going to be a shock to her—but he fixed it so that she was spared that particular shock. He took his chance, and he got away with it. Now I'm sorry I had you bring him in. He's been warned. And he'll fight. But we can't let him leave in the morning. Got any ideas?"

Mick grinned. The flattened nose and Neanderthal brows gave him the look of an amiable ape. "This won't be good for his nerves, boss, but I could sort of arrange it so he could overhear that the coroner has suspicions and is waiting for somebody to make a run for it."

"Good!" Park said. "Then he'll have to make an excuse to stay and that'll give me time to work out an idea."

The roar of the amphibian taking off from the protected basin in the lee of the island awoke Park the next morning. Carlos was being carted away to his rendezvous with the black beast from La Punta. At three o'clock, when it was four in Monterrey, he would pick up, on short wave, the report of the corrida. Park pulled on his trunks and went out onto the terrace. The dawn sun behind the house sent the tall shadow of the structure an impossible distance out across the gray morning sea. He stood and was filled with a sudden and surprising revulsion against the shoddy affair of Branneck and Laura Hale. Better to give it all up. Better to give himself to the sea and the sun, music and Taffy. Let the easy life drift by.

But he knew and remembered the times he had tried the lethargic life. The restlessness had grown in him, shortening his temper, fraying the nerve ends—and then he would read over a report from one of the investigators. "A psychiatrist shot in his office here last year. Three suspects, but not enough on any of them to bring it to trial. Think you could get all three down there for a short course in suspicion." And then the excitement would begin. Maybe Taffy was right. Playing God. Playing the part of fate and destiny. The cornered man is the dangerous man. The cornered woman has an unparalleled viciousness.

He saw a figure far up the beach, recognized Taffy's hair color. She was a quarter mile from the house, an aqua robe belted around her, walking slowly, bending now and then to pick up something. Shells, probably. He saw her turn around and stare back toward the house. She could not see him in the heavy shadows. She slipped off the robe, dropped it on the sand, and went quickly down into the surf.

Park grinned. In spite of Taffy Angus's modeling career, in spite of her very objective view of the world, she had more than her share of modesty. She would be furious if she knew that he had watched her morning swim au naturel. He glanced at the sixteen-power scope mounted on the corner of the terrace railing and decided that it wouldn't be cricket. The perfect gag, of course, would be a camera with a telescopic lens, with a few large glossy prints to . . .

He snapped his fingers. A very fine idea. One of the best.

At three o'clock in the afternoon, Mick was ten miles down the mainland beach. He was hot, sticky, and annoyed.

"Why do you have to be giving me arguments?" he demanded of the fat middle-aged tourist and the bronzed dark-haired girl.

The tourist looked angry. "Damn it! All I said was that if you stand so far away from us with that camera, you're going to get a bunch of nothing. We'll be a couple of dots on that negative."

Mick said heavily, "Mister, I know what I'm doing. I don't want your faces to show. This is an illustration for a story in a confession magazine."

The girl adjusted the suit that had belonged to Laura Hale. "This doesn't fit so good, Mr. Rogers," she said.

Mick sighed. "This time I want to get the blanket in, too. I'm going back up on that knoll. Now get it right. We got the marks in the sand across the beach where you dragged her. I want you, mister, to be hip-deep in that surf and dragging her by the hair. Don't look around. Girlie, you take yourself a deep breath and play dead.

"We're too far away from the camera," the man said sullenly.

Mick gave him a long, hard look. The man grunted and turned away. "Come on, sister," he said.

Mick arrived back at Grouper Island at six with the dozen prints. He found Park, O'Day, and Taffy on the lower terrace. Park stood up at once and they went upstairs.

"He still here?" Mick asked.

"Jittery but still around."

"How did Carlos do?"

"Too nervous. They threw cushions at him during the first bull. The second bull gave him a slit in the thigh. He's okay. Now let's see what you've got."

Park studied the pictures one by one. He laid three aside. "It's between these three. Nice job, Mick. The beach matches up pretty good. The girl seems a little small, but that man, from the back, is a dead ringer for Branneck. We can't use the ones with the blanket showing, because we can't be sure whether or not Branneck shook the sand off it before or after he took her into the water. And we don't know how he took her out. He could have dragged her by the wrists, hair, or ankles, or even carried her. But I'd bet on wrists or hair. Now let's see. These two here. The surf blanks it out so he could be holding her either way. We'll have to take a chance on her being on her back. Did you have enough money with you?"

"Plenty. Twenty apiece to the man and the girl and a ten-buck fee to get 'em developed fast. Am I going to be in on this?"

"It looks that way. Taffy drove Loomis over to Tampa this noon. She ought to be back within the hour. Townsend and O'Day are taking a swim. Branneck is tanking up at the terrace bar, and your good wife is fixing some food. Lew radioed that he'll be back by seven. You could bring him on up now . . . no. This'll be better. I've shot my bolt. I'll be in my room. Send Taffy up as soon as she gets back."

Taffy sat hunched on the hassock, the picture in her hand. Park finished the story. She said, "Once three of us had an apartment in New York. That was a long, long time ago. We had mice. One of the girls, Mary Alice, bought a mousetrap, a wire thing like a cage. Trouble was, it didn't kill the mouse. The idea was to catch one and drown him. I remember that first mouse. We got him, and he sat up on his hind legs and begged. He was a nasty little item and I drew the short straw and took him into the bathroom, but I couldn't do it. We finally got the janitor to do it for us. Then we bought another kind of trap."

"Laura was taking a nice peaceful sunbath."

"I know, Park. I know. Don't worry, I'll do it."

"We'll have the tape recorder on, and for good measure I'll be in your closet holding a gun on him."

Branneck came into Taffy's room and shut the door gently. His smile was very close to a leer. He said, "I've been watching you, Miss Angus. You don't belong here with this crowd of sharpies."

"I thought that we should get a little better acquainted, Mr. Branneck."

"Nothing would suit me better, believe me."

"I suppose, as an important businessman, Mr. Branneck, you have a hobby?"

"Eh? No, I don't have time for anything like that. Got to keep moving to stay ahead, you know. Say, I'm going to open my new motel in three weeks. Why don't you take a run over to Biloxi and be my guest? Be the first customer in one of the best suites. What do you say?"

"What would your wife say?"

"Hell, we can use you to take some publicity shots."

"I'm not as photogenic as I used to be, Mr. Branneck."

"Call me Carl. Anyway, I can tell the wife you're there for some photographs."

"That's my hobby, Carl. Photographs. I suppose it came from standing in front of so many cameras."

"Yeah? How about giving me a picture of you? Got any . . . good ones? You know what I mean."

"I've got one of you, Mr. Branneck. Nobody has seen it but me. I developed it myself. Of course, it isn't too good of you."

Branneck beamed. "Say, isn't that something! A picture of me!"

She walked slowly over and took it from the dresser drawer and walked back to him, holding it so that he couldn't see it. Her lips felt stiff as she smiled.

"I'll give you a quick look at it. Here!" She trust it out. His eyes bulged. As he reached for it, she snatched it back. "This is only a print, Carl."

"You . . . you . . ."

"I used a fine grain. You'd be amazed at how dead she looks when you use a glass on the print."

Branneck clenched his fists and studied his pink knuckles. He spoke without looking up. "You're smart, Taffy. I knew that right away. A smart girl. Smart girls don't get too greedy. They stay reasonable. They don't ask for too much."

"Isn't murder worth quite a lot?"

"Damn it, don't raise your voice like that!"

"Don't tell me I used the wrong word." Her tone was mocking.

"Okay. The word was right. I killed her because she wasn't smart, because she wasn't going to take a cut and shut up. She wanted the whole works. You can call that a warning."

"Don't scare me to death, Carl. Did she die easily?"

"You saw her. It didn't take long. It was too easy. What do you want for the negative?"

"Oh, I'm keeping the negative. I put it in a safety-deposit box in a Tampa bank today, along with a little note explaining what it is. I opened an account there, too. I think you ought to fatten it up for me. Say fifty thousand?"

"Say twenty."

"Thirty-five."

"Thirty-two thousand five hundred. And not another damn dime."

"A deal, Carl."

He stood up slowly and wearily, but the moment he was balanced on the balls of his feet he moved with the deceptive speed of most fat men. His hard-swinging hand hit her over the ear and she slammed back against the closet door, shutting it. He stood with the recaptured photograph in his hand. He gave her an evil smile.

"For this, honey, you don't even get thirty-two cents. I thought something was wrong with it. If it was me and Laura, there'd be a towel tied around my neck. Very clever stuff, but no damn good."

Taffy, realizing that the closet couldn't be opened from the inside, reached casually for the knob. Branneck, alert as any animal, tensed.

"Get away from that door!"

She twisted the knob. Park started to force his way out as Branneck hit the outside of the door, slamming it shut again. He caught Taffy when she was still four steps from the room door. He held her with her back to him. A small keen point dug into her flesh, and she gasped with the unexpected pain.

"Now walk out. Keep smiling and keep talking. This is only a pocketknife, but I keep it like a razor and I can do a job on that beautiful body before you can take two steps."

Park put his back against the back wall of the closet and braced both feet against the door. His muscles popped and cracked. There was a thin splintering sound, and then the door tore open so quickly that he fell heavily to the closet floor. There was an alarm bell in Taffy's room. He pushed it, raced to the side terrace in time to see Mick run out from the kitchen, a carbine in his hand, looking back over his shoulder. The causeway was blocked. Taffy appeared on the sand strip, Branneck a pace behind her, the sunset glinting on the small blade in his hand. Taffy stopped. He kept her in front of him and backed slowly out of sight.

Park cursed softly and raced from the terrace across the house. With a rifle he might have managed it. But the .38 didn't have a high enough degree of accuracy. Branneck pushed Taffy roughly down onto the cabin floor of the small twenty-one-foot cabin cruiser. As he ran to the bow to free the rope, Park risked a shot. Branneck flinched and scrambled aboard. The marine engine roared to life and Branneck swung it around in the small basin, crouching behind the wheel as he piloted it down the narrow mouth, dangerously close to the causeway where Mick stood. Mick leveled the carbine but did not dare risk a shot. The cruiser sped out in a wide curve in the quiet water between the island and the mainland.

Park gave a shout as Taffy jumped up and went over the side in a long, slanting dive. The cruiser swung back and Branneck stood at the rail, the light glinting blood-red on the polished metal of the gaff. Park's fingernails bit into his palm. Branneck raced to the wheel, adjusted the path of the cruiser, and hurried back to the rail. Taffy turned in the water. Branneck lunged for her with the gaff. Even at that distance, Park saw her hand reach up and grasp the shaft above the cruel hook. Branneck tottered for a moment, his arms waving wildly. Park heard his hoarse cry as he went overboard. Two heads bobbed in the water in the wake of the cruiser. Taffy's arms began to lift in her rhythmic, powerful crawl. Branneck turned and began to plow toward the mainland.

Park ran down and out the back of the house, across the patio to meet Taffy. Mick already had one of the cars started. He spun the tires as he yanked it around to head over the causeway and cut Branneck off.

The cruiser, with no hand at the wheel, came about in a wide curve. Park watched it. He saw what would happen. It swept on—and Taffy was the only swimmer. Mick stopped the car and backed off the causeway and parked it again. The cruiser continued on, missed the far shore, swung back, and grounded itself at the very end of Grouper Island.

Park went down into the water over his ankles. Taffy came out, the powder-blue dress molded to every curve. She shivered against him.

"He—he's swimming to the mainland."

"He was. Not anymore. The *Nancy* swung back and took care of that little detail."

"He tried to gaff me," she whispered.

"Come on. I'll get you a drink."

As they walked up to the house, she smiled up at him. Her smile was weak. "The next time you get me to help in any of your little games . . ."

"Branneck had a capacity for pulling off the unexpected."

"What will you do?"

"Accidental death. That widow he married may be a nice gal."

O'Day had left to accompany the girl's body back to Chicago. Park sat on his private terrace, with Taffy sharing the extra-wide chaise lounge.

Townsend came out and said, "Not that I want to be a boor, people, but it is nearly midnight and I've got to mark this case off my books and get back to work."

"Sorry it didn't work out," Park said.

"Better luck on the next one. 'Night."

He left and Taffy asked, "Who was that man?"

"Internal Revenue. He helped my investigator get a line on Branneck.

You see, when Branneck was calling himself by his right name—Krindall—he forgot to declare the money he squeezed out of Cauldfeldt as income. Branneck didn't know it, but all we were going to do was get satisfactory proof that he was Krindall. Penalties, back taxes, and interest would have added up to six hundred thousand."

"But Branneck had his own answer."

After the house was silent, Park Falkner took the woman's bathing suit, the dozen pictures, the permanent tape off the recorder and put them neatly and gently into a steel file box in the cabinet behind his bookshelves. Once the sticker with the date had been applied to the end of the box, it looked like all the others.

Falkner slept like a tired child.

When the Wedding Was Over

Author: Ruth Rendell (1930–)

Detective: Wexford (1964)

If a committee of crime-fiction experts was locked in a room and forced to reach consensus on the single greatest contemporary author in the genre, it might well come out battered and bloodied with the name Ruth Rendell. Beginning her career with relatively conventional, though superb, police novels about the Kingsmarkham team of Wexford and Burden, she has expanded into psychological suspense fiction under her own name and as Barbara Vine, while periodically satisfying the public and publishing demand for new cases for her police team.

"When the Wedding Was Over" is chosen to represent the series for several reasons. One, concerning as it does the wedding of Burden, it represents a milestone in the series. Two, its use of a central clue that might have appealed to Ellery Queen or Dorothy L. Sayers shows Rendell's allegiance to fairplay detection. Three, and perhaps most interesting, it represents in short-story form, one of the most interesting trends in recent detective fiction: the story set partly in the present and partly in the past, with a historical mystery reconsidered years later.

M atrimony," said Chief Inspector Wexford, "begins with dearly beloved and ends with amazement."

His wife, sitting beside him on the bridegroom's side of the church, whispered, "What did you say?"

He repeated it. She steadied the large floral hat that her husband had called becoming but not exactly conducive to sotto voce intimacies. "What on earth makes you say that?"

"Thomas Hardy. He said it first. But look in your Prayer Book."

The bridegroom waited, hang-dog, with his best man. Michael Burden was very much in love, was entering this second marriage with someone admirably suited to him, had agreed with his fiancée that nothing but a religious ceremony would do for them, yet at forty-four was a little superannuated for what Wexford called "all this white wedding gubbins." There were two hundred people in the church. Burden, his best man and his ushers were in morning dress. Madonna lilies and stephanotis and syringa decorated the pews, the pulpit and the chancel steps. It was the kind of thing that is properly designed for someone twenty years younger. Burden had been through it before when he *was* twenty years younger. Wexford chuckled silently, looking at the anxious face above the high white collar. And then as Dora, leafing through the marriage service, said, "Oh, I *see*," the organist went from voluntaries into the opening bars of the Lohengrin march and Jenny Ireland appeared at the church door on her father's arm.

A beautiful bride, of course. Seven years younger than Burden, blonde, gentle, low-voiced, and given to radiant smiles. Jenny's father gave her hand into Burden's and the Rector of St. Peter's began:

"Dearly beloved, we are gathered together . . ."

While bride and groom were being informed that marriage was not for the satisfaction of their carnal lusts, and that they must bring up their children in a Christian manner, Wexford studied the congregation. In front of himself and Dora sat Burden's sister-in-law, Grace, whom everyone had thought he would marry after the death of his first wife. But Burden had found consolation with a red-headed woman, wild and sweet and strange, gone now God knew where, and Grace had married someone else. Two little boys now sat between Grace and that someone else, giving their parents a full-time job keeping them quiet.

Burden's mother and father were both dead. Wexford thought he recognized, from one meeting a dozen years before, an aged aunt. Beside her sat Dr. Crocker and his wife, beyond them and behind were a crowd whose individual members he knew either only by sight or not at all. Sylvia, his elder daughter, was sitting on his other side, his grandsons between her and their father, and at the central aisle end of the pew, Sheila Wexford of the Royal Shakespeare Company. Wexford's actress daughter, who on her entry had commanded nudges, whispers, every gaze, sat looking with unaccustomed wistfulness at Jenny Ireland in her clouds of white and wreath of pearls.

"I, Michael George, take thee, Janina, to my wedded wife, to have and to hold from this day forward . . ."

Janina. *Janina?* Wexford had supposed her name was Jennifer. What sort of parents called a daughter Janina? Turks? Fans of Dumas? He leaned forward to get a good look at these philonomatous progenitors.

They looked ordinary enough, Mr. Ireland apparently exhausted by the effort of giving the bride away, Jenny's mother making use of the lace handkerchief provided for the specific purpose of crying into it those tears of joy and loss. What romantic streak had led them to dismiss Elizabeth and Susan and Anne in favor of—Janina?

"Those whom God hath joined together, let no man put asunder. Forasmuch as Michael George and Janina have consented together in holy wedlock . . ."

Had they been as adventurous in the naming of their son? All Wexford could see of him was a broad back, a bit of profile, and now a hand. The hand was passing a large white handkerchief to his mother. Wexford found himself being suddenly yanked to his feet to sing a hymn.

> "O, Perfect Love, all human thought transcending,
> Lowly we kneel in prayer before Thy throne . . ."

These words had the effect of evoking from Mrs. Ireland audible sobs. Her son—hadn't Burden said he was in publishing?—looked embarrassed, turning his head. A young woman, strangely dressed in black with an orange hat, edged past the publisher to put a consoling arm around his mother.

"O Lord, save Thy servant and Thy handmaid."

"Who put their trust in Thee," said Dora and most of the rest of the congregation.

"O Lord, send them help from Thy holy place."

Wexford, to show team spirit, said, "Amen," and when everyone else said, "And evermore defend them," decided to keep quiet in the future.

Mrs. Ireland had stopped crying. Wexford's gaze drifted to his own daughters, Sheila singing lustily, Sylvia, the Women's Liberationist, with less assurance as if she doubted the ethics of lending her support to so archaic and sexist a ceremony. His grandsons were beginning to fidget.

"Almighty God, who at the beginning did create our first parents, Adam and Eve . . ."

Dear Mike, thought Wexford with a flash of sentimentality that came to him perhaps once every ten years, you'll be OK now. No more carnal lusts conflicting with a puritan conscience, no more loneliness, no more worrying about those selfish kids of yours, no more temptation-of-St-Anthony stuff. For is it not ordained as a remedy against sin, and to avoid fornication, that such persons as have not the gift of continency may marry and keep themselves undefiled?

"For after this manner in the old time the holy women who trusted in God . . ."

He was quite surprised that they were using the ancient form. Still, the bride had promised to obey. He couldn't resist glancing at Sylvia.

". . . being in subjection to their own husbands . . ."

Her face was a study in incredulous dismay as she mouthed at her sister "unbelievable" and "antique."

". . . Even as Sarah obeyed Abraham, calling him Lord, whose daughters ye are as long as ye do well, and are not afraid with any amazement."

At the Olive and Dove hotel there was a reception line to greet guests, Mrs. Ireland smiling, re-rouged and restored, Burden looking like someone who has had an operation and been told the prognosis is excellent, Jenny serene as a bride should be.

Dry sherry and white wine on trays. No champagne. Wexford remembered that there was a younger Ireland daughter, absent with her husband in some dreadful place—Botswana? Lesotho? No doubt all the champagne funds had been expended on her. It was a buffet lunch, but a good one. Smoked salmon and duck and strawberries. Nobody, he said to himself, has ever really thought of anything better to eat than smoked salmon and duck and strawberries unless it might be caviar and grouse and syllabub. He was weighing the two menus against each other, must without knowing it have been thinking aloud, for a voice said:

"Asparagus, trout, apple pie."

"Well, maybe," said Wexford, "but I do like meat. Trout's a bit insipid. You're Jenny's brother, I'm sorry I don't remember your name. How d'you do?"

"How d'you do? I know who you are. Mike told me. I'm Amyas Ireland."

So that funny old pair hadn't had a one-off indulgence when they had named Janina. Again Wexford's thoughts seemed revealed to this intuitive person.

"Oh, I know," said Ireland, "but how about my other sister? She's called Cunegonde. Her husband calls her Queenie. Look, I'd like to talk to you. Could we get together a minute away from all this crush? Mike was going to help me out, but I can't ask him now, not when he's off on his honeymoon. It's about a book we're publishing."

The girl in black and orange, Burden's nephews, Sheila Wexford, Burden's best man, and a gaggle of children, all carrying plates, passed between them at this point. It was at least a minute before Wexford could ask, "Who's we?" and another half-minute before Amyas Ireland understood what he meant.

"Carlyon Brent," he said, his mouth full of duck. "I'm with Carlyon Brent."

One of the largest and most distinguished of publishing houses. Wexford was impressed. "You published the Vandrian, didn't you, and the de Coverley books?"

Ireland nodded. "Mike said you were a great reader. That's good. Can I get you some more duck? No? I'm going to. I won't be a minute." Enviously Wexford watched him shovel fat-rimmed slices of duck breast on to his plate, take a brioche, have second thoughts and take another. The man was as thin as a rail too, positively emaciated.

"I look after the crime list," he said as he sat down again. "As I said, Mike half-promised . . . This isn't fiction, it's fact. The Winchurch case?"

"Ah."

"I know it's a bit of a nerve asking, but would you read a manuscript for me?"

Wexford took a cup of coffee from a passing tray. "What for?"

"Well, in the interests of truth. Mike was going to tell me what he thought." Wexford looked at him dubiously. He had the highest respect and the deepest affection for Inspector Burden but he was one of the last people he would have considered as a literary critic. "To tell me what he thought," the publisher said once again. "You see, it's worrying me. The author has discovered some new facts and they more or less prove Mrs. Winchurch's innocence." He hesitated. "Have you ever heard of a writer called Kenneth Gandolph?"

Wexford was saved from answering by the pounding of a gavel on the top table and the beginning of the speeches. A great many toasts had been drunk, several dozen telegrams read out, and the bride and groom departed to change their clothes before he had an opportunity to reply to Ireland's question. And he was glad of the respite, for what he knew of Gandolph, though based on hearsay, was not prepossessing.

"Doesn't he write crime novels?" he said when the inquiry was repeated. "And the occasional examination of a real-life crime?"

Nodding, Ireland said, "It's good, this script of his. We want to do it for next spring's list. It's an eighty-year-old murder, sure, but people are still fascinated by it. I think this new version could cause quite a sensation."

"Florence Winchurch was hanged," said Wexford, "yet there was always some margin of doubt about her guilt. Where does Gandolph get his fresh facts from?"

"May I send you a copy of the script? You'll find all that in the introduction."

Wexford shrugged, then smiled. "I suppose so. You do realize I can't do more than maybe spot mistakes in forensics? I did say maybe, mind." But his interest had already been caught. It made him say, "Florence was married at St. Peter's, you know, and she also had her wedding reception here."

"And spent part of her honeymoon in Greece."

"No doubt the parallels end there," said Wexford as Burden and Jenny came back into the room.

Burden was in a gray lounge suit, she in pale blue sprigged muslin. Wexford felt an absurd impulse of tenderness toward him. It was partly caused by Jenny's hat, which she would never wear again, would never have occasion to wear, would remove the minute they got into the car. But Burden was the sort of man who could never be happy with a woman who didn't have a hat as part of her "going-away" costume. His own clothes were eminently unsuitable for flying to Crete in June. They both looked very happy and embarrassed.

Mrs. Ireland seized her daughter in a crushing embrace.

"It's not forever, Mother," said Jenny. "It's only for two weeks."

"Well, in a way," said Burden. He shook hands gravely with his own son, down from university for the weekend, and planted a kiss on his daughter's forehead. Must have been reading novels, Wexford thought, grinning to himself.

"Good luck, Mike," he said.

The bride took his hand, put a soft, cool kiss on to the corner of his mouth. Say I'm growing old but add, Jenny kissed me. He didn't say that aloud. He nodded and smiled and took his wife's arm and frowned at Sylvia's naughty boys like the patriarch he was. Burden and Jenny went out to the car, which had Just Married written in lipstick on the rear window and a shoe tied on the back bumper.

There was a clicking of handbag clasps, a flurry of hands, and then a tempest of confetti broke over them.

* * *

It was an isolated house, standing some twenty yards back from the Myringham road. Plumb in the center of the facade was a plaque bearing the date 1896. Wexford had often thought that there seemed to have been positive intent on the part of late-Victorian builders to design and erect houses that were not only ugly, complex, and inconvenient, but also distinctly sinister in appearance. The Limes, though well-maintained and set in a garden as multicolored, cushiony and floral as a quilt, nevertheless kept this sinister quality. Khaki-colored brick and gray slate had been the principal materials used in its construction. Without being able to define exactly how, Wexford could see that, in relation to the walls, the proportions of the sash windows were wrong. A turret grew out of each of the front corners and each of these turrets was topped by a conical roof, giving the place the look of a cross between Balmoral castle and a hotel in Kitzbuehl. The lime trees, which gave it its name had been lopped so many times since their planting at the turn of the century that now they were squat and misshapen.

In the days of the Winchurches it had been called Paraleash House. But this name, of historical significance on account of its connection with the ancient manor of Paraleash, had been changed specifically as a result of the murder of Edward Winchurch. Even so, it had stood empty for ten years. Then it had found a buyer a year or so before the First World War, a man who was killed in that war. Its present owner had occupied it for half a dozen years, and in the time intervening between his purchase of it and 1918 it had been variously a nursing home, the annex of an agricultural college and a private school. The owner was a retired brigadier. As he emerged from the front door with two Sealyhams on a lead, Wexford retreated to his car and drove home.

It was Monday evening and Burden's marriage was two days old. Monday was the evening of Dora's pottery class, the fruits of which, bruised-looking and not invariably symmetrical, were scattered haphazardly about the room like windfalls. Hunting along the shelves for G. Hallam Saul's *When the Summer is Shed* and *The Trial of Florence Winchurch* from the Notable British Trials series, he nearly knocked over one of those rotund yet lopsided objects. With a sigh of relief that it was unharmed, he set about refreshing his memory of the Winchurch case with the help of Miss Saul's classic.

Florence May Anstruther had been nineteen at the time of her marriage to Edward Winchurch and he forty-seven. She was a good-looking fairhaired girl, rather tall and Junoesque, the daughter of a Kingsmarkham chemist—that is, a pharmacist, for her father had kept a shop in the

High Street. In 1895 this damned her as of no account in the social hierarchy, and few people would have bet much on her chances of marrying well. But she did. Winchurch was a barrister who, at this stage of his life, practiced law from inclination rather than from need. His father, a Sussex landowner, had died some three years before and had left him what for the last decade of the nineteenth century was an enormous fortune, two hundred thousand pounds. Presumably, he had been attracted to Florence by her youth, her looks, and her ladylike ways. She had been given the best education, including six months at a finishing school, that the chemist could afford. Winchurch's attraction for Florence was generally supposed to have been solely his money.

They were married in June 1895 at the parish church of St. Peter's, Kingsmarkham, and went on a six-month honeymoon, touring Italy, Greece, and the Swiss Alps. When they returned home Winchurch took a lease of Sewingbury Priory while building began on Paraleash House, and it may have been that the conical roofs on those turrets were inspired directly by what Florence had seen on her alpine travels. They moved into the lavishly furnished new house in May 1896, and Florence settled down to the life of a Victorian lady with a wealthy husband and a staff of indoor and outdoor servants. A vapid life at best, even if alleviated by a brood of children. But Florence had no children and was to have none.

Once or twice a week Edward Winchurch went up to London by the train from Kingsmarkham, as commuters had done before and have been doing ever since. Florence gave orders to her cook, arranged the flowers, paid and received calls, read novels, and devoted a good many hours a day to her face, her hair, and her dress. Local opinion of the couple at that time seemed to have been that they were as happy as most people, that Florence had done very well for herself and knew it, and Edward not so badly as had been predicted.

In the autumn of 1896 a young doctor of medicine bought a practice in Kingsmarkham and came to live there with his unmarried sister. Their name was Fenton. Frank Fenton was an extremely handsome man, twenty-six years old, six feet tall, with jet-black hair, a Byronic eye, and an arrogant lift to his chin. The sister was called Ada, and she was neither good-looking nor arrogant, being partly crippled by poliomyelitis, which had left her with one leg badly twisted and paralyzed.

It was ostensibly to befriend Ada Fenton that Florence first began calling at the Fentons' house in Queen Street. Florence professed great affection for Ada, took her about in her carriage and offered her the use of it whenever she had to go any distance. From this it was an obvious step to persuade Edward that Frank Fenton should become the Winchurches' doctor. Within another few months, young Mrs. Winchurch had become the doctor's mistress.

It was probable that Ada knew nothing, or next to nothing, about it. In the eighteen-nineties a young girl could be, and usually was, very innocent. At the trial it was stated by Florence's coachman that he would be sent to the Fentons' house several times a week to take Miss Fenton driving, while Ada's housemaid said that Mrs. Winchurch would arrive on foot soon after Miss Fenton had gone out and be admitted rapidly through a French window by the doctor himself. During the winter of 1898 it seemed likely that Frank Fenton had performed an abortion on Mrs. Winchurch, and for some months afterward they met only at social gatherings and occasionally when Florence was visiting Ada. But their feelings for each other were too strong for them to bear separation and by the following summer they were again meeting at Fenton's house while Ada was out, and now also at Paraleash House on the days when Edward had departed for the law courts.

Divorce was difficult but by no means impossible or unheard of in 1899. At the trial Frank Fenton said he had wanted Mrs. Winchurch to ask her husband for a divorce. He would have married her in spite of the disastrous effect on his career. It was she, he said, who refused to consider it on the grounds that she did not think she could bear the disgrace.

In January 1900, Florence went to London for the day and, among other purchases, bought at a grocer's two cans of herring fillets marinaded in a white wine sauce. It was rare for canned food to appear in the Winchurch household, and when Florence suggested that these herring fillets should be used in the preparation of a dish called *Filets de hareng marinés à la Rosette,* the recipe for which she had been given by Ada Fenton, the cook, Mrs. Eliza Holmes, protested that she could prepare it from fresh fish. Florence, however, insisted, one of the cans was used, and the dish was made and served to Florence and Edward at dinner. It was brought in by the parlormaid, Alice Evans, as a savory or final course to a four-course meal. Although Florence had shown so much enthusiasm about the dish, she took none of it. Edward ate a moderate amount and the rest was removed to the kitchen where it was shared between Mrs. Holmes, Alice Evans, and the housemaid, Violet Stedman. No one suffered any ill-effects. The date was January 30 1900.

Five weeks later on March 5 Florence asked Mrs. Holmes to make the dish again, using the remaining can, as her husband had liked it so much. This time Florence too partook of the marinated herrings, but when the remains of it were about to be removed by Alice to the kitchen, she advised her to tell the others not to eat it as she "thought it had a strange taste and was perhaps not quite fresh." However, although Mrs. Holmes and Alice abstained, Violet Stedman ate a larger quantity of the dish than had either Florence or Edward.

Florence, as was her habit, left Edward to drink his port alone. Within a few minutes a strangled shout was heard from the dining room and a sound as of furniture breaking. Florence and Alice Evans and Mrs. Holmes went into the room and found Edward Winchurch lying on the floor, a chair with one leg wrenched from its socket tipped over beside him and an overturned glass of port on the table. Florence approached him and he went into a violent convulsion, arching his back and baring his teeth, his hands grasping the chair in apparent agony.

John Barstow, the coachman, was sent to fetch Dr. Fenton. By this time Florence was complaining of stomach pains and seemed unable to stand. Fenton arrived, had Edward and Florence removed upstairs and asked Mrs. Holmes what they had eaten. She showed him the empty herring fillets can, and he recognized the brand as that by which a patient of a colleague of his had recently been infected with botulism, a virulent and usually fatal form of food poisoning. Fenton immediately assumed that it was *bacillus botulinus* that had attacked the Winchurches, and such is the power of suggestion that Violet Stedman now said she felt sick and faint.

Botulism causes paralysis, difficulty in breathing, and a disturbance of the vision. Florence appeared to be partly paralyzed and said she had double vision. Edward's symptoms were different. He continued to have spasms, was totally relaxed between spasms, and although he had difficulty in breathing and other symptoms of botulism, the onset had been exceptionally rapid for any form of food poisoning. Fenton, however, had never seen a case of botulism, which is extremely rare, and he supposed that the symptoms would vary greatly from person to person. He gave jalap and cream of tartar as a purgative and, in the absence of any known relatives of Edward Winchurch, he sent for Florence's father, Thomas Anstruther.

If Fenton was less innocent than was supposed, he had made a mistake in sending for Anstruther, for Florence's father insisted on a second opinion, and at ten o'clock went himself to the home of that very colleague of Fenton's who had recently witnessed a known case of botulism. This was Dr. Maurice Waterfield, twice Fenton's age, a popular man with a large practice in Stowerton. He looked at Edward Winchurch, at the agonized grin that overspread his features, and as

Edward went into his last convulsive seizure, pronounced that he had been poisoned not by *bacillus botulinus* but by strychnine.

Edward died a few minutes afterward. Dr. Waterfield told Fenton that there was nothing physically wrong with either Florence or Violet Stedman. The former was suffering from shock or "neurasthenia," the latter from indigestion brought on by overeating. The police were informed, an inquest took place, and after it Florence was immediately arrested and charged with murdering her husband by administering to him a noxious substance, to wit *strychnos nux vomica*, in a decanter of port wine.

Her trial took place in London at the Central Criminal Court. She was twenty-four years old, a beautiful woman, and was by then known to have been having a love affair with the young and handsome Dr. Fenton. As such, she and her case attracted national attention. Fenton had by then lost his practice, lost all hope of succeeding with another in the British Isles, and even before the trial his name had become a by-word, scurrilous doggerel being sung about him and Florence in the music halls. But far from increasing his loyalty to Florence, this seemed to make him the more determined to dissociate himself from her. He appeared as the prosecution's principal witness, and it was his evidence that sent Florence to the gallows.

Fenton admitted his relationship with Florence but said that he had told her it must end. The only possible alternative was divorce and ultimately marriage to himself. In early January 1900, Florence had been calling on his sister Ada, and he had come in to find them looking through a book of recipes. One of the recipes called for the use of herring fillets marinated in white wine sauce, the mention of which had caused him to tell them about a case of botulism, which a patient of Dr. Waterfield was believed to have contracted from eating the contents of a can of just such fillets. He had named the brand and advised his sister not to buy any of that kind. When, some seven weeks later, he was called to the dying Edward Winchurch, the cook had shown him an empty can of that very brand. In his opinion, Mrs. Winchurch herself was not ill at all, was not even ill from "nerves" but was shamming. The judge said that he was not there to give his opinion, but the warning came too late. To the jury the point had already been made.

Asked if he was aware that strychnine had therapeutic uses in small quantities, Fenton said he was but that he kept none in his dispensary. In any case, his dispensary was kept locked and the cupboards inside it locked, so it would have been impossible for Florence to have entered it or to have appropriated anything while on a visit to Ada. Ada Fenton was not called as a witness. She was ill, suffering from what her doctor, Dr. Waterfield, called "brain fever."

The prosecution's case was that, in order to inherit his fortune and marry Dr. Fenton, Florence Winchurch had attempted to poison her husband with infected fish, or fish she had good reason to suppose might be infected. When this failed she saw to it that the dish was provided again, and herself added strychnine to the port decanter. It was postulated that she obtained the strychnine from her father's shop, without his knowledge, where it was kept in stock for the destruction of rats and moles. After her husband was taken ill, she herself simulated symptoms of botulism in the hope that the convulsions of strychnine poisoning would be confused with the paralysis and impeded breathing caused by the bacillus.

The defense tried to shift the blame to Frank Fenton, at least to suggest a conspiracy with Florence, but it was no use. The jury was out for only forty minutes. It pronounced her guilty, the judge sentenced her to death, and she was hanged just twenty-three days later, this being some twenty years before the institution of a Court of Appeal.

After the execution Frank and Ada Fenton emigrated to the United States and settled in New England. Fenton's reputation had gone before him. He was never again able to practice as a doctor but worked as the traveling representative of a firm of pharmaceutical manufacturers until his death in 1932. He never married. Ada, on the other hand, surprisingly enough, did. Ephraim Hurst fell in love with her in spite of her sickly constitution and withered leg. They were married in the summer of 1902 and by the spring of 1903 Ada Hurst was dead in childbirth.

By then Paraleash House had been renamed The Limes and lime trees planted to conceal its forbidding yet fascinating facade from the curious passersby.

The parcel from Carlyon Brent arrived in the morning with a very polite cover letter from Amyas Ireland, grateful in anticipation. Wexford had never before seen a book in this embryo stage. The script, a hundred thousand words long, was bound in red, and through a window in its cover appeared the provisional title and the author's name: *Poison at Paraleash, A Reappraisal of the Winchurch Case* by Kenneth Gandolph.

"Remember all that fuss about Gandolph?" Wexford said to Dora across the coffeepot. "About four years ago?"

"Somebody confessed a murder to him, didn't they?"

"Well, maybe. While a prison visitor, he spent some time talking to Paxton, the bank robber, in Wormwood Scrubs. Paxton died of cancer a few months later, and Gandolph then published an article in a newspaper in which he said that during the course of their conversations, Paxton had confessed to him that he was the perpetrator of the Conyngford murder in 1962. Paxton's widow protested, there was a heated correspondence, MPs wanting the libel laws extended to libeling the dead, Gandolph shouting about the power of truth. Finally, the by then retired Detective Superintendent Warren of Scotland Yard put an end to all further controversy by issuing a statement to the press. He said Paxton couldn't have killed James Conyngford because on the day of Conyngford's death in Brighton Warren's sergeant and a constable had had Paxton under constant surveillance in London. In other words, he was never out of their sight."

"Why would Gandolph invent such a thing, Reg?" asked Dora.

"Perhaps he didn't. Paxton may have spun him all sorts of tales as a way of passing a boring afternoon. Who knows? On the other hand, Gandolph does rather set himself up as the elucidator of unsolved crimes. Years ago, I believe, he did find a satisfactory and quite reasonable solution to some murder in Scotland, and maybe it went to his head. Marshall, Groves, Folliott used to be his publishers. I wonder if they've refused this one because of the Paxton business, if it was offered to them and they turned it down?"

"But Mr. Ireland's people have taken it," Dora pointed out.

"Mm-hm. But they're not falling over themselves with enthusiasm, are they? They're scared. Ireland hasn't sent me this so that I can check up on the police procedural part. What do I know about police procedure in 1900? He's sent it to me in the hope that if Gandolph's been up to his old tricks I'll spot what they are."

The working day presented no opportunity for a look at *Poison at Paraleash*, but at eight o'clock that night Wexford opened it and read Gandolph's long introduction.

Gandolph began by saying that as a criminologist he had always been aware of the Winchurch case and of the doubt that many felt about Florence Winchurch's guilt. Therefore, when he was staying with friends in Boston, Massachusetts, some two years before and they spoke to him of an acquaintance of theirs who was the niece of one of the principals in the case, he had asked to be introduced to her. The niece was Ada Hurst's daughter, Lina, still Miss Hurst, seventy-four years old and suffering from a terminal illness.

Miss Hurst showed no particular interest in the events of March 1900. She had been brought up by her father and his second wife and had hardly known her uncle. All her mother's property had come into her possession, including the diary, which Ada Fenton Hurst had kept for three years prior to Edward Winchurch's death. Lina Hurst told Gandolph she had kept the diary for sentimental reasons but that he might borrow it and after her death she would see that it passed to him.

Within weeks Lina Hurst did die and her stepbrother, who was her executor, had the diary sent to Gandolph. Gandolph had read it and had been enormously excited by certain entries because in his view they incriminated Frank Fenton and exonerated Florence Winchurch. Here Wexford turned back a few pages and noted the author's dedication: *In memory of Miss Lina Hurst, of Cambridge, Massachusetts, without whose help this reappraisal would have been impossible.*

More than this Wexford had no time to read that evening, but he returned to it on the following day. The diary, it appeared, was a five-year one. At the top of each page was the date, as it might be April I, and beneath that five spaces each headed 18 . . . There was room for the diarist to write perhaps forty or fifty words in each space, no more. On the January 1 page in the third heading down, the number of the year, the eight had been crossed out and a nine substituted, and so it went on for every subsequent entry until March 6, after which no more entries were made until the diarist resumed in December 1900, by which time she and her brother were in Boston.

Wexford proceeded to Gandolph's first chapters. The story he had to tell was substantially the same as Hallam Saul's, and it was not until he came to chapter five and the weeks preceding the crime that he began to concentrate on the character of Frank Fenton. Fenton, he suggested, wanted Mrs. Winchurch for the money and property she would inherit on her husband's death. Far from encouraging Florence to seek a divorce, he urged her never to let her husband suspect her preference for another man. Divorce would have left Florence penniless and homeless and have ruined his career. Fenton had known that it was only by making away with Winchurch and so arranging things that the death appeared natural, that he could have money, his profession, and Florence.

There was only his word for it, said Gandolph, that he had spoken to Florence of botulism and had warned her against these particular canned herrings. Of course he had never seriously expected those cans to infect Winchurch, but that the fish should be eaten by him was necessary for his strategy. On the night before Winchurch's death, after dining with his sister at Paraleash House, he had introduced strychnine into the port decanter. He had also, Gandolph suggested, contrived to bring the conversation around to a discussion of food and to fish dishes. From that it would have been a short step to get Winchurch to admit how much he had enjoyed *Filets de hareng marinés à la Rosette* and to ask Florence to have them served again on the following day. Edward, apparently would have been highly likely to take his doctor's advice, even when in health, even on such a matter as what he should eat for the fourth course of his dinner, while Edward's wife did everything her lover, if not her husband, told her to do.

It was no surprise to Frank Fenton to be called out on the following evening to a man whose spasms only he would recognize as symptomatic of having swallowed strychnine. The arrival of Dr. Waterfield was an unlooked-for circumstance. Once Winchurch's symptoms had been defined as arising from strychnine poisoning there was nothing left for Fenton to do but shift the blame on to his mistress. Gandolph suggested that Fenton attributed the source of the strychnine to Anstruther's chemist's shop out of revenge on Anstruther for calling in Waterfield and thus frustrating his hopes.

And what grounds had Gandolph for believing all this? Certain entries in Ada Hurst's diary. Wexford read them slowly and carefully.

For February 27, 1900, she had written, filling the entire small space: *Very cold. Leg painful again today. FW sent round the carriage and had John drive me to Pomfret. Compton says rats in the cellars and the old stables. Dined at home with F who says rats carry leptospiral jaundice, must be got rid of.* 28 February: *Drove in FW's carriage to call on old Mrs. Paget. FW still here, having tea with F when I returned. I hope there is no harm in it. Dare I warn F?* 29 February: *F destroyed twenty rats with strychnine from his dispensary. What a relief!* 1 March: *Poor old Mrs. Paget passed away in the night. A merciful release. Compton complained about the rats again. Warmer this evening and raining.* There was no entry for 2 March. 3 March: *Annie gave notice, she is getting married. Shall be sorry to lose her. Would not go out in carriage for fear of leaving FW too much alone with F. To bed early as leg most painful.* 4 March: *My birthday. 26 today and an old maid now, I think. FW drove over, brought me beautiful Indian shawl. She is always kind. Invited F and me to dinner tomorrow.* There was no entry for 5 March, and the last entry for nine months was the one for 6 March: *Dined last night at Paraleash House, six guests besides ourselves and the Ws. F left cigar case in the dining room, went back after seeing me home. I hope and pray there is no harm.*

Gandolph was evidently basing his case on the entries for 29 February and 6 March. In telling the court he had no strychnine in his dispensary,

Fenton had lied. He had had an obvious opportunity for the introduction of strychnine into the decanter when he returned to Paraleash House in pursuit of his mislaid cigar case, and when he no doubt took care that he entered the dining room alone.

The next day Wexford reread the chapters in which the new information was contained and he studied with concentration the section concerning the diary. But unless Gandolph were simply lying about the existence of the diary or of those two entries—things that he would hardly dare to do—there seemed no reason to differ from his inference. Florence was innocent, Frank Fenton the murderer of Edward Winchurch. But still Wexford wished Burden were there so that they might have one of their often acrimonious but always fruitful discussions. Somehow, with old Mike to argue against him and put up opposition, he felt things might have been better clarified.

And the morning brought news of Burden, if not the inspector himself, in the form of a postcard from Agios Nikolaios. The blue Aegean, a rocky escarpment, green pines. Who but Burden, as Wexford remarked to Dora, would send postcards while on his honeymoon? The post also brought a parcel from Carlyon Brent. It contained books, a selection from the publishing house's current list as a present for Wexford, and on the compliments slip accompanying them, a note from Amyas Ireland. *I shall be in Kingsmarkham with my people at the weekend. Can we meet? AI.* The books were the latest novel about Regency London by Camilla Barnet; *Put Money in Thy Purse,* the biography of Vassili Vandrian, the financier; the memoirs of Sofya Bolkinska, Bolshoi ballerina; and omnibus version of three novels of farming life by Giles de Coverley; the *Cosmos Book of Stars and Calendars;* and Vernon Trevor's short stories, *Raise Me Up Samuel.* Wexford wondered if he would ever have time to read them, but he enjoyed looking at them, their handsome glossy jackets, and smelling the civilized, aromatic, slightly acrid print smell of them. At ten he phoned Amyas Ireland, thanked him for the present and said he had read *Poison at Paraleash.*

"We can talk about it?"

"Sure. I'll be at home all Saturday and Sunday."

"Let me take you and Mrs. Wexford out to dinner on Saturday night," said Ireland.

But Dora refused. She would be an embarrassment to both of them, she said, they would have their talk much better without her, and she would spend the evening at home having a shot at making a coil pot on her own. So Wexford went alone to meet Ireland in the bar of the Olive and Dove.

"I suppose," he said, accepting a glass of Moselle, "that we can dispense with the fiction that you wanted me to read this book to check on police methods and court procedure? Not to put too fine a point on it, you were apprehensive Gandolph might have been up to his old tricks again?"

"Oh, well now, come," said Ireland. He seemed thinner than ever. He looked about him, he looked at Wexford, made a face, wrinkling up nose and mouth. "Well, if you must put it like that—yes."

"There may not have been any tricks, though, may there? Paxton couldn't have murdered James Conyngford, but that doesn't mean he didn't tell Gandolph he did murder him. Certainly the people who give Gandolph information seem to die very conveniently soon afterward. He picks on the dying, first Paxton, then Lina Hurst. I suppose you've seen this diary?"

"Oh yes. We shall be using prints of the two relevant pages among the illustrations."

"No possibility of forgery?"

Ireland looked unhappy. "Ada Hurst wrote a very stylized hand, what's called a *ronde* hand, which she had obviously taught herself. It would be easy to forge. I can't submit it to handwriting experts, can I? I'm not a policeman. I'm just a poor publisher who very much wants to publish this reappraisal of the Winchurch case if it's genuine—and shun it like the plague it it's not."

"I think it's genuine." Wexford smiled at the slight lightening in Ireland's face. "I take it that it was usual for Ada Hurst to leave blanks as she did for March second and March fifth?"

Ireland nodded. "Quite usual. Every month there'd have been half a dozen days on which she made no entries." A waiter came up to them with two large menus. "I'll have the bouillabaisse and the lamb *en croûte* and the *médaillon* potatoes and french beans."

"Consommé and then the parma ham," said Wexford austerely. When the waiter had gone he grinned at Ireland. "Pity they don't do *Filets de hareng marinés à la Rosette*. It might have provided us with the authentic atmosphere." He was silent for a moment, savoring the delicate tangy wine. "I'm assuming you've checked that 1900 genuinely was a Leap Year?"

"All first years of a century are."

Wexford thought about it. "Yes, of course, all years divisible by four are Leap Years."

"I must say it's a great relief to me you're so happy about it."

"I wouldn't quite say that," said Wexford.

They went into the dining room and were shown, at Ireland's request, to a sheltered corner table. A waiter brought a bottle of Château de Portets 1973. Wexford looked at the basket of rolls, croissants, little plump brioches, miniature wholemeal loaves, Italian sticks, swallowed his desire and refused with an abrupt shake of the head. Ireland took two croissants.

"What exactly do you mean?" he asked.

"It strikes me as being odd," said the chief inspector, "that in the entry for February twenty-ninth Ada Hurst says that her brother destroyed twenty rats with strychnine, yet in the entry for March first that Compton, whom I take to be the gardener, is still complaining about the rats. Why wasn't he told how effective the strychnine had been? Hadn't he been taken into Fenton's confidence about the poisoning? Or was twenty only a very small percentage of the hordes of rats that infested the place?"

"Right. It is odd. What else?"

"I don't know why, on March sixth, she mentions Fenton's returning for the cigar case. It wasn't interesting and she was limited for space. She doesn't record the name of a single guest at the dinner party, doesn't say what any of the women wore, but she carefully notes that her brother had left his cigar case in the Paraleash House dining room and had to go back for it. Why does she?"

"Oh, surely because by now she's nervous whenever Frank is alone with Florence."

"But he wouldn't have been alone with Florence, Winchurch would have been there."

They discussed the script throughout the meal, and later pored over it, Ireland with his brandy, Wexford with coffee. Dora had been wise not to come. But the outcome was that the new facts were really new and sound and that Carlyon Brent could safely publish the book in the spring. Wexford got home to find Dora sitting with a wobbly looking half-finished coil pot beside her and deep in the *Cosmos Book of Stars and Calendars*.

"Reg, did you know that for the Greeks the year began on Midsummer Day? And that the Chinese and Jewish calendars have twelve months in some years and thirteen in others?"

"I can't say I did."

"We avoid that, you see, by using the Gregorian Calendar and correct the error by making every fourth year a Leap Year. You really must read this book, it's fascinating."

But Wexford's preference was for the Vassili Vandrian and the farming trilogy, though with little time to read he hadn't completed a single one of these works by the time Burden returned on the following Monday week. Burden had a fine even tan but for his nose, which had peeled.

"Have a good time?" asked Wexford with automatic politeness.

"What a question," said the inspector, "to ask a man who has just come back from his honeymoon. Of course I had a good time." He cautiously scratched his nose. "What have you been up to?"

"Seeing something of your brother-in-law. He got me to read a manuscript."

"Ha!" said Burden. "I know what that was. He said something about it but he knew Gandolph'd get short shrift from me. A devious liar if ever there was one. It beats me what sort of satisfaction a man can get out of the kind of fame that comes from foisting on the public stories he *knows* aren't true. All that about Paxton was a pack of lies, and I've no doubt he bases this new version of the Winchurch case on another pack of lies. He's not interested in the truth. He's only interested in being known as the great criminologist and the man who shows the police up for fools."

"Come on, Mike, that's a bit sweeping. I told Ireland I thought it would be OK to go ahead and publish."

Burden's face wore an expression that was almost a caricature of sophisticated scathing knowingness. "Well, of course, I haven't seen it, I can't say. I'm basing my objection to Gandolph on the Paxton affair. Paxton never confessed to any murder and Gandolph knows it."

"You can't say that for sure."

Burden sat down. He tapped his fist lightly on the corner of the desk. "I *can* say. I knew Paxton, I knew him well."

"I didn't know that."

"No, it was years back, before I came here. In Eastbourne, it was, when Paxton was with the Garfield gang. In the force down there we knew it was useless ever trying to get Paxton to talk. He *never* talked. I don't mean he just didn't give away any info, I mean he didn't answer when you spoke to him. Various times we tried to interrogate him he just maintained this total silence. A mate of his told me he'd made it a rule not to talk to policemen or social workers or lawyers or any what you might call establishment people, and he never had. He talked to his wife and his kids and his mates all right. But I remember once he was in the dock at Lewes Assizes and the judge addressed him. He just didn't answer—he wouldn't—and the judge, it was old Clydesdale, sent him down for contempt. So don't tell me Paxton made any sort of confession to Kenneth Gandolph, not *Paxton.*"

The effect of this was to reawaken all Wexford's former doubts. He trusted Burden, he had a high opinion of his opinion. He began to wish he had advised Ireland to have tests made to determine the age of the ink used in the 29 February and 6 March entries, or to have the writing examined by a handwriting expert. Yet if Ada Hurst had had a stylized hand self-taught in adulthood . . . What good were handwriting experts anyway? Not much, in his experience. And of course Ireland couldn't suggest to Gandolph that the ink should be tested without offending the man to such an extent that he would refuse publication of *Poison at Paraleash* to Carlyon Brent. But Wexford was suddenly certain that those entries were false and that Gandolph had forged them. Very subtly and cunningly he had forged them, having judged that the addition to the diary of just thirty-four words would alter the whole balance of the Winchurch case and shift the culpability from Florence to her lover.

Thirty-four words. Wexford had made a copy of the diary entries and now he looked at them again. 29 February: *F destroyed twenty rats with strychnine from his dispensary. What a relief!* 6 March: *F left cigar case in the dining room, went back after seeing me home. I hope and pray there is no harm.* There were no anachronisms—men certainly used cigar cases in 1900—no divergence from Ada's usual style. The word "twenty" was written in letters instead of two figures. The writer, on 6 March, had written not about that day but about the day before. Did that amount to anything? Wexford thought not, though he pondered on it for most of the day.

That evening he was well into the last chapter of *Put Money in Thy Purse* when the phone rang. It was Jenny Burden. Would he and Dora come to dinner on Saturday? Her parents would be there and her brother.

Wexford said Dora was out at her pottery class, but yes, they would love to, and had she had a nice time in Crete?

"How sweet of you to ask," said the bride. "No one else has. Thank you, we had a lovely time."

He had meant it when he said they would love to, but still he didn't feel very happy about meeting Amyas Ireland again. He had a notion that once the book was published some as yet unimagined Warren or Burden would turn up and denounce it, deride it, laugh at the glaring giveaway he and Ireland couldn't see. When he saw Ireland again he ought to say, don't do it, don't take the risk, publish and be damned can have another meaning than the popular one. But how to give such a warning with no sound reason for giving it, with nothing but one of those vague feelings, this time of foreboding, which had so assisted him yet run him into so much trouble in the past? No, there was nothing he could do. He sighed, finished his chapter and moved on to the farmer's fictionalized memoirs.

Afterward Wexford was in the habit of saying that he got more reading done during that week than he had in years. Perhaps it had been a way of escape from fretful thought. But certainly he had passed a freakishly slack week, getting home most nights by six. He even read Miss Camilla Barnet's *The Golden Reticule,* and by Friday night there was nothing left but the *Cosmos Book of Stars and Calendars.*

It was a large party, Mr. and Mrs. Ireland and their son, Burden's daughter Pat, Grace and her husband, and, of course, the Burdens themselves. Jenny's face glowed with happiness and Aegean sunshine. She welcomed the Wexfords with kisses and brought them drinks served in their own wedding present to her.

The meeting with Amyas Ireland wasn't the embarrassment Wexford had feared it would be—had feared, that is, up till a few minutes before he and Dora had left home. And now he knew that he couldn't contain himself till after dinner, till the morning, or perhaps worse than that—a phone call on Monday morning. He asked his hostess if she would think him very rude if he spoke to her brother alone for five minutes.

She laughed. "Not rude at all. I think you must have got the world's most wonderful idea for a crime novel and Ammy's going to publish it. But I don't know where to put you unless it's the kitchen. And you," she said to her brother, "are not to eat anything, mind."

"I couldn't wait," Wexford said as they found themselves stowed away into the kitchen where every surface was necessarily loaded with the constituents of dinner for ten people. "I only found out this evening at the last minute before we were due to come out."

"It's something about the Winchurch book?"

Wexford said eagerly, "It's not too late, is it? I was worried I might be too late."

"Good God, no. We hadn't planned to start printing before the autumn." Ireland, who had seemed about to disobey his sister and help himself to a macaroon from a silver dish, suddenly lost his appetite. "This is serious?"

"Wait till you hear. I was waiting for my wife to finish dressing." He grinned. "You should make it a rule to read your own books, you know.

That's what I was doing, reading one of those books you sent me and that's where I found it. You won't be able to publish *Poison at Paraleash.*" The smile went and he looked almost fierce. "I've no hesitation in saying Kenneth Gandolph is a forger and a cheat and you'd be advised to have nothing to do with him in future."

Ireland's eyes narrowed. "Better know it now than later. What did he do and how do you know?"

From his jacket pocket Wexford took the copy he had made of the diary entries. "I can't prove that the last entry, the one for March sixth that says, *F left cigar case in the dining room, went back after seeing me home,* I can't prove that's forged, I only think it is. What I know for certain is a forgery is the entry for February twenty-ninth."

"Isn't that the one about strychnine?"

"*F destroyed twenty rats with strychnine from his dispensary. What a relief!*"

"How do you know it's forged?"

"Because the day itself didn't occur," said Wexford. "In 1900 there was no February twenty-ninth, it wasn't a Leap Year."

"Oh yes, it was. We've been through all that before." Ireland sounded both relieved and impatient. "All years divisible by four are Leap Years. All century years are divisible by four and 1900 was a century year. 1897 was the year she began the diary, following 1896 which was a Leap Year. Needless to say, there was no February twenty-ninth in 1897, 1898, or 1899 so there must have been one in 1900."

"It wasn't a Leap Year," said Wexford. "Didn't I tell you I found this out through that book of yours, the *Cosmos Book of Stars and Calendars?* There's a lot of useful information in there, and one of the bits of information is about how Pope Gregory composed a new civil calendar to correct the errors of the Julian Calendar. One of his rulings was that every fourth year should be a Leap Year except in certain cases . . ."

Ireland interrupted him. "I don't believe it!" he said in the voice of someone who knows he believes every word.

Wexford shrugged. He went on, "Century years were not to be Leap Years unless they were divisible not by four but by four hundred. Therefore, 1600 would have been a Leap Year if the Gregorian Calendar had by then been adopted, and 2000 will be a Leap Year, but 1800 was not and 1900 was not. So in 1900 there was no February twenty-ninth and Ada Hurst left the space on that page blank for the very good reason that the day following February twenty-eighth was March first. Unluckily for him, Gandolph, like you and me and most people, knew nothing of this as otherwise he would surely have inserted his strychnine entry into the blank space of March second and his forgery might never have been discovered."

Ireland slowly shook his head at man's ingenuity and perhaps his chicanery. "I'm very grateful to you. We should have looked fools, shouldn't we?"

"I'm glad Florence wasn't hanged in error," Wexford said as they went back to join the others. "Her marriage didn't begin with dearly beloved, but if she was afraid at the end it can't have been with any amazement."

Like a Lamb to Slaughter

Author: Lawrence Block (1938–)

Detective: Matt Scudder (1976)

By the time he created private eye Matt Scudder, Block was already regarded as one of the solidest and most versatile of mystery pros. But the Scudder series, with its depth of character and background, took him to new levels of both commercial and critical success. Born a drunken unlicensed private eye in *In the Midst of Death* (1976), Scudder later gets sober with the help of Alcoholics Anonymous and generally straightens out his life. One might have thought this newfound prosperity and relative happiness would destroy Scudder as a series character, but the later novels, including the Edgar-winning *A Dance at the Slaughterhouse* (1991), are among the best.

The title story of Block's 1984 short-story collection, "Like a Lamb to Slaughter," was first published in *Alfred Hitchcock's Mystery Magazine*, November 1977, as "A Candle for the Bag Lady." It's from early in Matt Scudder's career, but it captures his distinctiveness among contemporary private eyes.

He was a thin young man in a blue pinstripe suit. His shirt was white with a button-down collar. His glasses had oval lenses in brown tortoiseshell frames. His hair was a dark brown, short but not severely so, neatly combed, parted on the right. I saw him come in and watched him ask a question at the bar. Billie was working afternoons that week. I watched as he nodded at the young man, then swung his sleepy eyes over in my direction. I lowered my own eyes and looked at a cup of coffee laced with bourbon while the fellow walked over to my table.

"Matthew Scudder?" I looked up at him, nodded. "I'm Aaron Creighton. I looked for you at your hotel. The fellow on the desk told me I might find you here."

Here was Armstrong's, a Ninth Avenue saloon around the corner from my Fifty-seventh Street hotel. The lunch crowd was gone except for a couple of stragglers in front whose voices were starting to thicken with alcohol. The streets outside were full of May sunshine. The winter had been cold and deep and long. I couldn't recall a more welcome spring.

"I called you a couple of times last week, Mr. Scudder. I guess you didn't get my messages."

I'd gotten two of them and ignored them, not knowing who he was or what he wanted and unwilling to spend a dime for the answer. But I went along with the fiction. "It's a cheap hotel," I said. "They're not always too good about messages."

"I can imagine. Uh. Is there someplace we can talk?"

"How about right here?"

He looked around. I don't suppose he was used to conducting his business in bars but he evidently decided it would be all right to make an exception. He set his briefcase on the floor and seated himself across the table from me. Angela, the new day-shift waitress, hurried over to get his order. He glanced at my cup and said he'd have coffee, too.

"I'm an attorney," he said. My first thought was that he didn't look like a lawyer, but then I realized he probably dealt with civil cases. My experience as a cop had given me a lot of experience with criminal lawyers. The breed ran to several types, none of them his.

I waited for him to tell me why he wanted to hire me. But he crossed me up.

"I'm handling an estate," he said, and paused, and gave what seemed a calculated if well-intentioned smile. "It's my pleasant duty to tell you you've come into a small legacy, Mr. Scudder."

"Someone's left me money?"

"Twelve hundred dollars."

Who could have died? I'd lost touch long since with any of my relatives. My parents went years ago and we'd never been close with the rest of the family.

I said, "Who—?"

"Mary Alice Redfield."

I repeated the name aloud. It was not entirely unfamiliar but I had no idea who Mary Alice Redfield might be. I looked at Aaron Creighton. I couldn't make out his eyes behind the glasses but there was a smile's ghost on his thin lips, as if my reaction was not unexpected.

"She's dead?"

"Almost three months ago."

"I didn't know her."

"She knew you. You probably knew her, Mr. Scudder. Perhaps you didn't know her by name." His smile deepened. Angela had brought his coffee. He stirred milk and sugar into it, took a careful sip, nodded his approval. "Miss Redfield was murdered." He said this as if he'd had practice uttering a phrase that did not come naturally to him. "She was killed quite brutally in late February for no apparent reason, another innocent victim of street crime."

"She lived in New York?"

"Oh, yes. In this neighborhood."

"And she was killed around here?"

"On West Fifty-fifth Street between Ninth and Tenth avenues. Her body was found in an alleyway. She'd been stabbed repeatedly and strangled with the scarf she had been wearing."

Late February. Mary Alice Redfield. West Fifty-fifth between Ninth and Tenth. Murder most foul. Stabbed and strangled, a dead woman in an alleyway. I usually kept track of murders, perhaps out of a vestige of professionalism, perhaps because I couldn't cease to be fascinated by man's inhumanity to man. Mary Alice Redfield had willed me twelve hundred dollars. And someone had knifed and strangled her, and—

"Oh, Jesus," I said. "The shopping bag lady."

Aaron Creighton nodded.

New York is full of them. East Side, West Side, each neighborhood has its own supply of bag women. Some of them are alcoholic but most of them have gone mad without any help from drink. They walk the streets, huddle on stoops or in doorways. They find sermons in stones and treasures in trashcans. They talk to themselves, to passersby, to God. Sometimes they mumble. Now and then they shriek.

They carry things around with them, the bag women. The shopping bags supply their generic name and their chief common denominator. Most of them seem to be paranoid, and their madness convinces them that their possessions are very valuable, that their enemies covet them. So their shopping bags are never out of their sight.

There used to be a colony of these ladies who lived in Grand Central Station. They would sit up all night in the waiting room, taking turns waddling off to the lavatory from time to time. They rarely talked to each other but some herd instinct made them comfortable with one another. But they were not comfortable enough to trust their precious bags to one another's safekeeping, and each sad, crazy lady always toted her shopping bags to and from the ladies' room.

Mary Alice Redfield had been a shopping bag lady. I don't know when she set up shop in the neighborhood. I'd been living in the same hotel ever since I resigned from the NYPD and separated from my wife and sons, and that was getting to be quite a few years now. Had Miss Redfield been on the scene that long ago? I couldn't remember her first appearance. Like so many of the neighborhood fixtures, she had been part of the scenery. Had her death not been violent and abrupt I might never have noticed she was gone.

I'd never known her name. But she had evidently known mine, and had felt something for me that prompted her to leave money to me. How had she come to have money to leave?

She'd had a business of sorts. She would sit on a wooden soft drink case, surrounded by three or four shopping bags, and she would sell newspapers. There's an all-night newsstand at the corner of Fifty-seventh and Eighth, and she would buy a few dozen papers there, carry them a block west to the corner of Ninth and set up shop in a doorway. She sold the papers at retail, though I suppose some people tipped her a few cents. I could remember a few occasions when I'd bought a paper and waved away change from a dollar bill. Bread upon the waters, perhaps, if that was what had moved her to leave me the money.

I closed my eyes, brought her image into focus. A thick-set woman, stocky rather than fat. Five-three or -four. Dressed usually in shapeless clothing, colorless gray and black garments, layers of clothing that varied with the season. I remembered that she would sometimes wear a hat, an old straw affair with paper and plastic flowers poked into it. And I remembered her eyes, large guileless blue eyes that were many years younger than the rest of her.

Mary Alice Redfield.

"Family money," Aaron Creighton was saying. "She wasn't wealthy but she had come from a family that was comfortably fixed. A bank in Baltimore handled her funds. That's where she was from originally, Baltimore, though she'd lived in New York for as long as anyone can remember. The bank sent her a check every month. Not very much, a couple of hundred dollars, but she hardly spent anything. She paid her rent—"

"I thought she lived on the street."

"No, she had a furnished room a few doors down the street from where she was killed. She lived in another rooming house on Tenth Avenue before that but moved when the building was sold. That was six or seven years ago and she lived on Fifty-fifth Street from then until her death. Her room cost her eighty dollars a month. She spent a few dollars on food. I don't know what she did with the rest. The only money in her room was a coffee can full of pennies. I've been checking the banks and there's no record of a savings account. I suppose she may have spent it or lost it or given it away. She wasn't very firmly grounded in reality."

"No, I don't suppose she was."

He sipped at his coffee. "She probably belonged in an institution," he said. "At least that's what people would say, but she got along in the outside world, she functioned well enough. I don't know if she kept herself clean and I don't know anything about how her mind worked but I think she must have been happier than she would have been in an institution. Don't you think?"

"Probably."

"Of course she wasn't safe, not as it turned out, but anybody can get killed on the streets of New York." He frowned briefly, caught up in a private thought. Then he said, "She came to our office ten years ago. That was before my time." He told me the name of his firm, a string of Anglo-Saxon surnames. "She wanted to draw a will. The original will was a very simple document leaving everything to her sister. Then over the years she would come in from time to time to add codicils leaving specific sums to various persons. She had made a total of thirty-two bequests by the time she died. One was for twenty dollars—that was to a man named John Johnson whom we haven't been able to locate. The remainder all ranged from five hundred to two thousand dollars." He smiled. "I've been given the task of running down the heirs."

"When did she put me into her will?"

"Two years ago in April."

I tried to think what I might have done for her then, how I might have brushed her life with mine. Nothing.

"Of course the will could be contested, Mr. Scudder. It would be easy to challenge Miss Redfield's competence and any relative could almost certainly get it set aside. But no one wishes to challenge it. The total amount involved is slightly in excess of a quarter of a million dollars—"

"That much."

"Yes. Miss Redfield received substantially less than the income that her holdings drew over the years, so the principal kept growing during her lifetime. Now the specific bequests she made total thirty-eight thousand dollars, give or take a few hundred, and the residue goes to Miss Redfield's sister. The sister—her name is Mrs. Palmer—is a widow with grown children. She's hospitalized with cancer and heart trouble and I believe diabetic complications and she hasn't long to live. Her children would like to see the estate settled before their mother dies and they have enough local prominence to hurry the will through probate. So I'm authorized to tender checks for the full amount of the specific bequests on the condition that the legatees sign quitclaims acknowledging that this payment discharges in full the estate's indebtedness to them."

There was more legalese of less importance. Then he gave me papers to sign and the whole procedure ended with a check on the table. It was payable to me and in the amount of twelve hundred dollars and no cents.

I told Creighton I'd pay for his coffee.

I had time to buy myself another drink and still get to my bank before the windows closed. I put a little of Mary Alice Redfield's legacy in my savings account, took some in cash, and sent a money order to Anita and my sons. I stopped at my hotel to check for messages. There weren't any. I had a drink at McGovern's and crossed the street to have another at Polly's Cage. It wasn't five o'clock yet but the bar was doing good business already.

It turned into a funny night. I had dinner at the Greek place and read the *Post,* spent a little time at Joey Farrell's on Fifty-eighth Street, then wound up getting to Armstrong's around ten-thirty or thereabouts. I spent part of the evening alone at my usual table and part of it in conversation at the bar. I made a point of stretching my drinks, mixing my bourbon with coffee, making a cup last a while, taking a glass of plain water from time to time.

But that never really works. If you're going to get drunk you'll manage it somehow. The obstacles I placed in my path just kept me up later. By two-thirty I'd done what I had set out to do. I'd made my load and I could go home and sleep it off.

I woke around ten with less of a hangover than I'd earned and no memory of anything after I'd left Armstrong's. I was in my own bed in my own hotel room. And my clothes were hung neatly in the closet, always a good sign on a morning after. So I must have been in fairly good shape. But a certain amount of time was lost to memory, blacked out, gone.

When that first started happening I tended to worry about it. But it's the sort of thing you can get used to.

It was the money, the twelve hundred bucks. I couldn't understand the money. I had done nothing to deserve it. It had been left to me by a poor little rich woman whose name I'd not even known.

It had never occurred to me to refuse the dough. Very early in my career as a cop I'd learned an important precept. When someone put money in your hand you closed your fingers around it and put it in your pocket. I learned that lesson well and never had cause to regret its application. I didn't walk around with my hand out and I never took drug or homicide money but I certainly grabbed all the clean graft that came my way and a certain amount that wouldn't have stood a white glove inspection. If Mary Alice thought I merited twelve hundred dollars, who was I to argue?

Ah, but it didn't quite work that way. Because somehow the money gnawed at me.

After breakfast I went to St. Paul's but there was a service going on, a priest saying Mass, so I didn't stay. I walked down to St. Benedict the Moor's on Fifty-third Street and sat for a few minutes in a pew at the rear. I go to churches to try to think, and I gave it a shot but my mind didn't know where to go.

I slipped six twenties into the poor box. I tithe. It's a habit I got into after I left the department and I still don't know why I do it. God knows. Or maybe He's as mystified as I am. This time, though, there was a certain balance in the act. Mary Alice Redfield had given me twelve hundred dollars for no reason I could comprehend. I was passing on a ten percent commission to the church for no better reason.

I stopped on the way out and lit a couple of candles for various people who weren't alive anymore. One of them was for the bag lady. I didn't see how it could do her any good, but I couldn't imagine how it could harm her, either.

I had read some press coverage of the killing when it happened. I generally keep up with crime stories. Part of me evidently never stopped being a policeman. Now I went down to the Forty-second Street library to refresh my memory.

The *Times* had run a pair of brief back-page items, the first a report of the killing of an unidentified female derelict, the second a follow-up giving her name and age. She'd been forty-seven, I learned. This surprised me, and then I realized that any specific number would have come as a surprise. Bums and bag ladies are ageless. Mary Alice Redfield could have been thirty or sixty or anywhere in between.

The *News* had run a more extended article than the *Times,* enumerating the stab wounds—twenty-six of them—and described the scarf wound about her throat—blue and white, a designer print, but tattered at its edges and evidently somebody's castoff. It was this article that I remembered having read.

But the *Post* had really played the story. It had appeared shortly after the new owner took over the paper and the editors were going all out for human interest, which always translates out as sex and violence. The brutal killing of a woman touches both of those bases, and this had the added kick that she was a character. If they'd ever learned she was an heiress it would have been page three material, but even without that knowledge they did all right by her.

The first story they ran was straight news reporting, albeit embellished with reports on the blood, the clothes she was wearing, the litter in the alley where she was found and all that sort of thing. The next day a reporter pushed the pathos button and tapped out a story featuring capsule interviews with people in the neighborhood. Only a few of them were identified by name and I came away with the feeling that he'd made up some peachy quotes and attributed them to unnamed nonexistent hangers-on. As a sidebar to that story, another reporter speculated on the possibility of a whole string of bag lady murders, a speculation that happily had turned out to be off the mark. The clown had presumably gone around the West Side asking shopping bag ladies if they were afraid of being the killer's next victim. I hope he faked the piece and let the ladies alone.

And that was about it. When the killer failed to strike again the newspapers hung up on the story. Good news is no news.

I walked back from the library. It was fine weather. The winds had blown all the crap out of the sky and there was nothing but blue overhead. The air actually had some air in it for a change. I walked west on Forty-second Street and north on Broadway, and I started noticing the number of street people, the drunks and the crazies and the unclassifiable derelicts. By the time I got within a few blocks of Fifty-seventh Street I was recognizing a large percentage of them. Each mini-neighborhood has its own human flotsam and jetsam and they're a lot more noticeable come springtime. Winter sends some of them south and others to shelter, and there's a certain percentage who die of exposure, but when the sun warms the pavement it brings most of them out again.

When I stopped for a paper at the corner of Eighth Avenue I got the bag lady into the conversation. The newsie clucked his tongue and shook his head. "The damnedest thing. Just the damnedest thing."

"Murder never makes much sense."

"The hell with murder. You know what she did? You know Eddie, works for me midnight to eight? Guy with the one droopy eyelid? Now he wasn't the guy used to sell her the stack of papers. Matter of fact that was usually me. She'd come by during the late morning or early afternoon and she'd take fifteen or twenty papers and pay me for 'em, and then she'd sit on her crate down the next corner and she'd sell as many as she could, and then she'd bring 'em back and I'd give her a refund on what she didn't sell."

"What did she pay for them?"

"Full price. And that's what she sold 'em for. The hell, I can't discount on papers. You know the margin we got. I'm not even supposed to take 'em back, but what difference does it make? It gave the poor woman something to do is my theory. She was important, she was a businesswoman. Sits there charging a quarter for something she just paid a quarter for, it's no way to get rich, but you know something? She had money. Lived like a pig but she had money."

"So I understand."

"She left Eddie seven-twenty. You believe that? Seven hundred and twenty dollars, she willed it to him, there was this lawyer come around two, three weeks ago with a check. Eddie Halloran. Pay to the order of. You believe that? She never had dealings with him. I sold her the papers, I bought 'em back from her. Not that I'm complaining, not that I want the woman's money, but I ask you this: Why Eddie? He don't know her. He can't believe she knows his name, Eddie Halloran. Why'd she leave it to him? He tells this lawyer, he says maybe she's got some other Eddie Halloran in mind. It's a common Irish name and the neighborhood's full of the Irish. I'm thinking to myself, Eddie, schmuck, take the money and shut up, but it's him all right because it says in the will. Eddie Halloran the news dealer is what it says. So that's him, right? But why Eddie?"

Why me? "Maybe she liked the way he smiled."

"Yeah, maybe. Or the way he combed his hair. Listen, it's money in his pocket. I worried he'd go on a toot, drink it up, but he says money's no temptation. He says he's always got the price of a drink in his jeans and there's a bar on every block but he can walk right past 'em, so why worry about a few hundred dollars? You know something? That crazy woman, I'll tell you something, I miss her. She'd come, crazy hat on her head, spacy look in her eyes, she'd buy her stack of papers and waddle off all businesslike, then she'd bring the leftovers and cash 'em in, and I'd make a joke about her when she was out of earshot, but I miss her."

"I know what you mean."

"She never hurt nobody," he said. "She never hurt a soul."

"Mary Alice Redfield. Yeah, the multiple stabbing and strangulation." He shifted a cud-sized wad of gum from one side of his mouth to the other, pushed a lock of hair off his forehead, and yawned. "What have you got, some new information?"

"Nothing. I wanted to find out what you had."

"Yeah, right."

He worked on the chewing gum. He was a patrolman named Andersen who worked out of the Eighteenth. Another cop, a detective named Guzik, had learned that Andersen had caught the Redfield case and had taken the trouble to introduce the two of us. I hadn't known Andersen when I was on the force. He was younger than I, but then most people are nowadays.

He said, "Thing is, Scudder, we more or less put that one out of the way. It's in an open file. You know how it works. If we get new information, fine, but in the meantime I don't sit up nights thinking about it."

"I just wanted to see what you had."

"Well, I'm kind of tight for time, if you know what I mean. My own personal time, I set a certain store by my own time."

"I can understand that."

"You probably got some relative of the deceased for a client. Wants to find out who'd do such a terrible thing to poor old Cousin Mary. Naturally you're interested because it's a chance to make a buck and a man's gotta make a living. Whether a man's a cop or a civilian he's gotta make a buck, right?"

Uh-huh. I seem to remember that we were subtler in my day, but perhaps that's just age talking. I thought of telling him that I didn't have a client but why should he believe me? He didn't know me. If there was nothing in it for him, why should he bother?

So I said, "You know, we're just a couple weeks away from Memorial Day."

"Yeah, I'll buy a poppy from a Legionnaire. So what else is new?"

"Memorial Day's when women start wearing white shoes and men put straw hats on their heads. You got a new hat for the summer season, Andersen? Because you could use one."

"A man can always use a new hat," he said.

A hat is cop talk for twenty-five dollars. By the time I left the precinct

house Andersen had two tens and a five of Mary Alice Redfield's bequest to me and I had all the data that had turned up to date.

I think Andersen won that one. I now knew that the murder weapon
had been a kitchen knife with a blade approximately seven and a half
inches long. That one of the stab wounds had found the heart and had
probably caused death instantaneously. That it was impossible to determine whether strangulation had taken place before or after death. That
should have been possible to determine—maybe the medical examiner
hadn't wasted too much time checking her out, or maybe he had been
reluctant to commit himself. She'd been dead a few hours when they
found her—the estimate was that she'd died around midnight and the
body wasn't reported until half-past five. That wouldn't have ripened
her all that much, not in winter weather, but most likely her personal
hygiene was nothing to boast about, and she was just a shopping bag
lady and you couldn't bring her back to life, so why knock yourself out
running tests on her malodorous corpse?

I learned a few other things. The landlady's name. The name of the
off-duty bartender, heading home after a nightcap at the neighborhood
after-hours joint, who'd happened on the body and who had been drunk
enough or sober enough to take the trouble to report it. And I learned
the sort of negative facts that turn up in a police report when the case is
headed for an open file—the handful of nonleads that led nowhere, the
witnesses who had nothing to contribute, the routine matters routinely
handled. They hadn't knocked themselves out, Andersen and his partner, but would I have handled it any differently? Why knock yourself
out chasing a murderer you didn't stand much chance of catching?

In the theater, SRO is good news. It means a sellout performance, standing room only. But once you get out of the theater district it means
single room occupancy, and the designation is invariably applied to a
hotel or apartment house that has seen better days.

Mary Alice Redfield's home for the last six or seven years of her life
had started out as an old Rent Law tenement, built around the turn of
the century, six stories tall, faced in red-brown brick, with four apartments to the floor. Now all of those little apartments had been carved
into single rooms as if they were election districts gerrymandered by a
maniac. There was a communal bathroom on each floor and you didn't
need a map to find it.

The manager was a Mrs. Larkin. Her blue eyes had lost most of their
color and half her hair had gone from black to gray but she was still
pert. If she's reincarnated as a bird she'll be a house wren.

She said, "Oh, poor Mary. We're none of us safe, are we, with the streets full of monsters? I was born in this neighborhood and I'll die in it, but please God that'll be of natural causes. Poor Mary. There's some said she should have been locked up, but Jesus, she got along. She lived her life. And she had her check coming in every month and paid her rent on time. She had her own money, you know. She wasn't living off the public like some I could name but won't."

"I know."

"Do you want to see her room? I rented it twice since then. The first one was a young man and he didn't stay. He looked all right but when he left me I was just as glad. He said he was a sailor off a ship and when he left he said he'd got on with another ship and was on his way to Hong Kong or some such place, but I've had no end of sailors and he didn't walk like a sailor so I don't know what he was after doing. Then I could have rented it twelve times but didn't because I won't rent to colored or Spanish. I've nothing against them but I won't have them in the house. The owner says to me, Mrs. Larkin he says, my instructions are to rent to anybody regardless of race or creed or color, but if you was to use your own judgment I wouldn't have to know about it. In other words he don't want them either but he's after covering himself."

"I suppose he has to."

"Oh, with all the laws, but I've had no trouble." She laid a forefinger alongside her nose. It's a gesture you don't see too much these days. "Then I rented poor Mary's room two weeks ago to a very nice woman, a widow. She likes her beer, she does, but why shouldn't she have it? I keep my eye on her and she's making no trouble, and if she wants an old jar now and then whose business is it but her own?" She fixed her blue-gray eyes on me. "You like your drink," she said.

"Is it on my breath?"

"No, but I can see it in your face. Larkin liked his drink and there's some say it killed him but he liked it and a man has a right to live what life he wants. And he was never a hard man when he drank, never cursed or fought or beat a woman as some I could name but won't. Mrs. Shepard's out now. That's the one took poor Mary's room, and I'll show it to you if you want."

So I saw the room. It was kept neat.

"She keeps it tidier than poor Mary," Mrs. Larkin said. "Now Mary wasn't dirty, you understand, but she had all her belongings. Her shopping bags and other things that she kept in her room. She made a mare's nest of the place, and all the years she lived here, you see, it wasn't tidy. I would keep her bed made but she didn't want me touching her things and so I let it be cluttered as she wanted it. She paid her rent on time and made no trouble otherwise. She had money, you know."

"Yes, I know."

"She left some to a woman on the fourth floor. A much younger woman, she'd only moved here three months before Mary was killed, and if she exchanged a word with Mary I couldn't swear to it, but Mary left her almost a thousand dollars. Now Mrs. Klein across the hall lived here since before Mary ever moved in and the two old things always had a good word for each other, and all Mrs. Klein has is the welfare and she could have made good use of a couple of dollars, but Mary left her money instead to Miss Strom." She raised her eyebrows to show bewilderment "Now Mrs. Klein said nothing, and I don't even know if she's had the thought that Mary might have mentioned her in her will, but Miss Strom said she didn't know what to make of it. She just couldn't understand it at all, and what I told her was you can't figure out a woman like poor Mary who never had both her feet on the pavement. Troubled as she was, daft as she was, who's to say what she might have had on her mind?"

"Could I see Miss Strom?"

"That would be for her to say, but she's not home from work yet. She works part-time in the afternoons. She's a close one, not that she hasn't the right to be, and she's never said what it is that she does. But she's a decent sort. This is a decent house."

"I'm sure it is."

"It's single rooms and they don't cost much so you know you're not at the Ritz Hotel, but there's decent people here and I keep it as clean as a person can. When there's not but one toilet on the floor it's a struggle. But it's decent."

"Yes."

"Poor Mary. Why'd anyone kill her? Was it sex, do you know? Not that you could imagine anyone wanting her, the old thing, but try to figure out a madman and you'll go mad your own self. Was she molested?"

"No."

"Just killed, then. Oh, God, save us all. I gave her a home for almost seven years. Which it was no more than my job to do, not making it out to be charity on my part. But I had her here all that time and of course I never knew her, you couldn't get to know a poor old soul like that, but I got used to her. Do you know what I mean?"

"I think so."

"I got used to having her about. I might say 'Hello' and 'Good morning' and 'Isn't it a nice day' and not get a look in reply, but even on those days she was someone familiar to say something to. And she's gone now and we're all of us older, aren't we?"

"We are."

"The poor old thing. How could anyone do it, will you tell me that? How could anyone murder her?"

I don't think she expected an answer. Just as well. I didn't have one.

After dinner I returned for a few minutes of conversation with Genevieve Strom. She had no idea why Miss Redfield had left her the money. She'd received $880 and she was glad to get it because she could use it, but the whole thing puzzled her. "I hardly knew her," she said more than once. "I keep thinking I ought to do something special with the money, but what?"

I made the bars that night but drinking didn't have the urgency it had possessed the night before. I was able to keep it in proportion and to know that I'd wake up the next morning with my memory intact. In the course of things I dropped over to the newsstand a little past midnight and talked with Eddie Halloran. He was looking good and I said as much. I remembered him when he'd gone to work for Sid three years ago. He'd been drawn then, and shaky, and his eyes always moved off to the side of whatever he was looking at. Now there was confidence in his stance and he looked years younger. It hadn't all come back to him and maybe some of it was lost forever. I guess the booze had him pretty good before he kicked it once and for all.

We talked about the bag lady. He said, "Know what I think it is? Somebody's sweeping the streets."

"I don't follow you."

"A cleanup campaign. Few years back, Matt, there was this gang of kids found a new way to amuse theirselves. Pick up a can of gasoline, find some bum down on the Bowery, pour the gas on him and throw a lit match at him. You remember?"

"Yeah, I remember."

"Those kids thought they were patriots. Thought they deserved a medal. They were cleaning up the neighborhood, getting drunken bums off the streets. You know, Matt, people don't like to look at a derelict. That building up the block, the Towers? There's this grating there where the heating system's vented. You remember how the guys would sleep there in the winter. It was warm, it was comfortable, it was free, and two or three guys would be there every night catching some Z's and getting warm. Remember?"

"Uh-huh. Then they fenced it."

"Right. Because the tenants complained. It didn't hurt them any, it was just the local bums sleeping it off, but the tenants pay a lot of rent and they don't like to look at bums on their way in or out of their building. The bums were outside and not bothering anybody but it was the sight of them, you know, so the owners went to the expense of putting up cyclone fencing around where they used to sleep. It looks ugly as hell and all it does is keep the bums out but that's all it's supposed to do."

"That's human beings for you."

He nodded, then turned aside to sell somebody a *Daily News* and a *Racing Form*. Then he said, "I don't know what it is exactly. *I* was a bum, Matt. I got pretty far down. You probably don't know how far. I got as far as the Bowery. I panhandled, I slept in my clothes on a bench or in a doorway. You look at men like that and you think they're just waiting to die, and they are, but some of them come back. And you can't tell for sure who's gonna come back and who's not. Somebody coulda poured gas on me, set me on fire. Sweet Jesus."

"The shopping bag lady—"

"You'll look at a bum and you'll say to yourself, 'Maybe I could get like that and I don't wanta think about it.' Or you'll look at somebody like the shopping bag lady and say, 'I could go nutsy like her so get her out of my sight.' And you get people who think like Nazis. You know, take all the cripples and the lunatics and the retarded kids and all and give 'em an injection and Good-bye, Charlie."

"You think that's what happened to her?"

"What else?"

"But whoever did it stopped at one, Eddie."

He frowned. "Don't make sense," he said. "Unless he did the one job and the next day he got run down by a Ninth Avenue bus, and it couldn't happen to a nicer guy. Or he got scared. All that blood and it was more than he figured on. Or he left town. Could be anything like that."

"Could be."

"There's no other reason, is there? She musta been killed because she was a bag lady, right?"

"I don't know."

"Well, Jesus Christ, Matt. What other reason would anybody have for killing her?"

* * *

The law firm where Aaron Creighton worked had offices on the seventh floor of the Flatiron Building. In addition to the four partners, eleven other lawyers had their names painted on the frosted glass door. Aaron Creighton's came second from the bottom. Well, he was young.

He was also surprised to see me, and when I told him what I wanted he said it was irregular.

"Matter of public record, isn't it?"

"Well, yes," he said. "That means you can find the information. It doesn't mean we're obliged to furnish it to you."

For an instant I thought I was back at the Eighteenth Precinct and a cop was trying to hustle me for the price of a new hat. But Creighton's reservations were ethical. I wanted a list of Mary Alice Redfield's beneficiaries, including the amounts they'd received and the dates they'd been added to her will. He wasn't sure where his duty lay.

"I'd like to be helpful," he said. "Perhaps you could tell me just what your interest is."

"I'm not sure."

"I beg your pardon?"

"I don't know why I'm playing with this one. I used to be a cop, Mr. Creighton. Now I'm a sort of unofficial detective. I don't carry a license but I do things for people and I wind up making enough that way to keep a roof overhead."

His eyes were wary. I guess he was trying to guess how I intended to earn myself a fee out of this.

"I got twelve hundred dollars out of the blue. It was left to me by a woman I didn't really know and who didn't really know me. I can't seem to slough off the feeling that I got the money for a reason. That I've been paid in advance."

"Paid for what?"

"To try and find out who killed her."

"Oh," he said. *"Oh."*

"I don't want to get the heirs together to challenge the will, if that was what was bothering you. And I can't quite make myself suspect that one of her beneficiaries killed her for the money she was leaving him. For one thing, she doesn't seem to have told people they were named in her will. She never said anything to me or to the two people I've spoken with thus far. For another, it wasn't the sort of murder that gets committed for gain. It was deliberately brutal."

"Then why do you want to know who the other beneficiaries are?"

"I don't know. Part of it's cop training. When you've got any specific leads, any hard facts, you run them down before you cast a wider net. That's only part of it. I suppose I want to get more of a sense of the woman. That's probably all I can realistically hope to get, anyway. I don't stand much chance of tracking her killer."

"The police don't seem to have gotten very far."

I nodded. "I don't think they tried too hard. And I don't think they knew she had an estate. I talked to one of the cops on the case and if he had known that he'd have mentioned it to me. There was nothing in her file. My guess is they waited for her killer to run a string of murders so they'd have something more concrete to work with. It's the kind of senseless crime that usually gets repeated." I closed my eyes for a moment, reaching for an errant thought. "But he didn't repeat," I said. "So they put it on a back burner and then they took it off the stove altogether."

"I don't know much about police work. I'm involved largely with estates and trusts." He tried a smile. "Most of my clients die of natural causes. Murder's an exception."

"It generally is. I'll probably never find him. I certainly don't expect to find him. Just killing her and moving on, hell, and it was all those months ago. He could have been a sailor off a ship, got tanked up and went nuts and he's in Macao or Port-au-Prince by now. No witnesses and no clues and no suspects and the trail's three months cold by now, and it's a fair bet the killer doesn't remember what he did. So many murders take place in blackout, you know."

"Blackout?" He frowned. "You don't mean in the dark?"

"Alcoholic blackout. The prisons are full of men who got got drunk and shot their wives or their best friends. Now they're serving twenty-to-life for something they don't remember. No recollection at all."

The idea unsettled him, and he looked especially young now. "That's frightening," he said. "Really terrifying."

"Yes."

"I originally gave some thought to criminal law. My Uncle Jack talked me out of it. He said you either starve or you spend your time helping professional criminals beat the system. He said that was the only way you made good money out of a criminal practice and what you wound up doing was unpleasant and basically immoral. Of course there are a couple of superstar criminal lawyers, the hotshots everybody knows, but the other ninety-nine percent fit what Uncle Jack said."

"I would think so, yes."

"I guess I made the right decision." He took his glasses off, inspected them, decided they were clean, put them back on again. "Sometimes I'm not so sure," he said. "Sometimes I wonder. I'll get that list for you. I should probably check with someone to make sure it's all right but I'm not going to bother. You know lawyers. If you ask them whether it's all right to do something they'll automatically say no. Because inaction is always safer than action and they can't get in trouble for giving you bad advice if they tell you to sit on your hands and do nothing. I'm going overboard. Most of the time I like what I do and I'm proud of my profession. This'll take me a few minutes. Do you want some coffee in the meantime?"

His girl brought me a cup, black, no sugar. No bourbon, either. By the time I was done with the coffee he had the list ready.

"If there's anything else I can do—"

I told him I'd let him know. He walked out to the elevator with me, waited for the cage to come wheezing up, shook my hand. I watched him turn and head back to his office and I had the feeling he'd have preferred to come along with me. In a day or so he'd change his mind, but right now he didn't seem too crazy about his job.

The next week was a curious one. I worked my way through the list Aaron Creighton had given me, knowing what I was doing was essentially purposeless but compulsive about doing it all the same.

There were thirty-two names on the list. I checked off my own and Eddie Halloran and Genevieve Strom. I put additional check marks next to six people who lived outside of New York. Then I had a go at the remaining twenty-three names. Creighton had done most of the spade-work for me, finding addresses to match most of the names. He'd included the date each of the thirty-two codicils had been drawn, and that enabled me to attack the list in reverse chronological order, starting with those persons who'd been made beneficiaries most recently. If this was a method, there was madness to it; it was based on the notion that a person added recently to the will would be more likely to commit homicide for gain, and I'd already decided this wasn't that kind of a killing to begin with.

Well, it gave me something to do. And it led to some interesting conversations. If the people Mary Alice Redfield had chosen to remember ran to any type, my mind wasn't subtle enough to discern it. They ranged in age, in ethnic background, in gender and sexual orientation, in economic status. Most of them were as mystified as Eddie and Genevieve and I about the bag lady's largesse, but once in a while I'd encounter someone who attributed it to some act of kindness he'd performed, and there was a young man named Jerry Forgash who was in no doubt whatsoever. He was some form of Jesus freak and he'd given poor Mary a couple of tracts and a Get Smart—Get Saved button, presumably a twin to the one he wore on the breast pocket of his chambray shirt. I suppose she put his gifts in one of her shopping bags.

"I told her Jesus loved her," he said, "and I suppose it won her soul for Christ. So of course she was grateful. Cast your bread upon the waters, Mr. Scudder. Brother Matthew. You know there was a disciple of Christ named Matthew."

"I know."

He told me Jesus loved me and that I should get smart and get saved. I managed not to get a button but I had to take a couple of tracts from him. I didn't have a shopping bag so I stuck them in my pocket, and a couple of nights later I read them before I went to bed. They didn't win my soul for Christ but you never know.

I didn't run the whole list. People were hard to find and I wasn't in any big rush to find them. It wasn't that kind of a case. It wasn't a case at all, really, merely an obsession, and there was surely no need to race the clock. Or the calendar. If anything, I was probably reluctant to finish up the names on the list. Once I ran out of them I'd have to find some other way to approach the woman's murder and I was damned if I knew where to start.

While I was doing all this, an odd thing happened. The word got around that I was investigating the woman's death, and the whole neighborhood became very much aware of Mary Alice Redfield. People began to seek me out. Ostensibly they had information to give me or theories to advance, but neither the information nor the theories ever seemed to amount to anything substantial, and I came to see that they were merely there as a prelude to conversation. Someone would start off by saying he'd seen Mary selling the *Post* the afternoon before she was killed, and that would serve as the opening wedge of a discussion of the bag woman, or bag women in general, or various qualities of the neighborhood, or violence in American life, or whatever.

A lot of people started off talking about the bag lady and wound up talking about themselves. I guess most conversations work out that way.

A nurse from Roosevelt said she never saw a shopping bag lady without hearing an inner voice say *There but for the grace of God*. And she was not the only woman who confessed she worried about ending up that way. I guess it's a specter that haunts women who live alone, just as the vision of the Bowery derelict clouds the peripheral vision of hard-drinking men.

Genevieve Strom turned up at Armstrong's one night. We talked briefly about the bag lady. Two nights later she came back again and we took turns spending our inheritances on rounds of drinks. The drinks hit her with some force and a little past midnight she decided it was time to go. I said I'd see her home. At the corner of Fifty-seventh Street she stopped in her tracks and said, "No men in the room. That's one of Mrs. Larkin's rules."

"Old-fashioned, isn't she?"

"She runs a daycent establishment." Her mock-Irish accent was heavier than the landlady's. Her eyes, hard to read in the lamplight, raised to meet mine. "Take me someplace."

I took her to my hotel, a less decent establishment than Mrs. Larkin's. We did each other little good but no harm, and it beat being alone.

Another night I ran into Barry Mosedale at Polly's Cage. He told me there was a singer at Kid Gloves who was doing a number about the bag lady. "I can find out how you can reach him," he offered.

"Is he there now?"

He nodded and checked his watch. "He goes on in fifteen minutes. But you don't want to *go* there, do you?"

"Why not?"

"Hardly your sort of crowd, Matt."

"Cops go anywhere."

"Indeed they do, and they're welcome wherever they go, aren't they? Just let me drink this and I'll accompany you, if that's all right. You need someone to lend you immoral support."

Kid Gloves is a gay bar on Fifty-sixth west of Ninth. The decor is just a little aggressively gay lib. There's a small raised stage, a scattering of tables, a piano, a loud jukebox. Barry Mosedale and I stood at the bar. I'd been there before and knew better than to order their coffee. I had straight bourbon. Barry had his on ice with a splash of soda.

Halfway through the drink Gordon Lurie was introduced. He wore tight jeans and a flowered shirt, sat on stage on a folding chair, sang ballads he'd written himself with his own guitar for accompaniment. I don't know if he was any good or not. It sounded to me as though all the songs had the same melody, but that may just have been a similarity of style. I don't have much of an ear.

After a song about a summer romance in Amsterdam, Gordon Lurie announced that the next number was dedicated to the memory of Mary Alice Redfield. Then he sang:

She's a shopping bag lady who lives on
the sidewalks of Broadway
Wearing all of her clothes and her years
on her back
Toting dead dreams in an old paper sack
Searching the trashcans for something she
lost here on Broadway—
Shopping bag lady . . .

You'd never know but she once was an
actress on Broadway
Speaking the words that they stuffed in
her head
Reciting the lines of the life that she led
Thrilling her fans and her friends and her
lovers on Broadway—
Shopping bag lady . . .

There are demons who lurk in the corners
of minds and of Broadway
And after the omens and portents and
signs
Came the day she forgot to remember her
lines
Put her life on a leash and took it out
walking on Broadway—
Shopping bag lady . . .

There were a couple more verses and the shopping bag lady in the song
wound up murdered in a doorway, dying in defense of the "tattered old
treasures she mined in the trashcans of Broadway." The song went over
well and got a bigger hand than any of the ones that had preceded it.

I asked Barry who Gordon Lurie was.

"You know very nearly as much as I," he said. "He started here
Tuesday. I find him whelming, personally. Neither overwhelming nor
underwhelming but somewhere in the middle."

"Mary Alice never spent much time on Broadway. I never saw her
more than a block from Ninth Avenue."

"Poetic license, I'm sure. The song would lack a certain something if
you substituted Ninth Avenue for Broadway. As it stands it sounds a
little like 'Rhinestone Cowboy.'"

"Lurie live around here?"

"I don't know where he lives. I have the feeling he's Canadian. So many people are nowadays. It used to be that no one was Canadian and now simply everybody is. I'm sure it must be a virus."

We listened to the rest of Gordon Lurie's act. Then Barry leaned forward and chatted with the bartender to find out how I could get backstage. I found my way to what passed for a dressing room at Kid Gloves. It must have been a ladies' lavatory in a prior incarnation.

I went in there thinking I'd made a breakthrough, that Lurie had killed her and now he was dealing with his guilt by singing about her. I don't think I really believed this but it supplied me with direction and momentum.

I told him my name and that I was interested in his act. He wanted to know if I was from a record company. "Am I on the threshold of a great opportunity? Am I about to become an overnight success after years of travail?"

We got out of the tiny room and left the club through a side door. Three doors down the block we sat in a cramped booth at a coffee shop. He ordered a Greek salad and we both had coffee.

I told him I was interest in his song about the bag lady.

He brightened. "Oh, do you like it? Personally I think it's the best thing I've written. I just wrote it a couple of days ago. I opened next door Tuesday night. I got to New York three weeks ago and I had a two-week booking in the West Village. A place called David's Table. Do you know it?"

"I don't think so."

"Another stop on the K-Y circuit. Either there aren't any straight people in New York or they don't go to nightclubs. But I was there two weeks, and then I opened at Kid Gloves, and afterward I was sitting and drinking with some people and somebody was talking about the shopping bag lady and I had had enough Amaretto to be maudlin on the subject. I woke up Wednesday morning with a splitting headache and the first verse of the song buzzing in my splitting head, and I sat up immediately and wrote it down, and as I was writing one verse the next would come bubbling to the surface, and before I knew it I had all six verses." He took a cigarette, then paused in the act of lighting it to fix his eyes on me. "You told me your name," he said, "but I don't remember it."

"Matthew Scudder."

"Yes. You're the person investigating the murder."

"I'm not sure that's the right word. I've been talking to people, seeing what I can come up with. Did you know her before she was killed?"

He shook his head. "I was never even in this neighborhood before. *Oh.* I'm not a suspect, am I? Because I haven't been in New York since the fall. I haven't bothered to figure out where I was when she was killed but I was in California at Christmastime and I'd gotten as far east as Chicago in early March, so I do have a fairly solid alibi."

"I never really suspected you. I think I just wanted to hear your song." I sipped some coffee. "Where did you get the facts of her life? Was she an actress?"

"I don't think so. Was she? It wasn't really *about* her, you know. It was inspired by her story but I didn't know her and I never knew anything about her. The past few days I've been paying a lot of attention to bag ladies, though. And other street people."

"I know what you mean."

"Are there more of them in New York or is it just that they're so much more visible here? In California everybody drives, you don't see people on the street. I'm from Canada, rural Ontario, and the first city I ever spent much time in was Toronto, and there are crazy people on the streets there but it's nothing like New York. Does the city drive them crazy or does it just tend to draw crazy people?"

"I don't know."

"Maybe they're not crazy. Maybe they just hear a different drummer. I wonder who killed her."

"We'll probably never know."

"What I really wonder is *why* she was killed. In my song I made up some reason. That somebody wanted what was in her bags. I think it works as a song that way but I don't think there's much chance that it happened like that. Why would anyone kill the poor thing?"

"I don't know."

"They say she left people money. People she hardly knew. Is that the truth?" I nodded. "And she left me a song. I don't even feel that I wrote it. I woke up with it. I never set eyes on her and she touched my life. That's strange, isn't it?"

Everything was strange. The strangest part of all was the way it ended.

It was a Monday night. The Mets were at Shea and I'd taken my sons to a game. The Dodgers were in for a three-game series, which they eventually swept as they'd been sweeping everything lately. The boys and I got to watch them knock Jon Matlack out of the box and go on to shell his several replacements. The final count was something like 13–4.

We stayed in our seats until the last out. Then I saw them home and caught a train back to the city.

So it was past midnight when I reached Armstrong's. Trina brought me a large double and a mug of coffee without being asked. I knocked back half of the bourbon and was dumping the rest into my coffee when she told me somebody'd been looking for me earlier. "He was in three times in the past two hours," she said. "A wiry guy, high forehead, bushy eyebrows, sort of a bulldog jaw. I guess the word for it is underslung."

"Perfectly good word."

"I said you'd probably get here sooner or later."

"I always do. Sooner or later."

"Uh-huh. You okay, Matt?"

"The Mets lost a close one."

"I heard it was thirteen to four."

"That's close for them these days. Did he say what it was about?"

He hadn't, but within the half hour he came in again and I was there to be found. I recognized him from Trina's description as soon as he came through the door. He looked faintly familiar but he was nobody I knew. I suppose I'd seen him around the neighborhood.

Evidently he knew me by sight because he found his way to my table without asking directions and took a chair without being invited to sit. He didn't say anything for a while and neither did I. I had a fresh bourbon and coffee in front of me and I took a sip and looked him over.

He was under thirty. His cheeks were hollow and the flesh of his face was stretched over his skull like leather that had shrunk upon drying. He wore a forest green work shirt and a pair of khaki pants. He needed a shave.

Finally he pointed at my cup and asked me what I was drinking. When I told him he said all he drank was beer.

"They have beer here," I said.

"Maybe I'll have what you're drinking." He turned in his chair and waved for Trina. When she came over he said he'd have bourbon and coffee, the same as I was having. He didn't say anything more until she brought the drink. Then, after he had spent quite some time stirring it, he took a sip. "Well," he said, "That's not so bad. That's okay."

"Glad you like it."

"I don't know if I'd order it again, but at least now I know what it's like."

"That's something."

"I seen you around. Matt Scudder. Used to be a cop, private eye now, blah blah blah. Right?"

"Close enough."

"My name's Floyd. I never liked it but I'm stuck with it, right? I could change it but who'm I kidding? Right?"

"If you say so."

"If I don't somebody else will. Floyd Karp, that's the full name. I didn't tell you my last name, did I? That's it, Floyd Karp."

"Okay."

"Okay, okay, okay." He pursed his lips, blew out air in a silent whistle. "What do we do now, Matt? Huh? That's what I want to know."

"I'm not sure what you mean, Floyd."

"Oh, you know what I'm getting at, driving at, getting at. You know, don't you?"

By this time I suppose I did.

"I killed that old lady. Took her life, stabbed her with my knife." He flashed the saddest smile. "Steee-rangled her with her skeeee-arf. Hoist her with her own whatchacallit, petard. What's a petard, Matt?"

"I don't know, Floyd. Why'd you kill her?"

He looked at me, he looked at his coffee, he looked at me again.

He said, "Had to."

"Why?"

"Same as the bourbon and coffee. Had to *see*. Had to taste it and find out what it was like." His eyes met mine. His were very large, hollow, empty. I fancied I could see right through them to the blackness at the back of his skull. "I couldn't get my mind away from murder," he said. His voice was more sober now, the mocking playful quality gone from it. "I tried. I just couldn't do it. It was on my mind all the time and I was afraid of what I might do. I couldn't function, I couldn't think, I just saw blood and death all the time. I was afraid to close my eyes for fear of what I might see. I would just stay up, days it seemed, and then I'd be tired enough to pass out the minute I closed my eyes. I stopped eating. I used to be fairly heavy and the weight just fell off of me."

"When did all this happen, Floyd?"

"I don't know. All winter. And I thought if I went and did it once I would know if I was a man or a monster or what. And I got this knife, and I went out a couple of nights but lost my nerve, and then one night—I don't want to talk about that part of it now."

"All right."

"I almost couldn't do it, but I couldn't *not* do it, and then I was doing it and it went on forever. It was *horrible.*"

"Why didn't you stop?"

"I don't know. I think I was afraid to stop. That doesn't make any sense, does it? I just don't know. It was all crazy, insane, like being in a movie and being in the audience at the same time. Watching myself."

"No one saw you do it?"

"No. I threw the knife down a sewer. I went home. I put all my clothes in the incinerator, the ones I was wearing. I kept throwing up. All that night I would throw up even when my stomach was empty. Dry heaves, Department of Dry Heaves. And then I guess I fell asleep, I don't know when or how but I did, and the next day I woke up and thought I dreamed it. But of course I didn't."

"No."

"And what I did think was that it was over. I did it and I knew I'd never want to do it again. It was something crazy that happened and I could forget about it. And I thought that was what happened."

"That you managed to forget about it?"

A nod. "But I guess I didn't. And now everybody's talking about her. Mary Alice Redfield, I killed her without knowing her name. Nobody knew her name and now everybody knows it and it's all back in my mind. And I heard you were looking for me, and I guess, I guess. . . ." He frowned, chasing a thought around in his mind like a dog trying to capture his tail. Then he gave it up and looked at me. "So here I am," he said. "So here I am."

"Yes."

"Now what happens?"

"I think you'd better tell the police about it, Floyd."

"Why?"

"I suppose for the same reason you told me."

He thought about it. After a long time he nodded. "All right," he said. "I can accept that. I'd never kill anybody again. I know that. But—you're right. I have to tell them. I don't know who to see or what to say or, hell, I just—"

"I'll go with you if you want."

"Yeah. I want you to."

"I'll have a drink and then we'll go. You want another?"

"No. I'm not much of a drinker."

I had it without the coffee this time. After Trina brought it I asked him how he'd picked his victim. Why the bag lady?

He started to cry. No sobs, just tears spilling from his deep-set eyes. After a while he wiped them on his sleeve.

"Because she didn't count," he said. "That's what I thought. She was nobody. Who cared if she died? Who'd miss her?" He closed his eyes tight. "Everybody misses her," he said. "Everybody."

So I took him in. I don't know what they'll do with him. It's not my problem.

It wasn't really a case and I didn't really solve it. As far as I can see I didn't do anything. It was the talk that drove Floyd Karp from cover, and no doubt I helped some of the talk get started, but some of it would have gotten around without me. All those legacies of Mary Alice Redfield's had made her a nine-day wonder in the neighborhood. It was one of those legacies that got me involved.

Maybe she caught her own killer. Maybe he caught himself, as everyone does. Maybe no man's an island and maybe everybody is.

All I know is I lit a candle for the woman, and I suspect I'm not the only one who did.

The Witch, Yazzie, and the Nine of Clubs

Author: Tony Hillerman (1925–   )

Detective: Jim Chee (1980)

Hillerman's two Navajo police sleuths, Joe Leaphorn and Jim Chee, first appeared in a series of three cases each, then joined forces in subsequent novels in the series. Leaphorn has never had a case of less than novel length, while his younger cohort has either one or two, depending on how you choose to count.

Hillerman himself is not sure if he wrote his Jim Chee short story before or after the first Chee novel, *People of Darkness* (1980). The story exists in two quite different versions, both of which have been frequently anthologized. The other version is called "Chee's Witch." The version that follows, presumably the later (though it appeared in print first) and certainly the better of the two, won third prize in an international short-story contest sponsored by the Swedish Academy of Detection for the Third Crime Writers Annual Congress, held in Stockholm in 1981, and was first published with other winners in the British anthology *Crime Wave* (1981). Hillerman has put so much ingenuity and incident into this short tale, you must read it carefully to get its full impact.

All summer the witch had been at work on the Rainbow Plateau. It began—although Corporal Jimmy Chee would learn of it only now, at the very last—with the mutilation of the corpse. The rest of it fell pretty much into the pattern of witchcraft gossip one expected in this lonely corner of the Navajo Reservation. Adeline Etcitty's mare had foaled a two-headed colt. Rudolph Bisti's boys lost their best ram while driving their flocks into the high country, and when they found the body werewolf tracks were all around it. The old woman they call Kicks-Her-Horse had actually seen the skinwalker. A man walking down Burnt Water Wash in the twilight had disappeared into a grove of cottonwoods and when the old woman got there, he turned himself into an owl and flew away. The daughter of Rosemary Nakai had seen the witch, too. She shot her .22 rifle at a big dog bothering her horses and the dog turned into a man wearing a wolfskin and she'd run away without seeing what he did.

Corporal Chee heard of the witch now and then and remembered it as he remembered almost everything. But Chee heard less than most because Chee had been assigned to the Tuba City sub-agency and given the Short Mountain territory only six months ago. He came from the Chuska Mountains on the Arizona-New Mexico border three hundred miles away. His born-to clan was the Slow Talking People, and his paternal clan was the Mud Dinee. Here among the barren canyons along the Utah border the clans were the Standing Rock People, the Many Goats, the Tangle Dinee, the Red Forehead Dinee, the Bitter Waters, and the Monster People. Here Chee was still a stranger. To a stranger, Navajos talk cautiously of witches.

Which is perhaps why Jim Chee had learned only now, at this very moment, of the mutilation. Or perhaps it was because he had a preoccupation of his own—the odd, frustrating question of where Taylor Yazzie had gone, and what Yazzie had done with the loot from the Burnt Water Trading Post. Whatever the reason he was late in learning, it was the Cowboy who finally told him.

"Everybody knew there was a skinwalker working way last spring," the Cowboy said. "As soon as they found out the witch killed that guy."

Chee had been leaning against the Cowboy's pickup truck. He was looking past the Emerson Nez hogan, through the thin blue haze of Piñon smoke, which came from its smokehole, watching a half-dozen Nez kinfolks stacking wood for the Girl Dance fire. He was asking himself for the thousandth time what Taylor Yazzie could have done with $40,000 worth of pawn—rings, belt buckles, bracelets, bulky silver concha belts that must weigh, altogether, 500 pounds. And what had Taylor Yazzie done with himself—another 180 pounds or so, with the bland round face more common among Eastern Navajos than on the Rainbow Plateau, with his thin moustache, with his wire-rimmed sunglasses. Chee had seen Taylor Yazzie only once, the day before he had done the burglary, but since then he had learned him well. Yazzie's world was small, and Yazzie had vanished from it, and since he could hardly speak English there was hardly any place he could go. And just as thoroughly, the silver pawn had vanished from the lives of a hundred families who had turned it over to Ed Yost's trading post to secure their credit until they sold their wool. Through all these thoughts it took a moment for the Cowboy's message to penetrate. When it did, Corporal Chee became very attentive.

"Killed what guy?" Chee asked. Taylor Yazzie, you're dead, he thought. No more mystery.

The Cowboy was sprawled across the front seat of his truck, fishing a transistor radio out of the glovebox. "You remember," he said. "Back last April. That guy you collected on Piute Mesa."

"Oh," Chee said. He remembered. It had been a miserable day's work and the smell of death had lingered in his carryall for weeks. But that had been in May, not April, and it hadn't looked like a homicide. Just too much booze, too much high-altitude cold. An old story on the Reservation. And John Doe wasn't Taylor Yazzie. The coroner had put the death two months before the body was recovered. Taylor Yazzie was alive, and well, and walking out of Ed Yost's trading post a lot later than that. Chee had been there and seen him. "You see that son-of-a-bitch," Ed Yost had said. "I just fired his ass. Never comes to work, and I think he's been stealing from me." No, Yost didn't want to file a complaint. Nothing he could prove. But the next morning it had been different. Someone with a key had come in the night, and opened the saferoom where the pawn was kept, and took it. Only Yost and Yazzie had access to the keys, and Yazzie had vanished.

"Why you say a witch killed that guy?" Chee asked.

The Cowboy backed out of the pickup cab. The radio didn't work. He shook it, glancing at Chee. His expression was cautious. The bumper stickers plastering the Ford declared him a member of the Native American Rodeo Cowboy's Association, and proclaimed that Cowboys Make Better Lovers, and that Cowgirls Have More Fun, and recorded the Cowboy's outdated permit to park on the Arizona State University campus. But Cowboy was still a Many Goats Dinee, and Chee had been his friend for just a few months. Uneasiness warred with modern macho.

"They said all the skin was cut off his hands," the Cowboy said. But he said it in a low voice.

"Ah," Chee said. He needed no more explanation. The ingredients of "anti'l," the "corpse-powder" that skinwalkers make to spread sickness, was known to every Navajo. They use the skin of their victim, which bears the unique imprint of the individual human identity—the skin of palm, and finger pads, and the balls of the feet. Dried and pulverized with proper ritual, it became the dreaded reverse-negative of the pollen used for curing and blessing. Chee remembered the corpse as he had seen it. Predators and scavenger birds had left a ragged sack of bones and bits of desiccated flesh. No identification and nothing to show it was anything but routine. And that's how it had gone into the books. "Unidentified male. About forty. Probable death by exposure."

"If somebody saw his palms had been skinned, then somebody saw him a hell of a long time before anybody called us about him," Chee said. Nothing unusual in that, either.

"Somebody found him fresh," the Cowboy said. "That's what I heard. One of the Pinto outfit." Cowboy removed the battery from the radio. By trade, Cowboy was the assistant county agricultural agent. He inspected the battery, which looked exactly like all other batteries, with great care. The Cowboy did not want to talk about witch business.

"Any of the Pinto outfit here?" Chee asked.

"Sure," Cowboy said. He made a sweeping gesture, including the scores of pickups, wagons, old sedans occupying the sagebrush flats around the Nez hogans, the dozens of cooking fires smoking in the autumn twilight, the people everywhere. "All the kinfolks come to this. Everybody comes to this."

This was an Enemy Way. This particular Enemy Way had been prescribed, as Chee understood it, to cure Emerson Nez of whatever ailed him so he could walk again with beauty all around him as Changing Woman had taught when she formed the first Navajos. Family duty would require all kinsmen, and clansmen, of Nez to be here, as Cowboy had said, to share in the curing and the blessing. Everybody would be here, especially tonight. Tonight was the sixth night of the ceremonial when the ritual called for the Girl Dance to be held. Its original purpose was metaphysical—part of the prescribed re-enactment of the deeds of the Holy People. But it was also social. Cowboy called it the Navajo substitute for the singles bar, and came to see if he could connect with a new girlfriend. Anthropologists came to study primitive behavior. Whites and Utes and even haughty Hopis came out of curiosity. Bootleggers came to sell illegal whiskey. Jim Chee came, in theory, to catch bootleggers. In fact, the elusive, invisible, missing Yazzie drew him. Yazzie and the loot. Sometime, somewhere some of it would have to surface. And when it did, someone would know it. But now to hell with Yazzie and pawn jewelry. He might have an old homicide on his hands. With an unidentified victim and the whole thing six months cold it promised to be as frustrating as the burglary. But he would find some Pinto family members and begin the process.

Cowboy's radio squawked into sudden life and produced the voice of Willie Nelson, singing of abandonment and sorrow. Cowboy turned up the volume.

"Specially everyone would come to this one," Cowboy said toward

Chee's departing back. "Nez wasn't the only one bothered by that witch. One way or another it bothered just about everybody on the plateau."

Chee stopped and walked back to the pickup. "You mean Nez was witched?"

"That's what they say," Cowboy said. "Got sick. They took him to the clinic in Tuba City and when that didn't do any good they got themselves a Listener to find out what was wrong with the old man, and he found out Nez had the corpse sickness. He said the witch got on the roof—" (Cowboy paused to point with his lips—a peculiarly Navajo gesture—toward the Nez hogan)—"and dropped anti'l down the smokehole."

"Same witch? Same one that did the killing?"

"That's what the Listener said," Cowboy agreed.

Cowboy was full of information tonight, Chee thought. But was it useful? The fire for the Girl Dance had been started now. It cast a red, wavering light which reflected off windshields, faces, and the moving forms of people. The pot drums began a halting pattern of sounds that reflected, like the firelight, off the cliffs of the great mesa, which sheltered the Nez place. This was the ritual part of the evening. A shaman named Dillon Keeyani was the signer in charge of curing Nez. Chee could see him, a tall, gaunt man standing beyond the fire, chanting the repetitive poetry of this part of the cure. Nez stood beside him, naked to the waist, his face blackened to make him invisible from the ghosts that haunt the night. Why would the Listener have prescribed an Enemy Way? It puzzled Chee. Usually a witch victim was cured with a Prostitution Way, or the proper chants from the Mountain Way were used. The Enemy Way was ordered for witch cases at times, but it was a broad-spectrum antibiotic—used for that multitude of ills caused by exposure to alien ways and alien cultures. Chee's family had held an Enemy Way for him when he had returned from the University of New Mexico, and in those years when Navajos were coming home from the Viet Nam war it was common every winter. But why use it to cure Emerson Nez of the corpse sickness? There was only one answer. Because the witch was an alien—a Ute, a white, a Hopi perhaps. Chee thought about how the Listener would have worked. Long conversations with Nez and those who knew him, hunting for causes of the malaise, for broken taboos, for causes of depression. And then the Listener would have found a quiet place, and listened to what the silence taught him. How would the Listener have known the witch was alien? There was only one way. Chee was suddenly excited. Someone must have seen the witch. Actually seen the man—not in the doubtful moonlight, or a misty evening when a moving shape could be dog or man—but under circumstances that told the witness that the man was not a Navajo.

The Sway Dance had started now. A double line of figures circled the burning pyre, old men and young—even boys too young to have been initiated into the secrets of the Holy People. Among Chee's clans in the Chuskas ritualism was more orthodox and these youngsters would not be allowed to dance until a Yeibichai was held for them, and their eyes had seen through the masks of Black God and Talking God. The fire flared higher as a burning log collapsed with an explosion of sparks. Chee wove through the spectators, asking for Pintos. He found an elderly woman joking with two younger ones. Yes, she was Anna Pinto. Yes, her son had found the body last spring. His name was Walker Pinto. He'd be somewhere playing stick dice. He was wearing a sweatband. Red.

Chee found the game behind Ed Yost's pickup truck. A lantern on the tailgate provided the light, a saddle blanket spread on the ground was the playing surface. Ed Yost was playing with an elderly round-faced Hopi and four Navajos. Chee recognized Pinto among the watchers by the red sweatband and his mother's description. "Skinny," she'd said. "Bony-faced. Sort of ugly-looking." Although his mother hadn't said it, Walker Pinto was also drunk.

"That's right, man," Pinto said. "I found him. Up there getting the old woman's horses together, and I found him." Wine had slurred Pinto's speech and drowned whatever inhibitions he might have felt about talking of witch business to a man he didn't know. He put his hand on the pickup fender to steady himself and began—Navajo fashion—at the very beginning. He'd married a woman in the Poles Together clan and gone over to Rough Rock to live with her, but she was no good, so this winter he'd come back to his mother's outfit, and his mother had wanted him to go up on Piute Mesa to see about her horses. Pinto described the journey up the mesa with his son, his agile hands acting out the journey. Chee watched the stick-dice game. Yost was good at it. He slammed the four painted wooden pieces down on the base stone in the center of the blanket. They bounced two feet into the air and fell in a neat pattern. He tallied the exposed colors, moved the matchsticks being used as score markers, collected the sticks and passed them to the Hopi in maybe three seconds. Yost had been a magician once, Chee remembered. With a carnival, and his customers had called him Three-Hands. "Bets," Yost said. The Hopi looked at the sticks in his hand, smiling slightly. He threw a crumpled dollar on to the blanket. A middle-aged Navajo wearing wire-rimmed glasses put a folded bill beside it. Two more bills hit the blanket. The lantern light reflected off Wire Rims's lenses and off Yost's bald head.

"About then I heard the truck, way back over the ridge," Pinto was saying. His hands created the ridge and the valley beyond it. "Then the truck it hit something, you see. Bang." Pinto's right hand slammed into his left. "You see, that truck it hit against a rock there. It was turning around in the wash, and the wash is narrow there and it banged up against this rock." Pinto's hands recreated the accident. "I started over there, you see. I walked on over there then to see who it was."

The stick-dice players were listening now; the Hopi's face patient, waiting for the game to resume. The butane lantern made a white light that made Yost's moist eyes sparkle as he looked up at Pinto. There was a pile of bills beside Yost's hand. He took a dollar from it and put it on the blanket without taking his eyes from Pinto.

"But, you see, by the time I got up to the top of the rise, that truck it was driving away. So I went on down there, you see, to find out what had been going on." Pinto's hands re-enacted the journey.

"What kind of truck was it?" Chee asked.

"Already gone," Pinto said. "Bunch of dust hanging in the air, but I didn't see the truck. But when I got down there to the wash, you see, I looked around." Pinto's hands flew here and there, looking around. "There he was, you see, right there shoved under that rabbit brush." The agile hands disposed of the body. The stick-dice game remained in recess. The Hopi still held the sticks, but he watched Pinto. So did the fat man who sat cross-legged beside him. The lantern light made a point of white in the center of Yost's black pupils. The faces of the Navajo players were rapt, but the Hopi's expression was polite disinterest. The Two-Heart witches of his culture did their evil with more sophistication.

Pinto described what he had seen under the rabbit brush, his voice wavering with the wine but telling a story often repeated. His agile hands were surer. They showed how the flayed hands of the corpse had lain, where the victim's hat had rolled, how Pinto had searched for traces of the witch, how he had studied the tracks. Behind the stick-dice players the chanting chorus of the Sway Dancers rose and fell. The faint night breeze moved the perfume of burning piñon and the aroma of cedar to Chee's nostrils. The lantern light shone through the rear window of Yost's truck, reflecting from the barrels of the rifles in the gun rack across it. A long-barreled 30.06 and a short saddle carbine, Chee noticed.

"You see, that skinwalker was in a big hurry when he got finished with that body," Pinto was saying. "He backed right over a big chamisa bush and banged that truck all around on the brush and rocks getting it out of there." The hands flew, demonstrating panic.

"But you didn't actually see the truck?" Chee asked.

"Gone," Pinto said. His hands demonstrated the state of goneness.

"Or the witch, either?"

Pinto shook his head. His hands apologized.

On the flat beside the Nez hogan the chanting of the Sway Dance ended with a chorus of shouting. Now the Girl Dance began. Different songs. Different drumbeat. Laughter now, and shouting. The game broke up. Wire-Rims folded his blanket. Yost counted his winnings.

"Tell you what I'll do," Yost said to Wire Rims. "I'll show you how I can control your mind."

Wire Rims grinned.

"Yes, I will," Yost said. "I'll plant a thought in your mind and get you to say it."

Wire Rims's grin broadened. "Like what?"

Yost put his hand on the Navajo's shoulder. "Let your mind go blank now," he said. "Don't think about nothing." Yost let ten seconds tick away. He removed the hand. "Now," he said. "It's done. It's in there."

"What?" Wire Rims asked.

"I made you think of a certain card," Yost said. He turned to the spectators, to the Hopi, to Chee. "I always use the same card. Burn it into my mind and keep it there and always use that very same image. That way I can make a stronger impression with it on the other feller's mind." He tapped Wire Rims on the chest with a finger. "He closes his eyes, he sees that certain card."

"Bullshit," Wire Rims said.

"I'll bet you, then," Yost said. "But you got to play fair. You got to name the card you actually see. All right?"

Wire Rims shrugged. "Bullshit. I don't see nothing."

Yost waved his handful of currency. "Yes, you do," Yost insisted. "I got money that says you do. You see that one card I put in your mind. I got $108 here I'll bet you against that belt you're wearing. What's that worth?" It was a belt of heavy conchos hammered out of thick silver. Despite its age and a heavy layer of tarnish it was a beautiful piece of work. Chee guessed it would bring $100 at pawn and sell for maybe $200. But with the skyrocketing price of silver, it might be worth twice that melted down.

"Let's say it would pawn for $300," Yost said. "That gives me three-to-one odds on the money. But if I'm lying to you, there's just one chance in fifty-two that you'll lose."

"How you going to tell?" Wire Rims asked. "You tell somebody the card in advance?"

"Better than that," Yost said. "I got him here in my pocket sealed up in an envelope. I always use that same card so I keep it sealed up and ready."

"Sealed up in an envelope?" Wire Rims asked.

"That's right," Yost said. He tapped his forefinger to the chest of his khaki bush jacket.

Wire Rims unbuckled the belt and handed it to Chee. "You hold the money," he said. Yost handed Chee the currency.

"I get to refresh your memory," Yost said. He put his hand on the Navajo's shoulder. "You see a whole deck of cards face down on the table. Now, I turn this one on the end here over." Yost's right hand turned over an invisible card and slapped it emphatically on an invisible table. "You see it. You got it in your mind. Now play fair. Tell me the name of the card."

Wire Rims hesitated. "I don't see nothing," he said.

"Come on. Play fair," Yost said. "Name it."

"Nine of clubs," Wire Rims said.

"Here is an honest man," Yost said to Chee and the Hopi and the rest of them. "He named the nine of clubs." While he said it, Yost's left hand had dipped into the left pocket of the bush jacket. Now it fished out an envelope and delivered it to Chee. "Read it and weep," Yost said.

Chee handed the envelope to Wire Rims. It was a small envelope, just a bit bigger than a poker card. Wire Rims tore it open and extracted the card. It was the nine of clubs. Wire Rims looked from card to Yost, disappointment mixed with admiration. "How you do that?"

"I'm a magician," Yost said. He took the belt and the money from Chee. "Any luck on that burglary?" he asked. "You find that son of a bitch Yazzie yet?"

"Nothing," Chee said.

And then there was a hand on his arm and a pretty face looking up at him. "I've got you," the girl said. She tugged him toward the fire. "You're my partner. Come on, policeman."

"I'd sure like to catch that son of a bitch," Yost said.

The girl danced gracefully. She told Chee she was born to the Standing Rock Dinee and her father was a Bitter Water. With no clan overlap, none of the complex incest taboos of The People prevented their dancing, or whatever else might come to mind. Chee remembered having seen her working behind the registration desk at the Holiday Inn at Shiprock. She was pretty. She was friendly. She was witty. The dance was good. The pot drums tugged at him, and the voices rose in a slightly ribald song about what the old woman and the young man did on the sheepskins away from the firelight. But things nagged at Chee's memory. He wanted to think.

"You don't talk much," the girl said.

"Sorry. Thinking," Chee said.

"But not about me." She frowned at him. "You thinking about arresting somebody?"

"I'm thinking that tomorrow morning when they finish this sing-off with the Scalp Shooting ceremony, they've got to have something to use as the scalp."

The girl shrugged.

"I mean, it has to be something that belonged to the witch. How can they do that unless they know who the witch is? What could it be?"

The girl shrugged again. She was not interested in the subject nor, now, in Jim Chee. "Whyn't you go and ask?" she said. "Big Hat over there is the scalp carrier."

Chee paid his ransom—handing the girl two dollars and then adding two more when the first payment drew a scornful frown. Big Hat was also paying off his partner, with the apparent intention of being immediately recaptured by a plump young woman wearing a wealth of silver necklaces who was waiting at the fringe of the dance. Chee captured him just before the woman did.

"The scalp?" Big Hat asked. "Well, I don't know what you call it. It's a strip of red plastic about this wide [Big Hat indicated an inch with his fingers], and maybe half that thick and a foot and a half long."

"What's that got to do with the witch?" Chee asked.

"Broke off the bumper of his truck," Big Hat said. "You know. That strip of rubbery stuff they put on to keep from denting things. It got brittle and some of it broke off."

"At the place where they found the body?"

Big Hat nodded.

"Where you keeping it?" Chee asked. "After you're finished with it tomorrow I'm going to need it." Tomorrow at the final ritual this scalp of the witch would be placed near the Nez hogan. There, after the proper chants were sung, Emerson Nez would attack it with a ceremonial weapon—probably the beak of a raven attached to a stick. Then it would be sprinkled with ashes and shot—probably with a rifle. If all this was properly done, if the minds of all concerned were properly free of lust, anger, avarice—then the witchcraft would be reversed. Emerson Nez would live. The witch would die.

"I got it with my stuff in the tent," Big Hat said. He pointed past the Nez brush arbor. After the ceremony he guessed Chee could have it. Usually anything like that—things touched with witchcraft—would be buried. But he'd ask Dillon Keeyani. Keeyani was the singer. Keeyani was in charge.

And then Jim Chee walked out into the darkness, past the brush arbor and past the little blue nylon tent where Big Hat kept his bedroll and his machine bundle and what he needed for his role in this seven-day sing. He walked beyond the corral where the Nez outfit kept its horses, out into the sagebrush and the night. He found a rock and sat on it and thought.

While he was dancing he had worked out how Ed Yost had won Wire Rims's belt. A simple matter of illusion and distraction. The easy way it had fooled him made him aware that he must be overlooking other things because of other illusions. But what?

He reviewed what Pinto had told him. Nothing there. He skipped to his own experience with the body. The smell. Checking what was left of the clothing for identification. Moving what was left into the body bag. Hearing the cloth tear. Feeling the bare bone, the rough, dried leather of the boots as he . . .

The boots! Chee slapped both palms against his thighs. The man had his boots on. Why would the witch, the madman, take the skin for corpse powder from the hands and leave the equally essential skin from the feet? He would not, certainly, have replaced the boots. Was the killing not a witch-killing, then? But why the flayed hands? To remove the fingerprints?

Yazzie. Yazzie had a police record. One simple assault. One driving while intoxicated. Printed twice. Identification would have been immediate. But Yazzie was larger than the skinned man, and still alive when the skinned man was dead. John Doe remained John Doe. This only changed John Doe from a random victim to a man whose killer needed to conceal his identity.

The air moved against Chee's face and with the faint breeze came the sound of the pot drums and of laughter. Much closer he heard the fluting cry of a hunting owl. He saw the owl now, a gray shape gliding in the starlight just above the sage, hunting, as Chee's mind hunted, something that eluded it. Something, Chee's instinct told him, as obvious as the nine of clubs.

But what? Chee thought of how adroitly Yost had manipulated Wire

Rims into the bet, and into the illusion. Overestimating the value of the man's belt. Causing them all to think of a single specific card, sealed in a single specific envelope, waiting to be specifically named. He smiled slightly, appreciating the cleverness.

The smile lingered, abruptly disappeared, reappeared, and suddenly converted itself into an exultant shout of laughter. Jim Chee had found another illusion. In this one, he had been Yost's target. He'd been totally fooled. Yazzie *was* John Doe. Yost had killed him, removed the fingerprints, put the body where it would be found. Then he had performed his magic. Cleverly. Taking advantage of the circumstances—a new policeman who'd never seen Yazzie. Chee re-created the day. The note to call Yost. Yost wanting to see him, suggesting two in the afternoon. Chee had been a few minutes late. The big, round-faced Navajo stalking out of Yost's office. Yost's charade of indignant anger. Who was this ersatz "Yazzie"? The only requirement would be a Navajo from another part of the reservation, whom Chee wouldn't be likely to see again soon. Clever!

That reminded him that he had no time for this now. He stopped at his own vehicle for his flashlight and then checked Yost's truck. Typical of trucks that live out their lives on the rocky tracks of the reservation, it was battered, scraped, and dented. The entire plastic padding strip was missing from the front bumper. From the back one, a piece was missing. About eighteen inches long. What was left fit Big Hat's description of the scalp. His deduction confirmed, Chee stood behind the truck, thinking.

Had Yost disposed of Yazzie to cover up the faked burglary? Or had Yazzie been killed for some unknown motive and the illusion of burglary created to explain his disappearance? Chee decided he preferred the first theory. For months before the crime the price of silver had been skyrocketing, moving from about five dollars an ounce to at least forty dollars. It bothered Yost to know that as soon as they sold their wool, his customers would be paying off their debts and walking away with that sudden wealth.

The Girl Dance had ended now. The drums were quiet. The fire had burned down. People were drifting past him through the darkness on their way back to their bedrolls. Tomorrow at dawn there would be the final sand-painting on the floor of the Nez hogan; Nez would drink the ritual emetic and just as the sun rose would vomit out the sickness. Then the Scalp Shooting would be held. A strip of red plastic molding would be shot and a witch would, eventually, die. Would Yost stay for the finish? And how would he react when he saw the plastic molding?

A split second into that thought, it was followed by another. Yost had heard what Pinto had said. Yost would know this form of the Enemy Way required a ceremonial scalp. Yost wouldn't wait to find out what it was.

Chee snapped on the flashlight. Through the back window of Yost's pickup he saw that the rifle rack now held only the 30.06. The carbine was gone.

Chee ran as fast as the darkness allowed, dodging trucks, wagons, people, and camping paraphernalia, toward the tent of Big Hat. Just past the brush arbor he stopped. A light was visible through the taut blue nylon. It moved.

Chee walked toward the tent, quietly now, bringing his labored breathing under control. Through the opening he could see Big Hat's bedroll and the motionless outflung arm of someone wearing a flannel shirt. Chee moved directly in front of the tent door. He had his pistol cocked now. Yost was squatting against the back wall of the tent, illuminated by a battery lantern, sorting through the contents of a blue cloth zipper bag. Big Hat sprawled face down just inside the tent, his hat beside his shoulder. Yost's carbine was across his legs . . .

"Yost," Chee said. "Drop the carbine and . . ."

Yost turned on his heels, swinging the carbine.

Jim Chee, who had never shot anyone, who thought he would never shoot another human, shot Yost through the chest.

Big Hat was dead, the side of his skull dented. Yost had neither pulse nor any sign of breath. Chee fished in the pockets of his bush jacket and retrieved the conco belt. He'd return it to Wire Rims. In the pocket with it were small sealed envelopes. Thirteen of them. Chee opened the first one. The Ace of Hearts. Had Wire Rims guessed the five of hearts, Yost would have handed him the fifth envelope from his pocket. Chee's bullet had gone through the left breast pocket of Yost's jacket—puncturing diamonds or spades.

Behind him Chee could hear the sounds of shouting, of running feet, people gathering at the tent flap. Cowboy was there, staring in at him. "What happened?" Cowboy asked.

And Chee said, "The witch is dead."

Cat's-Paw

Author: Bill Pronzini (1943–   )

Detective: "Nameless" (1968)

When Pronzini introduced his unnamed pulp-collecting private eye in the short story "Sometimes There is Justice" (*Alfred Hitchcock's Mystery Magazine*, August 1968; later reprinted as "It's a Lousy World"), spies and secret agents were in the ascendancy and introducing a new traditional first-person dick-for-hire may have seemed quaintly retro. But the breed enjoyed a renaissance in the next couple of decades, and by the time "Cat's-Paw" appeared in a 1983 limited-edition chapbook, there was a whole organization of P.I. writers (Private Eye Writers of America) in existence to hand it a Shamus award for best short story.

As with the work of his wife, Marcia Muller, Pronzini's Nameless series owes some of its appeal to its well-realized San Francisco background. Thus, it's appropriate to represent Nameless with one of his best cases and one that uses as its setting a San Francisco institution: the Fleishhacker Zoo.

There are two places that are ordinary enough during the daylight hours but that become downright eerie after dark, particularly if you go wandering around in them by yourself. One is a graveyard; the other is a public zoo. And that goes double for San Fancisco's Fleishhacker Zoological Gardens on a blustery winter night when the fog comes swirling in and makes everything look like capering phantoms or two-dimensional cutouts.

Fleishhacker Zoo was where I was on this foggy winter night—alone, for the most part—and I wished I was somewhere else instead. *Anywhere* else, as long as it had a heater or a log fire and offered something hot to drink.

I was on my third tour of the grounds, headed past the sea lion tank to make another check of the aviary, when I paused to squint at the luminous dial of my watch. Eleven forty-five. Less than three hours down and better than six left to go. I was already half-frozen, even though I was wearing long johns, two sweaters, two pairs of socks, heavy gloves, a woolen cap, and a long fur-lined overcoat. The ocean was only a thousand yards away, and the icy wind that blew in off of it sliced through you to the marrow. If I got through this job without contracting pneumonia, I would consider myself lucky.

Somewhere in the fog, one of the animals made a sudden roaring noise; I couldn't tell what kind of animal or where the noise came from. The first time that sort of thing had happened, two nights ago, I'd jumped a little. Now I was used to it, or as used to it as I would ever get. How guys like Dettlinger and Hammond could work here night after night, month after month, was beyond my comprehension.

I went ahead toward the aviary. The big wind-sculpted cypress trees that grew on my left made looming, swaying shadows, like giant black dancers with rustling headdresses wreathed in mist. Back beyond them, fuzzy yellow blobs of light marked the location of the zoo's café. More nightlights burned on the aviary, although the massive fenced-in wing on the near side was dark.

Most of the birds were asleep or nesting or whatever the hell it is birds do at night. But you could hear some of them stirring around, making noise. There were a couple of dozen different varieties in there, including such esoteric types as the crested screamer, the purple gallinule, and the black crake. One esoteric type that used to be in there but wasn't any longer was something called a bunting, a brilliantly colored migratory bird. Three of them had been swiped four days ago, the latest in a rash of thefts the zoological gardens had suffered.

The thief or thieves had also gotten two South American Harris hawks, a bird of prey similar to a falcon; three crab-eating macaques, whatever they were; and half a dozen rare Chiricahua rattlesnakes known as *Crotalus pricei*. He or they had picked the locks on buildings and cages, and got away clean each time. Sam Dettlinger, one of the two regular watchmen, had spotted somebody running the night the rattlers were stolen, and given chase, but he hadn't gotten close enough for much of a description, or even to tell for sure if it was a man or a woman.

The police had been notified, of course, but there was not much they could do. There wasn't much the Zoo Commission could do either, beyond beefing up security—and all that had amounted to was adding one extra night watchman, Al Kirby, on a temporary basis; he was all they could afford. The problem was, Fleishhacker Zoo covers some seventy acres. Long sections of its perimeter fencing are secluded; you couldn't stop somebody determined to climb the fence and sneak in at night if you surrounded the place with a hundred men. Nor could you effectively police the grounds with any less than a hundred men; much of those seventy acres is heavily wooded, and there are dozens of grottoes, brushy fields and slopes, rush-rimmed ponds, and other areas simulating natural habitats for some of the zoo's fourteen hundred animals and birds. Kids, and an occasional grownup, have gotten lost in there in broad daylight. A thief who knew his way around could hide out on the grounds for weeks without being spotted.

I got involved in the case because I was acquainted with one of the commission members, a guy named Lawrence Factor. He was an attorney, and I had done some investigating for him in the past, and he thought I was the cat's nuts when it came to detective work. So he'd come to see me, not as an official emissary of the commission but on his own; the commission had no money left in its small budget for such as the hiring of a private detective. But Factor had made a million bucks or so in the practice of criminal law, and as a passionate animal lover, he was willing to foot the bill himself. What he wanted me to do was sign on as another night watchman, plus nose around among my contacts to find out if there was any word on the street about the thefts.

It seemed like an odd sort of case, and I told him so. "Why would anybody steal hawks and small animals and rattlesnakes?" I asked. "Doesn't make much sense to me."

"It would if you understood how valuable those creatures are to some people."

"What people?"

"Private collectors, for one," he said. "Unscrupulous individuals who run small independent zoos, for another. They've been known to pay exorbitantly high prices for rare specimens they can't obtain through normal channels—usually because of the state or federal laws protecting endangered species."

"You mean there's a thriving black market in animals?"

"You bet there is. Animals, reptiles, birds—you name it. Take the *pricei,* the southwestern rattler, for instance. Several years ago, the Arizona Game and Fish Department placed it on a special permit list; people who want the snake first have to obtain a permit from the Game and Fish authority before they can go out into the Chiricahua Mountains and hunt one. Legitimate researchers have no trouble getting a permit, but hobbyists and private collectors are turned down. Before the permit list, you could get a *pricei* for twenty-five dollars; now, some snake collectors will pay two hundred and fifty dollars and up for one."

"The same high prices apply on the other stolen specimens?"

"Yes," Factor said. "Much higher, in the case of the Harris hawk."

"How much higher?"

"From three to five thousand dollars, after it has been trained for falconry."

I let out a soft whistle. "You have any idea who might be pulling the thefts?"

"Not specifically, no. It could be anybody with a working knowledge of zoology and the right—or wrong—contacts for disposal of the specimens."

"Someone connected with Fleishhacker, maybe?"

"That's possible. But I damned well hope not."

"So your best guess is what?"

"A professional at this sort of thing," Factor said. "They don't usually rob large zoos like ours—there's too much risk and too much publicity; mostly they hit small zoos or private collectors, and do some poaching on the side. But it has been known to happen when they hook up with buyers who are willing to pay premium prices."

"What makes you think it's a pro in this case? Why not an amateur? Or even kids out on some kind of crazy lark?"

"Well, for one thing, the thief seemed to know exactly what he was after each time. Only expensive and endangered specimens were taken. For another thing, the locks on the building and cage doors were picked by an expert—and that's not my theory, it's the police's."

"You figure he'll try it again?"

"Well, he's four-for-four so far, with no hassle except for the minor scare Sam Dettlinger gave him; that has to make him feel pretty secure. And there are dozens more valuable, prohibited specimens in the gardens. I like the odds that he'll push his luck and go for five straight."

But so far the thief hadn't pushed his luck. This was the third night I'd been on the job and nothing had happened. Nothing had happened during my daylight investigation either; I had put out feelers all over the city, but nobody admitted to knowing anything about the zoo thefts. Nor had I been able to find out anything from any of the Fleishhacker employees I'd talked to. All the information I had on the case, in fact, had been furnished by Lawrence Factor in my office three days ago.

If the thief was going to make another hit, I wished he would do it pretty soon and get it over with. Prowling around here in the dark and the fog and that damned icy wind, waiting for something to happen, was starting to get on my nerves. Even if I was being well paid, there were better ways to spend long, cold winter nights. Like curled up in bed with a copy of *Black Mask* or *Detective Tales* or one of the other pulps in my collection. Like curled up in bed with Kerry. . . .

I moved ahead to the near doors of the aviary and tried them to make sure they were still locked. They were. But I shone my flash on them anyway, just to be certain that they hadn't been tampered with since the last time one of us had been by. No problem there, either.

There were four of us on the grounds—Dettlinger, Hammond, Kirby, and me—and the way we'd been working it was to spread out to four corners and then start moving counterclockwise in a set but irregular pattern; that way, we could cover the grounds thoroughly without all of us congregating in one area, and without more than fifteen minutes going by from one building check to another. We each had a walkie-talkie clipped to our belts so one could summon the others if anything went down. We also used the things to radio our positions periodically, so we'd be sure to stay spread out from each other.

I went around the other side of the aviary, to the entrance that faced the long, shallow pond where the bigger tropical birds had their sanctuary. The doors there were also secure. The wind gusted over the pond as I was checking the doors, like a williwaw off the frozen Arctic tundra; it made the cypress trees genuflect, shredded the fog for an instant so that I could see all the way across to the construction site of the new Primate Discovery Center, and cracked my teeth together with a sound like rattling bones. I flexed the cramped fingers of my left hand, the one that had suffered some slight nerve damage in a shooting scrape a few months back; extreme cold aggravated the chronic stiffness. I thought longingly of the hot coffee in my thermos. But the thermos was over at the zoo office behind the carousel, along with my brown-bag supper, and I was not due for a break until one o'clock.

The path that led to Monkey Island was on my left; I took it, hunching forward against the wind. Ahead, I could make out the high dark mass of man-made rocks that comprised the island home of sixty or seventy spider monkeys. But the mist was closing in again, like wind-driven skeins of shiny gray cloth being woven together magically; the building that housed the elephants and pachyderms, only a short distance away, was invisible.

One of the male peacocks that roam the grounds let loose with its weird cry somewhere behind me. The damned things were always doing that, showing off even in the middle of the night. I had never cared for peacocks much, and I liked them even less now. I wondered how one of them would taste roasted with garlic and anchovies. The thought warmed me a little as I moved along the path between the hippo pen and the brown-bear grottoes, turned onto the wide concourse that led past the front of the Lion House.

In the middle of the concourse was an extended oblong pond, with a little center island overgrown with yucca trees and pampas grass. The vegetation had an eerie look in the fog, like fantastic creatures waving their appendages in a low-budget science-fiction film. I veered away from them, over toward the glass-and-wire cages that had been built onto the Lion House's stucco facade. The cages were for show: inside was the Zoological Society's current pride and joy, a year-old white tiger named Prince Charles, one of only fifty known white tigers in the world. Young Charley was the zoo's rarest and most valuable possession, but the thief hadn't attempted to steal him. Nobody in his right mind would try to make off with a frisky, five-hundred-pound tiger in the middle of the night.

Charley was asleep; so was his sister, a normally marked Bengal tiger named Whiskers. I looked at them for a few seconds, decided I wouldn't like to have to pay their food bill, and started to turn away.

Somebody was hurrying toward me, from over where the otter pool was located.

I could barely see him in the mist; he was just a moving black shape. I tensed a little, taking the flashlight out of my pocket, putting my cramped left hand on the walkie-talkie so I could use the thing if it looked like trouble. But it wasn't trouble. The figure called my name in a familiar voice, and when I put my flash on for a couple of seconds I saw that it was Sam Dettlinger.

"What's up?" I said when he got to me. "You're supposed to be over by the gorillas about now."

"Yeah," he said, "but I thought I saw something about fifteen minutes ago, out back by the cat grottoes."

"Saw what?"

"Somebody moving around in the bushes," he said. He tipped back his uniform cap, ran a gloved hand over his face to wipe away the thin film of moisture the fog had put there. He was in his forties, heavyset, owl-eyed, with carrot-colored hair and a mustache that looked like a dead caterpillar draped across his upper lip.

"Why didn't you put out a call?"

"I couldn't be sure I actually saw somebody and I didn't want to sound a false alarm; this damn fog distorts everything, makes you see things that aren't there. Wasn't anybody in the bushes when I went to check. It might have been a squirrel or something. Or just the fog. But I figured I'd better search the area to make sure."

"Anything?"

"No. Zip."

"Well, I'll make another check just in case."

"You want me to come with you?"

"No need. It's about time for your break, isn't it?"

He shot the sleeve of his coat and peered at his watch. "You're right, it's almost midnight—"

Something exploded inside the Lion House—a flat cracking noise that sounded like a gunshot.

Both Dettlinger and I jumped. He said, "What the hell was that?"

"I don't know. Come on!"

We ran the twenty yards or so to the front entrance. The noise had awakened Prince Charles and his sister; they were up and starting to prowl their cage as we rushed past. I caught hold of the door handle and tugged on it, but the lock was secure.

I snapped at Dettlinger, "Have you got a key?"

"Yeah, to all the buildings. . . ."

He fumbled his key ring out, and I switched on my flash to help him find the right key. From inside, there was cold dead silence; I couldn't hear anything anywhere else in the vicinity except for faint animal sounds lost in the mist. Dettlinger got the door unlocked, dragged it open. I crowded in ahead of him, across a short foyer and through another door that wasn't locked, into the building's cavernous main room.

A couple of the ceiling lights were on; we hadn't been able to tell from outside because the Lion House had no windows. The interior was a long rectangle with a terra-cotta tile floor, now-empty feeding cages along the entire facing wall and the near side wall, another set of entrance doors in the far side wall, and a kind of indoor garden full of tropical plants flanking the main entrance to the left. You could see all of the enclosure from two steps inside, and there wasn't anybody in it. Except—

"Jesus!" Dettlinger said. "Look!"

I was looking, all right. And having trouble accepting what I saw. A man lay sprawled on his back inside one of the cages diagonally to our right; there was a small glistening stain of blood on the front of his heavy coat and a revolver of some kind in one of his outflung hands. The small access door at the front of the cage was shut, and so was the sliding panel at the rear that let the big cats in and out at feeding time. In the pale light, I could see the man's face clearly: his teeth were bared in the rictus of death.

"It's Kirby," Dettlinger said in a hushed voice. "Sweet Christ, what—?"

I brushed past him and ran over and climbed the brass railing that fronted all the cages. The access door, a four-by-two-foot barred inset, was locked tight. I poked my nose between two of the bars, peering in at the dead man. Kirby, Al Kirby. The temporary night watchman the Zoo Commission had hired a couple of weeks ago. It looked as though he had been shot in the chest at close range; I could see where the upper middle of his coat had been scorched by the powder discharge.

My stomach jumped a little, the way it always does when I come face-to-face with violent death. The faint, gamy, big-cat smell that hung in the air didn't help it any. I turned toward Dettlinger, who had come up beside me.

"You have a key to this access door?" I asked him.

"No. There's never been a reason to carry one. Only the cat handlers have them." He shook his head in an awed way. "How'd Kirby get in there? What *happened?*"

"I wish I knew. Stay put for a minute."

I left him and ran down to the doors in the far side wall. They were locked. Could somebody have had time to shoot Kirby, get out through these doors, then relock them before Dettlinger and I busted in? It didn't seem likely. We'd been inside less than thirty seconds after we'd heard the shot.

I hustled back to the cage where Kirby's body lay. Dettlinger had backed away from it, around in front of the side-wall cages; he looked a little queasy now himself, as if the implications of violent death had finally registered on him. He had a pack of cigarettes in one hand, getting ready to soothe his nerves with some nicotine. But this wasn't the time or the place for a smoke; I yelled at him to put the things away, and he complied.

When I reached him I said, "What's behind these cages? Some sort of rooms back there, aren't there?"

"Yeah. Where the handlers store equipment and meat for the cats. Chutes, too, that lead out to the grottoes."

"How do you get to them?"

He pointed over at the rear side wall. "That door next to the last cage."

"Any other way in or out of those rooms?"

"No. Except through the grottoes, but the cats are out there."

I went around to the interior door he'd indicated. Like all the others, it was locked. I said to Dettlinger, "You have a key to this door?"

He nodded, got it out, and unlocked the door. I told him to keep watch out here, switched on my flashlight, and went on through. The flash beam showed me where the light switches were; I flicked them on and began a quick, cautious search. The door to one of the meat lockers was open, but nobody was hiding inside. Or anywhere else back there.

When I came out I shook my head in answer to Dettlinger's silent question. Then I asked him, "Where's the nearest phone?"

"Out past the grottoes, by the popcorn stand."

"Hustle out there and call the police. And while you're at it, radio Hammond to get over here on the double—"

"No need for that," a new voice said from the main entrance. "I'm already here."

I glanced in that direction and saw Gene Hammond, the other regular night watchman. You couldn't miss him; he was six-five, weighed in at a good two-fifty, and had a face like the back end of a bus. Disbelief was written on it now as he stared across at Kirby's body.

"Go," I told Dettlinger. "I'll watch things here."

"Right."

He hurried out past Hammond, who was on his way toward where I stood in front of the cage. Hammond said as he came up, "God—what happened?"

"We don't know yet."

"How'd Kirby get in there?"

"We don't know that either." I told him what we did know, which was not much. "When did you last see Kirby?"

"Not since the shift started at nine."

"Any idea why he'd have come in here?"

"No. Unless he heard something and came in to investigate. But he shouldn't have been in this area, should he?"

"Not for another half hour, no."

"Christ, you don't think that he—"

"What?"

"Killed himself," Hammond said.

"It's possible. Was he despondent for some reason?"

"Not that I know about. But it sure looks like suicide. I mean, he's got that gun in his hand, he's all alone in the building, all the doors are locked. What else could it be?"

"Murder," I said.

"How? Where's the person who killed him, then?"

"Got out through one of the grottoes, maybe."

"No way," Hammond said. "Those cats would maul anybody who went out among 'em—and I mean anybody; not even any of the handlers would try a stunt like that. Besides, even if somebody made it down into the moat, how would he scale that twenty-foot back wall to get out of it?"

I didn't say anything.

Hammond said, "And another thing: why would Kirby be locked in this cage if it was murder?"

"Why would he lock himself in to commit suicide?"

He made a bewildered gesture with one of his big hands.

"Crazy," he said. "The whole thing's crazy."

He was right. None of it seemed to make any sense at all.

I knew one of the homicide inspectors who responded to Dettlinger's call. His name was Branislaus and he was a pretty decent guy, so the preliminary questions-and-answers went fast and hassle-free. After which he packed Dettlinger and Hammond and me off to the zoo office while he and the lab crew went to work inside the Lion House.

I poured some hot coffee from my thermos, to help me thaw out a little, and then used one of the phones to get Lawrence Factor out of bed. He was paying my fee and I figured he had a right to know what had happened as soon as possible. He made shocked noises when I told him, asked a couple of pertinent questions, said he'd get out to Fleishhacker right away, and rang off.

An hour crept away. Dettlinger sat at one of the desks with a pad of paper and a pencil and challenged himself in a string of tick-tack-toe games. Hammond chain-smoked cigarettes until the air in there was blue with smoke. I paced around for the most part, now and then stepping out into the chilly night to get some fresh air: all that cigarette smoke was playing merry hell with my lungs. None of us had much to say. We were all waiting to see what Branislaus and the rest of the cops turned up.

Factor arrived at one-thirty, looking harried and upset. It was the first time I had ever seen him without a tie and with his usually immaculate Robert Redford hairdo in some disarray. A patrolman accompanied him into the office, and judging from the way Factor glared at him, he had had some difficulty getting past the front gate. When the patrolman left I gave Factor a detailed account of what had taken place as far as I knew it, with embellishments from Dettlinger. I was just finishing when Branislaus came in.

Branny spent a couple of minutes discussing matters with Factor. Then he said he wanted to talk to the rest of us one at a time, picked me to go first, and herded me into another room.

The first thing he said was, "This is the screwiest shooting case I've come up against in twenty years on the force. What in bloody hell is going on here?"

"I was hoping maybe you could tell me."

"Well, I can't—yet. So far it looks like a suicide, but if that's it, it's a candidate for Ripley. Whoever heard of anybody blowing himself away in a lion cage at the zoo?"

"Any indication he locked himself in there?"

"We found a key next to his body that fits the access door in front."

"Just one loose key?"

"That's right."

"So it could have been dropped in there by somebody else after Kirby was dead and after the door was locked. Or thrown in through the bars from outside."

"Granted."

"And suicides don't usually shoot themselves in the chest," I said.

"Also granted, although it's been known to happen."

"What kind of weapon was he shot with? I couldn't see it too well from outside the cage, the way he was lying."

"Thirty-two Iver Johnson."

"Too soon to tell yet if it was his, I guess."

"Uh-huh. Did he come on the job armed?"

"Not that I know about. The rest of us weren't, or weren't supposed to be."

"Well, we'll know more when we finish running a check on the serial number," Branislaus said. "It was intact, so the thirty-two doesn't figure to be a Saturday night special."

"Was there anything in Kirby's pockets?"

"The usual stuff. And no sign of a suicide note. But you don't think it was suicide anyway, right?"

"No, I don't."

"Why not?"

"No specific reason. It's just that a suicide under those circumstances rings false. And so does a suicide on the heels of the thefts the zoo's been having lately."

"So you figure there's a connection between Kirby's death and the thefts?"

"Don't you?"

"The thought crossed my mind," Branislaus said dryly. "Could be the thief slipped back onto the grounds tonight, something happened before he had a chance to steal something, and he did for Kirby—I'll admit the possibility. But what were the two of them doing in the Lion House? Doesn't add up that Kirby caught the guy in there. Why would the thief enter it in the first place? Not because he was trying to steal a lion or a tiger, that's for sure."

"Maybe Kirby stumbled on him somewhere else, somewhere nearby. Maybe there was a struggle; the thief got the drop on Kirby, then forced him to let both of them into the Lion House with his key."

"Why?"

"To get rid of him where it was private."

"I don't buy it," Branny said. "Why wouldn't he just knock Kirby over the head and run for it?"

"Well, it could be he's somebody Kirby knew."

"Okay. But the Lion House angle is still too much trouble for him to go through. It would've been much easier to shove the gun into Kirby's belly and shoot him on the spot. Kirby's clothing would have muffled the sound of the shot; it wouldn't have been audible more than fifty feet away."

"I guess you're right," I said.

"But even supposing it happened the way you suggest, it *still* doesn't add up. You and Dettlinger were inside the Lion House thirty seconds after the shot, by your own testimony. You checked the side entrance doors almost immediately and they were locked; you looked around behind the cages and nobody was there. So how did the alleged killer get out of the building?"

"The only way he could have got out was through one of the grottoes in back."

"Only he *couldn't* have, according to what both Dettlinger and Hammond say."

I paced over to one of the windows—nervous energy—and looked out at the fog-wrapped construction site for the new monkey exhibit. Then I turned and said, "I don't suppose your men found anything in the way of evidence inside the Lion House?"

"Not so you could tell it with the naked eye."

"Or anywhere else in the vicinity?"

"No."

"Any sign of tampering on any of the doors?"

"None. Kirby used his key to get in, evidently."

I came back to where Branislaus was leaning hipshot against some-body's desk. "Listen, Branny," I said, "this whole thing is *too* screwball. Somebody's playing games here, trying to muddle our thinking—and that means murder."

"Maybe," he said. "Hell, probably. But how was it done? I can't come up with an answer, not even one that's believably far-fetched. Can you?"

"Not yet."

"Does that mean you've got an idea?"

"Not an idea; just a bunch of little pieces looking for a pattern."

He sighed. "Well, if they find it, let me know."

When I went back into the other room I told Dettlinger that he was next on the grill. Factor wanted to talk some more, but I put him off. Hammond was still polluting the air with his damned cigarettes, and I needed another shot of fresh air; I also needed to be alone for a while.

I put my overcoat on and went out and wandered past the cages where the smaller cats were kept, past the big open fields that the gi-raffes and rhinos called home. The wind was stronger and colder than it had been earlier; heavy gusts swept dust and twigs along the ground, broke the fog up into scudding wisps. I pulled my cap down over my ears to keep them from numbing.

The path led along to the concourse at the rear of the Lion House, where the open cat grottoes were. Big, portable electric lights had been set up there and around the front so the police could search the area. A couple of patrolmen glanced at me as I approached, but they must have recognized me because neither of them came over to ask what I was doing there.

I went to the low, shrubberied wall that edged the middle cat grotto. Whatever was in there, lions or tigers, had no doubt been aroused by all the activity; but they were hidden inside the dens at the rear. These grottoes had been newly renovated—lawns, jungly vegetation, small trees, everything to give the cats the illusion of their native habitat. The side walls separating this grotto from the other two were man-made rocks, high and unscalable. The moat below was fifty feet wide, too far for either a big cat or a man to jump; and the near moat wall was sheer and also unscalable from below, just as Hammond and Dettlinger had said.

No way anybody could have got out of the Lion House through the grottoes, I thought. Just no way.

No way it could have been murder then. Unless—

I stood there for a couple of minutes, with my mind beginning, finally, to open up. Then I hurried around to the front of the Lion House and looked at the main entrance for a time, remembering things.

And then I knew.

Branislaus was in the zoo office, saying something to Factor when I came back inside. He glanced over at me as I shut the door.

"Branny," I said, "those little pieces I told you about a while ago finally found their pattern."

He straightened. "Oh? Some of it or all of it?"

"All of it, I think."

Factor said, "What's this about?"

"I figured out what happened at the Lion House tonight," I said. "Al Kirby didn't commit suicide: he was murdered. And I can name the man who killed him."

I expected a reaction, but I didn't get one beyond some widened eyes and opened mouths. Nobody said anything and nobody moved much. But you could feel the sudden tension in the room, as thick in its own intangible way as the layers of smoke from Hammond's cigarettes.

"Name him," Branislaus said.

But I didn't, not just yet. A good portion of what I was going to say was guesswork—built on deduction and logic, but still guesswork—and I wanted to choose my words carefully. I took off my cap, unbuttoned my coat, and moved away from the door, over near where Branny was standing.

He said, "Well? Who do you say killed Kirby?"

"The same person who stole the birds and other specimens. And I don't mean a professional animal thief, as Mr. Factor suggested when he hired me. He isn't an outsider at all; and he didn't climb the fence to get onto the grounds."

"No?"

"No. He was *already* in here on those nights and on this one because he works here as a night watchman. The man I'm talking about is Sam Dettlinger."

That got some reaction. Hammond said, "I don't believe it," and Factor said, "My God!" Branislaus looked at me, looked at Dettlinger, looked at me again—moving his head like a spectator at a tennis match.

The only one who didn't move was Dettlinger. He sat still at one of the desks, his hands resting easily on its blotter; his face betrayed nothing.

He said, "You're a liar," in a thin, hard voice.

"Am I? You've been working here for some time; you know the animals and which ones are endangered and valuable. It was easy for you to get into the buildings during your rounds: just use your key and walk right in. When you had the specimens you took them to some prearranged spot along the outside fence and passed them over to an accomplice."

"What accomplice?" Branislaus asked.

"I don't know. You'll get it out of him, Branny; or you'll find out some other way. But that's how he had to have worked it."

"What about the scratches on the locks?" Hammond asked. "The police told us the locks were picked—"

"Red herring," I said. "Just like Dettlinger's claim that he chased a stranger on the grounds the night the rattlers were stolen. Designed to cover up the fact that it was an inside job." I looked back at Branislaus. "Five'll get you ten Dettlinger's had some sort of locksmithing experience. It shouldn't take much digging to find out."

Dettlinger started to get out of his chair, thought better of it, and sat down again. We were all staring at him, but it did not seem to bother him much; his owl eyes were on my neck, and if they'd been hands I would have been dead of strangulation.

Without shifting his gaze, he said to Factor, "I'm going to sue this son of a bitch for slander. I can do that, can't I, Mr. Factor?"

"If what he says isn't true, you can," Factor said.

"Well, it isn't true. It's all a bunch of lies. I never stole anything. And I sure never killed Al Kirby. How the hell could I? I was with this guy, *outside* the Lion House, when Al died inside."

"No, you weren't," I said.

"What kind of crap is that? I was standing right next to you, we both heard the shot—"

"That's right, we both heard the shot. And that's the first thing that put me onto you, Sam. Because we damned well *shouldn't* have heard it."

"No? Why not?"

"Kirby was shot with a thirty-two-caliber revolver. A thirty-two is a small gun; it doesn't make much of a bang. Branny, you remember saying to me a little while ago that if somebody had shoved that thirty-two into Kirby's middle, you wouldn't have been able to hear the pop more than fifty feet away? Well, that's right. But Dettlinger and I were a lot more than fifty feet from the cage where we found Kirby—twenty yards from the front entrance, thick stucco walls, a ten-foot foyer, and another forty feet or so of floor space to the cage. Yet we not only heard a shot, we heard it loud and clear."

Branislaus said, "So how is that possible?"

I didn't answer him. Instead I looked at Dettlinger and I said, "Do you smoke?"

That got a reaction out of him. The one I wanted: confusion. "What?"

"Do you smoke?"

"What kind of question is that?"

"Gene must have smoked half a pack since we've been in here, but I haven't seen you light up once. In fact, I haven't seen you light up the whole time I've been working here. So answer me, Sam—do you smoke or not?"

"No, I don't smoke. You satisfied?"

"I'm satisfied," I said. "Now suppose you tell me what it was you had in your hand in the Lion House, when I came back from checking the side doors?"

He got it, then—the way I'd trapped him. But he clamped his lips together and sat still.

"What are you getting at?" Branislaus asked me. "What *did* he have in his hand?"

"At the time I thought it was a pack of cigarettes; that's what it looked like from a distance. I took him to be a little queasy, a delayed reaction to finding the body, and I figured he wanted some nicotine to calm his nerves. But that wasn't it at all; he wasn't queasy, he was scared—because I'd seen what he had in his hand before he could hide it in his pocket."

"So what was it?"

"A tape recorder," I said. "One of those small battery-operated jobs they make nowadays, a white one that fits in the palm of the hand. He'd just picked it up from wherever he'd stashed it earlier—behind the bars in one of the other cages, probably. I didn't notice it there because it was so small and because my attention was on Kirby's body."

"You're saying the shot you heard was on tape?"

"Yes. My guess is, he recorded it right after he shot Kirby. Fifteen minutes or so earlier."

"Why did he shoot Kirby? And why in the Lion House?"

"Well, he and Kirby could have been in on the thefts together; they could have had some kind of falling-out, and Dettlinger decided to get rid of him. But I don't like that much. As a premeditated murder, it's too elaborate. No, I think the recorder was a spur-of-the-moment idea; I doubt if it belonged to Dettlinger, in fact. Ditto the thirty-two. He's clever, but he's not a planner, he's an improviser."

"If the recorder and the gun weren't his, whose were they? Kirby's?"

I nodded. "The way I see it, Kirby found out about Dettlinger pulling the thefts; saw him do the last one, maybe. Instead of reporting it, he did some brooding and then decided tonight to try a little shakedown. But Dettlinger's bigger and tougher than he was, so he used the recorder, the idea probably being to tape his conversation with Dettlinger, without Dettlinger's knowledge, for further blackmail leverage.

"He buttonholed Dettlinger in the vicinity of the Lion House and the two of them went inside to talk it over in private. Then something happened. Dettlinger tumbled to the recorder, got rough, Kirby pulled the gun, they struggled for it, Kirby got shot dead—that sort of scenario.

"So then Dettlinger had a corpse on his hands. What was he going to do? He could drag it outside, leave it somewhere, make it look like the mythical fence-climbing thief killed him; but if he did that he'd be running the risk of me or Hammond appearing suddenly and spotting him. Instead he got what he thought was a bright idea: he'd create a big mystery and confuse the hell out of everybody, plus give himself a dandy alibi for the apparent time of Kirby's death.

"He took the gun and the recorder to the storage area behind the cages. Erased what was on the tape, used the fast-forward and the timer to run off fifteen minutes of tape, then switched to record and fired a second shot to get the sound of it on tape. I don't know for sure what he fired the bullet into; but I found one of the meat locker doors open when I searched back there, so maybe he used a slab of meat for a target. And then piled a bunch of other slabs on top to hide it until he could get rid of it later on. The police wouldn't be looking for a second bullet, he thought, so there wasn't any reason for them to rummage around in the meat.

"His next moves were to rewind the tape, go back out front, and stash the recorder—turned on, with the volume all the way up. That gave him fifteen minutes. He picked up Kirby's body . . . most of the blood from the wound had been absorbed by the heavy coat Kirby was wearing, which was why there wasn't any blood on the floor and why Dettlinger didn't get any on him. And why I didn't notice, fifteen minutes later, that it was starting to coagulate. He carried the body to the cage, put it inside with the thirty-two in Kirby's hand, relocked the access door—he told me he didn't have a key, but that was a lie—and then threw the key in with the body. But putting Kirby in the cage was his big mistake. By doing that he made the whole thing too bizarre. If he'd left the body where it was, he'd have had a better chance of getting away with it.

"Anyhow, he slipped out of the building without being seen and hid over by the otter pool. He knew I was due there at midnight, because of the schedule we'd set up; and he wanted to be with me when that recorded gunshot went off. Make me the cat's-paw, if you don't mind a little grim humor, for what he figured would be his perfect alibi.

"Later on, when I sent him to report Kirby's death, he disposed of the recorder. He couldn't have gone far from the Lion House to get rid of it; he made the call, and he was back within fifteen minutes. With any luck, his fingerprints will be on the recorder when your men turn it up.

"And if you want any more proof I'll swear in court I didn't smell cordite when we entered the Lion House; all I smelled was the gamy odor of jungle cats. I should have smelled cordite if that thirty-two had just been discharged. But it hadn't, and the cordite smell from the earlier discharges had already faded."

That was a pretty long speech and it left me dry-mouthed. But it had made its impression on the others in the room, Branislaus in particular.

He asked Dettlinger, "Well? You have anything to say for yourself?"

"I never did any of those things he said—none of 'em, you hear?"

"I hear."

"And that's all I'm saying until I see a lawyer."

"You've got one of the best sitting next to you. How about it, Mr. Factor? You want to represent Dettlinger?"

"Pass," Factor said thinly. "This is one case where I'll be glad to plead bias."

Dettlinger was still strangling me with his eyes. I wondered if he would keep on proclaiming his innocence even in the face of stronger evidence than what I'd just presented. Or if he'd crack under pressure. as most amateurs do.

I decided he was the kind who'd crack eventually, and I quit looking at him and at the death in his eyes.

"Well, I was wrong about that much," I said to Kerry the following night. We were sitting in front of a log fire in her Diamond Heights apartment, me with a beer and her with a glass of wine, and I had just finished telling her all about it. "Dettlinger hasn't cracked and it doesn't look as if he's going to. The DA'll have to work for his conviction."

"But you *were* right about most of it?"

"Pretty much. I probably missed a few details; with Kirby dead, and unless Dettlinger talks, we may never know some of them for sure. But for the most part I think I got it straight."

"My hero," she said, and gave me an adoring look.

She does that sometimes—puts me on like that. I don't understand women, so I don't know why. But it doesn't matter. She has auburn hair and green eyes and a fine body; she's also smarter than I am—she works as an advertising copywriter—and she is stimulating to be around. I love her to pieces, as the boys in the back room used to say.

"The police found the tape recorder," I said. "Took them until late this morning, because Dettlinger was clever about hiding it. He'd buried it in some rushes inside the hippo pen, probably with the idea of digging it up again later on and getting rid of it permanently. There was one clear print on the fast-forward button—Dettlinger's."

"Did they also find the second bullet he fired?"

"Yep. Where I guessed it was: in one of the slabs of fresh meat in the open storage locker."

"And did Dettlinger have locksmithing experience?"

"Uh-huh. He worked for a locksmith for a year in his mid-twenties. The case against him, even without a confession, is pretty solid."

"What about his accomplice?"

"Branislaus thinks he's got a line on the guy," I said. "From some things he found in Dettlinger's apartment. Man named Gerber—got a record of animal poaching and theft. I talked to Larry Factor this afternoon and he's heard of Gerber. The way he figures it, Dettlinger and Gerber had a deal for the specimens they stole with some collectors in Florida. That seems to be Gerber's usual pattern of operation anyway."

"I hope they get him, too," Kerry said. "I don't like the idea of stealing birds and animals out of the zoo. It's . . . obscene, somehow."

"So is murder."

We didn't say anything for a time, looking into the fire, working on our drinks.

"You know," I said finally, "I have a lot of sympathy for animals myself. Take gorillas, for instance."

"Why gorillas?"

"Because of their mating habits."

"What are their mating habits?"

I had no idea, but I made up something interesting. Then I gave her a practical demonstration.

No gorilla ever had it so good.

Somewhere in the City

Author: Marcia Muller (1944–   )

Detective: Sharon McCone (1977)

Though technically preceded, by virtue of a short-story appearance, by Maxine O'Callaghan's Delilah West, Sharon McCone is generally regarded as the first of the new, relatively realistic, woman-created female private eyes. Though her debut in *Edwin of the Iron Shoes* (1977) made a relatively small impact, and was not followed by a second case until *Ask the Cards a Question* (1982), she continues to be one of the best-known and most skillful in the field. Of the top echelon of female private eyes, McCone is both the most active and the most effective at shorter-than-novel length.

One of the strongest attributes of the McCone series has been its sense of place, specifically San Francisco, so it seemed appropriate to represent her in a case involving a real-life trauma to that great city.

*A*t 5:04 *P.M.* on October 17, 1989, the city of San Francisco was jolted by an earthquake that measured a frightening 7.1 on the Richter Scale. The violent tremors left the Bay Bridge impassable, collapsed a double-decker freeway in nearby Oakland, and toppled or severely damaged countless homes and other buildings. From the Bay Area to the seaside town of Santa Cruz some 100 miles south, sixty-five people were killed and thousands left homeless. And when the aftershocks subsided, San Francisco entered a new era—one in which things would never be quite the same. As with all cataclysmic events, the question "Where were you when?" will forever provoke deeply emotional responses in those of us who lived through it . . . .

* * *

Where I was when: the headquarters of the Golden Gate Crisis Hotline in the Noe Valley district. I'd been working a case there—off and on, and mostly in the late afternoon and evening hours, for over two weeks—with very few results and with a good deal of frustration.

The hot line occupied one big windowless room behind a rundown coffeehouse on Twenty-fourth Street. The location, I'd been told, was not so much one of choice as of convenience (meaning the rent was affordable), but had I not known that, I would have considered it a stroke of genius. There was something instantly soothing about entering through the coffeehouse, where the aromas of various blends permeated the air and steam rose from huge stainless-steel urns. The patrons were unthreatening—mostly shabby and relaxed, reading or conversing with their feet propped up on chairs. The pastries displayed in the glass case were comfort food at its purest—reminders of the days when calories and cholesterol didn't count. And the round face of the proprietor, Lloyd Warner, was welcoming and kind as he waved troubled visitors through to the crisis center.

On that Tuesday afternoon I arrived at about twenty to five, answering Lloyd's cheerful greeting and trying to ignore the chocolate-covered doughnuts in the case. I had a dinner date at seven-thirty, had been promised some of the best French cuisine on Russian Hill, and was unwilling to spoil my appetite. The doughnuts called out to me, but I turned a deaf ear and hurried past.

The room beyond the coffeehouse contained an assortment of mismatched furniture: several desks and chairs of all vintages and materials, phones in colors and styles ranging from standard black touchtone to a shocking turquoise princess, three tattered easy chairs dating back to the fifties, and a card table covered with literature on health and psychological services. Two people manned the desks nearest the door. I went to the desk with the turquoise phone, plunked my briefcase and bag down on it, and turned to face them.

"He call today?" I asked.

Pete Lowry, a slender man with a bandit's mustache who was director of the center, took his booted feet off the desk and swiveled to face me. "Nope. It's been quiet all afternoon."

"Too quiet." This came from Ann Potter, a woman with dark frizzed hair who affected the aging-hippie look in jeans and flamboyant overblouses. "And this weather—I don't like it one bit."

"Ann's having one of her premonitions of gloom and doom," Pete said. "Evil portents and omens lurk all around us—although most of them went up front for coffee a while ago."

Ann's eyes narrowed to a glare. She possessed very little sense of humor, whereas Pete perhaps possessed too much. To forestall the inevitable spat, I interrupted. "Well, I don't like the weather much myself. It's muggy and too warm for October. It makes me nervous."

"Why?" Pete asked.

I shrugged. "I don't know, but I've felt edgy all day."

The phone on his desk rang. He reached for the receiver. "Golden Gate Crisis Hotline, Pete speaking."

Ann cast one final glare at his back as she crossed to the desk that had been assigned to me. "It has been too quiet," she said defensively. "Hardly anyone's called, not even to inquire about how to deal with a friend or a family member. That's not normal, even for a Tuesday."

"Maybe all the crazies are out enjoying the warm weather."

Ann half-smiled, cocking her head. She wasn't sure if what I'd said was funny or not, and didn't know how to react. After a few seconds her attention was drawn to the file I was removing from my briefcase. "Is that about our problem caller?"

"Uh-huh." I sat down and began rereading my notes silently, hoping she'd go away. I'd meant it when I'd said I felt on edge, and was in no mood for conversation.

The file concerned a series of calls that the hot line had received over the past month—all from the same individual, a man with a distinctive raspy voice. Their content had been more or less the same: an initial complaint of being all alone in the world with no one to care if he lived or died; then a gradual escalating from despair to anger, in spite of the trained counselors' skillful responses; and finally the declaration that he had an assault rifle and was going to kill others and himself. He always ended with some variant on the statement, "I'm going to take a whole lot of people with me."

After three of the calls, Pete had decided to notify the police. A trace was placed on the center's lines, but the results were unsatisfactory; most of the time the caller didn't stay on the phone long enough, and in the instances that the calls could be traced, they turned out to have originated from booths in the Marina district. Finally, the trace was taken off, the official conclusion being that the calls were the work of a crank—and possibly one with a grudge against someone connected with the hot line.

The official conclusion did not satisfy Pete, however. By the next morning he was in the office of the hot line's attorney at All Souls Legal Cooperative, where I am chief investigator. And a half an hour after that, I was assigned to work the phones at the hot line as often as my other duties permitted, until I'd identified the caller. Following a crash course from Pete in techniques for dealing with callers in crisis—augmented by some reading of my own—they turned me loose on the turquoise phone.

After the first couple of rocky, sweaty-palmed sessions, I'd gotten into it: become able to distinguish the truly disturbed from the fakers or the merely curious; learned to gauge the responses that would work best with a given individual; succeeded at eliciting information that would permit a crisis team to go out and assess the seriousness of the situation in person. In most cases, the team would merely talk the caller into getting counseling. However, if they felt immediate action was warranted, they would contact the SFPD, who had the authority to have the individual held for evaluation at S. F. General Hospital for up to seventy-two hours.

During the past two weeks the problem caller had been routed to me several times, and with each conversation I became more concerned about him. While his threats were melodramatic, I sensed genuine disturbance and desperation in his voice; the swift escalation of panic and anger seemed much out of proportion to whatever verbal stimuli I offered. And, as Pete had stressed in my orientation, no matter how theatrical or frequently made, any threat of suicide or violence toward others was to be taken with the utmost seriousness by the hot-line volunteers.

Unfortunately I was able to glean very little information from the man. Whenever I tried to get him to reveal concrete facts about himself, he became sly and would dodge my questions. Still, I could make several assumptions about him: he was youngish, reasonably well-educated, and Caucasian. The traces to the Marina indicated he probably lived in that bayside district—which meant he had to have a good income. He listened to classical music (three times I'd heard it playing in the background) from a transistor radio, by the tinny tonal quality. Once I'd caught the call letters of the FM station—one with a wide-range signal in the Central Valley town of Fresno. Why Fresno? I'd wondered. Perhaps he was from there? But that wasn't much to go on; there were probably several Fresno transplants in his part of the city.

When I looked up from my folder, Ann had gone back to her desk. Pete was still talking in low, reassuring tones with his caller. Ann's phone rang, and she picked up the receiver. I tensed, knowing the next call would cycle automatically to my phone.

When it rang some minutes later, I glanced at my watch and jotted down the time while reaching over for the receiver. Four-fifty-eight. "Golden Gate Crisis Hotline, Sharon speaking."

The caller hung up—either a wrong number or, more likely, someone who lost his nerve. The phone rang again about twenty seconds later and I answered it in the same manner.

"Sharon. It's me." The greeting was the same as the previous times, the raspy voice unmistakable.

"Hey, how's it going?"

A long pause, labored breathing. In the background I could make out the strains of music—Brahms, I thought. "Not so good. I'm really down today."

"You want to talk about it?"

"There isn't much to say. Just more of the same. I took a walk a while ago, thought it might help. But the people, out there flying their kites, I can't take it."

"Why is that?"

"I used to . . . ah, forget it."

"No, I'm interested."

"Well, they're always in couples, you know."

When he didn't go on, I made an interrogatory sound.

"The whole damn world is in couples. Or families. Even here inside my little cottage I can feel it. There are these apartment buildings on either side, land I can feel them pressing in on me, and I'm here all alone."

He was speaking rapidly now, his voice rising. But as his agitation increased, he'd unwittingly revealed something about his living situation. I made a note about the little cottage between the two apartment buildings.

"This place where the people were flying kites," I said, "do you go there often?"

"Sure—it's only two blocks away." A sudden note of sullenness now entered his voice—a part of the pattern he'd previously exhibited. "Why do you want to know about that?"

"Because . . . I'm sorry, I forgot your name."

No response.

"It would help if I knew what to call you."

"Look, bitch, I know what you're trying to do."

"Oh?"

"Yeah. You want to get a name, an address. Send the cops out. Next thing I'm chained to the wall at S.F. General. I've been that route before.

But I know my rights now; I went down the street to the Legal Switchboard, and they told me . . ."

I was distracted from what he was saying by a tapping sound—the stack trays on the desk next to me bumped against the wall. I looked over there, frowning. What was causing that . . . ?"

". . . gonna take the people next door with me . . ."

I looked back at the desk in front of me. The lamp was jiggling.

"What the hell?" the man on the phone exclaimed.

My swivel chair shifted. A coffee mug tipped and rolled across the desk and into my lap.

Pete said, "Jesus Christ, we're having and earthquake!"

". . . The ceiling's coming down!" The man's voice was panicked now.

"Get under a door frame!" I clutched the edge of the desk, ignoring my own advice.

I heard a crash from the other end of the line. The man screamed in pain. "Help me! Please help—" And then the line went dead.

For a second or so I merely sat there—longtime San Franciscan, frozen by my own disbelief. All around me formerly inanimate objects were in motion. Pete and Ann were scrambling for the archway that led to the door of the coffeehouse.

"Sharon, get under the desk!" she yelled at me.

And then the electricity cut out, leaving the windowless room in blackness. I dropped the dead receiver, slid off the chair, crawled into the kneehole of the desk. There was a cracking, a violent shifting, as if a giant hand had seized the building and twisted it. Tremors buckled the floor beneath me.

This is a bad one. Maybe the big one that they're always talking about.

The sound of something wrenching apart. Pellets of plaster rained down on the desk above me. Time had telescoped; it seemed as if the quake had been going on for many minutes, when in reality it could not have been more than ten or fifteen seconds.

Make it stop! Please make it stop!

And then, as if whatever powers-that-be had heard my unspoken plea, the shock waves diminished to shivers, and finally ebbed.

Blackness. Silence. Only bits of plaster bouncing off the desks and the floor.

"Ann?" I said. "Pete?" My voice sounded weak, tentative.

"Sharon?" It was Pete. "You okay?"

"Yes. You?"

"We're fine."

Slowly I began to back out of the kneehole. Something blocked it—the chair. I shoved it aside, and emerged. I couldn't see a thing, but I could feel fragments of plaster and other unidentified debris on the floor. Something cut into my palm; I winced.

"God, it's dark," Ann said. "I've got some matches in my purse. Can you—"

"No matches," I told her. "Who knows what shape the gas mains are in."

". . . Oh, right."

Pete said, "Wait, I'll open the door to the coffeehouse."

On hands and knees I began feeling my way toward the sound of their voices. I banged into one of the desks, overturned a wastebasket, then finally reached the opposite wall. As I stood there, Ann's cold hand reached out to guide me. Behind her I could hear Pete fumbling at the door.

I leaned against the wall. Ann was close beside me, her breathing erratic. Pete said, "Goddamned door's jammed." From behind it came voices of the people in the coffeehouse.

Now that the danger was over—at least until the first of the after-shocks—my body sagged against the wall, giving way to tremors of its own manufacture. My thoughts turned to the lover with whom I'd planned to have dinner: where had he been when the quake hit? And what about my cats, my house? My friends and my coworkers at All Souls? Other friends scattered throughout the Bay Area?

And what about a nameless, faceless man somewhere in the city who had screamed for help before the phone went dead?

The door to the coffeehouse burst open, spilling weak light into the room. Lloyd Warner and several of his customers peered anxiously through it. I prodded Ann—who seemed to have lapsed into lethargy—toward them.

The coffeehouse was fairly dark, but late-afternoon light showed beyond the plate-glass windows fronting on the street. It revealed a floor that was awash in spilled liquid and littered with broken crockery. Chairs were tipped over—whether by the quake or the patrons' haste to get to shelter I couldn't tell. About ten people milled about, talking noisily.

Ann and Pete joined them, but I moved forward to the window. Outside, Twenty-fourth Street looked much as usual, except for the lack of traffic and pedestrians. The buildings still stood, the sun still shone, the air drifting through the open door of the coffeehouse was still warm and muggy. In this part of the city, at least, life went on.

Lloyd's transistor radio had been playing the whole time—tuned to the station that was carrying the coverage of the third game of the Bay Area World Series, due to start at five-thirty. I moved closer, listening.

The sportscaster was saying, "Nobody here knows *what's* going on. The Giants have wandered over to the A's dugout. It looks like a softball game where somebody forgot to bring the ball."

Then the broadcast shifted abruptly to the station's studios. A newswoman was relaying telephone reports from the neighborhoods. I was relieved to hear that Bernal Heights, where All Souls is located, and my own small district near Glen Park were shaken up but for the most part undamaged. The broadcaster concluded by warning listeners not to use their phones except in cases of emergency. Ann snorted and said, "Do as I say but not . . ."

Again the broadcast made an abrupt switch—to the station's traffic helicopter. "From where we are," the reporter said, "it looks as if part of the upper deck on the Oakland side of the Bay Bridge has collapsed onto the bottom deck. Cars are pointing every whichway, there may be some in the water. And on the approaches—" The transmission broke, then resumed after a number of static-filled seconds. "It looks as if the Cypress Structure on the Oakland approach to the bridge has also collapsed. Oh my God, there are cars and people—" This time the transmission broke for good.

It was very quiet in the coffeehouse. We all exchanged looks—fearful, horrified. This was an extremely bad one, if not the catastrophic one they'd been predicting for so long.

Lloyd was the first to speak. He said, "I'd better see if I can insulate the urns in some way, keep the coffee hot as long as possible. People'll need it tonight." He went behind the counter, and in a few seconds a couple of the customers followed.

The studio newscast resumed. ". . . fires burning out of control in the Marina district. We're receiving reports of collapsed buildings there, with people trapped inside . . ."

The Marina district. People trapped.

I thought again of the man who had cried out for help over the phone. Of my suspicion, more or less confirmed by today's conversation, that he lived in the Marina.

Behind the counter Lloyd and the customers were wrapping the urns in dishtowels. Here—and in other parts of the city, I was sure—people were already overcoming their shock, gearing up to assist in the relief effort. There was nothing I could do in my present surroundings, but . . .

I hurried to the back room and groped until I found my purse on the floor beside the desk. As I picked it up, an aftershock hit—nothing like the original trembler, but strong enough to make me grab the chair for support. When it stopped, I went shakily out to my car.

Twenty-fourth Street was slowly coming to life. People bunched on the sidewalks, talking and gesturing. A man emerged from one of the shops, walked to the center of the street and surveyed the facade of his building. In the parking lot of nearby Bell Market, employees and customers gathered by the grocery carts. A man in a butcher's apron looked around, shrugged, and headed for a corner tavern. I got into my MG and took a city map from the side pocket.

The Marina area consists mainly of early twentieth-century stucco homes and apartment buildings built on fill on the shore of the bay— which meant the quake damage there would naturally be bad. The district extends roughly from the Fisherman's Wharf area to the Presidio— not large, but large enough, considering I had few clues as to where within its boundary my man lived. I spread out the map against the steering wheel and examined it.

The man had said he'd taken a walk that afternoon, to a place two blocks from his home where people were flying kites. That would be the Marina Green near the Yacht Harbor, famous for the elaborate and often fantastical kites flown there in fine weather. Two blocks placed the man's home somewhere on the far side of Northpoint Street.

I had one more clue: in his anger at me he'd let it slip that the Legal Switchboard was "down the street." The switchboard, a federally funded assistance group, was headquartered in one of the piers at Fort Mason, at the east end of the Marina. While several streets in that vicinity ended at Fort Mason, I saw that only two—Beach and Northpoint—were within two blocks of the Green as well.

Of course, I reminded myself, "down the street" and "two blocks" could have been generalizations or exaggerations. But it was somewhere to start. I set the map aside and turned the key in the ignition.

The trip across the city was hampered by near-gridlock traffic on some streets. All the stoplights were out; there were no police to direct the panicked motorists. Citizens helped out: I saw men in three-piece suits, women in heels and business attire, even a ragged man who looked to be straight out of one of the homeless shelters, all playing traffic cop. Sirens keened, emergency vehicles snaked from lane to lane.

The car radio kept reporting further destruction; there was another aftershock, and then another, but I scarcely felt them because I was in motion.

As I inched along a major crosstown arterial, I asked myself why I was doing this foolhardy thing. The man was nothing to me, really—merely a voice on the phone, always self-pitying, and often antagonistic and potentially violent. I ought to be checking on my house and the folks at All Souls; if I wanted to help people, my efforts would have been better spent in my own neighborhood or Bernal Heights. But instead I was traveling to the most congested and dangerous part of the city in search of a man I'd never laid eyes on.

As I asked the question, I knew the answer. Over the past two weeks the man had told me about his deepest problems. I'd come to know him in spite of his self-protective secretiveness. And he'd become more to me than just the subject of an investigation; I'd begun to care whether he lived or died. Now we had shared a peculiarly intimate moment—that of being together, if only in voice, when the catastrophe that San Franciscans feared the most had struck. He had called for help; I had heard his terror and pain. A connection had been established that could not be broken.

After twenty minutes and little progress, I cut west and took a less-traveled residential street through Japantown and over the crest of Pacific Heights. From the top of the hill I could see and smell the smoke over the Marina; as I crossed the traffic-snarled intersection with Lombard, I could see the flames. I drove another block, then decided to leave the MG and continue on foot.

All around I could see signs of destruction now: a house was twisted at a tortuous angle, its front porch collapsed and crushing a car parked at the curb; on Beach Street an apartment building's upper story had slid into the street, clogging it with rubble; three bottom floors of another building were flattened, leaving only the top intact.

I stopped at a corner, breathing hard, nearly choking on the thickening smoke. The smell of gas from broken lines was vaguely nauseating—frightening, too, because of the potential for explosions. To my left the street was cordoned off; fire-department hoses played on the blazes—weakly, because of damaged water mains. People congregated everywhere, staring about with horror-struck eyes; they huddled together, clinging to one another; many were crying. Firefighters and police were telling people to go home before dark fell. "You should be looking after your property," I heard one say. "You can count on going seventy-two hours without water or power."

"Longer than that," someone said.

"It's not safe here," the policeman added. "Please go home."

Between sobs, a woman said, "What if you've got no home to go to anymore?"

The cop had no answer for her.

Emotions were flying out of control among the onlookers. It would have been easy to feed into it—to weep, even panic. Instead, I turned my back to the flaming buildings, began walking the other way, toward Fort Mason. If the man's home was beyond the barricades, there was nothing I could do for him. But if it lay in the other direction, where there was a lighter concentration of rescue workers, then my assistance might save his life.

I forced myself to walk slower, to study the buildings on either side of the street. I had one last clue that could lead me to the man: he'd said he lived in a little cottage between two apartment buildings. The homes in this district were mostly of substantial size; there couldn't be too many cottages situated in just that way.

Across the street a house slumped over to one side, its roof canted at a forty-five-degree angle, windows from an apartment house had popped out of their frames, and its iron fire escapes were tangled and twisted like a cat's cradle of yarn. Another home was unrecognizable, merely a heap of rubble. And over there, two four-story apartment buildings leaned together, forming an arch over a much smaller structure . . . .

I rushed across the street, pushed through a knot of bystanders. The smaller building was a tumble-down mass of white stucco with a smashed red tile roof and a partially flattened iron fence. It had been a Mediterranean-style cottage with grillwork over high windows; now the grills were bent and pushed outward; the collapsed windows resembled swollen-shut eyes.

The woman standing next to me was cradling a terrified cat under her loose cardigan sweater. I asked, "Did the man who lives in the cottage get out okay?"

She frowned, tightened her grip on the cat as it burrowed deeper. "I don't know who lives there. It's always kind of deserted-looking."

A man in front of her said, "I've seen lights, but never anybody coming or going."

I moved closer. The cottage was deep in the shadows of the leaning buildings, eerily silent. From above came a groaning sound, and then a piece of wood sheared off the apartment house to the right, crashing onto what remained of the cottage's roof. I looked up, wondering how long before one or the other of the buildings toppled. Wondering if the man was still alive inside the compacted mass of stucco . . . .

A man in jeans and a sweatshirt came up and stood beside me. His face was smudged and abraded; his clothing was smeared with dirt and what looked to be blood; he held his left elbow gingerly in the palm of his hand. "You were asking about Dan?" he said.

So that was the anonymous caller's name. "Yes. Did he get out okay?"

"I don't think he was at home. At least, I saw him over at the Green around quarter to five.

"He was at home. I was talking with him on the phone when the quake hit."

"Oh, Jesus." The man's face paled under the smudges. "My name's Mel; I live . . . lived next door. Are you a friend of Dan's?"

"Yes," I said, realizing it was true.

"That's a surprise." He stared worriedly at the place where the two buildings leaned together.

"Why?"

"I thought Dan didn't have any friends left. He's pushed us away ever since the accident."

"Accident?"

"You must be a new friend, or else you'd know. Dan's woman was killed on the freeway last spring. A truck crushed her car."

The word "crushed" seemed to hang in the air between us. I said, "I've got to try to get him out of there," and stepped over the flattened portion of the fence.

Mel said, "I'll go with you."

I looked skeptically at his injured arm.

"It's nothing, really," he told me. "I was helping an old lady out of my building, and a beam grazed me."

"Well—" I broke off as a hail of debris came from the building to the left.

Without further conversation, Mel and I crossed the small front yard, skirting fallen bricks, broken glass, and jagged chunks of wallboard. Dusk was coming on fast now; here in the shadows of the leaning buildings it was darker than on the street. I moved toward where the cottage's front door should have been, but couldn't locate it. The windows, with their protruding grillwork, were impassable.

I said, "Is there another entrance?"

"In the back, off a little service porch."

I glanced to either side. The narrow passages between the cottage and the adjacent buildings were jammed with debris. I could possibly scale the mound at the right, but I was leery of setting up vibrations that might cause more debris to come tumbling down.

Mel said, "You'd better give it up. The way the cottage looks, I doubt he survived."

But I wasn't willing to give it up—not yet. There must be a way to at least locate Dan, see if he were alive. But how?

And then I remembered something else from our phone conversations . . . .

I said, "I'm going back there."

"Let me."

"No, stay here. That mound will support my weight, but not yours." I moved toward the side of the cottage before Mel could remind me of the risk I was taking.

The mound was over five feet high. I began to climb cautiously, testing every hand- and foothold. Twice jagged chunks of stucco cut my fingers; a piece of wood left a line of splinters on the back of my hand. When I neared the top, I heard the roar of a helicopter, its rotors flapping overhead. I froze, afraid that the air currents would precipitate more debris, then scrambled down the other side of the mound into a weed-choked backyard.

As I straightened, automatically brushing dirt from my jeans, my foot slipped on the soft, spongy ground, then sank into a puddle, probably a water main was broken nearby. The helicopter still hovered overhead; I couldn't hear a thing above its racket. Nor could I see much: it was even darker back here. I stood still until my eyes adjusted.

The cottage was not so badly damaged at its rear. The steps to the porch had collapsed and the rear wall leaned inward, but I could make out a door frame opening into blackness inside. I glanced up in irritation at the helicopter, saw it was going away. Waited, and then listened . . .

And heard what I had been hoping to. The music was now Beethoven—his third symphony, the *Eroica*. Its strains were muted, tinny. Music played by an out-of-area FM station, coming from a transistor radio. A transistor whose batteries were functioning long after the electricity had cut out. Whose batteries might have outlived its owner.

I moved quickly to the porch, grasped the iron rail beside the collapsed steps, and pulled myself up. I still could see nothing inside the cottage. The strains of the *Eroica* continued to pour forth, close by now.

Reflexively I reached into my purse for the small flashlight I usually kept there, then remembered it was at home on the kitchen counter—a reminder for me to replace its weak batteries. I swore softly, then started through the doorway, calling out to Dan.

No answer.

"Dan!"

This time I heard a groan.

I rushed forward into the blackness, following the sound of the music. After a few feet I came up against something solid, banging my shins. I lowered a hand, felt around. It was a wooden beam, wedged crosswise.

"Dan?"

Another groan. From the floor—perhaps under the beam. I squatted and made a wide sweep with my hands. They encountered a wool-clad arm; I slid my fingers down it until I touched the wrist, felt for the pulse. It was strong, although slightly irregular.

"Dan," I said, leaning closer, "it's Sharon, from the hot line. We've got to get you out of here."

"Unh, Sharon?" His voice was groggy, confused. He'd probably been drifting in and out of consciousness since the beam fell on him.

"Can you move?" I asked.

". . . Something on my legs."

"Do they feel broken?"

"No, just pinned."

"I can't see much, but I'm going to try to move this beam off you. When I do, roll out from under."

". . . Okay."

From the position at which the beam was wedged, I could tell it would have to be raised. Balancing on the balls of my feet, I got a good grip on it and shoved upward with all my strength. It moved about six inches and then slipped from my grasp. Dan grunted.

"Are you all right?"

"Yeah. Try it again."

I stood, grasped it, and pulled this time. It yielded a little more, and I heard Dan slide across the floor. "I'm clear," he said—and just in time, because I once more lost my grip. The beam crashed down, setting up a vibration that made plaster fall from the ceiling.

"We've got to get out of here fast," I said. "Give me your hand."

He slipped it into mine—long-fingered, work-roughened. Quickly we went through the door, crossed the porch, jumped to the ground. The radio continued to play forlornly behind us. I glanced briefly at Dan, couldn't make out much more than a tall, slender build and a thatch of pale hair. His face turned from me, toward the cottage.

"Jesus," he said in an awed voice.

I tugged urgently at his hand. "There's no telling how long those apartment buildings are going to stand."

He turned, looked up at them, said "Jesus" again. I urged him toward the mound of debris.

This time I opted for speed rather than caution—a mistake, because as we neared the top, a cracking noise came from high above. I gave Dan a push, slid after him. A dark, jagged object hurtled down, missing us only by inches. More plaster board—deadly at that velocity.

For a moment I sat straddle-legged on the ground, sucking in my breath, releasing it tremulously, gasping for more air. Then hands pulled me to my feet and dragged me across the yard toward the sidewalk— Mel and Dan.

Night had fallen by now. A fire had broken out in the house across the street. Its red-orange flickering showed the man I'd just rescued: ordinary-looking, with regular features that were now marred by dirt and a long cut on the forehead, from which blood had trickled and dried. His pale eyes were studying me; suddenly he looked abashed and shoved both hands into his jeans pocket.

After a moment he asked, "How did you find me?"

"I put together some of the things you'd said on the phone. Doesn't matter now."

"Why did you even bother?"

"Because I care."

He looked at the ground.

I added, "There never was any assault rifle, was there?"

He shook his head.

"You made it up, so someone would pay attention."

". . . Yeah."

I felt anger welling up—irrational, considering the present circumstances, but nonetheless justified. "You didn't have to frighten the people at the hot line. All you had to do was ask them for help. Or ask friends like Mel. He cares. People do, you know."

"Nobody does."

"Enough of that! All you have to do is look around to see how much people care about one another. Look at your friend here." I gestured at Mel, who was standing a couple feet away, staring at us. "He hurt his arm rescuing an old lady from his apartment house. Look at those people over by the burning house—they're doing everything they can to help the firefighters. All over this city people are doing things for one another. Goddamn it, I'd never laid eyes on you, but I risked my life anyway!"

Dan was silent for a long moment. Finally he looked up at me. "I know you did. What can I do in return?"

"For me? Nothing. Just pass it on to someone else."

Dan stared across the street at the flaming building, looked back into the shadows where his cottage lay in ruins. Then he nodded and squared his shoulders. To Mel he said, "Let's go over there, see if there's anything we can do."

He put his arm around my shoulders and hugged me briefly, then he and Mel set off at a trot.

The city is recovering now, as it did in 1906, and as it doubtless will when the next big quake hits. Resiliency is what disaster teaches us, I guess—along with the preciousness of life, no matter how disappointing or burdensome it may often seem.

Dan's recovering, too: he's only called the hot line twice, once for a referral to a therapist, and once to ask for my home number so he could invite me to dinner. I turned the invitation down, because neither of us needs to dwell on the trauma of October seventeenth, and I was fairly sure I heard a measure of relief in his voice when I did so.

I'll never forget Dan, though—or where I was when. And the strains of Beethoven's Third Symphony will forever remind me of the day after, which things would never be the same again.

Old Rattler

Author: Sharyn McCrumb (1948–)

Detective Spencer Arrowood (1990)

Though McCrumb is a short-story writer of consummate skill, her series detectives usually confine their efforts to novel-length works. There is one charming short story, "Love on First Bounce," about her entertainingly exasperating anthropologist sleuth Elizabeth MacPherson, but it proves to be a high school romance with neither crime nor detection.

Amusing as are her MacPherson novels and her satirical novels of the science-fiction world, *Bimbos of the Death Sun* (1987) and *Zombies of the Gene Pool* (1992), McCrumb's finest work is found in the Appalachian series about Sheriff Spencer Arrowood, beginning with *If Ever I Return, Pretty Peggy-O* (1990). "Old Rattler," the only short story to my knowledge about Arrowood, illustrates that series' fine use of background as well as its occasional brush with the paranormal.

She was a city woman, and she looked too old to want to get pregnant, so I reckoned she had hate in her heart.

That's mostly the only reasons I ever see city folks: babies and meanness. Country people come to me right along, though, for poultices and tonics for the rheumatism, to go dowsing for well water on their land, or to help them find what's lost, and such like, but them city folks from Knoxville, and Johnson City, and from Asheville, over in North Carolina—the skinny ones with their fancy colorless cars, talking all educated, slick as goose grease—they don't hold with home remedies or the Sight. Superstition, they call it. Unless you label your potions "macrobiotic," or "holistic," and package them up fancy for the customers in earthtone clay jars, or call your visions "channeling."

Shoot, I know what city folks are like. I coulda been rich if I'd had the stomach for it. But I didn't care to cater to their notions, or to have to listen to their self-centered whining, when a city doctor could see to their needs by charging more and taking longer. I say, let him. They don't need me so bad nohow. They'd rather pay a hundred dollars to some fool boy doctor who's likely guessing about what ails them. Of course, they got insurance to cover it, which country people mostly don't—them as makes do with me, anyhow.

"That old Rattler," city people say. "Holed up in that filthy old shanty up a dirt road. Wearing those ragged overalls. Living on Pepsis and Twinkies. What does he know about doctoring?"

And I smile and let 'em think that, because when they are desperate enough, and they have nowhere else to turn, they'll be along to see me, same as the country people. Meanwhile, I go right on helping the halt and the blind who have no one else to turn to. *For I will restore health unto thee, and I will heal thee of thy wounds, saith the Lord*. Jeremiah 30. What do I know? A lot. I can tell more from looking at a person's fingernails, smelling their breath, and looking at the whites of their eyes than the doctoring tribe in Knoxville can tell with their high-priced X rays and such. And sometimes I can pray the sickness out of them and sometimes I can't. If I can't, I don't charge for it—you show me a city doctor that will make you that promise.

The first thing I do is, I look at the patient, before I even listen to a word. I look at the way they walk, the set of the jaw, whether they look straight ahead or down at the ground, like they was waiting to crawl into it. I could tell right much from looking at the city woman—what she had wrong with her wasn't no praying matter.

She parked her colorless cracker box of a car on the gravel patch by the spring, and she stood squinting up through the sunshine at my corrugated tin shanty (*I* know it's a shanty, but it's paid for. Think on that awhile). She looked doubtful at first—that was her common sense trying to talk her out of taking her troubles to some backwoods witch doctor. But then her eyes narrowed, and her jaw set, and her lips tightened into a long, thin line, and I could tell that she was thinking on whatever it was that hurt her so bad that she was willing to resort to me. I got out a new milk jug of my comfrey and chamomile tea and two Dixie cups, and went out on the porch to meet her.

"Come on up!" I called out to her, smiling and waving most friendly-like. A lot of people say that rural mountain folks don't take kindly to strangers, but that's mainly if they don't know what you've come about, and it makes them anxious, not knowing if you're a welfare snoop or a paint-your-house-with-whitewash con man, or the law. I knew what this stranger had come about, though, so I didn't mind her at all. She was as harmless as a buckshot doe, and hurting just as bad, I reckoned. Only she didn't know she was hurting. She thought she was just angry.

If she could have kept her eyes young and her neck smooth, she would have looked thirty-two, even close-up, but as it was, she looked like a prosperous, well-maintained forty-four-year-old, who could use less coffee and more sleep. She was slender, with natural-like brownish hair—though I knew better—wearing a khaki skirt and a navy top and a silver necklace with a crystal pendant, which she might have believed was a talisman. There's no telling what city people will believe. But she smiled at me, a little nervous, and asked if I had time to talk to her. That pleased me. When people are taken up with their own troubles, they seldom worry about anybody else's convenience.

"Sit down," I said, smiling to put her at ease. "Time runs slow on the mountain. Why don't you have a swig of my herb tea, and rest a spell. That's a rough road if you're not used to it."

She looked back at the dusty trail winding its way down the mountain. "It certainly is," she said. "Somebody told me how to get here, but I was positive I'd got lost."

I handed her the Dixie cup of herb tea, and made a point of sipping mine, so she'd know I wasn't attempting to drug her into white slavery. They get fanciful, these college types. Must be all that reading they do. "If you're looking for old Rattler, you found him," I told her.

"I thought you must be." She nodded. "Is your name really Rattler?"

"Not on my birth certificate, assuming I had one, but it's done me for a raft of years now. It's what I answer to. How about yourself?"

"My name is Evelyn Johnson." She stumbled a little bit before she said *Johnson*. Just once I wish somebody would come here claiming to be a *Robinson* or an *Evans*. Those names are every bit as common as Jones, Johnson, and Smith, but nobody ever resorts to them. I guess they think I don't know any better. But I didn't bring it up, because she looked troubled enough, without me trying to find out who she really was, and why she was lying about it. Mostly people lie because they feel foolish coming to me at all, and they don't want word to get back to town about it. I let it pass.

"This tea is good," she said, looking surprised. "You made this?"

I smiled "Cherokee recipe. I'd give it to you, but you couldn't get the ingredients in town—not even at the health-food store."

"Somebody told me that you were something of a miracle worker." Her hands fluttered in her lap, because she was sounding silly to herself, but I didn't look surprised, because I wasn't. People have said that for a long time, and it's nothing for me to get puffed up about, because it's not my doing. It's a gift.

"I can do things other folks can't explain," I told her. "That might be a few logs short of a miracle. But I can find water with a forked stick, and charm bees, and locate lost objects. There's some sicknesses I can minister to. Not yours, thought."

Her eyes saucered, and she said, "I'm perfectly well, thank you."

I just sat there looking at her, deadpan. I waited. She waited. Silence.

Finally, she turned a little pinker, and ducked her head. "All right," she whispered, like it hurt. "I'm not perfectly well. I'm a nervous wreck. I guess I have to tell you about it."

"That would be best, Evelyn," I said.

"My daughter has been missing since July." She opened her purse and took out a picture of a pretty young girl, soft brown hair like her mother's, and young, happy eyes. "Her name is Amy. She was a freshman at East Tennessee State, and she went rafting with three of her friends on the Nolichucky. They all got separated by the current. When the other three met up farther downstream, they got out and went looking for Amy, but there was no trace of her. She hasn't been seen since."

"They dragged the river, I reckon." Rock-studded mountain rivers are bad for keeping bodies snagged down where you can't find them.

"They dragged that stretch of the Nolichucky for three days. They even sent down divers. They said even if she'd got wedged under a rock, we'd have something by now." It cost her something to say that.

"Well, she's a grown girl," I said, to turn the flow of words. "Sometimes they get an urge to kick over the traces."

"Not Amy. She wasn't the party type. And even supposing she felt like that—because I know people don't believe a mother's assessment of character—would she run away in her bathing suit? All her clothes were back in her dorm, and her boyfriend was walking up and down the riverbank with the other two students, calling out to her. I don't think she went anywhere on her own."

"Likely not," I said. "But it would have been a comfort to think so, wouldn't it?"

Her eyes went wet. "I kept checking her bank account for withdrawals, and I looked at her last phone bill to see if any calls were made after July sixth. But there's no indication that she was alive past that date. We put posters up all over Johnson City, asking for information about her. There's been no response."

"Of course, the police are doing what they can," I said.

"It's the Wake County sheriff's department, actually," she said. "But the Tennessee Bureau of Investigation is helping them. They don't have much to go on. They've questioned people who were at the river. One fellow claims to have seen a red pickup leaving the scene with a girl in it, but they haven't been able to trace it. The investigators have questioned all her college friends and her professors, but they're running out of leads. It's been three months. Pretty soon they'll quit trying altogether." Her voice shook. "You see, Mr.—Rattler—they all think she's dead."

"So you came to me?"

She nodded. "I didn't know what else to do. Amy's father is no help. He says to let the police handle it. We're divorced, and he's remarried and has a two-year-old son. But Amy is all I've got. I can't let her go!" She set down the paper cup, and covered her face with her hands.

"Could I see that picture of Amy, Mrs.—Johnson?"

"It's Albright," she said softly, handing me the photograph. "Our real last name is Albright. I just felt foolish before, so I didn't tell you my real name."

"It happens," I said, but I wasn't really listening to her apology. I had closed my eyes, and I was trying to make the edges of the snapshot curl around me, so that I would be standing next to the smiling girl, and get some sense of how she was. But the photograph stayed cold and flat in my hand, and no matter how hard I tried to think my way into it, the picture shut me out. There was nothing.

I opened my eyes, and she was looking at me, scared, but waiting, too, for what I could tell her. I handed back the picture. "I could be wrong," I said. "I told you I'm no miracle worker."

"She's dead, isn't she?"

"Oh, yes. Since the first day, I do believe."

She straightened up, and those slanting lines deepened around her mouth. "I've felt it, too," she said. "I'd reach out to her with my thoughts, and I'd feel nothing. Even when she was away at school, I could always sense her somehow. Sometimes I'd call, and she'd say, 'Mom, I was just thinking about you.' But now I reach out to her and I feel empty. She's just—gone."

"Finding mortal remains is a sorrowful business," I said. "And I don't know that I'll be able to help you."

Evelyn Albright shook her head. "I didn't come here about finding Amy's body, Rattler," she said. "I came to find her killer."

I spent three more Dixie cups of herb tea trying to bring back her faith in the Tennessee legal system. Now, I never was much bothered with the process of the law, but, like I told her, in this case I did know that pulling a live coal from an iron potbellied stove was a mighty puny miracle compared to finding the one guilty sinner with the mark of Cain in all this world, when there are so many evildoers to choose from. It seemed to me that for all their frailty, the law had the manpower and the system to sort through a thousand possible killers, and to find the one fingerprint or the exact bloodstain that would lay the matter of Amy Albright to rest.

"But you knew she was dead when you touched her picture!" she said. "Can't you tell from that who did it? Can't you see where she is?"

I shook my head. "My grandma might could have done it, rest her soul. She had a wonderful gift of prophecy, but I wasn't trained to it the way she was. *Her* grandmother was a Cherokee medicine woman, and she could read the signs like yesterday's newspaper. I only have the little flicker of Sight I was born with. Some things I know, but I can't see it happening like she could have done."

"What did you see?"

"Nothing. I just felt that the person I was trying to reach in that photograph was gone. And I think the lawmen are the ones you should be trusting to hunt down the killer."

Evelyn didn't see it that way. "They aren't getting anywhere," she kept telling me. "They've questioned all of Amy's friends, and asked the public to call in for information, and now they're at a standstill."

"I hear tell they're sly, these hunters of humans. He could be miles away by now," I said, but she was shaking her head no.

"The sheriff's department thinks it was someone who knew the area. First of all, because that section of the river isn't a tourist spot, and secondly, because he apparently knew where to take Amy so that he wouldn't be seen by anyone with her in the car, and he has managed to keep her from being found. Besides"—she looked away, and her eyes were wet again—"they won't say much about this, but apparently Amy isn't the first. There was a high school girl who disappeared around here two years ago. Some hunters found her body in an abandoned well. I heard one of the sheriff's deputies say that he thought the same person might be responsible for both crimes."

"Then he's like a dog killing sheep. He's doing it for the fun of it, and he must be stopped, because a sheep killer never stops of his own accord."

"People told me you could do marvelous things—find water with a forked stick; heal the sick. I was hoping that you would be able to tell me something about what happened to Amy. I thought you might be able to see who killed her. Because I want him to suffer."

I shook my head. "A dishonest man would string you along," I told her. "A well-meaning one might tell you what you want to hear just to make you feel better. But all I can offer you is the truth: when I touched that photograph, I felt her death, but I saw nothing."

"I had hoped for more." She twisted the rings on her hands. "Do you think you could find her body?"

"I have done something like that, once. When I was twelve, an old man wandered away from his home in December. He was my best friend's grandfather, and they lived on the next farm, so I knew him, you see. I went out with the searchers on that cold, dark afternoon, with the wind baying like a hound through the hollers. As I walked along by myself, I looked up at the clouds, and I had a sudden vision of that old man sitting down next to a broken rail fence. He looked like he was asleep, but I reckoned I knew better. Anyhow, I thought on it as I walked, and I reckoned that the nearest rail fence to his farm was at an abandoned homestead at the back of our land. It was in one of our pastures. I hollered for the others to follow me, and I led them out there to the back pasture."

"Was he there?"

"He was there. He'd wandered off—his mind was going—and when he got lost, he sat down to rest a spell, and he'd dozed off where he sat. Another couple of hours would have finished him, but we got him home to a hot bath and scalding coffee, and he lived till spring."

"He was alive, though."

"Well, that's it. The life in him might have been a beacon. It might not work when the life is gone."

"I'd like you to try, though. If we can find Amy, there might be some clue that will help us find the man who did this."

"I tell you what: you send the sheriff to see me, and I'll have a talk with him. If it suits him, I'll do my level best to find her. But I have to speak to him first."

"Why?"

"Professional courtesy," I said, which was partly true, but, also, because I wanted to be sure she was who she claimed to be. City people usually do give me a fake name out of embarrassment, but I didn't want to chance her being a reporter on the Amy Albright case, or, worse, someone on the killer's side. Besides, I wanted to stay on good terms with Sheriff Spencer Arrowood. We go back a long way. He used to ride out this way on his bike when he was a kid, and he'd sit and listen to tales about the Indian times—stories I'd heard from my grandma—or I'd take him fishing at the trout pool in Broom Creek. One year, his older brother Cal talked me into taking the two of them out owling, since they were too young to hunt. I walked them across every ridge over the holler, and taught them to look for the sweep of wings above the tall grass in the field, and to listen for the sound of the waking owl, ready to track his prey by the slightest sound, the shade of movement. I taught them how to make owl calls, to where we couldn't tell if it was an owl calling out from the woods or one of us. Look out, I told them. When the owl calls your name, it means death.

Later on, they became owls, I reckon. Cal Arrowood went to Vietnam, and died in a dark jungle full of screeching birds. I felt him go. And Spencer grew up to be sheriff, so I reckon he hunts prey of his own by the slightest sound, and by one false move. A lot of people had heard him call their name.

I hadn't seen much of Spencer since he grew up, but I hoped we were still buddies. Now that he was sheriff, I knew he could make trouble for me if he wanted to, and so far he never has. I wanted to keep things cordial.

"All right," said Evelyn. "I can't promise they'll come out here, but I will tell them what you said. Will you call and tell me what you're going to do?"

"No phone," I said, jerking my thumb back toward the shack. "Send the sheriff out here. He'll let you know."

She must have gone to the sheriff's office straightaway after leaving my place. I thought she would. I wasn't surprised at that, because I could see that she wasn't doing much else right now besides brood about her loss. She needed an ending so that she could go on. I had tried to make her take a milk jug of herb tea, because I never saw anybody so much in need of a night's sleep, but she wouldn't have it. "Just find my girl for me," she'd said. "Help us find the man who did it, and put him away. Then I'll sleep."

When the brown sheriff's car rolled up my dirt road about noon the next day, I was expecting it. I was sitting in my cane chair on the porch whittling a face onto a hickory broom handle when I saw the flash of the gold star on the side of the car door, and the sheriff himself got out. I waved, and he touched his hat, like they used to do in cowboy movies. I reckon little boys who grow up to be sheriff watch a lot of cowboy movies in their day. I didn't mind Spencer Arrowood, though. He hadn't changed all that much from when I knew him. There were gray flecks in his fair hair, but they didn't show much, and he never did make it to six feet, but he'd managed to keep his weight down, so he looked all right.

He was kin to the Pigeon Roost Arrowoods, and like them he was smart and honest without being a glad-hander. He seemed a little young to be the high sheriff to an old-timer like me, but that's never a permanent problem for anybody, is it? Anyhow, I trusted him, and that's worth a lot in these sorry times.

I made him sit down in the other cane chair, because I hate people hovering over me while I whittle. He asked did I remember him.

"Spencer," I said, "I'd have to be drinking something a lot stronger than chamomile tea to forget you."

He grinned, but then he seemed to remember what sad errand had brought him out here, and the faint lines came back around his eyes. "I guess you've heard about this case I'm on."

"I was told. It sounds to me like we've got a human sheep killer in the fold. I hate to hear that. Killing for pleasure is an unclean act. I said I'd help the law any way I could to dispose of the killer, if it was all right with you."

"That's what I heard," the sheriff said. "For what it's worth, the TBI agrees with you about the sort of person we're after, although they didn't liken it to *sheep killing*. They meant the same thing, though."

"So Mrs. Albright did come to see you?" I asked him, keeping my eyes fixed on the curl of the beard of that hickory face.

"Sure did, Rattler," said the sheriff. "She tells me that you've agreed to try to locate Amy's body."

"It can't do no harm to try," I said. "Unless you mind too awful much. I don't reckon you believe in such like."

He smiled. "It doesn't matter what I believe if it works, does it, Rattler? You're welcome to try. But, actually, I've thought of another way that you might be useful in this case."

"What's that?"

"You heard about the other murdered girl, didn't you? They found her body in an abandoned well up on Locust Ridge."

"Whose land?"

"National forest now. The homestead has been in ruins for at least a century. But that's a remote area of the county. It's a couple of miles from the Appalachian Trail, and just as far from the river, so I wouldn't expect an outsider to know about it. The only way up there is on an old county road. The TBI psychologist thinks the killer has dumped Amy Albright's body somewhere in the vicinity of the other burial. He says they do that. Serial killers, I mean. They establish territories."

"Painters do that," I said, and the sheriff remembered his roots well enough to know that I meant a mountain lion, not a fellow with an easel. We called them painters in the old days, when there were more of them in the mountains than just a scream and a shadow every couple of years. City people think I'm crazy to live on the mountain where the wild creatures are, and then they shut themselves up in cities with the most pitiless killers ever put on this earth—each other. I marvel at the logic.

"Since you reckon he's leaving his victims in one area, why haven't you searched it?"

"Oh, we have," said the sheriff, looking weary. "I've had volunteers combing that mountain, and they haven't turned up a thing. There's a lot of square miles of forest to cover up there. Besides, I think our man has been more careful about concealment this time. What we need is more help. Not more searchers, but a more precise location."

"Where do I come in? You said you wanted me to do more than just find the body. Not that I can even promise to do that."

"I want to get your permission to try something that may help us catch this individual," Spencer Arrowood was saying.

"What's that?"

"I want you to give some newspaper interviews. Local TV, even, if we can talk them into it. I want to publicize the fact that you are going to search for Amy Albright on Locust Ridge. Give them your background as a psychic and healer. I want a lot of coverage on this."

I shuddered. You didn't have to be psychic to foresee the outcome of that. A stream of city people in colorless cars, wanting babies and diet tonics.

"When were you planning to search for the body, Rattler?"

"I was waiting on you. Any day will suit me, as long as it isn't raining. Rain distracts me."

"Okay, let's announce that you're conducting the psychic search on Locust Ridge next Tuesday. I'll send some reporters out here to interview you. Give them the full treatment."

"How does all this harassment help you catch the killer, Spencer?"

"This is not for publication, Rattler, but I think we can smoke him out," said the sheriff. "We announce in all the media that you're going to be dowsing for bones on Tuesday. We insist that you can work wonders, and that we're confident you'll find Amy. If the killer is a local man, he'll see the notices, and get nervous. I'm betting that he'll go up there Monday night, just to make sure the body is still well-hidden. There's only one road into that area. If we can keep the killer from spotting us, I think he'll lead us to Amy's body."

"That's fine, Sheriff, but how are you going to track this fellow in the dark?"

Spencer Arrowood smiled. "Why, Rattler," he said, "I've got the Sight."

You have to do what you can to keep a sheep killer out of your fold, even if it means talking to a bunch of reporters who don't know ass from aardvark. I put up with all their fool questions, and dispensed about a dozen jugs of comfrey and chamomile tea, and I even told that blond lady on Channel Seven that she didn't need any herbs for getting pregnant, because she already was, which surprised her so much that she almost dropped her microphone, but I reckon my hospitality worked to Spencer Arrowood's satisfaction, because he came along Monday afternoon to show me a stack of newspapers with my picture looking out of the page, and he thanked me for being helpful.

"Don't thank me," I said. "Just let me go with you tonight. You'll need all the watchers you can get to cover that ridge."

He saw the sense of that, and agreed without too much argument. I wanted to see what he meant about having the Sight, because I'd known him since he was knee-high to a grasshopper, and he didn't have so much as a flicker of the power. None of the Arrowoods did. But he was smart enough in regular ways, and I knew he had some kind of ace up his sleeve.

An hour past sunset that night I was standing in a clearing on Locust Ridge, surrounded by law enforcement people from three counties. There were nine of us. We were so far from town that there seemed to be twice as many stars, so dark was that October sky without the haze of streetlights to bleed out the fainter ones. The sheriff was talking one notch above a whisper, in case the suspect had come early. He opened a big cardboard box, and started passing out yellow-and-black binoculars.

"These are called ITT Night Mariners," he told us. "I borrowed ten pair from a dealer at Watauga Lake, so take care of them. They run about $2,500 apiece."

"Are they infrared?" somebody asked him.

"No. But they collect available light and magnify it up to 20,000 times, so they will allow you excellent night vision. The full moon will give us all the light we need. You'll be able to walk around without a flashlight, and you'll be able to see obstacles, terrain features, and anything that's out there moving around."

"The military developed this technology in Desert Storm," said Deputy LeDonne.

"Well, let's hope it works for us tonight," said the sheriff. "Try looking through them."

I held them up to my eyes. They didn't weigh much—about the same as two apples, I reckoned. Around me, everybody was muttering surprise, tickled pink over this new gadget. I looked through mine, and I could see the dark shapes of trees up on the hill—not in a clump, the way they look at night, but one by one, with spaces between them. The sheriff walked away from us, and I could see him go, but when I took the Night Mariners down from my eyes, he was gone. I put them back on, and there he was again.

"I reckon you do have the *Sight*, Sheriff," I told him. "Your man won't know we're watching him with these babies."

"I wonder if they're legal for hunting," said a Unicoi County man. "This sure beats spotlighting deer."

"They're illegal for deer," Spencer told him. "But they're perfect for catching sheep killers." He smiled over at me. "Now that we've tested the equipment, y'all split up. I've given you your patrol areas. Don't use your walkie-talkies unless it's absolutely necessary. Rattler, you just go where you please, but try not to let the suspect catch you at it. Are you going to do your stuff?"

"I'm going to try to let it happen," I said. It's a gift. I don't control it. I just receive.

We went our separate ways. I walked awhile, enjoying the new magic of seeing the night woods same as a possum would, but when I tried to clear my mind and summon up that other kind of seeing, I found I couldn't do it. So, instead of helping, the Night Mariners were blinding me. I slipped the fancy goggles into the pocket of my jacket, and stood there under an oak tree for a minute or two, trying to open my heart for guidance. I whispered a verse from Psalm 27: *Teach me thy way, O Lord, and lead me in a plain path, because of mine enemies.* Then I looked up at the stars and tried to think of nothing. After a while I started walking, trying to keep my mind clear and go where I was led.

Maybe five minutes later, maybe an hour, I was walking across an abandoned field overgrown with scrub cedars. The moonlight glowed in the long grass, and the cold air made my ears and fingers tingle. When I touched a post of the broken split-rail fence, it happened. I saw the field in daylight. I saw brown grass, drying up in the summer heat, and flies making lazy circles around my head. When I looked down at the fence rail at my feet, I saw her. She was wearing a watermelon-colored T-shirt and jean shorts. Her brown hair spilled across her shoulders and twined with the chicory weeds. Her eyes were closed. I could see a smear of blood at one corner of her mouth, and I knew. I looked up at the moon, and when I looked back, the grass was dead, and the darkness had closed in again. I crouched behind a cedar tree before I heard the foot-steps.

They weren't footsteps, really. Just the swish sound of boots and trouser legs brushing against tall, dry grass. I could see his shape in the moonlight, and he wasn't one of the searchers. He was here to keep his secrets. He stepped over the fence rail, and walked toward the one big tree in the clearing—a twisted old maple, big around as two men. He knelt down beside that tree, and I saw him moving his hands on the ground, picking up a dead branch, and brushing leaves away. He looked, rocked back on his heels, leaned forward, and started pushing the leaves back again.

They hadn't given me a walkie-talkie, and I didn't hold with guns, though I knew he might have one. I wasn't really part of the posse. Old Rattler with his Twinkies and his root tea and his prophecies. I was just bait. But I couldn't risk letting the sheep killer slip away. Finding the grave might catch him; might not. None of my visions would help Spen-cer in a court of law, which is why I mostly stick to dispensing tonics and leave evil alone.

I cupped my hands to my mouth and gave an owl cry, loud as I could. Just one. The dark shape jumped up, took a couple of steps up and back, moving its head from side to side.

Far off in the woods, I heard an owl reply. I pulled out the Night Mariners then, and started scanning the hillsides around that meadow, and in less than a minute I could make out the sheriff, with that badge pinned to his coat, standing at the edge of the trees with his field glasses on, scanning the clearing. I started waving and pointing.

The sheep killer was hurrying away now, but he was headed in my direction, and I thought, *Risk it. What called your name, Rattler, wasn't an owl.* So just as he's about to pass by, I stepped out at him, and said, "Hush now. You'll scare the deer."

He was startled into screaming, and he swung out at me with some-thing that flashed silver in the moonlight. As I went down, he broke into a run, crashing through weeds, noisy enough to scare the deer across the state line—but the moonlight wasn't bright enough for him to get far. He covered maybe twenty yards before his foot caught on a fieldstone, and he went down. I saw the sheriff closing distance, and I went to help, but I felt light-headed all of a sudden, and my shirt was wet. I was glad it wasn't light enough to see colors in that field. Red was never my favorite.

I opened my eyes and shut them again, because the flashing orange light of the rescue squad van was too bright for the ache in my head. When I looked away, I saw cold and dark, and knew I was still on Locust Ridge. "Where's Spencer Arrowood?" I asked a blue jacket bending near me.

"Sheriff! He's coming around."

Spencer Arrowood was bending over me then, with that worried look he used to have when a big one hit his fishing line. "We got him," he said. "You've got a puncture in your lung that will need more than herbal tea to fix, but you're going to be all right, Rattler."

"Since when did you get the Sight?" I asked him. But he was right. I needed to get off that mountain and get well, because the last thing I saw before I went down was the same scene that came to me when I first saw her get out of her car and walk toward my cabin. I saw what Evelyn Albright was going to do at the trial, with that flash of silver half hidden in her hand, and I didn't want it to end that way.

Dalziel's Ghost

Author: Reginald Hill (1936–   )

Detectives: Dalziel and Pascoe (1970)

Over a near-thirty-year career, Hill has provided as much variety on as high a level of quality as any writer in the field, but his greatest achievement may still be the police team introduced in his first novel, *A Clubbable Woman* (1970). There are many examples of odd-couple police partnerships in fiction—Joyce Porter's Dover and MacGregor, Ruth Rendell's Wexford and Burden, Colin Dexter's Morse and Lewis—but the Yorkshire team of rude and crude senior cop Andrew Dalziel and his younger, posher, college-educated colleague Peter Pascoe may be the most interesting.

Short stories about Dalziel and Pascoe are relatively rare. Hill's off-beat story, "Auteur Theory," from the collection *Pascoe's Ghost* (1979), may remind you of the film versions of *The French Lieutenant's Woman* and *The Big Sleep*. Though the story can be recommended for the unique use it makes of the sleuthing pair, paradoxically they don't really appear. In the same collection is found the story that follows, in which they do appear and in solid form.

W ell, this is very cozy," said Detective-Superintendent Dalziel, scratching his buttocks sensuously before the huge log fire.

"It is for some," said Pascoe, shivering still from the frost November night.

But Dalziel was right, he thought as he looked around the room. It *was* cozy, probably as cozy as it had been in the three hundred years since it was built. It was doubtful if any previous owner, even the most recent, would have recognized the old living-room of Stanstone Rigg farmhouse. Eliot had done a good job, stripping the beams, opening up the mean little fireplace and replacing the splintered uneven floorboards with smooth dark oak; and Giselle had broken the plain white walls with richly colored, voluminous curtaining and substituted everywhere the ornaments of art for the detritus of utility.

Outside, though, when night fell, and darkness dissolved the telephone poles, and the mist lay too thick to be pierced by the rare headlight on the distant road, then the former owners peering from their little cube of warmth and light would not have felt much difference.

Not the kind of thoughts a ghost-hunter should have! he told himself reprovingly. Cool calm skepticism was the right state of mind.

And his heart jumped violently as behind him the telephone rang.

Dalziel, now pouring himself a large Scotch from the goodly array of bottles on the huge sideboard, made no move toward the phone though he was the nearer. Detective-superintendents save their strength for important things and leave their underlings to deal with trivia.

"Hello," said Pascoe.

"Peter, you're there!"

"Ellie love," he answered. "Sometimes the sharpness of your mind makes me feel unworthy to be married to you."

"What are you doing?"

"We've just arrived. I'm talking to you. The super's having a drink."

"Oh, God! You did warn the Eliots, didn't you?"

"Not really, dear. I felt the detailed case-history you doubtless gave to Giselle needed no embellishment."

"I'm not sure this is such a good idea."

"Me neither. On the contrary. In fact, you may recall that on several occasions in the past three days I've said as much to you, whose not such a good idea it was in the first place."

"All you're worried about is your dignity!" said Ellie. "I'm worried about that lovely house. What's he doing now?"

Pascoe looked across the room to where Dalziel had bent his massive bulk so that his balding close-cropped head was on a level with a small figurine of a shepherd chastely dallying with a milkmaid. His broad right hand was on the point of picking it up.

"He's not touching anything," said Pascoe hastily. "Was there any other reason you phoned?"

"Other than what?"

"Concern for the Eliots' booze and knickknacks."

"Oh, Peter, don't be so half-witted. It seemed a laugh at The Old Mill, but now I don't like you being there with him, and I don't like me being here by myself. Come home and we'll screw till someone cries *Hold! Enough!*"

"You interest me strangely," said Pascoe. "What about *him* and the Eliots' house?"

"Oh, sod him and sod the Eliots! Decent people don't have ghosts!" exclaimed Ellie.

"Or if they do, they call in priests, not policemen," said Pascoe. "I quite agree. I said as much, remember . . . ?"

"All right, all right. You please yourself, buster. I'm off to bed now with a hot-water bottle and a glass of milk. Clearly I must be in my dotage. Shall I ring you later?"

"Best not," said Pascoe. "I don't want to step out of my pentacle after midnight. See you in the morning."

"Must have taken an electric drill to get through a skirt like that," said Dalziel, replacing the figurine with a bang. "No wonder the buggers got stuck into the sheep. Your missus checking up, was she?"

"She just wanted to see how we were getting on," said Pascoe.

"Probably thinks we've got a couple of milkmaids with us," said Dalziel, peering out into the night. "Some hope! I can't even see any sheep. It's like the grave out there."

He was right, thought Pascoe. When Stanstone Rigg had been a working farm, there must have always been the comforting sense of animal presence, even at night. Horses in the stable, cows in the byre, chickens in the hutch, dogs before the fire. But the Eliots hadn't bought the place because of any deep-rooted love of nature. In fact Giselle Eliot disliked animals so much she wouldn't even have a guard dog, preferring to rely on expensive electronics. Pascoe couldn't understand how George had got her even to consider living out here. It was nearly an hour's run from town in good conditions and Giselle was in no way cut out for country life, either physically or mentally. Slim, vivacious, sexy, she was a star-rocket in Yorkshire's sluggish jet-set. How she and Ellie had become friends, Pascoe couldn't work out either.

But she must have a gift for leaping unbridgeable gaps for George was a pretty unlikely partner, too.

It was George who was responsible for Stanstone Rigg. By profession an accountant, and very much looking the part with his thin face, unblinking gaze, and a mouth that seemed constructed for the passage of bad news, his unlikely hobby was the renovation of old houses. In the past six years he had done two, first a Victorian terrace house in town, then an Edwardian villa in the suburbs. Both had quadrupled (at least) in value, but George claimed this was not the point and Pascoe believe him. Stanstone Rigg Farm was his most ambitious project to date, and it had been a marvelous success, except for its isolation, which was unchangeable.

And its ghost. Which perhaps wasn't.

It was just three days since Pascoe had first heard of it. Dalziel, who repaid hospitality in the proportion of three of Ellie's home-cooked dinners to one meal out had been entertaining the Pascoes at The Old Mill, a newly opened restaurant in town.

"Jesus!" said the fat man when they examined the menu. "I wish they'd put them prices in French, too. They must give you Brigitte Bardot for afters!"

"Would you like to take us somewhere else?" inquired Ellie sweetly. "A fish-and-chip shop, perhaps. Or a Chinese takeaway?"

"No, no," said Dalziel. "This is grand. Any road, I'll chalk what I can up to expenses. Keeping an eye on Fletcher."

"Who?"

"The owner," said Pascoe. "I didn't know he was on our list, sir."

"Well, he is and he isn't," said Dalziel. "I got a funny telephone call a couple of weeks back. Suggested I might take a look at him, that's all. He's got his finger in plenty of pies."

"If I have the salmon to start with," said Ellie, "it won't be removed as material evidence before I'm finished, will it?"

Pascoe aimed a kick at her under the table but she had been expecting it and drawn her legs aside.

Four courses later they had all eaten and drunk enough for a kind of mellow truce to have been established between Ellie and the fat man.

"Look who's over there," said Ellie suddenly.

Pascoe looked. It was the Eliots, George dark-suited and still, Giselle ablaze in clinging orange silk. Another man, middle-aged but still athletically elegant in a military sort of way, was standing by their table. Giselle returned Ellie's wave and spoke to the man, who came across the room and addressed Pascoe.

"Mr. and Mrs. Eliot wonder if you would care to join them for liqueurs," he said.

Pascoe looked at Dalziel inquiringly.

"I'm in favor of owt that means some other bugger putting his hand in his pocket," he said cheerfully.

Giselle greeted them with delight and even George raised a welcoming smile.

"Who was that dishy thing you sent after us?" asked Ellie after Dalziel had been introduced.

"Dishy? Oh, you mean Giles. He *will* be pleased. Giles Fletcher. He owns this place."

"Oh, my! We send the owner on errands, do we?" said Ellie. "It's great to see you, Giselle. It's been ages. When am I getting the estate agent's tour of the new house? You've promised us first refusal when George finds a new ruin, remember?"

"I couldn't afford the ruin," objected Pascoe. "Not even with George doing our income tax."

"Does a bit of the old tax fiddling, your firm?" inquired Dalziel genially.

"I do a bit of work privately for friends," said Eliot coldly. "But in my own time and at home."

"You'll need to work bloody hard to make a copper rich," said Dalziel.

"Just keep taking the bribes, dear," said Ellie sweetly. "Now when can we move into Stanstone Farm, Giselle?"

Giselle glanced at her husband, whose expression remained a blank.

"Any time you like, darling," she said. "To tell you the truth, it can't be soon enough. In fact, we're back in town."

"Good God!" said Ellie. "You haven't found another place already, George? That's pretty rapid even for you."

A waiter appeared with a tray on which were glasses and a selection of liqueur bottles.

"Compliments of Mr. Fletcher," he said.

Dalziel examined the tray with distaste and beckoned the waiter close. For an incredulous moment Pascoe thought he was going to refuse the drinks on the grounds that police officers must be seen to be above all favor.

"From Mr. Fletcher, eh?" said Dalziel. "Well, listen, lad, he wouldn't be best pleased if he knew you'd forgotten the single malt whiskey, would he? Run along and fetch it. I'll look after pouring this lot."

Giselle looked at Dalziel with the round-eyed delight of a child seeing a walrus for the first time.

"Cointreau for me please, Mr. Dalziel," she said.

He filled a glass to the brim and passed it to her with a hand steady as a rock.

"Sup up, love," he said, looking with open admiration down her cleavage. "Lots more where that comes from."

Pascoe, sensing that Ellie might be about to ram a pepper-mill up her host's nostrils, said hastily, "Nothing wrong with the building, I hope, George? Not the beetle or anything like that?"

"I sorted all that out before we moved," said Eliot. "No, nothing wrong at all."

His tone was neutral but Giselle responded as though to an attack.

"It's all right, darling," she said. "Everyone's guessed it's me. But it's not really. It's just that I think we've got a ghost."

According to Giselle, there were strange scratchings, shadows moving where there should be none, and sometimes as she walked from one room to another "a sense of emptiness as though for a moment you'd stepped into the space between two stars."

This poetic turn of phrase silenced everyone except Dalziel, who interrupted his attempts to scratch the sole of his foot with a bent coffee spoon and let out a raucous laugh.

"What's that mean?" demanded Ellie.

"Nowt," said Dalziel. "I shouldn't worry, Mrs. Eliot. It's likely some randy yokel roaming about trying to get a peep at you. And who's to blame him?"

He underlined his compliment with a leer straight out of the old melodrama. Giselle patted his knee in acknowledgment.

"What do *you* think, George?" asked Ellie.

George admitted the scratchings but denied personal experience of the rest.

"See how long he stays there by himself," challenged Giselle.

"I didn't buy it to stay there by myself," said Eliot. "But I've spent the last couple of nights alone without damage."

"And you saw or heard nothing?" said Ellie.

"There may have been some scratching. A rat perhaps. It's an old house. But it's only a house. I have to go down to London for a few days tomorrow. When I get back we'll start looking for somewhere else. Sooner or later I'd get the urge anyway."

"But it's such a shame! After all your work, you deserve to relax for a while," said Ellie. "Isn't there anything you can do?"

"Exorcism," said Pascoe. "Bell, book, and candle."

"In my experience," said Dalziel, who had been consuming the malt whiskey at a rate that had caused the waiter to summon his workmates to view the spectacle, "there's three main causes of ghosts."

He paused for effect and more alcohol.

"Can't you arrest him, or something?" Ellie hissed at Pascoe.

"One: bad cooking," the fat man continued. "Two: bad ventilation. Three: bad conscience."

"George installed air-conditioning himself," said Pascoe.

"And Giselle's a super cook," said Ellie.

"Well then," said Dalziel. "I'm sure your conscience is as quiet as mine, love. So that leaves your randy yokel. Tell you what. Bugger your priests. What you need is a professional eye checking on things."

"You mean a psychic investigator?" said Giselle.

"Like hell!" laughed Ellie. "He means get the village bobby to stroll around the place with his truncheon at the ready."

"A policeman? But I don't really see what he could do," said Giselle, leaning toward Dalziel and looking earnestly into his lowered eyes.

"No, hold on a minute," cried Ellie with bright malice. "The Superintendent could be right. A formal investigation. But the village flatfoot's no use. You've got the best police brains in the county rubbing your thighs, Giselle. Why not send for them?"

Which was how it started. Dalziel, to Pascoe's amazement, had greeted the suggestion with ponderous enthusiasm. Giselle had reacted with a mixture of high spirits and high seriousness, apparently regarding the project as both an opportunity for vindication and a lark. George had sat like Switzerland, neutral and dull. Ellie had been smilingly baffled to see her bluff so swiftly called. And Pascoe had kicked her ankle savagely when he heard plans being made for himself and Dalziel to spend the following Friday night waiting for ghosts at Stanstone Farm.

As he told her the next day, had he realized that Dalziel's enthusiasm was going to survive the sober light of morning, he'd have followed up his kick with a karate chop.

Ellie had tried to appear unrepentant.

"You know why it's called Stanstone, do you?" she asked. "Standing stone. Get it? There must have been a stone circle there at some time. Primitive worship, human sacrifice, that sort of thing. Probably the original stones were used in the building of the house. That'd explain a lot, wouldn't it?"

"No," said Pascoe coldly. "That would explain very little. It would certainly not explain why I am about to lose a night's sleep, nor why you who usually threaten me with divorce or assault whenever my rest is disturbed to fight *real* crime should have arranged it."

But arranged it had been and it was small comfort for Pascoe now to know that Ellie was missing him.

Dalziel seemed determined to enjoy himself, however.

"Let's get our bearings, shall we?" he said. Replenishing his glass, he set out on a tour of the house.

"Well wired up," he said as his expert eye spotted the discreet evidence of the sophisticated alarm system. "Must have cost a fortune."

"It did. I put him in touch with our crime-prevention squad and evidently he wanted nothing but the best," said Pascoe.

"What's he got that's so precious?" wondered Dalziel.

"All this stuff's pretty valuable, I guess," said Pascoe, making a gesture that took in the pictures and ornaments of the master bedroom in which they were standing. "But it's really for Giselle's sake. This was her first time out in the sticks and it's a pretty lonely place. Not that it's done much good."

"Aye," said Dalziel, opening a drawer and pulling out a fine silk underslip. "A good-looking woman could get nervous in a place like this."

"You reckon that's what this is all about, sir?" said Pascoe. "A slight case of hysteria?"

"Mebbe," said Dalziel.

They went into the next room, which Eliot had turned into a study. Only the calculating machine on the desk reminded them of the man's profession. The glass-fronted bookcase contained rows of books relating to his hobby in all its aspects from architectural histories to do-it-yourself tracts on concrete mixing. An old grandmother clock stood in a corner, and hanging on the wall opposite the bookcase was a nearly lifesize painting of a pre-Raphaelite maiden being pensive in a grove. She was naked but her long hair and the dappled shadowings of the trees preserved her modesty.

For a fraction of a second it seemed to Pascoe as if the shadows on her flesh shifted as though a breeze had touched the branches above.

"Asking for it," declared Dalziel.

"What?"

"Rheumatics or rape," said Dalziel. "Let's check the kitchen. My belly's empty as a football."

Giselle, who had driven out during the day to light the fire and make ready for their arrival, had anticipated Dalziel's gut. On the kitchen table lay a pile of sandwiches covered by a sheet of kitchen paper on which she had scribbled an invitation for them to help themselves to whatever they fancied.

Underneath she had written in capitals BE CAREFUL and underlined it twice.

"Nice thought," said Dalziel, grabbing a couple of the sandwiches. "Bring the plate through to the living room and we'll eat in comfort."

Back in front of the fire with his glass filled once again, Dalziel relaxed in a deep armchair. Pascoe poured himself a drink and looked out of the window again.

"For God's sake, lad, sit down!" commanded Dalziel. "You're worse than a bloody spook, creeping around like that."

"Sorry," said Pascoe.

"Sup your drink and eat a sandwich. It'll soon be midnight. That's zero hour, isn't it? Right, get your strength up. Keep your nerves down."

"I'm not nervous!" protested Pascoe.

"No? Don't believe in ghosts, then?"

"Hardly at all," said Pascoe.

"Quite right. Detective-inspectors with university degrees shouldn't believe in ghosts. But tired old superintendents with less schooling than a pit pony, there's a different matter."

"Come off it!" said Pascoe. "You're the biggest unbeliever I know!"

"That may be, that may be," said Dalziel, sinking lower into his chair. "But sometimes, lad, sometimes . . ."

His voice sank away. The room was lit only by a dark-shaded table lamp and the glow from the fire threw deep shadows across the large contours of Dalziel's face. It might have been some eighteenth-century Yorkshire farmer sitting there, thought Pascoe. Shrewd; brutish; in his day a solid ram of a man, but now rotting to ruin through his own excesses and too much rough weather.

In the fireplace a log fell. Pascoe started. The red glow ran up Dalziel's face like a flush of passion up an Easter Island statue.

"I knew a ghost saved a marriage once," he said ruminatively. "In a manner of speaking."

Oh, Jesus! thought Pascoe. *It's ghost stories round the fire now, is it?* He remained obstinately silent.

"My first case, I suppose you'd call it. Start of a meteoric career."

"Meteors fall. And burn out," said Pascoe. "Sir."

"You're a sharp bugger, Peter," said Dalziel admiringly. "Always the quick answer. I bet you were just the same when you were eighteen. Still at school, eh? Not like me. I was a right Constable Plod I tell you. Untried. Untutored. Hardly knew one end of my truncheon from t'other. When I heard that shriek I just froze."

"Which shriek?" asked Pascoe resignedly.

On cue there came a piercing wail from the dark outside, quickly cut off. He half rose, caught Dalziel's amused eye, and subsided, reaching for the whiskey decanter.

"Easy on that stuff," admonished Dalziel with all the righteousness of a temperance preacher. "Enjoy your supper, like yon owl. Where was I? Oh aye. I was on night patrol. None of your Panda-cars in those days. You did it all on foot. And I was standing just inside this little alleyway.

It was a dark narrow passage running between Shufflebotham's wool-mill on the one side and a little terrace of back-to-backs on the other. It's all gone now, all gone. There's a car park there now. A bloody car park!

"Any road, the thing about this alley was, it were a dead end. There was a kind of buttress sticking out of the mill wall, might have been the chimney stack, I'm not sure, but the back-to-backs had been built flush up against it so there was no way through. No way at all."

He took another long pull at his Scotch to help his memory and began to scratch his armpit noisily.

"Listen!" said Pascoe suddenly.

"What?"

"I thought I heard a noise."

"What kind of noise?"

"Like fingers scrabbling on rough stone," said Pascoe.

Dalziel removed his hand slowly from his shirt front and regarded Pascoe malevolently.

"It's stopped now," said Pascoe. "What were you saying, sir?"

"I was saying about this shriek," said Dalziel. "I just froze to the spot. It came floating out of this dark passage. It was as black as the devil's arsehole up there. The mill wall was completely blank and there was just one small window in the gable end of the house. That, if anywhere, was where the shriek came from. Well, I don't know what I'd have done. I might have been standing there yet wondering what to do, only this big hand slapped hard on my shoulder. I nearly shit myself! Then this voice said, "What's to do, Constable Dalziel?" and when I looked round there was my sergeant, doing his rounds.

"I could hardly speak for a moment, he'd given me such a fright. But I didn't need to explain. For just then came another shriek and voices, a man's and a woman's, shouting at each other. 'You hang on here,' said the sergeant. 'I'll see what this is all about.' Off he went, leaving me still shaking. And as I looked down that gloomy passageway, I began to remember some local stories about this mill. I hadn't paid much heed to them before. Everywhere that's more than fifty years old had a ghost in them parts. They say Yorkshiremen are hard-headed, but I reckon they've got more superstition to the square inch than a tribe of pygmies. Well, this particular tale was about a mill-girl back in the 1870s. The owner's son had put her in the family way, which I dare say was common enough. The owner acted decently enough by his lights. He packed his son off to the other end of the country, gave the girl and her family a bit of cash, and said she could have her job back when the confinement was over."

"Almost a social reformer," said Pascoe, growing interested despite himself.

"Better than a lot of buggers still in business round here," said Dalziel sourly. "To cut a long story short, this lass had her kid premature and it soon died. As soon as she was fit enough to get out of bed, she came back to the mill, climbed through a skylight on to the roof and jumped off. Now all that I could believe. Probably happened all the time."

"Yes," said Pascoe. "I've no doubt that a hundred years ago the air round here was full of falling girls. While in America they were fighting a war to stop the plantation owners screwing their slaves!"

"You'll have to watch that indignation, Peter," said Dalziel. "It can give you wind. And no one pays much heed to a preacher when you can't hear his sermons for farts. Where was I, now? Oh yes. This lass. Since that day there'd been a lot of stories about people seeing a girl falling from the roof of this old mill. Tumbling over and over in the air right slowly, most of 'em said. Her clothes filling with air, her hair streaming behind her like a comet's tail. Oh aye, lovely descriptions some of them were. Like the ones we get whenever there's an accident. One for every pair of eyes, and all of 'em perfectly detailed and perfectly different."

"So you didn't reckon much to these tales?" said Pascoe.

"Not by daylight," said Dalziel. "But standing there in the mouth of that dark passageway at midnight, that was different."

Pascoe glanced at his watch.

"It's nearly midnight now," he said in a sepulchral tone.

Dalziel ignored him.

"I was glad when the sergeant stuck his head through that little window and bellowed my name. Though even that gave me a hell of a scare. 'Dalziel!' he said. 'Take a look up this alleyway. If you can't see anything, come in here.' So I had a look. There wasn't anything, just sheer brick walls on three sides with only this one little window. I didn't hang about but got myself round to the front of the house pretty sharply and went in. There were two people there besides the sergeant. Albert Pocklington, whose house it was, and his missus, Jenny. In those days a good bobby knew everyone on his beat. I said hello, but they didn't do much more than grunt. Mrs. Pocklington was about forty. She must have been a bonny lass in her time and she still didn't look to bad. She'd got her blouse off, just draped around her shoulders, and I had a good squint at her big round tits. Well, I was only a lad! I didn't really look at her face till I'd had an eyeful lower down and then I noticed that one side was all splotchy red as though someone had given her a clout. There were no prizes for guessing who. Bert Pocklington was a big solid fellow. He looked like a chimpanzee, only he had a lot less gumption."

"Hold on," said Pascoe.

"What is it now?" said Dalziel, annoyed that his story had been interrupted.

"I thought I heard something. No, I mean really heard something this time."

They listened together. The only sound Pascoe could hear was the noise of his own breathing mixed with the pulsing of his own blood, like the distant sough of a receding tide.

"I'm sorry," he said. "I really did think . . ."

"That's all right, lad," said Dalziel with surprising sympathy, "I know the feeling. Where'd I got to? Albert Pocklington. My sergeant took me aside and put me in the picture. It seems that Pocklington had got a notion in his mind that someone was banging his missus while he was on the night shift. So he'd slipped away from his work at midnight and come home, ready to do a bit of banging on his own account. He wasn't a man to move quietly, so he'd tried for speed instead, flinging open the front door and rushing up the stairs. When he opened the bedroom door, his wife had been standing by the open window naked to the waist, shrieking. Naturally he thought the worst. Who wouldn't? Her story was that she was getting ready for bed when she had this feeling of the room suddenly becoming very hot and airless and pressing in on her. She'd gone to the window and opened it, and it was like taking a cork out of a bottle, she said. She felt as if she was being sucked out of the window, she said. (With tits like you and a window that small, there wasn't much likelihood of that! I thought.) And at the same time she had seen a shape like a human figure tumbling slowly by the window. Naturally she shrieked. Pocklington came in. She threw herself into his arms. All the welcome she got was a thump on the ear, and that brought on the second bout of shrieking. She was hysterical, trying to tell him what she'd seen, while he just raged around, yelling about what he was going to do to her fancy man."

He paused for a drink. Pascoe stirred the fire with his foot. Then froze. There it was again! A distant scratching. He had no sense of direction.

The hairs on the back of his neck prickled in the traditional fashion. Clearly Dalziel heard nothing and Pascoe was not yet certain enough to interrupt the fat man again.

"The sergeant was a good copper. He didn't want a man beating up his wife for no reason and he didn't want a hysterical woman starting a ghost scare. They can cause a lot of bother, ghost scares," added Dalziel, filling his glass once more with the long-suffering expression of a man who is being caused a lot of bother.

"He sorted out Pocklington's suspicions about his wife having a lover first of all. He pushed his shoulders through the window till they got stuck to show how small it was. Then he asked me if anyone could have come out of that passageway without me spotting them. Out of the question, I told him.

"Next he chatted to the wife and got her to admit she'd been feeling a bit under the weather that day, like the flu was coming on, and she'd taken a cup of tea heavily spiked with gin as a nightcap. Ten minutes later we left them more or less happy. But as we stood on the pavement outside, the sergeant asked me the question I'd hoped he wouldn't. Why had I stepped into that alley in the first place? I suppose I could have told him I wanted a pee or a smoke, something like that. But he was a hard man to lie to, that sergeant. Not like the wet-nurses we get nowadays. So after a bit of hemming and hawing, I told him I'd seen something, just out of the corner of my eye, as I was walking past. "What sort of thing?" he asked. Like something falling, I said. Something fluttering and falling through the air between the mill wall and the house end.

"He gave me a queer look, that sergeant did. "I tell you what, Dalziel," he said. "When you make out your report, I shouldn't say anything of that. No, I should keep quiet about that. Leave ghosts to them that understands them. You stick to crime." And that's advice I've followed ever since, till this very night, that is!"

He yawned and stretched. There was a distant rather cracked chime. It was, Pascoe realized, the clock in Eliot's study striking midnight.

But it wasn't the only sound.

"*There!* Listen," urged Pascoe, rising slowly to his feet. "I *can* hear it. A scratching. Do *you* hear it, sir?"

Dalziel cupped one cauliflower ear in his hand.

"By Christ, I think you're right, lad!" he said as if this were the most remote possibility in the world. "Come on! Let's take a look."

Pascoe led the way. Once out of the living room they could hear the noise quite clearly and it took only a moment to locate it in the kitchen.

"Rats?" wondered Pascoe.

Dalziel shook his head.

"Rats gnaw," he whispered. "That sounds like something bigger. It's at the back door. It sounds a bit keen to get in."

Indeed it did, thought Pascoe. There was a desperate insistency about the sound. Sometimes it rose to a crescendo, then tailed away as though from exhaustion, only to renew itself with greater fury.

It was as though someone or something was caught in a trap too fast for hope, too horrible for resignation. Pascoe had renewed his acquaintance with Poe after the strange business at Wear End and now he recalled the story in which the coffin was opened to reveal a contorted skeleton and the lid scarred on the inside by the desperate scraping of fingernails.

"Shall I open it?" he whispered to Dalziel.

"No," said the fat man. "Best one of us goes out the front door and comes round behind. I'll open when you shout. OK?"

"OK," said Pascoe with less enthusiasm than he had ever OK'd even Dalziel before.

Picking up one of the heavy rubber-encased torches they had brought with them, he retreated to the front door and slipped out into the dark night.

The frost had come down fiercely since their arrival and the cold caught at his throat like an invisible predator. He thought of returning for his coat, but decided this would be just an excuse for postponing whatever confrontation awaited him. Instead, making a mental note that when he was a superintendent he, too, would make sure he got the inside jobs, he set off round the house.

When he reached the second corner, he could hear the scratching quite clearly. It cut through the still and freezing air like the sound of a steel blade against a grinding stone.

Pascoe paused, took a deep breath, let out a yell of warning and leaped out from the angle of the house with his torch flashing.

The scratching ceased instantly, there was nothing to be seen by the rear door of the house, but a terrible shriek died away across the lawn as though an exorcised spirit was wailing its way to Hades.

At the same time the kitchen door was flung open and Dalziel stroke majestically forward; then his foot skidded on the frosty ground and, swearing horribly, he crashed down on his huge behind.

"Are you all right, sir?" asked Pascoe breathlessly.

"There's only one part of my body that feels any sensitivity still," said Dalziel. "Give us a hand up."

He dusted himself down, saying, "Well, that's ghost number one laid."

"Sir?"

"Look."

His stubby finger pointed to a line of paw prints across the powder frost of the lawn.

"Cat," he said. "This was a farmhouse, remember? Every farm has its cats. They live in the barn, keep the rats down. Where's the barn?"

"Gone," said Pascoe. "George had it pulled down and used some of the stones for an extension to the house."

"There you are then," said Dalziel. "Poor bloody animal wakes up one morning with no roof, no rats. It's all right living rough in the summer, but comes the cold weather and it starts fancying getting inside again. Perhaps the farmer's wife used to give it scraps at the kitchen door."

"It'll get precious little encouragement from Giselle," said Pascoe.

"It's better than Count Dracula anyway," said Dalziel.

Pascoe, who was now very cold indeed, began to move toward the kitchen, but to his surprise Dalziel stopped him.

"It's a hell of a night even for a cat," he said. "Just have a look, Peter, see if you can spot the poor beast. In case it's hurt."

Rather surprised by his boss's manifestation of kindness to animals (though not in the least at his display of cruelty to junior officers), Pascoe shivered along the line of paw prints across the grass. They disappeared into a small orchard, whose trees seemed to crowd together to repel intruders, or perhaps just for warmth. Pascoe peered between the italic trunks and made cat-attracting noises but nothing stirred.

"All right," he said. "I know you're in there. We've got the place surrounded. Better come quietly. I'll leave the door open, so just come in and give a yell when you want to give yourself up."

Back in the kitchen, he left the door ajar and put a bowl of milk on the floor. His teeth were chattering and he headed to the living room, keen to do full justice to both the log fire and the whiskey decanter. The telephone rang as he entered. For once Dalziel picked it up and Pascoe poured himself a stiff drink.

From the half conversation he could hear, he gathered it was the duty sergeant at the station who was ringing. Suddenly, irrationally, he felt very worried in case Dalziel was going to announce he had to go out on a case, leaving Pascoe alone.

The reality turned out almost as bad.

"Go easy on that stuff," said Dalziel. "You don't want to be done for driving under the influence."

"What?"

Dalziel passed him the phone.

The sergeant told him someone had just rung the station asking urgently for Pascoe and refusing to speak to anyone else. He'd claimed what he had to say was important. "It's big and it's tonight" were his words. And he'd rung off saying he'd ring back in an hour's time. After that it'd be too late.

"Oh, shit," said Pascoe. "It sounds like Benny."

Benny was one of his snouts, erratic and melodramatic, but often bringing really hot information.

"I suppose I'll have to go in," said Pascoe reluctantly. "Or I could get the Sarge to pass this number on."

"If it's urgent, you'll need to be on the spot," said Dalziel. "Let me know what's happening, won't you? Best get your skates on."

"Skates is right," muttered Pascoe. "It's like the Arctic out there."

He downed his whiskey defiantly, then went to put his overcoat on.

"You'll be all right by yourself, will you, sir?" he said maliciously. "Able to cope with ghosts, ghouls, werewolves, and falling mill girls?"

"Never you mind about me, lad," said Dalziel jovially. "Any road, if it's visitors from an old stone circle we've got to worry about, dawn's the time, isn't it? When the first rays of the sun touch the victim's breast. And with luck you'll be back by then. Keep me posted."

Pascoe opened the front door and groaned as the icy air attacked his face once more.

"I am just going outside," he said. "And I may be some time."

To which Dalziel replied, as perhaps Captain Scott and his companions had, "Shut that bloody door!"

It took several attempts before he could persuade the frozen engine to start and he knew from experience that it would be a good twenty minutes before the heater began to pump even lukewarm air into the car. Swearing softly to himself, he set the vehicle bumping gently over the frozen contours of the long driveway up to the road.

The drive curved round the orchard and the comforting silhouette of the house soon disappeared from his mirror. The frost-laced trees seemed to lean menacingly across his path and he told himself that if any apparition suddenly rose before the car, he'd test its substance by driving straight through it.

But when the headlights reflected a pair of bright eyes directly ahead, he slammed on the brake instantly.

The cat looked as if it had been waiting for him. It was a skinny black creature with a mangled ear and a wary expression. Its response to Pascoe's soothing noises was to turn and plunge into the orchard once more.

"Oh no!" groaned Pascoe. And he yelled after it, "You stupid bloody animal! I'm not going to chase you through the trees all bloody night. Not if you were a naked naiad, I'm not!"

As though recognizing the authentic tone of a Yorkshire farmer, the cat howled in reply and Pascoe glimpsed its shadowy shape only a few yards ahead. He followed, hurling abuse to which the beast responded with indignant meows. Finally it disappeared under a bramble bush.

"That does it," said Pascoe. "Not a step further."

Leaning down he flashed his torch beneath the bush to take his farewell of the stupid animal.

Not one pair of eyes but three stared unblinkingly back at him, and a chorus of howls split the frosty air.

The newcomers were young kittens who met him with delight that made up for their mother's wariness. They were distressingly thin and nearby Pascoe's torch picked out the stiff bodies of another two, rather smaller, who hadn't survived.

"Oh, shit," said Pascoe, more touched than his anti-sentimental attitudes would have permitted him to admit.

When he scooped up the kittens, their mother snarled in protest and tried to sink her teeth into his gloved hand. But he was in no mood for argument and after he'd bellowed, "Shut up!" she allowed herself to be lifted and settled down comfortably in the crook of his arm with her offspring.

It was quicker to continue through the orchard than to return to the car. As he walked across the lawn toward the kitchen door he smiled to himself at the prospect of leaving Dalziel in charge of this little family. That would really test the fat man's love of animals.

The thought of ghosts and hauntings was completely removed from his mind.

And that made the sight of the face at the upstairs window even more terrifying.

For a moment his throat constricted so much that he could hardly breathe. It was a pale face, a woman's he thought, shadowy, insubstantial behind the leaded panes of the old casement. And as he looked the room behind seemed to be touched by a dim unearthly glow through which shadows moved like weed on a slow stream's bed. In his arms the kittens squeaked in protest and he realized that he had involuntarily tightened his grip.

"Sorry," he said, and the momentary distraction unlocked the paralyzing fear and replaced it by an equally instinctive resolve to confront its source. There's nothing makes a man angrier than the awareness of having been made afraid.

He went through the open kitchen door and dropped the cats by the bowl of milk, which they assaulted with silent delight. The wise thing would have been to summon Dalziel from his warmth and whiskey, but Pascoe had no mind to be wise. He went up the stairs as swiftly and as quietly as he could.

He had calculated that the window from which the "phantom" peered belonged to the study and when he saw the door was open he didn't know whether he was pleased or not. Ghosts didn't need doors. On the other hand it meant that *something* was in there. But the glow had gone.

Holding his torch like a truncheon, he stepped inside. As his free hand groped for the light switch he was aware of something silhouetted against the paler darkness of the window and at the same time of movement elsewhere in the room. His left hand couldn't find the switch, his right thumb couldn't find the button on the torch, it was as if the darkness of the room was liquid, slowing down all movement and washing over his mouth and nose and eyes in wave after stifling wave.

Then a single cone of light grew above Eliot's desk and Dalziel's voice said, "Why're you waving your arms like that, lad? Semaphore, is it?"

At which moment his fingers found the main light switch.

Dalziel was standing by the desk. Against the window leaned the long painting of the pre-Raphaelite girl, face to the glass. Where it had hung on the wall was a safe, wide open and empty. On the desk under the sharply focused rays of the desk lamp lay what Pascoe took to be its contents.

"What the hell's going on?" demanded Pascoe, half-relieved, half-bewildered.

"Tell you in a minute," said Dalziel, resuming his examination of the papers.

"No, sir," said Pascoe with growing anger. "You'll tell me now. You'll tell me exactly what you're doing going through private papers without a warrant! And how the hell did you get into that safe?"

"I've got you to thank for that, Peter," said Dalziel without looking up.

"What?"

"It was you who put Eliot in touch with our crime-prevention officer, wasn't it? I did an efficiency check the other morning, went through all the files. There it was. Eliot, George. He really wanted the works, didn't he? What's he got out there? I thought. The family jewels? I checked with the firm who did the fitting. I know the manager, as it happens. He's a good lad; bit of a ladies' man, but clever with it."

"Oh, God!" groaned Pascoe. "You mean you got details of the alarm system and a spare set of keys!"

"No, I didn't!" said Dalziel indignantly. "I had to work it out for myself mainly."

He had put on his wire-rimmed National Health spectacles to read the documents from the safe and now he glared owlishly at Pascoe over them.

"Do you understand figures?" he asked. "It's all bloody Welsh to me."

Pascoe consciously resisted the conspiratorial invitation.

"I've heard nothing so far to explain why you're breaking the law, sir," he said coldly. "What's George Eliot supposed to have done?"

"What? Oh, I see. It's the laws of hospitality and friendship you're worried about! Nothing, nothing. Set your mind at rest, lad. It's nowt to do with your mate. Only indirectly. Look, this wasn't planned, you know. I mean, how could I plan all that daft ghost business? No, it was just that the Fletcher business was getting nowhere . . ."

"Fletcher?"

"Hey, here's your income tax file. Christ! Is that what your missus gets just for chatting to students? It's more than you!"

Pascoe angrily snatched the file from Dalziel's hands. The fat man put on his sympathetic, sincere look.

"Never fret, lad. I won't spread it around. Where was I? Oh yes, Fletcher. I've got a feeling about that fellow. The tip-off sounded good. Not really my line, though. I got Inspector Marwood on the Fraud Squad interested, though. All he could come up with was that a lot of Fletcher's business interests had a faint smell about them, but that was all. Oh yes, and Fletcher's accountants were the firm your mate Eliot's a partner in."

"That's hardly a startling revelation," sneered Pascoe.

"Did you know?"

"No. Why should I?"

"Fair point," said Dalziel. "Hello, hello."

He had found an envelope among the files. It contained a single sheet of paper, which he examined with growing interest. Then he carefully refolded it, replaced it in the envelope and began to put all the documents read or unread back into the safe.

"Marwood told me as well, though, that Fletcher and Eliot seemed to be pretty thick at a personal level. And he also said the Fraud Squad would love to go over Fletcher's accounts with a fine-tooth comb."

"Why doesn't he get himself a warrant then?"

"Useless, unless he knows what he's looking for. My tipster was too vague. Often happens with first-timers. They want it to be quick and they overestimate our abilities."

"Is that possible?" marveled Pascoe.

"Oh, aye. Just. Are you going to take that file home?"

Reluctantly, Pascoe handed his tax file back to Dalziel, who thrust it in with the others, slammed the safe, then did some complicated fiddling with a bunch of keys.

"There," he said triumphantly, "all locked up and the alarm set once more. No harm to anyone. Peter, do me a favor. Put that tart's picture back up on the wall. I nearly did my back getting it down. I'll go and mend the fire and pour us a drink."

"I am not involved in this!" proclaimed Pascoe. But the fat man had gone.

When Pascoe came downstairs after replacing the picture, Dalziel was not to be found in the living room. Pascoe tracked him to the kitchen, where he found him on his hands and knees, feeding pressed calves' tongue to the kittens.

"So you found 'em," said Dalziel. "That's what brought you back. Soft bugger."

"Yes. And I take it I needn't go out again. There's no snout'll be ringing at one o'clock. That was you while I was freezing outside, wasn't it?"

"I'm afraid so. I thought it best to get you out of the way. Sorry, lad, but I mean, this fellow Eliot is a mate of yours and I didn't want you getting upset."

"I *am* upset," said Pascoe. "Bloody upset."

"There!" said Dalziel triumphantly. "I was right, wasn't I? Let's get that drink. These buggers can look after themselves."

He dumped the rest of the tongue on to the kitchen floor and rose to his feet with much wheezing.

"There it is then, Peter," said Dalziel as they returned to the living room. "It was all on the spur of the moment. When Mrs. Eliot suggested we spend a night here to look for her ghosts, I just went along to be sociable. I mean, you can't be rude to a woman like that, can you? A sudden shock, and that dress might have fallen off her nipples. I'd no more intention of really coming out here than of going teetotal! But next morning I got to thinking. If we could just get a bit of a pointer where to look at Fletcher . . . And I remembered you saying about Eliot doing your accounts at home."

"Income tax!" snorted Pascoe. "Does that make me a crook? Or him either?"

"No. It was just a thought, that's all. And after I'd talked to Crime Prevention, well, it seemed worth a peek. So come down off your high horse. No harm done. Your mate's not in trouble, OK? And I saw nowt in his safe to take action on. So relax, enjoy your drink. I poured you brandy, the Scotch is getting a bit low. That all right?"

Pascoe didn't answer but sat down in the deep old armchair and sipped his drink reflectively. Spur of the moment, Dalziel had said. Bloody long moment, he thought. And what spur? There was still something here that hadn't been said.

"It won't do," he said suddenly.

"What's that?"

"There's got to be something else," insisted Pascoe. "I mean, I know you, sir. You're not going to do all this *just* on the off-chance of finding something to incriminate Fletcher in George's safe. There *has* to be something else. What did you expect to find, anyway? A signed confession? Come to that, what *did* you find?"

Dalziel looked at him, his eyes moist with sincerity.

"Nowt, lad. Nowt. I've told you. There'll be no action taken as a result of anything I saw tonight. None. There's my reassurance. It was an error of judgment on my part. I admit it. Now does that satisfy you?"

"No, sir, to be quite frank it doesn't. Look, I've got to know. These people are my friends. You say that they're not mixed up in anything criminal, but I still need to know exactly what is going on. Or else I'll start asking for myself."

He banged his glass down on the arm of his chair so vehemently that the liquor slopped out.

"It'll burn a hole, you stuff," said Dalziel, slandering the five-star cognac that Pascoe was drinking.

"I mean it, sir," said Pascoe quietly. "You'd better understand that."

"All right, lad," said Dalziel. "I believe you. You might not like it though. *You'd* better understand *that*."

"I'll chance it," replied Pascoe.

Dalziel regarded him closely, then relaxed with a sigh.

"Here it is then. The woman Giselle is having a bit on the side with Fletcher."

Pascoe managed an indifferent shrug.

"It happens," he said, trying to appear unsurprised. In fact, why was he surprised? Lively, sociable, physical Giselle and staid, self-contained, inward-looking George. It was always on the cards.

"So what?" he added in his best man-of-the-world voice.

"So if by any chance, Eliot did have anything that might point us in the right direction about Fletcher . . ."

Pascoe sat very still for a moment.

"Well, you old bastard!" he said. "You mean you'd give him good reason to do the pointing! You'd let him know about Giselle . . . Jesus wept! How low can you get?"

"I could have just let him know in any case without checking first to see if it was worthwhile," suggested Dalziel, unabashed.

"So you could!" said Pascoe in mock astonishment. "But you held back, waiting for a chance to check it out! Big of you! You get invited to spend the night alone in complete strangers' houses all the time! And now you've looked and found nothing, what are you going to do? Tell him just on the off-chance?"

"I didn't say I'd found *nothing,*" said Dalziel.

Pascoe stared at him.

"But you said there'd be no action!" he said.

"Right," said Dalziel. "I mean it. I think we've just got to sit back and wait for Fletcher to fall into our laps. Or be pushed. What I did find was a little anonymous letter telling Eliot what his wife was up to. Your mate *knows,* Peter. From the postmark he's known for a few weeks. He's a careful man, accountants usually are. And I'm sure he'd do a bit of checking first before taking action. It was just a week later that my telephone rang and that awful disguised voice told me to check on Fletcher. Asked for me personally. I dare say you've mentioned my name to Eliot, haven't you, Peter?"

He looked at the carpet modestly.

"Everyone's heard of you, sir," said Pascoe. "So what happens now?"

"Like I say. Nothing. We sit and wait for the next call. It should be a bit more detailed this time, I reckon. I mean, Eliot must have realized that his first tip-off isn't getting results and now his wife's moved back into town to be on Fletcher's doorstep again, he's got every incentive."

Pascoe looked at him in surprise.

"You mean the ghosts . . ."

"Nice imaginative girl, that Giselle! Not only does she invent a haunting to save herself a two hours' drive for her kicks, but she cons a pair of thick bobbies into losing their sleep over it. I bet Fletcher fell about laughing! Well I'm losing no more! It'll take all the hounds of hell to keep me awake."

He yawned and stretched. In mid-stretch there came a terrible scratching noise and the fat man froze like a woodcut of Lethargy on an allegorical frieze.

Then he laughed and opened the door.

The black cat looked up at him warily but her kittens had no such inhibitions and tumbled in, heading toward the fire with cries of delight.

"I think your mates have got more trouble than they know," said Dalziel.

Next morning Pascoe rose early and stiffly after a night spent on a sofa before the fire. Dalziel had disappeared upstairs to find himself a bed and Pascoe assumed he would still be stretched out on it. But when he looked out of the living room he saw he was wrong.

The sun was just beginning to rise behind the orchard and the fat man was standing in front of the house watching the dawn.

A romantic at heart, thought Pascoe sourly.

A glint of light flickered between the trunks of the orchard trees, flamed into a ray and began to move across the frosty lawn toward the waiting man. He watched its progress, striking sparks off the ice-hard grass. And when it reached his feet he stepped aside.

Pascoe joined him a few minutes later.

"Morning, sir," he said. "I've made some coffee. You're up bright and early."

"Yes," said Dalziel, scratching his gut vigorously. "I think I've picked up a flea from those bloody cats."

"Oh," said Pascoe. "I thought you'd come to check on the human sacrifice at dawn. I saw you getting out of the way of the sun's first ray."

"Bollocks!" said Dalziel, looking toward the house, which the sun was now staining the gentle pink of blood in a basin of water.

"Why bollocks?" wondered Pascoe. "You've seen one ghost. Why not another?"

"One ghost?"

"Yes. The mill girl. That story you told me last night. Your first case."

Dalziel looked at him closely.

"I told you that, did I? I must have been supping well."

Pascoe, who knew that drink had never made Dalziel forget a thing in his life, nodded vigorously.

"Yes, sir. You told me that. You and your ghost."

Dalziel shook his head as though at a memory of ancient foolishness and began to laugh.

"Aye, lad. My ghost! It really is my ghost in a way. The ghost of what

I am now, any road! That Jenny Pocklington, she were a right grand lass! She had an imagination like your Giselle!"

"I don't follow," said Pascoe. But he was beginning to.

"Believe it or not, lad," said Dalziel. "In them days I was pretty slim. Slim and supple. Even then I had to be like a ghost to get through that bloody window! But if Bert Pocklington had caught me, I really would have been one! Aye, that's right. When I heard that scream, I was coming out of the alley, not going into it!"

And shaking with laughter the fat man headed across the lacy grass toward the old stone farmhouse where the hungry kittens were crying imperiously for their breakfast.

The Watts Lions

Author: Walter Mosley (1952–   )

Detective: Easy Rawlins (1990)

Mosley's career got the same kind of push from President Bill Clinton as J.S. Fletcher did from Woodrow Wilson and Ian Fleming from John F. Kennedy. But Mosley and Easy Rawlins, who appears in *Devil in a Blue Dress* (1990) and subsequent novels with color-coded titles, would be major figures even without a boost from the Oval Office. There had been African-American fictional detectives before Rawlins, but most of them were the invention of white authors (Ed Lacy's Touie Moore, John Ball's Virgil Tibbs, Ernest Tidyman's Shaft), distinctly offbeat (Chester Himes' Coffin Ed and Grave Digger), or both (George Baxt's Pharoah Love). Easy Rawlins is both fully believable and fully black, and his placement in a well-realized 1950s Los Angeles gives extra interest to his adventures.

"The Watts Lions" is, to the editor's knowledge, the only Easy Rawlins short story, and in its elucidation of the subtleties of African-American society, it represents the series well. It first appeared in the anthology *The New Mystery* (1993), edited for the International Association of Crime Writers by Jerome Charyn.

I f you don't help, Mr. Rawlins, that RayJohn gonna kill us all," Bigelow said. He was the largest of the men sitting before us.

"That's right!" Mr. Mink shouted. "We gotta have us some p'otection from that crazy man!" He wore white painter's overalls and smelled strongly of turpentine.

Bledsoe, the third man, said nothing.

At the desk next to mine, Mofass lit a match on a piece of sandpaper nailed to the wall behind. In the flare his fat, black, and deeply lined face shone like a hideous tiki mask.

"You mean Raymond Johns?" I asked.

"He's gonna kill us, Mr. Rawlins. He already got Ornin." Mr. Mink spoke loudly enough to be heard across a football field.

"He means Ornin Levesque," Mofass said. The cool smoke of his cigar broke in a wave across my desk.

I nodded. Mofass stifled a cough.

"Well?" Bigelow asked.

"Well what?"

"What can you do to help us?"

I took a beat-up Lucky from my breast pocket.

"Gimme a light, Mofass," I said. And while he struck another match and leaned across the span of our desks, I asked, "Why would RayJohn wanna kill Ornin Levesque?"

" 'Cause he crazy, that's why!" Mr. Mink shouted.

"So go to the po-lice. It's they job t'catch killers. They do that kinda work fo' free."

"They been to the police, Mr. Rawlins," Mofass said. "But RayJohn moved out his house an' all the police said was that if he come around botherin' them again that they should call back then."

It was 1955 and the police weren't too worried about colored murders.

"Why would RayJohn wanna kill anybody? He ain't all that crazy," I said, but I knew that he was.

"He is now!" Mr. Mink squealed.

"Now I'm gonna ask you boys again," I said. "Why would this man wanna kill you?"

"We sinned against him," Bledsoe whispered. His quiet eyes were focused on a point far behind my head.

"Don't listen to him, Easy." Bigelow put up his hand like a boy in school. "He's so upset over this killin' that he's a li'l crazy hisself."

"That's alright," I said. "*You* tell me."

"We was mindin' our own business, man. We was at the Lions when he come bustin' in there . . ."

The Watts Lions was a social club that some colored "professionals" had formed. Electricians, plumbers, real estate men (like Mofass), and other tradesmen. They didn't want to hear from *street niggers* like me. Of course they didn't know that I owned more property than the three of them combined. Mofass represented my apartment buildings but I still pretended to be his "assistant."

". . . it was that Olson-Turpin fight," Bigelow was saying. "RayJohn said that he laid a bet on Olson wit' Ornin. Three hundred dollars at four to one."

"An' you didn't pay?" I asked.

"We thought he was lyin' at first!" Mr. Mink screamed. Maybe he thought that if he yelled loud enough I'd believe his lies. "An' then we thought that it was Ornin's bet! Why should we pay just 'cause Ornin lost a bet?"

I was wondering whether or not to call him a liar when the coughing started. Mofass had developed a smoker's cough over the years. I told him that all that smoke was going to kill him but he blamed his health on the smog. He hacked long and loud, sounding like an engine that wouldn't turn over.

"He intends t'kill them," Mofass whispered after a long while.

I motioned my head at Bigelow. "Who says?"

"He told us hisself when he come over to the Lions. Then they found Ornin . . ." Bigelow paused. He put his thumbs in the pockets of his vest and stared at the floor.

I knew what he saw there.

On page fourteen the *Examiner* had reported that Ornin Levesque was found tied up, naked, and spread-eagled, on his own bed. His mouth was stuffed full with cotton balls and taped shut. The flesh from his belly had been stripped off while he was still alive and plastered to the wall over his head. I could imagine RayJohn, the Louisiana half-breed, stripping off a patch of Ornin's stomach and then walking to the head of the bed where he held the flesh tight until the blood scabbed up enough to hold. All the while Ornin, in pain and fear, trying to rip free of the knots at his wrists and ankles.

Then RayJohn would pick up his straight razor and go back to his grisly revenge. The report said that Ornin died from a heart attack and not his wounds. Just another way of saying that he was scared to death.

"So what do you want from me?" I asked.

"Save us, man!" Mr. Mink begged. "Save my life. You know I got fam'ly t'look after."

"We know that you do . . ." Bigelow moved his hands around as if he were trying to pick words out of the air. "Things. Things to help people out when the cops cain't . . ."

"They need protection, Mr. Rawlins," Mofass wheezed. "An' they willin' t'pay off the bet now even if they didn't know 'bout it."

I shook my head and said, "I don't know. T'get me t'go up against RayJohn would cost you boys sumpin'."

"How much?" Bigelow asked. He reached for his back pocket to show me that he was serious.

"I don't know." I rubbed my chin. "Maybe a lifetime membership in the Lions."

The Watts Lions were all middle-class craftsmen and minor professionals. They could look at me, or the hundred thousand men just like me, and feel that they were better—superior.

They wore gold-plated rings with platinum-embossed onyx emblems of a roaring lion. They had the respect of churches and white businessmen. As a group they had climbed to a higher social level than any black people I'd known.

Everybody wanted something. Bigelow and Mink wanted to live a little longer. Bledsoe looked like he wanted his mother to slap his face and tell him that everything was okay. I wanted to share the knowledge of my success among the company of my peers.

"I thought you wanted money," Bigelow said.

"I don't need money that bad, man. Shit! Raymond Johns' one'a the baddest men in L.A. If you want me t'stop him, you gotta be willin' to get up off'a that membership."

"Let's do it," Mr. Mink whispered.

"Okay," Bigelow answered. I could barely hear him.

Bledsoe didn't say a word.

"An' maybe you could come across wit' five hundred dollars too," I said.

"Fi'e hunnert!" Mr. Bigelow roared.

"Listen, man, I need a li'l stake t'pay my dues."

They both agreed. They weren't happy though. I wasn't either.

My friends would have called me a fool. Three men in mortal danger, telling me what anybody could see was a lie and there I was blinded by the offer of their company.

I made a few calls and then invited my clients to come downstairs. We left Mofass hucking phlegm and wiping his tongue with a stained handkerchief. Mofass' office was on Hooper at the time. The street was empty at two o'clock on a Tuesday afternoon.

It was a glorious November day. The clouds were piled high on a mild desert wind. All the smoke and smog had blown away. The mountains were so clear that I could almost see the craggy valleys and pointy pines. I imagined that I could even hear a branch cracking . . .

"Get'own! Get'own!" I shouted.

The shots were weak echoes in the air. They sounded harmless, like a car backfiring down a country road. Mr. Mink shouted in fear and then, again, in pain. A sliver of granite, or maybe a ricochet, whizzed past my face.

"Goddammit!" Bigelow yelled and suddenly there was a .44-caliber pistol in his outstretched hand. He was behind Mofass' Pontiac, firing blindly in any direction the shots might have come from.

Mr. Mink was holding his calf. Thick blood oozed between his fingers. I tried to squeeze behind a bright yellow fire hydrant. It wasn't much, but it was all I could do.

Bledsoe didn't jump or try to hide. He just fell to his knees and let his head sag down.

Bigelow had shot all his cartridges and wasn't moving to reload. The streets were quiet except for Mr. Mink's moaning.

I got up into a crouch and sidled behind the Pontiac with Bigelow.

"You think I got 'im?" the fat man asked.

"Only if he gonna laugh to death; lookin' at you shootin' at shadows."

I hugged the side of Mofass' green car and caught a distorted glimpse of myself in the chrome. I looked like a grounded fish sucking at air. My eyes were big enough to see behind my head.

After a minute I stood up, cautiously. Bledsoe got up too. His navy blue pants were torn. His sad expression and raggedy knees made him look more like a boy than a man.

"You okay?" I asked him.

He just looked at me, the tears brimming in his sad eyes.

People were peeping out of their windows by then. A few brave souls ventured to their front doors. I hustled my future club brothers into my car and drove off before RayJohn came back to finish the job.

"What are we gonna do, Easy?" Mr. Mink cried. "That crazy man must be followin' us."

"Don't worry, Mink. I got places for all y'all." I drove on wondering how RayJohn knew to stake out Mofass' place.

I took Mr. Mink out to Primo Pena's house in the barrio. Primo's wife Flower knew how to dress a flesh wound.

I left Bigelow with Andre Lavender who had moved to Compton with his wife, Juanita, and their five-year-old boy.

I kept Bledsoe with me till last because I was worried about him and because I thought he was the one of them who might tell me the truth.

"What's wrong with you, man?" I asked Bledsoe. We were going down Avalon, to the safest place I knew.

"Nuthin'." With his knees hidden under the shadow of the dashboard and his dark blue suit and tie, Bledsoe almost looked like the notary public he was supposed to be.

"Then why didn't you hide when RayJohn shot at us?"

"Lord'll call me when I suffered enough to his will."

Bledsoe was a slight man. His dark blue suit seemed to be draped over wire. The bones of his eyebrows and cheeks protruded while the rest of his face drew back; black parchment stretched on a skull. He tried to smile at me but that failed.

"You wanna tell me why RayJohn is after you boys, Bled?"

"I'd like to thank you, Mr. Easy Rawlins, for he'pin' us brothers," he answered, then he nodded to himself. "Yes, I'd like to thank you, Mr. Easy Rawlins."

"Are you okay, Bled?"

He nodded in answer.

It was five-thirty by the time we made it to John Mckenzie's bar.

The side entrance to Targets was in an alley off of Cyprus. I led Bledsoe by the arm into the crowded bar. When I pushed open the swinging door that led to the private part of John's place the stony-eyed bartender looked up, but when he saw me he just waved.

Bledsoe and I went up to the second floor where we came to a small room that was adorned with an army cot, a straight-backed wooden chair and a sink.

"You stay here," I told the sad-eyed man. "John will bring you anything you need. Just ask'im when he comes up." I pointed in his face. "Now I don't want you to go nowhere, an' don't call nobody neither. Just sit in this room. Do you understand me?"

He sat down on the bed and nodded. It felt like I was talking to a dog.

Targets was a small bar but it was popular among my crowd: immigrants from southern Texas and Louisiana. The room, built to hold ninety, was populated by at least two hundred and fifty souls. People were drinking and shouting, blowing smoke and swaying to the tinny phonograph sounds of Billie Holiday. A woman yelled as I pushed open the swinging door. John was in the center of the room forcing Cedric Waters back by the lapels of his jacket.

"I'm'a kill the mothahfuckah, John! Ain't nobody gonna stop me!"

"You ain't gonna kill'im here, Cedric," John said firmly.

I noticed Jackson Blue leaning at the far end of the bar. Even though Jackson was a small man he stood out because he was blacker than waxed coal.

"Yes, I will!" Cedric shouted and at the same time he threw a wild punch at John's jaw. Unluckily for Cedric that blow landed true. John cocked his head with almost the look of surprise on his stone face. Then he hit Cedric with a short left jab.

Cedric collapsed as if some great magician had suddenly snatched the bones from his body.

"Get this man outta here!" John shouted. Cedric's friends dragged the comatose man away. John strode through the crowd back toward his place behind the bar.

I stopped him before he got back to work. I put my arm around his shoulder, restraining him in a friendly fashion, and spoke into his ear, "I need a li'l help fo'a couple'a days, John. I put Nathaniel Bledsoe in yo' extra room upstairs."

"What you want me to do with'im?"

"Give'im some food if he need it. An' if he leaves tell me 'bout it. I think Raymond Johns wanna kill'im."

John nodded and made back toward his bar. The prospect of RayJohn didn't scare him. He faced death nearly every day in his trade.

After John was situated behind the bar I went over to Jackson Blue. I pointed at Jackson's empty glass and John filled it with sour mash.

"Obliged to ya, Easy," Jackson said after he'd downed the shot.

I pointed again and John poured.

"You know anything 'bout Raymond Johns?" I asked.

"You don't wanna mess wit' that boy, Easy. RayJohn on the war-path."

"Over what?"

"Easy, you just bought me a drink. Why I wanna send you into pain?"

When John saw that we were talking he went away.

"I take care'a myself, Jackson. Just tell me what you know."

"Alright," the little man shrugged. "They sayin' RayJohn kilt Ornin Levesque. They say Ray ain't gonna rest till he get a couple'a more'a them Watts Lions."

"Anybody know why he killed Ornin?"

"One story is that he didn't pay on a bet."

"That true?"

"I don't hardly think so."

"No?"

"Uh-uh," Jackson shook his head. "The word is that RayJohn found out that them boys took advantage of his daughter, Reba. Raped her pretty good, I hear."

"That the truth, Jackson?"

"Well I don't rightly know, but I do know that it would take sumpin' like that t'get RayJohn that mad."

"You know where I can find Raymond?"

Jackson stuck out his bottom lip and shook his head. "Don't know, Easy. He's hidin'. But he's pretty well known down in the hobo jungle. When he ain't got no place t' stay, they say he gets a box down there."

"Where's Reba then?"

"She wit' Selma. They got a place down on Crenshaw." Jackson laughed. "You know Ray ain't lived wit' them in ten years, since Reba was five. I guess it takes a tragedy to bring a fam'ly back together."

The hobo jungle was a big empty lot behind Metropolitan High School, downtown. It was about four square blocks in area and undeveloped so the earth was soft enough for a man's back. The unfortunates who stayed there would go to the nearby Sears-Roebuck and find a cardboard box from a refrigerator or other large appliance and use that for their home.

I stood at the edge of the jungle at about midnight. Here and there faint lights outlined the cardboard structures but, by and large, the lot was dark.

"Hello, mister," someone said. It was a little man with a blanket wrapped around his shoulders. When he looked up, his face was revealed in the faint light. He was a brown man. Not a Negro but a white man who had spent so much time outside that he had weathered. He was hunched over and barefoot. His left eye winked at odd intervals and a coarse dank odor hung around him.

"Got a quarter for an old soldier?" he asked and winked.

"Maybe," I said. That got him to smile. "I might even have a dollar."

That got him grinning, winking, and smelling like a pig in shit.

"I'm lookin' fo' somebody," I said.

"No girls down here, mister. An' if there was you wouldn't want 'em."

"Lookin' for a man. A Negro, half-breed. Raymond Johns is his name."

The derelict grinned. He had a full set of teeth. They were as brown as his skin.

"RayJohn's a regular down here," he said. "He stays over on the colored side mostly. I could show you."

He held his hand out courteously and I went before him.

We made our way between the tents and flat beds of cardboard. Here and there a hand or foot stuck out. The smell of urine was everywhere. I could hear men scratching and moaning, snoring and talking. One man must have had a woman in his box, either that or he was dreaming pretty good about one.

The brown man kept talking about RayJohn and what a nice guy he was and how much he could use that dollar.

"Yeah, I sure could, sure could use a little Tokay right now," he said. "Eighty-nine cents buys you a whole quart. Bet you RayJohn would like that. Yeah, I sure . . ."

It was because he stopped talking that I turned around. I saw a man to my left throw something that looked like a brass globe. Somebody shouted, "Get 'im!" I ducked under the missile and heard the groan of a man on the other side of me. Two hands grabbed my ankles. I swung my fist downward but I don't know if I hit him because a board split itself on my back right then. There were at least five men on me. I kept swinging but they were at close quarters with me so the blows I threw were pretty much useless. Then there came a bright pain in the middle of my forehead and, for a moment, darkness.

"I got it," the brown man shouted. Suddenly I could see him running toward the outskirts of the jungle. I moved to run after him but tripped over the box that the sounds of love came from. The box ripped open and an angry, naked white man swarmed out at me. I grabbed half the plank I'd been hit with and brandished it. That slowed his pace.

I said, "Hey, man, listen, I'm sorry."

The torn crate revealed a slim brown girl. The white man hesitated and then crawled back into the box with her, pulling the tatters of cardboard over them.

The thieves were gone. So was my wallet. Sixteen dollars, a social security card, and my driver's license. I wasn't mad at being robbed. I was mad because I was a fool to be out there in the first place. I was a fool to protect rapists, to look for RayJohn. I was a fool to want to be a Watts Lion. Shit! I was a fool to be a black man in a white man's world.

Fool though I was I still rummaged around looking for the killer. I carried two half-pound stones, one in either hand, in case I was attacked again. But I went unmolested. I found the colored side of the jungle but RayJohn hadn't been there in weeks.

The next morning I checked on Bledsoe. He was in the same position he'd been in the night before; sitting on the cot and nodding. John told me he hadn't eaten but I didn't care if a rapist wanted to starve.

I drove out to Primo's next.

By then Primo and Flower had their dreamhouse. It was a two-story wood-frame house with a fake Victorian facade. Everywhere there were flowers. Roses, begonias, dahlias, asters, sweet pea vines on a trellis. Row after row of flowering bushes and trees.

I knew when I saw the police car parked across the street that Mr. Mink was dead. The policemen and a few civilians were in the Jewish graveyard that sat across from Primo's house. It was an old graveyard reflecting how the neighborhood had changed.

I walked in like the other curiosity seekers. Primo and I saw each other but we didn't talk. The short, stout Mexican looked at me apologetically.

Behind a great stone at the top of a hill they'd found Mr. Mink. His throat was slashed so terribly that the ligaments in his neck were severed. His head lay back from the open neck like the hinged lid of a trash can.

His clothes were torn and there were bruises on his face from the beating he got before he was killed. Flower's bandage was still wrapped around his calf.

The man climbing into the side window of the Lavender house wasn't tall but his short sleeves revealed the arms of a titan. I saw him reach to lift the window silently as I opened the car door. He raised his foot into the window as I raced as quietly as I could across Andre's lawn. It was just when RayJohn turned, his legs already in the house, that he saw me.

I grabbed his shirt and skin and yanked him from the house. He fell to the ground like a cat, rolling into his crouch. Then I hit RayJohn with a solid right hand.

I could have just as well socked a tree.

I saw RayJohn's fist coming but I didn't feel it. I was just opening my eyes, flat on my back, when I saw three things. The first was Ray standing over me still crouching, but this time he had the second thing I saw in his hand. That was a vicious-looking hunter's knife. Just when I knew that that knife would be my end I saw a big, fat, jiggly belly come running down the path to the side of the house. Then a yell full of fear and the belly collided with my death stroke.

RayJohn rolled away and kept on running. I watched him go down the street but I didn't go after him. We'd had our duel and I was a dead man. I even waved him good-bye.

"I'm cut!" Andre yelled. He stood there above me, nude to the waist and bleeding pretty well from his left forearm. Skinny little Juanita and porky Andre Jr. came to him and wrapped his wound in their own shirts. I wanted to get up and help but the strength had gone out of me.

When I knocked there was no answer so I began to work the lock with my pocket knife.

"Who's that?" a woman shouted when I almost had the door open.

"It's me, Selma, Easy Rawlins."

"Why you breakin' in my house, Easy?"

It wasn't really a house. It was a renovated storeroom above the rear of a pawnshop on Crenshaw Boulevard, but I said, "I'm tryin' t'keep some men from gettin' killed by that crazy old man'a yours."

The door opened a crack. Selma put her face there and I pushed my way in. She didn't fight it, just backed away hanging her head. Selma was a big woman. Rose-brown in color, she had Ethiopian features.

Reba was spread out on the couch. Her face bore the same marks as Mr. Mink. Bruises and cuts. Her hands were wrapped in blood-soaked gauze. Both eyes were swollen to slimy slits.

"Huh huh huh," she cried, a blind salamander dropped into the sun's harsh light.

"Shush now," Selma said, going to the girl, stroking her hair. "It's just Easy Rawlins. It's okay."

"They do this?" I asked.

"What you want, Easy?" Selma asked. I noticed that she had a mouse under her own eye.

"What happened to her?"

"Why? You wanna do sumpin' 'bout it? You wanna save her?"

"What happened?"

Reba moaned. She had her father's buff skin color and she was slight. I wondered that the violence perpetrated on that slim body didn't kill her.

"Shut up!" Selma said. She was talking to Reba. "Women get beat! Women get fucked! An' cryin' just make it worse!"

She kept stroking the girl tenderly as she ranted.

"You kept t'home wouldn't none'a this happened in the first place!" she cried. "But ain't no use in cryin' now!"

I noticed that the furniture in the house was overturned and that shards of broken plates littered the floor. On the far wall to my left someone had flung a plate of spaghetti. The red stain was scrawled over by drying pasta worms.

"Just shut up!" Selma told her daughter.

"Those men at the Lions do this?" I asked again.

"They did worse than that," a voice said.

I can't say that I was scared at that moment. I only feel fear when there is some chance that I might survive.

"I didn't know, RayJohn," I said to the man behind me.

"Daddy, no!" Reba cried.

"Get yo' ass outta here!" Selma stood in front of her daughter. She pushed her shoulders forward and put her hands behind her, wrapped in the folds of her housecoat.

"Calm down now, baby. I'm just here fo' Easy. He's gonna take me into Targets so I can have a talk with Nathaniel Bledsoe."

"No, Daddy. Please . . ." Reba got up from the couch holding her hands in front of her.

Selma went right up to RayJohn and started shouting.

"Get the fuck outta my house, niggah! Get out! Ain't you hurt her enough!"

It came clear to me that RayJohn had somehow found out about what happened to his daughter and he'd beaten her for being raped.

"Get outta my way, Selma." RayJohn sounded calm, but it was the kind of calm that preceded violence.

She bulled against him with her chest and shouted curses in his face.

I was hoping that she'd back off because I felt pretty sure that I could get the help I needed to stop the maniac at Targets. But I had no desire to take him on trying to save Selma's life.

"I say get yo' ass outta here!" Selma yelled.

"I'm'a have t'hurt you, girl. Stand back now."

"Hurt me! Okay! Yeah, hurt me! Put yo' coward's fist there!" Selma pointed at her own jaw. RayJohn obliged with a solid slap that would have killed a smaller woman, or man. But Selma simply listed to the side. She drove her hand deep into the pocket of her housecoat. Reba cried, "Momma!" The flash of the steak knife disappeared instantly, deeply into RayJohn's chest. The surprise on his face would have been comical in the movies. Maybe if he weren't surprised, if he had believed that a woman could fight to save her own, he might have survived. But while RayJohn was gaping that blade flashed four times, five, six. When he fell to the floor he was already dead. I didn't see any reason to pull her off.

Bledsoe sat with his back against the wall on the cot. He hugged his knees to his chest and nodded slightly.

I asked him, "Why?"

He smiled.

The police didn't take Selma to jail. When they saw Reba they figured that it was self-defense. I didn't argue with them.

"Why, man?" I asked again.

"What?" He grinned at me.

"You know, Bled. You the one called RayJohn an' told him 'bout

Reba. You the one told'im where t'find Biggs and Mink too. You the one had him waitin' outside Mofass' place. Had to be you."

"I told 'em when that girl started t'fightin' that it was wrong."

"They raped her, really?"

"She was playin' at first. It was late an' they had some drinks. But when Ornin started to pull at her dress she got scared. Then Bigelow exposed hisself . . . That ain't right." Bledsoe stared off into space again.

I don't know if they would have ever let me join the Watts Lions. I never asked. I went to the funerals though. Ornin Levesque and Gregory Mink were buried at the same service.

Raymond Johns was interred the next day. There were only four people there. Selma was dressed in a nice blue two-piece suit. Reba's eyes had opened like a newborn kitten's. I stayed in the back and watched Nathaniel Bledsoe with his arms around both ladies. I remember wondering which one he would marry.

Grace Notes

Author: Sara Paretsky (1947–   )

Detective: V.I. Warshawski (1982)

The two most famous female private eyes both appeared on the scene in 1982, Sue Grafton's Southern California sleuth Kinsey Millhone in *"A" is for Alibi* and Sara Paretsky's Chicago cop V.I. Warshawski in *Indemnity Only*. Similar as they are in quality, volume of output, and commercial success, the two writers and their characters are often bracketed together. But the differences between the two sleuths are as marked as the similarities. One contrast is the more overtly political spin of the Warshawski series. Paretsky is an outspoken liberal, and by her own account, the villains in the series are usually white-collar criminals who prey on or exploit the poor and less fortunate.

"Grace Notes," written for the 1995 collection of Warshawski stories, *Windy City Blues,* is the longest and possibly the best shorter case in the series. It illustrates one of the major differences between male and female private-eye fiction: while we know little or nothing about the family background of sleuths like Sam Spade, Philip Marlowe, and Lew Archer, for Sharon McCone, V.I. Warshawski, and many of the female sleuths-for-hire, family is a central part of their lives.

I

> **GABRIELLA SESTIERI OF PITIGLIANO.**
> Anyone with knowledge of her whereabouts
> should contact the office of Malcolm Ranier.

I was reading the *Herald-Star* at breakfast when the notice jumped out at me from the personal section. I put my coffee down with extreme care, as if I were in a dream and all my actions moved with the slowness of dream time. I shut the paper with the same slow motion, then opened it again. The notice was still there. I spelled out the headline letter by letter, in case my unconscious mind had substituted one name for another, but the text remained the same. There could not be more than one Gabriella Sestieri from Pitigliano. My mother, who died of cancer in 1968 at the age of forty-six.

"Who could want her all these years later?" I said aloud.

Peppy, the golden retriever I share with my downstairs neighbor, raised a sympathetic eyebrow. We had just come back from a run on a dreary November morning and she was waiting hopefully for toast.

"It can't be her father." His mind had cracked after six months in a German concentration camp, and he refused to acknowledge Gabriella's death when my father wrote to inform him of it. I'd had to translate the letter, in which he said he was too old to travel but wished Gabriella well on her concert tour. Anyway, if he were alive still he'd be almost a hundred.

Maybe Gabriella's brother Italo was searching for her: he had disappeared in the maelstrom of the war, but Gabriella always hoped he survived. Or her first voice teacher, Francesca Salvini, whom Gabriella longed to see again, to explain why she had never fulfilled Salvini's hopes for her professional career. As Gabriella lay in her final bed in Jackson Park Hospital with tubes ringing her wasted body, her last messages had been for me and for Salvini. This morning it dawned on me for the first time how hurtful my father must have found that. He adored my mother, but for him she had only the quiet fondness of an old friend.

I realized my hands around the newspaper were wet with sweat, that paper and print were clinging to my palms. With an embarrassed laugh I put the paper down and washed off the ink under the kitchen tap. It was ludicrous to spin my mind with conjectures when all I had to do was phone Malcolm Ranier. I went to the living room and pawed through the papers on the piano for the phone book. Ranier seemed to be a lawyer with offices on La Salle Street, at the north end where the pricey new buildings stand.

His was apparently a solo practice. The woman who answered the phone assured me she was Mr. Ranier's assistant and conversant with all his files. Mr. Ranier couldn't speak with me himself now because he was in conference. Or court. Or the john.

"I'm calling about the notice in this morning's paper, wanting to know the whereabouts of Gabriella Sestieri."

"What is your name, please, and your relationship with Mrs. Sestieri?" The assistant left out the second syllable so that the name came out as "Sistery."

"I'll be glad to tell you that if you tell me why you're trying to find her."

"I'm afraid I can't give out confidential client business over the phone. But if you tell me your name and what you know about Mrs. Sestieri we'll get back to you when we've discussed the matter with our client."

I thought we could keep this conversation going all day. "The person you're looking for may not be the same one I know, and I don't want to violate a family's privacy. But I'll be in a meeting on La Salle Street this morning; I can stop by to discuss the matter with Mr. Ranicr."

The woman finally decided that Mr. Ranier had ten minutes free at twelve-thirty. I gave her my name and hung up. Sitting at the piano, I crashed out chords, as if the sound could bury the wildness of my feelings. I never could remember whether I knew how ill my mother was the last six months of her life. Had she told me and I couldn't—or didn't wish to—comprehend it? Or had she decided to shelter me from the knowledge? Gabriella usually made me face bad news, but perhaps not the worst of all possible news, our final separation.

Why did I never work on my singing? It was one thing I could have done for her. I didn't have a Voice, as Gabriella put it, but I had a serviceable contralto, and of course she insisted I acquire some musicianship. I stood up and began working on a few vocal stretches, then suddenly became wild with the desire to find my mother's music, the old exercise books she had me learn from.

I burrowed through the hall closet for the trunk that held her books. I finally found it in the farthest corner, under a carton holding my old case files, a baseball bat, a box of clothes I no longer wore but couldn't bring myself to give away. . . . I sat on the closet floor in misery, with a sense of having buried her so deep I couldn't find her.

Peppy's whimpering pulled me back to the present. She had followed me into the closet and was pushing her nose into my arm. I fondled her ears.

At length it occurred to me that if someone were trying to find my mother I'd need documents to prove the relationship. I got up from the floor and pulled the trunk into the hall. On top lay her black silk concert gown: I'd forgotten wrapping that in tissue and storing it. In the end I found my parents' marriage license and Gabriella's death certificate tucked into the score of *Don Giovanni*.

When I returned the score to the trunk another old envelope floated out. I picked it up and recognized Mr. Fortieri's spiky writing. Carlo Fortieri repaired musical instruments and sold, or at least used to sell music. He was the person Gabriella went to for Italian conversation, musical conversation, advice. He still sometimes tuned my piano out of affection for her.

When Gabriella met him, he'd been a widower for years, also with one child, also a girl. Gabriella thought I ought to play with her while she sang or discussed music with Mr. Fortieri, but Barbara was ten years or so my senior and we'd never had much to say to each other.

I pulled out the yellowed paper. It was written in Italian, and hard for me to decipher, but apparently dated from 1965.

Addressing her as *"Cara signora Warshawski,"* Mr. Fortieri sent his regrets that she was forced to cancel her May 14 concert. "I shall, of course, respect your wishes and not reveal the nature of your indisposition to anyone else. And, *cara signora,* you should know by now that I regard any confidence of yours as a sacred trust: you need not fear an indiscretion." It was signed with his full name.

I wondered now if he'd been my mother's lover. My stomach tightened, as it does when you think of your parents stepping outside their prescribed roles, and I folded the paper back into the envelope. Fifteen years ago the same notion must have prompted me to put his letter inside *Don Giovanni.* For want of a better idea I stuck it back in the score and returned everything to the trunk. I needed to rummage through a different carton to find my own birth certificate, and it was getting too late in the morning for me to indulge in nostalgia.

II

Malcolm Ranier's office overlooked the Chicago River and all the new glass and marble flanking it. It was a spectacular view—if you squinted to shut out the burnt-out waste of Chicago's west side that lay beyond. I arrived just at twelve-thirty, dressed in my one good suit, black, with a white crepe-de-chine blouse. I looked feminine, but austere—or at least that was my intention.

Ranier's assistant-cum-receptionist was buried in Danielle Steel. When I handed her my card, she marked her page without haste and took the card into an inner office. After a ten-minute wait to let me understand his importance, Ranier came out to greet me in person. He was a soft round man of about sixty, with gray eyes that lay like pebbles above an apparently jovial smile.

"Ms. Warshawski. Good of you to stop by. I understand you can help us with our inquiry into Mrs. Sestieri." He gave my mother's name a genuine Italian lilt, but his voice was as hard as his eyes.

"Hold my calls, Cindy." He put a hand on the nape of my neck to steer me into his office.

Before we'd shut the door Cindy was reabsorbed into Danielle. I moved away from the hand—I didn't want grease on my five-hundred-dollar jacket—and went to admire a bronze nymph on a shelf at the window.

"Beautiful, isn't it." Ranier might have been commenting on the weather. "One of my clients brought it from France."

"It looks as though it should be in a museum."

A call to the bar association before I left my apartment told me he was an import-export lawyer. Various imports seemed to have attached themselves to him on their way into the country. The room was dominated by a slab of rose marble, presumably a worktable, but several antique chairs were also worth a second glance. A marquetry credenza stood against the far wall. The Modigliani above it was probably an original.

"Coffee, Ms."—he glanced at my card again—"Warshawski?"

"No, thank you. I understand you're very busy, and so am I. So let's talk about Gabriella Sestieri."

"*D'accordo.*" He motioned me to one of the spindly antiques near the marble slab. "You know where she is?"

The chair didn't look as though it could support my hundred and forty pounds, but when Ranier perched on a similar one I sat, with a wariness that made me think he had them to keep people deliberately off balance. I leaned back and crossed my legs. The woman at ease.

"I'd like to make sure we're talking about the same person. And that I know why you want to find her."

A smile crossed his full lips, again not touching the slate chips of his eyes. "We could fence all day, Ms. Warshawski, but as you say, time is valuable to us both. The Gabriella Sestieri I seek was born in Pitigliano on October 30, 1921. She left Italy sometime early in 1941, no one knows exactly when, but she was last heard of in Siena that February. And there's some belief she came to Chicago. As to why I want to find her, a relative of hers, now in Florence, but from the Pitigliano family, is interested in locating her. My specialty is import-export law, particularly with Italy: I'm no expert in finding missing persons, but I agreed to assist as a favor to a client. The relative—Mrs. Sestieri's relative—has a professional connection to my client. And now it is your turn, Ms. War-shawski."

"Ms. Sestieri died in March 1968." My blood was racing; I was pleased to hear my voice come out without a tremor. "She married a Chicago police officer in April 1942. They had one child. Me."

"And your father? Officer Warshawski?"

"Died in 1979. Now may I have the name of my mother's relative? I've known only one member of her family, my grandmother's sister who lives here in Chicago, and am eager to find others." Actually, if they bore any resemblance to my embittered Aunt Rosa I'd just as soon not meet the remaining Verazi clan.

"You were cautious, Ms. Warshawski, so you will forgive my caution: do you have proof of your identity?"

"You make it sound as though treasure awaits the missing heir, Mr. Ranier." I pulled out the copies of my legal documents and handed them over. "Who or what is looking for my mother?"

Ranier ignored my question. He studied the documents briefly, then put them on the marble slab while condoling me on losing my parents. His voice had the same soft, flat cadence as when he'd discussed the nymph.

"You've no doubt remained close to your grandmother's sister? If she's the person who brought your mother to Chicago it might be help-ful for me to have her name and address."

"My aunt is a difficult woman to be close to, but I can check with her, to see if she doesn't mind my giving you her name and address."

"And the rest of your mother's family?"

I held out my hands, empty. "I don't know any of them. I don't even know how many there are. Who is my mystery relative? What does he—she—want?"

He paused, looking at the file in his hands. "I actually don't know. I ran the ad merely as a favor to my client. But I'll pass your name and address along, Ms. Warshawski, and when he's been in touch with the person I'm sure you'll hear."

This runaround was starting to irritate me. "You're a heck of a poker player, Mr. Ranier. But you know as well as I that you're lying like a rug."

I spoke lightly, smiling as I got to my feet and crossed to the door, snatching my documents from the marble slab as I passed. For once his feelings reached his eyes, turning the slate to molten rock. As I waited for the elevator I wondered if answering that ad meant I was going to be sucker-punched.

* * *

Over dinner that night with Dr. Lotty Herschel I went through my conversation with Ranier, trying to sort out my confused feelings. Trying, too, to figure out who in Gabriella's family might want to find her, if the inquiry was genuine.

"They surely know she's dead," Lotty said.

"That's what I thought at first, but it's not that simple. See, my grandmother converted to Judaism when she married Nonno Mattia—sorry, that's Gabriella's father—Grandpa Matthias—Gabriella usually spoke Italian to me. Anyway, my grandmother died in Auschwitz when the Italian Jews were rounded up in 1944. Then, my grandfather didn't go back to Pitigliano, the little town they were from, after he was liberated—the Jewish community there had been decimated and he didn't have any family left. So he was sent to a Jewish-run sanatorium in Turin, but Gabriella only found that out after years of writing letters to relief agencies."

I stared into my wineglass, as though the claret could reveal the secrets of my family. "There was one cousin she was really close to, from the Christian side of her family, named Frederica. Frederica had a baby out of wedlock the year before Gabriella came to Chicago, and got sent away in disgrace. After the war Gabriella kept trying to find her, but Frederica's family wouldn't forward the letters—they really didn't want to be in touch with her. Gabriella might have saved enough money to go back to Italy to look for herself, but then she started to be ill. She had a miscarriage the summer of sixty-five and bled and bled. Tony and I thought she was dying then."

My voice trailed away as I thought of that hot, unhappy summer, the summer the city burst into riot-spawned flames and my mother lay in the stifling front bedroom oozing blood. She and Tony had one of their infrequent fights. I'd been on my paper route and they didn't hear me come in. He wanted her to sell something, which she said wasn't hers to dispose of.

"And your life," my father shouted. "You can give that away as a gift? Even if she were still alive—" He broke off then, seeing me, and neither of them talked about the matter again, at least when I was around to hear.

Lotty squeezed my hand. "What about your aunt, great-aunt in Melrose Park? She might have told her siblings, don't you think? Was she close to any of them?"

I grimaced. "I can't imagine Rosa being close to anyone. See, she was the last child, and Gabriella's grandmother died giving birth to her. So some cousins adopted her, and when they emigrated in the twenties Rosa came to Chicago with them. She didn't really feel like she was part of the Verazi family. I know it seems strange, but with all the uprootings the war caused, and all the disconnections, it's possible that the main part of Gabriella's mother's family didn't know what became of her."

Lotty nodded, her face twisted in sympathy; much of her family had been destroyed in those death camps also. "There wasn't a schism when your grandmother converted?"

I shrugged. "I don't know. It's frustrating to think how little I know about those people. Gabriella says—said—the Verazis weren't crazy about it, and they didn't get together much except for weddings or funerals—except for the one cousin. But Pitigliano was a Jewish cultural center before the war and Nonno was considered a real catch. I guess he was rich until the Fascists confiscated his property." Fantasies of reparations danced through my head.

"Not too likely," Lotty said. "You're imagining someone overcome with guilt sixty years after the fact coming to make you a present of some land?"

I blushed. "Factory, actually: the Sestieris were harness makers who switched to automobile interiors in the twenties. I suppose if the place is even still standing, it's part of Fiat or Mercedes. You know, all day long I've been swinging between wild fantasies—about Nonno's factory, or Gabriella's brother surfacing—and then I start getting terrified, wondering if it's all some kind of terrible trap. Although who'd want to trap me, or why, is beyond me. I know this Malcolm Ranier knows. It would be so easy—"

"No! Not to set your mind at rest, not to prove you can bypass the security of a modern high rise—for no reason whatsoever are you to break into that man's office."

"Oh, very well." I tried not to sound like a sulky child denied a treat.

"You promise, Victoria?" Lotty sounded ferocious.

I held up my right hand. "On my honor, I promise not to break into his office."

III

It was six days later that the phone call came to my office. A young man, with an Italian accent so thick that his English was almost incomprehensible, called up and gaily asked if I was his "Cousin Vittoria."

"*Parliamo italiano,*" I suggested, and the gaiety in his voice increased as he switched thankfully to his own language.

He was my cousin Ludovico, the great-great-grandson of our mutual Verazi ancestors, he had arrived in Chicago from Milan only last night, terribly excited at finding someone from his mother's family, thrilled that I knew Italian, my accent was quite good, really, only a tinge of America in it, could we get together, any place, he would find me—just name the time as long as it was soon.

I couldn't help laughing as the words tumbled out, although I had to ask him to slow down and repeat. It had been a long time since I'd spoken Italian, and it took time for my mind to adjust. Ludovico was staying at the Garibaldi, a small hotel on the fringe of the Gold Coast, and would be thrilled if I met him there for a drink at six. Oh yes, his last name—that was Verazi, the same as our great-grandfather.

I bustled through my business with greater efficiency than usual so that I had time to run the dogs and change before meeting him. I laughed at myself for dressing with care, in a pantsuit of crushed laven-der velvet, which could take me dancing if the evening ended that way, but no self-mockery could suppress my excitement. I'd been an only child with one cousin from each of my parents' families as my only relations. My cousin Boom-Boom, whom I adored, had been dead these ten years and more, while Rosa's son Albert was such a mass of twisted fears that I preferred not to be around him. Now I was meeting a whole new family.

I tap-danced around the dog in my excitement. Peppy gave me a long-suffering look and demanded that I return her to my downstairs neigh-bor: Mitch, her son, had stopped there on our way home from running.

"You look slick, doll," Mr. Contreras told me, torn between approval and jealousy. "New date?"

"New cousin." I continued to tap-dance in the hall outside his door. "Yep. The mystery relative finally surfaced. Ludovico Verazi."

"You be careful, doll," the old man said severely. "Plenty of con artists out there to pretend they're your cousins, you know, and next thing—*phht.*"

"What'll he con me out of? My dirty laundry?" I planted a kiss on his nose and danced down the sidewalk to my car.

Three men were waiting in the Garibaldi's small lobby, but I knew my cousin at once. His hair was amber, instead of black, but his face was my mother's, from the high rounded forehead to his wide sensuous mouth. He leaped up at my approach, seized my hands, and kissed me in the European style—sort of touching the air beside each ear.

"*Bellissima!*" Still holding my hands he stepped back to scrutinize me. My astonishment must have been written large on my face, because he laughed a little guiltily.

"I know it, I know it, I should have told you of the resemblance, but I didn't realize it was *so* strong: the only picture I've seen of Cousin Gabriella is a stage photo from 1940 when she starred in Jommelli's *Iphigenia.*"

"Jommelli!" I interrupted. "I thought it was Gluck!"

"No, no, *cugina,* Jommelli. Surely Gabriella knew what she sang?" Laughing happily he moved to the armchair where he'd been sitting and took up a brown leather case. He pulled out a handful of papers and thumbed through them, then extracted a yellowing photograph for me to examine.

It was my mother, dressed as Iphigenia for her one stage role, the one that gave me my middle name. She was made up, her dark hair in an elaborate coil, but she looked absurdly young, like a little girl playing dress-up. At the bottom of the picture was the name of the studio, in Siena where she had sung, and on the back someone had lettered, "*Gabriella Sestieri fa la parte d'Iphigenia nella produzione d'Iphigenia da Jommelli.*" The resemblance to Ludovico was clear, despite the blurring of time and cosmetics to the lines of her face. I felt a stab of jealousy: I inherited her olive skin, but my face is my father's.

"You know this photograph?" Ludovico asked.

I shook my head. "She left Italy in such a hurry: all she brought with her were some Venetian wineglasses that had been a wedding present to Nonna Laura. I never saw her onstage."

"I've made you sad, cousin Vittoria, by no means my intention. Perhaps you would like to keep this photograph?"

"I would, very much. Now—a drink? Or dinner?"

He laughed again. "I have been in America only twenty-four hours, not long enough to be accustomed to dinner in the middle of the afternoon. So—a drink, by all means. Take me to a typical American bar."

I collected my Trans Am from the doorman and drove down to the Golden Glow, the bar at the south end of the Loop owned by my friend Sal Barthele. My appearance with a good-looking stranger caused a stir among the regulars—as I'd hoped. Murray Ryerson, an investigative reporter whose relationship with me is compounded of friendship, competition, and a disastrous romantic episode, put down his beer with a snap and came over to our table. Sal Barthele emerged from her famous mahogany horseshoe bar. Under cover of Murray's greetings and

Ludovico's accented English she muttered, "Girl, you are strutting. You look indecent! Anyway, isn't this cradle snatching? Boy looks *young!*"

I was glad the glow from the Tiffany table lamps was too dim for her to see me blushing. In the car coming over I had been calculating degrees of consanguinity and decided that as second cousins we were eugenically safe; I was embarrassed to show it so obviously. Anyway, he was only seven years younger than me.

"My newfound cousin," I said, too abruptly. "Ludovico Verazi—Sal Barthele, owner of the Glow."

Ludovico shook her hand. "So, you are an old friend of this cousin of mine. You know her more than I do—give me ideas about her character."

"Dangerous," Murray said. "She breaks men in her soup like crackers."

"Only if they're crackers to begin with," I snapped, annoyed to be presented to my cousin in such a light.

"Crackers to begin with?" Ludovico asked.

"Slang—*gergo*—for '*pazzo,*' " I explained. "Also a cracker is an oaf— a *cretino.*"

Murray put an arm around me. "Ah, Vic—the sparkle in your eyes lights a fire in my heart."

"It's just the third beer, Murray—that's heartburn," Sal put in. "Ludovico, what do you drink—whiskey, like your cousin? Or something nice and Italian like Campari?"

"Whiskey before dinner, Cousin Vittoria? No, no, by the time you eat you have no—no tasting sensation. For me, Signora, a glass of wine please."

Later over dinner at Filigree we became "Vic" and "Vico"—"Please, Veek, no one is calling me 'Ludovico' since the time I am a little boy in trouble—" And later still, after two bottles of Barolo, he asked me how much I knew about the Verazi family.

"*Niente,*" I said. "I don't even know how many brothers and sisters Gabriella's mother had. Or where you come into the picture. Or where I do, for that matter."

His eyebrows shot up in surprise. "So your mother was never in touch with her own family after she moved here?"

I told him what I'd told Lotty, about the war, my grandmother's estrangement from her family, and Gabriella's depression on learning of her cousin Frederica's death.

"But I am the grandson of that naughty Frederica, that girl who would have a baby with no father." Vico shouted in such excitement that the wait staff rushed over to make sure he wasn't choking to death. "This is remarkable, Vic, this is amazing, that the one person in our family *your* mother is close to turns out to be *my* grandmother.

"Ah, it was sad, very sad, what happened to her. The family is moved to Florence during the war, my grandmother has a baby, maybe the father is a partisan, my grandmother was the one person in the family to be supporting the partisans. My great-grandparents, they are very prudish, they say, this is a disgrace, never mind there is a war on and much bigger disgraces are happening all the time, so—poof!—off goes this naughty Frederica with her baby to Milano. And the baby becomes my mother, but she and my grandmother both die when I am ten, so these most respectable Verazi cousins, finally they decide the war is over, the grandson is after all far enough removed from the taint of original sin, they come fetch me and raise me with all due respectability in Florence."

He broke off to order a cognac. I took another espresso: somehow after forty I no longer can manage the amount of alcohol I used to. I'd only drunk half of one of the bottles of wine.

"So how did you learn about Gabriella? And why did you want to try to find her?"

"Well, *cara cugina,* it is wonderful to meet you, but I have a confession I must make: it was in the hopes of finding—something—that I am coming to Chicago looking for my cousin Gabriella."

"What kind of something?"

"You say you know nothing about our great-grandmother, Claudia Fortezza? So you are not knowing even that she is in a small way a composer?"

I couldn't believe Gabriella never mentioned such a thing. If she didn't know about it, the rift with the Verazis must have been more severe than she led me to believe. "But maybe that explains why she was given early musical training," I added aloud. "You know my mother was quite a gifted singer. Although, alas, she never had the professional career she should have."

"Yes, yes, she trained with Francesca Salvini. I know all about that! Salvini was an important teacher, even in a little town like Pitigliano people came from Siena and Florence to train with her, and she had a connection to the Siena Opera. But anyway, Vic, I am wanting to collect Claudia Fortezza's music. The work of women composers is coming into vogue. I can find an ensemble to perform it, maybe to record it, so I am hoping Gabriella, too, has some of this music."

I shook my head. "I don't think so. I kept all her music in a trunk, and I don't think there's anything from that period."

"But you don't know definitely, do you, so maybe we can look together." He was leaning across the table, his voice vibrating with urgency.

I moved backward, the strength of his feelings making me uneasy. "I suppose so."

"Then let us pay the bill and go."

"Now? But, Vico, it's almost midnight. If it's been there all this while it will still be there in the morning."

"Ah: I am being the cracker, I see." We had been speaking in Italian all evening, but for this mangled idiom Vico switched to English. *"Mi scusi, cara cugina:* I have been so engaged in my hunt, through the papers of old aunts, through attics in Pitigliano, in used bookstores in Florence, that I forget not everyone shares my enthusiasm. And then last month, I find a diary of my grandmother's, and she writes of the special love her cousin Gabriella has for music, her special gift, and I think—ah-ha, if this music lies anywhere, it is with this Gabriella."

He picked up my right hand and started playing with my fingers. "Besides, confess to me, Vic: in your mind's eye you are at your home feverishly searching through your mother's music, whether I am present or not."

I laughed, a little shakily: the intensity in his face made him look so like Gabriella when she was swept up in music that my heart turned over with yearning.

"So I am right? We can pay the bill and leave?"

The wait staff, hoping to close the restaurant, had left the bill on our table some time earlier. I tried to pay it, but Vico snatched it from me. He took a thick stack of bills from his billfold. Counting under his breath he peeled off two hundreds and a fifty and laid them on the check. Like many Europeans he'd assumed the tip was included in the total: I added four tens and went to retrieve the Trans Am.

IV

As we got out of the car I warned Vico not to talk in the stairwell. "We don't want the dogs to hear me and wake Mr. Contreras."

"He is a malevolent neighbor? You need me perhaps to guard you?"

"He's the best-natured neighbor in the world. Unfortunately, he sees his role in my life as Cerberus, with a whiff of Othello thrown in. It's late enough without spending an hour on why I'm bringing you home with me."

We managed to tiptoe up the stairs without rousing anyone. Inside my apartment we collapsed with the giggles of teenagers who've walked past a cop after curfew. Somehow it seemed natural to fall from laughter into each other's arms. I was the first to break away. Vico gave me a look I couldn't interpret—mockery seemed to dominate.

My cheeks stinging, I went to the hall closet and pulled out Gabriella's trunk once more. I lifted out her evening gown again, fingering the lace panels in the bodice. They were silver, carefully edged in black. Shortly before her final illness Gabriella managed to organize a series of concerts that she hoped would launch her career again, at least in a small way, and it was for these that she had the dress made. Tony and I sat in the front row of Mandel Hall, almost swooning with our passion for her. The gown cost her two years of free lessons for the couturier's daughter, the last few given when she had gone bald from chemotherapy.

As I stared at the dress, wrapped in melancholy, I realized Vico was pulling books and scores from the trunk and going through them with quick careful fingers. I'd saved dozens of Gabriella's books of operas and lieder, but nothing like her whole collection. I wasn't going to tell Vico that, though: he'd probably demand that we break into old Mr. Fortieri's shop to see if any of the scores were still lying about.

At one point Vico thought he had found something, a handwritten score tucked into the pages of *Idomeneo*. I came to look. Someone, not my mother, had meticulously copied out a concerto. As I bent to look more closely, Vico pulled a small magnifying glass from his wallet and began to scrutinize the paper.

I eyed him thoughtfully. "Does the music or the notation look anything like our great-grandmother's?"

He didn't answer me, but held the score up to the light to inspect the margins. I finally took the pages from him and scanned the clarinet line.

"I'm no musicologist, but this sounds baroque to me." I flipped to the end, where the initials "CF" were inscribed with a flourish: Carlo Fortieri might have copied this for my mother—a true labor of love: copying music is a slow, painful business.

"Baroque?" Vico grabbed the score back from me and looked at it more intensely. "But this paper is not that old, I think."

"I think not, also. I have a feeling it's something one of my mother's friends copied out for a chamber group they played in: She sometimes took the piano part."

He put the score to one side and continued burrowing in the trunk. Near the bottom he came on a polished wooden box, big enough to fit snugly against the short side of the trunk. He grunted as he prised it free, then gave a little crow of delight as he saw it was filled with old papers.

"Take it easy, cowboy," I said as he started tossing them to the floor. "This isn't the city dump."

He gave me a look of startling rage at my reproof, then covered it so quickly with a laugh that I couldn't be sure I'd seen it. "This old wood is beautiful. You should keep this out where you can look at it."

"It was Gabriella's, from Pitigliano." In it, carefully wrapped in her winter underwear, she'd laid the eight Venetian glasses that were her sole legacy of home. Fleeing in haste in the night, she had chosen to transport a fragile load, as if that gained her control of her own fragile destiny.

Vico ran his long fingers over the velvet lining the case. The green had turned yellow and black along the creases. I took the box away from him, and began replacing my school essays and report cards—my mother used to put my best school reports in the case.

At two Vico had to admit defeat. "You have no idea where it is? You didn't sell it, perhaps to meet some emergency bill or pay for that beautiful sports car?"

"Vico! What on earth are you talking about? Putting aside the insult, what do you think a score by an unknown nineteenth-century woman is worth?"

"Ah, *mi scusi,* Vic—I forget that everyone doesn't value these Verazi pieces as I do."

"Yes, my dear cousin, and I didn't just fall off a turnip truck, either." I switched to English in my annoyance. "Not even the most enthusiastic grandson would fly around the world with this much mystery. What's the story—are the Verazis making you their heir if you produce her music? Or are you looking for something else altogether?"

"Turnip truck? What is this turnip truck?"

"Forget the linguistic excursion and come clean, Vico. Meaning, confession is good for the soul, so speak up. What are you really looking for?"

He studied his fingers, grimy from paging through the music, then looked up at me with a quick, frank smile. "The truth is, Fortunato Magi may have seen some of her music. He was Puccini's uncle, you know, and very influential among the Italian composers of the end of the century. My great-grandmother used to talk about Magi reading Claudia Fortezza's music. She was only a daughter-in-law, and anyway, Claudia Fortezza was dead years before she married into the family, so I never paid any attention to it. But then when I found my grandmother's diaries, it seemed possible that there was some truth to it. It's even possible that Puccini used some of Claudia Fortezza's music, so if we can find it, it might be valuable."

I thought the whole idea was ludicrous—it wasn't even as though the Puccini estate were collecting royalties that one might try to sue for. And even if they were—you could believe almost any highly melodic vocal music sounded like Puccini. I didn't want to get into a fight with Vico about it, though: I had to be at work early in the morning.

"There wasn't any time you can remember Gabriella talking about something very valuable in the house?" he persisted.

I was about to shut him off completely when I suddenly remembered my parents' argument that I'd interrupted. Reluctantly, because he saw I'd thought of something, I told Vico about it.

"She was saying it wasn't hers to dispose of. I suppose that might include her grandmother's music. But there wasn't anything like that in the house when my father died. And believe me, I went through all the papers." Hoping for some kind of living memento of my mother, something more than her Venetian wineglasses.

Vico seized my arms in his excitement. "You see! She did have it, she must have sold it anyway. Or your father did, after she died. Who would they have gone to?"

I refused to give him Mr. Fortieri as a gift. If Gabriella had been worried about the ethics of disposing of someone else's belongings she probably would have consulted him. Maybe even asked him to sell it, if she came to that in the end, but Vico didn't need to know that.

"You know someone, I can tell," he cried.

"No. I was a child. She didn't confide in me. If my father sold it he would have been embarrassed to let me know. It's going on three in the morning, Vico, and I have to work in a few hours. I'm going to call you a cab and get you back to the Garibaldi."

"You work? Your long-lost cousin Vico comes to Chicago for the first time and you cannot kiss off your boss?" He blew across his fingers expressively.

"I work for myself." I could hear the brusqueness creep into my voice—his exigency was taking away some of his charm. "And I have one job that won't wait past tomorrow morning."

"What kind of work is it you do that cannot be deferred?"

"Detective. Private investigator. And I have to be on a—a—"—I couldn't think of the Italian, so I used English—"shipping dock in four hours."

"Ah, a detective." He pursed his lips. "I see now why this Murray was warning me about you. You and he are lovers? Or is that a shocking question to ask an American woman?"

"Murray's a reporter. His path crosses mine from time to time." I went to the phone and summoned a cab.

"And, Cousin, I may take this handwritten score with me? To study more leisurely?"

"If you return it."

"I will be here with it tomorrow afternoon—when you return from your detecting."

I went to the kitchen for some newspaper to wrap it in, wondering about Vico. He didn't seem to have much musical knowledge. Perhaps he was ashamed to tell me he couldn't read music and was going to take it to some third party who could give him a stylistic comparison between this score and something of our grandmother's.

The cab honked under the window a few minutes later. I sent him off on his own with a chaste cousinly kiss. He took my retreat from passion with the same mockery that had made me squirm earlier.

V

All during the next day, as I huddled behind a truck taking pictures of a handoff between the vice president of an electronics firm and a driver, as I tailed the driver south to Kankakee and photographed another handoff to a man in a sports car, traced the car to its owner in Libertyville and reported back to the electronics firm in Naperville, I wondered about Vico and the score. What was he really looking for?

Last night I hadn't questioned his story too closely—the late night and pleasure in my new cousin had both muted my suspicions. Today the bleak air chilled my euphoria. A quest for a great-grandmother's music might bring one pleasure, but surely not inspire such avidity as Vico displayed. He'd grown up in poverty in Milan without knowing who his father, or even his grandfather were. Maybe it was a quest for roots that was driving my cousin so passionately.

I wondered, too, what item of value my mother had refused to sell thirty summers ago. What wasn't *hers* to sell, that she would stubbornly sacrifice better medical care for it? I realized I felt hurt: I thought I was so dear to her she told me everything. The idea that she'd kept a secret from me made it hard for me to think clearly.

When my dad died, I'd gone through everything in the little house on Houston before selling it. I'd never found anything that seemed worth that much agony, so either she did sell it in the end—or my dad had done so—or she had given it to someone else. Of course, she might have buried it deep in the house. The only place I could imagine her hiding something was in her piano, and if that were the case I was out of luck: the piano had been lost in the fire that destroyed my apartment ten years ago.

But if it—whatever it was—was the same thing Vico was looking for, some old piece of music—Gabriella would have consulted Mr. Fortieri. If she hadn't gone to him, he might know who else she would have turned to. While I waited in a Naperville mall for my prints to be developed I tried phoning him. He was eighty now, but still actively working, so I wasn't surprised when he didn't answer the phone.

I snoozed in the president's antechamber until he could finally snatch ten minutes for my report. When I finished, a little after five, I stopped in his secretary's office to try Mr. Fortieri again. Still no answer.

With only three hours sleep, my skin was twitching as though I'd put it on inside out. Since seven this morning I'd logged a hundred and ninety miles. I wanted nothing now more than my bed. Instead I rode the packed expressway all the way northwest to the O'Hare cutoff.

Mr. Fortieri lived in the Italian enclave along north Harlem Avenue. It used to be a day's excursion to go there with Gabriella: we would ride the Number Six bus to the Loop, transfer to the Douglas line of the el, and at its end take yet another bus west to Harlem. After lunch in one of the storefront restaurants, my mother stopped at Mr. Fortieri's to sing or talk while I was given an old clarinet to take apart to keep me amused. On our way back to the bus we bought polenta and olive oil in Frescobaldi's Deli. Old Mrs. Frescobaldi would let me run my hands through the bags of cardamom, the voluptuous scent making me stomp around the store in an exaggerated imitation of the drunks along Commercial Avenue. Gabriella would hiss embarrassed invectives at me, and threaten to withhold my gelato if I didn't behave.

The street today has lost much of its charm. Some of the old stores remain, but the chains have set out tendrils here as elsewhere. Mrs. Frescobaldi couldn't stand up to Jewel, and Vespucci's, where Gabriella bought all her shoes, was swallowed by the nearby mall.

Mr. Fortieri's shop, on the ground floor of his dark-shuttered house, looked forlorn now, as though it missed the lively commerce of the street. I rang the bell without much hope: no lights shone from either story.

"I don't think he's home," a woman called from the neighboring walk.

She was just setting out with a laundry-laden shopping cart. I asked her if she'd seen Mr. Fortieri at all today. She'd noticed his bedroom light when she was getting ready for work—he was an early riser, just like her, and this time of year she always noticed his bedroom light. In fact, she'd just been thinking it was strange she didn't see his kitchen light on—he was usually preparing his supper about now, but maybe he'd gone off to see his married daughter in Wilmette.

I remembered Barbara Fortieri's wedding. Gabriella had been too sick to attend, and had sent me by myself. The music had been sensational, but I had been angry and uncomfortable and hadn't paid much attention to anything—including the groom. I asked the woman if she knew Barbara's married name—I might try to call her father there.

"Oh, you know her?"

"My mother was a friend of Mr. Fortieri's—Gabriella Sestieri—Warshawski, I mean." Talking to my cousin had sunk me too deep in my mother's past.

"Sorry, honey, never met her. She married a boy she met at college, I can't think of his name, just about the time my husband and I moved in here, and they went off to those lakefront suburbs together."

She made it sound like as daring a trip as any of her ancestors had undertaken braving the Atlantic. Fatigue made it sound funny to me and I found myself doubling over to keep the woman from seeing me shake with wild laughter. The thought of Gabriella telling me "No gelato if you do not behave this minute" only made it seem funnier and I had to bend over, clutching my side.

"You okay there, honey?" The woman hesitated, not wanting to be involved with a stranger.

"Long day," I gasped. "Sudden—cramp—in my side."

I waved her on, unable to speak further. Losing my balance, I reeled against the door. It swung open behind me and I fell hard into the open shop, banging my elbow against a chair.

The fall sobered me. I rubbed my elbow, crooning slightly from pain. Bracing against the chair I hoisted myself to my feet. It was only then that it dawned on me that the chair was overturned—alarming in any shop, but especially that of someone as fastidious as Mr. Fortieri.

Without stopping to reason I backed out the door, closing it by wrapping my hand in my jacket before touching the knob. The woman with the laundry cart had gone on down the street. I hunted in my glove compartment for my flashlight, then ran back up the walk and into the shop.

I found the old man in the back, in the middle of his workshop. He lay amid his tools, the stem of an oboe still in his left hand. I fumbled for his pulse. Maybe it was the nervous beating of my own heart, but I thought I felt a faint trace of life. I found the phone on the far side of room, buried under a heap of books that had been taken from the shelves and left where they landed.

VI

"Damn it, Warshawski, what were you doing here anyway?" Sergeant John McGonnigal and I were talking in the back room of Mr. Fortieri's shop while evidence technicians ravaged the front.

I was as surprised to see him as he was me: I'd worked with him, or around him, anyway, for years downtown at the Central District. No one down there had told me he'd transferred—kind of surprising, because he'd been the right-hand man of my dad's oldest friend on the force, Bobby Mallory. Bobby was nearing retirement now; I was guessing McGonnigal had moved out to Montclare to establish a power base independent of his protector. Bobby doesn't like me messing with murder, and McGonnigal sometimes apes his boss, or used to.

Even at his most irritable, when he's inhaling Bobby's frustration, McGonnigal realizes he can trust me, if not to tell the whole truth, at least not to lead him astray or blow a police operation. Tonight he was exasperated simply by the coincidence of mine being the voice that summoned him to a crime scene—the nature of their work makes most cops a little superstitious. He wasn't willing to believe I'd come out to the Montclare neighborhood just to ask about music. As a sop, I threw in my long-lost cousin who was trying to track down a really obscure score.

"And what is that?"

"Sonatas by Claudia Fortezza Verazi." Okay, maybe I sometimes led him a little bit astray.

"Someone tore this place up pretty good for a while before the old guy showed up. It looks as though he surprised the intruder and thought he could defend himself with—what did you say he was holding? an oboe? You think your cousin did that? Because the old guy didn't have any Claudia whoever whoever sonatas?"

I tried not to jump at the question. "I don't think so." My voice came from far away, in a small thread, but at least it didn't quaver.

I was worrying about Vico myself. I hadn't told him about Mr. Fortieri, I was sure of that. But maybe he'd found the letter Fortieri

wrote Gabriella, the one I'd tucked into the score of *Don Giovanni*. And
then came out here, looking for—whatever he was really hunting—and
found it, so he stabbed Mr. Fortieri to hide his—Had he come to Chicago to make a fool of me in his search for something valuable? And
how had McGonnigal leaped on that so neatly? I must be tired beyond
measure to have revealed my fears.

"Let's get this cousin's name . . . Damn it, Vic, you can't sit on that.
I move to this district three months ago. The first serious assault I bag
who should be here but little Miss Muppet right under my tuffet. You'd
have to be on drugs to put a knife into the guy, but you know something
or you wouldn't be here minutes after it happened."

"Is that the timing? Minutes before my arrival?"

McGonnigal hunched his shoulders impatiently. "The medics didn't
stop to figure out that kind of stuff—his blood pressure was too low.
Take it as read that the old man'd be dead if you hadn't shown so pat—
you'll get your citizen's citation the next time the mayor's handing out
medals. Maybe Fortieri'd been bleeding half an hour, but no more. So, I
want to talk to your cousin. And then I'll talk to someone else, and
someone else and someone after that. You know how a police investigation runs."

"Yes, I know how they run." I felt unbearably tired as I gave him
Vico's name, letter by slow letter, to relay to a patrolman. "Did your
guys track down Mr. Fortieri's daughter?"

"She's with him at the hospital. And what does *she* know that you're
not sharing with me?"

"She knew my mother. I should go see her. It's hard to wait in a
hospital while people you don't know cut on your folks."

He studied me narrowly, then said roughly that he'd seen a lot of that
himself, lately, his sister had just lost a kidney to lupus, and I should get
some sleep instead of hanging around a hospital waiting room all night.

I longed to follow his advice, but beneath the rolling waves of fatigue
that crashed against my brain was a sense of urgency. If Vico had been
here, had found what he was looking for, he might be on his way to
Italy right now.

The phone rang. McGonnigal stuck an arm around the corner and
took it from the patrolman who answered it. After a few grunts he hung
up.

"Your cousin hasn't checked out of the Garibaldi, but he's not in his
room. As far as the hall staff knows he hasn't been there since breakfast
this morning, but of course guests don't sign in and out as they go. You
got a picture of him?"

"I met him yesterday for the first time. We didn't exchange high school yearbooks. He's in his mid-thirties, maybe an inch or two taller than me, slim, reddish-brown hair that's a little long on the sides and combed forward in front, and eyes almost the same color."

I swayed and almost fell as I walked to the door. In the outer room the chaos was greater than when I'd arrived. On top of the tumbled books and instruments lay gray print powder and yellow crime-scene tape. I skirted the mess as best I could, but when I climbed into the Trans Am I left a streak of gray powder on the floor mats.

VII

Although her thick hair now held more gray than black, I knew Barbara Fortieri as soon as I stepped into the surgical waiting room (now Barbara Carmichael, now fifty-two, summoned away from flute lessons to her father's bedside). She didn't recognize me at first: I'd been a teenager when she last saw me, and twenty-seven years had passed.

After the usual exclamations of surprise, of worry, she told me her father had briefly opened his eyes at the hospital, just before they began running the anesthetic, and had uttered Gabriella's name.

"Why was he thinking about your mother? Had you been to see him recently? He talks about you sometimes. And about her."

I shook my head. "I wanted to see him, to find out if Gabriella had consulted him about selling something valuable the summer she got sick, the summer of 1965."

Of course Barbara didn't know a thing about the matter. She'd been in her twenties then, engaged to be married, doing her masters in performance at Northwestern in flute and piano, with no attention to spare for the women who were in and out of her father's shop.

I recoiled from her tone as much as her words, the sense of Gabriella as one of an adoring harem. I uttered a stiff sentence of regret over her father's attack and turned to leave.

She put a hand on my arm. "Forgive me, Victoria: I liked your mother. All the same, it used to bug me, all the time he spent with her. I thought he was being disloyal to the memory of my own mother . . . anyway, my husband is out of town. The thought of staying here alone, waiting on news. . . ."

So I stayed with her. We talked emptily, to fill the time, of her classes, the recitals she and her husband gave together, the fact that I wasn't married, and, no, I didn't keep up with my music. Around nine one of the surgeons came in to say that Mr. Fortieri had made it through surgery. The knife had pierced his lung and he had lost a lot of blood. To make sure he didn't suffer heart damage they were putting him on a ventilator, in a drug-induced coma, for a few days. If we were his daughters we could go see him, but it would be a shock and he wanted us to be prepared.

We both grimaced at the assumption that we were sisters. I left Barbara at the door of the intensive care waiting room and dragged myself to the Trans Am. A fine mist was falling, outlining street lamps with a gauzy halo. I tilted the rearview mirror so that I could see my face in the silver light. Those angular cheekbones were surely Slavic, and my eyes Tony's clear deep gray. Surely. I was surely Tony Warshawski's daughter.

The streets were slippery. I drove with extreme care, frightened of my own fatigue. Safe at home the desire for sleep consumed me like a ravening appetite. My fingers trembled on the keys with my longing for my bed.

Mr. Contreras surged into the hall when he heard me open the stairwell door. "Oh, there you are, doll. I found your cousin hanging around the entrance waiting for you, least, I didn't know he was your cousin, but he explained it all, and I thought you wouldn't want him standing out there, not knowing how long it was gonna be before you came home."

"Ah, *cara cugina!*" Vico appeared behind my neighbor, but before he could launch into his recitative the chorus of dogs drowned him, barking and squeaking as they barreled past him to greet me.

I stared at him, speechless.

"How are you? Your working it was good?"

"My working was difficult. I'm tired."

"So, maybe I take you to dinner, to the dancing, you are lively." He was speaking English in deference to Mr. Contreras, whose only word of Italian is "grappa."

"Dinner and dancing and I'll feel like a corpse. Why don't you go back to your hotel and let me get some sleep."

"Naturally, naturally. You are working hard all the day and I am playing. I have your—your *partitura*—"

"Score."

"*Buono.* Score. I have her. I will take her upstairs and put her away very neat for you and leave you to your resting."

"I'll take it with me." I held out my hand.

"No, no. We are leaving one big mess last night, I know that, and I am greedy last night, making you stay up when today you work. So I come with you, clean—*il disordine*—disorderliness?, then you rest without worry. You smell flowers while *I* work."

Before I could protest further he ducked back into Mr. Contreras' living room and popped out with a large portmanteau. With a flourish he extracted a bouquet of spring flowers, and the score, wrapped this time in a cream envelope, and put his arm around me to shepherd me up the stairs. The dogs and the old man followed him, all four making so much racket that the medical resident who'd moved in across the hall from Mr. Contreras came out.

"Please! I just got off a thirty-six-hour shift and I'm trying to sleep. If you can't control those damned dogs I'm going to issue a complaint to the city."

Vico butted in just as Mr. Contreras, drawing a deep breath, prepared to unleash a major aria in defense of his beloved animals. *"Mi scusa, Signora, mi scusa.* It is all my doing. I am here from Italy to meet my cousin for the first time. I am so excited I am not thinking, I am making noise, I am disturbing the rest your beautiful eyes require. . . ."

I stomped up the stairs without waiting for the rest of the flow. Vico caught up with me as I was closing the door. "This building attracts hardworking ladies who need to sleep. Your poor neighbor. She is at a hospital where they work her night and day. What is it about America, that ladies must work so hard? I gave her some of your flowers; I knew you wouldn't mind, and they made her so happy, she will give you no more complaints about the ferocious beasts."

He had switched to Italian, much easier to understand on his lips than English. Flinging himself on the couch he launched happily into a discussion of his day with the "partitura." He had found, through our mutual acquaintance Mr. Ranier, someone who could interpret the music for him. I was right: it was from the Baroque, and not only that, most likely by Pergolesi.

"So not at all possibly by our great-grandmother. Why would your mother have a handwritten score by a composer she could find in any music store?"

I was too tired for finesse. "Vico, where were you at five this afternoon?"

He flung up his hands. "Why are you like a policeman all of a sudden, eh, *cugina?*"

"It's a question the police may ask you. I'd like to know, myself."

A wary look came into his eyes—not anger, which would have been natural, or even bewilderment—although he used the language of a puzzled man: I couldn't be jealous of him, although it was a compliment when we had only just met, so what on earth was I talking about? And why the police? But if I really wanted to know, he was downstairs, with my neighbor.

"And for that matter, Vic, where were you at five o'clock?"

"On the Kennedy Expressway. Heading toward north Harlem Avenue."

He paused a second too long before opening his hands wide again. "I don't know your city, cousin, so that tells me nothing."

"*Bene*. Thank you for going to so much trouble over the score. Now you must let me rest."

I put a hand out for it, but he ignored me and rushed over to the mound of papers we'd left in the hall last night with a cry that I was to rest, he was to work now.

He took the Pergolesi from its envelope. "The music is signed at the end, with the initials 'CF.' Who would that be?"

"Probably whoever copied it for her. I don't know."

He laid it on the bottom of the trunk and placed a stack of operas on top of it. My lips tight with anger I lifted the libretti out in order to get at the Pergolesi. Vico rushed to assist me but only succeeded in dropping everything, so that music and old papers both fluttered to the floor. I was too tired to feel anything except a tightening of the screws in my forehead. Without speaking I took the score from him and retreated to the couch.

Was this the same concerto Vico had taken with him the night before? I'd been naive to let him walk off with a document without some kind of proper safeguard. I held it up to the light, but saw nothing remarkable in the six pages, no signs that a secret code had been erased, or brought to light, nothing beyond a few carefully corrected notes in measure 168. I turned to the end where the initials "CF" were written in the same careful black ink as the notes.

Vico must have found Fortieri's letter to my mother stuffed inside *Don Giovanni* and tracked him down. No, he'd been here at five. So the lawyer, Ranier, was involved. Vico had spent the day with him: together they'd traced Mr. Fortieri. Vico came here for an alibi while the lawyer searched the shop. I remembered Ranier's eyes, granite chips in his soft face. He could stab an old man without a second's compunction.

Vico, a satisfied smile on his face, came to the couch for Gabriella's evening gown. "This goes on top, right, this beautiful concert dress. And now, *cugina,* all is tidy. I will leave you to your dreams. May they be happy ones."

He scooped up his portmanteau and danced into the night, blowing me a kiss as he went.

VIII

I fell heavily into sleep, and then into dreams about my mother. At first I was watching her with Mr. Fortieri as they laughed over their coffee in the little room behind the shop where McGonnigal and I had spoken. Impatient with my mother for her absorption in someone else's company I started smearing strawberry gelato over the oboe Mr. Fortieri was repairing. Bobby Mallory and John McGonnigal appeared, wearing their uniforms, and carried me away. I was screaming with rage or fear as Bobby told me my naughtiness was killing my mother.

And then suddenly I was with her in the hospital as she was dying, her dark eyes huge behind a network of tubes and bottles. She was whispering my name through her parched lips, mine and Francesca Salvini's. *"Maestra Salvini . . . nella cassa . . . Vittora, mia carissima, dale . . ."* she croaked. My father, holding her hands, demanded of me what she was saying.

I woke as I always did at this point in the dream, my hair matted with sweat. "Maestra Salvini is in the box," I had told Tony helplessly at the time. "She wants me to give her something."

I always thought my mother was struggling with the idea that her voice teacher might be dead, that that was why her letters were returned unopened. Francesca Salvini on the Voice had filled my ears from my earliest childhood. As Gabriella staged her aborted comeback, she longed to hear some affirmation from her teacher. She wrote her at her old address in Pitigliano, and in care of the Siena Opera, as well as through her cousin Frederica—not knowing that Frederica herself had died two years earlier.

"Cassa"—"box"—isn't the usual Italian word for coffin, but it could be used as a crude figure just as it is in English. It had always jarred on me to hear it from my mother—her speech was precise, refined, and she tolerated no obscenities. And as part of her last words—she lapsed into a coma later that afternoon from which she never awoke—it always made me shudder to think that was on her mind, Salvini in a box, buried, as Gabriella was about to be.

But my mother's urgency was for the pulse of life. As though she had given me explicit instructions in my sleep I rose from the bed, walked to the hall without stopping to dress, and pulled open the trunk once more. I took out everything and sifted through it over and over, but nowhere could I see the olivewood box that had held Gabriella's glasses on the voyage to America. I hunted all through the living room, and then, in desperation, went through every surface in the apartment.

I remembered the smug smile Vico had given me on his way out the door last night. He'd stuffed the box into his portmanteau and disappeared with it.

IX

Vico hadn't left Chicago, or at least he hadn't settled his hotel bill. I got into his room at the Garibaldi by calling room service from the hall phone and ordering champagne. When the service trolley appeared from the bar I followed the waiter into the elevator, saw which room he knocked on as I sauntered past him down the hall, then let myself in with my picklocks when he'd taken off again in frustration. I knew my cousin wasn't in, or at least wasn't answering his phone—I'd already called from across the street.

I didn't try to be subtle in my search. I tossed everything from the drawers onto the floor, pulled the mattress from the bed, and pried the furniture away from the wall. Fury was making me wanton: by the time I'd made sure the box wasn't in the room the place looked like the remains of a shipwreck.

If Vico didn't have the box he must have handed it off to Ranier. The import-export lawyer, who specialized in remarkable *objets,* doubtless knew the value of an old musical score and how to dispose of it.

The bedside clock was buried somewhere under the linens. I looked at my watch—it was past four now. I let myself out of the room, trying to decide whether Ranier would store the box at his office or his home. There wasn't any way of telling, but it would be easier to break into his office, especially at this time of day.

I took a cab to the west Loop rather than trying to drive and park in the rush-hour maelstrom. The November daylight was almost gone. Last night's mist had turned into a biting sleet. People fled for their home-bound transportation, heads bent into the wind. I paid off the cab and ran out of the ice into the Caleb Building's coffee shop to use the phone. When Ranier answered I gave myself a high nasal voice and asked for Cindy.

"She's left for the day. Who is this?"

"Amanda Parton. I'm in her book group and I wanted to know if she remembered—"

"You'll have to call her at home. I don't want this kind of personal drivel discussed in my office." He hung up.

Good, good. No personal drivel on company time. Only theft. I mixed with the swarm of people in the Caleb's lobby and rode up to the thirty-seventh floor. A metal door without any letters or numbers on it might lead to a supply closet. Working quickly, while the hall was briefly empty, I unpicked the lock. Behind lay a mass of wires, the phone and signal lines for the floor, and a space just wide enough for me to stand in. I pulled the door almost shut and stared through the crack.

A laughing group of men floated past on their way to a Blackhawks game. A solitary woman, hunched over a briefcase, scowled at me. I thought for a nervous moment that she was going to test the door, but she was apparently lost in unpleasant thoughts all her own. Finally, around six, Ranier emerged, talking in Italian with Vico. My cousin looked as debonair as ever, with a marigold tucked in his lapel. Where he'd found one in mid-November I don't know but it looked quite jaunty against his brown worsted. The fragment of conversation I caught seemed to be about a favorite restaurant in Florence, not about my mother and music.

I waited another ten minutes, to make sure they weren't standing at the elevator, or returning for a forgotten umbrella, then slipped out of the closet and down to Ranier's import-export law office. Someone leaving an adjacent firm looked at me curiously as I slid the catch back. I flashed a smile, said I hated working nights. He grunted in commiseration and went on to the elevator.

Cindy's chair was tucked against her desk, a white cardigan draped primly about the arms. I didn't bother with her area but went to work on the inner door. Here Ranier had been more careful. It took me ten minutes to undo it. I was angry and impatient and my fingers kept slipping on the hafts.

Lights in these modern buildings are set on master timers for quadrants of a story, so that they all turn on or off at the same time. Outside full night had arrived; the high harsh lamps reflected my wavering outline in the black windows. I might have another hour of fluorescence flooding my search before the building masters decided most of the denizens had gone home for the day.

When I reached the inner office my anger mounted to murderous levels: my mother's olivewood box lay in pieces in the garbage. I pulled it out. They had pried it apart, and torn out the velvet lining. One shred of pale green lay on the floor. I scrabbled through the garbage for the rest of the velvet and saw a crumpled page in my mother's writing.

Gasping for air I stuck my hand in to get it. The whole wastebasket rose to greet me. I clutched at the edge of the desk but it seemed to whirl past me and the roar of a giant wind deafened me.

I managed to get my head between my knees and hold it there until the dizziness subsided. Weak from my emotional storm, I moved slowly to Ranier's couch to read Gabriella's words. The page was dated the thirtieth of October 1967, her last birthday, and the writing wasn't in her usual bold, upright script. Pain medication had made all her movements shaky at that point.

The letter began *"Carissima,"* without any other address, but it was clearly meant for me. My cheeks burned with embarrassment that her farewell note would be to her daughter, not her husband. "At least not to a lover, either," I muttered, thinking with more embarrassment of Mr. Fortieri, and my explicit dream.

My dearest,

I have tried to put this where you may someday find it. As you travel through life you will discard that which has no meaning for you, but I believe—hope—this box and my glasses will always stay with you on your journey. You must return this valuable score to Francesca Salvini if she is still alive. If she is dead, you must do with it as the circumstances of the time dictate to you. You must under no circumstances sell it for your own gain. If it has the value that Maestra Salvini attached to it it should perhaps be in a museum.

It hung always in a frame next to the piano in Maestra Salvini's music room, on the ground floor of her house. I went to her in the middle of the night, just before I left Italy, to bid her farewell. She feared she, too, might be arrested—she had been an uncompromising opponent of the Fascists. She gave it to me to safeguard in America, lest it fall into lesser hands, and I cannot agree to sell it only to buy medicine. So I am hiding this from your papa, who would violate my trust to feed more money to the doctors. And there is no need. Already, after all, these drugs they give me make me ill and destroy my voice. Should I use her treasure to add six months to my life, with only the addition of much more pain? You, my beloved child, will understand that that is not living, that mere survival of the organism.

Oh, my darling one, my greatest pain is that I must leave you alone in a world full of dangers and temptations. Always strive for justice, never accept the second-rate in yourself, my darling, even though you must accept it from the world around you. I grieve that I shall not live to see you grown, in your own life, but remember: *Il mio amore per te è l'amor che muove il sole e l'altre stelle.*

My love for you is the love that moves the sun and all the other stars. She used to croon that to me as a child. It was only in college I learned that Dante said it first.

I could see her cloudy with pain, obsessed with her commitment to save Salvini's music, scoring open the velvet of the box and sealing it in the belief I would find it. Only the pain and the drugs could have led her to something so improbable. For I would never have searched unless Vico had come looking for it. No matter how many times I recalled the pain of those last words, *"nella cassa,"* I wouldn't have made the connection to this box. This lining. This letter.

I smoothed the letter and put it in a flat side compartment of my case. With the sense that my mother was with me in the room some of my anger calmed. I was able to begin the search for Francesca Salvini's treasure with a degree of rationality.

Fortunately Ranier relied for security on the building's limited access: I'd been afraid he might have a safe. Instead he housed his papers in the antique credenza. Inside the original decorative lock he'd installed a small modern one, but it didn't take long to undo it. My anger at the destruction of Gabriella's box made me pleased when the picklocks ran a deep scratch across the marquetry front of the cabinet.

I found the score in a file labeled "Sestieri-Verazi." The paper was old, parchment that had frayed and discolored at the edges, and the writing on it—clearly done by hand—had faded in places to a pale brown. Scored for oboe, two horns, a violin, and a viola, the piece was eight pages long. The notes were drawn with exquisite care. On the second, third, and sixth pages someone had scribbled another set of bar lines above the horn part and written in notes in a fast careless hand, much different from the painstaking care of the rest of the score. In two places he'd scrawled "da capo" in such haste that the letters were barely distinguishable. The same impatient writer had scrawled some notes in the margin, and at the end. I couldn't read the script, although I thought it might be German. Nowhere could I find a signature on the document to tell me who the author was.

I placed the manuscript on the top of the credenza and continued to inspect the file. A letter from a Signor Arnoldo Piave in Florence introduced Vico to Ranier as someone on the trail of a valuable musical document in Chicago. Signor Ranier's help in locating the parties involved would be greatly appreciated. Ranier had written in turn to a man in Germany "well-known to be interested in eighteenth-century musical manuscripts," to let him know Ranier might soon have something "unusual" to show him.

I had read that far when I heard a key in the outer door. The cleaning crew I could face down, but if Ranier had returned . . . I swept the score from the credenza and tucked it in the first place that met my eye—behind the Modigliani that hung above it. A second later Ranier and Vico stormed into the room. Ranier was holding a pistol, which he trained on me.

"I knew it!" Vico cried in Italian. "As soon as I saw the state of my hotel room I knew you had come to steal the score."

"Steal the score? My dear Vico!" I was pleased to hear a tone of light contempt in my voice.

Vico started toward me but backed off at a sharp word from Ranier. The lawyer told me to put my hands on top of my head and sit on the couch. The impersonal chill in his eyes was more frightening than anger. I obeyed.

"Now what?" Vico demanded of Ranier.

"Now we had better take her out to—well, the place name won't mean anything to you. A forest west of town. One of the sheriff's deputies will take care of her."

There are sheriff's deputies who will do murder for hire in unincorporated parts of Cook County. My body would be found by dogs or children under a heap of rotted leaves in the spring.

"So you have Mob connections," I said in English. "Do you pay them, or they you?"

"I don't think it matters." Ranier was still indifferent. "Let's get going. . . . Oh, Verazi," he added in Italian, "before we leave, just check for the score, will you?"

"What is this precious score?" I asked.

"It's not important for you to know."

"You steal it from my apartment, but I don't need to know about it? I think the state will take a different view."

Before Ranier finished another cold response Vico cried out that the manuscript was missing.

"Then search her bag," Ranier ordered.

Vico crossed behind him to snatch my case from the couch. He dumped the contents on the floor. A Shawn Colwin tape, a tampon that had come partially free of its container, loose receipts, and a handful of dog biscuits joined my work notebook, miniature camera, and binoculars in an unprofessional heap. Vico opened the case wide and shook it. The letter from my mother remained in the inner compartment.

"Where is it?" Ranier demanded.

"Don't ask, don't tell," I said, using English again.

"Verazi, get behind her and tie her hands. You'll find some rope in the bottom of my desk."

Ranier wasn't going to shoot me in his office: too much to explain to the building management. I fought hard. When Ranier kicked me in the stomach I lost my breath, though, and Vico caught my arms roughly behind me. His marigold was crushed, and he would have a black eye before tomorrow morning. He was panting with fury, and smacked me again across the face when he finished tying me. Blood dripped from my nose onto my shirt. I wanted to blot it and momentarily gave way to rage at my helplessness. I thought of Gabriella, of the love that moves the sun and all the other stars, and tried to avoid the emptiness of Ranier's eyes.

"Now tell me where the manuscript is," Ranier said in the same impersonal voice.

I leaned back in the couch and shut my eyes. Vico hit me again.

"Okay, okay," I muttered. "I'll tell you where the damned thing is. But I have one question first."

"You're in no position to bargain," Ranier intoned.

I ignored him. "Are you really my cousin?"

Vico bared his teeth in a canine grin. "Oh, yes, *cara cugina,* be assured, we are relatives. That naughty Frederica whom everyone in the family despised was truly my grandmother. Yes, she slunk off to Milan to have a baby in the slums without a father. And my mother was so impressed by her example that she did the same. Then when those two worthy women died, the one of tuberculosis, the other of excess heroin, the noble Verazis rescued the poor gutter child and brought him up in splendor in Florence. They packed all my grandmother's letters into a box and swept them up with me and my one toy, a horse that someone else had thrown in the garbage, and that my mother brought home from one of her nights out. My aunt discarded the horse and replaced it with some very hygienic toys, but the papers she stored in her attic.

"Then when my so-worthy uncle, who could never thank himself enough for rescuing this worthless brat, died, I found all my grandmother's papers, including letters from your mother, and her plea for help in finding Francesca Salvini so that she could return this most precious musical score. And I thought, what have these Verazis ever done for me, but rubbed my nose in dirt? And you, that same beautiful blood flows in you as in them. And as in me!"

"And Claudia Fortezza, our great-grandmother? Did she write music, or was that all a fiction?"

"Oh, no doubt she dabbled in music as all the ladies in our family like to, even you, looking at that score the other night and asking me about the notation! Oh, yes, like all those stuck-up Verazi cousins, laughing at me because I'd never seen a piano before! I thought you would fall for such a tale, and it amused me to have you hunting for her music when it never existed."

His eyes glittered amber and flecks of spit covered his mouth by the time he finished. The idea that he looked like Gabriella seemed obscene. Ranier slapped him hard and ordered him to calm down.

"She wants us excited. It's her only hope for disarming me." He tapped the handle of the gun lightly on my left kneecap. "Now tell me where the score is, or I'll smash your kneecap and make you walk on it."

My hands turned clammy. "I hid it down the hall. There's a wiring closet. . . . The metal door near the elevators. . . ."

"Go see," Ranier ordered Verazi.

My cousin returned a few minutes later with the news that the door was locked.

"Are you lying?" Ranier growled at me. "How did you get into it?"

"Same as into here," I muttered. "Picklocks. In my hip pocket."

Ranier had Vico take them from me, then seemed disgusted that my cousin didn't know how to use them. He decided to take me down to unlock the closet myself.

"No one's working late on this side of the floor tonight, and the cleaning staff doesn't arrive until nine. We should be clear."

They frog-marched me down the hall to the closet before untying my hands. I knelt to work the lock. As it clicked free Vico grabbed the door and yanked it open. I fell forward into the wires. Grabbing a large armful I pulled with all my strength. The hall turned black and an alarm began to blare.

Vico grabbed my left leg. I kicked him in the head with my right. He let go. I turned and grabbed him by the throat and pounded his head against the floor. He got hold of my left arm and pulled it free. Before he could hit me I rolled clear and kicked again at his head. I hit only air.

My eyes adjusted to the dark: I could make out his shape as a darker shape against the floor, squirming out of reach.

"Roll clear and call out!" Ranier shouted at him. "On the count of five I'm going to shoot."

I dove for Ranier's legs and knocked him flat. The gun went off as he hit the floor. I slammed my fist into the bridge of his nose and he lost consciousness. Vico reached for the gun. Suddenly the hall lights came on. I blinked in the brightness and rolled toward Vico, hoping to kick the gun free before he could focus and fire.

"Enough! Hands behind your heads, all of you." It was a city cop. Behind him stood one of the Caleb's security force.

X

It didn't take me as long to sort out my legal problems as I'd feared. Ranier's claim, that I'd broken into his office and he was protecting himself, didn't impress the cops: if Ranier was defending his office why was he shooting at me out in the hall? Besides, the city cops had long had an eye on him: they had a pretty good idea he was connected to the Mob, but no real evidence. I had to do some fancy tap-dancing on why I'd been in his office to begin with, but I was helped by Bobby Mallory's arrival on the scene. Assaults in the Loop went across his desk, and one with his oldest friend's daughter on the rap sheet brought him into the holding cells on the double.

For once I told him everything I knew. And for once he was not only empathetic, but helpful: he retrieved the score for me—himself—from behind the Modigliani, along with the fragments of the olivewood box. Without talking to the state's attorney, or even suggesting that it should be impounded to make part of the state's case. It was when he started blowing his nose as someone translated Gabriella's letter for him—he didn't trust me to do it myself—that I figured he'd come through for me.

"But what is it?" he asked, when he'd handed me the score.

I hunched a shoulder. "I don't know. It's old music that belonged to my mother's voice teacher. I figure Max Loewenthal can sort it out."

Max is the executive director of Beth Israel, the hospital where Lotty Herschel is chief of perinatology, but he collects antiques and knows a lot about music. I told him the story later that day and gave the score to him. Max is usually imperturbably urbane, but when he inspected the music his face flushed and his eyes glittered unnaturally.

"What is it?" I cried.

"If it's what I think—no, I'd better not say. I have a friend who can tell us. Let me give it to her."

Vico's blows to my stomach made it hard for me to move, otherwise I might have started pounding on Max. The glitter in his eye made me demand a receipt for the document before I parted with it.

At that his native humor returned. "You're right, Victoria: I'm not immune from cupidity. I won't abscond with this, I promise, but maybe I'd better give you a receipt just the same."

XI

It was two weeks later that Max's music expert was ready to give us a verdict. I figured Bobby Mallory and Barbara Carmichael deserved to hear the news firsthand, so I invited them all to dinner, along with Lotty. Of course, that meant I had to include Mr. Contreras and the dogs. My neighbor decided the occasion was important enough to justify digging his one suit out of mothballs.

Bobby arrived early, with his wife, Eileen, just as Barbara showed up. She told me her father had recovered sufficiently from his attack to be revived from his drug-induced coma, but he was still too weak to answer questions. Bobby added that they'd found a witness to the forced entry of Fortieri's house. A boy hiding in the alley had seen two men going in through the back. Since he was smoking a reefer behind a garage he hadn't come forward earlier, but when John McGonnigal assured him they didn't care about his dope—this one time—he picked Ranier's face out of a collection of photos.

"And the big guy promptly donated his muscle to us—a part-time deputy, who's singing like a bird, on account of he's p-o'd about being fingered." He hesitated, then added, "If you won't press charges they're going to send Verazi home, you know."

I smiled unhappily. "I know."

Eileen patted his arm. "That's enough shop for now. Victoria, who is it who's coming tonight?"

Max rang the bell just then, arriving with both Lotty and his music expert. A short, skinny brunette, she looked like a street urchin in her jeans and outsize sweater. Max introduced her as Isabel Thompson, an authority on rare music from the Newberry Library.

"I hope we haven't kept dinner waiting—Lotty was late getting out of surgery," Max added.

"Let's eat later," I said. "Enough suspense. What have I been lugging unknowing around Chicago all this time?"

"She wouldn't tell us anything until you were here to listen," Max said. "So we are as impatient as you."

Ms. Thompson grinned. "Of course, this is only a preliminary opinion, but it looks like a concerto by Marianne Martines."

"But the insertions, the writing at the end," Max began, when Bobby demanded to known who Marianne Martines was.

"She was an eighteenth-century Viennese composer. She was known to have written over four hundred compositions, but only about sixty have survived, so it's exciting to find a new one." She folded her hands in her lap, a look of mischief in her eyes.

"And the writing, Isabel?" Max demanded.

She grinned. "You were right, Max: it is Mozart's. A suggestion for changes in the horn line. He started to describe them, then decided just to write them in above her original notation. He added a reminder that the two were going to play together the following Monday—they often played piano duets, sometimes privately, sometimes for an audience."

"Hah! I knew it! I was sure!" Max was almost dancing in ecstasy. "So I put some Krugs down to chill. Liquid gold to toast the moment I held in my hand a manuscript that Mozart held."

He pulled a couple of bottles of champagne from his briefcase. I fetched my mother's Venetian glasses from the dining room. Only five remained whole of the eight she had transported so carefully. One had shattered in the fire that destroyed my old apartment, and another when some thugs broke into it one night. A third had been repaired and could still be used. How could I have been so careless with my little legacy.

"But whose is it now?" Lotty asked, when we'd all drunk and exclaimed enough to calm down.

"That's a good question," I said. "I've been making some inquiries through the Italian government. Francesca Salvini died in 1943 and she didn't leave any heirs. She wanted Gabriella to dispose of it in the event of her death. In the absence of a formal will the Italian government might make a claim, but her intention as expressed in Gabriella's letter might give me the right to it, as long as I didn't keep it or sell it just for my own gain."

"We'd be glad to house it," Ms. Thompson offered.

"Seems to me your ma would have wanted someone in trouble to benefit." Bobby was speaking gruffly to hide his embarrassment. "What's something like this worth?"

Ms. Thompson pursed her lips. "A private collector might pay a quarter of a million. We couldn't match that, but we'd probably go to a hundred or hundred and fifty thousand."

"So what mattered most to your ma, Vicki, besides you? Music. Music and victims of injustice. You probably can't do much about the second, but you ought to be able to help some kids learn some music."

Barbara Carmichael nodded in approval. "A scholarship fund to provide Chicago kids with music lessons. It's a great idea, Vic."

We launched the Gabriella-Salvini program some months later with a concert at the Newberry. Mr. Fortieri attended, fully recovered from his wounds. He told me that Gabriella had come to consult him the summer before she died, but she hadn't brought the score with her. Since she'd never mentioned it to him before he thought her illness and medications had made her delusional.

"I'm sorry, Victoria: it was the last time she was well enough to travel to the northwest side, and I'm sorry that I disappointed her. It's been troubling me ever since Barbara told me the news."

I longed to ask him whether he'd been my mother's lover. But did I want to know? What if he, too, had moved the sun and all the other stars for her—I'd hate to know that. I sent him to a front-row chair and went to sit next to Lotty.

In Gabriella's honor the Cellini Wind Ensemble had come from London to play the benefit. They played the Martines score first as the composer had written it, and then as Mozart revised it. I have to confess I liked the original better, but as Gabriella often told me, I'm no musician.